The Stonor Eagles

'My name is Cuillin,' she screamed into the storm, 'and I will fly!' Yet as she called out from the pride of generations, whose power was in her wings and whose courage was in the curl of her talons, she seemed to weaken again and sink powerlessly with the storm winds, down, down towards the sea, and the words she had cried out were hurled back at her as feeble pitiful cries: 'I am Cuillin, I am Cuillin . . .' and she bent her beak towards the sea, and let her wings go slack, for she knew it had been her last cry, the last of all the eagles from Skye . . .

Also by William Horwood

DUNCTON WOOD
DUNCTON QUEST
DUNCTON FOUND
CALLANISH
SKALLAGRIGG

The Stonor Eagles

A soaring epic of man and nature

William Horwood

ARROW BOOKS

Arrow Books Limited
20 Vauxhall Bridge Road, London SW1V 2SA

An imprint of the Random Century Group

London Melbourne Sydney Auckland
Johannesburg and agencies throughout
the world

First published in Great Britain by Country Life Books 1982
Hamlyn Paperbacks edition 1983
Arrow edition 1986
Reprinted 1987, 1989 and 1991

Printed and bound in Great Britain by
Cox & Wyman Ltd, Reading

ISBN 0 09 945540 4

Contents

For my mother
KYM HORWOOD
with love

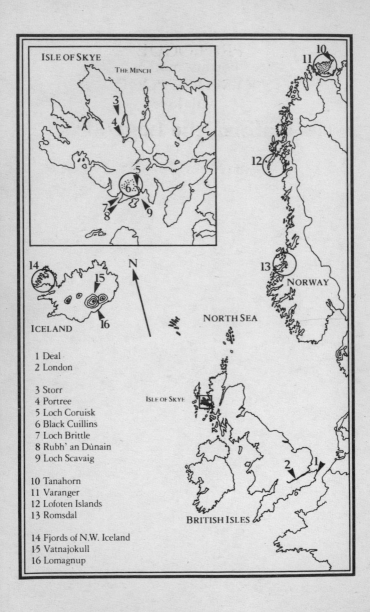

ISLE OF SKYE

THE MINCH

N

ICELAND

NORTH SEA

NORWAY

Isle of Skye

1 Deal
2 London

3 Storr
4 Portree
5 Loch Coruisk
6 Black Cuillins
7 Loch Brittle
8 Rubh' an Dùnain
9 Loch Scavaig

10 Tanahorn
11 Varanger
12 Lofoten Islands
13 Romsdal

14 Fjords of N.W. Iceland
15 Vatnajokull
16 Lomagnup

BRITISH ISLES

Haforn, the Legend

Haforn, the Legend

Haforn, the first sea eagle, was born when the skies still hung red with fire and volcanic dust, and the oceans ran wild with stress and hate. Her father was Land, her mother great Sea, but in their eternal quarrels neither wished that she be born. Sometimes Sea prevailed, lying deep and calm, but at other times Land thrust up, molten and enraged, to divide Sea and make her troubled and angry.

In the north it happened, before whale or seal roamed the ocean, or great skua and storm-petrel darkened a subarctic sky or cast their shadows on the waves and over the cliffs of the Island of ice and fire. For it was from the birth throes of that island that Haforn rose into the sky, and it was from Haforn that there came the first eagles that ever made true flight.

Today, only a remnant volcano remains on that northern island to mark the place where Haforn was born. It is called Mount Hekla, and still rises among the ice and lava deserts, half asleep and half awake, remembering, remembering . . .

For aeons Sea had been calm and untroubled, victor over Land. Then, suddenly, far beneath her lonely waves, there was a wrenching pain of heat, and the hidden depths split open. Blind, luminous creatures of the deep fled in vain the outpourings of red-hot lava which glimmered scarlet through the sea and sent hissing steam and sulphurous gases surging to the stormy surface.

At first this lava spread unseen across the sea-bed, but then it began to mount up on itself, and sent great concentric waves outwards to crash upon distant cliffs and shores. Sea-birds rose in flocks, then turned back again to prey on the dead fish that such upheavals bring.

For days the explosions and outpourings continued, as the surface of the sea was broken by great sparks which rose into the sky, then cooled, and fell back to the water as fragments of ash and lava, black as raven's wing.

By day, thick smoke and sulphur fumes overshadowed the sun; by night a fiery glow lit up the sky and cast strange colours across a lurid sea. Then Land thrust itself even higher, to form a tiny island of tephra, which the sea tore to destruction in hissing steam and crashing foam. But Land thrust up again, by day and night, and more lava rose above the sea again—and again the sea destroyed it.

For weeks, for months, the struggle continued until at last Land began to triumph, for Sea could no longer destroy its growing ramparts, only besiege them with great waves of wrath. Yet seeing that his new island might not last long, Land sent still more outpourings, until a black cone formed, rising

11

higher and higher. And down its sides flowed a great red-yellow river of lava to Sea below, which tore at it in steam and foam, turning it black as it cooled it, then broke bits off. By day the brightness of this lava rivalled the sun; by night it outshone the moon.

Months passed and the island built up steadily, the lava spreading first north, then south, then east, then west, to strengthen its walls against the sea. And by night, this lava river flowed bright red and yellow, but as the weeks went by, it cooled, and became more viscous and slow, till at night the colour changed to a duller, deeper red.

But soon Land grew tired of the fight already won, and the lava flow slowed till its cooling surface hardened even as it moved along, remaining bright and molten only at the centre.

Then strange, half-formed shapes began to appear on its surface, made up of the fiery reds of the molten lava and the darker colours of the cooling rocks: contorted, tortured shapes which thrust out the heads and limbs and aching mouths of blind, distorted half-life that struggled to be born. Sometimes, for an instant, one of these shapes took form which seemed to the birds hovering above like some extinct creature they vaguely remembered from the past, or, one which had plodded its way across the landscapes of their nightmares.

Among those birds that had flown out from neighbouring lands, were a number of black Corvidae – the family of the crow, of rook and of raven – who never take long to find a new source of prey; for they feed off the gulls unwise enough to fly into sulphur fumes and lose their grip on the air. Now the Corvidae observe all things as they go, black and darting on the darkest shores, watching and waiting and gossiping their news over great distances and down the vales of time until it finally reaches the knowledge of the Raven of Storr, in whom are all things told, and from whom no thing is hidden. And it was one of these who watched and saw what happened and later brought to Storr an account of the birth of Haforn, the first sea eagle.

Suddenly, from out of the red lava flow, a mass of cooler lava in the shape of an eagle's foot reached up and searched for a grip, struggling to pull its body's life from out of the molten earth. Then the foot slid back beneath the lava's surface, and when it next found strength to appear, it had been carried nearer to the waiting sea. Again its great dark talons reached around, but, finding nothing solid to grip on to, disappeared again. Then, briefly, the curve of a massive wing broke out, its great grey feathers of cool lava running with red drops of molten rock, before it, too, went under again.

Still the lava flowed on; still other half-formed creatures sought their twisted way to break from the clinging earth. Then, from out of the smoke and fumes, the great head of the eagle at last broke clear, its beak open with strain and its submerged wings beating desperately in the flowing lava to raise its body into the air, while its legs and talons pushed and heaved against the flow to raise the massive body clear before the lava flood carried it down to the sea, which had broken up other half-lives in its swirling waves.

For a moment the eagle's head sank low, but then, sensing that the sea was now dangerously near, it thrust up again—and first one wing and then another broke clear, great sprays of red lava shooting into the air as it slowly beat its wings and strove to lift its body upwards into life. Its beak was massive, its head so great that the sun, already dulled by the smoke and steam, seemed to slide in and out of eclipse as the eagle reared back and forth in its terrible struggle.

Yet neither Sea nor Land observed the eagle's attempt to escape, for they were busy arguing again.

'I always wear you down,' hissed Sea.

'And it is I who shape the oceans,' roared Land.

'And I who will be here long after I've worn you away back under,' said Sea, its great waves riding up the newly-formed land and breaking off lumps of lava from Land's flow.

So they only noticed the great eagle as its wings beat free and it slowly began to rise into the smoke-filled air in a final struggle to free its submerged talons. Appalled at the sight, Sea rose and fretted, while Land surged its lava up into great torrents, trying to drown the eagle back into its molten mass. But as waves of lava swept towards it, the walls of sea water rushed up the black beach, it beat its wings still more fiercely and at last its talons came clear. Then slowly, with a straining of wings, it began to rise.

But the sea surged even higher, sending great steaming waves over the lava to catch the eagle; and the land erupted its volcano again, to send masses of flaming magma down upon the great creature's back and wings. For a moment it sank down towards the swirling sea, its wings battered by falling lava and its tail sinking beneath the frantic waves. But then, with white surf pouring from its body, it rose again into the volcanic hail and beat its wings to rise higher and higher, until Sea could only surge in anger and Land roar with impotence. And the bird's great wings cast a massive shadow over Land and Sea, and the very sun seemed to disappear—as the first sea eagle rose slowly into the sky.

Then, as Sea and Land watched it soar, their anger turned to admiration of the great creature born out of their own struggle. They marvelled at its size and power, Sea feeling that its own powerful surges were mirrored in the rhythm of the eagle's flight, and Land claiming that the fact that it was bigger and slower than other birds reflected his own strength. So Land and Sea each claimed qualities in the eagle as their own, and began to bicker again.

Then Sea sighed and Land whispered, and they spoke as one: 'Her name shall be Haforn, which means sea eagle, and she shall have the gift of true flight. But her children and her children's children will have this gift only if they trust in Haforn's strength and power, and never forget the courage she showed in her struggle for life.

'Many will forget, or lack courage, and they will die. And we, Sea and Land, will harry her, for she has defied our strength and made us seem foolish and weak. We will seek to destroy her, as we have destroyed other creatures that defied us. And we will send a Doom of extinction on her, which will seek to destroy her kind. Wherever her kin travel over the dark sea, the Doom will find them. Only in true flight will they find salvation, and she must teach it to them. In repayment for life she has stolen from us, Haforn will have to teach each to trust her, and this labour of teaching will never cease, and many, many will be her failures, and great her agony. For her wings will only be as strong as the feathers of which they are made, and each feather will be an eagle, and many will be weak or fearful and unwilling to learn to fly true.

'But sometimes there will come sea eagles who will learn, and in them will great Haforn find pride and strength, and before them will the Doom retreat. From them will the wings of Haforn find new power to fight on against the Doom which has extinguished so many other life-forms before her.'

Then they seemed to take pity on her, for Land said 'Well, I'll give her a place where she can rest, and find better shelter and nesting sites . . .' At which Sea interrupted and said, 'And from me she'll have food of fish and food of birds.'

Haforn heard them and was grateful, but she never forgot − nor allowed any of her descendants to forget − that her white tail came from the wrath of Sea when she tried to suck her down into her cold depths; and the mottled brown of her great wings came from Land's anger when he threw great lumps of hot lava down on her to burn her struggling form.

And, though she found joy in her flight, she suffered as well, for so few of her offspring would listen, and her agony was that in their fear and ignorance, in their lack of courage, lay her Doom. As Land and Sea forecast, only rarely did great eagles come who learned to fly true and lightened the burden Haforn perpetually carried in her wings.

Time passed, ages flew, and Sea divided Land again, and Haforn's ancestors were separated. The strongest group settled along the coast of Norway and up to the tundra wastes called Varanger, facing the Barents Sea. A very few lived on the north-west coast of Scotland, where the Doom harried them and they lost strength and nearly all hope. While some remained in Iceland, the ancient land of ice and fire.

Between them flowed the dark sea, but the few survivors lost the courage or the urge to fly across its wastes until, at last, their separated populations began to dwindle and then, finally, to die.

This is the story of one of them, called Cuillin, the last sea eagle of west

Scotland, who was born in Skye and lived for a time in Shetland with Waulk, the last male. He taught her to trust in Haforn, but when he died and she was alone, she tarried there for years, hoping another would find her, so that perhaps the Doom that had come, but of which she did not know the name, would pass. She returned to Skye, and there the Raven saw her, and saw she had courage and faith, and he waited in his telling of the saga, on which the Doom had almost come. He waited in case the saga's end might change, and not be doomed. He waited. And she found courage to turn from her homeland and fly the dark sea to teach others how to fly true and conquer the sky and live off Land and Sea.

This is the telling of her story . . .

PART I

MacAskill

CHAPTER ONE

'In January 1917 the artist's father, Liam Hugh MacAskill, a corporal in the Highland Light Infantry at home on leave in Skye, visited the Storr, a grim series of basaltic cliffs on the east side of the island. He wrote in Gaelic, in his *War Diary* which is now in the archives of the Imperial War Museum, London: "Walked to Storr for a final time before taking the boat to the mainland tomorrow. There was a solitary female sea eagle there in poor condition—feathers awry, tail filthy. She was very tired and almost close enough to touch. She was not mobbed by the ravens, which is unusual."

Although the sea eagle officially became extinct in the British Isles in 1916, ornithologists now accept this as the final sighting. We know now that MacAskill, already shocked by his war service in France and Belgium, was deeply affected by it, and attached the guilt and horror he felt from his experiences on the Front Line, to the final destruction of the sea eagle in Scotland. In fact he appeared to feel directly responsible for it. MacAskill never settled back on Skye but moved to south-east England where he married and had four sons, of whom James MacAskill Stonor was the youngest. From his father's obsession with sea eagles, and the legends and stories he told about them, comes Stonor's own powerful interest in the species, which was to find such dramatic fusion in art and reality in the seventies and eighties when the sea eagle returned to Skye as a breeding species.

In this same period Stonor emerged as an artist of international stature, though the full story of the myths he created around the sea eagle may never be told . . .'

—Marion Poyser, exhibition director of the Museum of Modern Art, New York, in the catalogue for the retrospective of James MacAskill Stonor's work 1971/1996, shown Spring 1998.

April 1998

THE sheer glass doors of New York's Museum of Modern Art made the magnificent spring sky they reflected seem two-dimensional. Indeed, the eye skated over the reflection rapidly before pushing beyond, to the face that peered out from behind it.

Marion Poyser stood in the Museum's foyer, catalogue in hand, awaiting the arrival of Jim Stonor. She was nervous, excited and a little impatient as she watched the people in West 53rd Street, hoping to catch sight of him.

'What time's he coming?' called out Temple from the main office.

'Ten am,' she said for the fourth or fifth time.

Ms Poyser was short, dark and plump, and she spoke with a slight English accent which four years working at London's Tate Gallery had given her. Her suit was rich red, and the solitary earring she wore was black lacquer and based on a design from the Egyptian Collection in the Met. As she stood at the entrance, waiting, she watched the pedestrians go by, especially the youngsters who were wearing variations of the Nagi-thal look that had finally, two years late, reached New York from Madrid.

'It's *gone* ten,' said Temple.

She looked at the digital read-out above the door: 10.02 and forty-seven seconds. Forty-eight seconds. Forty-nine. Fifty . . .

It had taken her two years to get to be standing here waiting for Stonor, and it was the first major retrospective she had done for the Museum.

The previous evening she had stood outside to watch the extraordinary sight of a huge, awesome, holographic eagle, wingspan thirty metres – a work based on sketches of Stonor's famous lost *Tanahorn Eagle* – winging its way up Fifth Avenue and into 53rd as publicity for the show. *The Tanahorn Eagle* was the one which, in 1977, the sculptor had, for reasons very few people understood at the time, illegally erected on the dangerous and inaccessible cliffs of Tanahorn, in Varanger, north Norway. It was done with the help of two rock-climbers—against the wishes of the Norwegian Government and to the consternation of NATO authorities, near one of whose missile tracking bases the sculpture was based. It was a masterpiece of Conceptual art which had taken on a life in the public consciousness far beyond its actual physical existence—which was brief, since it was destroyed by Norwegian army personnel trying to remove it. The *idea* of *The Tanahorn Eagle* was what the work was about, and it marked Stonor's emergence as a major force in contemporary art.

The experience of seeing the holographic presentation of this now non-existent piece, combined with previews in several art magazines and coverage in almost every medium taking a serious interest in art – including the usual anti-notices in the left-wing press which always augured well for an 'establishment' show – added to Marion Poyser's excitement.

Stonor. She must be the only organiser of a retrospective of a perfectly healthy living artist who had never met the artist himself. Dammit, the man lived only sixty miles outside London, and yet, in the four years she had lived there, and on at least six trips since, she had never got to see him.

'He's nearly ten minutes late. Are you sure he's *in* New York?'

called out Temple again. 'I've got a meeting at the Whitney at 10.30.'

'He's kept to the letter of everything else he's arranged with us,' she called back, to stop him from actually getting out of his deputy administrator's chair and standing impatiently beside her. How could a man do a job like that and not like modern sculpture?

She smiled slightly. She had got so used to dealing with Stonor at second hand that in truth she herself could barely believe that he would turn up.

'. . . Finally, Jim says that he's glad it's the Museum of Modern Art, since it means he can come on a morning flight from Heathrow and be there for 10.00 am. He's minimising travel and hotel stops at the moment. His flight gets in to Kennedy at 7.30, so he'll be with you by ten. He'll bring the last piece with him, since it's not too large. As ever, Judith. Call if there's anything you need to know at the last minute.'

'Judith' was Judith Shure, director and owner of London's most prestigious and successful gallery for contemporary art, and Stonor's partner or lover; she never used the word wife and nor, apparently, did he.

It was Judith Shure who had overseen the sale of *Hafom*, the extraordinary piece that the Metropolitan Museum of Art in New York successfully acquired after bidding against London's Tate Gallery in 1992, establishing one of the highest prices ever paid, at that date, for a living British artist's work: $1.7 million. It was Judith Shure who intelligently, elegantly, and with infinite charm, protected Stonor from an importunate press and public. And it was Judith Shure – as Marion Poyser had only slowly come to understand – who had been behind the change in Stonor's personal life that led him at last to escape from the eagle imagery that might finally have reduced his art to a single vision.

Inevitably it was Judith who had been Marion Poyser's main guide and help in getting the retrospective off the ground. Even so, Marion now probably knew more facts about Stonor and his art than anyone, including Judith Shure, and certainly a lot more in some ways than Stonor did himself.

She and the committee which organised the show had rigorously pursued the date, origin, pedigree, title (or disputed title) of every one of the two hundred and seventy-three sketches, paintings, maquettes, constructions, sculptures and etchings in the exhibition. She had also written the definitive account of the making of the Eagle Series and its relationship to his post-1984 work, the date at which the Eagle Series so dramatically came to an end.

But, despite all her research, she knew that an historical account of the progenesis of works of art may tell little about the real, and sometimes irrational, creation of the works themselves. It was the myths about the sea eagle, first told by Liam MacAskill and then fabricated further by Stonor himself, which held the key to the Eagle Series. Like the early nineteenth-century English artist and poet William Blake, Stonor appeared to have found it necessary to create a mythology as a context for his work before he could find the energy and impulse to make it. A mythology, she suspected, that started as a profound and difficult search by a sensitive and inarticulate boy for human truths about the people who influenced him, starting with his father, Liam MacAskill.

Stonor had often told these stories to friends, most of whom Marion Poyser had interviewed – and in some cases counted as her own professional friends – but what they had told her was often fragmentary, lacked overall coherence and, most frustrating of all, rarely seemed to relate to those important moments in Stonor's personal and professional development of which the myth-making was clearly such a crucial part.

She had tackled Judith Shure about this, and asked why Stonor was so reluctant to talk personally with her, or answer her written questions about such basics as the naming of some of the pieces: *Haforn* she understood, but *Sleat*? What was he, or she? And Stonor's most famous piece, *The Raven of Storr*, a copy of which was later erected on top of the Tanahorn by a conciliatory Norwegian Government and remained one of the very few contemporary works in public collections which had the power to inspire awe, and in some cases real fear—who was the Raven?

Judith Shure maintained that Stonor no longer thought it important—it was the works themselves that mattered, not their genesis. For him to go through the myths again, even assuming he could remember them, would be like repeating an old anecdote in the same company twice, and he had no wish to do it. Yet Marion Poyser hoped that today at least she might have the opportunity of getting him to talk about it all, so that, even though it was too late to include anything in the catalogue, yet her own understanding – and theories – might be improved. And she took heart from what so many people had told her, for example Vi Clarke, one of his old college friends: 'He's a charming, open, intelligent man, not the secretive, uncommunicative person he might seem from the fact that he's so rarely seen publicly in the art or gallery world. He prefers working to socialising, that's all.'

Suddenly Marion Poyser saw him, standing on the far side of West

53rd and presumably staring up at the banner hoarding above the Museum, which she could not see from inside the doorway. He was staring at his own name. She knew him immediately from photographs Judith had sent and the pictures her researchers had turned up: medium height, stocky, short grey hair and bearded, with grey at the sides and black below the mouth. He looked relaxed in well-cut blue trousers and a less elegant grey woollen jacket with a red woollen pullover underneath. No coat, no hat. Just a black hold-all in which he was carrying something bulky.

He was waiting patiently, and with an amused expression for the heavy traffic to clear so he could cross the street. His easy stance, looking around at the buildings as he waited, was not that of a New Yorker but of someone who lived in civilised countryside where things went at a slow pace. She liked him immediately.

He crossed the road and, seeming to make her out through the glass doors, he smiled openly. The doors parted automatically, he came in, stretched out his hand, and said, 'Marion Poyser, I presume?'

'How did you know?' she said ironically.

'It's that earring you're wearing,' he replied immediately, and she did not know why she laughed.

'Nice to be back,' he said.

'When were you last here?'

He looked marginally shamefaced. 'Well, last year, for the Jasper Johns show, as a matter of fact. Just an anonymous visit,' he added in explanation of why he had not made contact with her.

'You're impossible!' said Marion, surprised to find he made her feel so relaxed and familiar.

'Between you and me, it's Judith who's impossible, completely impossible. They're sharks, those gallery owners, Miss Poyser. Never fall in love with one. They improve your credit rating but ruin your integrity!'

When Temple appeared, he and Stonor made polite introductory talk for a few minutes, before Stonor grew bored, smiled, and said, 'I expect you have a lot to do, Mr Temple, but I appreciate you giving me this opportunity for a private view. It's not often an artist gets a chance to see his work all in one place . . .' His voice tailed off and he sounded a little less relaxed than before.

As Temple left them, Stonor turned to Marion.

'I'm terrified,' he declared. 'Have you any idea . . .?' She nodded, and seeing that she clearly understood, he said no more. He was about to come face to face with his life's work.

'Let's get it over with,' he said, and she led him towards the first gallery of the five in which his works were on show. He walked rapidly, swinging the object in the bag as he went.

'Shall I take it?' she ventured. 'I mean, I assume that's the piece you were going to bring . . .'

'Yes it is, but I'll hang on to it for a bit, if you don't mind.'

She accompanied him to the gallery entrance to clear him with security. He went inside and she followed him for a few steps. He stopped for a moment, looking towards the only one of the Eagle Series that was out of sequence. But it was too big to put anywhere else, and this gallery was open to two floors, with a balcony on one side of the mezzanine floor so you could look down into it.

It was the darkest, the biggest, the most looming piece of all, and its reputation was such that after its installation some of the office staff had not been prepared to walk into its dark depths alone. It was also the only one not explicitly 'eagle' in imagery.

It was *The Raven of Storr*. Exhibit 123 in the catalogue, 1983. Five massive vertical walls that each bent and curved or overhung this way and that, and that interlocked to form a maze in the centre of the gallery. It was smooth and shining black on the outside, but, inside, the walls were intricately carved and moulded into the beaks and talons and suggestions of wings of hundreds of thousands of ravens, whose outlines formed silhouettes above, and whose shadows interlocked darkly across the floor below. The walls towered eleven feet high, but Stonor's extraordinary handling of their slants gave them an awesome power to suggest, as one looked up to the 'sky' above, that they rose for hundreds of feet.

The work was intended for outdoors, and it said a great deal for Stonor's thorough approach that he had, with the original commission, prepared detailed lighting instructions in case one of the three casts should be shown – 'against my better judgement' – in artificial light. The lights simulated the changing light of an arctic sky at the end of summer.

Stonor stood for a moment outside an entrance to *The Raven of Storr* room and then, suddenly, was lost inside it. And Marion Poyser turned away, back into the foyer, feeling restless and uneasy.

An hour later, the stillness in the gallery was broken abruptly by the urgent buzzing of a security alarm.

A security guard appeared from the offices, smiling. 'It's all right. He's only trying to steal one of his own works,' he said ironically. She followed him back into the special security room and he pointed to a camera. It showed Stonor, in colour, standing before a drawing in Room 2 of the exhibition. He was looking around for the source of the alarm sound.

'Have you been watching all the time?' asked Marion acidly.

'That's our job.'

'Turn it off,' she said sharply.

'The alarm?'

'That and the cameras.'

The security man started to protest, but a look from Marion Poyser stopped him in mid-flow.

'I'll tell him to stop touching his own work,' she said, a little sarcastically, rather glad to have a reason to go into the room where Stonor was.

She went through the galleries to find him, feeling as if she was trespassing. He was still in the same room, and obviously waiting for someone to tell him things were all right.

'I'm sorry, I . . .' he said, shrugging his shoulders.

He turned to the drawing and said: 'I haven't seen that for twenty-five years. It was the first one, you know . . .'

She didn't. It was one of the series of raven/eagle drawings he had done when he lived in New York in the early seventies, and like several others was a discard, judging by the creases and crumple marks on it. It was one of the thirty or so that Judith Shure herself had loaned. There was a slight tear at the top, as if he had started to destroy it and then had second thoughts, and from the evidence she had dated it March 1974. It showed a raven flying, but cut across by the great sweep of an eagle's wing.

'The first . . .?' she began, hoping he would go on.

He nodded silently, his hand still reaching out towards the sketch while his head turned and his eyes wandered around the sculptures spread through the centre of the gallery. His attention seemed to have travelled on.

Then, ignoring her, he walked the few yards to *Haform* and put out his right hand to touch it, and then his left. She stood uncertainly, reluctant to leave but deciding she must to give him privacy. Then he said softly, his eyes slowly running ahead of his hands over the sculpture: 'Not the first in the sense of me never having made such images before, but the first time I began to make them with the same power as I felt them, the first time that making them began to release them from me.'

Then, dropping his hands to his sides, he turned abruptly towards her, as if to focus his full attention on the ideas her question seemed to have provoked.

'There are as many theories about making art as there are artists, and like most artists I leave them to the critics and art historians. When you're starting, there's a natural tendency to want to talk about your work, especially the work you're about to do, partly out of the sheer excitement and interest you feel for it, but also because you need the support a sympathetic listener will give—especially one who is also an artist. But I noticed as a student that when I talked about my work – which often grew into great works of original genius in conversation – essential energy actually to make them would evaporate. I would try, but my mind had drifted on to a new idea and my hands were bored with the old one. It was only when I tried to articulate the idea through the process of making it that I really began to work effectively. I did the sketch that activated your security alarms when I renewed my friendship with Judith Shure in New York in the early seventies. Something she said – quite unconsciously – pushed me to try again at the eagle theme I had been carrying with me all my life. I was thirty then, and it was at a time when I had virtually given up any notion of being an 'artist' with a capital 'A'. I was working in an advertising agency. It would be too simplistic to say I was suffering, because the feelings I had were not really negative. I had the sense, as my eagles had, that I was at the edge of a dark sea, without the strength or courage to fly over it. Yet if I didn't, I would stay where I was and be isolated and – I don't think I'm being too dramatic about it – become extinct.'

He fell silent, staring at her, and Marion Poyser was acutely conscious that this moment was the only one she was ever likely to have to get him to talk.

She was tempted to reach out and touch *Haform* as he had done, hoping that in a fellow feeling of touching and sympathy he might continue, but it didn't feel right.

Then suddenly she stopped trying, and in stopping she found the tiny key she needed. 'The dark sea'—it was a phrase Judith had used of that period in Stonor's life, but she understood now that, in the myths of the eagles he had made, it reflected reality.

'So in the first eagle piece you made . . .'

'For the British Nature Conservancy Council. Rather tame I'm afraid.'

'1976.'

'You know more facts than I do probably.'

'That's the problem, I *don't* and I want to,' she said with a smile.

He smiled warmly at her. 'I'm sorry. I haven't made it very easy for you at all, Miss Poyser. I mean, this' – and he waved a hand at the catalogue she had given him – 'is a great honour for me. I'm deeply grateful. Now, you were saying . . .' and she saw that he didn't mind her being there, and would answer her questions, and wanted to tell her whatever he could.

So she continued: 'That first one, *Eagle*, gave me the impression of a creature at the edge of something it feared—the dark sea, perhaps?'

' "It" was a she. Her name was Cuillin*, and I would have called the piece that but the committee that commissioned it would have made no sense of the name.'

He looked around the gallery, and then pointing and saying 'Over there', he led her to *Eagle*, the most representational piece he had ever made, technically quite superb but without the grace and power of most of the other pieces.

'I'm glad you get a sense of her fear from this piece, because that is exactly what she felt, or I felt: me and the eagles were always the same. In retrospect it's right that she was rather still and formal, unyielding, ignorant—brittle if you like. It's what I was like then. After all, it's like most young people are for a while, though at the time they would say they were just the opposite and it's the rest of us . . .' He laughed and so did she. It was how *she* was sometimes, even now.

'What do you know about Cuillin? Is she mentioned in your account of the making of the pieces?' he asked.

'Not much. A few of the people I spoke with remember you telling them things about her. She was the last one on Skye . . .'

'She was the one my father saw, and it was my father who gave her her name. Cuillin is the name of the mountain range on Skye which he used to walk as a boy, and where he saw the last sea eagle pair in the British Isles flying and nesting.'

He sounded suddenly rather tired, and sat down on a bench on one side of the gallery where he had put the bag he had been carrying. She waited for a moment and then went and joined him.

'It started as a simple story he told me about the first sea eagle, Haforn, who was born out of the volcanic upheavals that were to form Iceland. Of course, children are infinitely more perceptive than most adults give them credit for, and though they may not be able to articulate what's going on around them, they know perfectly well when an adult's saying something that matters. So I understood, without being able to say so, or even *think* so, that the story about Haforn mattered in some deep way to my father. I also enjoyed it. I suppose I was five or six then.

'Well, he started making up these eagle stories more and more, moving away from a god eagle to one I could more easily identify with—Cuillin, the last one. He had taken me to London's Natural History Museum, I remember, and I was greatly affected by the dinosaurs and being told that they became extinct. It seemed

* pronounced *Coo-lin*

27

impossible that something so big . . . it seemed like a doom of some kind. If *they*, which towered skeletally above me into the heights of the Museum's vaulted ceilings, were doomed, what about me? I really was frightened. I think my father unconsciously understood my fear and so made a story that would not only comfort me but also projected his own experience into something he, too, could face.

'Cuillin was young and ignorant, afraid and gawky—she couldn't fly very well. She . . .' Jim Stonor laughed again, his eyes softening with the memory of it. 'And there was the Raven who lived in Storr, an extraordinary series of cliffs and pinnacles on Skye, and about whom there was an incredible secret.'

He leaned forward conspiratorially and said in a low voice: 'Do you know what it was?'

'No,' she whispered, joining in his game.

'Well, at first I thought the Raven was one bird, old and wise and so on. But in fact it was a group of birds that lived in the dark Storr and communally carried all knowledge. When one died, another came forward from outside to join them. The Raven was eternal and carried forward a distillation of all gossip and news into legend and saga. At first, to me, my father was the Raven, but later I came to understand that it was all much more profound than that, and that one day I would be part of the Raven's knowledge.' It was no longer a game for Stonor, nor research for Marion Poyser. It was real and rather awesome.

'Cuillin was banished from Skye by her mother, after her father had been shot and a sibling male strangled. Events which really took place, incidentally. The mother drove her away with another sibling from an earlier brood, whose name, as I recall, was Torrin. Torrin, being stronger and more experienced, and also knowing more of the legends, was ordered to fly north over the dark sea to find "the land of ice and fire" which sea eagles in Skye had lost all touch with. There he might find other sea eagles. While Cuillin was sent over the dark sea to the east, towards Norway, where she, too, might find another population of sea eagles.

'In the story, Cuillin lost her courage and ended up for a long time in the Shetland Islands, where she found a mate whose name was Waulk. From him she learned a kind of wisdom and he taught her to fly and made her understand that for an eagle the greatest thing is true flight, which is flight that pays heed to the natural harmony between land and sea and sky. Of course, these elements are always changing, so, to remain true, such flight has to take account of the changes. Failure to fly true ultimately leads to extinction, but as it's so hard, it only needs one or two eagles in a generation to achieve it for the rest to survive. I remember I used to leap off my bed flapping my arms trying to fly true! Only later did I understand that the notion also had a far deeper meaning than its literal one, a meaning that became fundamental to my work as an artist.

'After Waulk was shot, Cuillin stayed on Shetland for a long time, for years, in fact, trying to summon up the courage to fly the dark sea as her mother had ordered. In my father's stories it was only "the coming of the grey ships to Shetland", in other words, the First World War, that provoked her to make a move. Still uncertain, she finally flew back to Skye in 1917 to visit her nesting homesite on the Cuillins near Lock Coruisk, and, I suspect, to visit Storr and the Raven. It was the imagery he evoked then that was really the precursor of *The Raven of Storr* . . .'

★　★　★　★　★

Flight-tired and worn, Cuillin flew wearily across the Minch, the narrow stretch of grey sea that separates the mainland of north-west Scotland from the island of Skye. Behind her the steep hills and mountains of the Scottish coast fell into a dull afternoon's grey, while ahead, to her right, the points and jumbles of the rocks of Storr began to become distinct at last.

Below, the oily surface of the water turned into swelling surf against rock, and the rock lost itself under drab heather by the shore as Cuillin reached land once more and wheeled north for the final stretch of the journey.

Tiring suddenly, she plunged down and settled briefly on top of a leaning fence-post whose weight was no longer taken by the peat into which it had been driven long ago, but by the rusting barbed wire it was meant to support. It swayed slightly as she flapped and untidily ruffled her wings, and the rhythmic motion of the sway made her whisper: 'We are the Raven of Storr and in us are all things told.'

She peered towards Storr, and the fear that had so long prevented her from starting this terrible journey returned again. On the road to her left, two hooded crows pecked at some carrion they had found. A wind hissed in the heather, swirled up the post, ruffled a feather below her right wing, and then lost itself northwards along the barbed wire of the fence.

With a heavy push she followed it, briefly sinking down towards the heather before her wings gained the air again. Then she was flying steadily, rising to no more than a hundred feet above the ground as she quickly made passage to Storr before her nerves caught up with her courage.

The Raven of Storr. In whom all things are told. Most feared, most respected, most awesomely loved and most mysterious of all the Corvidae: the carrion crow, the hooded crow, the magpie, jay and chough; and the rook, and the raven. Wherever they flapped or stole, or darted their beaks, wherever they peered with their black eyes, wherever they fed off death or whispered their news and passed on their gossip, the Raven was somewhere close behind them, or at their side; or listening above.

Cuillin knew it was to the Raven of Storr on far-off Skye, across the mountains and beyond the seas, that all things came and all things were told. For crow told crow who told rook who whispered to chough who told raven; and raven passed on the distillation of stories and news about all the birds until what remained was what the Raven needed to know; and then the Raven was told.

Why was she coming back to Storr, which she had only ever seen briefly in the distant years before, with her mother on her passage off the island? What was the Raven to eagles?

Suddenly the dark and treacherous cliffs of Storr rose before her, dark as parts of her own wings, but without the redeeming sheen. No greys in the grim sky were reflected in the Storr's jagged rises; no softer slopes of rock or lighter strata cheered its bleak surfaces.

She faltered to a momentary hover and, unwilling to go straight in among the cliffs, dropped to a stance on scree. She looked this way and that at the steep confusions of rock ahead. They rose irregularly but massively into a murky line of blackness against the sky, and she looked vainly for some sense of a centre or shape to their formations which would guide her to where the Raven might be.

The cliffs were made of black basaltic lava whose rough and unpredictable surface was lightened only by the white crystals and encrustations of feldspar, its shine only bright where recent rockfall had exposed a fresh surface. The cliffs once formed a sheer majestic face, but thousands of years of landslip and erosion had broken them up into buttresses and isolated rocks, deep fissures and jutting promontories, so that it was hard to discern even where they started, or quite where they reached a summit. But in front of what seemed the main bulk of cliff there stood a series of great tapering, isolated pinnacles, narrow and sharp from a distance, but rough as a shower of hail close to. At the bases of these pinnacles and cliffs were great falls and slides of hundreds of feet of mucky scree.

As Cuillin took in the scene, she heard the occasional hiss and clatter of rockfall, and once a fragment of basalt shot down from the height above and smashed into the scree slope below, echoing softly among the damp cliffs.

The whole place had the faint smell of dead embers, and reminded her of a patch of forest destroyed by fire over which she had once flown, except that here there was a sense of great age mixed with the black decay.

There was a croak, and the scutter of claws on rock somewhere ahead among the cliffs, and for the briefest of moments she saw a massive and aged raven fly out of shadow, before she lost sight of it behind one of the basalt pinnacles. And then, just as she was beginning to think *that* must be the Raven, she heard a grumbling croak come from somewhere else, and then the sound of another raven from a third place. Silence. She waited. Another raven moved, on another high turret. The brightness of an eye in shadow.

'Come nearer!'

The voice was authoritative, and came from a fourth direction, or a fifth, and she peered uneasily forward, loosing her wings and shifting her weight from one foot to the other in nervous uncertainty.

'Nothing to be afraid of here,' said a different voice.

She had no idea where to go or where to perch, so she flew boldly towards the turret where she had seen the first raven disappear, only winging aside from it when she was feet away and turning towards another one, before which she again stalled and swung around towards a third rock pinnacle. There was darkness, and the confusing cliffs of rock all around, and the comforting sky seemed a long, far way above her.

'Well?' cried out another voice.

It felt wrong to perch up high among the rocks, though she would have felt safer doing so, but respect demanded that she drop down to the scree between the pinnacles and find a stance there. Now that she was finally inside the Storr, with the Raven somewhere very near, she did not feel afraid. But she did not altogether know why she was there.

'I'm not sure why I came . . .' she began feebly.

'Just tell us what you fear,' said a voice.

'. . . and why,' said another.

'. . . and when.'

'Tell us it as it is . . .'

'. . . and might prove to be.'

Their voices were those of mature birds, and though she looked hard at the shadowed rock faces and overhangs all around, and caught sight of a beak in darkness here, two shining claws there, and the droop of an old wing somewhere else, she never quite seemed to see a whole raven, or feel that any one of these was *the* Raven.

But as their voices swung around her, she realised suddenly that *they* were the Raven. For the Raven of Storr was not one bird but many, and as she knew it, she also understood why: for how could one raven remember all sagas and tales? How could one raven be the Raven-that-never-died? But several, even many, coming together in this dark place, listening wisely to what others saw and came to tell, could distil the truth and hand it on to one another, old to young, on and on until the stories became tales and time distilled the tales to sagas.

So, understanding that what she was about to tell was part of something that stretched far back and would reach far, far forward, she settled herself down, tidied her wings, and quietly began to tell her story: of how she was the last one, of how she had settled in Shetland, and her mate had been killed as once her father and sibling were, of how she was alone now and lost and did not know what to do or where to go. She told the Raven all she knew of her kind, of what sagas her mother had told her, and of the nature of true flight as Waulk had tried to explain it.

The afternoon moved on towards night as she spoke, until, when she had finished, she noticed that the sky beyond the pinnacle above was cleared of the heavy cloud cover, and held a gentle evening light. In the silence that followed the end of her telling, there was a croak or two from the Raven, and a rustling of wings. And then one asked her about her journey to Storr, and another about Shetland, questions which seemed unimportant to her. But when she had answered them, one of the voices said 'Welcome' and another voice echoed it: 'Welcome, welcome, welcome, welcome . . .', their voices lightly running into each other, and circling as one voice among the rocks on Storr.

Then one of them said: 'Long have we waited in the shadows of Storr. Long have the sea eagles fought with their weakness and loss to find their courage to survive and renew. Long have we feared this end to your saga. Long have . . .'

Then Cuillin mantled her great wings and pulled them into a posture of pride and anger, and cried out into the shadows: 'It is not over, it is not finished, for I am alive still and I can fly. I came here for help, for advice, because I thought . . .'

'Because you thought we could give you courage,' interrupted the Raven, 'and could lead you towards where you must go. But we cannot, Cuillin, nor ever will, for we watch and report, distil and abstract, without fear or favour of the things we see. We cannot advise you.'

'But . . .' whispered Cuillin, afraid and feeling low again.

'But we know of the sea eagle and of the Doom it has always

32

faced, and we remember feats of courage and flights of faith, and it is from those inherited memories, told in your sagas, that you must find your advice and guidance. When any creature is cast low, and fears it is lost, it had best ask itself what it fears most of all, and then turn to face it.'

There was a deep silence in the Storr until, in a softer voice, the Raven asked: 'And what do *you* fear, Cuillin?'

'The dark sea,' she whispered, 'which my mother told me to fly. I fear its size and unknown dangers.'

'Are you sure?' asked the Raven. 'Are you sure that it's your greatest fear?'

'No,' she whispered at last. 'No . . . I fear myself, for I have not the strength in my wings to make such a flight. I cannot judge the sea and land and sky as Waulk did, or the great eagles of legend. I cannot fly true.'

'True flight, Cuillin, may finally lie in the knowledge that your wings *are* weak and that you do *not* have the courage or the skill. Have you faith and trust?' asked the Raven.

'In what?' she asked.

'Do you not know?' whispered the Raven from a thousand shadows.

Cuillin looked down at the dark rocks of her stance and, not daring to look up towards the sky, she nodded and said, so quietly that it seemed the barest whisper, 'Haforn, the Great One.'

The Raven was silent.

'Will she protect me?' asked Cuillin.

But the Raven stayed silent.

Suddenly the Storr seemed empty, and the shadows vacant, and she knew she was alone and that none was there with her. She was alone with herself.

So she groomed her feathers for a few minutes, stretched her wings, sighed, and flew up towards the evening sky, leaving the Storr and its pinnacles and mysteries far below her as she circled around, thinking matter-of-factly: Well, there's really nothing for it but to try to make the flight over the dark sea. Perhaps I'll find other sea eagles beyond it, if Haforn guides me there, and I can tell them about Skye where once sea eagles lived.

Then she flew south to Loch Coruisk to take a final look at the mountain of Gars Bheinn on whose eastern side, where it rose above the sea loch of Scavaig, was the most ancient nesting site of Skye—where she herself had been born, and from where she had first been taught to fly. There she tarried a day or two, no longer doubting what she must do, but enjoying, for the last time, the place which was her ancestral home, surrounded by the great Black Cuillin mountains and the sea.

Until one day, quietly, as the tide of a calm sea turns unseen, she left Loch Coruisk and flew north again, to follow the coast of Scotland to the Shetland Islands, and from there to start the great flight she had feared so much.

* * * * *

Jim Stonor stood up and stretched.

'Even with jet-lag hypnosis I still feel tired after that transatlantic flight. Not so bad as it was in the old days though—could knock you out for a couple of days then.'

'Did your father tell you the eagle stories throughout your childhood?' asked Marion Poyser.

'No, no, it wasn't like that. He left home when I was four or five, or rather my mother drove him out. But I can remember him coming back once when she was away and I was ill, and he told me a story then. And another time up on the Dunes to the north of the town, where he often went walking, and where I went as well.

'But after that I began to make up the stories for myself, following on where he had left off. It happened rather haphazardly over two decades. The eagles would leave me for a while, for years sometimes, and then suddenly come back. There was a time at art college, for example, when I went with Vi Clarke, one of the students . . .'

'I met her,' said Marion.

'I know. She told me,' said Jim Stonor with a grin. 'Anyway, we went to the Natural History Museum and saw some eagles in a glass case—that provoked a bit more of the story. There was another time, after college, and I was working as an art teacher in Camden on a painting called *Portrait of Miss Campbell* . . .'

'It's in the show,' said Marion Poyser.

'Ah, yes. But it really all started to come to a head in my final few months in New York at an agency, when Judith Shure came over and we met again. That's when everything changed really, and the story escalated and somehow became entangled with intense and painful memories of my childhood of the kind that perhaps all of us have to go through. It was provoked partly by my near breakdown in New York, and also by a crisis with my father.'

He stopped, and then suddenly asked: 'Could I have a coffee? Is it possible to get one round here somewhere?'

'Of course,' she said, and went to get him one. When she came back he was standing by one of the famous portraits of Liam Hugh MacAskill. Though he appeared to have led a sad and undistinguished life, yet his eyes and face, and dejected way of standing at an angle to the wind and staring out across the rises and falls of a desolate sea, became known to thousands of people all over the world through his son's portraits of him.

Marion Poyser could see that even now, after so very long, Jim Stonor was still deeply affected by the images he had made of his father. He had loved him as deeply as any son can.

Stonor smiled wryly and took the coffee. 'I was going to show you this final sculpture I brought with me and which I've been so mysteriously hiding from you, but perhaps, after all, I had better tell you a little more about the real background first.

'My father's name was Liam and he was a MacAskill. But you know that, don't you?'

She nodded.

'Well,' he continued, 'I'll tell you something you probably don't know. The MacAskills were in the employ of the MacLeods on Skye, for whom they were the official watchers over the sea—or the dark sea, as they traditionally called it. They were watchers after enemies, watchers after doom, and what I instinctively knew when my father told me those stories was that his heart had never left his ancestral home. And nor, you see, had Cuillin's.'

CHAPTER TWO

'ARTIFACTS (**** don't miss it/*** worthwhile/** of passing interest/
*boring) At the Museum of Modern Art this month (ending 3 June), is
the much vaunted Stonor Retrospective which majors on his self-
indulgent Eagle Series of sculptures. Falling clumsily between abstract
and representational art and failing to get the best out of either, this
exhibition is likely to bore even the most ardent exhibition freak. It
has some interest for those interested in the development of an artist's
ideas, hyped up though these particular ones have been for so long
by the Art establishment. But it's going too far to include the avian
scribbles the nine-year-old Stonor drew for his Daddy on wallpaper
when so much art by socially committed American artists still fails to
get any official support or showing in New York or anywhere else in
America . . . A one-star rating.'

—Review in *Art Scene*, April 1998.

December 1953

A bitter easterly wind drove ever heavier waves against the
grey concrete piles of Deal pier, on the south-east coast of
Britain, and it carried the resulting spray in hissing flights across the
deserted lower deck. This had been closed just before noon, for the
tide was coming in and the sea so heavy that frightening runs of
white spray spurted up between the gaps in the planks that formed
its floor, as the storm-risen waves ran along underneath it.

The pier attendant had run the storm notices out across the two
sets of wooden steps down to the lower deck: 'CLOSED TO ALL
FISHING UNTIL FURTHER NOTICE' these read, swaying and creaking on
the rusting chains that secured them between the railings on either
side of the steps.

The upper deck, twelve feet above, which housed the club-house
bar and tourist café, finally had to be closed at 2.15 as the weather
worsened, and the few who were there went grumbling out into the
bitter wind again, pulling on woollen mitts with the finger ends
cut off so their wearers could bait the hooks and retie traces.

Other fishermen stood in familiar huddles, bait boxes full of lug
and ragworm open on the seats in the tiny shelters that were spaced
regularly along the pier, tackle boxes on the pier's concourse. Some
wore yellow oilskins, some dark duffle coats, while most kept their
heads warm with woolly hats and stumped the pier deck in black

wellington boots. As they talked monosyllabically about weather and cod, about a coming beach competition and the chance of stray pollock, they drank thick thermos-flask tea and watched, always watched, the tips of their straining rods for the sudden tug-tug that signalled a bite; while the sea rolled inshore beneath them, rollers sucking at the piles of the pier.

Some reeled in, some cast out, one knelt on the concourse untangling red seaweed from his tackle. Most of the time they just stood and watched and waited, keeping their backs to the wind and their faces to the darkening shore.

They peered across the sea to North Deal and watched the waves driving heavily up the shingle. Here and there, in the old houses that lay behind the promenade above the sea-wall, a light had come on. Then, every few minutes, another was switched on, so that in the twenty-minute interval between casting out, reeling in, rebaiting and casting again, the dead-looking seafront became alive with people's domestic lights, while Christmas tree decorations occasionally lit up an odd window. Sometimes the shape of someone standing at a window looking out at the grim sea showed against the lights; sometimes a curtain was drawn suddenly.

The waves that surged in towards the shore beneath them were getting bigger—though now almost lost in the dark, except where the pier lights caught them and, as the tide rose along the shore, the waves broke more heavily, for the shingle steepened near the high-tide mark beneath the sea-wall. Then they piled up within themselves before crashing down with a thump and confusion of wet, brown pebbles and seaweed, and sending out walls of foaming water that pushed the shingle up the beach, and then tore it back again. As the December afternoon darkened, the foam showed whiter and whiter against the dull shore.

Deal faces east, towards the Continent, and the part to the north of the pier is its oldest district, for it was here, in the seventeenth century, that fishermen and boatmen first established themselves on the pebbly shore to service the growing shipping trade of London, which used the Channel as its route out into the world, or for the final run home. In rough weather, sailing ships would shelter in the sanctuary of the Downs, the stretch of water six miles wide between the shore and the treacherous Goodwin Sands, in whose shifting darkness more treasure lies lost than is contained in the Bank of England itself.

As evening falls and a gale builds up, the sky behind the stretch of eighteenth-century houses facing the promenade turns dark, and the ancient silhouette of chimney and red-tiled roof, of dormer window and gables, of street gaps and pub-signs, is clear for only a brief moment before it is lost in the dark—and only the lighted windows remain.

Only one building stands on the promenade itself: the massive, square-built Royal Hotel, along whose creaking wide corridors and by whose back stairs, front stairs and side stairs visitors for two centuries have climbed wearily up to their rooms, out of the salty cold.

On evenings like that, indeed, on an evening like this particular one, when a fisherman waits on the pier for a bite and begins to think of supper, the warm lights of the Royal are welcome, and the sudden pull-to of bedroom curtains a prompting that it might be as well to give up and go home.

Also on the promenade there are three shelters, spaced out at intervals and giving older folks and young lovers a view out to sea and shelter from the wind. Two of them were built in the late 1940s, of cement and concrete painted dull yellow, and they have the same flat planes and curving lines as pre-war cinema architecture. They are built to an oval design, with slatted wooden seats in cubicles on all sides. The more popular of these two shelters is a hundred yards north of the Royal Hotel, and stands opposite one of Deal's oldest seafront pubs: the Bosun's Mate.

In the winter few people use it, except fishermen from the beach sheltering from a sudden squall of rain, or a couple of kids who want a quiet cuddle between the pub and getting home. In the summer, old folk use it all the time, and sit wrapped up in their woollies to watch the summer crowd walking the promenade or clambering down the concrete steps in the sea-wall a few feet away, to the beach.

In the winter especially the shelter seems to attract all the litter on the promenade, as the driving wind is caught, turned, and twisted into mini-hurricanes among the empty seats. These little swirls of wind seem to suck in any passing litter on the road or promenade, or from the beach—dried seaweed, empty cigarette packs, the red and white gobstopper that a boy let fall from his mouth and had the sense to leave alone, a Superman picture on the waxed wrapper from a piece of bubblegum, and greasy newspaper used to wrap fish and chips from Skillet's, down in Middle Street.

The litter is always there, along with a few storm-tossed pebbles from the beach, but its nature changes with the years. One year may be that of the green and orange pack of Woodbines; three decades later the Woodbines have been replaced by the black and gold of John Player Special, and the packet of ten by a packet of twenty.

That year, that December, it was Woodbines; and the cardboard of the pack was soggy with sea spray. There was a torn cigarette card among the litter, and the newspaper wrapping from Skillet's was a bit of the local *East Kent Mercury*, advertising next week's film as *Shane*, with Alan Ladd, Jean Arthur, Van Heflin, Jack Palance and Brandon de Wilde. Programmes starting at 1.10, 4.35 and 7.40. This crumple of paper skidded about the shelter, and then out on to the front, and then, along with a tangle of worn nylon fishing line, rounded the corner of the shelter and blew back under a seat again until it came to a grimy stop at a man's feet.

He sat huddled against one of the little walls of the shelter, facing across Beach Street to the Bosun's Mate. He was waiting for it to open, and could see that he had some time to go yet, for Jamie Chunter, the landlord, had not even turned on the light in the bar, let alone opened the door.

Spray from the pounding sea beneath the sea-wall behind him spattered against the glass of the shelter as a street-light finally went on and illumined the spot where he was sitting.

He looked sixty, his face gaunt and worn. His hair was thin and dishevelled, caught as it had been in wind and spray. It might once have been red, but it was now a sandy grey. He wore a cheap dark raincoat that was blue where the light caught it, but black elsewhere. His shoes were black and had rings of salt on the instep where they had dried out and not been cleaned. He kept his hands in the pockets of his coat and, though he huddled back, there was a curve to his neck as he stared intently forward. His eyes, rather sunken and lost beneath furrowed and worried brows, were fixed on the swinging, creaking sign that hung above the window of the Bosun's Mate.

His face was pale, with only the faintest touch of colour in his cheeks. His nose was slightly hooked, and beneath it his lips kept up a continual murmur as if his worried thoughts could not contain themselves inside him.

His gaze shifted slowly to the right of the pub and along Beach Street. There lay Compass Street. Its name was on a metal street-sign, white letters on black, and the narrow street sloped down from the seafront and out of sight.

As a gust of wind flurried at his hair and caught fiercely at the swinging pub-sign, he looked back towards it. It showed a poorly executed and long-faded painting of a jolly sailor's face, whose colour had all gone but for white teeth which grinned back and forth as the sign swung in the wind.

The man in the shelter suddenly grinned back, except that his eyes stayed lost and worried. The grin might have been pinned on by a child playing an identikit game with a cut-out face in which smiles and grimaces can be exchanged at will. But, thus temporarily smiling, his eyes lost their hesitancy and took on a look of feeble determination.

'I will,' he muttered. 'I *will* . . . And Mrs Frewin will give me a cup of tea. And Jamie Chunter will get his sign repainted next spring. Aye, and I'll take the boy up to London again one day to feed the pigeons, whatever she may say.'

He stood up and stepped from the shelter into the wind, which whipped his hair forward from behind and over his forehead, and replaced the temporary smile with a grimace against the weather, and everything else that troubled him. He wore no gloves and only one of the buttons on his raincoat was done up, but the cold didn't seem to worry him. What did was his shirt collar, which he tried to pull more tidy and straight as he crossed the street and was blown by the driving wind round the corner of the Bosun's Mate and down into Compass Street.

The same wind, indeed the very same gusts, caught at the grubby lace curtains of the boys' room on the second floor of Number 11. This was because the old sash window was so warped by decades of salt sea wind that it no longer closed properly, and though now jammed as best it could be with two wodges of paper from the *Daily Telegraph*, it still rattled in the wind and let the stronger gusts in. The house itself was taller than its neighbours, the boys' room overlooking the red-tiled roof of the Grimmonds' house opposite. For Number 11, so it was said, had been built by a sea captain in the eighteenth century, and its proportions were on a marginally more elegant and extravagant scale than those of the fishermen's cottages and pilots' houses, now all joined together for lack of any spare space, which the street comprised.

Perhaps because of this, the boys' room caught more wind than most other second-floor rooms down the street. However it was, there was a strong sense of an impending gale inside the room itself. Not only did the curtains stir with wind, but the door on to the landing was ill-fitting as well, and its simple cast-iron catch rattled softly in time with the curtains; while the very room itself occasionally shook and vibrated with the crash of a particularly large wave on the shingle of the nearby beach. Because there was a light on the landing, and a tiny rectangular window cut into the partition wall by the door, the room was dimly lit; but, anyway, a certain amount of light came through the window from a lamp down at the bottom of the street. The room formed an askew rectangle, for the house was built to fit the wedge-shaped site which the long-dead sea captain had purchased for it.

The door out on to the stairs was made of thin planks, and there was another leading into an adjacent room. Both had the same simple iron latches, painted black in gloss paint.

The floor was covered with cracking linoleum, and a homemade rug of cast-off rags across the space between the beds. Opposite the window was the mantelpiece of a tiny fireplace, now boarded up, and in front of it a small, white-painted chest of drawers, chipped from children's toys and from being opened and closed in a hurry.

The room was tidy of toys because Mrs Frewin, the home help, had cleared it up—but she had not touched the wooden battleship that lay immediately under the window, for she knew enough about small boys to realise that, to the child who had placed it there, the ship was still asteam and astir across the North Sea where it had been sent on wartime patrol.

Its funnels were two wooden cotton reels; its railings were a crude line of pin-nails normally used for picture framing, with thread wound between them; its guns were four two-inch nails and they were very carefully ranged towards one of the legs of an unused bed that stood against the wall to the left of the window, and around whose corner—in the last instalment—the entire German fleet was about to sail. And in the gloom of the evening, the fantasy was not so hard to realise, for the fretting and shifting of the lace curtains above the ship cast sombre changes of shadow that might have been the heavy swell of the North Sea in the dark days of the Second World War—the sea whose rushing, driving sound now came in from the seafront through the ill-fitting window.

The mattress on the unused bed was covered with a thin, worn counterpane which once might have looked quite elegant. A boy's clothes were piled on it: grey corduroy shorts, a grey flannel shirt, a pair of white pants, a pair of grey woollen socks, a white vest, and a dark blue pullover. School uniform, in fact.

In the second bed lay its owner, Jim MacAskill Stonor, ill, hair lank, blankets and sheets awry, mouth and lips dry, breathing shallow and short, face white veering to violet in the murky light. His right eye was quite closed but his left was just a little open, though he was asleep, and the white of his eyeball showed. He was lost in the beginnings of a nightmare – a repeated nightmare – whose sounds were the terribly distorted howl of wind and tremor of wood against window-sill, and whose vibrations were the amplified thumps of the crashing surf seventy yards away on the seafront. He was on the beach and running, or trying to, up a shingle bank whose heavy looseness pulled him back and stopped him getting away. His hands were struggling to grab the steepening bank and help him up. And what was behind him, and coming for him, was infinitely more terrible than the feel of the fronds of dead seaweed against a little boy's legs when he's learning to swim. His small fists were clenching, one of them caught in the folds of a sheet, and his legs were stirring, and his breathing was becoming heavier and more desperate.

There was a knock at the front door, far, far away, a thumping of the heavy knocker, and the tread of feet to answer it—from the distant ground floor below, where there were bright lights and a coal fire and Mrs Frewin to make soft bread fingers to dip in boiled egg yolks. But in the nightmare the sounds transmuted into a shaking and roaring beyond the rise of shingle whose summit he was so desperately trying to reach, and whose safety seemed suddenly to hold worse terrors. And he began, at first imperceptibly, to shake with fear, as he tried to drag himself out of sleep and into safety.

Down below, Mrs Frewin opened the door.

'Hello, Liam. I had a thought it might be you. Come in out of the cold and I'll make you a cup of tea.'

He stood on the doorstep staring at her.

'It's all right, dear,' she said softly. 'She's gone. Went up by train this morning. Won't be back till Sunday night, and Granny's still away as well, so I'm holding the fort. Come on in and have some tea.'

He went in, a guest in his ex-wife's house, and stood waiting for instructions. To take off his raincoat, to sit by the fire, to hold a cup of tea in his long fingers and watch the steam rise and disappear in the firelight, to stop fretting for a moment now.

'Jimmy's not very well,' said Mrs Frewin. 'All hot and feverish. He got out of bed after lunch and turned the electric fire off. Something going round at school, I expect. Poor mite.'

Then they heard him crying, calling, and after a very short silence, and before Mrs Frewin could move, they heard him come down the spiral stairs and along to the back sitting-room door from which he peered in at them—half-asleep, terribly afraid, and his whole body shaking.

Mrs Frewin held him for a little while, going on her knees to do so, and only the top of his tousled head showed over her shoulder. 'Come on, my love,' she said very gently, 'it's all right now. It's all right. See, your Dad's here. It's all right.' She led him back upstairs, for she found him too heavy to carry now, and his shaking voice, and her gentle one, grew softer as they went back to the top of the house.

Liam Hugh MacAskill, who hadn't stirred at all from his seat, stared at the door where they had been. 'Not very nice things, nightmares,' he said aloud. 'I've had a few in my time! Mmm.' But he was thinking about his son, and that calling sound he had made. 'I know what I'll give him,' he said to himself quite loudly. 'He's the right age now.' So he set off upstairs and said, 'Yes, yes, it is,' when he heard Jim ask Mrs Frewin, 'Is that Daddy coming upstairs?' The voice was afraid—not of his Daddy but that it might be someone from a nightmare. He wanted to know whose footsteps they were.

'Yes, yes, it's your Daddy,' said MacAskill, entering the room and ducking a little under the door frame. 'Don't be afraid of nightmares. We all have them, even me. I'm going to give you something, Jim. Do you know what it is?'

Mrs Frewin looked a little askance. Liam MacAskill often talked about giving his children something or other, but rarely did. The others knew—but Jim and Michael were still young enough to be disappointed. Perhaps it was as well *she* had sent Michael off to boarding school, now he was ten.

Jim nodded his head from the bed to which Mrs Frewin had returned him; the sheets now tidy and his hair brushed straight again. It was lovely having grown-ups in the room. He felt safe again. He wanted to keep them there.

'My binoculars! Solid brass. Army issue. Very good.'

Jim could barely understand what he meant, but clutched at any straw to keep him there. 'What are they for?' he asked feebly.

'Right, Mrs Frewin, you leave Jim to me. I'll talk to him for a bit.'

'Don't keep him awake too long,' she said, pleased that he had ventured this far into one of his children's lives again. 'Don't tell him any of your stories.'

When she had gone they stayed silent: Jim very limp in the bed; Liam MacAskill sitting awkwardly on it, facing the window. He could see that the light from the corridor was painful to Jim, so he pushed the door to and sat down on the bed again, Jim's hand feeling for his leg to make sure he was there.

'Daddy?'

'Yes?'

But that was all Jim wanted to know. The window rattled and the curtains stirred. MacAskill leaned over and picked up the wooden battleship he had made years before for Oliver. That was when he was on observation duty at Dover harbour during the war.

'What were you afraid of?' he asked.

'I don't know, Daddy,' said Jim, but then he remembered something of the nightmare.

His mouth opened and his forehead puckered up as he remembered it, and as he reached out a hand to feel for his father he fell into a half-sleep, still breathing heavily from the effort of going downstairs and up again. There were all kinds of half-shapes and colours in his mind, and a feverish disturbance through which the sound of his own crying came back . . . and he was standing on the wet shingle of a vast beach, his legs skinny and scratched inside black wellington boots, and his knees shaking with cold, or fear, as he tried to get out of the way of the white walls of rough sea-water coming up the beach towards him. So he stood still—and cried because his legs ached so much . . . and his hand seemed caught . . . he couldn't seem to untangle it, where it was, over there where he was going back in the room . . . then his hand was nice now, held by his Daddy's hand.

There are moments when sound and sight and touch and smell combine again to recall something long forgotten—a moment long past. For Liam Hugh MacAskill, a feeble man whom people shied away from because he almost smelt of his own lost roots, this was one. The wind that rattled at his son's bedroom window was the one that had rattled at an old church in Belgium which was once a field hospital at the end of the First World War; the pale face was his own, aged by fatigue and shock, and also those of soldiers he had never seen before, who were dying by his side or relaxing suddenly in the knowledge that their bodies' wounds had taken them from the Front; while the very faint smell of some medicine that Jim had taken earlier took him back through decades of loss to the touch of a hand that had once held his, unknown but there, pulling him out of his own shell-shock, and exploding nightmares of black faces under strange helmets which rose from dug-outs and rushed smoothly towards him, across the mud in which he floundered.

He had never sat with any of his children before, never really held their hands. *She* had made him feel he couldn't. Made him feel awkward.

'I expect you're too tired to want to know about the binoculars,' he whispered in a voice much warmer than his normal nervous, troubled one.

Jim said nothing.

The bedroom door rattled with the draught against its frame; the catch rose a little and then dropped again. The curtains stirred, and sounds of sea and wind clattered around the narrow street outside the window. The room was a little cold, but Jim's hand was feverishly hot.

MacAskill must have stirred—and Jim must have thought his

father was leaving. For, to keep his father from ever going, he said urgently, 'What can you use binoculars for?'

'Seeing things. They make things bigger. Things that are far off come nearer.'

'What things?' asked Jim.

'Well, anything you want to look at. Like boats. Or seagulls.'

'Daddy, do you know something? Seagulls eat fish. Mrs Frewin told me, and I've seen them.'

'I've seen something better than seagulls, laddie. I've seen an eagle through these binoculars. Not only sleark – that's golden eagles – but a sea eagle, too. Probably the last sea eagle ever to fly in the whole of Britain.'

Jim settled back comfortably, his breathing easier. His father was going to tell him a story, just like Mrs Frewin did, and *she* did sometimes.

It was a female. And years later he discovered that it was probably the one reported as being last seen in 1916. He had read about it in 1939, the year the Second World War started and he began service with the Observation Corps at Dover.

It was a female and it was tired, and there was something about the way it had finally flown up into the wind and above the black cliffs of Storr as it searched for something that later, after the war was over, MacAskill felt he, too, had lost.

His father had always begun his stories traditionally: '*Dhe naoimhe na firinn, Dhe chaoimhe na trocair . . .* Oh holy God of Truth, Oh loving God of Mercy . . . take the fear from my story and bring your peace at its ending . . .'

Holding on to his son's hand for support, he said the words very quietly, as if he was intruding on some ancient privacy in which he no longer had the right to share. Certainly, to an outsider, the sight and sound of this ageing and gaunt man, who in daylight looked little more than a tramp, talking Gaelic to an ill little boy in a room as far from Gaelic Scotland as it is possible to get in the British Isles, was at best bizarre—at worst sinister. MacAskill looked and sounded as if he was uttering an incantation over a child's corpse.

Before Jim could stir and question him about this foreign language, MacAskill quickly reverted to English and continued his story.

* * * * *

For days Cuillin had remained at a stance on the high cliffs at the easternmost part of the Shetland Islands, facing the dark sea. She had groomed, she had stared, she had hunted; now another dawn had come, and she knew there could be no further delay or excuse.

Occasionally the wind caught at her pale, brown feathers, bending them away from her body and making her look unkempt. Sometimes it buffeted her harshly and she moved head and body to keep balance, but mainly she stayed still and set, her eyes fixed on the distant horizon, as she tried to think herself into a flight which, if she erred, would be her last.

How vast and grey the sea looked, how treacherous its swells and dark places, how fearful the day! Hours changed to minutes, and then the moment itself came when the world at her back – which had been her home and her life – was now a void. And the void ahead had to be made into a world for her to fly into, and cast her shadow upon as best she could. An upward gust, a pull at her feathers, and she opened her wings wide to it and said aloud the simplest of all prayers: '*Gaoth an iar liom a comhnadh . . .* Wind from the west, protect me!' And with that, and without one single circle back to take a last look towards the seas and islands she had loved, Cuillin started out across the unknown sea, to find a race of her own kind who had been lost from time immemorial in the shadow of legend and tale.

She flew at 350 feet, and within an hour the coast-bound fulmar were behind her and she was alone over the sea. It stretched ahead, frighteningly vast, and she could only close her mind to what lay behind her, and commit herself to its care.

At about midday, when the murky sun had shifted beyond her right-wing side, the wind began to bluster and break up. It made her flight infinitely harder, for she constantly had to reply to its changes, and concentrate more on keeping her eastward bearing. Her course became more erratic as she took advantage of wind flows that were in her general direction until, when they faltered, she pulled herself back on course.

The last tip of land had long gone when the first bout of real tiredness hit her; then she found her altitude sinking down to less than 200 feet, and could hear the sound of the choppier waves below as the wind caught their tops and overspilled them into foam. A spar of driftwood. A dead cormorant . . . *too far out!* Its head flopped under the green water, its wings floated loosely at its sides.

A black shape ahead, jagged and moving. Not land but a ship, from whose funnel the wind blew smoke. Blacks and greys and murky whites and green, and a darkening sky as evening approached. She veered to the left of the ship for fear of danger, but how longingly she eyed its solid shape, for on it she might have rested . . . One last glance and then forward again with the steady, low beat of mindless, deadening flight.

The sky gloomed over, and suddenly with each laboured wing-beat, it seemed that yet more of the light was going. The foam on top of the bigger waves – white before – was now violet, and had lost its brightness. The horizon disappeared into one trackless run between sea and sky, and it was only behind her, to the west, that the sky remained white. Even that was turning grey. When she looked back she saw its grey reflected in certain angles of the waves, and she had the sense that she was fleeing day for night.

Which was true, for night lay ahead. The ship she had passed was now far, far behind to her left, and it suddenly showed a light, tiny and yellow. Then it was gone. She strained her eyes ahead to make out if land lay near, but there was nothing but darkness, and a terrible tired despair crept over her. The wind had weakened but it was now moist with spots of rain, and this added to her sense that she was lost forever over an endless sea—and soon the sea itself would take her, and none would know.

She was as tired as she had ever been, and sometimes her mind slipped into a half-sleep in which the waves in the blackness below rose up towards her, and the ones behind, over which she had flown, were coming back for her, high walls of green, grey, sea, curling at the top into foam to catch her and roll her, wings drowned under their weight as they came down upon her and she was lost among them. She was on the sea, or just inches above it, flying – or trying to – up the hill of a wave whose rolling looseness was attempting to pull her down and stop her flying away. Yet what was behind her, coming for her, was infinitely more terrible than this sea; for it was reaching out for her and had a great black beak and a hundred black eyes, and it was coming, it was coming . . . She was woken by a flash of lightning that lit the tops and sides of driving waves and showed her what she was flying straight towards.

It was the roaring and running foam of a great sea wave, and its sound might have been that of the thunder that followed the lightning, and her great wings seemed mere shadows against its towering, black face as it bore down upon her. She beat and floundered her wings desperately to rise above it, turning vertically up to escape, and then around, trying to find purchase in the confused air among the storm waves. As it crashed down upon her, the foam leaping forward out of darkness to take her, she rose back through the spray and dead air, and into the storming wind that she had entered in her tiredness, and one of whose down-draughts had so nearly sucked her to death. Now the wind picked

47

her up again and, holding her wings stiffly against it, she let it carry her out of the waves' reach—though the sea's spume still glistened with lightning among the feathers of her legs.

Cartwheeling, turning, soaring upward into an appalling night, on a wind that was at once her friend and foe, and into a sky that showed a racing moon now here, now there, behind swirling clouds. Then a flash of lightning again, and she was into the glorious freedom of a storm that took her as one of its squalls or clouds and drove her before it so that she surrendered to its power, up and down in the confusion of its powerful driving winds, blowing rain and thunderous light, and a moon that seemed to be lost the moment it was found. A vast wild sea below, and a towering sky above.

'My name is Cuillin,' she screamed into the storm, 'and I will fly!' Yet as she called out from the pride of generations, whose power was in her wings and whose courage was in the curl of her talons, she seemed to weaken again and sink powerlessly with the storm winds, down, down towards the sea, and the words she had cried out were hurled back at her as feeble pitiful cries: 'I am Cuillin, I am Cuillin . . .' and she bent her beak towards the sea, and let her wings go slack, for she knew it had been her last cry, the last of all the eagles from Skye.

As Cuillin plunged downward into darkness, the skies opened up with great streaks of lightning . . . until the whole sky was shattered in light and dark, and the towering wind-mad clouds and rain seemed to open and widen and shape themselves in a form that she never saw, but which a raven caught in the same storm never forgot. For in that moment of blackness, broken by lightning and vibrating with thunder, the clouds became wings that joined in a massive body and the dark falls between lightning-strikes turned into talons, and a great eagle, as powerful as sea and sky, who had once wrestled with life as Cuillin now did, stooped down for her and took her up gently from the very surface of the sea where she was lost, and carried her through the storm and on through the night.

Until at last the wind weakened and the lightning was gone, as ahead the sky began to brighten into dawn, and Cuillin saw far, far away a shadow and substance, a shadow that was land . . . And gathering her rain-drenched, storm-tossed wings together for that final effort, Cuillin broke clear of the storm and headed for safety.

Three seagulls veering away, welcome seaweed tossing in the sea below, spars of wood that had fallen from a ship—land was near. Her wings were heavy with rain and tiredness but she flew on proudly, for now it was possible some eagle might see her, and she must in no way look weak and beaten like those vagrants of whom she had been told.

She was from Skye, she was the last—but to them, now and on into the legends they made after she was gone, she was the first. And so she flew towards land, slowly and with strength, veering a little to the right when its shapes became more concrete, and she could see an opening to a great cliff-bound fjord. On one of its scree-filled sides she could see the tangle of wood and sticks that pair on pair of birds had used to build up a nest through the decades. An old nest site, an ancient race.

Behind her, almost at her tail, the storm still raged, seeming to drive her landwards. A broken sun was rising beyond the far end of the fjord, and as it did so, and its rays caught the skerries at the mouth of the fjord, she suddenly saw three eagles perched and still. As she drew nearer she saw they were juveniles and that they were afraid. One was crouched ready and mantling; another, a female by its size, was starting her head this way and that as if looking for help or support. While a third just stared.

She flew more strongly, ever more boldly with each wingbeat . . . for was she not Cuillin who had flown from Skye? And was she not there to demand their help? She flew as she intended always now to fly, though before the storm she had never flown that way before. She flew as only an eagle who has flown to the very void and back again can fly, with a power born of having known an ultimate fear and faced it, and gone safely beyond it; for she was Cuillin and *at last she had flown true.*

As she approached them out of the storm, her wings bedraggled but her flight more awesomely powerful than anything they had ever seen, the three juveniles stumbled and faltered at their perch on the skerry. Waves from the rough sea rose and reached out towards them but their eyes were fixed only on the looming approach of this strange sea eagle, who was paler than any they had ever seen, and seemed to have come out of the very heart of the storm. Instead of rising up and fleeing to the sides of the great fjord, they hesitated and stayed where they were, and she flew on over them and they heard the swish of her wings in the strong wind.

They watched as she moved further into their fjord, and watched as other eagles, the adults, began to rise up at sight of her and fly forward threateningly, gathering their force.

Cuillin saw them on all sides of this fjord whose cleft walls rose into the distance all around, black against the pale, sunlit sky. She saw one adult eagle after another rise up from perch or eyrie and circle round on the wind to come out towards her. Not two, not five, but ten . . . or fifteen . . . more eagles than she had ever seen.

And she heard their cries on the wind, though whether of fear or anger it was hard to tell, for their language was strange. But there was one word that sounded through, one startled surprised call, and it sounded to her like '*Fremmed . . . Fremmed*'.

They were a great dread of eagles, but not one flutter of fear touched her wings, for she drove hard towards their very centre, and ever higher to take the initiative of flight from them. She was sure of her power at last and proud of it, and *theirs* was the honour, not hers.

And theirs seemed the fear. For she came out of the wind and rain of the stormy North Sea, which had kept them stooped and waiting, bedraggled at their perches, and she was the great white female their legends spoke of, the Fremmed – the strange one – and there was strength and wildness in her wings just as the Doom of Weir predicted; just as the ravens had whispered. So they had gathered, so they had waited—and here she was. And they were afraid. For it was said that she was going to demand more of them than they ever had to give, and that those that were proud in their strength and vain in their glory would suffer; and those that were weak would flourish.

*   *   *   *   *

While far from the fjord, far, far away in distance and time the dark sea roared and shook, and the wind fretted and fumed at a window-sill, and ran under the loose frame to billow out a lace curtain as MacAskill's voice, already down to the barest whisper, finally died in the room and there was stillness, but for a boy's deep breathing.

'Jim?' whispered his father, leaning close to him. 'Jim?' But his boy was asleep, his last child was sleeping and he hardly dared move for fear of waking him: a pale face lost with a small hand in a crumple of sheets and blankets. MacAskill gently pulled the blanket over Jim's side, whence it had ridden clear, so he wouldn't get cold, and he stood up. He looked again and wished he could do something to stop the violence of the wind. But a father can never do that, and can only pray that a laddie like Jim will be all right.

Jim woke briefly at dawn and turned to look at the grey light at the window. The curtain was still now, and he could hear from the distance of the waves' roar on the shingle that the tide was out and the storm had died. His head felt clear though he was a little weak. He propped himself up on his elbow just to look at the door on to the landing and check that all was safe. It was. The light was on and his Daddy had left a slipper in the door to stop it shutting.

He remembered an eagle quite clearly, and a word called Fremmed. And how his Daddy had said she had flown somewhere to safety, and she was all right. But she wasn't. He knew she wasn't, though he could not say why. But his Daddy had told him a story and seen him asleep and that was all right, as good as cooking chestnuts at a coal fire with Mrs Frewin. He fell asleep again.

In the days that followed he slowly recovered from his 'flu, if that was what it was. He played down in the kitchen in his pyjamas and dressing-gown and pretended that the armchair by the fire was a great cliff, and the rug beyond it a great sea, and the folded paper in his hand was an eagle, bigger than the room itself.

At the weekend *she* went away again, and Mrs Frewin came to look after him. He asked if he could draw something and have a go with Michael's old painting set. He made a painting on the back of an old bit of wallpaper Mrs Frewin found in the cellar. Black for the cliff, grey for the sea, blue for the sky; white for the eagle. He sat quietly at it, giving up bothering with the tiny brush in Michael's set in favour of a much bigger one which Mrs Frewin found for him. He clenched it among his fingers and sat head bent, and lost.

'What is it?' asked Mrs Frewin when he had finished, and he took it to where she sat with a cup of tea by the fire, knitting a scarf for her niece's Christmas present.

'It's the eagle,' he said.

They looked at it for a while, and she knew better than to ask what eagle. It was the one his father had told him about to send him to sleep that night he was so feverish. Always one for tales which were too powerful was Liam MacAskill.

'What will you do with it?' she asked.

'Give it to Daddy,' he said indifferently. It no longer interested him. It was outside him. There were other things crowding in, so many. But Mrs Frewin was not sure about giving it to Liam. *She* might not approve. Come to think of it, she wouldn't. Mrs Frewin sighed: it was all such a waste of lives, those two, MacAskill and Mrs Stonor; Liam and Margaret. Silly some folks were.

On the other hand, Liam might like it, poor man. Though whether he would know what to do with a child's picture, she doubted.

'You'll have to write something to go with it,' she said, remembering his need to improve his writing. 'Or at least write your name on it.'

His letters were still weak, so he wrote simply along the bottom

51

of the picture, taking longer than it had to paint it: '*For Daddy, love from James MacAskill Stonor*'. He wrote his full name because that was the way they had to write it on exercise books at school. And, anyway, he had practised it so much that it was what he could write best. Even so, the '*Stonor*' got a bit bent because he ran out of space.

'Now run off to bed with you,' said Mrs Frewin, 'and I'll be up to say goodnight in a quarter of an hour, when you've washed your hands and face!'

'And don't forget to clean your teeth properly,' she called, following him to the parlour door.

She looked up the corridor after him with a smile, then turned back into the room. He was happier than he had been for days. Back to school for him, come Monday, she thought.

She found a buff envelope of the kind Margaret Stonor used for sending bills, and folded up the painting as best she could to make it fit, and then put it in her bag so she wouldn't forget to pop it in the door of the house where Liam had a room, over in West Street. Better not leave it lying around, else *she* would find it, and Mrs Frewin wasn't going to get involved in all that again! Of course he'd be pleased, poor man! Not much like that had ever come Liam's way.

Then she tidied away the paint set and cleaned the big brush, and finally wiped the table clean where Jim had spattered some of the colours of rocks and sea, eagles and sky, far beyond the edges of his painting.

CHAPTER THREE

'The sandhills to the north of Deal – we call them "the Dunes" – form one of the best natural golf-courses in England. But it's a strange, desolate sort of place really, and the Dunes seem to attract strange people—funny people. Old MacAskill was one of them. He used to lean his bike against the ramparts of old Sandown Castle, where the road ended, take off his bicycle-clips, and walk up on to the great shingle bank which runs north of the town, eventually to Sandwich Bay. Many times I've seen him there! Many times! He always just sort of leaned into the wind and stared out to sea. His son Jim Stonor started coming when he was nine or ten, but never with his father. Of course they didn't live with their Dad, the boys. Lot of stories about it, but I ignored them. Still, one day I did see them together. The old man had come first, and Jimmy came a bit later, saw his Dad up on the shingle, watched him for a while, and then went up to him. Don't know why I remembered it so well, but I got a hell of a shock when I went up to that exhibition of Jimmy's in London and there was a tall thin sculpture leaning over. Jamie Chunter who went with me said, "Load of rubbish this stuff is. You can't see what it is at all!" But I said different because though the sculpture didn't exactly have a head you could call a head, or hands you'd call hands, if it wasn't old MacAskill standing up there that day I saw them together, then my name's not Sandy! So I just said, "That's Liam MacAskill you bloody fool." '

—Sandy Watts, assistant greenkeeper of the Royal Cinque Ports Golf Club as quoted in *Three Modern Sculptors*, Anthony Cunliffe Gallery catalogue, 1983.

September 1957

HIS father turned towards him, though some time after he must have first heard the laboured crunch of feet up the shingle bank. MacAskill was grinning without smiling, his eyes filled with tears from the wind and his skin taut and strained. He was frightening. Seeing him like that made Jim Stonor wish he had followed his impulse to sneak away across the Dunes behind him and go over to Sandwich Bay, as he had planned, to see if the terns there were breeding yet. But somehow he couldn't. Not just like that.

MacAskill was dressed in his usual stained dark raincoat, the shot-silk lining of it loose at the hem and fraying, his greased hair untidy from the wind. He was grinning, and his lips mouthed something at Jim before he reached him.

'Rough day,' his father said.

Stonor felt awkward and muttered, 'Yes, it is,' and he hunched himself into the wind beside his father and looked out to sea, hands deep in the warmth of his green gabardine anorak as the wind drove the material of his beige-coloured trousers against his legs. He was twelve, nearly thirteen, and had recently been coming more often to the Dunes, where he didn't feel so awkward or at such a loose end as he did at home. He could lose himself along the shingle beach with the wind at his ears and no one to see him but the seagulls and terns. He relaxed there. So it felt uncomfortable meeting his father like this, the more so because some of the kids at school laughed about 'Old Man MacAskill', and Jim didn't know whether to join in or punch them; or hide from embarrassment.

He was now only a foot shorter than his father, and a lot stockier and tougher-looking. MacAskill seemed to grow thinner and more stooped with each passing week. From a distance, such as from where Sandy Watts stood watching them unseen over on one of the greens, the lad looked solid and firm, while his father seemed frail and impermanent, with his grey trousers flapping at his legs.

They exchanged pleasantries for a few minutes before Jim saw a dead gull on the ridge of wet shingle that was the day's high-tide mark. It was a herring-gull, and its belly was tarred and one wing bent and loose. The eyes were no longer fresh, and the pink mark on its lower bill, of which he did not yet know the significance, was already faded.

'Big birds,' said his father.

'Usually it's the black-heads and razorbills you see like this,' said Jim, more to himself than to his father. The herring-gulls were the kings of the air around here, and infinitely more impressive in flight than the blackheaded gulls or even the great black-backs. A dead herring-gull made him feel uneasy. He walked over to it and picked it up. He held it by the bad wing and ran his right hand over the head, feeling the curious soft hardness of it and cupping it for a moment in his palm. He ran his fingers through its grey-pink scaly feet, pressing their digits back and releasing them to watch the muscle spring them back, even in death. If he had been alone he would have put the bird back on the shingle, taken out his sketch-pad and tried to draw it. But that was a private thing.

'Cormorant?' said MacAskill, face screwed up against the wind as he stared about five hundred yards out to sea to where the black arrowed shape was flying swiftly north, just above the waves. Jim squinted out at it and nodded. 'Could be a shag,' said his father.

'Here, have a look.' And he removed the binoculars from around his neck and gave them to Jim. They were heavy and the focusing adjustment in the middle was a little loose.

Jim held them awkwardly, and in his rush to get the bird into view, pulled them out of focus. His father stretched out from behind and Jim could hear his breathing at his ear and smell the dry smell of him and his cigarettes. He didn't move but he didn't like it.

'Get the left eye in focus first by turning the lens, and then get the right into line with it using the central adjustment.'

His father ended up holding them, and Jim watched the cormorant disappear across the waves into the shadows of the cliffs of the Isle of Thanet—not an island at all but an eastward promontory that formed the northern arm of Sandwich Bay.

As MacAskill raised the binoculars to his face, Jim looked at the lines and wrinkles around his eyes and his bleak mouth with curiosity, and unobserved. When his father looked around to say something, Jim pretended to be looking out to sea.

'No good any more. Canna seem to see so well with them as I used to. Here, you have them!' It was said so quickly, and the binoculars were thrust so awkwardly at him, that had he not taken them and stepped back, he might have fallen over.

'Oh!' said Jim, unsure what to say. The binoculars felt good and heavy in his hands, and he had sometimes wished he had a pair now he visited the Dunes more. Reluctance to take anything from his father, and so owe him something, gave way to acquisitive delight.

'I've had my time with them,' said MacAskill quietly, fearing Jim's reluctance. 'Don't need them now.' And he turned back to look out to sea with his mouth muttering in the wind, '. . . had them for a long time, since before the First World War. But I dinna need them now . . .'

Jim thanked him rather formally and raised them dutifully to his eyes to look through them and show he liked them. But really he wanted to sit somewhere with them by himself and read the writing on their side and feel their weight and so make them his. That could wait.

'As a matter of fact, Jim, they're really yours. I once promised to give them to you when you were quite small, but you were too young and I doubt she would have liked it. You know.'

Jim nodded. He knew. But he couldn't remember them having been promised him.

'It was when I told you one of the eagle stories. I canna recall the last time we had one of those! Remember them?'

Jim nodded and his father looked pleased. 'Cuillin . . .' he whispered, that was it. That was the name he made. The last one. The last sea eagle. *Haliaeetus albicilla*.

Jim remembered. It was a secret only Mrs Frewin knew, and she had probably forgotten it by now. His mother never knew. Most of the stories were gone now, except for the storm and a great cliff and other eagles shouting something, calling something that set her apart. She had stayed in his mind, somewhere in its shadows, but coming out into light sometimes and each time more massive, and as the years had gone by she was invested with a sense of loss whose sources lay in the strands and dereliction of feeling that any growing child may sense in the adult world about him, but be quite unable to articulate.

'What happened to her?' he asked quietly, unwilling to look at his father and staring instead out to sea.

★   ★   ★   ★   ★

They called her Fremmed, which in their language meant 'the Strange One'. And at first they honoured her, giving her precedence, and fighting to take stance near her, and watching the strange lines of her flight in awe, for it was quite unlike anything they had ever seen.

But their respect did not last long. For she could not understand their language and paid no heed to the simplest advice or suggestion, and spoke in turn a strange and primitive-sounding language that had no rhyme or reason to it. Their respect withered even more when she began to stay clear of them and perch out at the seaward end of the great fjord which was at the heart of their territories. What was worse, she began to forage for carrion with the juveniles who had been driven out to the skerries. And some began to say that though she might be a fremmed, she was not *the* Fremmed, the one who played such a significant part in the Doom of Weir.

For her part, Cuillin was shocked, appalled, to find she could not make herself understood. It was not only their language, harsh and primitive as it was, that she had trouble with; it was their flight as well. It seemed to have no code or coherence, and was so quick and slovenly that had Waulk been there, with his special punctiliousness about the timing of turns and soars, he would have stooped upon them to get them to do things properly. Their flight was, quite simply, uncouth, and it soon gave her no pleasure at all to overfly them, or try to soar with them, for their slow responses and careless ways gave her no stimulus.

So after some weeks she chose to perch quite apart from them out at the seaward end of the bay, where the roaring of heavy seas

56

and the sight of a horizon helped, just a little, to ease the homesickness she felt. She had been alone so many years. Such *hopes* had driven her over the vast North Sea! Hopes of companionship, hopes of friends, hopes, finally, of a mate. But all she found was fear at her coming, for the only males left after the pair-formation and territory-taking of January and February were juveniles.

Once clear day she stood watching the three juveniles who seemed always to stick together out on the skerries at the great fjord's mouth. They had a lot to learn! There were two males and a female; and the female, who should have known better, still seemed to have trouble finding a true balance in the face of rising waves. How she started up in alarm, when any eagle could see *that* wave would not reach her. As for the males, one was so pathetic that she was surprised he had survived, while the other was a nondescript, judging from his boring flight-lines and soarings. None of the adults ever bothered to talk to them.

Curiosity, boredom . . . perhaps more truly the need for companionship drove her off her perch and in a long and finely-judged swing down towards them. Not one of them dared mantle at her, and while the female's thin and worried head started this way and that, the two males stopped and hunched down in gestures of submission.

'Why, they're truly afraid,' she said to herself in surprise. 'Of me!'

And so she flew slowly and unthreateningly over them, into a flight of friendship that Waulk had often flown, which took as its counterpoints the two heads of the fjord, and their skerry, and used as its theme the distant horizon from which she had come. The female watched from the start, but the two males at first stayed stooped—until one of them, the less pathetic of the two, bent his head sideways to look, and she saw with pleasure that he was watching. She turned the flight into one of real joy.

When she had finished – and surely not even the most timid juvenile would think that it was anything but a friendly flight – she settled back down near them and said softly, 'My name is Cuillin, and I am from Skye. Cuillin. My name is Cuillin . . .' But they only looked at her in alarm. It was the male, the one who had surreptitiously watched her, who eventually spoke. And though he seemed to be trying hard, she could not make it out . . . except the word 'Fremmed, Fremmed'.

'I'm not Fremmed,' she said suddenly, her despair at not being understood again turned to anger. 'I'm not Fremmed. I'm Cuillin'. She could not help but cry out the name harshly and a little angrily, for she was frustrated . . . and as she did so they grew afraid and backed away, so she flew away from them high over the fjord.

There, she saw an eider duck beneath her and stooped suddenly on it in one powerful, long-swung movement, which left spray hanging in the air as she rose, crushing her prey in her talons.

Yet the following day she was surprised to see the female juvenile flying over the water towards her—or sort of. It was an indirect flight which pretended not to be coming near her as it scouted along the rocky fjord edge and hesitated here and there. But come she did, until, to Cuillin's regret, she sheered off, having apparently lost her nerve.

It happened again a couple of days later, and Cuillin did her very best not to look intimidating—to encourage the female. But again she seemed to lose courage.

A bleak depression settled over Cuillin, for whichever way she turned she seemed unable to escape her loneliness. And the coming of early summer, with the first sparkling wild flowers up on the fjells above the fjords, and the running of elk and fox, and the flight of eider and gull all caught in a glistening sun and sending their calls at dawn and dusk across the wilderness, only increased her sense of being apart. For they were calls of mating and companionship, the cries of mothers for their young, and of young for their discovery of living. And none of them had anything to do with her.

So, cast down, huddled in shade, wings untidy, not knowing how to find a friend, she did not at first notice that one day the juvenile female was again trying to find the courage to fly over the fjord towards her. She flew slowly, with a nervous, jerky movement of wings which took her only obliquely towards Cuillin, while she cast continual and stolen glances to her left to where 'the Fremmed' had taken stance. And then, summoning up her courage in both wings, and finally committing herself to a course of action she had planned, dreamt of, and failed to execute for weeks, she threw caution aside finally and flew straight towards the space immediately in front of the Fremmed's perch.

It was there that Cuillin now again took notice of her, the strange female flying about over the cliff-face above her, and flying in a way that she had never seen one of these sea eagles fly before. It was not like one of their brief and slovenly flights which paid no regard to the rhythm of rock or sky or sea, but neither did it have much coherence. It was ragged and a little desperate, and certainly very self-conscious, and . . . Cuillin found it interested her and she was watching and beginning to want to call out, 'No . . . No . . . Fly more slowly and take your line from the clouds on the horizon out to sea, and don't turn yet . . . no . . .'

Then Cuillin saw with a gasp what she was trying to do, and her wings fell loose from the huddle they were in and pushed strongly back, and she raised her head and looked up full-square at the hesitant female.

'Why,' she gasped, 'she's trying to copy my flight of friendship! She's trying to talk to me . . .' And with a push out into the void before the cliff, Cuillin turned and flew upward and began to copy the youngster's flight and then improve it, two eagles trying to fly as one. At the sight of her, the female's flight suddenly grew more assured, and she looked down at Cuillin and beyond, down to the surface of the sea on which the sun cast the distant sliding shadows of two eagles, her shadow and the Fremmed's!

There came a moment when Cuillin crossed in a gyre to move above the juvenile, and as she did, she heard her make a hesitant call in the wind which at first Cuillin could not make out. 'Kooring . . . Koor . . . ing . . .?'

Oh! And Cuillin knew what she was trying to say! As she took the flight over and gyred above, leading the juvenile ever higher, she called out with joy 'Yes, yes . . . my name is Cuillin . . .' And the other called excitedly, 'Koolin . . . Coolin . . . CUILLIN!' At which Cuillin quite lost her line, and the cliff-face and horizon and sea beneath blurred as she flattened her wings and slid and skeltered down the breeze to touch her wingtip on the other's as they swung back high over the bay as one. For it was the first time in nearly a decade of loneliness that Cuillin had heard another eagle call her name.

The juvenile's name was Mizen, and it was from her, and from the two males she foraged with, Weever and Clew, that Cuillin was to learn about the language, the customs, and the country to which she had come.

Though she was the only female, Mizen was not really the leader of the three. She was timid by nature and looked more like a frightened squirrel than a female eagle, for her head always jerked around this way and that as if she feared that behind every rock or wave an enemy lurked. Her beak had a slight down-turn at the end, and the pattern of feathers over her eyes had a worried touch, giving her a sad air.

Yet this unpromising appearance hid a heart so warm, so caring, that her name remains one of the most beloved of all the sea eagles in the sagas that the ravens tell. And even in the dark recesses of Storr, the Raven's voice softens at the name and memory of Mizen.

Weever, the bigger of the two males, and the one who had surreptitiously watched Cuillin when she first did a friendship flight over the three of them, was sturdy and rather matter-of-fact. Although when Cuillin first met him he was still a little timid and unsure of himself, which was not surprising in a second-year juvenile, once he had gained confidence she saw that he had a firm way of carrying himself in any circumstances; and though his flight was a little unimaginative, at least it got him there efficiently. He was quick to grasp Cuillin's desire and need to learn their language, and understood better than Mizen that what was needed was repetition of basic nouns, verbs and simple structures so that she might understand the rudiments of what they were saying.

From the pattern of his feathers, the other male, and the smallest of the three, appeared much younger than Cuillin later discovered him to be. He was, in fact, a fourth-year juvenile, and his name was Clew; but from his stance and appearance he might have been a first-year, at best a second. He had the dappled paleness of a young bird, and it took some time for Cuillin to understand the others' attachment to him, for it happened that when she first got to know them, he was in one of his periodic moods of introspection and disinclined to talk or even look at them. Yet Cuillin soon understood that he had some deep need of their company, for he was always nearby; and if they moved he would soon follow, gliding down to settle close to them—not too close, but near enough to be a part of their group.

His silence might have been taken for the same kind of sadness as Mizen's, except that it was punctuated by seemingly irrelevant questions whose full import only dawned on the others some time after he had asked them. She began to see that his silence was not a vacant sadness but a busy mind, searching for something she could not easily understand.

Indeed, the first time he spoke to Cuillin directly was with a question, 'Do you know of Haforn the First One?' he had asked. But because the question was then too difficult for her – she had trouble understanding the words – Weever had had to step in and try to rephrase the question. When she had stumblingly tried to answer, Clew had shaken his head and said, 'Let it wait, I will ask you again.'

Which he had, some weeks later, when she was better able to reply. She told him what she knew: of how Haforn had been born from a struggle between the molten earth and the raging sea, and of how, through her, the race of sea eagles came to have white tails and mottled brown backs.

She learned that the great fjord she had come to was Romsdal, home of an ancient race of sea eagles.

Seaward of it lay a scatter of islands and islets which spread miles out to sea, and north and south along the coast. Most were occupied or controlled by pairs of sea eagles, and it was an area into which Cuillin and the others did not venture, for etiquette demanded that they did not disturb pairs who were raising broods; and common sense as well—because if they did venture into occupied territory, the adults swung swiftly along the surface of the sea and rose powerfully on some convenient air-current to menace intruders.

So she preferred to keep to the neutral waters of the skerries and shoreline north and sorth of Romsdal. The fjord itself narrowed steadily inland, and its walls grew higher and more forbidding. Cuillin herself never ventured into it for fear of upsetting eagles which held territory there or on the adjacent fjells, but Clew seemed to know a lot about it.

'It continues inland for about ten miles and then narrows so suddenly that it looks almost like a wall across the fjord. There's a narrow gap there with treacherous unflyable winds, and from beyond it there drive never-ending runs and clouds of spray from the great waterfall that flows there, which is called the Storrin.'

At the very mention of the name Weever looked awed and Mizen quite terrified.

'What is this Storrin?' asked Cuillin, curious.

'It is a holy place, a fearsome place, within whose unknown depths is the most ancient and revered nesting site in Romsdal. It is said that once the Weir nested there, centuries ago, and that from there was the Doom of Weir declared.'

'The Doom? The Weir?'

But Clew too was frightened now, and none of them would answer any other questions, however much she tried to persuade them.

Summer deepened, August came, and with it the clear, warm days of earlier weeks began to give way to more unsettled weather in which the occasional mist drifted in from the sea, and the odd summer thunderstorm flurried the inland fells and mountains. Cuillin and her friends saw more and more first-year juveniles journeying out of their home territories, as the adult pairs began to relax from the long season of rearing their young, and the more adventurous members of the broods began to roam free and find their wings.

Other birds, too, began to fly more freely, and the sky and sea were scattered with terns and guillemots, kittiwakes and ducks enjoying a month or so of relaxation before the year turned them back towards the concerns of autumn and the start of the long subarctic winter.

Cuillin herself began to explore more widely, and she sensed that the other adults, less burdened now by responsibility, and learning that she could talk their language, might stop ostracising her as they had done for so many months. How she wanted to talk to them, and find answers to some of the mysteries the three juveniles had faced her with! The 'Weir', for instance, the sinister 'Doom of Weir' which Clew had once mentioned in an unguarded moment; and this habit of calling her 'Fremmed'—how did it all hang together?

The September days shortened. As the mists became more frequent and the sun began to pale, autumn was coming at last, and now each day brought more and more migrants flying south: the leisurely heron and powerful swan, the busy mallard and tufted duck, and the swift runs of scaup and teal and geese. It was an unsettling time for Cuillin, for these migrations reminded her that her own roots lay far off, and gave her the urge to fly—not south, but west, back across the grey North Sea . . . And she took to perching for hours on end up on one of the headland entries into Romsdal, and looking out across the sea beyond the islands to the empty, dark horizon beyond which was the world she had left behind. But for what? Why had she ever come? The answer, she knew, lay in the sense of duty and pride that her parents and Waulk had instilled into her. So she returned again and again to memories of her parents and Waulk, as if seeking confirmation that what she had done was right, and that the restless loneliness she now felt was worth something. And she heard again, as if across a very great distance, her mother's voice when she drove her and her brother off Skye: '*You, Torrin, will fly directly north . . . beyond the outer limits of your strength, to where Haforn the Great One was born . . . as you know more of the legends and will remember them. You, Cuillin, will fly across the dark sea to teach them our language so that it will not be lost, and teach them to fly as we have taught you . . .*'

But why? And in the answer, she knew, would be the key to her present restlessness. For she knew in her heart that the past months had been but a quiet time to learn a new language and something of a new land, to prepare her . . . oh, she wished she knew for what!

As the evenings drew in she fell to seeing what legends and poetry of her language she still remembered, by recounting some of them to the other three. But when she lapsed into the language itself, Mizen soon grew bored, and sighed and flew off to pretend to be one of the great females Cuillin had inspired her imagination with. But often it was then that Clew would settle quietly nearby, though never too near, and listen to her strange words with half-closed eyes, as if in some strange way he could understand them . . .

> A Mhuir beannaich mo bhonntaigh
> > Beannaich fein na bheil ann;
> A Mhuir beannaich mo chuideachd
> > Beannaich fein mo chonntadh . . .
> Oh sea bless my best site
> > Bless thou all therein
> Oh sea bless my kindred
> > Bless thou my substance.

'What language is that?' It was a high voice, a male voice, and she reared round, a little more threateningly than she might normally have done, because, being lost in her own reverie and thinking the eagle perched nearby was Clew, she was taken by surprise.

Clew had silently gone, and in his place was an old and frail-looking eagle whose tail feathers were worn and split and whose talons were blunted by age and long summers. His wing feathers were raggedy, and he looked as if he had seen a long hard season taking care of a brood for a mate who had spent most of her time sitting pretty. However, he did not seem especially afraid of Cuillin's size or anger, showing the well-tried patience of a male who had seen it all before.

'Sorry. Didn't mean to disturb you, but I've been waiting a long time to have a chat with you. And, what with a brood to bring up and a mate who is, to say the least of it, demanding, it hasn't been easy. And anyway . . .' He rattled on as if afraid she would herself start talking and never let him get another word in. 'And anyway, there was a general consensus of opinion hereabouts that it was best to leave you well alone. You know—an unknown quantity. And also . . .'

He stopped. But before she could draw breath to reply – indeed, before she could even work out what possible reply there might be – he continued: 'The thing is, you're a bit of a mystery, aren't you? I mean, they've been saying for years that a fremmed would come, and would be very important to the future of all of us. So when you flew in out of a gale at sea expectations ran somewhat high. Unfortunately you did not live up to them. Oh no, certainly not. Cavorting about with three useless juveniles, sulking up here all by yourself . . .' At this Cuillin made a determined effort to interrupt, but he raised a talon and continued ever faster. 'And even venturing over other adults' territory when they had not yet got their broods off the nest. In fact, generally being thoroughly disobliging and threatening. It really will not do!' With which he stopped abruptly, looked at her with a twinkle in his wrinkled eye, and burst into a high, cackling kind of a laugh that was so infectious that Cuillin's sense of outrage gave way to laughter, too, as she realised that he did not really believe a word of what he had just been saying. In fact, he laughed so much, and his tottery legs wobbled about so, that, had he not flailed his decrepit wings about rather desperately for a moment or two, he might very easily have fallen off his perch and disappeared from sight.

'Idiots!' he said finally, in a rather different voice. 'I tried to tell them, but—well, if you'll forgive me saying so, *females*! So vain, so proud, so ready to jump to the wrong conclusions and do foolish things. So unwilling to *listen*!'

There was a long silence, during which he stared at her, and she at him.

'My name's Cuillin,' she said finally.

'Yes, I know,' he said. 'Clew told me.' Then he leaned forward and asked, 'What do you think of Clew?'

'He's very clever,' answered Cuillin, 'and I think one day he may be able to fly as an eagle should.'

'You're right. He's my son. But I'm afraid we're the only two who think he shows promise. However, time will tell; it usually does—though of course pointing *that* out to the females round this place . . . well, they'll never admit they're wrong anyway.'

Cuillin felt at peace suddenly, with the same sense of purposeful silence she had often enjoyed with Waulk.

'What's your name?' she asked eventually.

'Finse, as in "fish"—you don't pronounce the "e". Now, listen. I'm not going to waste time, because there isn't much of it left. I've no doubt that *she'll* be going on about me being away from the nest so long, but more important than that, if you are who I think you are, and things are as bad for us as I fear they may be, what with sleark sneaking up on all sides and more humans building houses along the fjords this year than ever before, which can only mean one thing for sea eagles, then . . .' and he paused for emphasis, 'there is not much time.'

'There are things you'll have to do which will be hard, and for which you may not get much support. The trouble is, for you to understand it all, you'd need to have lived here all your life, but – and this is the contradiction – it's the very fact that you *haven't*, and you *don't* know us, and are *not* weighed down by all the ideas and traditions and fears *we* have, that will make it possible for you to get on with your task. Now stay where you are and don't move, because there isn't time!'

With which he launched himself off into the dusk at an angle to the distant setting sun—an angle governed by the position of a great bank of cirrus to the right, and modified by the white foam around some skerries down in the darkening sea. In short, a line of difficulty and precision—from which, and without more ado, he performed a ritual flight of welcome that was so complex, so born of wisdom and love, that she itched to follow his lead and take to the air. But she heeded his instruction and stayed where she was, watching in admiration as her respect for him deepened with each soar and patterned turn.

When he landed back at her cliff site, he settled his old wings against his body graciously, and she stayed silent as a mark of respect until he spoke. 'Now I did that,' he began very seriously, 'because I want you to understand that there are some of us, though not many now, who know how to fly, which may help you to take what I'm about to say seriously. Most of us left who can fly are old and male, and so without much influence. And we were able to learn what we know in a time when the sleark was less prevalent on the coast, and our territories included both land and sea, where there was a range of sites and air-currents that made flying easier and less harried.

'But humans are coming, and in my lifetime I have seen more and more of them arrive—up the fjords by boat, across the land by roads. Once they start they never stop. Those of us whose forebears lived in the southern fjords and were killed or driven away can tell you that. They never stop. So the cunning sleark has taken our place on the southern coast, wherever he is able to, coming down from his traditional haunt on the mountains. Being quicker and more compromising, sleark can cope with humans better.' He paused, and then asked her: 'Has Clew mentioned the Doom of Weir?'

Cuillin nodded. She began to see that, whatever it was, the 'Doom' might make far more sense to her than she had suspected. For did she not also know about shooting and trapping, and about the extermination of eagles? And could she ever forget Waulk's long plummet of death down into the sea?

'He mentioned Weir,' she explained, 'but could not, or would not, explain it.'

'He was wise,' said Finse, 'for he could only have caused harm by trying to do so.'

'Is Weir this place where we are?' she asked.

Finse looked at her with surprise.

'Oh no,' he said, 'Weir is not a place. It is the title of an eagle, a sea eagle. He – and I say "he" only because the present Weir is a male – is an eagle of very great importance, perhaps the most important of us, though without us he is nothing.

'There is a great misunderstanding about what the Weir truly is, for each generation tries to invest the Weir with its own purpose and hopes, and most seek to make the Weir holy or powerful, and sometimes both. And a true eagle knows that these are qualities carried only in Haforn, the Great One, and only caught sometimes by an individual in a moment of true flight — for they are not permanent qualities. No, Cuillin, the Weir is best thought of as a centre from which, at the right time, the inspiration for right action flows. Decades may pass without word or sight of the Weir, for the Weir's home is far, far away to the north, where the winter is black and without sun and where in the summer the sun never sets. There – where most creatures cannot live all the year, and migrate away – is a place warmed by sea currents and protected from harsh wind, where the Weir lives. Its name is Tanahorn. And it is to Tanahorn that you must go.' He looked to the north, from where so many flocks of birds were now fleeing, and Cuillin looked there too, and shuddered.

'But what is the Doom of Weir?' asked Cuillin.

'It is a warning, a mystery, a rhythm of words and flight which was given us by one of the greatest of the Weirs, whose name was Fjara. In all her long years after flying north, she was seen again only once, and she flew back to speak her warning near this spot, up in the narrows at the head of Romsdal—by Storrin the waterfall, of which you may have heard. It is said that she quelled the waterfall with the power of her wings and, in the silence that followed, the sound of her warning was heard echoing about the fjord, and so passed on, and her flight was remembered by all who saw it. It is said that she learnt the words of the Doom from the Great One herself, having flown north-east to Haforn's island.

'How is the Weir chosen?' asked Cuillin, who was growing increasingly curious and awed at the same time.

'The Weir choose themselves,' he said quickly, and in a kind of closed voice that suggested it was best not to pursue that question further.

'The Doom is a warning which members of each generation should know and reconsider. But times have changed, and now the Doom of Weir is beginning to be forgotten, and many scoff at it as part of an old saga so obscure and difficult to interpret that really it has no worth. So those of us who do remember pass it on only with discretion, choosing to tell only those of our children who may have the integrity and courage to understand its seriousness.'

'Did you tell it to Clew?' asked Cuillin quietly.

'It is not exactly something you tell like a story. It is something you show—though the "telling" part of the Doom has to be learnt. But, yes, Clew was "told" it.'

'Well, what is it? What does it say?' asked Cuillin, who was now becoming frustrated with all this mystery.

'It warns of a terrible danger to our race—a danger we may not know of until too late. It gives strange warnings: that our enemies may be our friends, and that to survive them and profit from them we will have to be even more cunning than sleark and wiser than ravens. It warns that most of us will not believe it or trust it, and that only tragedy and suffering will change our minds . . . and even then maybe not for long enough. And it says that the start of the Doom will be marked by the coming of a fremmed, a stranger, who will speak a language only a few will understand. And she will suffer. She will suffer terribly.'

He bowed his head, no longer looking at her, and stayed silent for a long time, until Cuillin began to sense that he was suffering something for her, and that, for all his lightness and humour earlier, there ran through him a deeper, more serious current whose ripples had aged and harrowed him. As she felt this, she felt a sense of unreality creep over her, for did they not call *her* the Fremmed? It couldn't be so. Yet she looked down at her talons, already becoming worn with age, and understood that, yes, she had suffered far more deeply perhaps than she had ever admitted to herself. Years of loneliness, years of loss.

'There is so much you need to know, Fremmed, so much', he continued, 'but the cold winds of autumn are upon us and the migrations have begun, and there is no time to lose if you are to make a journey which I fear you must make.'

'But where to?' she asked feebly, as if lost—but knowing that Finse was a guide who would lead her to the right place. 'Where shall I go?'

'Fly north, Cuillin, against the migrations. Fly north into the blizzards and cold, and then yet further north to Tanahorn. There you will find the Weir, and when you do, trust him and remember, Fremmed, that he needs you for your help and guidance.'

'But I know nothing,' said Cuillin.

'Clew will help you, and those others. Trust them and trust yourself. It is said in the Doom that you will go when the winter comes,' and he looked northward past her, his wings opening a little and his legs straining at his perch, as if he wanted to lead her himself but knew in his heart he did not have the strength any more.

'Take Clew,' he said again, and she saw that it was his greatest wish, and she felt that he was giving over to her a burden he had carried for so long.

'I will,' she said.

'Good,' he said, great peace upon him. 'May Haforn be with you, Fremmed.' And then he was gone.

But later that evening Clew joined her, and soon after Weever, and finally Mizen, uncertain quite where to find them up there at night, and showing the state of her nerves by missing her footing twice before landing properly.

'That old male, Finse, told me to come. He said to obey you and go with you . . .' Mizen looked beseechingly at Cuillin, as if to say that, yes, she would go with her, but please not to make it a difficult journey or a long one.

'Yes,' said Cuillin. 'Yes, we are all going together, for I need your help and your guidance to fly north.'

As she looked northward and was lost in her own thoughts, they followed her gaze, though there was now little to see in the dark, and only the sound of the sea beneath them. They each looked a little afraid, but their fear gave way to pride as they gazed at Cuillin's great wings and powerful back. And they recalled that she said she needed their help, and that was an honour, so they were ready to do their best.

The night passed, dry and cold, and as dawn came over the cliff, Cuillin shook her wings, looked round at each of them encouragingly and, with a nod of her head, turned her beak north and opened her wings to the air.

While, in the rocks above them, an old male eagle watched the empty space between the headland and the northern horizon where the sea, light with the dawn sky, heaved and swelled. Until at last he saw four eagles, three juveniles and an adult, who flew a little behind and above them, heading north to find far-distant Tanahorn and the Weir who lived there.

* * * * *

His old eyes were wrinkled and his face bore the marks of time and worry, and of passages juveniles could never know. The wind came off the sea, and the sea itself rushed up the shingle and then pulled back down the slope to meet itself in a white confusion of foam that hesitated for a moment before being driven back up the shore by the following wave—as Liam MacAskill watched his youngest son walk on along the shingle bank that separated the sea from the Dunes. He was off to look at the tern colony on Sandwich Bay, he had said, and had even invited MacAskill along with him, but Liam shook his head. So the boy had gone crunching off with the wind in his hair, and looking back after forty yards to give his father a jerky, embarrassed wave.

CHAPTER FOUR

'I was interested to read Johnson Cook's review of the Stonor Retrospective currently showing at the MoMA in New York (*Artscribe*, June 1998) and soon to visit London at the Hayward. He describes the exhibition catalogue by Marion Poyser as "scholarly and exhaustive" and suggests it "goes as far as any work is ever likely to in analysing the seminal influences at work on Stonor's famous Eagle Series of paintings and sculptures, and in dating its creation". Not quite, it doesn't.

'I was at the London School of Art with James MacAskill Stonor from 1963 to 1966, and remember an occasion in March 1965 when he drew eagles, which is some eighteen months *before* Ms Poyser's "exhaustive" catalogue dates the first major eagle drawing. Stonor, as was often his way, got fed up with a sketching project in the Victoria and Albert Museum ordered by our tutor, and suggested to me we break off and go and have some tea in the nearby Natural History Museum canteen. Afterwards, wandering through the ornithological section, he stopped suddenly at the raptor cases, looked along them very intently, and pointed out a sea eagle to me. He told me his father had seen them before their extermination in Scotland before the end of the First World War, and he repeated some legends about them that he knew. He also sketched that particular one from as wide a range of positions as the showcases would allow, two of which I still have, and, even more interesting, wrote down two legendary names for me: Mizen and Sleat. Although there is no visual link between the drawing I have and the infamous *Sleat* sculpture in the Tate Gallery, the dark menacing tone of the drawing gives some hint of what was to come. The trouble with scholarship is that it never ends, and I'm sure that there is a lot more to know yet about Stonor's "seminal influences", as Johnson Cook puts it, and some of it will never get into print. Which is just as well, since the art is always more important than the artist.'

—Violet E. Clarke, Senior Lecturer in Fashion Design, Manchester Polytechnic. (Extract from a letter to *Artscribe*, November 1998.)

March 1965

'My goodness. It's Jim Stonor!'

Harold Ginnan, RA, head of Sculpture at the London School of Art, sometime exhibitioner with the Royal Academy, sometime acquaintance of an aging Constantin Brancusi, Henry Moore and Oscar Nemon, and most other twentieth-century sculptors active, or at least alive, after 1925, looked with exaggerated paternal interest at his pupil. 'Welcome!' he said ironically.

Stonor looked pale and tired, and felt irritable. He had spent most of the night in Opie's grotty Camden Town flat, in a bed that was too small, sleeping with Vi Clarke. He was irritable because they had turned up late and together at Ginnan's morning class, and because of this he knew that the others knew, or could guess, the what and the when, and probably the where – since half of them had been at Opie's twenty-first – of the past twelve hours. To make it worse, Vi Clarke looked blooming, and not only entered the class with a smug, selfconsciously nonchalant way about her, but smiled possessively back at Stonor so the others could see. A guarded and reluctant smile of acknowledgement passed briefly over Stonor's face, as if the sun had shone momentarily on the city of London and the spot it happened to light up was Pentonville Prison. Stonor did not like being possessed, so, sitting down as far from Vi Clarke as he could, he listened to Ginnan's project talk all dark and broody, trying to get printer's ink from yesterday's etching session out of his nails with a palette-knife.

Ginnan's project, deliberately sprung on the group as a surprise and change from the normal studio life-work, was for them all to go to the Victoria and Albert Museum and do something so academic that it was almost nineteenth-century: draw traditional figurative sculpture, and in particular concentrate on Roubiliac's *Handel* and the copy of Michelangelo's *David*.

'Hands and feet, my friends. Concentrate on hands and feet. See how they use the extremities to express the soul of their figures. Don't waste time on detail or gloss. Just bring me back nice free drawings, in which I expect a great deal of thought to have been paid to hands and feet *before* you set pen, pencil, charcoal, or crayon, to paper!' Ginnan finished and, sitting down in a black plastic armchair which was usually used by life models, he gazed with a beaming smile at them all. For a long moment no one moved, unsure quite when they should start.

'Well! Off you go! No need to come back at four to discuss the work, because for once I won't be here. Thursday morning, promptly. Anyway, not much point travelling back all this way, since some of you no doubt live down in fashionable Chelsea. Crumpets and tea, hands and feet!'

His good humour was infectious and most of them were smiling and chattering as they got up to leave. He watched them with affection.

71

Only a year or so, and most of them would be gone. He had watched them grow up and seen faces that had been young and uncertain when he had first set eyes on them, two years before, become shadowed and firmer as the bloom on some had gone, and the purposefulness of others had appeared.

These were at least a good year. Derek Gordon with his short, neat hair and pinched mouth and grinning eyes, who looked like a Walt Disney animal when he was huddled over a piece of work, and who, whatever he did after this, would get and give enormous pleasure with the classic medium at which he was best: water-colour. He would make a bit of money at it, too, if he painted the right things and stayed in Britain!

Gerald Opie, tall and agangle, his mind quick but his words pedantic, so he tended to fumble desperately for the precise word, though everyone soon got to know it was worth waiting for. He was the one who was inclined to utter half-words and finish sentences for others, and let his eyes wander, and generally race ahead of them because so often he knew, more or less, what they were going to say. What would he do? Not art, no. Ginnan did not know.

Vi Clarke who, by the look of it, had finally got Stonor into bed. Personally he would not have thought it needed much prompting. For her today's outfit was yesterday's, or rather last night's, when Opie had held his birthday party to which Ginnan had briefly gone. From which Ginnan, like a few others no doubt, drew the obvious conclusion. So, today's outfit is a tight grey polo-neck sweater shot through with silver foil; a tightish mini-skirt shot through with sex appeal; a pair of off-white stockings and silver and gold boots which she probably picked up for 57s 6d at Biba's down in Kensington. She had graduated in the last two years to softer make-up, though for Ginnan's taste, not that he had ever meddled with students except for the one he married in 1930, the eyes were still a bit overdone. She wanted to be a fashion illustrator but he suspected that she would end up teaching the subject, and not too well.

David Farrell, who had already lined himself up a job at Pember-ton's Advertising, and would probably end up as an art director; Gary Scheymer, half-American and a little older than the others, also for advertising, but in New York. Judith Shure, classier but less willing to spend money on clothes than Vi Clarke. Not a strong artist and one who had not really fulfilled her promise, and yet . . . well, she loved the subject. Knew more about art history than Ken Clare who did the lectures. She invited him round to dinner once to meet her father, Max Shure, one of the most influential gallery owners in London. She was a cut above some of the long-legged, well-heeled Chelsea set the London School was getting into the habit of taking. Most needed to be sent packing with a kick up the arse. Not Judith Shure, though.

Jim Stonor, who was just beginning to show a depth in his work, just a touch of something. You can't tell much from students' work; at least you can't tell which ones are going to succeed at making things that are true and uncompromised, because most are still so influenced. Ginnan had thought him a bit flash when he first came, one of those superb draughtsmen with a portfolio that's got real style, but who so rarely develop anything more. Yet he was impressed that Stonor had taken the trouble, off his own bat, to go on a day trip to Calais to see the famous Rodin. 'Why?' he had asked, but the answer was monosyllabic, and all that Stonor did was move his hands about in the air over their desk and look desperately out of the window for the words. His drawings had shown, as they say, great facility. Clearly he would do.

But now, eighteen months later, Harry Ginnan was becoming certain that, of all the students of that year, perhaps of all the years he had taught, Jim Stonor had the qualities that might, just might, make him a very great artist. It was not just his superb technical ability, for each year there were always two or three who possessed that. It was a deeper intelligence and sensitivity to experience, finding expression sometimes in the things he had made, which most marked him out.

Sitting there in the emptying teaching studio, Ginnan remembered the time he had first seen the passion and originality in Stonor's work.

One Monday morning, drunk or drugged from the weekend and looking terrible, which was unusual for him, Stonor had come to Ginnan's studio and hung around, morose and bitter. Ginnan ignored him, provocatively so. Stonor picked up some clay and bullied it. He made a coffee and looked at the clay. His childish monosyllables turned to silence. Ginnan could feel the heaviness of a storm-to-come in the air, and sensed Stonor's silent battle to control it and direct it. Ginnan worked on his own piece breathlessly, his back to Stonor but his heart with him in the love and peace that the dullest-seeming student sensed in their teacher, and which led them to make the trek to Ginnan's door and knock on it, without knowing why.

Stonor quietly took up the clay and began to shape and model something that Ginnan would like to have looked at, but in which he thought it best not to show too great an interest. But he could see, from the corner of his eye, that there was a terrible concentration in what Stonor was doing, a kind of passionate control, as if he was moving something which was far bigger than himself, but which yet was delicate, and if it overbalanced and he lost control of it, might smash. And when it did just that, he found a piece of wood and some wire and made a simple armature for it, to support the wet clay. Then he pushed and slapped the clay back on, wetting it untidily with water from a cup, and kneading the tiny thing with a strength and power a man might take to control a wild stallion. Still Ginnan did not turn to look, and he only relaxed at last when he heard Stonor's breathing grow slower and he sensed that the model was nearly done.

Finally, when Stonor had finished, he stood back and looked at the maquette; and the way he relaxed and smiled apologetically showed that he wanted Ginnan to look now.

'*The Cormorant's Memorial*,' he said flippantly. They both looked at the model, which was ten or eleven inches high. It was thin and stark, reminiscent of a Giacometti, but it had a broken sweep at its top which savagely cut short the vertical shape of the piece. There were curious, haunting, circled shadows behind the harsh lines. It was unlike anything Stonor had done for Ginnan before. Unlike anything any student had ever done.

It had a sense of space about it that suggested, more than anything else, a place, a real place that Ginnan knew he had never been to, but to which – by some alchemy – Stonor had, in his tiny sculpture, transported him. A desolate place where this object, of which it was part, and whatever it was, must stand. It was a sculpture pulled by a man out of the very ground on which he stood—and suffered. It was an expression of what had been, and what that place had made him feel. It was a sculpture for landscape, not for a gallery or a Camden Town studio. And yet, there it was, and there around it was the power of that place, and that strange suffering it suggested.

'It was about nine feet high,' said Stonor, quietly. 'I had to stand on a breakwater to finish it. To the left, as we look at it, there were brown and black pebbles of flint embedded in the sand. To the right, where the pebbles stopped, was the sand itself, revealed only at low tide and quite firm to walk on. The sandbank stretched out under the sea. All around was the grating rush of flat but heavy water . . .

'There was a wind, and he stood at a kind of angle into it, as if it was stronger than it really was, as if he distrusted it. So he set his feet firm into the beach so that if the wind dropped suddenly, or blew even stronger, he would be ready for the change . . .

'Like the soldiers in one of those old war memorials who stand eternally at the ready for the enemy. It *was* a memorial . . .' And there was a shakiness in Stonor's voice that made Ginnan look away from the model to Stonor himself, and he saw that Stonor's eyes were staring at the model, and far beyond it, and his mouth was a little open and trembling not to cry. But he was crying, or weeping, or whatever men did. There were tears on his unshaven and now washed-out face. Then he turned to Harry and said, 'I had a letter from my mother this morning. My grandmother died last week but my mother didn't phone to say. They buried her in Canterbury on Thursday. I didn't even know.' Before Harry could say anything, Jim simply turned and left.

But the clay model stayed where it was, and alone of all his students' work, through all the years, Ginnan was to take it to his country cottage and place it at the window where the ivy trailed outside and blew in the wind, and rippled with young shine in the sunlight in spring. For he was sure for the first time, from the power of that strange sculpture, of the power and force inside the student who had made it. And he knew the unspoken compliment he had been paid by Stonor making it there in his studio, and he treasured it more than all the letters, and words, and speeches, and gifts four decades of students had given him.

There was still the look of awe and pleasure now on Ginnan's face as the memory faded and he brought himself back to the present, and to the studio in which he had just been teaching.

The sound of the students had finally faded away and the studio was silent and still, except for the slight swing of Ginnan's blue-corduroyed leg from the chair. To his right the great windows, slanting inwards up from the floor, were grey. They faced north. The walls of the studio were an untidiness of dried paint around empty rectangles, where students had stuck paper up to paint on and overrun the edges on to the wall; there was a paper sculpture of a horse coloured red in poster-paint lying on its side by the sink. The sink, a deep old glazed one built up on bricks and added as an afterthought, had once been white, but its sides and inside were so marked, chipped and stained by generations of students washing their hands, or taking water, or mixing paint in it, that it was now grubbiness incarnate. All around it were paper cups which someone had brought in for some construction exercise, and which had been taken over as water holders. The wooden floor was covered with paint and colour like a faded Jackson Pollock.

Around where Ginnan sat, at the centre of the wall at one end of the studio, the floor was clear. But along the other three walls extended a tangle of plywood and tubular-steel chairs, also paint-splashed, three easels, and several long, low seats with four slanting

75

legs for stability and an easel stand at one end of them—donkeys. Just another teaching studio.

The chairs and donkeys faced his way, the easels had their backs to him. So many students' faces and bodies sitting or standing, watching or listening, looking and drawing, eyes up, eyes down, hand still, hand moving, making image after image. It was not in a studio they became artists, but outside it in streets or rooms or fields—and by reaching out a hand to touch each other, or to reach themselves. But studio work helped! Ginnan smiled ruefully and got up: he was not a philosopher with words, but with his heart he had to be. *His* reaching out was to students first and to media second, and they loved him, though most only realised it when they left the school. In those moments when they needed him and his words came back, or the meaning in what he had once said was suddenly clear, they remembered Harry Ginnan.

They did not expect him in the V & A, because he had not told them he would be there. A few of them weren't around, having probably scarpered when they had done a minimum of work. Well, the year was ending. But he found Vi Clarke, Opie, Stonor and David Farrell in the Michelangelo room, busily at work—on hands and feet! He came in quietly, and since the Museum was fairly busy and they had grown used to people coming up behind them and looking at their work, they did not notice him.

Stonor had taken a stance some way back from Michelangelo's *David*, and though he appeared to be drawing from it, in fact Ginnan saw with a smile that he was sketching the other three, or rather caricaturing them. He had obviously grown tired of hands and feet, but then, being Stonor, he had probably already done what Ginnan had asked of them.

Which was true. For Stonor was now feeling better, and having done enough of Ginnan's project to satisfy himself, he was doing some quiet sketching while waiting for Vi Clarke to finish off. After a lunch away from her, with Opie and a pork pie and a pint of brown, he was feeling more enthusiastic about her than he had in the morning.

In fact, though he stood sketching Opie, who was standing near her, he was half thinking of Vi at the same time, whose mini-skirt and the thighs beneath it held him captivated. She was, he happened to know, wearing stockings. In fact, he had helped her put them on, twanging the suspender strap against the inside of her thigh with one hand while holding her down on the bed with the other, until laughing made him too weak to continue. But he gave up on the Opie drawing, suddenly taken by the sight of all three of them with their backs to him drawing industriously away, all bums, legs and elbows. On the left I give you Opie's bum, gaunt of cheek and highest of altitude, covered in the old pair of Burton-tailored dark-grey trousers that he wore for painting as a sort of protest against his father who had bought them for him on his sixteenth birthday. Whenever he went home he left the trousers in the flat because even now he felt slighly guilty about misusing them.

Next to Opie's bum, though a shade lower and infinitely rounder, plumper and nicer, was Vi's—and I give it to nobody, thought Stonor. He drew it carefully, but got the real contrast into the shapely potential of her thighs, whose secret upward meeting was suddenly cut off by the hard line of her mini-skirt. To her right, and anybody's who cared to take it, was 'Farrell's farter', as Opie had called it last night when he was very drunk. It was slightly nondescript, but there was a ribbed pattern to David Farrell's trousers which Stonor accentuated to give the bum, which was marginally plump, a curiously round, sculptural form, like a Henry Moore bum. Farrell had a Marks & Spencer pullover on, the one he got for Christmas, though now across its back was a slanting line of red paint to enliven the beige, acquired when leaning against an inking stone in the print department. From their bums, Stonor moved up to their backs, and then their elbows: Vi's plump and loose, Opie's awkward and angled, Farrell's boring. Their necks leaned at different angles, with Opie's more hairy than Stonor had noticed before, and Farrell's rather hollow in the middle. While Vi's was covered by her long, crinkly fair hair, which he let his pencil flow into so that the tips of it slunk all the way down her back to the roundest, nicest two spots on her bum, where they rested fondly, like fingers.

He extended Opie's nascent right hand, which had been rather weakly extended towards the Michelangelo foot they were drawing, into a groping, lustful set of fingers which ended up caressing the tip of Vi's left breast. It was a sent-up version of the nearly touching hands of Michelangelo's *God and Adam* in the Sistine Chapel. Beyond them all he drew a massive, heavy foot from the copy of *David*, as solid in the air as a steamroller on ground. And in capital letters along the bottom he wrote: 'A NICE BIT OF CRUMPET, HANDS, AND FEET!'

'Mmm,' murmured Ginnan over his shoulder. 'Mmm. That's your day's work is it?'

He was smiling, and as Stonor quickly turned the pages of the sketch-pad to show what he had done, he smiled too. 'Good,' said Ginnan simply, and went off to look at the others' work.

Stonor and Vi Clarke finally headed off for tea a little earlier than the others, Stonor insisting that they cross Exhibition Road to the Natural History Museum so they could avoid everybody else. It just made life simpler. Vi took his arm across the road and he felt her left breast – the one he had drawn Opie groping for – pressing against him. He liked it.

The massive Victorian yellow-brick museum towered above them beyond black iron railings, and Stonor stopped to look at it, moving just a little away from Vi to be alone with himself. It was thirteen years since he had been there, and he was even more excited now than he was then.

'I came here once when I was a kid,' he said. 'My father took me.' And had Vi Clarke known the background, she might have understood the excitement in his voice.

It was 8 November, 1952. Remembrance Sunday. He had a red poppy in the lapel of his blue school raincoat. He had bought the poppy for 3d from a lady in Trafalgar Square, with his own pocket money. They had come here by tube, and when they reached the Museum had gone up the steep steps to the great swing-doors. He walked into the foyer and his father took his coat and gave it to somebody while he stood beneath the gothic arches and shadows of the Museum's antechamber. The main hall opened before him, lit by a range of grubby clerestory windows high above everything. A couple of steps and he was there, standing with open mouth before the gaping, grinning, fossil teeth and fierce eye cavities of the huge extinct Diplodocus, whose relatively tiny and delicate head seemed to hang poised in the air little higher than his own, but at only the lowest end of a steep hill of vertebrae which went back, and up, and higher towards the distant ceiling, until they joined huge flattened scapulae, whose strange curves and sculpted shapes riveted him to the spot as his eyes travelled past them, higher for a moment, and then sliding and turning and contorting through the vertebrae to the great rounded cage of hanging blackened ribs, which could have held ten little James MacAskill Stonors, with stumpy rises of bone above each one, the whole forming a great warm shape, far beyond which the spine curved down and down to back legs that were bent and walking forwards. His eyes got lost among the bones, some of which were bigger than he was, and all of which seemed to fit together to make a thing so whole that it seemed almost alive, but wasn't any more. And eight-seven feet long.

His Daddy was behind him, but Jim hardly noticed as he started the long walk around it, the great curved bones changing shape all the time as they swooped up towards the lancet windows above, or down into the front legs and through them powerfully to the feet, which rested like his own on the ground, until he got back to the point he had started from, and simply stood and stared and searched until his eyes finally rested back at the great heavy skeletal feet of the extinct creature. His own legs were thin and brown from sun and sea-wind, and scratched from hunting for fossils in the chalk scree by the cliffs. He was wearing a grey-flannel school uniform, freshly pressed, but his woollen socks had collapsed into untidy folds around his ankles, and beneath them, solid on the ground – like the feet of Diplodocus – his black school shoes stood still, battered and scuffed.

'Daddy, why did they become ecsinkt?' he asked.

'They got too big and couldn't support themselves any more.' But even then this explanation somehow did not satisfy him. It was too simple for the enormity of it, that great life gone, lost for ever— and there must have been one last one raising its head, this head with its eyes, and looking into a world where it was all alone. It left him uncomfortable, and that same night it became a nightmare in which the doom of extinction was chasing him over a shingle beach he could not seem to run on . . .

It felt wrong being there with Vi Clarke, and Stonor wished he was alone so he could lose himself again in front of the creature.

'Let's go,' he said finally, cold and indifferent. She feared he had lost interest in her, and did not want her there. She sneaked a look at his face to see if it gave her any clue about how to react. It was dark, the eyebrows dark, the eyes clear and cold, and they were looking away from her. Stonor looked a little tired. To Vi he looked her age, any age—a man she fancied and who she thought last night she knew but knew this afternoon she didn't.

It was chance that took them past the raptor showcase: marsh harrier; hen harrier; red kite; buzzard; pair of osprey, the male a juvenile. Stonor stopped and peered heavily at its spread of wing, which was all white and fluffy at the body end. He did not like stuffed birds. There was something very grim about the cliff-edge settings with distant heather-clad hills in the background, and the occasional badly-painted sea. And something terrible about the starling, skylark or brown rat caught pathetically in their talons, where a taxidermist had placed them for added realism, for ever.

The cases ran down the wall and turned a corner to the door, so he reluctantly followed them. He could see his reflection in them now. His eyes readjusted to the inside of the case and, oh dear God, she was there, next to a golden eagle, but bigger, with her full yellow beak massive and hooked, her wings rounded and powerful, and her thrusting head whose great clear eyes were staring straight at him. But it was what she was standing over that stopped him still and turned him quite cold, so that whatever Vi Clarke was saying just faded away to outside the glass inside which he felt himself to be standing.

Vi must have seen the change in him by the sudden shock on his face, for she started forward to ask what was wrong, and then, when his back stayed firmly towards her and she could see he wasn't listening, just staring, and his face white, she withdrew and pretended to look at another case.

He stepped slowly forward at last, peering down below the horror at her feet, to read the museum label. It was written in round, neat copperplate, black fading to brown: '*Haliaeetus albicilla – White-tailed, or Sea Eagle. Female and brood.*'

The four chicks were a downy beige, their pale black beaks pathetically prominent in their nearly bald heads. The weight of their heads was supported, but only just, by frail, shaky bodies whose every bone and angled line of little wing showed through the thin down that covered them. They were clustered together in a small nest of bleached twigs, and whatever the museum label might say, they had never been a brood together, since broods of four were very rare. They probably came from two different eyries, possibly three, and there would have been no need to shoot them to take them, as their 'mother' had been shot. Some bastard of a Scottish gamekeeper or bailiff had probably stalked their nests for weeks until each brood was hatched. Then he had disturbed the parents, frightened them off, or killed them, and climbed up to the nests. It would not have been difficult, since sea eagles have a preference for low, flattish sites, often at the foot of cliffs above the scree-line. So he had climbed up the scree with the smell of the moor about him and the distant sound of sea in his ears, and the terrified chicks would have been waiting. They could not fly, and instinct would have made them lie still and ape dead. So, with one of the adults circling and calling frantically above the cliff, he would have picked them up and cupped them in his hand. With their tiny talons scrabbling in the air, or against green Scots tweed, he would have squeezed the life out of them gently, and felt a last flutter of life through the down before they lay still. Their eyes would have been gouged out and replaced with glass, their innards cut out from under the wing and replaced with cotton and sawdust; and the muscle that now held them up with beaks agape, in an eternity of waiting for food, was wire.

The female who stood over them protectively, her talons almost as big as each individual chick, stared forward and up into the recesses of a nineteenth-century gothic ceiling, where there were no clouds to take a flight-line on, no cliffs to find an upcurrent by. Her feathers had long ago lost their true lustre, and wind had not touched them in seventy years or more. And the last time they moved was when a hand, or trained retriever, picked her up by legs or body, and her wings flopped open and dragged along the ground.

Vi then came to his side and looked at the sea eagle and the golden eagle next to it. 'Aren't they magnificent!' she said.

Stonor ignored her, willing her to leave him alone for a bit, and she got the message. A little piqued she said, 'See you in the Museum bookshop,' and went off. But she looked back just before she left the gallery, and there he was, already kneeling by the case with sketch-book out and drawing the eagles.

She grew bored in the bookshop and finally, after nearly three-quarters of an hour and feeling a little annoyed, she came back. He was still there but, thank God, he was putting his sketching things away. And, praise the Lord, he actually smiled when she came up to him.

'My father saw almost the last one of these alive in Britain,' he started, and he continued as she steered him hopefully out of the Museum across Cromwell Road, through Thurloe Square, and beyond it towards the flat she shared in South Kensington. He was telling her stories about the eagle he had been drawing, stories which his father had told him, and she let him, because she was going to get his arms round her again, and her all around him, like last night.

* * * * *

They had flown into winter, and ahead of them the snows of north Norway lay ever more solid, while the grey sea seemed ever colder, as the days shortened into only a few hours of heavy cloud or occasional dim sunlight. The air was often so heavy and still with cold that even along cliffs and hills, where normally a few helpful upcurrents of air might be found, it became an effort to fly.

So their journey had begun to slow and Mizen especially had begun to tire, so that Cuillin had to take account of her growing weakness and make the flight stages as easy as possible.

Inland the ground was now white and silent with snow, and only the tracks of reindeer in search of food or arctic hare and fox broke its smooth, endless surface, except when sometimes a rise of vertical black rock thrust through it, or the stunted points of coniferous trees stood still and deep, and dark green, ranking reluctantly up a hillside until they petered out into nothing but rock, ice pools and snow wilderness. So they kept to the west, to the coast, feeding on the resident duck, which were mainly boring eider, or the odd gull, and an occasional seal corpse.

Until now the juveniles had been happy to take the lead, with Cuillin content to follow behind, keeping an eye on them and feeling herself pulled along by their enthusiasm and excitement in the journey. But now, as the days grew darker and heavier, and they began to weaken so that even Clew, who though not as strong a flier as Weever yet proved to have a dogged resilience, was slowing. Often now, when they stopped, they perched together in silence, too tired even to talk.

Eventually it was always Cuillin who would lead them, chivvying them along, beating steadily through the air at a pace that was too slow for her but one they could all keep up with. She was proud of them, for there had not been a single word of complaint, and even Mizen, who was beginning to suffer, had never suggested that they might stop or slow down. One more day; and one after that. And then . . . a day came when she knew she would have to leave them and go on alone. As she pressed through the air ahead, or led them along the best routes over the cliffs, she began to look for a place where there would be food for them through the winter, and they would be safe while she flew on to Tanahorn where the Weir was said to be. The wind, at least, was in the right direction, from the south-west; and without this prevalence they would never have got so far. But now she was feeling the urge to fly inland and away from the islands and sea, over the fells and towards the dangerously high mountains which towered above deep snow-bound valleys where nothing moved but rivers—and they were beginning to freeze.

They came at last to a great and complex bay, to the north side of which – well away from where they took a stance – was a small fishing station. A few lights in the winter murk to mark its location. Cuillin knew she had no need to go further north than this, and looking seaward, at skerry and island, she knew it was the place to leave them over winter.

'A rich place,' said Cuillin, 'and one I think we should explore for a few days.' She hesitated, but they knew her so well by now that they sensed she was going to want to part from them soon. They knew their strength was failing, but there was not one of them who would willingly have said so.

'The days are drawing in, and if we're going to get to Varanger and find the Weir we can't afford to waste time . . .' It was Weever who said this but his voice, usually so strong, did not carry much conviction. He was as glad to rest as the others.

'The truth is, we are all growing tireder and weaker, and now we must turn east to cross the mountains where the flying will be more difficult and food very scarce. I do not think it wise, or right, that I should ask you . . .' Cuillin hesitated.

'It's me who's holding you back!' declared Mizen miserably, her head all jerky and the errant feather above her left eye springing this way and that. 'It's me who's slowing you. But I *do* have the strength to go on, if only we keep to a steady pace and you don't mind waiting sometimes.'

Cuillin moved nearer to Mizen and shook her head sympathetically. 'As you know, my dear, I'm as much in the dark as you all are about what we're really doing here and precisely where we should go. But my instinct tells me that I must turn east, and I sense that you have all done as much as you can for the moment. There will be other things for you to do, far more important things, and ones that may demand more of you than even the great courage you have already shown. We shall explore this place and see if it's a good base for you all to winter in.'

'Oh, leave me behind,' cried out Mizen, very upset. 'I can cope by myself until you all come back. It's not safe for you to go alone, Cuillin, for there may be no food, and inland there are sure to be sleark who will attack a solitary sea eagle, and you don't really know where to go . . .'

'No, Mizen, I must go alone.'

To their surprise Clew suddenly nodded his head and shook his wings philosophically and said, with a touch of irony that they had never heard from him before: 'Well, it's probably all in the Doom, if only we could make sense of it. Or at least if only *I* could. And what's obvious is that, if Cuillin is the Fremmed, then she's not going to die quite yet. And if she isn't, then we must all be mad! It cannot be far now to Varanger, where the Tanahorn is, and she'll know where to find us when she returns.'

'But how long will you be gone?' asked Mizen, looking nervously at Cuillin . . . and the discussions went on until Cuillin had convinced them all that she was right, and they must trust her.

As night lengthened and the stars began to fade, the distant grey of dawn began to appear. She felt in her wings the strength of the Weir who had flown this way and made the Doom, and she knew she was indeed a part of it, as Finse had believed. But her own country was part of her as well, a most beloved part which had no time now for bitterness or loss. She felt a great strength and purpose overtaking her, and more and more clearly realised that she would have to make for them a dream and a memory of Skye, so that they or their children would have a guide – as the Doom had guided her – to lead them back to where she had come from. She would have to tell it in word and in flight year after year after year so that none of them would forget, and one or two might listen who would have the strength to go back there and start again.

Dawn came. And as the distant horizon lightened, the jagged tops of islands began to show that the day would be clear, and so the light would last a little longer than it had on some previous days. A good day for her journey.

So she shook her wings into the light wind and stretched. And feeling at peace and greatly rested, she turned to the others and said, 'Without you all I could not have got this far, nor have had the strength to press on to find the Weir—as it has been said I must. You have given me more support than you can know. I will return in the spring, for these mountains will be far too dangerous to fly back over once winter finally takes hold and the eternal night sets in. But I am the Fremmed, and you are nearly adults now and will remember what we have talked about and what you have learnt from me.' She spoke with strength, and all three realised a change had come over her. They looked at her in awe. 'We have been born at an end and at a beginning,' she continued 'and I am the last and the first, and each one of you is a fremmed as well, for this journey you have made is the start, and it is in the years ahead that you must triumph. The storms are coming from the west . . .' As she quoted the lines from the Doom that Finse had spoken to her, she looked towards her own distant country, which the storms had already passed through, and her voice grew ever more powerful in their ears. And they were almost as fearful of her as they had been when they first saw her, because she was raising her great wings with a strength they had not seen before, and they knew that she, Cuillin, *was* the Fremmed, and that she had honoured them.

'The time has come for me to turn from the safety of these shores and fly inland to the hidden sea where the Weir will be found, and by whose wisdom we may all be guided. Trust in each other as you have trusted in me, and I in you. Learn from each other in the dark night ahead. Forge a bond between each other which nothing, and no eagle, can break in the future; for what the Fremmed will ask of you will demand far more than you will ever realise you have strength to give. And may the power of Haforn be with you always.'

With that, Cuillin leaned forward into the void and took off, her great wings aslant in the air to make a passage east, towards the inland mountains and beyond them to Varanger and fabled Tanahorn.

Hope. Purpose. Trust. Strength . . . These were the feathers that made up the wings of courage which carried Cuillin away from Weever, Clew and Mizen, and inland towards the dark mountains whose edge they had been skirting for so long. The wind was directly behind her, so she tacked her way north-east in the hope it would take her to Varanger, of which she knew nothing reliable—really only what little Finse had been able to tell her: that it was almost an island but not quite, and that beyond it there was nothing for eagles but a wide and freezing sea. But most important of all, somewhere on it was Tanahorn and there, or near there, she would find the Weir.

The short day was already growing dark when the mountains ahead began to loom and she reached their first steep rises. As she did so, she found that the wind stiffened behind her, growing more blustery and uncertain, and she saw that ahead, where it had risen over the first mountains, thin cloud had formed, so that beyond them there was little to see except the occasional black jag of rock-face across which mist was racing.

It was time to stop. The air was cooling rapidly and the wind felt threatening—and, to add to her sudden concern, she saw the remnants of a sleark eyrie off to her right beneath an overhanging cliff-face. On the ground below it was a litter of birch sticks and bleached prey fur, and bones of small mammals. She looked fiercely about, her wings battling to maintain balance and her tail fanning as she searched the site for evidence of recent activity. But in so cold and bleak a place, where she did not know the prey too well, it was hard to say.

She found a well-protected roost on a cliff facing west, the way she had come. This gave her a wide view, and kept her tucked well out of sight of any sleark that might happen out of the mist on the mountains above. As evening fell the wind from the west strengthened, and she could tell from the tang of it that it had come off the distant sea. She had probably been flying ahead of it for the last few hours, and its violence was no doubt stirring up the sea and dashing it against the rocks where Mizen, Weever and Clew were roosting. She huddled her wings forward against the wind, puffed them out a little to gain more warmth, lowered her head into her body, and started the long wait for dawn. Tomorrow would come. Tomorrow she would have the strength to cross the mountains. Tomorrow . . .

She flew on next day, with the wind stronger, the mountain

ridges now steeper, the valleys deeper but higher, the ice thick and trees a thing of the past. Barren and cold. The air was growing stiller and forcing her down along the corries and cliff-sides, unable to beat any easy route upward. She perched for a few moments by a steep rock gulley, to take stock, but the place was heavy with cold darkness and she could hear a rumble of rock or slithering ice all around. The cliffs were so high above her that for a moment she lost her sense of direction, then used up energy to start powering up, but it was like flying through water, each upward pull of her wings feeling heavier, each down-glide less controlled, her legs beginning to lose tone and hang looser and out of true, the face of wretched rock moving slowly by only feet away from her. She felt she would never rise up out of this rock-bound gully.

It was then, when she was weak and struggling and lost, that they came. One from the right, one from the left. Dark stoopings of sleark—two adults, and then, beyond them, a juvenile male. She heard them before she saw them—their wings hissing with the power of their dive towards her, and the sudden harsh calls of instruction from the female. Cuillin turned urgently to locate them – the air too still to give her any real purchase – and the male was on her, his stoop a real one and not merely a warning.

The sky above her was suddenly dark brown with his feathers, and then black with the stabbing of his talons, and she turned instinctively on to her side, her own talons thrusting up towards him. The effort of it sent a gasp of strain from her which rode round the fastness of rock gullies in which she seemed suddenly trapped. He shot by, his trailing talons catching her left leg—not only ripping her flesh but spinning her out of control. As she struggled to regain balance, the sleark now swinging away below her was replaced by the female stooping down from above and buffeting the side of her head, while her own talons were struggling to give her the balance she needed to regain control. The blow hurt and angered her, but this combined with shock to give her the strength she needed to plan a move, and make it. She was in an almost fatal position. On either side were the sheer walls of the gully, and its natural exit was above her. But this air-space was controlled by the sleark, so the only other route – one they would know of – was down along the bottom of the gully and away. But that way was narrow and cold, and it would be easy for the sleark to follow her passage and continually stoop on her till she grew exhausted trying to rise, and eventually fell prey to their talons . . . Yet what else could she try?

She folded her wings behind her and started to fall through the chill air, the treacherous cliff-face only feet away as she plummeted down. It was a gamble on the wind—but a way of escape. As the scree below began to loom nearer, and the cliff-face to blur, she summoned up all the strength of the moment, and the experience of recent months, and opened her wings slowly into the air-stream, bringing her feet out in front of her, sliding slightly sideways, and so wheeling swiftly out and away from the cliff. So she rode back up on the power of her fall and some weak upcurrent she almost forced out of the air. As she made this spectacular dive and swoop upward, with the sound of the wind in her feathers hissing around the rocks, she gained time to see where the sleark were now positioned, and what their strength was. One, the juvenile, circled high above them all, the occasional flap of its wings telling her there was at least a little air to find up there. The second, the male who had just struck her, was swinging above her, level-pegging around the top of the gully. The third, the female, was out of sight, and Cuillin suspected she was perched on a rock terrace above her, whence she could observe any low dive out to escape—and prevent it.

Cuillin slowed, in control again. She swung across the face, right under the overhang, so as to be out of the sight of the female. She dismissed the juvenile as no immediate danger. Then she swung back across the face, to test the response of the male. He was fast and dark, his feathers more black than brown, and their noise was a soft and vicious hiss compared with her rougher, more rippling sound. Being sleark they would probably expect her to attack, since there was no way she could flee. She played for time and settled gently on to a narrow ledge, wide enough only for her to sit sideways. The male immediately arced round towards her, to see exactly where she was. Then he flew along the cliff-face towards her, just far enough out to lure her off the ledge if she wanted to attack, but not so far that she could gain any speed if she did. He leisurely stretched out a talon towards her as he went by – for the pleasure of it – and she heard the hiss of it in the air before she felt the sudden gust from his flight past.

He swung round for a second run, leisurely and slow, looking round first to get a good line, and a quick glance up at the female Cuillin could not see, who was perched waiting on the ledge a hundred feet above her. The juvenile even higher swung out of her sight as well, for the cliff behind her was steep and curving, so the view was very limited for any eagle above her. So now the only sleark who could see her was the male now powering towards her, and a cold calm descended on her as she realised this might be the best, perhaps the only moment, for attack. She was not going to fall prey to sleark. She was the Fremmed . . . and she was going to find the Weir. And suddenly she was cool and clear of thought—and made a decision then which might have given her ancient race, and her mother, and Waulk himself, great pride. For she realised that if she could surprise the male coming towards her, she could effectively surprise all three and, in their surprise, make her escape.

Cuillin ostentatiously cowed back against the ledge to lure the sleark even nearer the face. He looked arrogant and vicious, and there was a cruel pleasure of the moment alight in his dark wings. Seeing her cower, he turned nearer and, with her back half to him because of the narrowness of the ledge, he risked swinging into the cliff, talons out to scare her and hoping to dislodge her.

He was almost on her, moving very fast. And when she was sure he was committed, and the sky above still clear of other sleark, she pushed sideways off the ledge, opened and mantled her wings as fully as she could, presenting her talons, and did the unthinkable: she grappled on to him. There was a scream of surprise as her huge talons, far more powerful than his, locked into his—and he shot over the top of her, and then was stopped dead in the air by her plummeting weight as she swung down and around. His own wings opened wide as he struggled desperately to pull his talons free and regain control. But caught in her much more powerful ones, they were being crushed, broken, pierced, and he was now screaming with the pain of it as they swung over—and to him the world was becoming a nightmare, a rushing circle of racing sky, and cliff-face, and looming gully floor. As they bolassed in a grapple, over and over each other, and the speed of it increased as they descended, Cuillin brought down her great beak in vicious hammer-blows on his neck and she began to feel him shudder and weaken with pain.

Now she felt increasingly powerful and in control, and she slowed their whirling fall by opening her wings. She had done the same with Waulk in mating grapples high over the Shetland Isles, and had found that it was possible, by wing control, to swing the other viciously round and down, while slowing her own pace. The problem then was to unlock talons high enough over ground or sea for both to escape.

But that was with Waulk. And this was with sleark. She had no wish for him to escape and she was full of anger, and full of a power that, though she could not see it, had taken the female sleark high above them totally by surprise. All she could do was watch in horror as her mate – so recently in control – was swung in a grapple down into the sharp and jagged depths of the dark gully beneath.

They swung down and down, head over talons, until the rock

and ice of the scree were dangerous feet away; and Cuillin, in complete control, coldly and deliberately timed the final swing so that at the last moment she came up out of it and opened her wings and released him from her talons; and he, only half-conscious from the pain and the surprise, crashed terribly into the ice and rock below her. And before he could even feebly start to raise himself, she dropped hugely on him, her wings wide and full, her talons crushing, as her beak came down in one fatal lunge at the top of his head. Then, with blood on her beak and his body dead beneath her, she looked up, her pale eyes like cold suns; and even if there had been a hundred sleark above her, instead of one female and a juvenile, she would have risen to face them all.

For she was the Fremmed, and she was going to find the Weir— and sleark had done too much harm to her race to be allowed to do more. Let them see from the start of this new time – of which she was so much a part – that sea eagles *could* overfly sleark.

She rose into a clear sky—the remaining sleark having beaten a retreat south, where they circled at a distance as she flew on over the highest mountain ridge and down towards foothills that some deep instinct told her would lead her to Varanger at last.

It was perhaps an hour later that she suddenly saw another sea eagle high, high above her in the wind of the light storm that was enveloping them, his great wings caught in the light of the strange sky, his fiercesome eyes watching, his flight more forbidding in its power and purpose than any she had ever seen.

While Cuillin, borne up by a sense of strength in the wind and on a wonderful line through the total confusion of the sky, called out, 'I am the Fremmed!'

As she did so, the eagle far above – now silhouetted by bright, diffused light at the edge of a boiling dark cloud – folded his wings above him, tilted forward and fell into a stoop towards her. And she heard his voice crying out as if it, too, was the thunder, 'And I am the Weir, and in me will all things be told . . .'

Then Cuillin rose towards him, not to meet him but to pass him in flight, as a balance to his downward plunge, and there came over her a sense that at last she was flying with an eagle she could never overfly but with whom, if she trusted, she could fly in powerful harmony, as the sky and the earth and the distant sea became centred on their flight.

And as the Weir's downward flight turned up into a gyre into whose vortex Cuillin felt herself drawn, her wings were no longer tired, and her spirit soared as their words mingled in the sky into ancient words of power:

Power of the Raven be thine
Power of the Eagle be thine,
Power of the Fiann

and one of them repeated in the ancient language

Feart fithich dhuit
Feart fiolair dhuit
Feart Feinne . . .

but which one spoke which language neither knew, for one was the
Fremmed and one was the Weir, and which might be which, or
who might be who, mattered not as they flew each other's flight
northward in the strange sky, with the clouds of Varanger in their
wings, and the light of the sun and the lightning on them, so that all
eagles, all ravens, all sleark might know that this was their land; and
that the sea eagle had found its power once more.

* * * * *

'Who told you those legends?' asked Vi Clarke, for even she had
lost her physical need for Stonor in the story that he told, and had
listened sitting on her bedsit floor in front of an electric fire as her
coffee grew cold in her hands. 'Can I see those sketches you did,
again?' she went on, undaunted, though seeing that he was silent
and rather morose. He passed her his sketch-pad. A great flank of
wing; a curving beak, massive; the subtle feathers over the eye
which gave the chicks a ferocious look to hide their feebleness;
curling talons on a long-dead oak branch. A museum case. A label:
Haliaeetus albicilla.

'My father told them to me,' said Stonor. 'He saw the last one
and never forgot it.'

'Where is Varanger?' she asked.

He did not really know—north Norway, beyond the Arctic
Circle? She did not have an atlas but in a history of European art
they found a map of sorts and peered at it together. Stonor's finger,
still grubby with printer's ink, followed a line from north Scotland
to the Shetlands, and then across to the Faroes, and from there to
Norway and up its coast to . . .

'That's it,' he said firmly, but not really sure. It spoilt the impact
of the story, the fact that he didn't know. Yet how well he
remembered his father telling him.

'His name is Liam Hugh MacAskill,' said Stonor.

'Oh, I thought he was dead,' she said in genuine surprise. And
seeing his look of alarm verging on anger, she added, 'Well, you

always seemed to talk as if . . .' And quickly changing the subject, but getting deeper into trouble, she asked, 'If he's a MacAskill, why are you named Stonor?'

He looked even more angry for a moment, but there was something about her obvious alarm that caught his sympathy. It wasn't her fault. Anyway, he felt released from something, with the story out of him; and there was the way she was sitting with the book open on her knees, so he could see a hint of her pants, soft and pale, and her rounded thighs.

Oh, he's smiling, thought Vi Clarke with gratitude. Thank Christ for that! And she opened her arms to him, and her legs as well.

A few days later Harold Ginnan had a visit from Stonor at his Camden Town studio—and in a mood not much different from the one when he had created the cormorant piece.

Ginnan made him a coffee, and let Stonor morosely take up some wet clay, monosyllabic, frowning, searching. He left the lad to it while he got on with something in an adjacent studio.

Stonor let the clay swallow his hands, so that they became part of it as it slipped among his fingers and over his wrists, cold for a moment, like the first dip in a summer sea. He was searching for a shape in the clay which began not with the sweep of a wing, or thrust of a claw, or hook of a great beak, but deep inside the bird whose lonely agony he had felt at last—a core of feeling on which he would build the shape of the eagle.

For days since talking to Vi Clarke, he had struggled to see her and been forced to discard drawing after drawing, for they seemed only to express the confusions he felt about her. Then he was flying with her, who was Cuillin, and she with him—and great wet hands of clay that moved with life gave her great talons and a spread of wings greater than she had ever had, for they took in Coruisk, and Cuilce, and Storr and all the lochs of Skye; they took in the dark sea and Romsdal, and the flight north to Tanahorn; they gave her a faith to conquer her fear; they gave her a hope to weigh against loss.

They put into her flight the sadness of a language nearly lost, and a pride that had died, or nearly died, into nothing, with only a memory of Haforn and her mother's words to keep it alive. Scalpels and fingers, spatulas and thumbs, wet clay and a strewn surface of remnants out of which she had risen and started to fly. The winds across the sea where he stood on shingle, a cormorant's broken wing, the crunch of lonely shingle and a little boy's wet boots. He put them in her. Behind him the curve of the beach hid the houses, and ahead the black and dull-yellow shore of shingle and sand, stretching north, and more north, into sky. The strength to remember, the strength to fly forward; one day the strength to meet the Weir; the strength for some eagle to come back by Haforn's grace.

Stonor stood still at last, his hands wet and heavy with clay, and hanging by his side. His breathing fast but slowing at last into peace. A cup of coffee, cold and with skin on its surface, stood to one side of the work surface on which the maquette of the eagle stood. Or flew. Or pulled its very heart out of the Loch na Cuilce from which it was departing.

'OK, Harry. I'm safe now,' he called.

Ginnan came out from the other, smaller studio and looked from Stonor to his work. Stonor watched him.

'Make me a coffee,' said Ginnan finally.

And as Stonor went into the kitchen and grumbled about finding milk and instant coffee, and having to wash a couple of mugs, Ginnan looked for the first time at work which he had hoped, one day, Stonor might produce. It was a sea eagle, the last one, which had been seen at the end of the Great War. And it was Stonor, or part of him.

Ginnan just sat on a stool and looked. And he saw the maquette, as one day so many others would see it, not small and studio-bound, but massive and bronze, dark against open sky, with a sweep of wings so great and powerful that they would smash a studio's walls into falling fragments as it rose up into the sky.

CHAPTER FIVE

Interviewer: You met Jim Stonor at the London School of Art in the early sixties where you were both students. Did you realise then that he might become one of the outstanding artists of his generation?
Judith Shure: (Laughs) No. No. Students don't think in such grand terms. He was technically outstanding, the only one of us who had total command of what was then a neglected skill: drawing and composition. Things have swung back again now but in the sixties art in London was all social concern, found materials, and concepts. Skill as such was almost *de rigueur*. I did not know him well personally. I was only twenty or twenty-one, and he was a year younger; and I was a well-brought-up young lady, while he seemed to me rather a lout. That didn't stop me rather fancying him, as we used to say. At the same time, on the rare occasions I heard him talking about art – usually with Gerald Opie who was our contemporary (now chairman of the Royal Arts Commission) – I was impressed with his ideas. He was critical of the poverty of public sculpture in Britain at that time, with people like Nemon producing dull effigies of Churchill and Montgomery for Westminster sites; while the powerful St Martin's School, led by Anthony Caro, produced cold, non-referential, non-passionate, cerebral steel work which I know Jim disliked intensely. His views were mine, so naturally I was impressed!

—From the transcript of an interview with Judith Shure transmitted in *The Making of Modern Art*, ITV 2, 1995.

June 1965

JUDITH Shure sat in sudden darkness with her back to the engine as the carriage pulled out of Waterloo Station and into the short tunnel beyond it. She sat quietly, with a basket full of picnic and drawing things beside her, but her chest was heaving. Not that she had been late for the train – in fact she had been early – but rather because she had a sense of boldness and adventure about what she was doing. For she was taking a step out into a void whose depths she could not know.

As the train pulled back into daylight, a distorting rectangle of bright sunlight fell across the seat opposite, travelling around the carriage as the train stressed its way round a wide bend to find a route east among the warehouses of the River Thames. Until finally, and contrarily, the sun settled, hot and unwavering, upon her—her eyes having to screw up to protect themselves, but warm and pleasant on her dark hair, cheeks, and lips.

All her life Judith had sat with her back to the engine—ever since an uncle had observed that a little girl did not feel so travel-sick that way. Thus she had sat, neat and still, looking out of carriage windows, her feet dangling above the carriage floor until one day they touched it, and on another day she crossed them consciously, and on a third they took shape, and stockings, and later tights. And her skirts, always expensive, changed back and forth with fashion, except that they were never so short and never so long as the extremes of the day. She wore her very slight out-of-dateness well. This day, her dress was a two-year-old summer frock from Liberty's, though she had raised the hemline a little, and it now settled at her knees.

That morning she had woken in her flat feeling lighthearted and in need of change. The other girls had gone off for the weekend and she was alone. She had looked again at a crumpled drawing of herself made by Stonor—one he had done during a life class when he had got bored with the model and started to sketch other people in the studio. It showed her in half-profile, standing at the easel she preferred to work at. He had made the painting apron she always wore – to protect her clothes – look homely, as if she was cooking a meal rather than drawing a nude; and for some reason he had put the face of Ginnan behind her, though it was not Ginnan's class.

At the end of the class she had walked over to see what he had done, and he had muttered, 'It's not any good', though in fact she thought it *was* very good. She wanted to laugh at the straight way he had portrayed her, for she *was* like that in a way, though she had never been made to see it quite so clearly before. Yet he coursed his pencil across it in irritation, as he so often did, and ripped it off the pad and dropped it, crumpled, on the floor.

She had lingered until they all left and the studio was empty, then, with her heart beating as if she was stealing something, she had picked it up and stuffed it in among her paints, not daring to look at it again until she got back to her flat. The guiltily innocent start to what was to become the greatest collection of Stonor's work in private hands. As she looked at it again that Saturday morning, she had wanted to know more about the place he came from, and, oh, she had wanted to know more about him. She had fantasies about him, relatively innocent ones, for though she knew he had slept with one or two of the other girls, she did not yet have the experience or the freedom to imagine the reality of him being with her, his face near hers and his lips and mouth on hers, but gently, not wild—not yet. Vi Clarke probably has a double bed!

94

she had thought to herself, laughing at her own silly jealousy. She *didn't* really want him . . . Oh, but she did! So her thoughts had waxed and waned, and she had looked at herself undressed at the mirror in her bedroom and wondered what he might think of her . . .

In fact, though she did not know it, she was the object of interest and envy among many of the other students at the art school. There was something assured and uncluttered about her and her voice, clear and clearly spoken, which contrasted with the slurs and affectations of so many of the students who pretended to a working-class culturelessness they did not possess, and which showed itself in monosyllabic pseudo-cockney, but uttered in a slightly embarrassed, half-convinced way that made them sound false and unpleasant.

Judith's father was a German and ran the Shure Fine Art Gallery in Cork Street, W1. Her mother, who was Jewish, came from London, and together they had brought her up to wear their wealth like a very good perfume: it was there, but subtle and inconspicuous. Her decision to go to art college rather than to university was her own, and against her father's wish, but he knew and loved her well enough to know that she had his own tough will. She mixed little with the other students, sharing her flat with two friends from the boarding-school she had gone to, and her weekends usually with family friends.

The fantasies she reluctantly had about Stonor were what lay behind the feeling of restlessness she woke up with that particular Saturday. Her flatmates went off for the weekend; mid-morning came, and her sense of restlessness deepened. She looked at the sketch of her he had done, and then, impulse gave way to action . . . carried forward by circumstance and something in the warm summer air that told her to get out of London and away to somewhere she had never been, she put a few things together and was off.

So, neat, unaffected, a little innocent, and with a certain girlishness to her excitement as the Deal train wound out among East London suburbs, Judith made one of those insignificant changes of habit that may mark a very significant moment in someone's life. She suddenly got up and sat down in the opposite seat and for the first time in her life enjoyed the pleasure of going forward to meet the town and country ahead, rather than watch passively as it slipped away behind.

It was a train of many stops, for the day-trippers had gone on faster trains to the coast, and now older couples were going down the line to see their grandchildren for the day, and boarding the train shakily for a ride of two or three stations. She talked to some of them, or rather they talked to her—she wasn't as intimidating as some of the girls of her age, with their mini-skirts and blonded hair, and heavily made-up eyes that looked like they were lost in a coal-scuttle. This one smiled as they sat down and even helped them with their bags when they were too heavy.

The train rattled through the summer-drowsy Kent countryside, passing stretching orchards, rising escarpments of green pasture, and rural villages with red-tile roofs, until, one and a half hour: after leaving London, and now half-asleep, Judith suddenly saw the sea. Folkestone, with its hotels and boarding-houses; tunnels through the chalk to Dover, and there a high, square castle overlooking the town; a station announcement at Dover Priory saying 'Train for Martin Mill, Walmer, Deal and Sandwich' and the train was into a tunnel again and heading for Stonor's home town.

Judith was awake and nervous, wondering what she was doing on the train at all. As she took her ticket out of her purse, her fingers were perspiring. Eighteen minutes and two tiny country stations later, the train pulled into Deal—and she was committed.

First impressions. How powerful and lasting they can be. Stonor had said once his home town was a 'wild, cold place, with a wind that drives the gulls down on to the wet shingle beach', and into this image he had somehow contrived to create expectations of tar, and boats, and Force Eight winds; along with old fishing cottages, and adult faces, hard and lined.

Judith's first impression, and the one that ever after showed through the overlays of later loving impressions she gained, was the fresh sea air of a quiet resort, rather off the beaten track, which was taking a rest for Saturday lunch.

A ticket-collector gave her directions to Compass Street—'Out of the station, down Queen Street, cross the High Street at the traffic-lights and up to the front, left past the Pier and the Royal Hotel, and it's along the promenade on the left, not far past the Bosun's Mate.'

What had seemed a good idea in London, now seemed close to madness, here in Stonor's home town. If she looked a little flushed and her hair a little frowzy, it was because she felt it—quite apart from having been in a train with the window open on a hot day. Her dress, green cotton with flowers on and short sleeves, felt well round her breasts and pleasant at her hips; her legs were just a little pale and her sandals a good quality, pale dyed leather.

Queen Street turned out to be little more than a hundred yards long and, apart from the cinema which was showing *How to Murder your Wife* with Jack Lemmon, there was just a little gift shop with shiny china dogs and horses in it, a food store, a couple of banks, and the *East Kent Mercury* offices, with old news photographs in the window showing, among other things, a Deal Wanderer scoring a goal against Tilmanstone Colliery on a snow-covered pitch, a group of young swimmers holding a trophy, the marriage picture of Mr Anthony Upton and Miss Elizabeth Grant.

Across the High Street and on up Broad Street, which rose steeply beyond the traffic-lights; and over its brow she could see the top of some boat masts. Past the wall of the last building – the Crystal Café – and a cooling sea breeze drove into her legs. Ahead of her was a narrow promenade, and beyond that a line of fishermen's boats, and beyond them, at last, within sight and sound and smell, was the sea.

She crossed the road and stood by the boats, looking down to the shoreline at last. There was no one on the stretch of shingle between the boats and the sea, but then it was covered with fishermen's gear—oily planks, a clutter of ropes, and beaten-up lobster-pots.

She turned north towards the pier, into the breeze, the same breeze that on a winter's night in Deal can blow up to a gale in a couple of hours and have a full-grown man clutching at the promenade benches for support. But Deal's weather, benign that day, felt pleasantly cool where it played at her bare neck and up her short sleeves.

Jamie Chunter, publican for thirty-seven years, secretary of the Royal National Lifeboat Institute (Deal branch), father of a merchant seaman (whom he loved but never mentioned), and an accountant in London (whom he disliked yet often talked about favourably), and secret owner of two guest-houses along the front of North Deal – which explained why he was able to run a second-hand Jaguar – saw Judith before she saw him.

But then, young girls with flushed cheeks and an innocent air about them, rarely hesitated with puckered brows outside the smoky windows of the Bosun's Mate wondering whether or not to come in.

The pub was well filled, mainly with men. There was a cheery and friendly liveliness about their conversation born of long familiarity with each other and with the special pleasure of a lunchtime drink on Saturday. Most of them were getting on in years, and many had been coming to the Bosun's Mate, a free house, ever since Jamie took it on in 1947, after the war.

The place was traditional and old and its cream-gloss painted walls and ceilings had a patina of cigarette smoke and pipe tobacco which had turned it a pleasant mellow yellow that blended better with the varnished, high-backed wooden benches and old, rutted wooden tables than any interior designer from London could have managed.

Judith stepped in from the light of sunshine, into the pub's warm murkiness. 'I was looking for Compass Street,' she said, addressing Jamie himself, since he was the most obviously in charge.

'Looking for anyone in particular?' asked Jamie with a smile. 'And while you're thinking about it, have a drink. On the house.'

It was one of those days, and without any demur Judith said, 'Half a pint of shandy, please.' She did feel very hot. But she insisted on paying.

'I was looking for Mr Stonor, James Stonor's father. I'm a friend of his from London.'

'Mr *Stonor*? You mean Mr MacAskill,' said Jamie. 'That's his Dad. *Mrs* Stonor is his mother, mind, if that's helpful.

'Albert!' called Jamie. 'Albert, there's someone here who knows Jimmy Stonor. You come on over and put her right.'

One of the old men looked up and, with a polite word to his friends, rose and came over towards them. As he did so, he dug into the sagging pocket of the old tweed jacket he was wearing and pulled out a yellow tobacco-pouch and a pipe.

He looked at Judith quizzically for a moment before nodding his head and saying, 'So you know Jimmy Stonor, do you? Well! And how is he?'

Despite his thinning white hair, the great number of wrinkles around his eyes, and a certain gauntness to his neck, there was a strong sense of solidity and vigour in the gaze he fixed on Judith. He was small and slim, and his jacket hung about him rather loosely and had worn leather patches on its elbows and cuffs. There was a curiously thick pencil in his breast pocket which reminded her of something that she could not quite place—until a day or two later she remembered suddenly and irrelevantly that it was the same kind of pencil tht Stonor himself sometimes used for drawing: a carpenter's pencil, with thick lead for scribing on wood.

'He's very well—and doing well at the School. He's one of the best students of his year . . .'

'Good,' said Albert, nodding in a friendly way that cut her off mid-sentence. 'Good. He's plenty of friends, has he?'

'Well, yes. He . . .'

'And you're one of them?' There was real pleasure in his voice and, had she known him well enough, she would have heard relief as well . . . but she felt she was getting into deep water and could not say, as she wanted to, 'I don't really know him at all well, and I'm not even a friend of his really, and I don't know why I'm here but . . .' But she couldn't, and she groped for the shandy on the bar and sipped at it rather desperately, suddenly embarrassed by his gaze.

'He used to work with me,' said Albert. 'Used to call himself my apprentice. I'm a cabinet-maker, a carpenter, and he used to help me in my workshop.'

Judith smiled and nodded ambiguously, as if to say that, yes, Stonor must have mentioned him but, no, she didn't know all *that*, and she began to feel even more that she was trespassing on private property and rapidly putting herself into a very false position indeed.

'She's got a message for Liam MacAskill,' interrupted Jamie, beginning to sense that the girl – the young lady – did not want all of them crowding about and asking questions about Jimmy. 'Haven't seen him, have you?'

Albert Chandler, the cabinet-maker, looked at them, turned slowly to look at the half pint he had left on the table, looked down at his pipe and, weighing it all up, one thing with another, decided to take her down to Number 11 himself. He could see she was a little embarrassed, and he had to remember that Jimmy was his own man now, and his people were his own. Prickly lot, youngsters, if you got to be too interfering. Just like fresh-cut wood: best left to mature at its own pace. One day it came right, and so would they. But whatever it was that concerned the girl, and he could see something did, he was more pleased than Judith could ever have known that there was someone like her in Jimmy's life.

He could see she didn't know Jimmy too well, or else she would have known about Margaret Stonor and Liam. He ached to know how the boy was, for those times when Jimmy had hung about his workshop, sometimes talkative, often silent, touching wood and holding tools, and letting Albert put his hands round his and show him how to take a grip and stand so a saw stayed straight and a chisel would not overcut had been among the happiest of his long life. So Albert really wanted to talk to Judith and ask her if Jim was all right, and if he had found something at least of what would always leave him unsettled and discontented until he found it.

'Finish your drink, lass, and I'll take you there. It's not far down to the street, but these houses can be a bit confusing with their funny old doors. Good place to live, though. Snug in a north-easter.'

Eventually they came to a narrow turning, and walked down into the shadows of an eighteenth-century street whose period doors and windows eyed each other in a higgledy-piggledy way across a fifteen-foot gap. The narrow street was little more than twenty old cottages and houses long, with a pavement on either side girded by old-fashioned granite kerbstones. The pavements were so narrow that it was easier and more natural to walk down the middle of the street, which is what Albert automatically did. Compass Street was quite empty, apart from a tortoiseshell cat that lay on a window-sill halfway down it; and the doors were all shut, though one or two of the first-floor windows were a little open to air the bedrooms. Although there were scarcely any gaps between the buildings, the houses did not give the air of being uniformly terraced. Each was different, and each gave a different sense of space and size, colour and feeling, in the few seconds it took to pass them by.

Most of the buildings were what estate agents – then beginning to advertise them in classy Sunday newspapers in the hope that Londoners might buy them as weekend retreats – dubbed 'fishermen's cottages'. And so, once upon a time, they may have been— but here and there, stuck boldly between them with only a built-over alleyway dividing them off, were taller, more elegant, houses built at the turn of the eighteenth century, when British marine power was nearly at its height and ship captains, Channel pilots and customs officials needed something a little more substantial than 'fishermen's cottages'. Most had a second floor, though noticeably meaner in scale – the windows being narrower in all directions – for these were the rooms those old sea-dogs set aside for a servant or two, or to accommodate the occasional sailor friend awaiting embarkation on the Downs. The street was empty now, but in its shadows still rumbled the ghost wheels of carts carrying sailing gear and tackle, timbers and tar, and a man's personal possessions in a sea-chest, up to the front. And in the summertime shade there walked with Judith and Albert a gang of men so motley, drunk and lively, so full of the sea and a rough, tough life, that had some trick of time brought them all out into the open, Albert would have felt it necessary to take her arm and hurry her on down towards the safer, wider pavements of the High Street.

Sun caught the red-tiled edges of some of the cottage roofs, and halfway down the street, where there was a gap between them, the sun shafted through on to the house opposite, its sand-coloured paint and peeling brown woodwork warm and peaceful. It was just before this, on the left and in the shade, that Albert halted, and Judith found herself outside Number 11. It was here, with a nod and a smile, that he left her, and Judith felt there was nothing for it but to raise the knocker. It was one of the taller houses, built of a very dark brick but flecked with yellow. Above the windows it had been faced with a softer, deep-red brick, beautifully pointed. The door had two white marble steps before it, and an unpolished brass overlay on the top level of the upper one.

Judith knocked twice and waited. Somewhere inside a nearby house, a power drill whined to a start and suddenly stopped. Children shouted up on the nearby front, and she heard the sound of a rubber ball bouncing across the top of the street. There was some perceptible but unidentifiable movement inside the house, a sinking of floor-boards perhaps, a run of air under the door as some other interior door was opened. She stepped back and down on to the pavement, feeling rather too close, and involuntarily ran her fingers through the fringe of her hair. She quickly dropped her hand to her side as the door opened, and a woman of sixty or so looked down at her.

'Hello.' The voice was friendly and the woman had a pleasant dumpiness about her, was wearing a floral housecoat over a light blue dress.

'Mrs Stonor?' started Judith.

'No, she's not here. Mrs Frewin's my name. I'm just cleaning the place a bit, and feeding the cat and watering the garden. Mrs Stonor's in London. Is it something urgent?'

'Well, not exactly, but you may be able to help. I'm a friend of James in London and . . .' But she was not allowed to finish the sentence. At the mention of his name, Mrs Frewin's face, already friendly, opened into real pleasure, and she stepped back to gesture Judith into the house, as if she had been waiting a very long time for just this moment.

'You're a friend of Jimmy's! Oh! Well! You must come in.' And brushing aside Judith's hesitance, she stepped forward again almost to pull her off the street and up the steps.

Judith's discomfort was steadily increasing as she found herself pushed ahead of Mrs Frewin and guided down a corridor of white-painted wood towards a door glazed with squares of bottled glass, and into a kitchen parlour. It was long and narrow, one door to the far left leading to a scullery and kitchen, another to the right, wide open to a tiny walled garden. The sun's warmth hung in the garden and filtered into the parlour, along with the sounds of bees buzzing at flowers and of sparrows somewhere nearby.

To the right of the garden door were three thick shelves of wood, painted gloss-white and carrying a jumble of objects so various, so contradictory, that had they been the contents of a handbag, a psychologist would have had a field day—and proved almost anything about the owner. There were books: three Georgette Heyer historical romances in torn and battered hardback covers; a *Concise Oxford Dictionary*, whose spine, inexplicably, bore a teacup ring mark; Eve Garnett's *Family from One End Street*; volume VIII of Arthur Mee's *The Children's Encyclopedia*, circa 1924; an ordnance survey map of East Kent; a lovely but now ruinous edition of Herbert's *Poems*; and several others.

The biggest book, the Arthur Mee, was propped at an angle against the others to hold them up; and by its side was a light-bulb, blackened and internally broken. There was a piece of pale, thin driftwood, whose whorls and veins came to an abrupt halt in more white gloss, now congealed, where it had once been used to stir a pot of paint.

A leaved oak table stood against the left-hand wall, taking up a third of the free space in the room. It had the same exhausted but beloved air as the books, and on it was cup of tea and a *Daily Telegraph* folded lightly to the horse-racing section. Selections had been made and marked, and the ballpoint pen that marked them lay on the table as well. On the wall next to the scullery door was a fireplace tiled in cheap 1930 brown tiles, screened by a piece of corrugated cardboard over which some wallpaper of an elegant and stylish green-leaf pattern had been spread and folded, then sello-taped down. Between the fireplace and the wall opposite the scullery door was an arched alcove painted cream; and the small shelves inside it were the only part of the entire room that had any semblance of order. They held a selection of small, blue and white china cups, delicate and beautiful, and a coffee-pot of the same pattern, which spoke of rooms and houses and a time that had been elegant and peaceful, when tea was served at five o'clock on table-cloths of starched white linen, and french windows were open on to lawns.

Mrs Frewin wiped her hands on her housecoat and said, with real good cheer: 'Well, this is unexpected! A friend of Jimmy's from London! Well, now!'

And as she spoke she looked on Judith with curiosity and interest, pleasure and delight, and with many more good feelings besides. And how could Judith know that she was the very first 'girlfriend' of Jim's (as Mrs Frewin supposed) who had ever come into the house? Or how could she tell that one of the reasons Mrs Frewin still came to Number 11 – though it was hardly worth it, what with bus fares up and only an hour's work a week which Mrs Stonor would let her do – was to hear something of what the boys were up to, and especially Jim? Nearly two years he had been gone now, and his room empty of him but for a couple of days in the holidays when he came down to take books and a few things back to London—by all accounts, looking terrible and tired. Two Christmases and not a card from him, except to his mother. Two years and the house empty and damp upstairs and the windows still rattling and wet with sea salt. Two years, and him out in the world with such hurts and loves hidden down deep inside of him.

Well, here was flesh and blood at least! And she looked as good as apple and blackcurrant pie, with a pot of best cream standing by. So Mrs Frewin smiled at Judith and told her she needed, and was going to have – despite her polite refusal and general shifting about – a glass of freshly-made orange squash. And she got it immediately, the water straight from the tap in the scullery, and had to drink half of it at least before Mrs Frewin would let her say what her business was. Which, once she had started, did not stop easily, since a body that does not know quite where it is going takes longer to get there than a body that does.

The child's name was Judith. She did not know Jim quite as well as Mrs Frewin might have hoped, and a lot less than she might have expected, having come all this way. And she was here on some wild-goose chase to see the boy's father, bless the poor man, who, she seemed to think, might be interesting to talk to, whatever that might mean. Jim's father, according to what Judith said, knew some legends about eagles, and these interested Judith.

Without much difficulty or cunning, Mrs Frewin switched the conversation to what she herself wanted to talk about, which was Jimmy; and she soon discovered that Judith did not know very much about him, and she wanted to know more. Well, no harm in that.

'Always been one to draw and model he has,' she said. 'Used to lose himself in it completely up in his room. Wouldn't see him for hours, but it was the devil's own job to get him to show you what he'd been up to. Hated anyone to see until it was finished. Soldiers, boats, driftwood armies, drawings of the pier—you name it, he did it . . .'

She offered to go and fetch some of the drawings, but Judith – rightly sensing that this would be an invasion of privacy which Stonor would not like (as if this whole day wasn't a terrible invasion, she thought ruefully) – said she didn't feel it would be right.

'As for his father, well, that's something you'd best not start *me* on, and Margaret Stonor knows what I feel about *that*. Mind you,

I'm not so conventional as to think that there's not right *and* wrong on both sides, but when a man and woman wed it's for better or worse, and if more couples stuck by their guns and saw it through they would find, as I have in my own time and others I've known, that in the long run it pays.' She paused and smiled before falling serious again to add: 'But maybe there are some for whom it pays only in grubby halfpennies and a wasted life. Maybe that was how it would have been with her, so she threw him out. Anyway, my dear, I don't think that's something for you to think about in this case, since once I start I'm sure I'll never stop, because if there's a single most daft house full of stuff and nonsense in the whole of Deal this is it. And in my work I've seen a few, I can tell you.'

'Would you like to see his room,' asked Mrs Frewin, herself feeling just a little emotional that Jimmy had such nice friends, 'now you're here?'.

But Judith said it was best not to, and Mrs Frewin agreed, and she fell to giving directions about how best to track down Liam MacAskill, Jim's father, who would either be sitting on a green wooden public bench on the promenade by the Coastguard Station, with his mac on despite the warm weather, or up at the allotments at the end of Golf Road, on the way to the Dunes. Then they said goodbye at the door with a warm glow of fellow-feeling that left them both sure that, one way or another, they would one day see each other again.

She went back up to the front, on to the promenade. The tide had turned and gone some way out since when she had first seen it, so the piles of the pier were now more exposed as it stood much higher out of the water. Ahead of her was another of those 1940-style shelters, like the one near the top of Compass Street, and a few feet beyond it the edge of the sea-wall which formed one side of the promenade.

She saw the Coastguard Station not far along, and the row of coastguard cottages behind it which Mrs Frewin had described. Judith examined the occupants of the benches facing the sea to find an old man in a mac.

One bench, a second, then another . . . she walked slowly through the summer afternoon, content to enjoy the view.

She was tempted to sit down, feeling suddenly too warm, but this bench was full, and the next had a couple of kids on it mucking about, and the next thing was a shelter. She didn't fancy sitting inside it, out of the sun and breeze, but as she came abreast of it she suddenly saw him: an old man in a mac.

He sat in a corner, away from an elderly couple on the other side, and he sat upright, hands on his knees, looking out towards the sea as if he was ill at ease and should not be there. His head was tilted forward as if against a wind—which, in a sense, it was. For the tips of his white hair were caught by a breeze and fell across his forehead. His face was long and thin, his nose a little hooked, his skin pale-brown and sallow, without a trace of health in it. His eyebrows thin, his mouth open. His mac was blue, or possibly black, certainly old, and at his neck she could see an open pale shirt. She paused in hesitation, and the elderly couple looked up momentarily as if they expected her to say hello to them. He stayed still. Suddenly resolute she went up to him and said: 'Excuse me. Are you Mr MacAskill?'

His eyes lifted a little and screwed up to peer at her. He looked as if he had heard a voice from a quarter of the compass he had not reckoned on, and did not understand why it was his name that was being called.

'Mr MacAskill?' she repeated. And if her voice faltered and she looked uncertain, it was because she had not expected such an old man, or one who looked half-mad, or half-lost at least. Stonor's *father*? It didn't seem possible.

He grinned or grimaced, and half rose from the bench to greet her, but then he seemed to think again and sat back, one hand still behind him awkwardly on the seat from which he had intended to lever himself up.

'Yes,' he said—and it might have been a question and it might have been an answer, but whatever it was, it expressed surprise, as if he suspected Judith must have the wrong man.

'I'm a friend of Jim's. And Mrs Frewin said I might find you here.'

The fact that she was Jim's friend, which had had such a telling impact on Albert Chandler and Mrs Frewin, had no obvious effect at all on Mr MacAskill.

He made a sort of sound of acknowledgement, similar to 'Ah' but with a touch of 'Mmm' in it, and looked out to sea. Finally he grimaced again and said, 'Of Jim's?' Then he made another sound that ended with '. . . do you?'

She looked puzzled.

'You know him, do you?' he said more clearly.

'He's at college with me in London, the art college . . .' but she paused because she found she was speaking a little loudly, and beginning to repeat things as if he was deaf or stupid or backward. It was hard to say quite what he was. The sun might have been shining on Deal all day, and on the sea and East Kent as well, but it did not seem to have favoured him with its light. He looked like a plant lost in shade and short of water. His hands were thin and pale;

his shoes black and worn, but clean. In fact, his mac was clean, but didn't look it merely because it was so old.

Suddenly, almost violently, he turned to her and – as if the good news that here, indeed, was a friend of Jim's had finally sunk in, and with pleasant effect – he sat up straight and smiled in that grimacing way, and said, 'Are you? A friend of Jim's? Well, that's interesting. Haven't heard from Jim for a long time, though Margaret got a Christmas card from him, because Mrs Frewin showed it me. What's the lad want? Money?' And he laughed, quite genuinely though rather excessively, and Judith was aware of the elderly couple looking curiously at them. So she smiled with him, and glanced at them for a moment, and they looked away, pretending they had not been looking at all.

'No,' said Judith, 'I don't think he wants your money.'

'Haven't got any,' he said, the smile fading as fast as it had come, and replaced by the grimace again, which might have been a scowl or might have been the beginnings of another laugh. 'What's he want, then?'

'Nothing. He doesn't know I'm here. It was just an impulse to come down to Deal for the day, and as he'd mentioned you, I thought it wouldn't do any harm to say hello. It was just an impulse.'

This brief and seemingly harmless explanation had a profound effect on MacAskill. His brow creased and furrowed, his mouth opened and whispered to itself, his eyes screwed and unscrewed as if struggling to see something beyond the horizon, and his hands fretted and worried at his knees. He made a sound, a groaning, half-formed sound of speech, which eventually resolved itself into the last half of some fretful thought of his own: '. . . impulse. It was just an impulse.'

She noticed then that there was a faint shake to his head, little more than a shimmer among his white hairs. Then his gaze moved away from her again and out towards the sea, and she saw that his eyes were troubled—and for the first time, as she stared at him, Judith saw an echo, some faint and distant hint that in the old, gaunt face on the seafront was another face, a younger, darker, stronger one, which she had only ever seen in a studio in a London art college and across a canteen table. The echo was not in the features so much as the gaze, as if MacAskill and Stonor, father and son, were both searching a distant horizon in the hope of catching sight of the very same thing.

As she looked she saw, too, that there was something in the fineness of the old man's blowing hair, and perhaps in the lines around the eyes, that did, after all, have a semblance of Jim Stonor.

And she wanted to sit a little closer to him and reach out her hands and touch him and say things whose importance she was still too young to know.

But it was Liam MacAskill who spoke, and not Judith.

'If you came on impulse,' he said, 'there's no much point in asking you why you came, for ye'll not know quite yet awhile.' And he shook his head slowly as if thinking about what he had said, and then, with the slightest of smiles and still gazing out to sea, he whispered, 'Well, now, I came on impulse, too, and have never yet got away to my home again. Nor never will.' And his head shook a little, leaning forward a shade, and his eyes were lost even to the far horizon, for they were seeing instead a distant, still picture from a battered archive, where the film is monochrome and the people walk funny, and the sound is long gone: Whitehall, London, 11 November 1920—Remembrance Day.

She wanted him to tell her, she wanted to hear him talk . . . and there was something about the way she sat close to him, smiling and peaceful, a woman like his mother in the photograph on a mantelpiece in childhood, that made him start to describe and experience again the images that had haunted him for so many years.

Corporal Liam MacAskill of the Highland Light Infantry! Aye, that's who he was, and no older than this young lass at his side. And as he began to talk and whisper to himself, his hand reaching out sometimes to touch her arm as if to be sure she was still there, she sensed that he would not mind if she took out her sketching things and began to draw him.

CHAPTER SIX

'All day beyond the line in a fruitless push forward, but I never saw the enemy once: only rifle fire off to the west, towards Roeselare. The noise of shelling the loudest I have yet experienced, and signals were visual. But our chaps had no trouble keeping in touch. Towards the end I got separated with a few of my fellows from the main battalion, and we came across a corporal of the Highland Light Infantry standing stock-still at the edge of a crater, badly shocked but looking towards the enemy lines. He had dropped his rifle and was filthy with mud and blood. At first we thought him injured but he was not. I spoke to him myself and he told me he was "a MacAskill" and that he was "watching over the sea for the bloody Macdonalds". He seemed right enough after some tea in our trenches, and I decided against reporting the incident and told him so. He thanked me as if I was a War Lord himself and not another soul as liable to break as he himself. God knows, any one of us could lose our senses for a time like he did, and perhaps many of us have! The lice are already back with most of us . . .'

—From *Mons Ypres and the Somme:* an unpublished war diary of Lieutenant (later Lieutenant-Colonel) H. C. Fleck, MC, DSO, in the archives of the Imperial War Museum, London.

March 1919

THE white cliffs of Dover are not so white on a grimy day when an oily sea heaves and sways the ship, and the months of waiting, first in Belgium and then in France, ever since November 1918, when the war was meant to have finished, are drawing to their last few moments. And your eyes are puckered with tiredness and you lean with your mates on a wet hand-rail just to see the cliffs through the drizzle and join in the cheer. At last.

London. Money in a grey-flannel trouser pocket. A good malt whisky and dreadful laughter in the night with a mate and a girl whose suspenders were pink, whose hair smelt of fish and chips, and whose thighs were bigger, wider, so much bigger than your own. She took the money first, outside a doorway darker than a dug-out, and said she didn't want her hair-do crushed, and he was hardly finished but she was off the bed and wiping herself clean of him, and he felt grubby yet just wanted to sleep in the warmth of where they'd so briefly been. He was just twenty-two.

108

Trains and changing stations and a final goodbye to a man called Ross he never saw again, but whose last smile, as the train left, was the only one he could ever remember again of the hundreds, the thousands, on the file on file of faces he had seen, and whose tired, blank eyes and grimy, unshaved cheeks were his own.

He woke reluctantly for a hundred-thousandth time, dragged up from dark sleep, and found himself alone in a carriage, staring out at a wasteland of moor at dawn. Wraiths of mist ran on a blustering wind and slid untidily around the rocks of the hillocks the train pulled by. In a lochan near the line, four tufted duck bobbed against chilly wavelets as he reached out an automatic hand to check that his kitbag was safe, the canvas marked in black: Cpl L. H. MacAskill, HLI.

Three of the tufted duck were black with sharp white sides: males. The other was browner and duller: a female. Occasionally one or other of them turned sideways on to the wind to peck at something on the surface of the lochan, and the wind caught the longer feathers at the back of its head and pushed them sideways and forward so they looked raggedy. Many a time he had hidden among the long grass by the side of Loch Fada, north of Portree, while his father and uncle cut peat, and watched the tufties bobbing on the water and seen a heron he had disturbed earlier, now standing over on the far shore. The sight of the tufties made him feel he was getting nearer home, so why did he still feel so numb and lost, and why did his eyes watch them so blankly?

The train was moving very hesitantly, as if frightened that the moor around it would swallow it up, and MacAskill swayed very gently back and forth on the slatted wooden seat. He looked right and left out of the compartment windows watching the rusty brown shapes of the moorland and the grey slivers of silver lochan with black edges of peat around them. He observed these images through the frames of the windows as if they were two cinematographs on either side of him, and in colour, at that. He could not engage himself with the landscape and felt he was quite alone, and that the compartment he was in, which had no corridor or means of escape until the train reached a station, was all by itself in the moorland space without engine in front or other carriages behind. He was in a cell, moving across a landscape, and it was not his own world he saw. Tufties, cloud, the mist on distant rock, the remnants of a bank of bog asphodel in some water by the track . . . were all sepia pictures from the past. He was numb.

But not yet lost. As he sat unresponsive, watching the desolate landscape of Rannoch Moor slide by, and with his eyes on the middle distance of rocky knolls and brown, faded heather, he saw a hint of a movement, the flexing of a wing, that had him sitting suddenly straight up with his heart pounding, and then moving forward to pull at the strap of the window and drop it down with a thump and to lean out and search more closely . . . The train swayed slightly back and forth, its wheels creaking on the tracks below, and he stared and stared out at the heather-bound rocks, until the spot where he thought he had seen it had dropped away behind him, and he felt tired again and slumped back hopelessly on to the seat, staring.

Then he saw it through the window, black as night in the sky. A golden eagle. A sleark, as his father had once jokingly referred to it in a story he told. And it was not sliding away beneath the horizon, or distant in the clouds, but soaring along parallel with the train, its head turning towards him, its wings so large and beautifully flexed in the wind that, Oh Lord, he wanted to lean out into the sky and touch it. He went to his kitbag and took out the binoculars he had kept by him throughout the war, and standing with his thigh to the door frame for stability, turned the binoculars on the sleark and framed it in their circle, the dark browns of its back, the yellowing of its beak, the trailing of its talons all quite clear as it looked sometimes over towards the train, and sometimes down at the ground beneath it for food.

There Liam MacAskill might have stayed until the sleark veered left and he lost view of it, but there was such freedom in its flight, and it gave him such a sense of its power, that when he saw that some of its tail feathers were still pale and he realised that it was hardly more than a juvenile, like himself, the pain and suffering that had been so deep inside him and which he had controlled so long, began to well up and surface. The line of his mouth became uncertain, he began to see less clearly, and his breathing came faster and ever more gulping, and knowing that he was quite alone, quite unseen, and there were no chums to think of, or father to disapprove of him giving way, he gave way. His hands with the binoculars dropped slowly from his terrible, troubled eyes, his gaze lost its focus, a gulping and gasping came to his mouth and he turned from the lost freedom of the eagle into the greyness of the carriage, and putting the binoculars on the seat in front of him, his legs gave way to kneeling and he began to weep. And for lack of any human being to hold on to, who might have put their arms around him and whisper the words of love and reassurance he so needed to hear, he put his arms around his own kitbag, his forehead puckering into its hardness, his tears and mouth wet against the black lettering of his own name.

While the image that came before him, and through whose terrible sequences he travelled with his tears, was not of anything he had seen in his years with the army, but was something he should have cried over long, long before, but which he had let stay silent and explosive in his heart.

He had been thirteen or fourteen, and being a MacAskill and his cousin having sheep over by Loch Brittle, he got to know Rubh' an Dùnain where the ruins of the MacAskill stronghold lay—as desolate as any peninsula on Skye until a boy gets to know the way the rocks run, and to know where the driftwood will be and the sun hangs warm on a summer's day. There, all by himself, over past An Sgùman to the seaward side of the Cnoc Leathan, among the remnant birch and confusing cliffs, he watched the last sea eagle nest. He knew it was the last because his cousin said so, and told him to leave them be. 'It was their land before it became ours or the Great Sheep's,' he had said.

Others saw them but only *he* knew where they set talon to ground and made an eyrie secret as two lovers' smiles. He was young and tousled, and no more noticeable than an individual rock or a stand of heather on an island slope. He saw them, the male and female, and watched them circle one on one and up out of sight, and saw them mate down by the sea. Once, just once, he crept near enough to look right into the nest of the eyrie and see two great round white eggs, bigger than his hands. February, to March, to April, through storm and sun, through drizzle and racing rain, he said he was out with his cousin; and his cousin smiled and stayed silent, for he knew there were times ahead when the laddie would work hard, so let him be now with his games over Rubh' an Dùnain.

When one of the eggs hatched, he was lost in wonder at the comings and goings as their wings beat back and forth with food and sticks for the nest. And their flight took them out over Loch Scavaig, and round towards Loch na Cuilce, and up between the magic falls of Loch Coruisk, where deer ran and sleark kept their distance over the heights of the Black Cuillins. The sea eagles made their ground seem magical to him.

One day, at school, when Donald Munro was taunting him about something, he said he had a secret, better than all they had, but he wasn't going to tell. But Donald made him, and cunning Alec Nicolson found out, and *his* father knew what the information was worth to the laird's factor, Mr Creag. They had gone to his own father, who said, what they said, that the sea eagle got lambs and was a pest and had all but gone, and would go anyway. Better

111

clean and neat than trapped or poisoned, eh, lad? He nodded his head because he had no words to express why they were wrong, for how can a child express beauty and love when all he's done is be part of it and has never watched it from a distance like an adult does?

So he led them out over his ground, with only his cousin to understand it was wrong, and crept along the slippery scree and took them to where they could see. But they didn't see, not as he had, because their time did not run like the wind through heather and grass, or dally with the swirls of clear water in the rock pool of a burn; but rather it ticked away like a chronometer, and was caught in the godly, marbled march of the minister's clock on the mantelpiece.

Sudden as a splinter under your nail, Mr Creag, the factor, raised his gun and fired, and the male fell, hardly fluttering on to the scree below. Then, slow and certain, Mr Creag climbed down to the sacred nest which Liam knew he had profaned, and the female rose threateningly, before soaring away and above to watch fearlessly from the sky as a shot missed her. Mr Creag went to the nest where a young juvenile hissed and shook its puny wings. Its threat failing, it laid its neck on the white sticks in the eternal gesture of submission, and Mr Creag picked it up and broke it in his hands, and gave it to a bailiff to have stuffed as a souvenir.

'You're a good lad,' Mr Creag said to Liam MacAskill, but Liam stood stock-still and staring, white and shocked by what he had done. And only one thing gave him any hope on that day: an older juvenile – the first that had been hatched, and which had been coming near to flight in the last few days – was not there, and there was none of them seemed to know it except his cousin, who was staring at him and willing him to silence. And he looked up from the empty nest and out across Soay Sound towards Loch Scavaig, and prayed so hard that it was like writing black ink on the sky, that the other juvenile would stay away, because it carried in its frail wings his only hope.

'You shouldn't blame yourself, Liam,' said the minister later, uncomprehending, and his black clock ticking. 'It was inevitable they should go. Killed a lot of sheep in their time, attacked a lot of lambs—and weren't lambs the symbol of Christ's work? Eh? Well, then?' and a yellow-toothed smile.

While the laird himself, to mark the occasion when the last breeding sea eagle on Skye was shot, had the bright idea of sending the wee laddie a gift, and it was Mr Creag himself who brought it, calling on Liam's father and then summoning him to the front room. A bright new pair of German-made binoculars. He took them very willingly, though feeling black deep down; yet he couldn't wait to show them to his schoolmates and see the look on the face of Donald Munro. But it was years before he ever went anywhere near Rubh' an Dùnain again, or wandered along the cliffs to Cnoc Leathan.

And it was years after that he put those same binoculars on the wooden-slatted seat of a train lost across Rannoch Moor, and went on his knees to cry at last for the pain of what he had done.

They said back at home on Skye Liam MacAskill was touched by the war like so many others had been; and some even went so far as to suggest that it might have been better if more had been taken, for all the good they were now, mooning about and thinking things nobody needed to hear—memories, like him crouched and waiting, somewhere in Belgium, looking past his men to the others on the road, all waiting, and his own breath a whimper which he himself could not hear because of the noise of barrage.

Down the road there was a movement and an arm raised in signal, an officer's watch ticked and moved, and a whistle was blown, but no one among MacAskill's party heard it. But the signal was clear enough, and he was up automatically, leading, if it could ever have been called that. And they were all up, with hands grasped on their rifles, and the verge of the road above them nearer and bobbing towards them as their boots stuck hard into the earth and muddied grass, and their left hands grabbed what they could to lever them up and forward into the stark air of exposure. A long line of men suddenly on an horizon, one of them already falling before all of them were over the top.

Minutes were hours, and yet hours were seconds, as time cartwheeled with them across the battered, slimy, chalky plain; and they watched ahead for craters filled with water and mud, and their feet slipped and felt heavy. And you noticed the bend in a stray strand of Jerry barbed wire and heard the scream and flunk of shells, and something spattered mud on your cheek.

A banging flash and MacAskill found himself blank-minded and standing near the torn-off head and left shoulder and arm of a man that might once have been Aonas MacEachlan, moments before. He could see the ear, perfect, and the hair still brushed and greased above it just as Aonas had brushed it that morning. But an inch beyond, the hair melted into red flesh and white skull, and that melted into mud. The neck became a confusion of red rag; the arm, the torso, the legs and feet had all gone. There was no rifle. The left hand was there, on the ground by the part-of-head. It was Aonas MacEachlan, who had come from Uist – where once he had gutted

113

fish, and had sung the songs of his mother Mary – to look like he did now.

Not a scratch or a mark on MacAskill's body, though, but the blast of the shell had stopped his hearing, so that he stood in a world of violent silent lights, watching ahead of him a stage or canvas where figures, not men, could be seen, and black smoke and dirt rose in slow explosions, while over to the right he saw Donald Wilson go down slowly, as untidy as a heron landing. There was a German dead in the crater to the left, grey uniform and grey hanging-open face. Liam let his rifle slip out of his hands and into the mud, though he would have to clean it extra special for doing that, but he didnae wanna be bothered wi' a gun right now, when the sea beyond the black smoke was smoothing and the MacDonald men might come. Not far though they wouldna. There's an eagle, but don't you tell a soul, and her wings are black and fierce out of the smoke and fire, and her head is raised and staring in the sky, her eyes yellow and bright through the smoke and swirling mist in front, and her talons massive over the ground, and she'll take the MacDonalds and she'll take the MacAskills, because they're all there down in the mud where they're struggling.

He stared up into the great eagle's eyes, yellow changing to red now, and his legs started to shake a little because his hearing was coming back and he could begin to hear the terrible sounds of battle again. Her black wings were massive across the sky, and she was neither sea eagle nor sleark, but all-eagle and, please, could she take him and leave the bloody MacDonalds to their own kind of death . . .

He was as weak as a nestling in a high eyrie, but no rough boot crunched over the scree towards him, no rough hands came down out of the sky to break him. Just a gentle hand at his shoulder and a distant mouth speaking words he could hardly hear yet.

'Come on then. You're all right, mate. Come on, chummie . . . it'll be a bit safer if you come with us . . .' And he understood the bravery of the soldier who stood there so patiently, and then bent down to pick up his muddy rifle, when the best thing to do would have been to run like hell out of it.

'Come on, mate.' He was led back to his own lines and the gentle touch on his arm again . . . as he left the black eagle wings to fold and writhe across the sky, and ceased to look into the staring eyes of fire. So a year passed by.

The Government announced that on 11 November, the year of 1920, they would be burying an unknown British warrior in Westminster Abbey, along with kings and queens and poets. Why, the dead warrior might be any one of the men he had known: a Scot, a Skye-man. He might have been one of Liam's mates, killed at his side in the war. Aonas MacEachlan or Donald Wilson, or one of those men who had reached out a hand to him, to help him, though they spoke with an English accent. Surely it would be one of them. Whatever anyone said or did, he would go—not that anyone said anything much, least of all his mother who stood bareheaded to the wind in Portree habour when the boat left, with him on it at the rail, and took on to herself a dark look of loss as if it was a coat she had expected to wear, as so many of her kind had done.

But it was not the sight of his mother that he finally recalled as his last memory of Skye, but of the Black Cuillins rising into their bleak and inaccessible peaks from out of the very heart of his homeland, black against the grey clouds that settled over the island on 9 November 1920. He already knew that he would never come back.

Judith suddenly felt a little chilly, and dug into her basket for the white cardigan she had brought along. Stonor's father had fallen silent for a while, staring out to sea, but his hand rested on the bench between them, where it had slipped gently after he had once more reached out and touched her. Her sketch-pad now lay on her knees, the pencil loose in her hand. The couple in the shelter when she had first arrived were long gone, and the sun was beginning to fade a little, its rays softening behind them to the west, and the shadow of the shelter, which had skirted their feet when she first arrived, had now shifted all the way to the sea-wall and over it. The tide was most of the way out, and the few sunbathers had migrated down the beach in its wake, for the sea-wall threw a shadow on the beach and it was chillsome there for old folk. In the last half hour most of the bathers had gone.

MacAskill sat very still, his head bent and his shoulders a little slumped, and Judith noticed that his chest hardly moved when he breathed. His mouth was a little open and he looked frail and hurt. Involuntarily she reached out her hand to his and touched him for a moment as if to remind him he was not alone, and that someone cared. She did it quite without embarrassment for she felt a strength in herself she had not felt before, and she knew it was all right to touch him—much more than that, it was *right* to.

He looked slowly round at her, his eyes no longer so blank and staring as when she had first seen them, but softer and younger, though bound by the lines and darkness of approaching old age.

She smiled gently, wondering why she wanted to do more, to hold him, and yet not knowing how to start.

'How old are you, lass?' he asked.

'Twenty-two,' she said.

'Ye're a fine girl,' he said, 'to listen to an old man as ye've done.'

'What was it like, the Remembrance Day you went to?'

'It was . . .' But his voice cracked and he could not finish, and it was all he could do not to have his face break up and start weeping, but he didn't want to in front of the lass. So he looked again out to sea and tried to tell her what it was like, and why it had made him come to Deal. Though how could her generation, born only at the end of the Second – and infinitely different – World War, ever know?

He had finally reached Glasgow station at midday on 10 November, and immediately went to buy a ticket to London. There were queues, silent and sombrely dressed—and mainly women. So silent was the crowd, so still. A sense of shared purpose. An occasion when you could hear the long dresses of some women rustling on the station platform as they slowly turned.

He got a ticket finally for a train that would get him to London overnight, reaching Euston Station in good time to get across the city and be somewhere near the Cenotaph or Abbey by nine o'clock to watch the funeral procession. Meanwhile he had time to kill, for the great black clock in the station showed that it was not yet 3.30.

There was a sudden and special hush among the many who, like himself, were waiting for trains to London, and who had read the official schedule for the return of the body of the Unknown Warrior to British shores. He might have died in the mud of Flanders, or by the bullets on the Somme. He might have been a gunner, an infantryman, a platoon sergeant or an officer: he might have been a doctor or a stretcher-bearer.

Whoever he was, wherever he came from, however he died, whatever part of the British Commonwealth he called his home, he was being returned now to its very heart: to its capital and its church, and into the hearts and remembrance of its people. So that he was all of them who died, or any individual; and the mothers and wives, sisters and brothers, and comrades who waited now in silence in stations like Glasgow or Edinburgh, Birmingham or Manchester, Plymouth or Canterbury, to travel to London to pay homage and respect, might tell themselves that he was one they had known and loved—a son, a brother, a husband, a father, a man or a boy who went to war and left behind a photograph.

Twenty-nine minutes past three, and down at Dover the sky was gun-metal grey and the sea deathly calm. The British Destroyer *Verdun*, chosen because of her association with the battle of 1916 in which 700,000 men fell on a Front extending only fifteen miles, came out of the mist over the Channel and into the eastern entrance of Dover harbour. Not the western entrance, where the passenger ships go through, but the smaller, eastern entrance, in memory of the hospital ships and carriers of the dead which always used that access. As the *Verdun* approached in silence, there was a nineteen-gun salute from the ramparts of Dover Castle, high on the chalk cliffs above. Watchers from the shore said she seemed almost a ghost ship, for no one walked or moved on deck; all had been ordered below. Except the two men who took over the ropes and tied her at last to the dock-side.

The coffin was brought ashore draped in a Union Jack, and four men stood guard over it for one and a half hours. Then six bearers took it aboard a special single-coach funeral train, each a warrant officer from one of the main services; each had seen much action in the war, and each might just as well have become the man they carried. As the train left the dock-side station, the only sound over Dover was the sound of gulls on the cliffs, calling and wheeling in the grey light of November.

One officer and fifteen men travelled on the train with the Unknown Warrior to Victoria Station, and all along its route men and women stood, and mothers took their children from play and held them up in their arms as the train went by, saying: 'Look. Remember. It is the train of the Unknown Warrior.' And women stood who had no children now, for they had been lost forever to them on the fields where the warrior himself had walked, and rested and fought. Folkestone, Ashford, Pluckley and a distant farm; Headcorn and the string of harvested hopfields; Paddock Wood and orchards whose fruit had long been picked. On to Tonbridge and Hildenborough, where a minister and members of his congregation stood in silence on the station platform as the train rumbled by, through the evening dark, only the white petals of the flowers at the windows of the single carriage where the body lay, reflecting light—lilies, laurels, palms, and roses, and white chrysanthemums. Then by slow and solemn degree to Victoria, where a crowd of officials and soldiers, bowler hats and peaked military caps, bent heads and grey hair, waited for the train to stop, as its grey steam billowed and buffeted among the arc-lamps, and died in the silence of its vaulted ceiling. And there—a coffin amidst flowers, and a train among the people – the silence and stillness in the capital began, as the long wake throughout the night began.

Metal on racing metal, wheel after metal wheel, the trains ran down the spokes of Britain towards the capital throughout the night of 10 November. If people talked, it was softly and in peace; if people stayed in silence, it was deep and uninterrupted. Some, a mum and dad, a father and son, went together for comfort and support; but many travelled alone, as Liam MacAskill did. And though many other ex-soldiers were also dressed in civilian clothes, it was not so very hard to tell which were the soldiers, and which the relatives. The soldiers were so young, yet so prematurely old. They had about their eyes a look of suffering seen and horrors committed; their eyes would never quite be able to catch again the innocence that once was theirs.

MacAskill had learnt enough about travel to bring his own food, and for a blanket at night he used the thick dark tweed coat his father had given him, sitting still and only half asleep with one shoulder the prop for an old woman, the other propped against an old man.

If the hush of the previous evening at Glasgow Station had been real, at Euston on the morning of the 11th it was deep and almost tangible. People looked into each other's eyes and understood. Mothers were helped along, and young men gave place to old; the healthy gave way to the maimed. A bus-conductor wore a black armband. A ticket-collector told a couple not to worry that they couldn't find their ticket—'Go on, my love,' he said, 'and you, sir.'

By ten past eight, MacAskill had made his way to Trafalgar Square, and might have pressed on down into Whitehall but that the crowd was already so thick that they had closed the barriers. But he could just see the draped flags over the tall Cenotaph opposite Downing Street, and beyond that the turrets of the Houses of Parliament.

MacAskill was then twenty-two, a young man who had been hurt by the war, one of hundreds of thousands, perhaps of millions, who bore no visible scars but carried other wounds—some shadow of which he would pass on to his children and to those, like Judith Shure, whom he touched for a moment with his heart.

What did he tell her? What could he remember of that day which changed his life—if a single day can ever change a life? Odd moments. Big Ben striking nine in the morning, and only forty minutes to go before the start of the procession. Officials walking in the empty streets beyond the crowds, solemn and with umbrellas furled. Patient policemen. A flag at half-mast over the National Gallery.

Then ten o'clock struck, and out of sight the cortège was on its slow, impressive way to Hyde Park Corner and Wellington Arch.

The sky cleared and the air grew light, and the day developed into as perfect a November's winter day as there ever was. The crowds strained to see past Admiralty Arch, down the Mall, as the slow and distant beat of drums came through to them, and they stood even more silent.

So slow to come, so swift to pass by. Ranks of slow-marching feet in boots, the clip-clop of the black horses, and there between the four great, shining wheels of a gun-carriage lay the coffin, with the famous Padre's Flag, stained at Vimy Ridge, Bully Grenay, Hill 60 of the Ypres Salient, the Messines Ridge, Cambrai, Béthune and Epernay; with the blood of men it had seen to burial, woven with the frail sound of men's prayers before battle, touched by the sacrament of the faithful, revered by men with nothing left but hope that other men might die but them; folded and kept, hidden and touched, shaken out and torn by the spikes of war—here now, in front of Liam MacAskill, drawn past in a moment when all else faded away, a flag draped over the coffin of a man perhaps like him. Involuntarily he whispered a Gaelic prayer as the gun-carriage went slowly by.

There was a deep hush as it turned to enter Whitehall and then started its slow progress down to the Cenotaph where King George V and Prime Minister David Lloyd-George waited in silence, and Queen Mary watched from the window of one of the Government buildings.

The procession stopped at the monument, and only the occasional sound of the metalled hoof of one restless horse on the street broke the silence. All the way down to Parliament Square, all the way up to Trafalgar Square, men and women stood still as prayers were said under the Cenotaph, where the gun-carriage had been pulled abreast of that monument hung with the folds of great Union Jacks. Of all the thousands who watched, only one man – it was said later – kept his hat on; and if many people noticed, most must have understood that it was not from disrespect but from forgetfulness in the moments of silence, remembering. 10.37.

Then a cord was pulled and MacAskill saw the great flags on the distant Cenotaph begin to slide and billow and tumble, and it seemed that the monument rose up from them into light whiteness of sky as they continued their descent down to the street. He wanted to travel up with the monument, up and over the buildings, up and beyond them into the sky, where the air was light and the blue so deep, and the cold as pure as any man or woman could ever know. A sob, and somewhere behind him in Trafalgar Square a terrible, terrible cry; one woman's grief and the same sense of helplessness that he had so often felt in the sight of terrible injury and fearsome death.

The gun–carriage moved on, the King and Prime Minister and soldiers and generals behind, and then others, more and more of them, as the procession continued the final few hundred yards to its destination: the western entrance to Westminster Abbey, where the Dean and his attendants waited for the final ritual and burial. At the ancient arched entrance a shadow fell, and slowly, so gently, they came with the coffin on their shoulders, bareheaded old men of state or war who might have found it hard to converse with the man whose body they now carried, had he once walked their way. For he might have had an accent or brogue they would find hard to understand; and he might have had a manner they would call rude; and he might have found it hard to say quite what it was which he was now becoming the symbol of in so many different hearts. The organ sounded and the words he would have known, dear Lord, dear God, rang out: *'Oh God Our Help in Ages Past.'* Prayers, ritual, words to God, and the Abbey's space of vaulted ceilings and lengthy floors and serried seats, and faces hung so quiet that the precentor's voice could be heard in its every part. Then the words of the reading from Revelations: *'For the Lamb which is in the midst of the throne shall feed them and shall lead them unto living fountains of waters; and God shall wipe away all the tears from their eyes'*.

Their eyes, the people's eyes, were serious, and stared down the length of Whitehall, or Parliament Street, or across Parliament Square, to the Cenotaph and the porch of the Abbey where, one by one, men and women, wives and fathers, prepared to go in silence, then follow the way the warrior had gone, to stand for a moment at the hush of his grave in the Abbey. They went in their thousands, dark clothes and pale faces, with flowers for the Cenotaph and prayers for the grave, after waiting patiently hour by hour for admittance past the barriers. And then on to the spot where they might leave behind their own special sense of loss—and hope.

Liam MacAskill was lucky, for he was in the right place to be among the first to file past the Cenotaph, and just among those who gained admittance to the Abbey before its doors were finally closed at 8.00 pm that day.

There he filed behind a young woman with her father, both in black, and there – oh God whose help seemed ages past – he walked and stood before the flowers and the sword and the King's wreath on the grave itself: *'In proud memory of those who died unknown in the Great War. Unknown and yet well known as dying, and behold they live. George R. I. November 11, 1920'*.

And, behold, MacAskill's memory melts for a moment into another as he sees again his son Frank, the first by Margaret, so much older than Michael and Jim as to be in grey shorts and a little blue belted raincoat when war started again nineteen years later. His legs thin but brown from August sun, and holding in his hand a gas-mask they had issued as he stood on the platform at Deal, ticketed and ready to be evacuated, and laughing with a friend. They try on the gas-masks and MacAskill watches from a distance, Margaret nearer-by, and Frank stares across at him, his body that of the child, his face transformed by the heavy monster mask into that of men MacAskill had seen squatting like animals in mud trenches; and God did not wipe away all the tears from his eyes.

It was nine when he left the Abbey, and Big Ben was striking again, twelve hours since he had first arrived at the other end of Whitehall, and the change that had started when he first arrived at Dover after the war, and crept up on him in the silences and misunderstandings over the kitchen table at his parents' home in Portree, to gather force in the clouds over the black Cuillins, now finally carried him forward to make a break with his past. He walked away . . . stumbled in a daze from the Abbey, as so many others did that night, not knowing where to go. To avoid the crowd still standing in Whitehall, he turned down to Westminster Bridge, and the night grew deep and cold for him, and he slept where he found himself, taking a pullover from his case to warm his legs. He shivered, hearing the moans of another man on a seat nearby. He slept. There was no place now. Skye did not exist, his home was no more, and the sky was empty of eagles to help him. Like so many others in those days, he was lost from any place he might once have known. Morning came stiffly, and with it more crowds, and he wandered back towards Whitehall. But finding it still full of crowds of mourners defying their fatigue to gain admittance to the Unknown Warrior's grave in the Abbey, he headed back to Trafalgar Square. And there he might have stayed, but he got cold and crossed the road to a Lyons Corner House for tea. Full up, more queues. He wandered the few yards to Charing Cross Station to find the station buffet, his face pale and his heart and energy quite gone.

He queued for his tea for a while—but the queue did not move, and he stepped away and stood like others there, staring and lost. And Skye seemed lost to him. Platform one, platform two, platform three . . . His eyes followed the numbers and the destinations, and read them, hardly noticing platform six: Tonbridge, Folkestone, Dover and stations beyond to Sandwich.

It was just an impulse, that was all, but if a day can change a life, that was it. A train was scheduled to leave for Dover at 4.17 and MacAskill decided he would be on it. And so he was, and if the journey was long, and he grew more and more tired as the evening darkened and the train rattled on, yet somehow he was lighter and freer in himself. He felt no responsibility for his own home, and wished to cast himself as far from it as he could and yet still be in his own country; and Dover and stations beyond seemed as good a place as any. He did not get out at Dover, nor at Martin Hill, nor at Walmer Station. But at Deal the train stopped still for a while and he opened the window and could smell the sea in the air and it was dark outside but there were lights on, and a railwayman was sitting under a gas-light beyond a half-open door, looking out at the line and sipping tea from a metal mug which Liam recognised as army issue. He leaned forward in his seat, the train stressed, he hesitated, the train began to heave, he stood up, the train shuddered, he took his case off the rack and opened the door, a voice shouted, he climbed quickly down on to the platform and slammed the door behind him. A voice shouted, 'Close the doors and stand clear!' MacAskill stood still on the platform, a whistle blew and a green lantern waved, and the train pulled heavily past him, creaking and blowing steam and gathering speed.

Then it was gone, and he found himself in a strange town whose air smelt of the familiar sea and in whose unknown streets and along whose unfamiliar shore he would begin to search for something he had lost.

* * * * *

Cuillin hung effortlessly in the cold air, the Weir nearby, high, high over the sheer faces of the Tanahorn, the highest and most northerly tip of the Varanger in Norway, where the Weir of the sea eagles lived.

To the distant north stretched the Arctic Ocean, beneath her now, the wastes and chilly depths of the Barents Sea; to the south-east the rocky tundra of Russia spread out greyly into darkness; while to the south-west the familiar coastline up which she had flown. Only to the west and south-west did she find any sense of friendliness and lightness in the sky, because that was the only quarter in which some sense of distant sunlight remained. There, too, far, far out of sight, almost beyond imagining any more, lay her own lands of Scotland and Skye, and somewhere north of them was the fabled land of Haforn, land of ice and fire, too distant for eagles to reach unless their wings held Haforn's power. But these places were far away, and beneath her now was the rocky, frozen tundra.

'So you're surprised, are you, Fremmed? Surprised at what I

am?' The Weir pulled his wings back a little more behind himself to begin the long, slow descent to the top of the Tanahorn.

Yes, she was. The eagle she had come so far to find, and of whom she hoped so much, was indeed very different from what she had expected. She had thought he would be old and grey, slow and wise of speech, gentle and kind in his humour. But he was none of these things: he was a juvenile.

Yet he spoke like a mature, and without further ado made her a telling of how he had become the Weir, the first surprise of which was that the old eagle Finse was his father, and that Clew, her companion on the flight to the north, was his brother.

'When I was less than a year old and before Clew was born, for he came two years after I did, Finse recited the Doom of Weir with other males who still believed it important for juveniles to hear; though many of the females, including my mother, were against it, regarding it as a thing of the past.

'He took me to within sight of the Storrin and the falls, where even the strongest female flies in danger unless she has the strength of Haforn in her wings . . . Have you been near there?' And Cuillin nodded, and he saw that she understood the awesome nature of the place he described.

'There, with the thunder of Storrin in my ears and the rushing of conflicting winds down the fjords, my father Finse told me the Doom, and even as he started the first words I knew what it would be and that it was true.

'It was as if I was in the sky and set on a flight which I had flown long, long before, and whose dangers I knew and had suffered, and yet I could not quite remember it and feared I no longer had the courage to face it. Oh, I was frightened as each scene and image of the Doom unfolded, and soon I was lost in the flight of his words, the words of the Doom, and I saw the reality of the terrors that are coming for all sea eagles, and which threaten us all wherever we are. We think we are strong. We fly, and we cannot think there may be a time when our wings will be weak; we eat and we cannot believe that someday there may be no food; but, most important, we mate and brood our young, and can never, never believe that one day it may be impossible to rear young . . . We never even doubt it.

'As he recited the Doom, I lost myself in its power, as if I saw the terrible blackness coming—and it was engulfing me, so that my own father nearby could not reach out a talon and help. Even *he* could not see what I knew, what I felt was there. And I . . .' The Weir faltered and stopped for a moment, and Cuillin could feel the terror in him, as if he was taking on his wings the terror for all of them, and trying to carry it, and somehow fight it for them all. So she moved nearer to him and stretched a wing over him for a moment, and he whispered, 'Yes . . . yes . . . that's how it was. For out of that darkness and from across the unknown sea to the west, there came a fremmed, *the* Fremmed, and though she did not know who she was or what her strength was, yet she came to protect and give hope. She spoke to me and told me what I needed to know to survive. Then I grew stronger and realised that there was light beyond the horror, and I started to laugh at the danger that I had felt, and I remember Finse grew angry with me . . . until another, darker, more terrible thing came that threatened us in a way we could not understand . . .'

The Weir's voice grew higher and more chanting, and his head began to sway from side to side with his eyes half-closed, as if he could see across the darkness of the sea the images he was describing. And Cuillin herself almost fancied that in the strange light of the arctic winter she too could make out flickerings and changings of something dark and menacing . . .

'And though the Fremmed told me things I should know, I would need to know, yet I didn't listen. Then, when the second darkness came, the Fremmed was suddenly gone, and there seemed nothing left but me alone, carried along by the horror and fear of it, which I knew threatened each one of us. Feeling terribly afraid and lost, I called out for the Fremmed, but she was not there. Then I tried to remember the things she had told me, knowing too late that I needed to know them, for in them lay a clue to the future, the key to a safe passage through . . .'

He fell silent but his fear was so real, and the sense of his suffering so potent, that Cuillin herself felt frightened, and she looked up menacingly into the dark and flickering sky as if to say, 'This is the Weir that you threaten, and though I too am afraid, yet I am strong and will fight to protect him, for he carries in him so much that we need.'

The Weir started speaking again, more slowly, more clearly, almost in a whisper: 'I remember Finse's voice carrying rhythmically on and on, like the sound of rock falling down a cliff-face and echoing on after the rocks are still. It echoed and became part of the great waterfall of the Storrin, and out of his words, which were the words of the Doom, I seemed to see the form and shape of a new eagle, very powerful, who had courage and purpose, and seemed to be battling up through the waterfall itself. That is impossible, and yet there it was, great wings beating back and forth darkly through the never-ending stream of white water, and its great beak straining up and up through the torrent . . . And I felt I was there, too, and though in such terrible danger, yet so safe. And I followed behind, up through the water, the great height of the Storrin towering above us. But no sooner did I feel safe behind it than I realised that this eagle, who seemed part of the Fremmed and yet different, this eagle was growing visibly older and frailer with each great beat of its wings, and its progress through the water was slowing. And my fear came back a hundredfold, because *I* was now the one who was strong; but I did not have strength enough for the force that was against me. And the eagle before me, who had been my saviour, was suddenly dependent on *me*. It was slipping back, its feathers older and older, its beating wings frailer. While around, up, above and below, beyond the Storrin, lay the final darkness, and it was closing in on us. It was the final Doom, and I remember I shouted, "Fremmed help us, oh, help us," and then an even greater cry as I called out above the roar of the waterfall, "Haforn, oh Great One! Help us, help us!" for I knew now what the Doom was.

'There, flying out of the white waterfall, and in the icy darkness all around, were the lost ones, and they were calling for me to join them. Sometimes I could glimpse their terrible, archaic shapes, their primitive beaks and scaly wings, and their calls seemed like wails, and yet seemed enticing, for they made me want to escape from the waterfall which was at once my final enemy and my only friend. Some had misshapen beaks, others feet so heavy they would weigh you down in flight, and others had wings with no strength for the changing winds and pressures of the seaside cliffs I knew. They called out their names: *Skimir . . . Sindri . . . Tofa . . .*'

As he repeated these names Cuillin shuddered in real fear, for she understood at last what the darkness was, and who were the strange half-eagles calling out to the Weir to join them. They were the lost ones whose forms were dead and gone, but whose shadows remained cast upon every sea eagle and sleark—sometimes in the rounding of a talon, sometimes in the heavier form of a beak, or in the cast of a wing . . . They were the lost ones of legend, about whom every juvenile is told tales: how Skimir offended the sea, and he and all his race were drowned; how Sindri dared question the earth, and she and all her race were starved; how Tofa dared ignore the sun, and she was blinded with all her children, and their children and theirs after that, one by one, until they could not fly and the spiteful terns and Corvidae came and took them, and they were destroyed . . . Until only the cunning ones remained, secretly and cleverly, the ones which the sea and earth and sky could not bother with, breeding in the mountains, and lurking in the shadows— the ones who became the sleark. While from out of Sea and Earth had come Haforn, the Great One, who was stronger than the Skirnir and wiser than the Sindri and more loving than the Tofa, and from her came . . . Cuillin hardly dared think on, for if what the Weir was saying came true, then the Doom meant that all the sea eagles descended from Haforn would die and her race become extinct.

'Extinct.' The Weir whispered the word as soft as wind on a summer evening, and yet it hung over them as great as the flickering night itself, heavy as a storm to come. That was, finally, the Doom they faced.

'I felt as if I was all the sea eagles alive, and that I was being destroyed. I felt that I was the last. I felt the Doom itself upon me, and I know I cried out again and again for my father to stop, so that I could escape the darkness and the terrible waterfall. But his voice seemed to grow yet stronger, and the rhythm of the words of the Doom gripped me more firmly in its power. Then, from far beyond the darkness in which the lost ones flew and shrilled, there came a distant light—the eyes of an eagle whose form was not sleark or sea eagle, but both, and more. Its light seemed to be searching for something, and I knew its was the only way to go. For now I was carrying the older eagle in my talons, to save it from the Doom where the last ones flew, but my wings were heavy with tiredness and I was nearly lost. But I knew that if the light broke through our darkness, we would be safe. So I called out to it to guide us from where I was caught by the rushing of the waterfall and my own growing weakness. I saw the light trying to find us . . . yet sometimes fading away as if it did not want to help us after all . . .'

The Weir fell terribly silent, hunched and shivering—almost shimmering in the curious flickering dark that had settled over the sky above Tanahorn.

'Then my father ended his narration of the Doom, and I seemed forever lost in its rhythmic grip, carried forward towards something terribly dangerous for each one of us, and before which we would need all our trust and faith and courage.

'For days afterwards I did not feed, and was hardly conscious, for I was caught in a shaking rigor through which I seemed to see all the images the Doom had summoned up, and calling out for Finse to help me, or the Fremmed, or Haforn the Great One—my voice so weak and pitiful against the roar of the Storrin and the winds that ever surround it. And I heard my father murmuring over me, and others who had gathered round . . . and my own words stammering that it was true, the Doom was true, and whispering its warnings from my half-consciousness, repeating it word by word, line by line. Even as I spoke, I heard other voices muttering, "He is the Weir. He is the chosen one. Finse, your son is the Weir." And I knew that that, too, was true—but that surely no eagle was ever given such a burden when so young and afraid . . . And they marvelled that I remembered all the ancient words of the Doom after hearing them only once. They did not know that I had *lived* them and *felt* each one of them.'

Afterwards, Cuillin was never sure whether the Weir told her this story in one telling or in many, for she lost all sense of time in the arctic night, where the cliffs and tundra, wastes and sea seemed covered in pale grey electric light or shadows, and few creatures roamed.

Sometimes she was aware of the Weir's need of her presence, at other periods, lasting days or even weeks, she barely saw him move from some meditative stance he had taken, seeming not to wish her near him.

Until the days began to lighten, the ice on the sea beneath the cliffs to whiten with some struggling, unseen sun. Winter was going, and spring was on the way.

'You will leave me soon,' he said then. 'And you will teach the eagles of Romsdal what you can, however reluctant they may be to learn it. Teach them to trust in Haforn. Teach them to fly true.'

'But I cannot fly true myself,' she whispered, 'so how can I teach others?'

'Watch,' he said gently. 'Watch and remember . . .'

Then he leaned over the edge of the Tanahorn and into the void, and the grey light of the cliffs and ice about them seemed to catch at his wings and lift them, and he flew a flight for her that seemed to carry in its great harmony the line of the horizon, the run of the clouds and the rise of a new sun; while in its circles and falls it seemed to echo the coming of spring, the rising of summer, and the decline into autumn before the dark fall into winter.

He flew no more as a juvenile, but as a mature who had wintered into age, and whose flight could forever hover between the joy and the suffering in life and the search for true flight.

'Remember that all eagles may fly true, Cuillin, for each has that power in their wings, however slight or weak or clumsy they may seem. Trust Haforn, and trust me, for we will be there when we are needed, at those moments when courage or hope may falter into fear and despair. So return to your friends now, and teach them to trust . . .'

And the sky itself over the Tanahorn seemed to be enchanted with the wings of the Weir, so that he himself was gone and only the spirit of him was there with her, and the wind whispered at the rocks and dwarf birch at her feet, saying, 'Remember, Cuillin, and trust. And fly now—for Haforn's grace is in your wings.'

Then, as the grey skies cleared and a brighter spring day rose up, she found the strength to say farewell, and raise her wings into the wind and gyre out above the great Tanahorn, before she turned back south to start the creation of a dream that would give them something to fight for when the Doom came at last.

* * * * *

The sun was low, and sinking lower, when Judith Shure finally closed her sketch-pad and laid it, with charcoal and pencil, in the open basket to her right. On her left sat Liam MacAskill, who had told her about how it was he had come to live in Deal, and having asked her if his son Jim had ever mentioned eagles, recounted to her a story, at times only half coherent, which he said he might have told Jim himself, had he been there.

In the last hour, as the sun's bright light had melted into a warm, orange-yellow, people had come up from the beach to go home. Some wearing just bathing trunks, others carrying their towels and wet costumes in baskets, and dressed again in their summer clothes. Their faces showed the warm health of a little too much sun, and the wrinkles round their eyes were more prominent for being paler than the skin that had caught the sun's full glare. Even the children moved quietly, and it seemed that, as Liam MacAskill finished talking, the very last of these beach people went slowly past them, and they were alone.

A tanker out at sea was faded orange in the evening sun; the sea stretching out to it was flat and calm. Over to their right the piles of the pier caught evening light on one side, so that they appeared black and green in the shadow, orange in the light. And the water out to the pier took on a curious luminous green where it lapped quietly at the shore-line, far down the pebbly beach at the low-tide mark.

Indeed, the tide was so far out that here and there great chunks of concrete and brick stuck out of the calm water, covered in limpets and barnacles. They were blocks of masonry from a building that had once stood on the seafront, and had been blown up in the fifties because it was a danger to the children who climbed up to play on it. Off to their left a great, round, rusting iron drainage pipe exposed by low tide emerged from the shingle and ran into the sea, where suddenly it stopped—sheared off and left useless by a gale. Thereafter they had to take the sewage another way, and processed it now on the marshes adjacent to the Dunes. But the great pipe remained and kids liked to play on it, walking down its slippery, curving length and out over the waves. A little boy did that now, and when he got to the end he lay down and looked back up into its mysterious darkness. Then he called out a muffled 'Hello!' which echoed and boomed up to where they were sitting.

Liam MacAskill sighed, unusually calm and at ease with himself. If he had been less tired he would have talked some more—as he had really only just begun. He looked shyly round at Judith and wondered quite what it was about her that made him talk so much. She was a well-made lass, and one of Jimmy's friends. So young she was, and yet when, right at the beginning, she had stretched out her hand and touched his arm, she had felt so strong to him, so solid, that . . . well, she couldn't have known he was close to tears. Margaret never liked that—a man crying. But strangely enough, Margaret had sometimes sketched him as this girl had done, sketched him when he was talking. And for a moment his lips parted to say Margaret's name, and talk a bit about all that—but he stopped. Too tired. Time to go. Not sure what to say to the lass.

It was Judith who got up first, to take leave of the old man—who wasn't quite so old that she felt she could suggest without embarrassment that she see him home. She felt her time in Deal was over for now, and she wanted to go back and sit quietly on the train and look at her sketches and think of what Jim Stonor's father had been saying.

He looked up at her with as much of a smile as his caught and tortured face could manage, and he started to mumble something or other by way of saying that he had enjoyed meeting her, and please forgive him if he didn't get up quite so fast as he used to. But her smile was so genuine and warm that he felt he had no need to say more, and he couldn't have managed it anyway because she involuntarily bent down and kissed him where the wind had been blowing his hair. And all he could do was sit there and look blindly out to sea, and wonder why her young kiss was still with him long after she had gone off down the promenade back towards the station; and why tears came to his eyes now she was gone; and why he suddenly had a mental picture of his mother standing on the harbour at Portree, a picture that had troubled him for nearly fifty years. For he thought to himself that it would not have been so hard for him to kiss his mother gently then, as Jim's girl had just kissed him. It would have given his mother such pleasure. So why hadn't he?

The little boy who had been playing on the beach came up the concrete steps by the shelter, holding three pebbles. Ignoring Liam MacAskill, he threw them one by one high into the air, and they fell in a great arc down towards the sewage pipe. One of them hit it, and the sharp crack died out in an echo.

The boy turned and ran down the promenade the same way Judith had gone. MacAskill gazed after him, and then beyond, to see Judith, but she had gone. The boy ran on, and MacAskill, wiping his eyes, slowly got up and turned to follow them.

CHAPTER SEVEN

'You could do a PhD on Stonor's *Portrait of Miss Campbell*—in fact
one of you American art historians probably will. I think it's one of his
most interesting "early major" works. I have personal cause to remember it being made, because he suddenly walked out of the flat
we were sharing after announcing he had his own studio – in fact a
seedy little basement room with bad lighting – and started work on
it. Not many people realise that the dark background, serrated at the
left-hand edge, is in fact a sea eagle's wing. Protective or threatening?
Ask Jim! Bits of it don't work, and I suspect that if Judith Shure hadn't
stepped in and rescued it, he would have left it to rot in my flat. I
sometimes shudder to think what works have been lost to the world
in damp basements and leaky attics . . . Rembrandts, Picassos . . .'

> —Gerald Opie, Chairman, Royal Arts Commission, in conver-
> sation with Marion Poyser for an article published in *Art in
> America*, 1994.

Spring 1968

FOR nearly two years after finishing their time at the London
School, Jim Stonor and Gerald Opie shared a flat in Camden
Town. Gerald took a job teaching art on a part-time basis at a
college of further education, while Jim began to make good money
working freelance for a couple of advertising agencies. Together
they ran art classes at the Camden Town Adult Education Institute.
Good times, irresponsible times, times when they bought a car
together – an old Morris Minor – and times when Jim began to see
the realities that lay beyond his dreams of being an artist: hawking
portfolios around West End galleries, fighting the fact that it was
easier to make money working for an advertising agency to strict
and generally uncreative briefs, than by selling original work.

The only thing that Jim held on to was his habit of sketching and
drawing wherever he went, whatever he did. Inverness Street
market, the Greek restaurant where they often had supper, the
cinema, Regent's Park . . . he would make images of them almost
compulsively. The oil painting he had done at college he gave up;
but he did continue water-colours as an adjunct to his drawing,
perfecting his technique but resisting all Gerald's entreaties for him
to make a serious attempt to show his work.

'It's a dead medium these days, Gerald, even if I *could* sell them and make a few bob with a show in the public library or something. It's not what I want to achieve seriously . . .'

But what *that* was, he did not seem to know.

But in the January of 1968 it all changed for Jim. The endless parties, the different girlfriends, the jokes and drinking, the occasional pot, the never-ending untidiness of the flat reached into him and depressed him.

He began to talk morosely of finding a studio better than his bedroom and borrowed premises, and doing some 'real' work. He grew unsettled, and Gerald's good humour, which had once cheered him, now seemed to touch only a raw spot.

Then Gerald let one of the old School students, David Farrell, move into the sitting-room, and space became even more cramped, and their relationship deteriorated even more. An era was ending. They were all growing up and beginning to need their own space, and to live in their own way.

It was about then that something occurred that gave Stonor the impetus to make the change that had been building up inside him.

It was during a life class he had organised for his evening-class group. He noticed that one of the students, a young Scots girl who drew in a tense, hard line, was visibly upset at the sight of the naked model. The girl, Janet Campbell, seemed scarcely able to draw her, and at the break time was unwilling even to go off with the others for a cup of tea.

The model's body had shocked Miss Campbell. The whole thing had shocked her, the more so because she had missed the previous session, when the life class was announced. For it was not a normal part of the course, but Harry Ginnan had taught Jim that good teachers occasionally surprised their pupils.

So, for Miss Campbell, the model had appeared like a sudden nightmare, completely unexpected, in a class in which she expected to draw nice things, safe things. The girl had sat down, taken off her jacket, got herself ready, looked up towards the end of the studio, and a woman, old and tired with unkempt hair, had stepped out from behind a screen wearing a creased silk dressing-gown. And before Miss Campbell could catch her breath, she had taken it off and stood for a moment of stillness naked before them, with gaunt thighs and breasts that seemed to hang asymmetrically, one a little higher than the other, and with nipples and aureoles which were stretched and haggard. There was a white scar on her stomach, and when she sat down the flab on her bottom squashed out sideways beyond the bony knees. The model, quite unaffected by the horror that she was (as it seemed to Miss Campbell), moved

132

around to find a position and opened her legs quite naturally so that she showed all of . . . well . . . it was horrible.

But Miss Campbell's horror went deeper than merely the full-frontal fact of what a body looks like. For she sensed what Stonor knew: that the model was poor, needed money, had problems, and was a vessel used and broken, a woman discarded. She did not know, as Stonor did, that these sessions not merely earned her money but gave her a time to sit and think, and to be still in a way so very few of the people who drew her ever were. Nor could Miss Campbell conceive that she took professional pride in doing the job well.

The fact was that Miss Campbell had seldom really looked at her own body, and it was therefore a shock to be shown one so unlike what she might have imagined of herself, or any woman. It wasn't a body a man would want. It was not a body she could bear to have herself, though the dear Lord and sweet Mother Mary knew that Miss Campbell had, from time to time, stood profile to a mirror and asked herself if her breasts were normal or her thighs too fat. As for her sex, or 'it', as she called it, she had never really looked at it, nor anyone's.

Of these thoughts Stonor knew little, and sensed less. But he unerringly felt her distress, for there were things that had bruised him as much, and shocked him into confronting himself. He wanted to help her in some way—but there was no way. You could not put your arms around a student, even if you thought of it. There are taboos on comforting. Yet how powerful his sense of her distress was, and how much it needed expression.

'How can you paint or draw that?' she had asked him, as these thoughts flashed through his mind.

'You don't really draw what you see,' he said at last. 'Because, if that's all you did, you would produce a technical drawing like an architect's or an engineer's, or a black-and-white photograph. Drawing is selecting things and investing your line with feeling for what you see. I don't know what you've seen of women before, or men come to that,'—Miss Campbell looked down for a moment, and then back at him—'but the model has a name, and it's Dora, and she's a friend of the best art teacher I ever had. She's a person. She's a woman. Maybe things you see in her body aren't the same as things she knows about. Models are often very relaxed about their bodies, which is why they can sit naturally for hours on end and let people dissect every muscle and bone, every shadow, every hair, every blemish. I don't think *I* could do it.'

Stonor pointed to the harsher, stronger lines in one or two places on Miss Campbell's skimpy drawing. 'Do it that way, if you like.

133

Remember that she's a person just like you or me, Miss Campbell. As a matter of fact, I think she has a rather fine body; she knows how to carry it. I've seen chocolate-box blondes with perfect figures who look ugly when they try to do what our model's doing for us . . .'

When the class started again, Stonor began to draw the model himself, and as he did so, an idea for a project began to overtake him, and an excitement not felt for months began to come back. So that in the days which followed he began to search for an image whose purpose and meaning he could not quite define . . . Its essence lay in the shock he had seen in Miss Campbell when she was confronted by a vision of what her body might become, and the despair she evidently felt at the inevitability of ageing.

But the idea did not find final form or substance until a few days later when Jim impulsively decided to visit London Zoo, in nearby Regent's Park. He had avoided it for years, not liking zoos or the caging of wildlife. He had been to the Zoo once as a child, and that had been enough.

Now, wandering around its cages, his prejudices were confirmed and he found himself unable to draw – his original intention – but merely cast into a profound gloom at the grim sight of trapped animals.

It was in this frame of mind that he found himself confronted, quite unexpectedly, with great black Victorian aviaries in which, to his horror, he saw great eagles caged.

Aquila chrysaetos, Golden Eagle . . . *Aquila heliaca*, Imperial Eagle . . . *Aquila rapax*, Steppe Eagle . . . *Haliaeetus vocifer*, African Fish Eagle . . .

They stared out into the February afternoon, unmoving, their wings heavy and useless, their tails grubby, their lot hopeless. Their great talons gripped the perches they had taken. Only one seemed to move, and that was the golden eagle – sleark – which tore at a piece of meat in its cage. Above the cages, great sycamore trees, bare of leaves, stressed and bent a little with a winter wind, a wind which not one of those eagles would ever feel upon its open wings.

Jim stood motionless as they were, staring, his face white, his eyes horrified, and then tearful. By some process of association he saw his father caged by fears and unknown experiences of the First World War, forever trapped now in a town and by a shore not his own. He saw Miss Campbell and felt again her sense of despair at time passing and age coming, these old eagles, trapped by men, staring at him. With even more haunting eyes. The Doom had taken them. It was then he had the image he must make, and then that he decided to leave Opie's flat, find a studio, and start working seriously again.

Harry Ginnan, always helpful, found him a basement studio he could afford, which, though damp, was serviceable. Stonor would have taken anything, so great was his need now to work.

He became a man possessed by an idea and an image he sought to define and trap within the confines of a canvas: an image of the fear of ageing, and of death, which sought escape in the act of flying, and failed to find it.

Spring gave way to the beginnings of summer. The student demonstrations that year, against the war in Vietnam, left him untouched. There was strident aggression in the air as his own generation began to revolt against the system that had formed them. University professors were hissed on campus, buildings occupied, conservative student bodies gave way to left-wing groups.

Alone, Stonor worked in his studio, feverishly, day after day, his small kitchen a mess, his time begrudged for anything but this work. And sometimes late at night, after another day sketching out ideas, walking down nearby Parkway desperately lonely, but unable to find the strength to knock at Gerald Opie's door, or Harry Ginnan's.

His preliminary sketches became bigger and more boldly compositional, for he had the elements now, and he pursued them with passion. He wanted to take that feeling he had sensed in Miss Campbell, and hold it up across the sky so that people could see it, and know it as sometime their own. Your body grows old, your breasts sag, your pubic hair turns grey and thin, the bottom that was ogled or fondled grows gaunt and yellow. But your spirit can still soar, it can gyre away from the body that grows tired, and it can carry the aged up into the clouds and resurrect them as the blues of a bright sky, and the clear white of distant clouds; and they can feel again the pinks and greys of a rising sun.

He began the picture impulsively one morning, the canvas ready, as it had been for weeks. He sketched lightly with a thinned-down black and a medium brush, his hand fast and sure. He knew he had most of the elements, most of the ideas; and if something was missing, as he knew it was, it would come—he knew it would come. The thinking had been done, and he wanted now to *make* it and move on. There was a smell of paint in the air, mingled only slightly with the musk of damp, and he didn't care about the bad light because he knew how to compensate for it. He just wanted to get on.

Miss Campbell . . . soon he knew her head far better than his own. There was no colour to start with, just monochrome black and grey, and some white to accentuate the forward bend of her head. But there was more than just a head; there were the vague forms of people: Mrs Frewin, Mrs Angel, Peter his childhood friend whom he had not seen for so long now, his father . . . Strange hints of people, but behind them all an eagle . . . and he grew angry, and his brush more powerful then. Colour crept in on the fourth day, in sunrise pink and a curious green behind one of the hands.

If he talked to himself, as he usually did, he barely noticed it, the sound of his voice mingling with the hum of traffic on the street above the window, or the patter of the well-dressed kids who went to the little prep school round the corner, morning there and mid-afternoon back. There was an ice-cream van over to the north in the afternoons, playing the first few bars of *Greensleeves*.

He felt powerful and vulnerable at the same time, and whispered curious things as he worked: 'Soddit! . . . raven . . . the Raven of Storr . . .' And the eagle flew in his mind, heavy on the background of the canvas, comforting or threatening, depending on his mood.

One day, unaccountably, he found himself crying by the picture, unable to continue for a while. He had seen it was part of himself he was painting, although the images were taken from other people. It was dark and black in places, lighter blue and white in others, and although he could not have drawn a whole eagle – for that would have meant showing its face and eyes, and he could not do that yet – yet there was the great shadow of its wing, or perhaps the wing itself—the final background, protector of Miss Campbell, behind her unseen and powerful. Or was it threatening?

He did not really know.

That day, on impulse, he went over to see Opie, banging on the door rather than letting himself in, and putting a great smile on his face.

'You look bloody awful,' said Opie, when he opened the door. 'Come in, you stupid bugger.' Farrell was hovering in the corridor by the kitchen, and said: 'Talk of the devil!'

Farrell had moved in for good, which was a kind of relief for Stonor who took it as a sign that a move had been due. Life had changed.

'What are you going to do when summer's over?' Jim asked Opie.

'There's a teaching job out at Hackney I got on to through a mate—you know, that technician, Sandra, at Central. Starting next term.'

'I'm getting a promotion in the agency—which means wearing

136

a collar and tie again, just like at school,' said David Farrell. 'Only temporary, mind you. I've still got art in mind. I mean, there's space to work here . . .'

But the space left in David Farrell's voice was filled with uncomfortable things which Stonor could see more clearly and feel more deeply than any of them. It was a space where hopes were raised but no images made; a space in which bored but patient girls listened to the 'interesting' things said, and their men – if men they were – smoked a little and drank a bit and put their energies into the same talking that Stonor, too, had once enjoyed.

He did not want to look into David's disappearing hopes of making things, because, now that this latest picture was so nearly finished, he seemed to have nothing left of his own hopes. He felt suddenly tired and lonely because he felt he could not share whatever it was that possessed him, nor could he bear to carry it alone much longer.

Gerald sensed that something was not right, and told David Farrell to go and get them some fish and chips and beer—Newcastle Brown and nothing else. 'None of that Bull's Blood wine rubbish you produced last time!'

'Why didn't you come round before?' Gerald asked aggressively after Farrell had gone. It was his way of reaching out to Stonor. Jim said nothing but just sat on the other side of the kitchen table looking uncomfortable. Gerald saw that he had bags under his eyes, and his face was pale and drawn. There was a little cut below his ear where he had caught himself when shaving. He was wearing paint-covered brown corduroys; a rough, green shirt poked itself uncomfortably out of the neck of the polo-neck pullover he habitually wore. It was ribbed and black. He had a little khaki satchel from a shop which sold army rejects, and sticking out of it were a couple of pencils and the tin box in which he carried charcoal.

'Still drawing and sketching all the time?' asked Gerald. There was well-hidden admiration in his voice. 'Can I see?'

Stonor picked up the satchel, pulled out his current sketch-book, and handed it to Gerald. They often did this when they didn't want to talk. It was the quickest way to discover what each other had been doing. Gerald leafed through the pages.

'Can I come and see what else you've been doing, Jim?' he asked finally.

Perhaps it was, after all, why Stonor had come. He was ready to show someone. Yet, if that was so, the feelings he had as the three of them walked through Camden Town to his basement studio contradicted it. He knew with grim and terrible certainty that they would not like the picture he had made; and in a way he half understood that it was important that they didn't. He had no wish to be obscure; indeed, the terrible effort of the past weeks had been directed at making as clear a statement as his skill and heart allowed of that confrontation as a young girl faced the inevitable decay of her body and looks . . . except it wasn't that. Dear God above, he couldn't *say* what his picture was about. It simply *was*.

But he knew they wouldn't like it. It was so old-fashioned as to be nearly archaic. It was a painting, for a start. Not a collage, or a construction, or kinetic, or pop-based. It was in oils, of all things— not acrylic or silver foil or powder. It was figurative, humanistic and emotional—not mechanistic and controlled. It was . . . not what it should be. Not what any of them, himself included, had been making.

Yet what it was – or was beginning to be – was an image of so many things he loved and hated, and which, for better or worse, had enriched his life. There was always the sea in it, in the shifting, coursing lines around her thighs, for if she could be like that, back and forth with an eternal rhythm, she had no need to fear decay; there was, finally, an eagle's wing, though why it held such power over him he did not know; there were the eyes and face of Janet Campbell now made exquisite—and gazed at not by the cruelty of the world she imagined to be around her, but by the timid eyes of a little boy in wellington boots, which chafed at his calves as he struggled against a wind on the shingle shore below the Dunes. While behind him across the canvas, with only the wild wind now to give life to its wings, lay the black body of a cormorant whose life he had himself been forced to take.

These powerful images, which meant so much to him, were no more than echoes on his portrait, sources of power and feeling which invested each stroke and touch with a life someone else could read their own way. Why should anyone ever understand what the cormorant had meant to him? How could anyone else ever know what your own thin legs in a boot half-filled with swilling sea-water had to do with a nineteen-year-old girl from Edinburgh looking at the reality of an ageing body for the first time?

But these were Jim's sources—and not the raunchy, glittering, hopeful, piss-taking mood of the sixties that had until now so dominated him. Its colours and brightness were there in places; but the skill of the composition and line, the sense of space and the feel of the tears, were born on the foreshore at Deal and in the flight of eagles in a sky over the Dunes, where no eagles had flown—not over coffee and beer, or with a pinch of dope, in a London flat.

The picture was wet on the canvas, still bright and glistening in the top left-hand corner where he had done some work that morning. Gerald and David stared at it, aghast. It seemed to them to show none of the technical skill and élan of Jim's final year's work. It was so old-fashioned. And in their silence something in Jim finally died; some great iron gate finally swung across a road he had spent so long coming down, and back up which he would now never be able to return. He felt cast down, and he felt angry, and then tired, for his cries were on the canvas and not at his mouth.

'I . . .' and Gerald said something noncommittal. And through his terrible, hopeless isolation Stonor wished that his brother Michael might have been there, or his friend Peter, or Albert Chandler. He would not have had to defend it to them. Whether or not they would have understood it, they trusted him. And if he had said, 'I made it and it's right; it's as it is,' they would have said, 'Yes, yes, it is', and they would have felt no need to talk about it.

'What does this part represent, assuming it's figurative?' asked Gerald Opie, waving an embarrassed hand, its fingers at sixes and sevens, over the great, surging primary feathers of the eagle's wing that swept into the portrait from behind, and framed the head and torso in darkness and light. Jim could find no answer, but merely stared into the desolation of the canvas.

★ ★ ★ ★ ★

Winters passed, and springs came, and slowly Romsdal eagles began to forget that a fremmed had been among them and had then flown north, taking three juveniles with her. None had heard of her, nor had any vagrants down from the north brought news of her.

There was, in any case, more interesting news, which excited the aggressive youngsters in Romsdal, but disturbed the wiser eagles who had seen many years through and knew when news may mean trouble.

More than one vagrant coming up from the south brought stories of the eagles of Hardanger fjord, long notorious for their vicious toughness. There was about them a stockiness and darkness of feather, and a peculiar directness of flight, which contrasted with the Romsdalers who – though they had seemed crude in flight to Cuillin – were by comparison with the Hardangers positively subtle.

These stories said that humans were spreading up the Hardanger fjord and had begun systematically to destroy sea eagle nests, resulting in a rapid decline of the Hardanger eagle population. Now a young male was gathering together the few strong eagles that remained there and was beginning to raid other fjords to the north of Hardanger, as a move towards colonising other, safer territory. The name of this eagle was Sleat.

Eagles like Finse knew well what this could mean, for such a strong and proud stock as Hardanger would not be satisfied with any insignificant fjords for a homeland base. Their target might even be Romsdal, which was as grand and formidable a place as Hardanger, and had the additional prestige of including the holy nest site of the Storrin, of which the Romsdalers were the traditional protectors—a role which now seemed defunct, but one which still added pride to their wings.

Then, one fresh spring day, when the grass and trees at the fjord were glistening with new growth, and the eider and tufted duck were back along the skerries, and eagle after eagle was flying mating flights and beginning to mark out territories for breeding, a young but strong female, with a Hardanger eagle's look to her flight, flew into the fjord. Without any preliminary deference or caution she settled herself up near the Storrin Gap, a traditional meeting place for the old eagles.

She settled there quietly, but there was no mistaking the fact that she would, if necessary, fight hard for her place. She had evidently come with a purpose, and over a period of several hours after her arrival, various of the more important Romsdal females slowly came and gathered nearby—not around her, for that would have suggested either deference or aggression; but near enough for her to have full opportunity of saying her piece, but leaving her in no doubt that if that was not convincing, she would be driven from Romsdal.

There was a curious coldness about her, enhanced by the extreme neatness of her feathers and her movements, and the sleek health in her colour.

Eventually – when she seemed satisfied that enough had assembled, and just before irritability among some of the prouder eagles erupted into anger – she turned full towards them, raised her wings into the wind from the fjord, and flew a long, slow flight past them, and back, and then higher. All knew that it was a flight of significance, but only a few recognised the flight for what it was and were able to recall the legends and stories that attended it.

One of these was Finse, the old male wise in traditional ways, and so often spurned by the females who called him weak and doting, and though a good father and mate, yet a fool to himself with all his poetic mutterings and talk of the Doom over Storrin. But he was father of the Weir. As the strange female flew the flight high above them now, and their whispers of curiosity and trepidation increased, it was Finse to whom they finally turned for an explanation.

'It is the flight of a herald, which summons great eagles to meet and discuss. It is flown only at a time of danger. Do you not remember the tale of Olve, who dared fly such a flight, though a male, to summon eagles to Maeren in the legends of old . . .?' But they did not, and he wondered for a moment if he had been lost too long in the stories of the past. Could they not see the importance of what was happening—that this was one more sign that the Doom was coming? Could they not see that the important question was which eagle had sent the herald?

'This is a sign that there is to be a Gathering, and it will be here in ancient Romsdal, within sound of the mighty Storrin, and its purpose will be to talk of ourselves as we have not done for generations . . .' But his voice faded, for the female now came closer and, flying before them, spoke in such a way that her voice could be heard by all up and down that stretch of the fjord.

'This old male speaks the truth. There has been much fear up and down the land, as fjord after fjord has seen the lights of men shine through the winter, and has suffered strange casualties. Have you not had eagles die here from no cause? Eagles who were strong . . .' and she hardly bothered to wait for their surprised and eager nods of affirmation, before continuing. 'And there is one living in Hardanger, where so many have died this spring, who demands that there should be a Gathering . . .' And as she said this ancient word, which most had heard only in the old stories, there was a gasp of surprise and awe among them all, and they looked at each other silently and in fear. All of them, even the dimmest and most territory-bound, began to see that they were entering an unusual time, and a dangerous one. And most of them had the sense to see that there might be a link between this call for a Gathering and the strange things that had been happening for so long, in which the lights, the coming of Cuillin, and so many other things seemed to play a part. And many there made a vow to seek out Finse, the old one, alone, and ask him to repeat just for them the Doom, because there was some distant echo in their memory of it which told them a Gathering had been predicted at the start of the Doom itself.

The female watched their reactions and, seeming satisfied that she had impressed them with the seriousness of her mission, she continued. 'There is one in Hardanger who has the power to call such a Gathering. You, who live here in such remoteness, may not yet know his name. But eagles in the south, who live so near to continual danger from man, know of his wisdom and cunning and have faith in his power to lead sea eagles back to the course from which they have so far drifted. His name is Sleat.'

So the terrible name that had only been a rumour now became fact, and echoed through Romsdal, and if it seemed to slide and sleer around its walls, like dripping water from thawing ice which courses down black rock and turns from crystal clearness to the blackest colour of night, then such was the name itself. Sleat of Hardanger. Sleat the Powerful. Sleat the Saviour . . . name after name would attach to him in the years and decades that now lay so dreadfully before them. Sleat.

Only one of those who heard it recognised that danger lay in its sound—not hope. And that courage and faith in Haforn would be needed when he came—not blind trust and weak optimism. But who listened to Finse? Who really listened, even now that so many started coming to ask him about the Gathering? And who could he properly trust with his knowledge?

But when the female had gone – northward to other fjords, to inform others that there would be a Gathering at Romsdal, within sound of the Storrin, since this location was central for all of them – Finse flew inland through the shadows of the cliffs, towards the Storrin itself. He flew resolutely, for the winds there were always treacherous, and had caught many younger, more arrogant eagles in their grip and sucked them down into the swirling depths beneath the great waterfall.

So Finse flew on, his aged wings seeming no match for the spray-filled wind that came rushing and bursting around the dark corner at the end of the main fjord, and yet showing in every turn of his body and parry of his wings that the older he got, the wiser and more powerful became his flight. The fjord narrowed as its two sides veered towards each other to form what eagles called the Gap of Storrin. The waterfall was beyond it, out of sight, but at the Gap, which rose sheer and intimidating above the waters, an eagle could see the run of driving spray from the Storrin itself. Here the winds were treacherous – sometimes they blew out from the Gap, sometimes sucked terribly in – and few eagles dared venture there. Here, now, Finse came to find a stance among the cliffs, all wet and slippery from spray, and dangerous too, with sudden winds and cross-currents that seemed to come from within the fractured rock behind him. But there he stayed.

'Sleat . . . Sleat . . .' he muttered the name into the spray-sodden wind, which seemed to take it from him and swirl it away—*sleet, sleet, sleet . . .* And he called out aloud to Haforn to guide all of them in the trial that was coming. 'Send the Fremmed back to us,' he called. 'Let her come and show us the way. Let her come and lead us, and show us how to resist this Sleat. Let her bring the Weir himself to help us. Oh, Haforn, who have seen so much of our strength go, and our old power disappear, show us now where our pride lies, and how to fly again as we should. Show us.'

One thousand miles to the north, the spring that was already turning into early summer in Romsdal had only just begun. Snow and ice lay thick and encrusted on the ground, and only in the most sheltered places – and then only along the coastal edge where the warm currents swept up from the south – were plants and scrub beginning to show life. Here the shining green leaf of dwarf birch was beginning to uncurl; there the first buds of northern willow were starting to break; whilst down among the scattered rocks, fragmented by thousands of years of freezing and thawing, tiny mosses and lichens glistened secretly, red and yellow, strange metallic blues and greens, shiny with water and condensation from the pale air.

Yet, while the plants began their acceleration into spring, the coastal birds were already active. The drear rafts of eider, their green feathers no more than watery shadows through the winter, were suddenly in brighter, finer plumage. Common and herring-gull, which had quite disappeared from sight through the winter, arrived with every new wind, wheeling and cutting into the frail light of the start of an arctic spring, their wings sharp white against the dark, wet cliffs down which meltwater dripped and ran.

Along the flatter stretches of the shore, on ancient hallowed ground, groups of great skua began to break up into pairs, their communal flight disrupted now by the sudden grim-eyed, lunging flight of the bigger, stronger ones, seeking to establish territory every fifty or sixty yards at some point of rock or nesting rubbish from the year before. The air was filled with the sudden swish of their dives, the sky blackened by their dark-brown wings, back and forth; and they peered fiercely from ground perches this way and that, to divide and demarcate—and eventually protect.

Here too had Weever and Mizen long held territory, their love growing through the winter when Cuillin was with the Weir, and finally leading them over the skerries on her return, to mark out territory and mate, and start the long round of raising young.

Sometime then, gently from an inland sky, Cuillin returned to them from her stay with the Weir, and together the four of them lived near each other in peace.

Springs passed and winters came, and Cuillin and Clew stayed more together, not as mates but in friendship, and Cuillin passed on to Clew all she had learnt from his half-brother the Weir, and he in his turn built up her trust in the youth of which he was a part. And often the four eagles, and Mizen's young, would come together in the winter months, to feed along the shore and talk, as eagles should, of tales and legends, of fears and of hopes.

Then did Cuillin begin to sow a dream. For then did she remember the place she had come from, and wanted to tell again of a distant island across the dark sea, where the winters were mild and the winds were fair and the food was good across the moorland hills and the sea lochs. Then would she whisper the names she had loved, of Loch Coruisk, of Loch Scavaig, of Rubh' an Dunain, and the mountainside of Gars-bheinn, where she was born, which over-looked the tiny Loch na Cuilce, and was overlooked in its turn by the jagged rises of the Black Cuillins, and the rounded tops of the Red Cuillins opposite.

'It was from the side of Gars-bheinn that I learned to fly,' she would tell them, 'and from there that my mother led me and my half-brother, Torrin, north past the Storr, where the Raven lives, of which I have told you, and then towards Shetland, where she turned back into the wind to end her days on the island I loved.'

'Was it hard flying over the dark sea?' Mizen would ask. But she knew the answer, and only wished that her young might share with Cuillin her sad and courageous flight away from her home-land. And remember.

It was spring, another spring, and that year Cuillin was unsettled and restless, so that Clew, who knew her well, was unsettled also.

'What is it?' he would ask.

'I'm not sure, but I know our time here is coming to an end, and I am afraid. These years of peace and of learning are over. We must travel again.'

'Where to?' he would ask. But she did not know, only looking silently southwards and wondering what doom was approaching there.

Inland the lakes lay under snow, only their featureless flatness revealing what they were, in contrast to the rougher, rocky ground that rose between them. But sometimes a crack in the ice appeared, and in lower valleys where lakes lay caught among the drift of glacial moraine and drumlins, a bright aquamarine pool of water might spread quietly across the ice, with only the dark reflection of a passing eagle's wing to stir its face. A wing that seemed filled with grey light, and that flew without flying, crossing the face of the sky, as light fills it at dawn.

He came on them at twilight when they were talking, and not one of them seemed to see him before he spoke, for his voice seemed but wind in the dwarf birch, or the soft sea spray on the rocks below.

'Cuillin, your time here is ended. Fly south now to where you are needed. Take Clew with you, for you will need him, and he has strength now to help you. Leave Mizen and Weever here for they are still learning how to nurture, how to protect, and in time, too, all their skill will be needed. You will know when to call them to you. Go soon, and know that the peace of Haforn is with you, and that she will grace your wings and give you strength . . .'

Then almost before they were aware that he had spoken, the light of the Weir's wings had gone, and black night had fallen.

The following day Cuillin decided to leave. She knew they would all follow her if she wished it, but that was not how it would be. There were years ahead of them yet, and their time would come – as hers had – in unexpected, unplanned ways. Clew would come with her, but Mizen and Weever would stay where they were – as she was sure Haforn wished them to – to learn those things of love and duty which they could learn from no eagles but themselves.

So, with the briefest of farewells but much affection, Cuillin and Clew began to turn their backs on the north.

'Oh, surely you don't have to go! I mean, I know we're together, Weever and I, but the summer's coming and there's plenty of territory here, and Weever says he's never seen as good a place for food down south. And not many humans about here, either . . .' So Mizen sought to keep them there. And when Cuillin said she *must* go, as there were things brewing down south, though she had no idea what they were, Mizen looked even more concerned and, with her head going this way and that and her eyes wide, she said: 'But will you be all right, Cuillin? I mean, they never liked you down there in Romsdal, and it didn't do you any good being with us three because that made them respect you even less. I suppose you can speak our language now, so that's something! But . . . but it doesn't feel *right*. All this talk of the Doom makes me worry about you, even though *I'm* not much good to anyone. Will you be all right?'

Cuillin went close to her, wing to wing. 'You're worried about yourself really, aren't you, Mizen? Rearing young and establishing a territory is a task that will never end.' Mizen fell silent and looked down at the sea beneath them, swirling back and forth, at the foot of the cliffs. Cuillin saw that she had guessed right.

'Well, don't worry. Plenty of eagles have done it before you! And there'll be plenty yet to come! When you see the weakness of the very young and begin to observe their strength, their everlasting strength, you'll realise something about your own. You're doing something I've never done . . .' And indeed it was true, though to Mizen Cuillin seemed so strong and patient, so experienced, that she somehow could not believe that she had never had young of her own.

So, in friendship and a growing sense of loyalty and love between them, the four eagles separated. There were few words, and no special flight of farewell. When the moment came – and Cuillin decided when it was – she simply raised her wings into the air and swept away, with Clew behind her, and they turned their backs on Mizen and Weever, and the north, to begin the long flight south to Romsdal. While, down on the sea, groups of eider and fulmar grew alarmed and scattered, as above them against the white sky, beyond the highest cliff, two great eagles swept slowly by, and the two of them seemed to carry in their great dark wings a sense of purpose and destiny.

Summer came and one by one, sometimes by night, sometimes by day, sometimes in pairs, sea eagles began to arrive at Romsdal and over its surrounding fjells.

Whatever may have been the intent of the dark, strange female who had first announced it, the feeling she left behind her was one of menaced excitement. Among the Romsdal eagles themselves, arguments raged about who should be at the Gathering, and what it should discuss. There was no doubt, for instance that concern would be voiced about the growing onslaughts of the sleark, stories of whose raids reached Romsdal with increasing frequency from the strange eagles who appeared in the area, and who said they had come for the Gathering at the bidding of Sleat. From north and south they came, from mountain and skerry, from fjell and coastal reach. Some came from so far off that it took time for the Romsdal eagles to understand what they said, for their accents seemed strange and different. Some adopted a proud and distant manner, mantling if another eagle came too close; others were friendly, and only too eager to pass the time of day. Most, naturally, were females, for the males could hardly leave their territories at such a time of year, when the young were still inexperienced fliers and needed protection from their own foolishness and uncertainty in hunting and, perhaps, from opportunistic sleark.

As for the Romsdal eagles themselves, two females emerged as the ones who seemed best able to voice the fears and feelings of the rest—Hild of Sigvat and Aiman of the Jarlsfjord. Both were powerful fliers and both were willing to speak their minds. As the days went by, a third eagle emerged as one who had the trust of the others—and that was the aged Finse. He had lived his life quietly for many years, fathering a succession of broods by different mates, dutifully protecting his territory and feeding his young, but there were many who saw that he held wisdom in his flight, and knew that nearly alone of them – bar one or two of the inland eagles – he knew the ancient Doom and many of the forgotten legends. He it was who explained that there were many precedents for Gatherings from the past. He it was who could explain the seriousness of what might be happening. And when others had finished speaking, it was Finse who could quietly advise how they might act now that the talking was over.

So, over the space of a few days, the great Gathering began to assemble, and the air was filled with rumours and talk. Occasionally fights broke out between two eagles, each proud, each fierce, and more than once Hild or Aiman had to intervene to stop one of the Romsdal eagles objecting with violence to the settling on its territory of some stranger who had come for the Gathering. Fortunately, it being mid-summer, food was in good supply, or else the Gathering might well have broken up in an anarchic scramble for space and food.

Most of the eagles preferred to roost down by the fjord-side, often where one of the rivers drove its way down the steep cliffs and into the fjord; and many flew seawards daily to take what food they could from among the skerries and along the coast. The sky over Romsdal had never been so dark with eagles' wings, nor so heavy with talons.

The day came when annoyance and grumbling overtook the excitement, and many began to say that if this Sleat wasn't going to turn up, they might as well get on with it. 'I mean, where is he, and where are the Hardanger eagles as a whole? It's not right, somehow . . .'

For the most talked-about eagle of the gathering, Sleat, had not even shown a wing-tip in the sky. And those mysterious heralds of his – for several had been reported in different areas – had not been seen again in Romsdal either. So it was not surprising that conflicting rumours about Sleat spread around. Some said he was kind, some said he was cruel, some that he had killed sleark, others that his flight was as swift as a skua's and as powerful as the Storrin itself . . . But whatever extravagances the talk produced, one simple fact was agreed: whenever he had been seen, it was in company with at least three, often more, of those efficient, dark and powerful females of Hardanger; and though he was smaller than they, yet it was to the line of his flight, and in the shadow of his wings, that the others flew. 'So close that they seem as one giant eagle' in the words of one who claimed to have seen Sleat.

The tension grew, and as it did, the weather began to deteriorate. Romsdal was cast down with summer mists and rain, lightning lit its sides, and awkward, blustering winds bent the trees of the forests back and forth. And crows, who watched the arrival of the eagles with curiosity and alarm, struggled to keep on their perches, or skulked away to the protection of the dark interior of the forest, beneath the canopy of the trees, like blackbirds in undergrowth.

The waters of the main fjord grew ruffled, and then rough, and white mares' tails spread seaward down its length before the cold wind that started to blow viciously from the direction of the great mountains beyond the fjells. The eagles now began to gather closer together, flying in from the sea coast and skerries where they had been congregating, and forgathering at the head of the main fjord, near the Gap, not far beyond which, though out of sight, the great Storrin fell. They took the north side of the fjord, for the power of the wind was such that it carried chill white spray from the crashing falls out into the fjord and over to its southern side. One by one they came together, their great wings hunched and huddled, a grouping of more eagles than had been seen in living memory—or, indeed, heard of in legend. Thirty, forty, fifty . . . their great wings nearly touching, their beaks shiny wet with the damp air, their talons mainly worn and rough, for most were old females who had lived many years out. Among them were a few males—mainly ones like Finse who had gained a place there by their knowledge and wisdom. A few eagles were there neither for their knowledge nor wisdom but because – as others had found from the last few days' exchanges – they represented the very last of their families in the valleys or along the coastal fjords where they lived, the rest having been killed or driven out by the twin pressures of humans encroaching and the advance of sleark.

Any eagle could tell which these were: they held their wings low and they seemed frail, battered and a little lost, as if the world had somehow passed them by. Finse could not help thinking that they reminded him of an eagle who had once been among them and he prayed might return. For had not the Fremmed looked as lost as these when she first came to Romsdal?

But he shook his head silently as he waited for whatever was going to happen, and thought that perhaps *she* had been different: there was always true pride in her flight, always courage. But these eagles . . . And he wondered fearfully if they might be a fore-shadowing of what was to come to the rest of them. Seeing them he understood what extinction might mean.

The weather stayed grey and wet, and the wind did not abate. There was a sudden sense that at last the Hardanger eagles would be coming, and with them Sleat. Below, the fjord waters looked dark and angry. They waited. The wind blew. The air was heavy with wild spray. Talons pressed and stressed at the rocky stances they had taken; heads turned impatiently this way and that. Impatience grew. Until, at last, Aiman, the proud Romsdal eagle, called out, 'It is time for us to begin. If the Hardanger eagles who called this meeting don't care to come to it, then . . .'

But whatever it was she was going to say, they never heard. For as she spoke, and they craned forward to see her, there was a murmur and a ruffle, an intake of breath and then a half-mantling of wings, the sound of a gathering of eagles spread around and forth—for they suddenly saw them coming, by ones and two and fours. Not, as they had expected, from the west. Nor over the tops of the fjord, which might have been another route, but from the east, from the direction of the mountains, borne fast and massively along on the cold wind, a chill rain at their feathers and the angry grey of the fjord far below their hanging talons. High over the spray of the Storrin they came, round the corner of the great north wall of the fjord . . . three, or four . . . eight . . . nine . . . great dark eagles, most of them females, their wings strong and massive, the power of their flight sufficient to still the wind itself. The eagles of Hardanger. And, in their midst, yet never lost, for it seemed that the others radiated from him, flew a male eagle whose power and fiercesome majesty was such that no eye looked on anything but him.

He flew just marginally ahead of the others, as if he was the head and the rest were his wings. His tail was pure white, his feathers more grey than brown—though, in the poor light and with spray on them, they seemed more black than any colour.

'Welcome!' he said, his voice firm and sharp. 'We are the eagles of Hardanger, the only ones left. We have called this Gathering and we are glad that you have come. My name is Sleat of Hardanger, and there are many things I wish to say . . .' And though he did not speak loudly, Finse could not help noticing that, despite the noise of Storrin and the wind, there was not one of them that seemed to have any trouble in hearing what he said. His voice was as treacherous as ice on black rocks.

Then Finse knew that, whatever doubts there may have been in the past, whatever warnings ignored, there was no doubt at all that the Doom had now started. And he wished more than anything else that the Fremmed, who called herself Cuillin, who had flown the dark sea, who had flown north so long before, was here now to witness it.

★ ★ ★ ★ ★

'Come in, come in, *come in!*' Gerald Opie beamed, his arms wide, and greeted Judith Shure with exaggerated disbelief.

It was a Saturday morning, nearly six years since Stonor had completed the *Portrait of Miss Campbell*. Unheralded and unannounced, and because she was 'just passing', Judith had knocked on the door of Gerald's flat in Camden Town.

'You're lucky to find me,' said Gerald, making a cup of coffee for her and setting it on the familiar old red formica surface of the kitchen table. 'It's my last week here. The world must be coming to an end!' It was early 1974, and the job he had been angling for at the Royal College of Art had finally come through. Gerald Opie was to be a principal lecturer complete with his own studio. He was on his way up at last, towards the top in art education administration.

'Yes, I heard you had a post at the Royal College,' she said. 'Well done!' He shook his head as if it was an insignificant thing, and they both looked at their coffees for a moment—old acquaintances with a lot of catching up to do.

Gerald looked up at Judith. She looked older and her dark hair was shorter than he remembered from the last time they met, three years before, at a preview party at the Whitechapel Gallery. She looked *better*, and somehow harder. They had held a brief and facile conversation then—'How *are* you?' 'Where have you *been*?'—and there was drink and noise, and he recalled that Judith, of old, had never been one to enjoy them much. Since those days she had begun building an international reputation as a gallery dealer, and had expanded Shure Galleries into Europe.

Now, seeing her here in his flat, smiling just a little embarrassedly into her coffee cup, he thought, My God, she's changed, meaning that she looked attractive.

And to Gerald she seemed not merely attractive, but intimidating as well. She wore a two-piece suit, lilac-blue and very well cut; she looked smart and somewhat of a contrast to most of the girls he had ever known.

'I'm getting married,' he said; and when she looked surprised, he added, 'It's true!'

'Who . . .?'

'Oh, you don't know her. She's nothing to do with the art world at all. As a matter of fact, and between ourselves, and don't tell

150

anyone until the announcement in *Computer Weekly*, she's a programmer with IBM!'

Judith laughed and leaned across the table and touched his arm and, smiling at him, said, 'Really?' her eyebrows raised and questioning.

Gerald nodded, and for once said nothing. He was smiling, too, and looked happier than she ever remembered him.

'Congratulations,' she said.

And then they started to talk, not preview party talk at which she had never been any good, but the real talk between people who would have known each other better had circumstances, and their own fears, allowed.

His fiancée's name was Nina. She was half-American and stood no nonsense when it came to Gerald's mishandling of life or money—'In other words, she watches what I do and spend, and frankly I can't say I mind.' She was, it seemed, almost perfect.

And what about you, Judith, whom none of us ever really got to know; who led such a mysterious, rich life; whose family was in the business; who knew more about art and all the shows than we did—what about you?

'I hear you're doing very well,' he said.

She had been in Munich and Paris, helping in her father's business. 'I was brought up to it, you know, and I never really thought I'd do anything else. I'm good at it. I'm running one of the galleries now, the Paris one, but I don't think my father will let me take over the London one yet. He likes nineteenth century; I think there's potential in contemporary work. Anyway he wants the best for me, which means he wants me married. He's sweet really.'

'Any chance of that?' asked Gerald. 'I mean . . .' He didn't want to pry or anything, step on any toes, but, 'For Chrissake is there a man in your life? Was there ever?'

Judith laughed again. 'I'm not as pure as I may seem,' she said rather too seriously. Then she told him. The man was Patrick Chanay, and he ran an advertising agency in Paris, specialising in television commercials.

'I thought the French couldn't make TV commercials. I thought the business was all in London and New York.'

'It is, most of it. Patrick did time at J. Walter Thompson in New York and then Leo Burnett in London. Now he's on his own. He wants me to marry him. He'll do very well, you know. He has already.'

She spoke of him as if he was over there and she was here, which was indeed the truth. She did not say, and barely knew, that she had come back to London to get away for a while. The ostensible reason was a deal involving Lord Matley's private collection which a US dealer wanted, and which her father felt she should handle best. The dealer liked her, and her father was a realist. Judith needed to go to New York.

'That's why I've come back to London,' she said. 'I'm going to New York.'

'Very logical,' said Gerald drolly. 'Have a double bourbon! What's your father think of him?'

'Oh, he likes him, of course. He's everything he ever wanted for me except . . .' Except he wasn't everything she ever wanted for herself. She did not voice these thoughts, but Gerald suspected what she was thinking.

'Jim Stonor's over in New York, isn't he?' she continued innocently . . .'

She tried to sound offhand, but that wasn't her. Dear Lord, she wanted to know how he was and where he had been. There were shows he should have been in. Where was his work? Where was *he*?

Gerald looked at her. He was beginning to be a good judge of people, and light dawned on him quickly. It was Jim Stonor she was really interested in. Jim! And looking at her and her sophistication and gentle charm, and the obvious intelligence and toughness in her, all he could think was, Jim and Judith? Why the hell not?

'He went over three years ago, and I haven't heard a single bloody word from the silly sod. God only knows what he's doing. No, I tell a lie: I had a Christmas card last month, with "Happy Christmas, wish you were here" on it, and no address. I think he was with McCann's, the advertising agency people. You know he left this flat to go into some so-called studio – a damp basement – and got into his Van Gogh period . . .' Gerald stopped. He stared at Judith bloody Shure sitting opposite him with her legs crossed. Why was he suddenly so angry?

He got up, paced about, and then said: 'Look, I'll show you'. She followed him into a surprisingly tidy bedroom, with a neat counterpane over the bed and a long white cotton nightie folded over the back of the chair. The room smelt of Calèche. Gerald had been taken over, and he obviously liked it.

On the mantelpiece over a blocked-up fireplace was a jumble of cards and invitations, a couple of gallery catalogues and a newly-framed sketch of himself at the kitchen table at which they had just been sitting. Judith stopped and stared, for she recognised it immediately as Jim Stonor's work. He had caught Gerald's gangling energy perfectly, and the curious angle of his head, too, as he leaned forward in that plastic-covered chair, to say something. There was a beer mug on the table in front of him; not a coffee cup.

'That's Jim's of course,' he said. 'Nina found it in the cupboard and has just had it framed.' It wasn't this he wanted to show her, but the Christmas card. She saw he had put it right in the centre of the mantelpiece, in pride of place. He picked it up and ran his hand along its edge, and then gave it to her. It was a single card stuck over the front of a Christmas card, and she turned to the writing inside: 'Gerald. Happy Christmas. Wish you were here. Jim'.

'Look at the picture,' said Gerald.

It was hardly a Christmas card. The picture was from the New York Museum of Natural History, and it showed the blackened fossil skeleton of an extinct eagle, found in the famous tar-pits of Arizona. The words underneath read *'Haliaeetus mortuus. Extinct'*.

It shook Judith to see it, and it moved her to see his writing. She had never seen it before. It was strong and interesting. She wondered why he was over there and so far away, and she knew it wasn't right. None of it was right. But they were so ridiculous, these feelings. She felt she had no right to them.

'Why did he go?'

'How the hell do I know,' said Gerald irritably. But she knew it was not because of her but because he missed Jim.

'He left this flat to do some painting. He did it. When he finished, or soon after, there was something with his brother Michael which upset him. I said he was just tired and he told me to fuck off, if you'll forgive me repeating it. I put all his moods down to the effort he had made that summer on *Miss Campbell* . . .' Judith looked questioning, but Gerald went on quickly. 'He got offered a job by McCann's, with whom he had done a bit of freelance just to make ends meet, and he took it. I told him not to be a silly sod – like I often did – and that it would be the ruin of his art, and he said I was talking crap. We often had conversations like that. Only this time it was serious. He left a week or two later, and I haven't seen him since. I haven't even heard of him since, except for this card.'

'What was the work he was doing? You said "*Miss Campbell*".'

'*Portrait of*,' said Gerald. 'Want to see it? He couldn't leave it in that stupid basement so he brought it here, along with a million other things. They're in the broom cupboard, prosaically enough. We have a rather large one. What the hell I'm going to do with it all when we move, I don't know. Nina wants the place sorted out.'

'Can I see it?' asked Judith, suddenly feeling unaccountably nervous. But really she knew perfectly well why. She had fantasised about Stonor's work for years now, and one way or another had collected bits of it from friends, as a magpie collects gold rings if it can find them.

They came out of the cupboard one by one, unlooked at for several years. Sketch-pads, loose charcoal studies—the body of a summer's work. Sketches which had nothing to do with *Miss Campbell*, and yet, taken together and looked at retrospectively, they all led to the canvas at the back, which Stonor himself had propped up against the far wall in the dark, and which had not been looked at since. When it came out at last, having been heralded by bold and exquisite and angry works one after another, Judith just stared blankly. She knew immediately what she was looking at, and she saw it in the context of the sixties in which it had been made. She was not surprised that Gerald did not fall over himself with wonder at it. But for herself, she could hardly contain her sense of excitement and triumph. The *Portrait of Miss Campbell* was a major and original work, and as she looked at it, other things that had happened and were beginning to happen in the art world – Britain, Germany and America – fell into place.

She did not try to talk of them to Gerald, for they were distant things, vague and so far inarticulate. They would one day, no doubt, be seen as a movement, a revolt against abstraction; not back to realism but into an art that took account of both. But if it was a revolution it was a strange one, for it was fought in silence and by individuals alone, struggling to find the weapons and the visual language to steer through an abstraction in art which had begun to die, and a conceptualisation in sculpture and painting which had lost touch with love and feeling. Stonor's *Portrait of Miss Campbell* might, in some ways, have been painted in Germany, around 1920. It was figurative, expressionist and emotional. But the colour, which seemed to transform Gerald's dowdy flat, and the movement and the strange, stressed energy were what made it more than merely contemporary.

Judith was never one to talk too much about art, for she had learnt that the key to seeing truth lay more in feeling and living than in explanation to the sceptical. Yet she was so excited to see the canvas, and the other work associated with it, that she said: 'I think it's marvellous and original and I think it must have been very hard for him to make. A young spirit in an old body: I don't know who Miss Campbell was or is, but I know what her feelings represent for me.' She stood in silence again, lost for words and not really wishing to find any. They were merely a means of expressing feelings before art you liked or disliked, and always an inadequate one.

154

But faced by her obvious enthusiasm, Gerald looked at the canvas anew, wondering why he had never seen its worth when Stonor first showed it to him. He didn't exactly like it, but it made him think of things he might himself make, things he had been struggling with. Dammit, where the hell was Jim? Christ, he wanted to talk to him again!

'If you've nowhere to keep it – them – I'm sure my father will provide storage space. You should keep them somewhere safe. You don't mind if I make a record of each item and then give you a receipt?' She sounded strong and forceful, and rather reminded him of his own Nina. Of course, she could look after it all better than he could, and if she felt it was that good . . .

He let the details slip away. Judith could take care of them. He was looking at the canvas again, and at the jumble of work propped up along the walls of the corridor. Judith was looking at him, willing him to see, with a strange pride and relief in her eyes. She was thinking that she had, after all, been right in her assessment of Stonor; and she was wondering why, for the first moment in a long time, she felt such sudden purpose and determination. She had a pen in her hand, and a notebook, and she was beginning to write things down and get an idea of what was there. And as she put her handbag down and went on her knees and grubbed her lilac suit on the edge of the dusty sketch-pad, Gerald was looking for a fourth or fifth time at the canvas.

Was that how Miss Campbell had been? Was *that* the quality she had had? Why hadn't Jim said what he was about? But then Gerald told himself off for being a fool; he probably hadn't known. He just made it while the rest of them, David Farrell and himself and those others, just talked.

He could remember Miss Campbell, strange girl, and remembering her through the language Jim had created he began slowly to see, as Judith Shure already obviously did, what his friend might be—possessed and lost as well.

'If you're going to New York you might track him down and tell him what you've done with the work,' he said.

Judith nodded. 'McCann's, you said?' She had a reason to find him now. Extinct eagle, indeed. And for the briefest moment Gerald thought she muttered something under her breath which sounded like 'Silly sod!'—but surely he was wrong, because Judith Shure didn't speak like that, did she?

CHAPTER EIGHT

'I don't know why I'm writing to you again or what I want to say. The reason I thought of you, I suppose, is because yesterday I went into St Patrick's Cathedral after some stupid row in my department, and just sat there. I wanted to light a candle like you told me you used to, but though I put some money – a dollar note – in the box I couldn't do it because it felt wrong, like a blasphemy. I sat there wondering how you were, what you were doing, wishing you were there with me. . .

'I haven't done any of my own work for months now, perhaps even years. I feel unhealthy and am constantly doing, doing, doing nothings here in a city I once thought wonderful and believed had everything London did not have. I get so tired though. I find I get pangs of missing things—the seafront at Deal, Gerald Opie whom I can't bring myself to write to, you.

'Did you ever get my last letter or did I only imagine I sent it? Months ago now. I haven't spoken to anyone personally since Patti went back to San Francisco two months ago. I feel dead inside, unable to draw even, let alone paint or sculpt.

'I'm writing to you because I know you can't really reply, so it doesn't matter what I say. I feel I've hurt someone, Michael, but I don't know their name and I can't say I'm sorry. I think I'm writing to you because for the first time in my life I want someone to pray for me . . .'

—Letter from James MacAskill Stonor to his brother Michael, of the Order of St Benedict, 20 February 1974. (Never sent)

February 1974: New York

OUTSIDE it was bitter cold, and a light blizzard was blowing silently against the window, individual snowflakes hanging against the glass, scurrying up and down the pane before whirling again into a million others. The snow was thickening, the sky grey-mauve and darkening, and the gloom seeming darker than it was because the office lights were beginning to flick on, hundreds by the minute. The snowflakes drove wildy down the street, and the building opposite, filtering through, looked soft and airy, and seemed to tilt into the blizzard. Over to the left, five blocks down, Stonor could still just see the twin spires of St Patrick's, grey-blue now against the snow's white.

Inside it was warm, almost hot, and smoke curled up from

Charlie Stahl's cigarette, which lay untouched and had burned almost through since he had first lit it. He had been making a judicial statement, designed to pull together into one harmonious whole the the discordant oil-and-water verbal exchanges of the last two hours. The seventeenth-floor conference room of Everett, Stahl and Kassin was suffering another (but probably the last) meeting with Ben Tenning, marketing chief of Maljo Electrics. Accounts were represented by Charlie Stahl himself, with Ray Moor in tow; creative by Sue Cassio and Jim Stonor; media by Clark Rinstein.

Stonor happened to know that the meeting – which was a hastily cobbled-together marketing presentation for idea options for the autumn – was a total waste of time. His own secretary knew it from Dina Wilmott of Maljo, Ben's present sleeping partner. He had had lunch with Ted Zappin of Kramer's yesterday, and agreed to switch the whole of the $7.25 million billing for the major autumn campaign. Bastard!

So now they were playing games, and when they all lost them, Stahl would haul people all over the place for a week or two before announcing, with a special memo to everyone, that they had won Talmon Computers against fierce opposition, and let it be known that his own personal influence had . . . And Stonor's eyes went back to the window, and he put down the cigarette he had lit after making his own contribution. It had been clear and concise, and not what anyone traditionally expected of creative men, which is why they used him to front so many presentations. When it came to the marketing and media sell, of course, his English accent was a disadvantage: the British did not have that kind of reputation. But for creativity Stonor could not be beaten, within the agency at least, and especially on press-orientated campaigns. That's why Stahl had poached him from McCann's. The face Jim wore was contemplative-creative with a distant bonhomie about it. He wore a moustache Zapata-style; and Mrs Frewin, who kept a picture of him and Michael on the beach when they were seven and ten respectively, would not have recognised him. Then his legs had been skinny and his face a little pinched; his hair was tousled and his skin browned by the sun over the months; his bathing costume hung rather loosely over his middle because it was one of Michael's cast-offs, and was wet.

Twenty-four years later, in a New York winter, beached up in an overheated office, Stonor looked terrible. The hair was fuller, the one-shilling short back and sides from the Royal Marine barber's was now a twenty-eight dollar trim in 'Scissors', East 44th. His face was unpleasantly chubby, his eyes tired as if they had watched an orgy all night in which he himself had not had the energy to take part. He wore a uniform: well-cut suit, neat, handmade leather shoes, a brass-buckled leather belt, and a cotton shirt, with a forty dollar silk tie just a little undone. A close inspection of the belt would have shown that it was fixed by the second hole in the leather, but that once upon a time he had regularly used the third, for it was indented and rubbed grey by the buckle. Had Mrs Frewin come through the door after all and eventually recognised him, then it might have been the hands she knew first and not the face. They were the same: strong, supple, brown, workaday. They fidgeted on the conference table, now restless, now idle—then suddenly still.

Stonor was studying the snow outside the window, now getting fiercer. He was watching the last faint image of St Patrick's disappear behind the white flurries and, indeed, any person who had not been watching it as he had, would not now be able to pick it out. The light was fading fast and he found it almost impossible to conceive that so violent a phenomenon as the blizzard outside had been reduced to silence by double-glazing. He imagined what it might be like to stand in that blizzard—not down in the shelter of the streets with an overcoat and hat on, and with the protection of skyscrapers about; but up here, this high, on one of the ledges round the building where birds roosted in summer, and in the thin clothes he now wore. He tried to imagine the wind on his cheeks and whipping at his hair. He tried to imagine the cold biting at his hand and penetrating his legs. He attempted to imagine his eyes screwed up and watering with cold.

But the mute window won, and he could not really imagine any of it. Some distant urge in his hands fretted at him to draw it, twin cathedral towers tilting into snow, a simple study in pencil. But he felt tired and frustrated, and the feeling swamped the urge. Ben Tenning was now droning on, talking utter bullshit in view of the fact that he was about to remove the account from the team which he was now calmly complimenting. Stonor dug a couple of fingers into the pocket of his jeans and eased out a page torn from a memo pad.

'Miss Judith Shure of Shure Galleries phoned.' It gave her number—until 5.00 pm. He felt no real emotion at the sight of her name. Perhaps distant curiosity. He remembered her, of course; he could have probably drawn a likeness. But he was tired and just didn't want to think. He wondered how she had tracked him down.

The snow swirled; the light outside finally faded. It was evening, and twenty to five, and office lights were taking over from snowflakes. He got up suddenly, rudely, smiled smoothly to cover himself, said he wouldn't be a moment, urgent phone-call, would be back. He stood there coping with his own sudden move, the paper with her name on it in his hand, and as he countered Stahl's slightly raised brow, and did a marginal genuflection in the direction of Tenning, the window at their backs seemed suddenly much bigger. If it blew in suddenly, exploding forward, and the blizzard came into the room where they sat, ice-cold rushing wind and driving snow; if it happened, it might be . . . quite interesting. A blizzard along the beach south of Deal had once nearly killed him.

Stahl watched him go with a sideways twist of his eyes. Perhaps what they were beginning to say about Stonor was right: he was beginning to crack up. Wonderboy fails. Shit, thought Stahl, we're going to lose this bloody account. He watched Stonor leave. Did he know something Stahl didn't, for once?

They met in the lounge of the Doral Inn Hotel on Lexington, and Judith did not recognise him. He even had the trace of an American accent, or the covering of a mid-Atlantic drawl.

'Hi!' he said. 'It's got to be Judith Shure. It's really great to see you, Judith.' He held out a hand, steady and strong. She took it, the disbelief in her eyes slipping into a look of warmth, which faded rapidly into a look of surprise she held for only microseconds. Stonor noticed none of this: his eyes were smiling in a fixed kind of way, and he was looking over her head towards the bar and saying, 'What'll you have?' Then he slipped into a pseudo-cockney accent and said, 'There ain't no Newcastle Brown Ale here, you know.' She didn't respond. He switched back into smoothness—the quip was just a joke, a nothing, forget it. He could see this was going to be heavy weather.

He got them drinks. She had a straight gin and tonic, ice and lemon; he had something called a San Louis Twist, with a bottle green dye in it.

They finally sat down and stared at each other. He looked terrible. Overweight and pasty-faced. She was at a loss for words, though, God knows, she had said enough of them to him in her mind over the past weeks. The reason she had come to see him, the ostensible reason, was to tell him that the work she had removed with Gerald Opie's blessing to her father's store-room, behind his Cork Street gallery, was accounted for and safe. But there was so much about it she had wanted to say, that she felt she could not now say to this stranger, that she found it hard to know where to begin. He seemed to be having difficulty, too.

'Well,' he said, 'where do we start?' For a moment he smiled, almost laughed, and briefly the old Stonor was there underneath, staring out at her as if caught in a gaol. The puffy eyes then resumed their adman's warmth and the look was gone. He took a pack of cigarettes from his pocket and offered her one. The packet was good-quality and stiff: Fribourg and Treyer; the lighter was one of the new popular plastic kind from France, bottle-green.

'No, thank you,' she said.

'No, I didn't think you did. Bad habit. You're right not to.' He lit up, and she looked at him as he did so, thinking she had never seen him nervous before, but then she hardly knew him. She felt a confusion of things, most of them an anger born of disappointment. He was an adman, not an artist.

They talked. He asked her what she had been doing, and, as she told him, his eyes flicked about the hotel bar, his hands playing at the cigarette he had lit, his legs crossed and uncrossed. Yet he looked at her intently as he sipped his cocktail, as if to say, 'I'm listening! I'm listening! What you're saying is really interesting.' And occasionally, as she told him about something she had done in Paris or London, something of which she might feel proud, he muttered encouraging noises like 'Great, great' and 'Superb'.

To her first question, about what he was doing in New York, he reacted immediately, almost before she had finished the question, with a smile and another quick sip at his drink. And his answers were flip: 'It's not everyone's city this, the Big Apple. But the energy here's great, really great, and once you get to know how to survive here, well . . .' Words failed him, it was so great. 'It's your first time, is it? Well, you must let me show you a few places I know, places you might not get to see. Of course, the place for the galleries is SoHo in Lower Manhattan, between Houston and West Broadway. I've got a good friend down there who's just . . .'

Stonor rattled on, and seemed to have friends everywhere, though from the lost look in his eyes neither they nor the Big Apple gave him much satisfaction.

So the first hour of their meeting passed by, until Stonor asked if she was busy that evening and if not, which she wasn't, having quickly postponed an engagement she had made so that she might see him with the freedom to go on and do something after a drink, would she like to join him? He knew a place, 'a great place,' on West Houston Street, Italian, great chums with the owner Rick Calvino, lot of artists went there. He phoned ahead for a table. They went by cab, Stonor suddenly animated, but she felt like a tourist being taken round a strange city by an uncle over-eager for his niece to enjoy herself and see the real thing. When they arrived, Rick Calvino was indeed there to welcome them, looking like a jovial Matisse, and greeting everyone, and not especially Stonor, as an old, dearly beloved, long-lost newly-found intimate-confessorial friend. For two minutes, anyway. As they took their table, Stonor waved a noncommittal 'Hi'!' to someone whom it was great to see, and they sat down. The food was rich and beautiful, with a red pepper salad as glossy as plastic, and lettuce leaves and chives as green and shiny as fresh oil-paint. There was a hum and a hubbub, the rushing about of people and waiters that Judith expected of New York, and such an impossibility of conversation that it reduced most of what they said to irrelevance. Stonor was glad to hear about London, and he fell quieter and less ebullient when she told him how Gerald was, and that he was marrying someone called Nina.

'No, can't say I know her. Mind you, I'm not surprised he's getting married. He always chose girls to look after him a bit, even if some of them were a bit bossy for my taste . . .'

There was silence between them, so far as the increasingly boisterous crowd in the restaurant allowed it, and they remained uninterrupted by the whizzing, singing waiters. *Riso con spinaci, si; fegato alla veneziana, si, si; zuppa inglese*, shove off mate. One might have thought that, at that moment, only a Gerald Opie could have broken through the mask that Stonor was so unhappily wearing. But quietly, and without really meaning to, Judith did it.

'What kind of girls do you like, then?' she asked jokingly, a little flip; and if he had smiled and shrugged and offered her more wine (though all she wanted was San Pellegrino), and bucked the question, she would have smiled and shrugged as well, and they would have carried on as they had so far.

But for no apparent reason the question floored Stonor. He started to say something, something quick and easy, but he could not continue with it.

'Well, I . . . I don't know really. I . . .' and at each pause she was staring at him, Judith Shure, and he felt suddenly deeply sickened by himself because the smile in his eyes was not real, and the girl he wanted, the kind he would have liked, was the one who did not exist. She would have said, 'Come on, my love,' as gently as sea at pebbles on a summer's day. 'Come on, let's go out into East 55th, because I know a little place where I can take you by the hand, and you can turn a corner and there aren't any buildings there, my love, no buildings turned into galleries and restaurants, no bars and people rushing forward at you and saying things you can't hear.' The one he needed was the one who would take him in her arms and let him rest awhile, where the air was fresh and the food was made with love, and she was the someone in the next room humming a tune as she changed, or as she sat and turned the pages of a Sunday paper.

The way he had known them, girls had not been like that, or women either. And all he saw of them now, as such a wave of desperate longing overcame him, was images of rolling breasts and nipples that he'd touched, and fanny cunts all dark and opening again and again as if he, who had invited himself in, was really a servant caught in the act of service. The girl he wanted had her clothes on, and she opened her arms to him, and the bodies underneath were not what it was about. Then the woman he wanted was going to help him start to rest, after so many long years caught in a gaol he did not yet have the strength to destroy.

Of this Judith knew nothing. She saw him hesitate, she saw his mouth weaken for a moment, she saw a sudden loss in his eyes, which disappeared so fast that she had no time to pinpoint where she had seen it before, or realise how closely at that moment James MacAskill Stonor, adman and former artist, resembled his father.

Nor could she see then, though she recognised it easily much, much later, that now those hands of his – playing with a fork and stressing themselves at it, and then falling still and resigned – were so like his mother's hands. She could not know what images he saw, or that one single touch across the table, one momentary and caring caress of his hand, or cheek, or neck would have had him crying for loss.

'. . . Well, you know,' he smiled. 'I've just had the odd girlfriend here in New York now and then,' he said, falling into an uncomfortable silence again.

She was silent, too. There seemed nothing to say. It didn't seem she was spending the evening with Stonor, but with a stranger she didn't much like. And her disappointment was the greater because she had made something of a fantasy of him, and one that had compensated for the asphyxiating affair in Paris with Patrick Chanay, from whom this trip to New York was to have been such a relief. She had thought, in those moments when hopes make a myth that forgets reality, that perhaps, somehow, by meeting Stonor there might be a new course, a different course. He had seemed once to have a quality which made him special and precious, and there had been something in his work that she knew was strong and truthful, and different from the thousands of images she saw each week that went by. Canvas after canvas, sculpture after sculpture, installations, spaces, mobiles, constructions, performances, new happenings . . . and through it all the work that he started to make as a fellow student had stayed with her, talking to her with a voice that he himself seemed no longer to possess.

She was not one to be depressed. She never looked it—her dark hair healthy and well-groomed, her clothes always smart, and her complexion clear and bright without much make-up. But at that moment she felt terribly sad and alone.

She looked across the table at Stonor, wondering if he perhaps was about to say something. Dammit, two successful, assured people, young and bright, and with a desperate silence between them.

He was looking round for a waiter, except really it was because he had nowhere else to look. She was startled to see that in profile, and with that adman's smile now gone from his face, he looked remarkably like what she remembered of his father. She wondered if perhaps she could mention all of that, and how she had gone down to Deal . . . but Stonor looked back, and then down at the table, his hands moving towards the cigarettes and then stopping as he seemed to think better of it. Someone at the next table was served a bright fish salad with a flourish by a waiter who said simultaneously to Stonor, 'I won't be a moment, *Signore*.' Stonor smiled slightly and looked intently at the red-checked tablecloth, lost for words.

Judith found her breath caught up and her heart racing, because she wanted to do what she had dared do once before—put out a hand, touch an arm. She had done so with Stonor's father, instead of just walking away from him in Deal. She had kissed him. It had been all right. You can touch someone without hurting yourself. There's no harm in it. And now, for no reason she understood, she wanted to reach across the table and lay a hand on his. But she couldn't breathe, and couldn't move, and a waiter would come and Jim would take it the wrong way, and she couldn't, she just couldn't, she had never done that before, and she did not have the courage, and . . . and Judith looked at his face, and the eyes that could not seem to look up at her, and the set smile on his face, and she reached out a hand and touched his. He looked up at her slowly, not surprised or horrified or retreating, but shakily, as if he might be close to tears.

'I owe you an apology,' she said.

Then he did look surprised and his hand slid from under hers and on top of it and he was suddenly holding on to her tightly and she felt him hot and shaking and Stonor was breathing through the mask of his own face and he was saying in his turn, 'I'm sorry, I'm sorry . . .' And because she saw he was about to cry, and because she didn't want him to, not here, with the waiters in their red shirts singing and coming past, and where she couldn't reach out to him, she said quickly, 'I once did something I shouldn't!' It sounded quite ridiculous, yet they stared at each other desperately until, a moment later, the waiter did come. '*Si, Signore?*'

Stonor looked around at him, took his hand from Judith's, started to smile, and said, 'Two coffees, white and . . . white. And why not give us *zabaglione* with it? It's very good, Judith'.

The waiter went away. Still smiling, Stonor looked back at her and repeated quietly, 'You once did something you shouldn't?' and began to laugh aloud at the end of it, and so did she. And they said more to each other in those moments of laughter, contemplating the unimaginable awfulness of whatever it was that Judith Shure had done, than they had in the previous two hours.

But whatever it was Judith had done, they did not get round to talking about it, because as the laughter died away and the coffees came, and later the *zabaglione*, Judith said, 'It's not been so easy for you in New York, has it?'

And for the first time in a long time – since Patti had left him for the West Coast just before Christmas – he began to talk. He did it reluctantly and hesitantly, and if his words had been brush strokes or fingers at clay, the image or form they might have produced would have been a timid and hesitant thing but, for all that, one with feeling and a terrible, lonely passion.

Patti had left him at Christmas—not that she had lived with him, or even been exclusively his. She would never have agreed to that, and as he got used to the idea that she came and went with different men, he wasn't so sure he would have wanted her living there. She stayed when she felt like it.

'She's beautiful really, not just physically but mentally. I mean . . . Hell, its difficult . . .' And it was painful, too.

Judith listened sympathetically, though some of it was not what she wanted to hear. The woman was a freelance make-up artist who worked with models at the agency photo sessions. She was 'free' and, as Stonor put it, 'very into self-awareness'. It seemed she slept with different men quite openly and told the others. It seemed Stonor had loved her. It seemed her mother had forced her to sleep with one of her lovers when she was fourteen, and that her father had assaulted her for doing so. It seemed she was very beautiful indeed—Judith shifted a little uncomfortably in her chair as Stonor went on about her beauty, mental and physical and spiritual, wondering not unnaturally how far up the scale, or down it, she herself might come.

It seemed that Patti – and here Judith had trouble relating the name to the paragon of virtue that was being described with such quiet desperation by Stonor, for 'Patti' sounded sort of light somehow – it seemed Patti had a child by a man she had slept with once, and that he had been married to someone else. It seemed, or rather it emerged as a slight shock, that Patti the Paragon was thirty-five. It seemed she had agreed to spend Christmas with Stonor but some sudden whim – 'spiritual need' was the phrase Stonor used – had carried her off to San Francisco for the festivities, and back to her son's father. A telegram on New Year's Day announced she was staying there for good.

Stonor spoke quickly, urgently, reliving the loss and the wonder which the relationship had given him. She had invited him to a party at her apartment, and when he got there there was no party, just her. He fancied her and she was beautiful, and when she said, 'Do you want to make love to me?' and he had said, with a deep and heartfelt seriousness, 'Yes,' as if they were agreeing to take Communion together, she had said, 'Why didn't you say straight out?'

This confrontation, it seemed, had been important for Stonor who said that, until that moment and for the previous decades of his life, he had never said outright what he wanted.

It seemed . . . and to Stonor it seemed that he had not talked for years so openly and directly, as Judith listened on the other side of the red and white checked table-cloth, and poured him more coffee from the flask they had left at the table.

Patti had taken him by the hand and through a door at whose threshold he had not even been aware he was hesitating. She said he was everything in the universe, he was beautiful, he was Superman, he was everything wonderful he did not believe he ever would be. He could fuck her, rape her, do everything to her, because that was him, whatever he did. And the days and nights were full of pain and wonder, and the ones when she was somewhere else with someone else were full of fear and jealousy.

'What do you feel?' she would say afterwards when she came back, her hands at him again, her breasts worlds for him to love. Oh, New York was beautiful where she was. And sometimes it was evil and terrible. Sometimes he lay beside her crying and crying for the hurt that began to surface and come out at last. And she ever wise and knowing, and he there to worship and not feel possessive because that's selfish and destructive.

'How do you feel, Jim?'

Silence.

'Try and say how you feel.'

Beginning of tears.

'I know, I know. It's something we all have to grow through.'

I feel like killing the fucking bastard. That's how I feel, you silly cow. But he never said that because Patti was wonderful, the Perfect One, and such passions were selfish, and mere cravings. Yet he was a man, he had balls, and she took them in her hand and stroked them, and kissed them, and sighed at them, and whatever else she was and might well be – and only as he spoke of it now to Judith did the very first seeds of doubt begin to grow in the good earth of his trust in Patti – she had made him feel a man, a king, a joyous human being. She helped him begin to break some of the chains of prejudice and fear and conditioning forged in the wild sea air of Deal.

But she made him suffer, too, because when he began to get angry over her being out of his sight with other people, and to ask her, hesitantly, if, well, if she had, you know, well, had she been with someone else, in bed, you know . . .

'You mean did we sleep together?'

And he didn't mean that. He meant did she bloody well get screwed by some other bastard . . .

'Well?' and she confronted him with his own question and he was forced to ask it.

'Did you?'

'Yes,' she said, neither soft nor harsh, but simply, like saying she went to the theatre last night.

'And did you enjoy it? I mean like we enjoyed it, when I thought it was special to us, to you and me. And did you caress him like you did me, and could you have given him something with your arms all special around him, like they were about me, and your hair to be soft and rough against, and your lips and your breasts and your nipples which I've loved so well—did he have them too?'

'Yes,' she said.

So the streets of New York, and the sky, and the sun in the hair of the passers-by, all of which had seemed so golden and rich and full of love, seemed suddenly dank and bleak, and dark as the pitch they used to put on Deal luggers at the start of the season, when he was a boy. And he found that such obvious joys he had failed to see in the world about him were suddenly expressed with her and through her, while in the very same breath, it seemed, the sufferings came out as well.

It was then that his interest in his job at Everett, Stahl and Kassin began to creep away, for his mind was overtaken by a storm of sun and ice, and there was no meaning any more in the things they would have him do. She had taken him over the threshold to a world he had not been able to see, so chained had he been, but from which he could see very well the world he had left, and see it as different and worthless. Each day of knowing her brought him wonders and horrors by turn; which to anyone else – and at this moment to Judith Shure – might easily seem trivial and slight. A glass of fresh orange juice is but a glass of fresh orange juice, until you make it with love for someone who has just held you, and who drinks it before starting to hold you again. A walk in the early morning down an empty street with steam rising from a manhole and new light beginning to slant on the city and your body still smelling of hers may be but a trivial, forgotten moment, until you share it, hand in hand, with someone whose love has given you new sight to see it.

For him, each day then was a crisis in which he confronted demons and angels whose names he had heard called out before, but which he had thought would never breathe their fire on him: ego, animus, jealousy, possessiveness, the way, the dark night, the vale of tears, craving, always craving, male chauvinism, being, being free, letting go, taking responsibility—dear God, can you hear me calling? For the Lamb which is in the midst of the Throne shall feed them and lead them into living fountains of waters. And each demon he faced, each one he conquered, he had thought would be the last, and beyond it would be a sun-filled field in which they could lie, she and he, he and she, and there would be no need to suffer there.

But after the sun had shone for only a moment, in which she said, 'Good, I knew you would see, I felt you would understand, I love you, I love you, you are a King and my master my servant and now . . .'

And now say hello to the new demon, and start to cry because, no, I won't be free tonight, and you've more suffering to do alone. *Ciao*! Bye-bye!

Stonor had tried to paint and sculpt then, retreating to the blank space of paper and canvas and the freedom of clay, to construct a world he could define for himself and make safe, or one which would put a face and form to the sun and ice that raged inside him.

But not for long, for his hand was not still, nor were the mind and heart that moved it. Nor did he find he could draw – as he had for so long, rejoicing in the freedom of line and composition – with the simplest of all materials, and perhaps the most durable: pencil or pen, and a pad. The streets he had seen and drawn when he first came to New York no longer looked the same, nor stayed still enough before him to make it possible to address them. The people he had observed for so long, catching with such wit and joy and anger their natures, or foibles, or what he perceived as *theirs*, though they might often have been his own, he no longer wanted to observe. He wanted to engage them in a different way, to ask them if they felt the things he did, to touch them, to sing and cry with them, to fly with them. Not merely to draw them.

Then suddenly, at Christmas time, after he had conquered the great demon of possessiveness, she dispossessed herself of him and was gone to San Francisco. He spent his Christmas with people he did not love, working alone in his apartment in the morning and opening a present or two over a cup of tea that gave him no comfort. The paper torn and crackling in the silence, the room sounding with his tears of self-pity. And a present from her of a book that did not have arms to hold him. Christmas lunch with friends as solitary as he: another Englishman, an Australian, three women not one of whom was Patti or had her hair or eyes or laugh, as he stared beyond them at the decorations bought and not made as he would have made them, had she been there. Trying to smile and enjoy the drink. Saved only by a sudden decision to visit St Patrick's for the evening service—a church and a city and a people not his own. Yet someone there smiled at him, and someone said 'Happy Christmas,' and he thought of Michael, his brother, lost to him forever, and prayed that he might pray for him.

Winter came, the bitter New York winter which seemed worse than any winter an eagle may face in northern Norway. He lived in fits and starts, dreams and hopes, and without her to guide him through the dark night. Then did Cuillin come back to him, as she had at other times, and through her he could touch something he had lost, and bear the terrible rise and fall of his joy and suffering. For Cuillin was strong and could bear him, and sometimes he could put himself at her beak and talons, or feel some power in the beat of her wings. She bore him away from the confusion of the world, in which he felt he could only ever walk or run, and never fly, as the demons of suffering and joy, and the sirens of hope, pulled him off balance. Sometimes, with Cuillin, he could fly again with other things, and people of so long ago, half-hidden from him even when they had been close by. His father, Liam Hugh MacAskill, Michael his brother who left him for a monastery, Peter his friend who had left him, Albert Chandler his friend he left, Mrs Frewin his friend he left, and more, so many more, and his mother Margaret Stonor whose name was as chill and bitter to him as the sleet that drove through a New York embattled with winter. Sleet. And he went again to the map of Skye he had looked at in those days, to see, for the first time, where it was his father had come from.

Portree, Storr, the Cuillins, Black and Red, and an ugly spit of land to their south, indented and windblown, bleak and bitter in winter, and of which his father only ever said harsh words. A place called Sleat.

* * * * *

Sleat of Hardanger, caller of the Gathering, gazed dispassionately from his place near the top of the Romsdal cliffs at the other eagles who endlessly discussed what he had said. Behind him the spray of the Storrin came from round the corner of the cliffs that held it, in great blowing swathes, spreading across the deep, dark fjord and on to the far cliffs, which were dark with wet.

To Sleat's side, and a little behind him and above him, were the other Hardanger eagles, dark and big and mostly females. Their eyes glanced coldly this way and that, in silence. No eagle came forward to discuss who might be in charge of the Gathering, or what might be its rules. No eagle seemed to question or doubt that this strange and powerful male, who had flown in from the direction of the mountains where the sleark lived and not from the sea, was in charge of the Gathering, or at least the one to whom the lot of summing up might fall.

What he had said to them seemed familiar enough. More humans were advancing from the south with each year that went by, and the first thing they did when they built their houses and put in their mooring posts, or drove their dirt tracks through the forests from one fjord to the next, was to kill eagles.

'It is not only us who have suffered, but all creatures. Last season, for example, it was not just sea eagles in Hardanger, but sleark as well. When I saw what was happening in other parts of the fjord region, I retreated to the mountains and not to the skerries—for there were sea eagles already established who would not have welcomed me, and some of them are here now and know my words are true. I retreated and decided against establishing a territory, or trying to take a mate this year . . .' And when he first said this, there was an audible gasp among the eagles listening, for traditionally an eagle's greatest duty, important beyond all else, was to breed and protect a brood.

For the male especially, whose job it was to establish a territory and choose nest sites, this was particularly important. But Sleat said it matter-of-factly and without apology, for . . . 'I sensed there were bigger and more important things to consider. Some of the older Hardanger eagles have been saying for years that the Doom of Weir is on us, and there have been rumours that the Fremmed has come. These things I considered, and those who you see with me now – who were loyal to me and prepared to follow the route I took – helped me to find the truth of it. I do not know if the eagle who flew from the dark sea is the Fremmed, though I personally doubt it. The legends warn us that claimants would come who would lead us astray, and we must approach this Fremmed, if indeed she is still alive, with caution and care.'

In making this attack on Cuillin, Sleat was on safe ground, for most of the females listening did not want to believe she was the Fremmed, and it was only a few of the older eagles, and mainly males like Finse, who shook their heads and mantled their wings to indicate there was another point of view.

Then Sleat moved back to a theme and a question he had raised earlier: what was going to happen to his own group? And his suggestion was bold, and immediately controversial. 'You will not have failed to notice that we of Hardanger approached this Gathering from the east, from the land of the sleark and the mountains. We have done this for two reasons: first to show our respect for other eagles whose territory we might otherwise have crossed, and secondly to show our pride and strength. The sleark is not invincible, though he is a powerful opponent and stronger in individual flight than we are. It might be conceivable for an individual sea eagle to conquer sleark in battle,'—and at this he was interrupted by a powerful murmur of dissent, for in living memory no sea eagle had ever defeated sleark, and even the legends which delighted in victory over sleark always assumed that it was done by trickery and cleverness, not by outright flight power or sheer fighting ability. 'I say it *may* be possible, and there are some who believe that such a day is not far off, for unless we gain our courage and show that we are the daughters and sons of Haforn, then what, after all, are we? What I am getting at is that we eagles of Hardanger have shown that, by sticking together and flying powerfully as one, we have been able to cross sleark territory again and again and without trouble— so much so that, as you have seen, some of us come and go at will across their territory.

The other Hardanger eagles mantled and pushed wing to wing, looking out at the rest a little insolently. Sleat's voice suddenly hardened. 'We propose now to occupy together the landward end of Romsdal, from the fjells above Storrin and halfway towards its seaward end. We have no wish—' But he was interrupted by a gasp of surprise from most and anger from all of the Romsdal eagles. Sleat's voice powerfully overrode them. 'We have no wish to start an internecine fight between eagles at a time when all of us are under pressure from the problems we're all familiar with, but we have considered the matter carefully. Why Romsdal? It is at the centre of eagle territory—or at least at its traditional centre. It holds the power and mystery of the Storrin, which no sea eagle can fathom or understand: not the wishy-washy rune magic of the Weir and his followers, but the wild and savage power from which Haforn herself was born. To this place, at this hour of need, we of Hardanger have come.

'And there is one more thing I will say, and I utter it with the power of Storrin at my back.' As he said this, he opened his wings so they were stark against the great white wraiths of the Storrin behind him. 'We believe that the Romsdal eagles have forfeited any right to hold sole sway in these great and legendary fjords. This devolves back to us who, all of you know, were once the guardians here. It is said that the present Weir – whose absence from this Gathering is so marked – came from Romsdal. It is said that the Fremmed may have come and chosen this very place to learn our ways, except that the Romsdal eagles, who seemed to reject the idea that she was indeed the Fremmed (as I do myself), did not have the pride or the wit or the courage to deal with this Fremmed in the obvious way—giving her the choice of returning over the dark sea from which she claims to have come; or subjecting her to the Flight of Storrin, which surely would quickly have proved her claims; or by killing her and those pathetic juveniles who chose to be her disciples, when they would have done better to learn what their elders could teach them. But then,' – and here Sleat looked everywhere but to where the Romsdal eagles were waiting to say their piece and fuming with rage and assaulted pride – 'perhaps these juveniles realised that their elders had little left to teach them'.

It was a bold and effective speech, and one which Finse, watching from the back, realised was carefully considered. He realised that at any moment Hild of Sigvat or Aiman of Jarlsfjord, the two representatives of Romsdal, would take leave of common sense and try to assault Sleat, or at least overfly him. It was to prevent this that Finse came forward to a place of prominence, and slowly looked around him for silence.

'Sleat of Hardanger has spoken well,' he began judiciously, 'and I think sincerely. He has brought our attention to things which all of us, yes, all of us, have ignored for too long. It would be surprising if we agreed with all he said, and even more so if we eagles of Romsdal accepted either the spirit or the intent of his words concerning his own group and Romsdal . . .' As he said this there was a sudden commotion, and Hild of Sigvat flew violently forward muttering, 'Come off it, Finse. The only thing these overbearing idiots understand is aggressiveness, so let's give it 'em. If you think the Romsdal eagles are going to perch about the place letting the Hardanger lot take over, you've got another think coming . . .'

Finse was well aware that an argument between him and Hild was precisely the kind of thing Sleat would welcome, and doubted in fact if the Romsdal eagles could take on the rest of the Gathering, who were now beginning to thrust their heads and beaks forward. So he swiftly started on another tack, raising his voice and flying a little above them all. 'My colleague and friend is right. There will indeed be violence among us if the Hardanger eagles follow the course Sleat is suggesting, and there are other considerations than their territory and ours to take into account. Sleat has mentioned sleark, and the threat they now pose . . .'

'That's right, he has. Let's talk about sleark, and come back to this quarrel over Romsdal later,' shouted out one of the skerry eagles, who had no interest in Romsdal, but a lot in the safety of his own territory which, being in the south, was more threatened by the advance of sleark than most.

'That's right,' shouted another. 'While we're arguing here, Haforn knows what the sleark may be up to . . .' And in the mêlée of voices and hubbub that followed, Finse managed to restrain Hild, who was mantling fiercely towards Sleat, behind whom the bitter yellow eyes of the Hardanger group, and their wings, were thrusting forward malevolently, as if eager for a fight.

So, in some confusion and anger, the long discussions of the Gathering continued, and no eagle could have said after the first day what their outcome was. Sleat stayed silent now. Having set the arguments going, it seemed to Finse that he was listening, as an eagle hangs over living prey, waiting to see which way it might go and to follow it until it tires of being chased, and can easily be taken.

By the end of the second day of the Gathering it was clear that there was no general or particular agreement on anything, except that sea eagles were about to face dangers of a kind they had never faced before. Eagle after eagle reported the incursion of humans in their territory, of shooting, of boats and ships disturbing breeding by landing near nesting sites, of fumes and chemicals near towns. Others reported that the sleark were beginning to join forces with each other, so that a sea eagle might be ambushed by groups where once they were attacked only by individuals. And despite the cries of shame and outrage that greeted these stories, Finse – and those like him – could not help but observe that such outrageous tactics were precisely what the Hardanger eagles had themselves used to fly through the inland to get to Romsdal—and that some of the juveniles here seemed likely to copy them.

But the question of whether the Hardanger eagles were going to stay in Romsdal remained unresolved—and tension was growing over it.

It was on the evening of the second day that a rumour spread around which delighted Finse, and gave him new hope. The Fremmed, it said, was on her way. She was coming, and she was not alone.

The third day broke to a clear sky, but a cold east wind blew off the mountains. The eagles were tired now, and tempers short again. There was a sense of an ending and beginning, a feeling it was time that Sleat – referred to now as 'he who wisely called the Gathering', and 'Sleat who has Storrin at his back', and 'Sleat the Sensible' – spoke again. At the same time, however, there hung over them all the possibility that this rumour might be true, and that the so-called Fremmed might put in an appearance, which would be more than interesting.

There was a flurry of activity in the middle of the hard day, which brought to a sudden halt a discussion on whether eagles south of Hardanger should now move a little northward and abandon territory already only loosely held against sleark. A couple of eagles arrived from the fjells and talked urgently in low voices to one of Sleat's minions who, after only a moment's pause, divulged the news to Sleat. The Gathering heard him say, 'Yes, I understand,' and 'Are you sure they saw it?' And he moved a little away from them all, as if to ponder something important.

Slowly Sleat looked around at the Gathering, and in his eyes there was such cold power that an eagle there could not but feel its chill. All waited, and Finse, for all his growing distrust of this Sleat, had to admire the way he controlled the Gathering with not a word said.

'I have listened, I have heard,' he said finally. 'I have said nothing. While you have talked and argued and debated, my friends have kept eyes and ears open to see what is happening away from Romsdal. Rumours have flown that the so-called Fremmed is coming with words from the Weir.' There was a ripple of excitement over the Gathering.

'And so she will. But she is not the Fremmed. She is not to be trusted. She is friend of sleark, friend of no sea eagle. Just listen to her harsh tongue that cannot speak our language. See her worn talons, when the legend says the Fremmed will come with youth and beauty on her wing. See how old and lacking in pride she is. Trust not her words, for they are woven with sleark.

'You of Romsdal think we are the danger—we who have come here to warn you, and have had the courage to summon the

Gathering. We ask for only a little, but if necessary we will take it. But first, we will show you the true danger.'

At this, he turned up the side of the cliffs and, with his group at his sides, suddenly powered his way into the sky above them, and their wings were louder than the roar of Storrin in their hissing through the dark fjord air. And then they were gone, off to the north over the fjells.

For a long time the Gathering was held together only by its own stunned silence. Then, one by one, they began to ask each other what he meant, was it some trick, what should they do now, was the Gathering over? While, alone among them, Finse, marvelling at the evil he had seen in the flight of the Hardanger eagles, noticed that at the end of the fjord, where the wind had been driving the spray of Storrin out into the fjord, the wind was suddenly still. What had been white with fine water was now dark and still with cold air. And the babble of eagles' voices fell away from him as he saw that it was there all would come to pass.

* * * * *

53rd, 52nd, 51st, and the air was bitter cold, and Stonor running through the night, his hands in his coat pockets and tight to his body. Two red lights of a car, a wind at the snow piled in the gutter; and the sky so far away above him—grey, swirling clouds caught high by city lights—was calling, calling, and now he was the man in the wasteland. It was his turn now.

He had given up waiting for a cab outside the Doral Inn, after saying goodnight to Judith Shure. When they came they were full, or taken by older men who wore warmer clothes, and women who laughed and did not seem to feel the cold. Anyway, the evening had left him angry and impatient, and frustrated. He and Judith had come close together, but towards the end they had both withdrawn again—as if embarrassed by their sudden intimacy. After the swing-doors swung him out into the cold, he prowled about the pavement, watching for an empty cab. He clutched his hands in his pockets, staring at other people's faces in angry discontent. His hands burned to make again the images his life had made him turn away. A hundred images that called out for help now—and down at his apartment a studio that smelt only of dust, and not of the oil and clay and spirits that were there closed up in bottles and tubes, dried up now from non-use. So he turned finally into the wind and the night, and fuck the muggers and the waiting, because he would go back now, and now, and now, fast through the night.

38th, 37th, 36th, and where had the streets gone? Round to the left, down another street and past dark alleys and bleak store-fronts.

Snow uncleared, feet wet with slush, and his face all white and staring in the dead windows he passed by. He was chilled to the bone, but his face sweated and he raced to get back, to open the door to the studio, to switch on the light, to start again so that when he met her next and she asked, as she might, 'Have you been working?' he would shout and cry out, 'Yes, oh yes!' because he had. Images, at his hands, the eagles flying there, their great wings black and angry at his hands, their sweep up past his bitter, lonely face, their talons hanging powerful by his desperate eyes.

Old men in doorways, huddled close for warmth, a paper at their trouser legs and cardboard at their heads. And he felt his legs and feet on the ground and heard the wet patter of his shoes, and wished he was back already.

24th, 22nd, and turning now, and up and round past the shop of Joe, and keys awkward in his cold hands, and a door. Up the stairs. Dear God, help me, for I am afraid, and all you ghosts come out and help. Dear places lost, where this urban wind would smell instead of sea and of pebbles strewn by waves across the asphalt of a promenade. He wasn't what their evening had made him seem; and he had nearly cried because it wasn't him who smiled at her, not him, not I—and help me, Judith; help me, anyone. And then her hand at last across the table, reaching out from the dark sea and showing him a distant light. He had wanted to cry and kneel at her feet, not because of who she was, but for what she showed him far away: a light, and warmth, a human touch.

Liam Hugh MacAskill is my father and he stands on the shore at Deal leaning into the desolate wind, and he'll lean that way forever because no one's touched *him* and led him from the dark sea he is in. Stonor fumbled at the second key, trying it this way and that, and in the darkness by the door to his apartment, where no one could see and a mugger had best beware for he was in a mood and had a power to kill, he started to cry, his mouth open and ugly to the dark cold, his feet wet and his forehead grey with sweat.

I am not me, I am not me, he was saying, and he wanted to call out aloud into the night, up and over the great buildings, past the island city that bound him, out into the Atlantic and across, across the grey seas and the bleak currents, to where the few who knew him as he was, might be. Peter and Michael and Mrs Frewin and old Albert Chandler, whose hands had held his own when young, to show him how to cut a joint in wood so that it was true.

The studio door was across from his apartment's, some left-over room no one wanted, which got attached as a bonus to his rent. The key to it was in his hands, and an image in his mind, the one that had stayed throughout his walking run down here: Cuillin,

Finse, MacAskill and Clew . . . all of them. And spreading his black wings was Sleat; he was there, or she, for who, after all of it, was Sleat? The key was in his hands, and he opened the unused door he had avoided so long, and flooded on the light, and took off his coat, though it was bitter cold, the window never quite closing in that poky room. My God, it was cold! And he was shaking. But it was from fear that he was shaking, not cold, as at last he took up a pad of paper and spread it over the mirror he had used for oils, so long ago when he last worked. And taking anything, it didn't matter what, taking up this tube of black paint, he crashed it spurting on to the paper and put his hand in it to feel it and see a shape. And wiping his hand and crumpling up that first sticky piece of cartridge paper, he took up charcoal and desperately reached out a hand from his body—a body that was not his. And up from the dark water of the fjord it came, breaking violently through the still surface in spray and white water, reaching up blindly to the cliffs and sky high above. Searching—a hand risen out of water to where the eagles fly.

* * * * *

Ahead, not far now, the first dark fjells of Romsdal showed, and Cuillin breathed out in relief, and leaned yet harder across the wind. To her right the dark sea was touched by a setting sun, to her left the inland mountains rose far, far away; below, the tedium of the fjell, with its pockets of shrub, and last nooks of snow and the endless boggy lakes where creatures drank and waited for their prey.

But ahead was Romsdal, and in her wings Cuillin felt the beat of time and legend, and knew the weight of burdens yet to come.

Behind her, flying just a shade higher, flew Clew, eagle of Romsdal, adult now, and her companion for all the long days past. No words between them now. None was necessary. Each day had seen him shed his past and find his strength, each day he had learned the power of her flight and tried to show it in his wings. No words uttered between them for nearly two days; and only the sound of the wind in their wings, and a belief in the Doom of Weir.

Territory after territory had been deserted or unkempt, and eagles who should have threatened them seemed to hide away, their broods huddled like wet eider among the rocks, staring down—not out at the sky like eagles should. While time after time they saw sleark inland, in twos and threes, and sensed the threat of them, the curse. They flew at the sea's edge on a bearing of south-south-west, and Cuillin could feel how Clew absorbed her flight and learned her ways. To him she could begin to be quite open.

'Shadows have fallen over this land, as they once did over Skye. There they came slowly, too. But as they came first there, so will they go first thence; and there you will find a land to teach your children's children how to fly. Oh Clew, if only I could tell you of the beauty that lies there, or make you see the sun caught in a thousand rippling waves across the face of Coruisk; or make you know the great winds of the Cuillins, Black and Red!

'I begin to see that the Doom is not a sudden thing, a single danger to be vanquished. The legends simplify the dangers which eagles face, and only in the Doom are its many faces seen. Ones of fear or horror, ones of triumph, many on many—and each one full of hope and fear, and each one touched by all the grief and joy that every heart can know. Oh Clew, can you see it coming now as it has come for decades before I came, and will come on when I am gone? Our stance is at the very edge of extinction now, and we may lose as others have, and all our words be gone—living only in the beak of the Raven who tells it in the shadows of Storr. We can fly again over the Black Cuillins, fly in Romsdal's depths with joy and not fear; or sink into the slow and dreadful Cleft of Straumen and linger briefly on, a dying generation followed by a dead one.'

Clew heard her words in awe, and knew she was the Fremmed, and felt her flight upon his wings. And sometimes, as she flew ahead of him towards Romsdal, he dared to wonder what he could give her in exchange. Ah, but she was the Fremmed and strong, and what had he to give? Yet give he did, not knowing how, by words he said and the comfort of his silent, growing presence. He told her stories of his own, and how his father Finse had uttered the Doom to him and he had pretended not to hear; and he thought that Finse believed he did not know, and then found that all the time he knew he knew, which made Cuillin laugh, and helped her fly on and on, knowing young Clew was there and learning how to fly alone. It made her feel, as she listened to her and learned from her and made her flight a pattern of his own, that she might, after all, have had a brood of her own, and that he might have been her son: Finse her mate. For was not Waulk much like Finse, and had not Finse entrusted her with Clew, so could she not pretend, just for a while, that Clew was hers, and something to show from the bleak years that she had known?

So Cuillin and Clew, separated from Mizen and good Weever, flew at last to Romsdal.

As they rounded the seaward end of the fjord they felt that the air was heavy with danger and anger, and they knew that they had needed to come. Ahead there was eagle on eagle, circling up near

Storrin far ahead, and soon they would be seen—and possibly attacked.

'Follow me closely,' said Cuillin, 'and don't be afraid. Fly with all the pride you can, and take the wind as yours, and feel my strength. The Weir spoke of this and said a Gathering would come. There is danger here now, and here it will stay. Here fear will show itself in dark wings, and each one of us will have cause to be ashamed. Fly close, and remember always that I will need you, Clew, as I need the others—and one day you, too, will need them. Fly close . . .' And he felt that she, too, was afraid and did need him, and it helped him fly with pride up Romsdal's depths towards the ancient Storrin.

★　★　★　★　★

Some time in the night, when the blizzard came back to beat at his studio window and the coffee he had started to drink grew cold, Stonor stopped work. The drawings he had made had started flat and strongly compositional, but now they were changing into rounds and shadows of sculpted shapes, and he realised it was a form and mass he was trying to make come out of the paper, not the illusion of three dimensions in two. He had started in black, in strong and dusty charcoal, but now was using pastel crayon in ochres and reds, and where the form tried to break free and rise from the paper, he put no mark at all, or heightened it only with white, as if the light had fallen on the elbow of an eagle's wing, or caught at its thrusting beak and frightened brow.

From the sky and the fjord something reached out – a talon, a wing, the encirclement of flight – to touch and aid and reach across and help this eagle that flew above its wasteland home.

He stopped as suddenly as he had started, and sat quite still. He took the latest sketch and placed it on the floor by his chair, revealing again the mirror underneath with the congealed spurts of oil-paint at its edge. He picked it up and placed it on the table to his side, and looked at himself. My God, he looked tired and white, and where his cheeks had once been shaven a shadow had appeared. He looked at himself expressionlessly, searching the face that was his own, and seeing in the eyes a touch, a spark and distant hint of flame. He had worked again.

He thought of Judith and of her reaching out across the table to him. He took a fresh sheet of paper and, with an ochre colour he had just been using, drew a swift self-portrait. The lines were free and strong and he drew the tiredness, the fear, the close-to-tears fragility, and, somewhere distant in the eyes, the pride. He used charcoal as well for the shadows and the black, and he wrote on the

178

bottom of it 'For Judith Shure', and rolling it in another sheet to protect it, took it across the landing to his apartment and propped it by the door so he would not forget to deliver it to her hotel in the morning. And the face that looked at him later from the bathroom mirror, wet and with soap in its moustache, was different from the one he had drawn, different again from the one she had first seen that day. It smiled a little at itself, and, sighing, he turned out the bathroom light and went to bed at last to sleep.

✴ ✴ ✴ ✴ ✴

After Sleat so suddenly left the Gathering, the only sound heard among the eagles—apart from the distant, muted roar of Storrin—was the muttering of old Finse, his pale, scraggy feathers looking ungroomed and loose. He seemed to have been much affected by the pressures of the Gathering, and now had taken a stance apart and was swaying slightly back and forth, and whispering. For hours they waited.

Then a talon at rock, a great yellow beak turning suddenly inland, a widening of a yellow eye, a sudden setting of shoulders and wings as if for flight—and Sleat was back, his flight an ugly hiss of wind and feathers, and at his tail the great sweep of his group.

'Look and see what it is we face!' he cried, as sudden as hail striking at a mountain face.

The eagles gasped and shuddered at what he brought with him, for, hovering above them, one of the Hardanger females displayed in her talons the body of a male sea eagle, limp and dank with water. Then another came round the cliff-face and into view, and then a third . . . each carrying a dead eagle.

'Look and see the sleark's destruction. This one' – and Sleat nodded briefly at the first body – 'was Dovre of Namdal . . .' And as he said this, a terrible cry went up from Talin, for Dovre was her mate. 'And this was Hjorek of the brood of Storde from Stokksund . . .' and Fjail mantled and gasped – for was it not one of her brother's brood? 'And this' – and he nodded towards the third body, a female, much torn about the head and breast – 'we do not know, and none was there when we found her, to give her a name.'

'Look at her . . .' And the female who carried her flew with the body before all of the Gathering, and every eagle there bent forward to look, some in fear, some in dreadful expectation. All shook their heads; she was not theirs. And in the terrible excitement of that moment none noticed that Finse had stopped whispering and was looking at the body, and then up and beyond Sleat and his gang, for he alone knew who she was: an old female who lived as far inland as any of them had ever ventured, and who had won some

179

respect from sleark, who never troubled her. She eked out a living from some forgotten lake and river, one of the forgotten ones who lived alone in the pride of memory. It was she.

'Where did you find her, Sleat?' Finse asked suddenly.

'Along the coast where even now sleark roam in twos and threes. There we found her . . .' And Finse could not but notice that Sleat did not like to be questioned, and that as he answered his talons stressed and squeezed at the rock on which he stood. Then Finse was filled with anger and horror, for he knew that this was not sleark work, but Sleat's. But he felt powerless before them all, and desolate, because these murdered birds were the first. The battle had begun, and sea eagles had killed their own. Killing, lying, treachery—they had come at last to Romsdal.

'Look and see the danger we now face,' cried Sleat. And as he did so, the three eagles soared into the air and, one by one, dropped the stricken bodies from their talons, down and down, and far on down, into the fjord below. The noise of the splash took time to reach back up to them, and long before it did, three black-throated diver down on the fjord had heard it, and beat frantically at the surface, their feet racing, their wings catching the water in white spray as they took off in fright and circled round to the far side, and then pointed their black beaks towards the distant sea, fleeing westwards.

Interrupted, Sleat looked after them to watch them go, and then back at the stunned gathering, well satisfied to see the effect his gesture had made. And he might have then continued with his warnings and threats, had not Finse started forward suddenly and cried out, 'Yes, great eagles, now look and see!' And there, against the light, western sky, with the fleeing divers below them to their left and the black trees to their right, not many feet above the surface of the fjord, two adult eagles came, steady and sure, heavy flight in the heavy air. Finse knew one, for he had taught him to fly—though never had he seen his Clew fly like this. And Finse guessed who the other, bigger one, must be. And his heart filled suddenly with pride and relief, the anger in him came forth, and a sense of legend and of time flowed into his wings and gave them an aged strength.

Some deep and fearsome sound came from him and he began a flight of Doom over the Gathering, subtle and skilled, weaving words in its turns, and images into its shapes and form, and the others fell back and gasped anew, and Sleat fell still and staring.

They heard Finse start to speak, the words coming out with the power of some mighty river that flows from a distant place that none can see.

> For then the bleak black rocks will break
> And sorrow come, and death; and all your words
> Will fall . . .

The watching eagles shuddered and scuttered at their stances, and some of the older ones whispered, 'The Doom—he is flying the Flight of the Doom . . . the Doom is starting, for only from it comes the power to fly this Flight and speak out these words . . . the Doom . . .'

While behind him, to the west, their flight quite different in its power—steady and sure—the two sea eagles came ever nearer. Now the Romsdal eagles recognised Clew, and soon they saw that flying at his side, and not ahead of him, was Cuillin, the eagle from the dark sea, the one they called the Fremmed . . . both flying steadily towards them, black against the dark water. And with the flight of Finse before them, they seemed as mighty as the sky itself.

> And sorrow come, and death; and all your words
> Will fall to silence in the waters deep.
> The strongest wings will flee, the weak will face
> The threat, and call to Haforn for their strength,
> And you will cry, and in your tears
> Where then will courage go?
> Where true flight? Where loyalty then, where life?
> One with black wings will fly high,
> One with weak wings know the sky,
> And then the Fremmed will grow weak
> And seem to die, where Storrin falls.

Some of the words were lost, some unclear, some in a language too old for them to understand, but through it all the flight described a frame and a stage into which Cuillin the Fremmed and Clew son of Finse were now flying, and before which Sleat and his companions – and all the great eagles there – would have to set themselves.

Nearer and nearer came Cuillin and Clew, their wings beating in time, and soaring only where such wind as there was over the fjord gave them space. Now the colour of their backs and wings and breasts could be seen: rich brown for Cuillin, and her tail pure white; greyer and more mottled for Clew, his wings sleeker and frailer. Their beaks were strong, thrusting forward; their heads swayed marginally up and down with each stroke of their wings; and it seemed to the eagles who watched them with such awe that they had control of time within their wings, and everything had stopped before their flight.

Meanwhile old Finse, eagle from the past, his talons long worn down and his feathers all grey and dry, entrapped them all with his Flight of Doom, making a line of sky and fjord and distant mountain, seeming to centre the very world itself, in place and time, on this long moment. 'Your talons weak, your wings awry, the Weir will hear your words and cry . . .' he seemed to fill the sky with the flight of his words.

Did you fail to see the Fremmed's flight?
And did you think the sleark would care?
And did you hope that men would go?

Now all your land is bare; the wind an enemy,
The sea a foe, the sky a desert place
Whose lines once clear are lost in haze.

She came, the Fremmed, and yet you saw it not,
And when she's gone, too late you'll see her then,
Yet still be blind. You saw her not
Nor what she left behind . . .

The ancient words faded, his flight began to fail, though whether from fatigue or despair was hard to say. Yet, had it failed? For now the very cliffs on either side of the great fjord, the distant sound of the Storrin, the gloom of the sky in the east over the mountains, and the fading light in the west whence the two eagles came, all seemed linked as one, the space between them as solid as any eagle's stance. And in its theatre now were Sleat, and Cuillin, Clew and Finse, watched by all the others of the Gathering.

'Are you she who calls herself the Fremmed?' called out Sleat, bold and threatening.

'I am she whom the Weir has called the Fremmed,' replied Cuillin, strong as rock, her words causing the others to stir and mutter because it meant she had seen, or would claim to have seen, the Weir.

It was one thing for Sleat to doubt and mock the Weir in debate, another to face out his avowed representative. But Sleat did so boldly, though never so directly or contemptuously as to seem overly disrespectful to those listening who might be overawed by the Fremmed—for all were beginning to accept that Cuillin must be she—and whose support he would one day need.

'If you are the Fremmed, then dare you inspire us, lead us, show us the power of the Weir, by making the Flight of Storrin?' It sounded reasonable, for if she was the Fremmed, then she must be able to fly true; and it was said only those who could fly true could make the fearsome Flight into the wind and spray beyond the Gap of Storrin.

Cuillin looked at Sleat, and saw in his black wings and icy gaze not the enemy, but the face of the enemy that was in all of them, and of which the Weir had warned her. She saw, too, in the stance of the other great eagles gathered there, the frailty of their hope and the bleak despair in themselves that had created it.

She saw Finse, and in his face the fear that she now might make the wrong move. And she understood so well the nature of the burden she carried: for being Fremmed did not make her a god like Haforn, able to do all things. She felt no stronger than the others, and knew the rocks and treacherous air currents she must face were ten times worse than theirs. There was no immediate answer to Sleat's challenge.

'What has this Gathering decided?' she asked. 'And will one of you be kind enough to tell me the name of this eagle who so directly demands proof of Haforn's power, when proof exists on every side for any eagle of faith and trust to see?'

'Sleat of Hardanger, *late* of Hardanger, is my name,' said Sleat. And he let others do the telling. And she marvelled at how all the elements of danger and doom of which the Weir had warned her – not merely of sleark and men, but of a seeking for power and envy of territory – had surfaced so soon, and in Romsdal. She felt, too, the fear of knowing that what would happen was not preordained, as events in the legends often were. They were but eagles, sea eagles, and on their decisions and from their courage or treachery would flow the course of the Doom. They would cast their own fate. They held the very life of their children, and their children's children, in their talons and only if their flight was true would they honour it.

Cuillin listened to their account of the Gathering, but when it was over she felt that Sleat's challenge still hung over her. A cold wind blew, darkness was falling, in the distant Gap the billows of white spray, now turning grey, were forming again. They all waited for her to speak, all curious except Clew, who had taken a stance at her side and now stared aggressively out at the rest of them, protective, powerful, loyal.

'The Flight of Storrin is not a game,' she began, 'subject to challenge by any eagle. It is a sacrament of Haforn, made by her will and through her strength. It is not to be made when eagles war with each other. Yet I accept that, being Fremmed, such a flight must be made by me. And so one day it shall. But the moment will be my choice, and subject only to Haforn's will. Until that hour I will take my territory here; and Clew of Romsdal, who is yet young and has not been involved in your debates and wrangles, will be its guardian. Seaward of this territory will remain the Romsdal eagles' land. Inland of it, and over the bleak fjells, the eagles of Hardanger may make their territory. I, who come from another place, will favour neither side, nor any other eagle. But any eagle that may threaten Clew will face my wrath, and the displeasure of the Weir himself. The Gathering is over.'

As she said these historic words, Cuillin mantled her wings and flew the brief space over to where Sleat and his companions had taken their stance, and for the first time before them all he was forced to back away. He seemed to smile, if smile it was that looked like growing hate, and with a signal to his companions, who seemed ready to face out Cuillin and start a fight, he retreated into the sky.

Then Cuillin turned and faced the rest of the Gathering and they, too, backed away, even old Finse. For a few minutes the air was heavy with the sound of departing eagles' wings. Then everything fell silent and still, while to her side, a little higher than her, at a stance near where his father had alighted after the Flight of Doom, Clew waited, watchful and protective. He had a task at last, and felt he had the strength. In the silence of the night he asked that Haforn might put the power of Storrin in his wings and help him give help to Cuillin, the Fremmed, who had come across the dark sea from Skye.

* * * * *

Stonor did not see Judith Shure again for weeks. New York's grubby snow gave way to a watery sun, bitter winds to squalling rain. Easter approached.

They tried to meet. But both their diaries seemed full, and Judith had to cancel once and Stonor twice, for business meetings that he, or she, couldn't quite get out of. But the truth was not that simple. Both were reluctant to meet. Patrick Chanay had flown in to New York from Paris a few days after Judith had seen Jim and, in a strange city with so much to see, the oasis of their old familiar relationship let her forget its desert horizon. Patrick was there for ten days, a time in which Judith would have been confined to hotel rooms in any case, until she took over an apartment from one of her father's friends who was visiting the West Coast. They wined and dined as they had in Paris, they tried and rejected the French restaurants of New York. Patrick was the perfect escort to the many art show functions that Judith found herself invited to. And for a time, after their separation, he seemed exciting again in bed.

As for Stonor, he had no real wish to see her, though he said on the phone that he did, and 'It's a helluva nuisance we can't get together, but I've been working for months on this presentation, and now it's been brought forward . . .' But the truth was different for him, too. Since the night he had seen her he had felt shamed by his past laziness over 'work', and now suddenly it was starting again. He owed her nothing, and seemed to set no store by her opinion, and yet he did not want to meet her again until he felt that if she should ask again 'Have you been working?' he could look directly at her and without equivocation say 'Yes. Yes. Yes.'

Patti came back briefly, for two nights, and could she stay? He buried himself in her arms, and his face in her long hair which seemed to him to smell of sea and wildness. She took his kisses as if they were honey, but during the day she saw people he didn't know, and did things he felt it wrong to ask about. On the last morning he found, that as she put on her pants beside his bed, singing softly to herself, for the first time he was seeing things about her body that he hadn't seen before—she held her stomach in when he was looking at her, and he caught her profiling herself in the mirror and reacting rather angrily when he watched her. He found that she was, perhaps, human after all—like himself.

When she was gone – and she kissed him goodbye more like a sister than a lover – he felt relieved and free, and returned with a passionate intensity to the work he had been doing in the early mornings and into the night. Oh, dear God, his hand could draw again and feel the lines flowing ahead of his pencil or charcoal or crayon, and see the mountains and valleys, nooks and crannies, light and shade of the forms he had started to paint.

Now he grew even more tired and weary of the work at his office, and less willing and able to direct his staff, who passionately believed that what they were doing actually mattered. For as they sat talking through some repetitive flat-plan, or bringing out old ideas with a fervour that suggested they believed they were new, he found it simply tiring and boring—while the games he had to play with Stahl and the others were becoming intolerable.

His mind was a flight of eagles now, and he saw the world as if it was Romsdal and the dark sea. And for the first time in his life he was beginning to wonder what the island of his father was really like, and to turn it into a dream, as the Weir had bid Cuillin do for the eagles of Romsdal. He was also beginning to arrive at the office with printer's ink under his nails, and the skin on his hands dry from the spirit he used to clean his brushes.

'The man's cracking up, just like I said he was months ago,' said Charlie Stahl one day. 'Is he going to a shrink? He's *not*? Well he should be, for Chrissake.' It was, in a way, fair comment. The change in Stonor was evident to more than just Patti.

His secretary, formerly totally loyal, told Chérie Mason, account executive on BrimCorp, which Stahl personally handled, that 'Sometimes he scares me. He stares for *hours* out of the office window and draws things.'

'What things?' whispered Chérie, fascinated, though there was no one to hear in the women's room.

'I don't know what they are. Dark things . . . Have you tried that Estée Lauder I gave you?'

'You mean pictures? People?'

'Things,' said his secretary. 'He's never been for analysis, you know. Laughs at it.'

'Laughs?' shouted Chérie, voice cracking among the mirrors.

'Oh, *he* wouldn't go for analysis,' she told Stahl later. Not Stonor.

He ripped Albi Steadman's scheme for BrimCorp to bits, literally, shouting down the office. And he seemed so shaky at one client meeting that he spilt coffee on the table. His nails were dirty, his hair unwashed. 'He doesn't have the confidence of any of the older creative people at all, and you need that,' said someone eventually.

So, suddenly, Stonor's stock at the agency began to fall, and if he was aware of it most of the time, he did not give a damn. His mind was aflame again, the office was an intrusion, and the strain of keeping a straight face and straight mind between the hours of nine and five, or thereabouts, was beginning to tell.

One day, only five weeks after the meeting with Judith, he found he had lost sufficient weight to take in a hole on his belt: back to base. Another day, he saw himself in the men's room mirror and couldn't believe it was him: so pale and drawn. His inclination was to sit down and draw himself, fascinated, like he once drew dead birds he found on the beach. That was the afternoon he ripped Albi's scheme to shreds. Silly smart little bastard!

He found himself less and less willing to make an effort with friends—if such they were—who didn't help when he most needed them. Acquaintances, then, he told himself, and sometimes he met them here and there in bars or over some snatched meal, and told them that, yes, he was working again, and couldn't they see the lies that their jobs made them live? Didn't they bloody well care, then? While sometimes – more often than not – he found himself listening reluctantly to what they were saying so pointlessly (because it missed the *point*, for Chrissake), his eyes wandering, and his hands and arms itching to get back to work again. Sometimes he refused

186

to answer the phone, irritated by its ringing where once he would have reached for it swiftly as he put a smile into 'Hi, Stonor here.'

The smell in the corridor changed. It was alive now with oil and paint, and cleaned brushes, and the tap of a hammer and the soft sound of clay. While sometimes he played music as he worked, humming tunelessly to it as he did some loving chore: cutting paper or mixing the inks he was trying out.

The night he had gone back into the studio, that night he had seen Judith, months ago it seemed, it had looked tidy and dead. Untouched canvas leaning against the wall. Pads unburred at their edges, their covers clean. Some clean rags at the back of the table—even its surface clean, apart from dust. Now, weeks later, the place was a mess, the walls alive with colour, not a space left for drying canvases. Here a curious maquette in cardboard and blue paint—the cardboard from out of a bin at the clothes shop on the corner of his block. A failed maquette, collapsed clay on wire, had tumbled on to the window-sill and was the prop now for a spray of ink colours on a sheet of paper, rolled on with no thought for shape, but to see how the colours might blend. Except that some devil of energy in him made him work round them with crayon one night, and the colours were, the picture was, the shape became an outstretched hand and then a wing.

And yet, for all this mess, there was an order. The new sketches and drawings broke down into three clear groups. There was the New York he had now begun to draw again, the people in it. Different from the drawings he had made there when he arrived three years before—neat then, ordered, very accurate, very fast, clear of line and savage in their detail. These now were heavier, less sure in detail, but the feet of the men and the women he drew now seemed more solid on the ground, as if the whole weight of their bodies drove down into their feet; and their heads were heavier, too, cast on their shoulders as solid as rock, as if their bodies could never escape them. While their hands seemed to weigh down the tables or knees or window-ledges they rested on, into the very earth itself.

Then there was a whole series of raven drawings, done from memory and from books he owned, and so a little mythological and much less realist. Were ravens' wings ever so large? Were their eyes ever so intelligent? Were their beaks and black claws ever so searching? These studies, covering sheet after sheet, were done in black charcoal and ink, and as the pages flew past and days turned to weeks, they became more complex and more fragmented. For these were the first studies for Stonor's monumental *Raven of Storr*, in whom are all things told. And as he worked at these, his whole body seemed to change, his very hand to grasp differently the medium he was using, clasping it tightly and with points to his fingers, his eyes peering at the paper, the light seeming to dim.

The third group of work contained the eagles, and it was with these that he talked and whispered, sometimes thinking that their great wings and broad yellow beaks and staring eyes were there with him and at his shoulder, and were his own; not fearsome, or at least not often, nor merry, but serious and hopeful, distraught and lost in turns.

One evening Judith phoned. He picked up the phone quite willingly, because he had nearly finished something and was tired, and fancied someone being on the other end of the phone. Outside the city was roaring and he wouldn't mind being a part of it again, just for a moment's conversation.

'Hello?' An English voice and one he didn't know.

'Jim?'

'Yup!'

'It's Judith, Judith Shure.'

'Hello, Judith.' His voice was friendly and warm, a lot more so than when she had spoken to him ten days before, to change a date and arrange another.

'Are we seeing each other tonight?' she asked.

Oh, my God. Um. Ah.

'You've forgotten, haven't you?'

Nine weeks before he would have denied it, saying that of course he hadn't, and of course they were meeting, and he was glad she had called because he was about to call her, and all that bullshit.

He laughed lightly. 'Well, yes, as a matter of fact.'

There was a long pause. Finally he said what he felt. 'It's nice to hear your voice.'

'I'm going back to England next week,' she said rather chilly, 'and it would be good to see you again before I go. I haven't thanked you for the self-portrait.'

Was it the voice, which carried that accent and sound of so many others he had loved and seemed to have lost? Was it the thought of home? Was it the simplicity of what she said, after all that crap in his office? He was suddenly tired and wishing she was there to have a coffee with, or a drink, and talk. Last time they had spoken – to cancel a meeting – they had pencilled something in their diaries. This must be it.

'Come over,' he said quickly. 'I'm just finishing something, and I'll be through by the time you're here.'

'Half an hour,' she said.

'Please,' he said, just as Patti sometimes had.

188

What it was that he finished was something that he had not started. It was a letter to Michael he would probably never send. He suddenly missed him terribly and just wanted to say that 'I seem to have been over a dark sea for months now and have often wished you were here to talk to. I've been working again, drawing things and painting things. Well, eagles. *You* know. Remember the games we played around father's stories?'

He looked at the words he had written, head bowed and his hand quite still, with the ballpoint pen held gently in it. Only the light over the desk was on, and it held him in its circle. The rest was dark, and austere. Gerald Opie would never have recognised the neatness and sparseness of it. Brother Michael, his brother Michael, now Brother—and for the first time since that day he had watched him go through the ordination, alone because his father didn't want to know and his mother wouldn't come, though Michael wrote to her and as near begged her as he could, he knew how much he missed him. Michael, protector and bully, enemy and beloved friend, and brother, had turned his back on all of them, and him as well.

Judith arrived soon, and when he offered her a drink she asked for good old gin and tonic. She was well dressed, with shiny high-heeled shoes and tights and a blue skirt, well cut, topped by a white silk blouse and soft wool cardigan. Her hair was swept back loosely behind her head, and held by a comb and clip, dark red; and he thought to himself that she had class and style. Her mouth was strong, and fuller than he remembered, and his eyes fell to her breasts, which were full under the blouse, the line of a bra just showing through. He stared at her, his drink untouched, until she raised her glass and said, 'Cheers!'

'Well,' she said finally. 'Well!'

'I've been working,' he said, 'like . . .' and he hesitated and then smiled and continued, 'like a black, as my father used to say quite wrongly, but then he was culturally conditioned against everyone but the Scots—being a Scot.'

'I'm glad that you've been working again. I mean, it's important, isn't it?' With artists she dealt with she had learnt that it was best to let them talk in their own way about their work. It was a gentle art, but a fraught one, to winkle out of artists what they had actually been doing. Some took your interest as intrusive, others were so insecure about what they did that silence was an affront; some wanted to show you everything, while others kept it hidden away and suddenly surprised you with it, or parts of it.

Her father had never learnt this art, which was why he dealt mainly in second-hand work by dead artists. Judith preferred the living work, living artists, and as the years went by, she got better and more astute at dealing with them all.

But with Stonor her normal, cool professionalism, friendly but objective, enthusiastic but realistic, was replaced by something more basic, passionate and demanding. She wanted to know what he had been doing, she wanted to see and touch.

'Yes, it's important, I suppose, to me,' he said. 'I don't know what I was doing all those months. Something was happening, though, because it was all there waiting to show itself.' He was relaxed in the way that the tired but fulfilled often are, his speech slower than when she had last seen him, and his movements gentler. It was Judith who was unrelaxed this time, and she who kept sipping at her drink, her heart and mind at odds with her body, her shoes uncomfortable for the first time in weeks.

'What have you been doing with yourself since we saw each other?' he asked.

'Business. Seeing shows and work. New York, you know . . .'

'Have you got a boyfriend here?' he asked next, his eyes searching, his face smiling and relaxed.

'Well, no. I mean not what you mean by that, I suppose. There was somebody from Paris who came a few weeks ago—just after I saw you, as a matter of fact.'

'Are you lovers?'

'Well, yes, we are. Were. I mean . . . But I don't see . . .'

'No, I'm sorry,' said Stonor. 'Just me being inquisitive. It's an American habit, asking things outright. Quite a good one actually. Saves a lot of bother. The British are incredibly reserved really, aren't they?'

Judith sipped at her drink, feeling a lot less composed than she looked.

'You must see a lot of work,' said Stonor, 'and a lot of contemporary work. Probably a damned sight more than I do. Who have you seen in New York who impressed you?'

She put down her drink and looked up at him slowly. 'I don't think of it that way. I try not to articulate it too much because finally, whatever anyone says, it is instinctual rather than conceptual. But as the weeks have gone by here, I've returned to two or three artists' work several times. I knew about David Smith before I came, but it wasn't until I went down to Butler's Wharf and saw the things he made, that I realised his importance. Of course he puts Caro in perspective: a warm, untidy human against a cold, technocratic one, in terms of their art, that is. I hadn't realised the potency of minimalism until I came here, but I don't know . . . It leads away from making to talking. People don't buy words in the air.'

'They soon will,' said Stonor.

'I think some of the work being done with light now is probably important—people like Larry Bell, John McCracken, Robert Morris, you know?'

Stonor did and he nodded. It interested him. He longed to talk about it, but when it came to it he had no energy left. Techniques, not movements, were what he was interested in. What was going on in New York now did not interest him much as art, so far as one could generalise about it. Minimalism, conceptualism—though it stimulated him none of it made him feel warm. But then, he wasn't meant to feel warm, someone had told him. He was meant to think, to be aware of his responsibilities, to work for the proletariat, to tell people how to see. What his period in New York had done was to wake him up to the potency of artists like Pollock, Barnett Newman and Clyfford Still. And introduce him to a range of sculptors like David Smith and Christo, and superb realist painters like Andrew Wyeth.

Yet as he expressed these thoughts he began to hear himself sound irritable, and he suddenly stopped and offered Judith another drink. She didn't want one, but she said yes, because maybe he would go on. There had been a terrible fire in his words.

There was now silence between them, but the sound of traffic and police sirens came into the room. The room, she saw, was austere and rather dull. A light over a desk, a new-looking carpet, plain. Serviceable sofa and armchair. An out-of-sorts coffee-table. Why did men live so plainly? she wondered, thinking it was either that or rolled-up dirty socks on the bathroom floor. Stonor sat opposite her in an armchair, looking tired, and thinner than she remembered. She noted with pleasure that his hands were stained with ink. There was a dab of red paint on his forearm.

'I'd like it if you looked at some of the things I've been doing,' he said quietly—adding facetiously, 'and tell me what movement they belong to!' They laughed nervously and he wished he hadn't said that. Then his calm was gone and hers had returned. Why had this impulse come to show her? What was it he wanted her to see? His hand was quite literally unsteady as he took out the key to open his studio across the corridor. It wasn't that he was unsure of what he had done, for he was not, but rather that he was opening a door upon himself which he had never, to his knowledge, opened before to anyone, except perhaps Albert Chandler all those years ago in Deal. But why now?

As he turned on the light he saw the studio was not really his any more, and that he had left it. Whatever it was he had been doing there was complete, and this was almost a last look, a final visit. He felt terribly tired and emotional again, and stood with his back to one side of the door to usher her in.

Yet, perhaps the showing was not quite so impulsive as he believed. For some reason, that evening he had stacked the eagle work in such a way that it could not be seen without pulling off covers and moving back an easel and chair. He had, in effect, hidden it.

He did not show it now, and was nervous lest she should try to ferret down there and look at it. That was not finished yet; there was so much more to do.

But the latest New York drawings were there to show her, and he spread out a crude portfolio of them on his table, one after another, sketch after drawing after filled-up page. So much.

While Judith, saying nothing, her heart beating at being there with him where he worked, stared at the drawings, unbelieving. Their technical skill and range she took for granted and barely bothered with. It was the faces and the compositions that she saw, faces she had seen for weeks past, one after another; for years past in London; in cities everywhere. Not just the lost and derelict people beloved of social artists whose work was angry and slight, but living faces of people for whom the city was not a wasteland of despair but a place of small delights, and greater pleasures, of struggles and obstacles overcome, of life. A sequence of joggers in Central Park made her laugh out loud, so heavily they bore their aching legs, so vain their stylish athletic wear. A woman on a bus looking with love at . . . what? No clue—but something there. Shoppers walking past a café window into a blizzard wind, an office man staring out with coffee and a pretzel in front of him, warm as toast, and they all huddled battling by.

Not all were straight realist. In some Stonor had added elements of his own which were not New York: a sudden view of a rolling sea between familiar skyscrapers. No pebble beach and running surf ever lashed at the base of the Chrysler building before; no skylark from the Dunes ever hovered light and frail in the sunshine shafting down past the twenty-second floor of the Empire State.

'Actually, it's too high,' he explained. 'They're not normally much more than sixty or seventy feet off the ground, but in situ they seem much higher. I was interested to show the real scale of the building by having a skylark hover by it, but when I tried the true height the bird got lost, so she's higher than she should be.'

Image after image, Stonor's own New York, where the smell of old Deal took over for a while the harsh, busy streets of the Big Apple, and the spirit of Jamie Chunter smiled benignly at the bars of 42nd Street; and Mrs Frewin, who had only ever been to London for the Coronation – except once for her daughter's best friend's wedding in Surbiton, and that's hardly London – was here in America, buying a vacuum cleaner in Bloomingdales. There, by the grace of Stonor's love. And Michael and Peter, though Judith did not know it then, tucked away in the crowds, but only in profile, for they were walking away and would soon be gone.

What could she say with Stonor standing there, his chunky, strong hand pulling out one drawing after another, too fast for her to see them all and take them in, talking too much as a cover for his waiting for her reaction?

They're wonderful? They're superb? They . . . She found she had nothing to say except, 'I'm so glad. I'm so pleased you're working . . .'

'They're all right, aren't they?' he said at the end.

'Yes, they're all right,' she said ironically. 'They'll do!'

The studies for *The Raven of Storr* were there at the far end of the studio, and he showed them to her. 'Fantasy, I'm afraid. It would cost too much to cast the way I want it done. It'd have to be good old-fashioned bronze or nothing'.

The drawings were extraordinary, and quite different in style and intent from the New York ones. The lines were thick and curved, in places fragmented, as he tried to show a sense of mass and form and space between the different elements of the piece.

'How big?' she asked.

'Eleven or twelve feet each one, though they'll seem much, much more. But it can't be right yet, because I've never been there.'

'Where?'

'Storr on Skye, where my father lived. Storr is where the Raven lived and . . .' And he remembered she didn't know! How could anyone not know? Except that in a way she did, for as he spoke she remembered something that his father had told her, and was thinking that he didn't know she had been to Deal and seen MacAskill, had never had the chance to tell him. Would he be angry? She had tried to tell him that evening they went out, but it got lost. It got lost again.

He was grubbing around for a book of pictures of the Islands and Highlands of Scotland, and showing her a dark and cavernous picture of a place with pinnacles of weathered rock beneath great looming cliffs. 'The Raven of Storr, in whom all things are told, lives there,' he said, 'but don't ask me to tell you more right now.'

She saw, propped against the remains of a maquette on the window-sill a drawing, or rather an essay in printer's inks with a drawing daubed around it. A . . . a wing! The primary feathers of a great wing.

'What's this?' she asked.

'Nothing,' he said, his face suddenly dark. 'Let's go and eat.' And the private view was over.

Two days later Stonor heard indirectly that Charlie Stahl was using an aggressive freelance creative shop specialising in animation, to prepare press-work for the new Talmon Computers account which Stahl himself had brought to the agency, just as Stonor had told Sue Cassio he would. Stahl was playing games again, and heard out Stonor's anger that they were sending out work which his department should be directing, should have *known* about, hadn't even been consulted on.

'For fuck's sake, Jim, Talmon was using these boys before we came in. We've got the account on our media strength, not creative. Maybe we'll swing that side into the agency . . .' Stahl got up, moving rapidly into second and third gear for his planned assault on Stonor. He had been brooding on it for weeks. Stonor had been going downhill, and his department, so long the star sideshow of the agency, was now in a mess. Ill-rumour was rife.

'You need to take a vacation, Jim,' said Stahl.

'Fuck vacations,' said Stonor. 'That's irrelevant. The Talmon account is what I'm here to talk about . . .'

'It's part of a wider issue,' smiled Stahl, expansive, his slitty eyes silky again, his mood shifting from Stalinesque to avuncular. 'Some of us have lost confidence in your creative department's ability to handle certain accounts. The loss of Maljo, for example . . .'

Stonor was getting very angry, and when he did, his coherence began to break down. Not that he said anything now; it was all such bullshit what Stahl was on about. Dear God above, the Maljo account went for very different reasons than creative, like the cock-up over last autumn's radio media schedule.

'. . . But if an organisation can't cater for its staff's needs, then it isn't worth anything, Jim. I don't know what crisis you're going through at the moment . . .'

Crisis? For Christ's sake.

'. . . But all I feel is that you need to take a bit of time off, and as Easter is coming, and the department has no need to handle this extra business, I was thinking . . .'

The phone rang, Stahl flicked a switch to remote and, still standing and not moving his head towards the machine at all, said, 'Yes Rona?'

'Call for Mr Stonor, I'm afraid. Personal and urgent, she says.'

Stahl smiled winningly, his office at Stonor's service, his chair and desk Stonor's. Stonor could have whatever he wanted, couldn't he?

'Like to take it in private, Jim?' he asked sarcastically.

Stonor darted a furious look at Stahl and picked up the receiver, his hand over the mouthpiece.

'Sorry about this,' he said, suddenly very British. 'How do you switch off the loudspeaker thing?'

Stahl smiled again, leaned elaborately forward and clicked another switch. 'There!' he said softly and with a sigh, like a doctor who had just given a patient an injection he had been making rather too much fuss about.

'Hello?' said Stonor, flustered and wrought. 'Hello?'

His third 'Hello' clashed with a female voice at the other end, which also said 'Hello', and it was only at his fourth attempt, and her second, that they made contact.

'Hello, is that you, Jimmy?'

Then Stahl was gone, and his office and all his games, and the view out of his windows across Manhattan, and all else but the beloved voice that spoke to him.

'Hello, Jimmy, it's Mrs Frewin. I'm phoning from Deal and it's been so hard to get hold of you, I thought I never would.'

'Hello,' he said. 'Is anything wrong?' There was a long pause at the end of the line, but he could hear her breathing, as if she had climbed a flight of stairs. When she started speaking again, her voice seemed distant and frail, not like the Mrs Frewin he had once known.

'Hasn't your mother been in touch with you?' she asked.

'No,' he almost shouted out. 'What is it, Mrs Frewin?'

'I think you had better come home.' She said it as simply as if he lived in the next village down the road. 'It's your father. I think one of you should be here.'

Jim Stonor turned his back on Stahl and sat on the desk, and whatever the expression on his face as he did so, it shut Stahl up and had him retreating down his own office.

'What's happened to him? Is he ill?'

'They found him in his rooms again. Well, if she's not been in touch at all, then I'd better tell you that he had a turn about three months ago, up on the front. They found him on one of the benches, but it wasn't drink. Then a big one again two weeks ago. And about three days ago, when your mother was away again, they found him in his room—near death he was. They took him to hospital.'

'Where is he now?' His voice was stronger, more controlled.

'Still there.'

'Where is she?' His voice was angry now.

'At Compass Street.'

'Has she been to see him?'

'No, my dear, she hasn't,' said Mrs Frewin. 'I have. I think one or other of you boys should come home. It's all he wants. They don't want to send him back to his room because, of course, he can't look after himself. But your mother won't have him. I don't think he's got long, Jim. Can I tell him you're coming?'

Stahl was sitting on the hi-tech armchair, by a steel-tube table on which a TV monitor was placed. He was looking at Stonor with a puzzled look of concern—a face that could slide into total sympathy at the slightest hint that that was where it was meant to be. The whites of his legs were showing above short silk socks.

'Yes, tell him that. It'll take me a day or two. Thank you for calling me, Mrs Frewin.' He put down the phone.

'How do I make an international call with this thing?' he asked, authoritatively. Stahl called Rona and she made the call. Two minutes later the phone rang again. He picked it up.

'Hello. Yes, it's Jim. Yes, I'm all right Mother. I'm in New York. I'm coming home today and you'll take Father out of hospital and you'll put him somewhere comfortable at home.' There was a long pause as Margaret Stonor said something. 'I don't care a bugger about that,' said Jim. 'Just do it.'

Then, with a long and cold glance at Stahl, he said, 'You're on. I'm going on vacation.' And he was gone.

Judith found him at his apartment an hour after he phoned her. Why her? He had tried Patti but there was no answer. There was no one else.

She heard the strain in his voice, told him to pack a few things – it didn't matter what – and she would get tickets. She was going back herself in two days' time, so she would cut her stay short and accompany him to Heathrow.

'Not necessary,' he said.

But she changed her tickets all the same.

They were out of Kennedy at about eight that night, TWA Flight TWA700 LHR, boarding, boarding. He had the window seat, she the middle one, no one in the aisle seat. The flight was half-empty, and he said nothing at all as they waited and taxied and took off. Then she turned to him and said 'You know, Jim, I met your father. I feel so ashamed because I never told you. It seems so false . . . now.'

'Tell me,' he said. And the young student she had been, and the boy he must have been then, seemed decades away in the past, and both of them grown-up. She told him as best she could about that day with MacAskill on the seafront, and towards the end he was looking out of the window at the dark, his face reflected in it, his mouth unsteady.

He looked round at her at last, and though his face was old and tired, it was a boy who was beginning to cry, and a lost child whose head she was cradling as once she might have cradled his father's.

'There's so much,' she eventually understood him to be saying, 'So much,' and as the long flight started across the dark sea, she held his hand and he began to tell her.

PART II

Stonor

CHAPTER NINE

July 1949

THEY stood on their own doorstep, the front door just shut on them, Michael seven and Jim nearly five. She didn't want them back until 4.30, so they could go into Victoria Park to play.

'I don't want *him* with me,' Michael had said, because there were friends of his own age he was meeting and he didn't want Jimmy tagging along.

'Well, you'll have him,' she had said, 'and that's that. Now go on. And don't come back until tea-time. I won't open the door before then.' Because it was Sunday, and she wanted two hours to herself away from all the children. The big boys had already gone, and Michael and Jim had lurked about with nothing much to do, arguing, making the noise boys do, tapping tins and sticking a bamboo cane between the paving stones in the yard.

It was a hot summer's day, drowsy with bumblebees and sleepy traffic up on the front, and she didn't want them there. Some sudden final straw, and she was wrenching Michael by the ear and hair to the front door, and shouting that Jimmy could follow as well, because he was as much to blame, and the door was shut on them and they were left standing on the edge of the alien world to wait until tea-time to get back to safety again.

'Well, if you have to come you can stay at least ten steps behind me, and if you come nearer I'll leave you to find your own way home,' said Michael spitefully. So Jim tagged along, keeping the distance, fearful of the dark alleys and shadowy doorways he had to pass alone. Then Michael found two friends from his class, and they stared back at Jim and muttered and moaned, 'Why?' ''Cos she said.' 'Why not leave him here and get him later?' ''Cos I can't.' 'Well he's not playing with us.' 'He'll be all right—he won't get in the way.'

They did boy things along the street on the way to the park, rolling a milk bottle down into the gutter, and watching a line of ants going round some dry and dusty barley-grass that grew between the pavement and a house wall. 'Look, they're carrying things.' 'Food I 'spect.' And then Tommy Chunter, last of the Chunter boys, wheeled away with his arms outstretched, being a RAF fighter plane and shooting up Jim, who backed into the wall and gazed at the bigger boy with no expression on his face.

'C'mon, Tommy! We'll go to the park the secret way.' 'Not allowed any more—the Keeper's wired it up.' 'We'll go and see. Come on!' And they ran off, and Jim found he had to run fast to keep up with them, his grey-flannel shorts all hot at his thighs and the sun beginning to hurt his head, so he screwed up his eyes to see where they were going, round corners, their feet running faster than his could. *'Michael!'*

'Oh come *on*, Jimmy,' Michael was calling, reluctantly stopping at the corner as the others ran on. 'Come on, we're going into the park.' And by the time Jimmy got there all he saw was the last leg of one of them, foot in a grubby plimsoll, disappearing through some barbed wire which was all entwined round the upright iron posts that formed the park perimeter. Just here, ages ago, a car had hit the fence while reversing, and children had been using the gap to go back and forth ever since.

In his anxiety to keep up with Michael and not be alone, Jim ran across the road without even looking, and, panting, tried to pull himself through the barbed wire. It caught at the crutch of his shorts, it tagged at the back of his shirt, he had to pull back on to the pavement and start again, and when he finally got through, and ran out of the shrubbery inside the fence, they were gone. Not a sign of them.

He ran into the park searching for them: green grass stretching, and trees here and there; dips in the ground and a symmetrical flower-bed to the right, full of great rose bushes and the bright reds and yellows of roses full out.

He couldn't see Michael, or Tommy, or the other big boy. He ran forward and suddenly, ahead, one of the rose bushes became a big man, and he was carrying something in his hands and looking angry.

'You! Get off there! Get off there now! Can't you read?'

No, he couldn't not very well yet, only Book Two where Bobby had a shilling all his very own; should he buy a toy top, or an ice-cream cone?

KEEP OFF THE GRASS. He stood still and frightened, because he didn't know where he should go not to be wrong, and the man pulled himself clear of the bushes and was very big and coming towards him.

'You clear off, and stop standing on my new-sown grass, or do you know what I'll do?' And he waved the grey sharp thing in the air and said, 'I'll cut off your ears with my garden shears.' And Jim knew he would, and could feel the cutting at his ears and the terrible blood, so he turned from fear and started to run away, across the park towards the gates. Quick, quick, because the big man was coming after him to cut him, the shears coming down out of the sky. And he was running so fast to get out of the park, down along Camber Road, then up by the corner shop past a wooden fence, running, afraid of the man who was coming.

While in the park, a nineteen-year-old youth, who was just doing a weekend job on the Corporation gardens, watched baffled as the little boy disappeared from sight. 'Bloody kids,' he muttered, working his way along the grass edge with his shears.

But the big man was coming to hurt him, so Jimmy ran on, panting painfully, his eyes frightened, until at last he was in his own street, Beach Close, and at his own front garden. Up the concrete path and banging on the door because the man was coming. 'Mummy, Mummy, Mummy!' Terrible despair because, looking through the letter-box and up the dark stairs, he could see her bedroom door was opened and then closed again, and he knew she had heard him but wasn't going to come, and the man would be there first. Oh, she wasn't going to help him.

Round the side of the house to the tall green gate of the yard, but he knew it was locked and too high to climb. Yet he rattled at the iron catch. 'Let me come back in. Let me in.' Because the man was coming now to cut off his ears. And he started to cry and shake with fright, because the man was behind him and he was cowering down against the hot gate, and a shadow falling on him. 'Mummy, Mummy'.

It was Michael's hands that came gently down on to his shoulders, and when Jim looked round and saw him and Michael said, 'Don't cry. I'm sorry I left you. Don't tell Mummy,' Jim was so relieved he would have done anything for Michael. But he couldn't stop crying and Michael seemed a bit tearful himself, having a cut on his cheek from when Tommy Chunter had pushed him too hard and he had fallen off the roundabout in the park. So Michael went to the front door and looked fearfully through the letter-box and called out, 'Mummy, is it time yet? Can we come in?'

A door slammed. They could feel the heaviness of her angry steps down the stairs and through the house, even out there in the front garden. The back gate crashed open.

'No, it's not,' she said, and Margaret Stonor stood there, black cardigan draped over her shoulders even though it was boiling hot, her eyes cold and angry. 'No, it's not time,' she said savagely, 'and I said . . .' And she hit Michael across the head so he fell through the gate, and shouted at him, 'You go to bed now, now this instant. And you as well, Jimmy, because you came back first. *Now!*'

And Michael was crying, and humiliated, and as he ran through the kitchen door, with Jimmy crying behind him, Michael was shouting, 'It's not fair, it's not fair,' and Jim could almost smell the anger of her coming in below. He didn't want her coming up and hitting him as well, nor to see the sight of her hating and angry, with the dead sleeves of the cardigan flapping at her shoulders in the sky as he stood weak and hopeless. So he stumbled up the stairs as fast as he could.

That was the summer of 1949, the same year she told Daddy to leave, because she didn't mind if he was a danger to himself with drink and idleness but he wasn't going to be one to her and the children. That was while they were still in Beach Close, three years before they moved to Compass Street, and in the period before Granny came back home.

Jim couldn't remember Granny then. She had gone out to South Africa to be with Aunt Mary after the war, for her health. Her health had improved and Mary's had got worse, and Mummy got a letter saying it was time she did her bit; Mary couldn't look after Granny any more. Then Granny wrote and said she had decided to come home and would be travelling down to Deal via London on 27 September, arriving at 5.23, and she had no wish to be met but a taxi must be arranged. A taxi was imperative.

A taxi! The boys had looked at each other in disbelief, and all Jim knew was that it cost a lot of money and was black. It carried your luggage and you got into it for special journeys.

Daddy's room was made into Granny's room, and a plumber put a sink and kitchen things in the little room next to it, so Granny would be able to look after herself. She sent money for a carpet and Jim watched them laying it: red with patterns on, and the edge of black, polished floorboard showing all around. Granny had furniture sent from the Pickford warehouse in Canterbury where it had been stored: a dark oak book-case, a single bed with dark Victorian wooden ends, a writing desk which was all old and polished and with brass bits where the keyholes were, a footstool with a raffia top, an umbrella stand, a folding table and two chairs. An armchair. Mummy had the gas-fire mended so all the white ceramic burners were intact again—Daddy had once broken two of them while making toast, Mummy said.

Daddy was gone and Granny yet to come, and while the others were downstairs, Jim went into her room by himself and stood there. It smelt of mothballs and lavender polish, and was now the cleanest, tidiest place in the house. He touched her writing desk and pulled one support bar out a little way, which had a brass knob screwed to its end. He looked out of the window on to the street below. He was a little afraid of what she would be like.

The taxi came when the clock was nearly at six o'clock. The big boys had ordered Michael and Jimmy upstairs to wait—though to wait for what, neither quite knew. Mummy had gone to the station on foot because she wanted to meet Granny alone. She had arranged for a station taxi to bring them back.

Down the stairs, round the door, over by the window, the big boys started to shout, 'They've come! They're here!' And Michael and Jimmy, hearing their excitement, waited, fascinated, at the top of the stairs outside Granny's room. They had on their school clothes, ironed and neat, and for some reason Mummy made Jimmy put on his school tie, with his top button done up, so he stood to attention all awkwardly in the half-light of the landing.

Downstairs the front door opened and light filtered up to where they were, and they leaned over the banisters to look. Comings and goings at the front door—and a red case, and then a blue case, and then a trunk were carried in by the taxi driver.

'Thank you, ma'am,' he said. 'Thank you.' You tipped taxi drivers Oliver had said. 'More than you get in pocket money, just for one journey!' he had told Michael. Michael got 6d, Jimmy 3d. 'More than *you* get?' asked Michael, because Oliver got 9d. 'No, not *that* much,' said Oliver.

The door closed and there was a hush. They heard Mummy speaking in the voice she used when other people were in the house. 'I think it best for you to go upstairs first, Mother, to your room. I expect you'll want to relax after the journey. When you're ready, we'll have tea together with the boys. Ah . . . now this is Oliver who's twelve now, and this is Frank who's just fourteen. Where are the others?' The question was asked more quietly, and in her normal, quicker voice—and Michael and Jim realised that Granny being deaf, as Mummy said, meant you had to speak up so she could hear. They pulled back from the banisters so they wouldn't be seen watching.

'They're upstairs waiting for Granny,' said Frank, and then loudly, 'Hello, Granny.' It was all very formal down below.

Then Granny started up the stairs and Jimmy got a first glimpse of her head. The hair was white and crimped, and covered, fascinatingly covered, by a thin, delicate net. She was thin and slightly bowed, and Jim could see she had a pale grey sort of face, all old and withered. She wore gloves, and a red coat. He wanted to say hello. For some reason, no reason he ever understood, he darted forward to the banisters and in one swift, impulsive moment leaned over and plucked the hair-net from her head and held it in the half-light, feeling it to be like cobweb only stronger, falling gently across his hand. Mummy didn't see, and Granny didn't react at all, she just came on inexorably up the stairs, and then round the corner and was facing them. She was smaller than Mummy, but bigger than she had seemed when climbing the stairs. He had touched her writing desk and felt its shine and age, and somehow she was like that, too. Her eyes were sharp and light-coloured, her gaze strong behind spectacles, and as she looked at him he knew she was all right. She looked at Michael.

'You're Michael, aren't you?' she said and stretched out a hand. He reached for it rather formally to say, 'How do you do?' like they did to strangers. But he was right to hesitate, for she merely patted his shoulder and half-smiled.

'You're James, then,' she said, and all he did was to reach out to give her back her hair-net feeling very foolish.

'Thank you, my dear,' she said, and quite calmly she raised it over her head with her gloved hands, a brown crocodile-skin bag in the crook of her arm, and fixed it back on slowly, as if to put herself completely to rights before entering her own domain, upright, proud and, to Jim—or James, as Michael sneeringly called him for a while – very impressive.

She declined tea, taking a rest instead. But at 6.45 she asked to see them all in her room, and they came and stood obediently in a line, even Frank—the first time for years that the four brothers had been together doing the same thing at the same time, peacefully.

She made a kind of speech but Jimmy did not concentrate enough to listen to it, because he was fascinated by four little boxes wrapped up in brown paper on her desk, which now lay open. Presents. They were little ivory souvenirs from Africa, white and black, and angular, and Jim didn't like his. It soon got broken.

Two or three days later he was called to her room, and it was only the second time he had really seen her.

'Sit down, James,' she said, pointing to a high, hard chair on one side of the fireplace and taking the armchair on the other side. The gas-fire was on and there was the smell of butter and crumpets in the room.

'Your mother says you can't read yet,' she said.

He shook his head. 'Not very well,' he muttered.

'Why not?' It was an impossible question to answer, even though she asked it in quite a pleasant way. Her shoes were shiny blue and laced, and she wore a patterned blouse with a big brown brooch on it. He stared down at her shoes.

'Well,' she said, 'reading is very enjoyable. It is also very interesting. Do you know what this is?' He looked up from her shoes and saw what she was holding, and he knew the answer.

'It's a newspaper,' he said.

'No, my dear, it's *The Times*. If you can read this properly you can go anywhere in the world that's worth going to every day of the week, except Sundays, when of course they don't print. Being able to read is like having a ship which will take you there, so you see its importance. Now I'll read you something.' And she did; and as he gazed at her bent head, the light from the window across it and showing the lines in her face and catching the dark skeins of the net in her hair, he relaxed back into the chair, his feet dangling towards the floor but not touching it. It was about Africa and something happening there, and though he understood barely a word and got no particular sense out of it, yet she gave him then a longing, deep and terrible, to be able to read as she did and travel out where she had been, so far away. He looked at the bleak, black columns of print and saw that, after all, they might be penetrable. He could find a way through them.

The room had changed. There was a bag by the window and the two cases were piled on top of the wardrobe, almost touching the ceiling. There was a picture over the bed, quite small, and as she read on, he found himself looking at it and then into it. It was dark round the outside and then all yellow and light on the inside, and he saw it was a man in white knocking at a door. He was holding a lamp whose warm light was flooding outwards. In Granny's room, with her reading, there was peace.

'Do you like it?' she asked suddenly.

He looked caught out and she smiled a little, and said, 'You can take it off the wall if you like, and look at it.'

He did so, only just tall enough to raise the picture sufficiently to disengage the cord from the picture-hook. 'It was your grandfather's favourite picture. It is called *The Light of the World* and is very famous. That is a copy. The original – the first one, the one the artist painted – is really quite big. One day you shall see it, I expect.'

But he wasn't listening. He was looking at and seeing the face, and though he understood it was religious and thought he might have seen it before, it was the way the light was shining that captured him, for he understood that there was a difference between darkness and light.

'Your mother says that at least you like drawing, and that's a first step to writing,' she said. He nodded. 'Would you like to draw me something?' He nodded. She got him some paper and a pencil. He put the picture face-down on the table and climbed off the chair and, choosing the hard floorboards beside the fireplace to lean on, he started to draw straight away.

'What are you drawing?' she asked after a few minutes, surprised at his speed and concentration.

He did not answer directly but sort of panted, and raced to finish it. She looked at the seriousness of his face, and the way his hand grasped the pencil so firmly and he put everything into what he was doing. He did not see her glance soften, and her eyes grow a little younger; nor how she glanced across at the picture he had been looking at, and looked herself at its back, where the framing had been finished off with a sheet of framer's paper. She was thinking how like his grandfather Jimmy looked, and remembering him writing, with just the same concentration in his face, the words she read now on the picture he once gave her: '*For dearest Laura with my love, 16 April 1908*'.

With difficulty she went down on her knees on the floor by Jimmy to see what he had drawn.

'That's Michael, that's Oliver, that's Frank with his rugger vest, that's Mummy and that's Daddy,' he said. 'It's the family,' he added.

'And where are you, my dear?'

'Oh, I forgot me,' he said. And before she could stop him he took the paper and pencilled a drawing of himself, sort of running into Michael at one side. 'Oh dear,' he said, when one of his feet ran off the paper. Then: 'That's Mummy's hat, and that's a taxi there which you came in.'

He could not know how long she stared at the drawing after he was gone, nor with what new-found pleasure she hung up her picture again, remembering the day her husband had taken her to see the picture in Oxford.

Nor did he know for how long she stood by the window looking down at a darkening street, holding his drawing in one hand, the other stretched out for the curtain, but reluctant to pull it. Nor how she did not pull it, but finally sat down again in her armchair, the light fading about her from dull grey to mauve, back straight but head a little bowed.

She was thinking that a room and a kitchen in an unhappy house is not much to end a life with. And yet there were Frank and Oliver, Michael and James, and in a way, in a certain way, they had become hers and it was something to be proud of and to want to fight on just a little longer for.

Yet, in the weeks and the months that followed, as Jim forgot that Granny had never been there, who can say that he did not know such things? Who dares guess what ancient secrets passed between them, when he put his young hand in her old one to cross the road and go for a walk by the roses in Victoria Park?

*　*　*　*　*

Old Finse was older now, an eagle of forgotten words and drifting silences. Young ones saw him up in the cliffs, in stances their parents no longer bothered with. The years had passed by so quickly since the great Gathering, when Romsdal was divided between the Hardanger eagles and the Romsdalers who had always lived there, but had not the strength to resist the new.

Cuillin lived there still—who some said might be the Fremmed, but others said was just a vagrant eagle from another place, sent by the Weir to occupy the central point and prevent a feud. Clew, Finse's last son, was the guardian of her territory, and fierce in its defence against Hardanger and Romsdal eagles alike. Both camps found it a convenience to have these two strange eagles between them, but none save old Finse bothered much with them any more. And few bothered much with Finse, except to point him out and say he was the last, apart from the Weir perhaps, who knew all of the Doom; and the only eagle living who had flown the Flight of the Doom. Then they would laugh and wheel away to find food, or teach their young to fly.

But Finse, decrepit and haggard, his feathers a greying, fraying, ragged mess, his beak and talons worn, without territory now of his own, watched and wondered. Whole weeks went by when he spoke to no eagle, and even when he took it into his head to fly over towards Cuillin, he barely spoke to her. So, years had gone past unnoticed, one after another, in which fear of an imminent disaster had faded and been almost forgotten.

But Finse watched and saw, and often thought that if great Haforn had spared him so long, though now he often yearned to fly out to the sea where the winds were kind and an eagle lost himself in Haforn's flight . . . well, if Haforn had spared him it must be for a reason.

It did not take an eagle such great wisdom to see that time was on Sleat's side—and it would be to the sleark's advantage to have him on theirs. For the day would come when he would push seaward, taking Romsdal for his own, and the skerries seaward of it, and yielding territory to sleark, including the sacred but now rarely visited Falls of Storrin.

Finse saw this, and other things—far worse things, which might lead to the Doom he knew was still coming. For one thing, almost imperceptibly, eagle broods were getting smaller. Once, three young in each brood – sometimes four – had been common enough; and the sight of fretful, tired parents, desperate to keep them fed and well, was common too. Now, one or two was the rule and, worse, there were years when many pairs did not breed at all. Or other years in which they bred, but their eggs were addled or broken, often by the female—as if some death wish had come over them. This Finse saw and feared, and understood as one result of the spread of humans inland and northwards, from the more populated fjords in the south-west. They were coming and could never be stopped, and wherever they came they attacked and disturbed sea eagle and sleark alike. But it was the sea eagles that suffered most, for their flight was slow and their defences poor, and the humans seemed always to come at the start of the breeding season, just when an eagle, alarmed from its nest, might leave its eggs unwarmed too long and return to find them dead and cold. So brood after brood was lost, dead even before hatched.

Finse had hoped that Cuillin and Clew might breed, for whether or not she was the Fremmed, she was a great female and one to whom a brood a year would have been natural. Yet it seemed she had never had one successfully before she flew the dark sea, and it occurred to Finse that an eagle cast down with the stress and pressures of survival, such as Cuillin had always been, might find it harder to breed than one who lived free of worry or excessive fears.

This may have been true, for though Clew and Cuillin had never bred, it was not wholly Cuillin's fault; there were times when she saw the glossy, powerful flight of Clew, and much desired him.

But it was a bittersweet desire, born of distant memory of how she had loved Waulk of Shetland, her first and perhaps only mate, and dulled into affection by the knowledge that Clew was always awed by her, forever remembering that she was the Fremmed and could not be touched by such as he. Once or twice they had come near to grappling high, high in the sky, presenting talon to talon, racing in a fair wind, joyful in their flight . . . but always one or other backed away. He seemed forever too young to her, and she forever too awesome to him.

And occasionally old Finse flew with her. Once or twice in those long years they even circled together over the Storrin, and then Finse pointed out to her the holy nesting site of the white rock, where no eagle had had the strength to nest in living memory; and none had even tried. Protected from above by a grim overhang, and below by the spray and winds of the Storrin, it seemed a bleak and desolate place to rear a brood. Yet still some forgotten eagle in the past had made a nest there, and its sticks and remnants were still there, bleached white by time.

Only to Finse did she confide her fears about the Flight with which Sleat had challenged her. Had she been rash to promise it? Was she guilty of pride and vanity?

'No, my dear, you answered as your heart told you, and wisely, too, for have we not had peace of a kind these long years? Better not to fight among ourselves, and so be weak and defenceless as a group when the Doom finally comes. One day, at the right moment, Haforn will give you the strength, and then all things will be clearer.' So spoke Finse.

It was in the twelfth or thirteenth year after the Gathering that things began to change again, and for the worse. The Hardanger eagles began to press seaward, in twos and threes, always with the juveniles they had reared over the years since their arrival. They seemed deliberately provocative, heading towards the very heartland of some eagle's space, disturbing others just at the critical time of breeding when the eggs must not be left alone, or the female must not feel unsettled.

Sleat himself was never seen in these invading parties, and there seemed to be a policy among them not to encroach on the area occupied by Clew and Cuillin—beyond the normal harassment it was their pleasure to mete out to them.

But that changed, one day at last, when a group of Hardanger eagles, led by Sleat, suddenly bore down on the heartland of their territory on the edge of the Romsdal fjord. And Sleat said, 'We have waited a long time for you to meet the challenge of the Flight, Cuillin who calls herself the Fremmed, and still you have not done it. You may be thinking now that time is running out, and we may be thinking you are right. We have left you in peace these long years, but now our patience is beginning to fail against the need we have for space. So take heed, and prepare yourself.'

He seemed to turn away, then came back and said with a sneer, 'Of course, should you make the Flight, by Haforn's will, I, Sleat of Hardanger, will be your most humble servant. Ha!' And all his minions laughed, their mockery greyer than slush beneath a thawing slope of scree.

Now the eagles of Romsdal, depleted by the years, seemed to grow older and more fearful; and as time went by, they began to lose their communal strength: eagle vied with eagle, juveniles squabbled, siblings fought and sometimes killed each other. Time was running out at last. And even Clew and Cuillin and Finse grew out of sorts with each other, for Clew said that they must give leadership to the Romsdal eagles, and turn and face those led by Sleat. While Cuillin said that wasn't the way, they should wait and see, Haforn would guide them; and neither was satisfied with

Finse's reaction, which was to sink into an even deeper silence and huddle for hours in the darkest, wettest places near the Storrin, muttering and whispering, mantling his feathers at the ghosts of the past.

Until one day, driven by frustration, Clew flew over to face him, where he had been perched for days, and said, 'You taught me the Doom, Father, which declares that only by courage and true flight, by trusting action and the power of Haforn, will we be saved. And yet you do nothing but moan and grumble in silence, the laughing-stock of all who see you, an eagle without pride of flight.'

'My dear Clew,' said Finse, reluctantly drawing himself out of his meditation, 'those are brave words and well spoken, and you a fine eagle, but you should listen to Cuillin a bit more. Trust her. She . . .'

'I *do* trust her. I *do* listen to her. I've been bloody well listening to her for years on end, and all I get is the same old story—time will tell and there's a place across the sea called Skye where she came from, and what good does *that* do? And then she goes on about *true* flight, but when I ask her what that is, she does not seem to know. Do you?'

And Finse responded patiently: 'I don't know where the secret of true flight lies—or even what it is. As you know, few eagles ever achieve it, unless it be right that in an honourable and courageous death, an eagle flies a true line to where the sky and sea and earth meet as one, and enters the wings of Haforn. Be that as it may, a few eagles are said to achieve true flight in their lifetime. Your half-brother, the present Weir, achieved it while still a juvenile, but that was Haforn's will and she had her reasons, I suppose. Do you remember your half-brother?'

Clew nodded, a little sadly. Yes, he did, for how could an eagle forget the Weir? He remembered the peace in him, and how the light seemed to catch in his wings and blend them with the sky. He remembered . . . or was it just a memory of what he had been told by Finse, so vivid that it had become reality to him?

'They say, that when *you* were young you flew true, and there never was a more powerful male in flight. They often told me that,' said Clew, the very deep love and the awe he felt of Finse now clear in his voice.

'It may have seemed so, but I have never yet flown true. I tried too hard, I was too proud, I fathered many a brood from pride, born of vanity and fear. Others, even less wise than me – and I was pretty stupid in my time – could not see anything but the outward show of my flight, and so good was it that it is all they remember.'

'They told me the very sky seemed to stop still when you flew,' Clew persisted.

'Did they?' said old Finse quietly, no longer able to look his son in the eyes and turning away for fear he might seem weak and emotional. 'Did they?' he whispered to himself, and he looked at Cuillin who was flying then far across the fjord, thinking of the broods he had watched over and fed and taught to fly, during the long years when peace and stillness reigned in Romsdal, and an eagle did not have to look over his wing all the time. He remembered then his mates, one by one, some proud as he was, some having to learn how to be still, some never quite being what they might have been—but each one loved by him, and cherished. Most were dead now, some long gone away, some changed and hardly recognisable—as his children had changed and gone, until only Clew remained, and that special one who had become the Weir, whom he had taught so much.

'Father . . .' began Clew, but Finse was leaning into the wind, and heading off across the fjord, flying now towards great Cuillin who seemed to have seen him. And as he flew, it seemed to Clew, who watched them both, that the buffets they took from the wind, and the lapses in line – which he had seen before as weakness and age – were gentle and true, and behind them lay a lifetime's strength and trust. And as Clew watched more intently, he grew suddenly excited by their flight and felt in awe of it, for as they got nearer to each other, far across the fjord, it seemed that Cuillin had seen old Finse and the line of her flight was suddenly as one with his, and the link between what had gone before was suddenly strong, as if she had know, long, long before she flew that way, that one day she and Finse might, with Haforn's power, fly as one. For there was joy in their flight above the fjord, and power as well—as, to Clew's astonishment, Finse flew a gentle flight of welcome over the centre of the fjord, as if he was greeting a young female who had made some long and lonely flight in search of a territory and a mate, and that here, at Romsdal, he hoped she had found both.

Finse's flight was simple and elegant, and in its frame of reference – Clew was even more astonished to see – he drew not only on the sides of the great fjords but on the dread Gap of Storrin itself. Yet his astonishment changed to awe and then concern when he saw Cuillin respond with her own flight of welcome which said 'This is not your territory or mine, but it is one for us to make together in a place in which no eagle lives'. And she rose higher than Finse, and drew a line inland, first to the spray of Storrin itself and then, subtly yet quite distinctly, beyond it, towards the sacred nesting site itself. It was only a line not a flight, a hint not an act, a future not a present, but the air over the fjord was suddenly vibrant with a sense of history being made, and Clew watched them with love.

But after a while he sensed he was not the only one who saw. To his right, at the seaward end of the great fjord, there was movement in shadow, darting and winging in flight, as other Romsdal eagles watched the great flight of Cuillin and Finse, and knew that more than a mating was taking place. Fathers called to juveniles, mothers to young, to come and see, come and know, for Cuillin the Fremmed, after so many years of stillness and silence, was flying a special flight; and old Finse of Romsdal, wisest of them all, who was laughed at and mocked by some, was showing that he had the power to fly with her. So they started to flock and travel down the fjord. But as they came, Clew was filled with dread and fear, and turning back to avoid them he flew up to watch from over the inland fjells.

A trick of light? A sudden storm cloud? None knows, but legends tell of how the fjells fell into darkness as over the fjord the light grew stronger, where Cuillin and Finse flew in great high sweeps. Light and dark . . . and out from the darkness Clew saw the wings of power beat forth, grey sky on bleak feather, lost light in dark beak, yellow eye from sunless fjell. The Hardanger eagles were flying, not in twos and threes as over the past months, but rather as one, as when they first came to Romsdal, a great flight of black eagles – or seeming black – and at their head flew one more powerful than the rest: grim Sleat.

Had Cuillin not said that a battle must be avoided—and had not Finse agreed? As Clew turned towards the inland fjell, pride, fear, trust, a thousand confusions in his breast gave his wings a flight of strength to intercept, to try to prevent the feud becoming war.

When the Hardanger eagles first arrived in Romsdal years before, there had been only nine of them; now there were thirty or more. They flew as one. Some of the older ones had gone, but though the group had a younger and more juvenile profile than that of Romsdal, yet they flew with a strength and power that suggested strong discipline. It was an ugly flight, harsh and quick, which ignored the curving lines of lake and lee which the more traditional eagle might take. It rose hard across the country, sleark-like, and seemed to make a virtue of powering through contrary winds and flashing out of shade and into light.

'Well, well!' called out Sleat, seeing Clew approach. 'It is the guardian of this ancient realm, young Clew!'

'You trespass, Sleat, and those who fly with you,' cried Clew. 'Not for the first time this season, and I suppose not for the last.'

'Oh, this is the last for you, Cuillin's minion. This is the last time

214

you will see us here!' And with that, and at a quick signal from Sleat who never seemed to engage in a fight for himself, two of the others came suddenly forward, one from the right and one from the left, and made for Clew.

They drove him steadily north-eastwards, towards the wild spray of the Storrin, and its deeps. And as they did so, the other Hardanger eagles flew on into Romsdal fjord, to confront the gathering of eagles there who had come in awe at the great flight Finse and Cuillin were making high, high above them all.

Now the two groups of eagles bore down on each other, Sleat at the head of the dark eagles of Hardanger, while Hild and Aiman led the Romsdalers. One group swift and purposeful, the other slow and seeming unsure—the peace that Cuillin and Clew had wrought about to be broken at last?

So it was that Clew's struggles with the two eagles went unseen as he tried to escape their remorseless pursuit, driving him towards the Storrin. And in the stress and fear of that moment, his desperate losing battle with his pursuers took him ever closer to its dark deeps and treacherous winds, where no eagle could fly and survive but those graced by Haforn.

'Fly now,' roared great Aiman meanwhile. 'Strike at will when Sleat's eagles approach, but stay close together, for otherwise they will have an edge on us and catch us one by one and cast us into the waters.'

'Retreat or die!' called Sleat ahead of them. 'Retreat and save yourselves, for this fjord is ours now, and this pathetic mating flight by dying eagles high above our wings is a mockery of this venerable place. Retreat!'

No words came from Aiman or Hild, but rather their flight became more compact and guarded, as the gap between the groups narrowed. Three hundred yards . . . two hundred and fifty . . . two hundred . . . And now the air was whirring and hissing with the cutting of wings, and the scutter of talons. Aiman's beak was open, her eyes fierce; Hild drew back her talons the better to strike forward with them; Sleat slipped slightly to his left, for the fjord jutted out from the north face and he wanted to keep his eagles centred and let none pass.

While high above their heads, unwatched, Cuillin had reached the highest she could fly in so slight a wind, while Finse, by some miracle of ancient strength, overflew her yet again, and they laughed with joy in the heavens and turned talon to talon on to each other, talons open with love and desire, knowing that their destiny was one, and the sky was flying in their wings.

215

Yet one eagle there did see the mating cartwheel fall of Cuillin, the Fremmed, and Finse of Romsdal. Not one that fought but one that wrestled in the air for life, drifting now dangerously low and close to Storrin, chased relentlessly by two of Sleat's eagles. Clew it was who saw their flight, and seeking to distract his foe and summon help and give himself a space in which to turn and strike and win his pride, caught for a moment's glimpse the cartwheel fall, their talons interlocked with love and desire, the sun caught in their feathers. He saw more than that, far more, and saw that beneath them, where they would have to stop their fall, was the Gap of Storrin where great winds blew and no eagle dared. There they would be, ungrappling and at risk—unless what he saw beyond their fall was what he had hoped and prayed might one day come.

'The Flight! The Fremmed has begun the Flight!' He called out the words not as Clew the pursued but as Clew the guardian, son of Finse and protector of great Cuillin's peace, and the words were carried on the winds, swifter than ten eagles' flight, and tumbled at the Gap and echoed out: 'The Flight. The Flight . . . Flight!'

Eagle disengaged from eagle, and eyes were cast up and saw in the sky above them, bearing down as powerful as a gale, Cuillin and Finse, their whirl together so fast that even the clearest eye could not see which was which, except that both were one, and that *one* was greater than that all that watched. They fell in sunshine, against a bluff of angry cloud and storm which drove down from the distant mountains.

'They're locked,' said one. 'They cannot break free from each other.'

'They'll drown in the fjord, for no eagle is strong enough to arrest such a fall.'

'The Flight is doomed,' whispered a third in horror.

But as these words were whisked away in the scurrying winds of the fjord, and when the two great eagles were no more than a hundred feet above the fathomless dark water, they broke free of each other, averted their wings, extended their talons for balance, and swung down and round, and round again, hardly clear of the water itself. And, indeed, some of those who were nearest said afterwards that the wing-tips of Cuillin broke the dark surface of the fjord into two great white columns of spray before she arrested her fall to turn back up again—so near to disaster did the Flight bring her.

But it was the smaller Finse who turned the tighter circle and headed first for the terrible winds beyond the Gap itself, and he looked older now and frail, as if his task was almost done. While

216

beyond him, raging between the two great cliffs, could be seen the rush of spray and dark winds, into which no eagles could fly unless their wings were graced by Haforn's strength.

'He'll never do it!' said one.

'He should leave the Fremmed to fly alone, now he has done what he can.'

If Finse even heard their doubting words he ignored them, taking a line directly on the centre of the Gap, and flying, as it seemed to many, with an ageless grace that might have stilled a hurricane.

Some say they heard him speak to Cuillin, others that they could read a flight of encouragement in his old, wise wings; and a very few older ones, from Romsdal and Hardanger alike, would afterwards say that what they saw in those brief and final seconds was the true flight of an eagle filled with courage, with faith, and with trust. However it was, in between the fearsome cliffs Finse flew, and close behind him followed Cuillin, her great wings as peaceful in flight as his own, and her white tail the last thing any of them saw of the Flight, before great curtains of rain moved over the Gap from the storm off the mountains and all was suddenly lost from sight.

But it was not quite over yet. Inside the Storrin's nightmare cliffs Clew was caught and falling towards death. Then out from the spray and violent wind he saw two eagles flying with Haforn's strength. They came towards him, and over the roar of the great waterfall he heard them speak. 'Fly, Clew, fly. For now is the Doom nearer and now our final act begins. Fly with Haforn's strength in your wings, and never forget what you have seen. Watch us and take strength from the Flight. Watch and then fly. Seek out Mizen and Weever. Seek them and urge them here, for their help will soon be needed, and the years will have given them strength. Seek them now, for this is your final act of guardianship.'

Then strength came to his wings, and courage to his heart, and Clew turned his back on the Storrin and headed for the Gap—and he burst out of its grim darkness into the circling confusion of the eagles of Romsdal and Hardanger, whose battle had been averted by the Flight itself.

Ignoring all of them, Clew set course westwards up the fjord, to reach the coast and then start the long flight north to find the two eagles Cuillin and Finse had asked for.

While Sleat circled and gyred near the Gap, deploying his eagles to drive the Romsdalers back to the coast, so that he and his kind might watch over the Storrin and its inmates, and see what harm he could bring them.

And fast in the protection of the Storrin itself, given hope and strength by old Finse, Cuillin settled down at last to prepare for what she knew would be her final task as Fremmed. For now she would brood and make young, and she and Finse would pray that great Haforn – who had granted them the strength to make the Flight – would give one or other of her brood the strength to show others how, in times of trial, when the Doom was come, and sleark encroached, and Sleat was in control of Romsdal, and humans threatening, an eagle may fly true.

★ ★ ★ ★ ★

On the first day of spring term in 1952, Michael and Jim had a fight in the playground. They often had fights and wrestles, sometimes goodnatured, sometimes not. Michael always won because he was bigger. This fight was different.

'I can jump off the sea-wall and twelve feet out on to the shingle,' Michael had claimed to a group of boys boasting of physical feats they could do. One had hung for seventeen minutes off the edge of his banisters at home. Another had kept a football bouncing on his foot fifty-eight times. Another . . . Then Michael had staked his claim.

'Cor,' said Tommy Chunter, 'that's good, but I bet you can't *that* far.'

'I can!'

'Twelve feet?'

'Probably more,' said Michael.

'You can't,' said Jim who was listening. 'You jolly well can't.' Nor could Michael, for the fact was it was Jim himself who could do it, and who had done it, and whose personal discovery it was. Maybe Michael could do it now, but it was Jim who did it first and he who could do it furthest. He did it one day by himself, after teetering on the edge all morning watching older fishermen's boys try it. Then he showed Michael, and at first Michael wouldn't do it. Then he did. But then Jim ran helter-skelter for the wall and jumped the twelve feet, landing in a cloud of shingle on the sloping bank, where the tide had built it up. That was the secret, and he worked it out himself: if you jumped on to a sloping bank where it was steep, you didn't hurt yourself. So it was a lie, what Michael said.

'I *can*,' said Michael, angry, threatening. He turned on Jim and pushed him over, and then jumped down on him, on to his shoulders, on the ground. But Jim knew he couldn't, and he knew it was unfair.

'Can't I?' said Michael threateningly.

218

'No,' whispered Jim. 'No.' So Michael had to hit Jim to make him say yes, and suddenly a lot of things piled up in Jim's head and made him say 'No.' Then more things piled up and he was pushing hard against Michael because it was unfair what he had said, and that he should get the credit. I did it first and furthest, thought Jim angrily.

So he pushed up in anger and frustration, and as he did so, he felt Michael beginning to give. Just a little, just an inch—their faces sweating and contorted as one sought to hold the other, to fight free. Jim continued pushing, and wriggled his middle where Michael was sitting to make him lose his balance, and then pushed harder. Michael began to weaken. Then, to his astonishment, Jim sensed that Michael couldn't really hold him down. First one shoulder came up, then another, then both a little way. He knew that with an effort, and if he wriggled around enough, Michael would give up, and he wouldn't have to agree to a lie. So he pushed harder and harder, concentrating all his energy on pushing at Michael's left shoulder to force him away. He could feel Michael's shoulder shaking with the effort, hot and sweaty, and his face was strange and angry, and just a little lost. It was suddenly important for Jim to win, so he pushed harder and harder, his legs free and kicking at Michael's back, thump, thump, and Michael weakening, his thin white arms contrasting with Jim's which were scratched by brambles up by the glen and brown where the sun had caught them. Michael was unstable, rocking above him, and with a further push at his shoulders, and twist of his body, Michael was off him—and Jim, triumphant but angry, over on to him, to pin him down and make him admit that . . . but Jim never completed the move. For as he turned over on top of Michael, his body over his face, he saw a terrible look of fear in Michael's face as if he was asking him, pleading with him, not to win—not in front of the other boys. The two of them would know for always, but not them, not the likes of Tommy Chunter. The look was almost painful to Jimmy, for he saw that his brother could suffer like he often did, and he felt no sense of triumph in that, only wanting to protect him, like Michael sometimes had protected him. He knew he was stronger than Michael, not physically but in himself, and it didn't matter if he lost. So he rolled over, and let Michael come back on top of him, triumphant, pinning his shoulders down with new strength.

'Can't I?' shouted Michael.

'Yes,' whispered Jim, terribly, terribly sad. 'Yes.' But it was a lie, and something was wrong with Michael that it mattered to him that he claimed it. Because it was Jim who did the jump first and best. It *was*.

After that, Michael never again picked a physical fight with Jim, using words instead, at which he was better and which hurt more, and something changed between them, and Jim felt stronger in himself.

It was soon after this, in the spring 1952, that Margaret Stonor announced they were moving. There had been whispers in the house, talk and pieces of paper with printing on, and pictures of houses which Frank and Oliver and she had looked at.

'Mummy's buying a house under her own name,' said Frank importantly, and whatever that meant, it was different and better. And so it was: for Margaret Stonor, realising that there was no point in paying rent if you could buy, had somehow taken all the savings, which Grandfather willed to her, out of the bank and put them into a building society—which she built up, despite Liam's spending in the war years. She had borrowed fifty pounds from Granny and fifty pounds from Aunt Mary, seventy-five pounds from Uncle Richard, and she borrowed the rest from the society. Then she bought the house and told them all they would be making plans to move, which would involve most of them staying with people for a few weeks over the Easter holidays while she arranged things. Frank and Oliver were going to stay at the home of Bailey I, who was one of the house captains and a senior prefect, like Frank was. To Jim there was something important and exalted about all that: the big boys staying with a prefect. He never saw them anyway, because they came home late at night and went to bed late, and often never seemed to be there at breakfast even. They rarely spoke to him or to Michael. Once Frank stayed a whole week in London, with a friend, and he had been to France. He was very big and dark, and could pick up Jim and Michael together, one under each arm, and hold them there with his legs apart, and Jim would feel his hairy arms pressing against his chest, and his great hand at his hip where he held him. He smelt big.

When the move came, the big boys went off for three weeks, so Mummy could pack up things in peace. They would come back on the day of the move itself. Michael was going to someone in Canterbury who would give him coaching as well, in History and French. He was going to come back for one weekend, the weekend before the move, because the man he was staying with would be away then. Afterwards he would go back and stay there two more weeks. As for Jim, Granny said she would take care of him on the day of the move, and keep him out of the way when the men came. He would be all right. 'No need for him to go away,' said Granny.

220

Oh, thank God, Jim sometimes thought in the years after. Thank God. In view of what happened to Michael.

The house Mummy was buying in Compass Street was going to cost eight hundred pounds, plus nearly two hundred pounds for the roof, which the building society said had to be done. Also, Mummy was paying Bailey I's mother four pounds a week to cover the cost of food and things ('And even more proportionally for Michael because he's having lessons,' said Granny.) Money calculations were in the air.

There were lists on the table, with pounds signs on them, and penny signs as well. A whole lot of tea-chests were delivered by the removal men, so Mummy could begin to put things in them, and Jim was allowed to help. The tea-chests had bright, shiny silver paper lining them which broke and cut nicely if you touched it. It crinkled up into heavy, silvery, jagged nuggets, but when you opened them out again the silver paper wasn't nicely smooth any more. The chests smelt of tea, just as if you'd put your nose in a packet of Typhoo. It was a different world where tea was packed in the cases, and Granny said it was a long, long way away across the blue expanse of an atlas page. 'Look! Look! Mummy, look!' because there was a picture of men on a boat in a harbour in a children's history book, and it said underneath '*The Boston Tea Party*'. With tea-chests the same as they now had in their corridors and sitting-room. The same! Look!

But Mummy was busy and so Jim showed it to Granny, and she said 'Yes,' and talked a bit about the picture. The men wore white rags on their heads.

Two weeks after the chests came, Granny and Jim went down to the station to meet Michael off the Canterbury train for his weekend back home. When he got off and stood there, looking up and down for them, Jim saw he looked different. He wasn't Michael any more. He was strange and pale. It wasn't Michael.

Granny went up to him and said 'Hello' and kissed him, but he didn't really look at Jim. It wasn't Michael there in Michael's clothes and with Michael's blue case for his things, but Granny didn't notice.

When they got home, Michael didn't seem to understand it was his home, because everything he had ever known had been moved and was in packing cases, except his bed was the same—well, not quite, because the red coverlet had been packed. He went up to their room at the back of the house and didn't come down for a long time, even when Mummy called out, 'Lunch, everybody, lunch.' So she asked Jim to go and tell him to hurry up, and Jim found him by his bed, his case open, and putting all his things from the case on to the bed very neatly: black shoes, two grey-flannel shirts, a plastic bag with toothbrush and Gibbs' toothpaste, pants and vest and socks. All arranged. There were exercise books and some other books and a pencil-box, all arranged. He had never arranged things carefully like that before.

'It's lunchtime,' said Jim.

'I *heard,*' said Michael.

'Mummy's going to serve it up now,' said Jim.

'I'm coming.'

Jim went up to Michael's bed to look at the pencil-box which he had not seen before.

'Don't touch it. It's mine,' said Michael when Jim tried to pick it up. 'Don't you touch anything here at all.' Then he ran out past him and downstairs, with Jim following, confused. It *wasn't* Michael any more. He even stood differently, all awkward and ready for something.

There was also something awkward about the way Michael changed into his pyjamas for bed that night. He did it in the bathroom, which he had never done before. He got into bed quickly, without taking a book from the little book-shelf, as he usually did. He asked Jim to turn off the light before time, which he had never done, so when Mummy shouted up the stairs, 'Lights off, boys!' they were already off. Jim lay in darkness and could hear Michael's breath: it was hard and nervous—though then he only thought of it as strange.

Jim had a dream—there was a stirring and shouting in it, and he woke up forgetting it immediately. It was the first light of dawn and in its dead pale grey-blue he could see Michael across the room, lying tummy-down, his arms around the pillow, his face towards Jim, mouth open. He was fretful in sleep. Jim fell asleep again, the shout dying from his memory, but never quite dead, never ever. It was years before he worked out that it was Michael's nightmare shout that had woken him. He was calling for help and Jim hadn't known.

Michael wouldn't go to the Royal Marine swimming baths where they had been learning to swim, even though Mummy tried to insist because it would mean they were out of the way most of the morning. Before he had been sent away, Michael had always been the one to want to go there, and the one who was going to be the first to swim a length.

But Michael wouldn't go, and when he put down his head and said 'No, I won't go,' Mummy said that if Granny would take him shopping with her, he needn't go. Granny agreed. That was the morning Jim swam his first length, but he didn't tell anyone because, with Michael changed, it didn't feel right. He kept it to himself.

That night, the Saturday night, the night before the Sunday when Michael was going back to Canterbury for the last two weeks of the holiday, he was strange. He kept arranging things all neatly at the foot of his bed: books and shoes and things. He gave Jim two stones with holes in which he had found, and which Jim knew he liked.

'Are you sure, Michael?' he asked.

Michael only nodded, silent and miserable.

Jim woke the following morning very early again, the light still grey. He lay awake, but tied to the bed by tiredness as if he had not slept. He wanted to go to the toilet.

'Are you awake, Jim?' Michael asked out of the gloom.

'Yes,' said Jim. 'I'm going to the lavatory.'

When he got back he went to pull off the blankets to get into bed, but the strangest thing: Michael was in his bed, curled into the place where he had been, curled into his own familiar warmth. He was deep asleep. Even by the dawn light Jim could see that where his pyjama top had ridden up there were terrible black-blue bruises on his back and down towards his bottom. Very gently Jim put the blankets back and tucked him in. Then he went over and got into Michael's bed. It felt bitterly cold and a long, long way away from where Jim was used to being in the room.

When it was morning properly and they were getting up, Jim asked Michael, 'Why have you got bruises on your back? Who hit you?'

Michael said, 'You shouldn't have seen them. Promise you won't tell Mummy. Promise!'

'I promise,' said Jim.

'Schoolboy's honour!' ordered Michael.

'Yes,' said Jim. 'But what are they for. What did you do wrong?'

'If you say anything I'll . . . I'll . . .' and he searched for the most terrible thing he could do to Jimmy. 'I'll tear up your picture,' he said finally. And Jimmy knew from the way he said it that he would. It was the picture that Granny had given him, a copy of the one over her bed, with the lamp and the man. *The Light of the World*. He loved it more than anything.

At tea-time, before Michael was due to go, he caused a scene. He deliberately broke a tea-cup, crashing it down on to a saucer. Jim was not surprised: he had never been Michael from the time he came back.

'If you weren't going away shortly I would send you to bed,' shouted Mummy. 'Now stop behaving as you have, and shut up.

You'll be gone soon, thank God, and we'll have some peace and quiet.' Then she changed her voice a bit and said, 'Anyway, the lessons are good for you.

'Jim's no better than I am in his form at French and History,' said Michael bitterly. 'I don't want to go back.'

He started to cry and shout, and Mummy suddenly got up and grabbed him viciously by the arm and pulled him from the room and into the sitting-room.

'Drink your tea,' said Granny to Jim.

Jim did, but he listened as well, and heard screams and shouts and sobbing. He heard Michael plead finally, 'Please don't send me back, Mummy. Please don't send me back there!' And he said it in the same way that he had looked at Jim in the playground when Jim had been winning the fight.

Jim wanted to run into the sitting-room and say, 'Mummy, he's got bruises on his back he won't let you see,' but Michael had made him promise not to. Maybe he could mention them in some way to Granny, somehow or other. He started to try but never finished, because Mummy came back into the room, hair wild and breathing heavily. She was white in the face, and angry-looking. 'He's being very naughty indeed, and the sooner he goes off for the train the better. You had better take him, Mother. And you . . .' and Jim stopped trying to talk to Granny as he had been, 'had best shut up. I don't want any more fuss from either of you'.

The atmosphere was so unbearable that, as soon as tea was over, Jim got down and went upstairs to the bedroom. Michael's bed was stripped, the blankets folded ready for packing in a tea-chest. His case was packed, the lid propped open for some last thing to be put in.

Then Jim knew what he should do for Michael, and searched his own possessions to put something deep in the suitcase, so Michael would have it when he got where he was going. Something in exchange for the two stones with holes in. He searched through his things, his books, his marbles, the two cars and the stones he had collected. Then he saw the picture he loved best of all, and lifting up the shirt and things, he put it carefully down at the bottom of the suitcase where it wouldn't be seen.

Then Mummy came up carrying a pair of plimsolls she had whitened, to put in the case. Jim watched, heart in his mouth, as her great hands patted and delved at the suitcase contents, praying she wouldn't find it. He would have to explain. He couldn't explain.

She found it, hands puzzled at the hard edge of the frame, fingers delving beneath grey flannel and past grey corduroy, fingers

224

flinging and pulling out. Back straightening and head turning, face surprised and angry.

'Michael!' She shouted the name, and the anger of it pierced Jim through as if he was being beaten. He knew what she was thinking.

'He didn't take it, Mummy. He didn't honestly. I put it there. It's a present.'

She looked at Jim, weighing it all up: she knew the boys protected each other from her.

'If you did, you shouldn't. Your grandmother gave it to you.' She said it with distaste. 'You can't give a present away.'

But if Granny knew, she wouldn't mind, he was thinking desperately, mind racing against the fact that Michael was coming slowly up the stairs in answer to Mummy's terrible call. It was his way of saying something to Michael, but he couldn't explain.

'Now take it back and I'll forget all about it,' his mother said.

'Don't tell Michael,' he said. Because that would make it worse somehow. She could at least not tell Michael.

She did not agree or disagree, but when Michael came in the picture was back up, and all she finally said was, 'Here, take this downstairs. You're big enough to carry your own case now.' Jim watched him helplessly. It seemed he was so beaten down, his older brother Michael, so frightened and pale, that he would hardly be able to bear the burden of the suitcase and would fall under the weight of it. And Jim wanted to carry it for him. But Mummy wouldn't let him.

That night Jim slept alone, and had the first experience of a nightmare that was to trouble him for years. It was dusk and he was running up wet shingle from the sea, because a great wave was coming for him, and his black wellingtons were slipping and giving him no grip, and the wave was turning black and rising into the sky over him, and it had dark wings and he knew that if only he could raise his arms and fly he could escape the shingle that dragged him down—escape the thing that was looming over him from behind and would lose him in its terrible darkness.

'It was always the same, always the same . . .' whispered Jim Stonor to Judith, her hand in his hair, caressing him. 'I couldn't fly. I didn't know how . . .' The lights were low because they were about to show the film, and anyway Judith had long since switched off the reading lights on the rack above their heads. The plane being half-empty, the seats before and behind were unoccupied, and Stonor was talking, barely looking at her, almost talking to himself, and she felt the huge need he had of someone and she felt strong and calm and old as the sea. Because he had found her, and didn't mind needing her, and he was talking to her of things he had never talked of to anyone.

The film flickered to its start, silent, because you only heard the words through earphones. When they were handed out, she had waved the stewardess away and turned back to Jim, arms round him.

'But you tried to . . . you tried,' she whispered again, knowing how inadequate it was to say that.

'But it was never enough, just to try,' he said. 'It's *never* enough.'

Then he was talking again, and she holding, and they beginning to share something important in the long flight over the dark sea.

CHAPTER TEN

March 1952

ON the day before the move to Compass Street, a man came to the house in a black, shiny car to see Mummy. Jim saw the car come to a stop and saw the man get out. He was wearing a grey hat and a grey overcoat against the wind, and he had a white shirt and tie, and black shoes, shiny like the car.

Mummy took off her apron and straightened her hair when Jim came to tell her the man was there. She looked kind of different, sort of afraid. She went out and led the man into what was left of the sitting-room, and Jim could hear her voice apologising and the man's voice saying it really didn't matter, Mrs Stonor, before the door closed on them and the voices were lost.

Later, Jim heard the man leaving and Mummy saying goodbye. Then there was silence. He went to look for her and found her on a chair in the sitting-room, looking out of the window. In her hand was a buff envelope with big black writing on it. She looked round when he came in and smiled faintly at him, as if from a distance, from another world.

'Hello,' she said.

'Who was that man?' he asked.

'My solicitor,' she said. It sounded important.

He looked at the envelope. 'What's in it?' he asked.

'You can open it, if you like,' said Mummy. 'Go on. You open it, my dear.'

He did. It was a yellow brass Yale key for a front door.

'It's a key,' he said.

'Yes,' she said, and he had never heard her speak like that. She took it from him, and held it, feeling it and turning it in her fingers, just like he sometimes touched and held one of his favourite things.

'It's the key to Number 11 Compass Street,' she said. And suddenly she reached out and clumsily took him in her arms, him half-falling over her thigh, and there she held him. He didn't like it and felt embarrassed. When he pushed away and was standing upright again, looking at her, he saw she was crying, or that there were tears in her eyes.

'I'm sorry,' she said. 'I'm not always a very good mother, am I? You're confused, aren't you? But don't worry, I expect you'll understand one day. This is the most important day of my life.'

Jim didn't understand and just stared.

That afternoon, Mummy had another argument with Granny. The whole house seemed desolate and miserable. 'It's not much to ask of you, even if it doesn't suit you, Mother. I'm not leaving Jim alone in the house today. Take him for a walk or something. I want the afternoon to myself, just to myself. Just until tea-time. Please, Mother.'

It was despairing, defiant, strong, weak, and to Jim, downstairs, it seemed the disembodied voice of some lost spirit he could not see. Round a corner, through a door, up the stairs, at an open door into Granny's room . . . that's where the spirit's cry came from. Then the familiar thump downstairs, and Mummy had gone out without saying goodbye.

Margaret Stonor's progress, from Walmer down into Deal and then along the front to North Deal, was deliberately slow. She was not going to let her rage at her mother spoil the moment. Bloody, bloody woman. She did not have to make her pay for everything she did. She did not have to deliberately set out to spoil this moment like she had spoilt so many others. She . . .

It was a warm day, a lovely day, and once she was up on the front by the green near the lifeboat and heading north, the rage began to melt away and she began to forget. She began to think instead of . . . of . . . not things she had to do, or things, or children, or her mother, or of Liam, poor man, or what money they did not have, but of what she was feeling. Of what *she* was feeling.

She was forty-seven, nearly forty-eight. She was getting on for fifty. What she was feeling was relief, and enormous tiredness. In her bag was the key to Number 11 Compass Street, an object she had marvelled about ever since Mr Wittle gave it to her so simply that morning. Twenty years, thirty years . . . well, nearly fifty in all honesty, and finally, finally, she reached out her hand and took hold of her freedom.

Oh, the sun was shining, and out to sea she could see ships on the horizon of the blue and sparkling water, and to their right the dim outline of France. Oh, she was on the way, and the sun was among the brown pebbles of the beach, and the boats were steaming, and France, or anywhere, was there. It was there. She stopped still, quite still, without a shopping bag in her hand, or the need to go somewhere for some loathsome child, or the need to get home to make something for someone or meet some demand, and she looked out at a horizon that was suddenly hers. *Je suis comme je suis, je suis faite comme ça, Quand j'ai envie de rire, Oui je ris aux éclats!*

She whispered the lines to herself and, though she did not laugh out loud, as the poet she loved and read sometimes when the house was quiet, might himself have done, her eyes smiled secretly with joy, because she was walking along the front, and there was still time left to live after the past dark years.

They had all been against it, but she liked the old fishermen's houses of North Deal, even if no one else did. They were lived in, and somehow *real*. Grubby, old, damp in the winter no doubt, subject to flooding when heavy rain coincided with a northerly gale and high tide . . . 'Really, Mrs Stonor, we do not recommend you to purchase one of these houses, even if the price does seem very reasonable. You have to bear in mind the high costs of getting them into some kind of habitable order . . . and the society will almost certainly withhold some money until necessary repairs to windows and roof are made . . .' So said the building society man.

'But I know it's right,' she had said, weakly at first, almost willing to be dissuaded, until some demon in her, some tiny spirit of rebellion and protest, strengthened her resolve, and one by one she persuaded the people who could lend her the money to part with it. 'Really, Margaret, do you think it wise? I mean, you can hardly rely on Liam's support long-term, and the money you got from Father won't last that long. Wait until the children are off your hands,' said her brother. But by then it would be too late, and she too old. And the price would have gone up. And since asking directly didn't seem to work, she resorted to a kind of blackmail. 'If you don't trust me and can't afford it, Richard . . .' and he had lent her seventy-five pounds. Bit by bit, pound by pound, she got the money together. It would be her place, and if they didn't like the location she had chosen, down there where real people lived, and where the houses were old and beloved; then . . . then . . . well, it would be sad.

She was nervous. What was she now? A mother of four boys whose marriage had broken. A house-owner! The word seemed incredible. *Mais je suis que je suis* . . . and she finished the line with the thought that, whatever else she was, she was now, as a house-owner, liable under the law to jury service. She smiled to herself at the burden of it! But she was nervous, because there was Coppin Street, soon Farrier Street, and not far past that, just where the sign of the Bosun's Mate hung over Beach Street, after Silver Street was the turning down into Compass Street.

Round the corner and out of the light, into the narrow street itself, feeling so conspicuous and sure that everyone was looking out at her from behind their lace curtains. The key, the door, the lovely eighteenth-century door which would be hers—was hers.

Mr and Mrs Barnes had left the day before, and she didn't want to know about them. The house was to be a fresh piece of paper on which she might make one of those drawings she used to make before she had married Liam. Drawings of a provincial spinster, daughter of a domineering, sanctimonious seaside vicar and his indomitable, loyal wife, Laura. The house was a new page, a new sketch-book, and as she put the key to the lock, her hands were shaking, and her eyes squinting with strain through her glasses.

The door opened loosely into the hollow, dry sound of an empty house. She stepped quickly over a couple of letters and closed it behind her, to stand, at last, in the privacy of her own home. She closed her eyes, and breathed deeply, her mouth a little open, her face rather pale. One of her stockings was snagged, and her hair, which was done up round a ring made from an old stocking, just as they had done throughout the war, looked straggly. It was beginning to grey. She had in her bag a pencil, a pen, and a sketch-pad on which she intended to make drawings and lists of things to do. But still she stood, not moving, not walking, looking up the unfamiliar wood-panelled corridor to the kitchen door, which was glazed with old bottle-glass through which she could make out the distortions of a distant wall and mantelpiece.

No noise. No Frank and Oliver arguing; no Michael whining on, as he often seemed to these days. No Jim. No Mother looking at her from the stairs. Peace to be herself.

On down the corridor, she turned into what she supposed would now be the sitting-room, which had a window on to the garden—if garden it was that was only a strip of red-bricked walled courtyard, all higgledy-piggledy but with lovely eighteenth-century red-tiled roofs peeping over it to right, to left, to centre. The room smelt musty, and of oiled shelf-paper. Mr Barnes had kept his tools in it, and the old tool cabinet was pinned against what must, she supposed, be a fireplace. The room seemed bigger than she remembered and she went and stood by the window, looking out at the garden. It was a total mess. Old shelves rotted at one end of it. There was a pile of mouldering black war blinds against a wall, a dustbin on its side in the middle. A few grimy shrubs here and there among the rubble, and a rampant lilac to cast mauve colour and shade. There were some rotted lobster-pots beneath the window itself, and along the left wall, which was the kitchen and had a door set in it, was an old brass bedstead, the iron bits rusty.

'We won't be able to clear out the garden, I'm afraid,' Mrs Barnes had said on the second visit, after the solicitor had passed on her offer—a daring fifty pounds beneath the asking price but already more than she could really afford. 'But if you've got boys they'll be able to sort it out for you.'

'It doesn't matter, you know. I'm sure I can manage,' Margaret Stonor had said, for it didn't. They had accepted her offer! She was committed. It might soon be hers! And they could leave it exactly as it was, because it didn't matter, it really didn't.

Now, three months later, she pushed open the door into the kitchen. The sun was shining into it, dust floating in a shaft over the brown-red linoleum they had left there.

Beyond it was the brown tiled fireplace which, Mrs Barnes had told her, they had put in themselves, taking out the old one. It was ugly and mean—very thirties. She had smiled and nodded her head as if impressed, but she had been thinking Thank God, they didn't take out any of the others, for they were carved wood and pine, old and very beautiful beneath their cream or brown paint and chips and scars. Merely unloved, that was all. And an unloved thing withers, and wilts, but it needn't die. No, it *needn't*.

There was an old pottery jam-jar on the mantelpiece, and underneath it a note. It read: 'Dear Mrs Stonor, in jar is key to back door, and key to back gate. This opens with a shove. Coal cellar shutters dangerous and need fixing. Albert Chandler of Union Road is a good carpenter known to me who charges fair prices. R. Barnes.' This was written in a firm, tight hand. Underneath, written in a looser, round hand was the following: 'Have left half a pint of milk standing in cold water in sink, and some tea and a kettle and a cup we will not need. Also matches so you can make yourself a cup of tea when you come. We have been very happy in Number Eleven, I hope you may be. Bless you and good luck in your home. Rosalee Barnes'.

She looked at the note a long time, leaning heavily against the mantelpiece and fighting the urge to cry. She had never really done anything very right and was nearly fifty now. But she felt the past few years, when she had suffered so much with the change of life, were fading away and that here she would have her own place in her own way. No, she wouldn't cry.

She made a cup of tea and, there being no chair, sat in the sun on the step down into the little garden. The old bed-frame and the dustbin began to go, and the broken glass and pebbles to fade away, and in their place, and over where the war blinds lay in a heap, and even as far as the forgotten broken window-frames, eglantine and an apple tree, primroses and toadflax, string-beans and the greenest, prettiest foliage and flowers that ever a house-owner saw, began to grow. While deep, deep inside her and despite the disappointment she found with Liam, and the long years and broken nights of the children, and the desperate war years, and years since with so little money, and the sense that she was growing older and slower now and she had almost died away to nothing in these last years, despite all this, something that was not quite dead moved and stretched and reached out from her and felt the warmth of the sunshine all around.

* * * * *

For weeks past, ever since the long dark days of January, Mizen, mate of Weever, lost friend of Cuillin, once of Romsdal like Clew, had been restless and uneasy. The harsh years in the north, where they had felt bound to stay by some sense of duty and prophecy, had calmed her and made her look more self-assured. Her tail was quite white now, her wings strong, but her face still wore the hint of anxiety and she still jerked her head this way and that, only falling quite still and calm when Weever was nearby in flight or at stance. They had had a brood most years, and their young were spread far and wide now—some out to the skerries, some south towards Lofoten—loved for a year or two, and then gone one day, usually in late summer. Then another brood, and more work and care, with Weever to mark out the nest sites and guard the home and territory, and she to brood; and then, once they were hatched, fly further afield for the bigger prey and food. The previous lot of young fading away and forgotten in the creation of the new.

Some years they had not bred. They had always tried, but disturbance at the wrong time, some misfortune with the eggs, some sudden freezing storm . . . and the pattern was broken. Still, in those years, the juveniles from previous broods stayed near, and they spent the summer roaming in company or resting, looking out at the western horizon and remembering things they once knew of Romsdal, which they loved, or of Cuillin who had taught them both so much in that long flight together from the south.

But Mizen's restlessness this year was different and Weever found it hard to understand. He grew a little impatient, for his urge was to make young, to find a site, to search out new prey for the young . . . and all this sitting about glooming on the past did not wear well with his practical sturdy nature. To make it worse, the previous year's brood – two males – had both gone with the approach of winter to find their fortunes in Lofoten, and so they were alone here but for the gulls and the perennial eider. Yet his impatience was not very deep. He loved Mizen with a feeling as great as the sky, and barely a day went by that he did not – though he rarely showed it – feel the honour of being her mate. For though she was nervous and sometimes awkward, yet how deeply she

232

nurtured and cared for her young; and how she understood his own need for care. How beautiful she was! How . . . and as he thought such things, she herself thought the same about him. For what male would put up with her worried ways, and not seem to mind when she looked and looked again, and looked for the thousandth time, to see if he was back yet, and yet had nothing much to say when he was!

So though impatient, her strange restlessness this year, which gradually deepened and took ever greater hold of her, brought out the depth of his love. He made sure to be always near, and when she grew alarmed or angry at nothing, he was there to point out prey, or some new flight among the ragged cliffs of the coast which might give her pleasure. And if all else failed, he would tell her stories of Romsdal in his own brief and matter-of-fact way, and would say, 'Yes, I'm sure it's so . . .' and 'Yes, Mizen, that must be!' when she wondered aloud if the Storrin still flowed, or the waters of Romsdal were still as dark as peat until the sun caught them and the sky shone its blue into them. 'Aye, it'll still be like that. But that's in the past. Now come, my dear, I've something to show you over by . . .'

There came an early morning in the spring, when the sun was still hidden over to the east behind the mountains and the world was mute under a layer of mist. On the ground itself the new growth of dwarf arctic trees was wet with dew, the dark cliffs softened by grey, misty light, everything cold and still. If creature stirred or bird flew, or seal rolled in the flat sea, it was silently, as if at a great distance. The world was waiting on the morning, and the morning waiting for none knew what. And Mizen was huddled and quiet.

Suddenly, almost violently, she could take the stillness no longer, and she was off from their stance and up into the mist, to fly up through it to where the light and sun must be, with a call of desperation.

And Weever was after her, for she was suffering and he did not know why. So that together they broke up out of the layer of mist, its grey fronds rolling off their wings as their heads and beaks broke into the pale sunlight, and their dark flight was the only movement for tens of miles of stillness in the secret sky.

'What is it, Mizen, what is it?' called out Weever.

'I can feel, oh, I *know*, out there somewhere there's a calling, but I don't know where or why. It's there now, Weever, and we should not be here. I don't know whether to fly south, or north, east for the mountain, or west . . .' and she turned seawards '. . . towards where Cuillin came from, towards Skye.' But no, it wasn't from there.

All day she was unhappy and tortured by the need to fly to where the feeling came from, but where that was she did not know. So Mizen suffered still, crying out sometimes as if she was hurt, or one of her young was in pain—though there were no young now. And Weever stayed close by, despairing in flight and at stance, feeling only pain but not understanding from where it came, or why.

'Something . . . somewhere,' whispered Mizen. 'Oh, my love, perhaps one of our young has been hurt . . .'

In the late afternoon, when the air was growing colder, what they had been waiting for all day finally came. A movement became a distant, hazy shape, the shape a form, the form an eagle, and it flew up from the south towards them, slowly in and out of the great sea cliffs, searching the skerries and the secret stances.

Weever saw it first, and Mizen knew immediately who it was. Clew had come back. From the south he had come, and he had come for their help; she knew it and she feared the news he would bring. The long years of growing and learning were over.

So she flew forward to meet him, with Weever at her side, the grim western sky to her right and the cold murky inland sky to her left, where even shadows could no longer be seen.

As the broken cliff-line became visible, they saw Clew turn sharply towards them in the air and the pace of his wings quicken as a distant call came up to them.

Yet before they could speak their greetings and joy, even before they began a circling flight of welcome, a greater voice seemed to come from among the inland cliffs whose depths they could not quite make out.

'Mizen! Weever! Clew! Now are you met, and now begins your task . . .' And as they looked into the murk to the east, where the cliffs were, there flew a raven, its wings blacker than the dark sky, and it cut beneath them, totally ignoring them, to set a passage seaward, towards the western horizon.

'For now is the Doom begun, and now are your ways prepared. For you were always the chosen ones, to help the Fremmed and to see her task fulfilled.' And as the voice continued, they peered deep into the gloom where the raven had been, and somewhere amongst it they saw the flight of an eagle's wings, shining with reflected light from the setting sun behind them, an eagle whose breadth of wing seemed like the land itself, and whose flight was immeasurable. And as it came nearer, it rose higher above them, and its feathers seemed aflame with the distant sun.

'Do not wait, or hesitate. Fly by night and by day. Fear not the dark or the sun's bright rays. Long years was the Doom in the making and long has the Fremmed carried its burden alone. Now she is weakened and failing, and has one task only left to fulfil—and you three will go to her by the Storrin. You, Mizen, have learnt much of caring and protecting, and now you will use your knowledge. And you, Weever, know of guarding, and of seeking out the places where life can be made and food found. Use this knowledge, pass it on. Teach them, teach them what you know. And you, Clew, so long the guardian, you will have to find your own way through . . .' And then the voice changed, and the great and terrifying flight above them seemed to waver, and then, for a moment, the briefest of moments, the eagle seemed less fearsome, less brilliant with light, and infinitely frailer. And then they knew, each one to himself, that above them flew the Weir, whom Cuillin herself had once known, and they knew that he, too, carried the burden in his wings.

'Clew . . .' he called out, as if he also needed help—and Clew remembered his brother and looked at him in awe and terror, for where he flew his wings would not take him, and what he spoke seemed the very Doom itself.

'Cuillin has made the Flight of Storrin,' continued the Weir, 'and in its site and by its protection she will bring to life her first and only young. One of them will take her work on into the very Doom itself, and will live her dream, and make her dream turn into the rock and raging sea and fire of reality. Which one it will be, none knows—not even Haforn can know, not even she. But one of them will fly truly. And you three are the chosen, and you will protect them and teach them, at whatever cost or sacrifice. It will be hard, but you will trust them whatever they are, and show them all that Cuillin, the Fremmed, who braved the dark sea, has shown you. For in that one will lie salvation, in that one's wings will all of us be blessed, and in that one's flight will all our strengths and weaknesses fly. So fly to the Fremmed now to help her, and when . . . and when the time comes, teach them.'

The Weir fell silent and Mizen cried out, 'But is Cuillin all right? Will she be all right?'

'Fly to her, Mizen, and let her know that you will help her young to learn the dream she told you of, of a land where the winter is mild and the wind is fresh, and the light as bright as birch leaves in the sun.

'And what of you?' called out Clew, suffering as he sensed his brother suffered. 'What of you?'

'Cuillin knows that I fly as the Raven will one day tell it, for in the Raven are all things known. Let her tell you, and may Haforn give each one of us the strength we need.' And with that he turned in the sky, his wings still shining with the dying sun's light, and he followed the line that the Raven had set: seaward, westward, towards the empty sea. And Clew understood something that Cuillin had told him, that one day the Weir would answer a calling to make his own flight across the dark sea—not to Skye but to Haforn's land where there was ice, and fire to burn an eagle's wings.

And then they, too, turned to fly south, neither Mizen nor Weever looking back at the territory they had known for so long, which now fell into darkness behind them. And Clew leading them, to journey as far as they could before darkness forced them down.

★ ★ ★ ★ ★

That spring, that strange spring when they moved, everything did change. Jim had the room at the top of the house, facing out on to the narrow street and opposite the Grimmonds' house—which was a little lower than theirs, so his window looked out at their red-tiled roof. Michael had a bed on one side of the room, and Jim on the other, except that she, Mummy, decided to send Michael to boarding school. He had still seemed strange when he came back from his stay in Canterbury, all cold and defensive. And a friend's son was already going to the boarding school, so Michael went as well. It meant he was only home in the holidays, so they saw each other much less, and moved apart from each other.

As for the big boys, they never seemed to come to Compass Street much. They did for a while, but then Frank got a place at university and Oliver was boarding for a while as well. They were there in the holidays sometimes, but then there was always arguing, and Frank used to refuse to do things and have arguments with Mummy.

There was a corner shop at the foot of Compass Street, where it met Middle Street. Mr Allenby ran it with his wife and daughter, who was fat and vague. Mummy told him to be nice to her; she was simple.

Next-door to Number 11, in a basement flat, lived Mrs Angel. She couldn't walk very well, but on a warm day she sat at the gate in the wall that led to her flat, and sometimes asked Jim to just run and fetch her something from Mr Allenby's: a small sliced loaf; half a pint of milk; a peck of butter, as she put it. 'Ee, lad, tha's strong for your size, and time'll make you stronger.' Mummy liked her and explained she came from Lancashire, up north.

'Why does she speak funny like that?' Jim asked.

'To her, we speak funny. If you went to her home town, they'd think you odd.'

'So why did she come here?'

It was marriage brought her, a man she met who had a job here, so she moved. It was then that Jim asked about Daddy because, after all, he spoke funny as well.

'He's from the north-west of Scotland, an island called Skye.'

Mummy found some maps and showed him. Scotland was yellow and England was red, and where Daddy came from was further away than France.

Occasionally Liam MacAskill came, and only slowly did Jim work out that it was always when Granny was out. He would come to the door and Mummy would try to shoo Jim away into the garden, or down to Mr Allenby's, but Daddy would say, 'Hello lad, how ye keeping?' and Jim would say 'All right, thank you, Daddy,' and then they would talk about something together. His Daddy grinned in a funny way, without laughing, and now that he was living down in North Deal, Jim saw him more often—up on the front on a seat, waiting for something, or going into the Bosun's Mate, or dawdling along the High Street.

'What does Daddy do exactly?'

'He works in Correll's Market Garden out near Eastry, near where Michael is at school.' And once, when Mummy took Jim over to the school because it was Michael's concert where he was playing the recorder with some other boys, he saw Correll's Market Garden. He saw the big name of it near a road, by some glasshouses: painted on wood in red and black paint. Mummy didn't point it out; he saw it himself.

'Is that where Daddy works?'

'Yes,' said Mrs Stonor.

'Would he be there now?' asked Jim.

Sometimes Mummy didn't mind talking about Daddy; sometimes she did—and this was one of those times.

'I don't know,' she said shortly and he watched her tugging at the horrible white gloves she was wearing for the concert.

That was the spring when so many things happened, and the world seemed to change. North Deal was so different from Beach Close where they had been, but it was really Jim himself who changed. He was standing at the threshold of so many different doors, and stretching out his hand and tentatively pushing them open to see what lay beyond.

He took over Oliver's old bicycle then, and one day, soon after they moved, cycled all the way north of the town, along the front to where the promenade and buildings ended sharply at the ruins of Sandown Castle. These were now no more than a few low buttresses and walls, interwoven with concrete steps put in by the Council, and some rockery plants. They formed the northern end of the sea-wall, and it was the sea itself that had over the years undermined and ruined the castle. That was the first time, Jim parked his bike and climbed up the steps to have a look. He stood there, twenty feet above the beach, on top of the castle and looked north and saw the Dunes.

The air was free, and for a long time he just stared at the low hillocks of sand and grass, with the fluttering flags of the golf-course poking up among them into the distance, and the shingle beach stretching interminably northward, separating sea from dune.

Away across the water, north-east of the beach, a jut of land known as the Isle of Thanet stretched out, too distant to seem more than a hazy peninsula coming to a stump end. He had seen it at night lit up with lights: Ramsgate, Cliftonville and Margate.

Jim stood there staring down from the castle ruins, thinking he would like to go on to the Dunes, but he didn't dare. Perhaps you weren't allowed on because it was the golf-course.

But that wasn't true, because there were boys down there playing around on bicycles. Big boys. That was why he didn't want to go there. Yet how he stared across the myriad rises and falls of the Dunes, where birds flitted up into the sky and landed back again, invisible among the long grass. One step on to them and he felt he might be free of whatever it was behind him in the town that was beginning now to hang so heavy.

He stared. And then turned for his bicycle to go home for lunch.

That was the spring when there was a storm, and he went up on the seafront and saw a couple of boys and a man standing on the shingle beneath the sea-wall, near the concrete steps. They were searching for something among the sand and pebbles—heads down, this way and that, watching out for the waves, which were high and dangerous, and drove up nearly to the sea-wall itself. When bigger ones came the boys darted back to the wall and, when very big, they hopped up on to the steps.

Sometimes they bent down to pick things off the beach, rubbing them in their hands and studying them closely. Jim darted back home to get his black wellingtons, so he could join them.

They were beachcombing. At certain tides – when they were high with the full moon, and if the wind was over Force Five and driving from the north – the great waves washed in and stripped the shingle away which other more constructive seas had put there.

Great swathes of water came sweeping in at an angle to the beach, filling themselves with pebbles and dragging them roaring and swishing out and under the water. In a minute, tens of tons would move. In an hour the beach might be laid bare. Under the shingle, six or seven feet beneath its normal depth, was a hard-mix sand, mud and shingle, and on this, by some alchemy of specific gravity, and tidal force, metal objects would collect. Small things: the broken buckle from a belt; a shelf angle; a rusted screw; the handle of a Gillette safety razor, turned green with corrosion. And coins. Threepenny bits encrusted with sand and minute brown pebbles; a halfpenny. Pennies. Lead discs which were uncorroded and ancient—medieval trading discs from nearby ports. A Spanish coin. Curious, mysterious objects, mostly worthless, too worn for collectors to be interested in; but a world of tiny, exciting, sea-washed doors which Jim, one day, in wellington boots, discovered beneath a sea-wall, and in the face of an angry, deliciously dangerous sea.

Head bent like the others, windcheater hood put up to stop his eyes watering in the wind, ear and eye cocked for the sound of the pulling waves up the beach which was stripped of sand and shingle, and looking for the hints of green corrosion, or a smooth, round edge that wasn't natural, which had him bending over and digging with his fingers, and grasping, before running up towards the sea-wall, never quite sure if the wave would come all the way up to it and drench him. His brown hair tousled by the wind and spray, and shedding salt when it dried by the coal fire at home. Salt in his eyebrows and sand in his socks.

One day, that way, he met Peter. A succession of storms, early-morning beachcoming one weekend, and a check-out of the beach when the tide came back in the afternoon, waves each fractionally higher up the beach than the last; and he was being pressed back towards the sea-wall ever further until he got a bootful of water from a big wave, and saw a whole succession of them piling up towards him. One last search of the swilling sand, a grab at a shape that was a coin, and with a handful of wet sand and something worth looking at, he turned and ran up the concrete steps whose very foundations had been exposed by that tide—and was grasping at the spray-wet railing up to the top, the next angry wave already foaming and pouring over the steps he had just climbed.

'What're you doing?' A boy he hadn't seen before stood in a neat, clean anorak by the railings, looking at him.

'Beachcombing.'

'What for?'

'Money.'

The boy looked in total disbelief at the exposed beach beneath them.

'I *am*!' said Jim, and held out his clenched hand. He opened it and they looked together at the exciting mush of wet sand, small pebbles, and the latest thing he had picked up. By some great good fortune it was not an unrecognisable farthing, or remnant key, but a whole florin, hardly eroded at all.

'Crumbs,' said Jim. 'That's the best thing I've ever found.'

He looked up at the boy for approval, and in the way he looked at him the boy gave it. Gosh! The boy was dark, very dark, and his eyebrows met in the middle, giving him a fierce, studious look, intensified by the round, dark-brown spectacles he was wearing. He had a big head, held on one side, and he was taller than Jim by two or three inches. He stood awkwardly, his legs thin and gawky beneath his shorts; and his hair was so thick that it didn't go all over the place in the wind the way Jim's did.

'Do you live near here?' asked Jim.

'No, up Walmer. Just moved here. I was exploring on my bike.'

'What's your name?' asked Jim proprietorially, because this bit of sea-wall was his territory.

'Peter. What's yours?'

'James MacAskill Stonor. Jim.'

'What school d'you go to?' Jim asked.

'Don't know yet,' replied Peter.

'I go to Upper Walmer Primary,' said Jim, 'and my brother Michael goes to a prep school in Betteshanger.'

'That's where the colliery is,' said Peter.

'Yes,' said Jim. 'And a market garden,' he added, not to be outdone with information.

The waves below slackened for a moment, and Jim wanted to get back. Peter was wearing school shoes and grey socks and couldn't come down. 'I'll have another look—but *you* can't come with shoes. You'll get wet'.

'Yes, I can,' said Peter and came down the steps, the sea-wall towering behind them and above.

'You stand near the steps then, in case a big wave comes,' shouted Jim against the sound of wind and sea. 'They come jolly fast.'

Jim showed him what to look for, pushing him towards the steps when a bigger wave came, then standing up by the wall if he was certain it wasn't going to swamp him. He had never enjoyed judging the waves so much, judging some of them to mere inches so that their foam literally died on the toes of his boots.

Peter didn't seem so good at finding things—he had to take off his glasses and rub them dry because of the spray, and the salt mucked them up. And several times Jim saw things under his nose which some protective, friendly sense made him point out rather than grab for himself.

'Jim! Jimmy!'

He looked up, and his mother was on top of the sea-wall, her head in a scarf against the wind.

'Come on, you'll be late for lunch, and Granny's coming downstairs for it today. Come on.'

'I'm just coming.'

'Not more than five minutes, else I'll serve it up!' And she meant it.

'Got to go,' said Jim, and they raced for the steps together, for some reason suddenly each wanting to get to the top before the other. Jim was first and Peter was flushed and breathing heavily. His neat black shoes were covered in wet sand, his socks falling down. His anorak had a rust mark from the railings by the steps.

'Bye,' said Jim, and he ran towards Compass Street. But when he reached it, he turned and looked at Peter, who was just pushing his bike out of the shelter and on to the road. Jim waved, and Peter cycled off into the wind towards the Royal Hotel and Walmer.

They met a fortnight later on the front.

'Hello,' said Peter.

'Want to come to the Dunes?' asked Jim.

'What are they?' asked Peter. Jim told him.

'Sounds all right,' said Peter. 'Haven't been there before.'

'I'll get my bike,' said Jim, and off they went.

Was it that day, that spring, when the wind was blustering and warm days alternated with cold—was it then Jim first heard a skylark above the dune-hills? Was it then they first lay in wait by number seven hole and watched the golfers lose their golf-balls in the long grass behind it, which flooded if there was rain? Was it then they lay in the grass and Peter said, 'I can smell onions', and Jim ferreted around in the grass and they found wild garlic for the first time? Or was it the following summer, or another, when they took their bikes right across the Dunes towards Sandwich, and Peter's mother gave them sandwiches, so they ate them up on the shingle among dried seaweed beached after some freak high tide? When they held their arms against each other's to see who was brownest, and played a game jumping off a hillock into loose sand, and Peter cut his hand on glass? Was it then they came across the mysterious frightening stone on the ancient highway to Sandwich, near the Dunes, and reading it they were caught by the memory of Mary Bax, foully done to death on that spot on an August day two hundred years before . . . and there was the purple of upright vetch in the grass, and the yellow and dark red of birds-foot trefoil tucked in under it, and they raced across the golf-course and up the shingle to see who could be first to touch the sea? Was it then?

* * * * *

Finse knew the eggs were near to hatching the moment he flew in with prey for Cuillin and she bridled and mantled over them, hissing and threatening him. Oh, so many times he had seen it, and knew the ritual and the rules, and felt the final pride of guardianship as his mate waited out the last hours, changing her stance so the pressure was off the eggs and the tiny, unseen creatures might carry on their desperate tap-tap-tapping at the shell that now entrapped them, and beyond which they could sense light, and life.

So Finse took a watching stance fifty yards off, waiting and searching the sky above for danger, though he had little fear that any would come there. The nesting site was the best protected he had ever known, with the Storrin itself to one side, a great and towering overhang above, and a sheer dangerous cliff to the side where the winds continually whirled and raced, filled with spray and blustering power. Only where he now stood on the cliff-face, was he safe. As he looked to his right he could see Cuillin close to the rock, the sticks of the ancient nest beneath and about her, a lip of rock to her front, and raging beyond her to her right, the rushing, crashing, fascination of the waterfall which flowed so powerfully from above that it fell clear of the cliff-face and flowed down for thirty yards before the winds caught at it, and the cliff pushed out, and it crashed on the rocks in the initial stage of its long fall down the cliff surface to the fjord waters so far beneath it. Out where he watched, the sound was massive, but he knew that where Cuillin was, at the nest, by some trick of acoustics there was a silence of peace and stillness: the cliff-face and rocks to her right protected her from the sound of the Storrin.

The spot was not as inaccessible as he had always thought, nor as the danger of the Flight might have made an eagle suppose. There was a route out, away from the winds, along the stratum level on which he had taken a stance, in among the clefts and dykes which faults and weather had etched into the cliffs. It was a dangerous route, and nearly impossible to find except from the nesting site of Storrin itself—for several of the aerial manoeuvres involved flights across voids and vacuums of space where, if an eagle for one moment lost control or was unsteady, then the sucking currents would have him down, down into the racing emptiness below, and lost forever in the winds and spray which had so nearly caught Clew when forced into them by the Hardanger eagles.

It would have been nearly impossible to work out the route into the nest from outside; but once having made the Flight itself, Finse was able to create an outward route. This route, or series of routes, Finse showed to Cuillin; and in the weeks when they had been brooding the eggs – when they had needed to go back and forth for food and nesting material – both of them had grown used to its dangers and difficulties, though each time it taxed their concentration to its limit.

Now, for the time being, Cuillin would be making no more flights. One of the chicks was nearly through and the other on its way, and she would stay nearby until she was sure that life was safely theirs. So now Finse waited, watching over the nest and Cuillin, and thinking that no mate of his had ever been so special – such an honour to him – as Cuillin, the Fremmed, who came from a place where no sea eagles now flew, but to which, with her stories and her dreams, she had begun to make many eagles want to fly.

Cuillin had indeed mantled when Finse came so near with food. Beneath her, at her belly, she could feel the cracking vibrations in the first egg begin to grow stronger. The second was still, and some days younger, and though there had been a third, it had been cold and dead, and she had cracked it open and eaten its contents, disposing of the shell over the edge of the nest. She stood higher on her feet now, to give the egg space and freedom for its final hours. Sometimes she shifted to one side to look and check, and always at these moments Finse would look her way, attracted by the sudden flash of white from the nest as she moved to reveal, for just a moment, the two white eggs.

She would bend her neck and look fiercely down at them, her beak like a great carved rock above their fragile forms. And yet, they were not so fragile. For to the chick inside, tapping away, falling still, and then tapping again, the egg must have seemed infinitely strong. Until, at last, Cuillin saw that a crack had appeared at one point, and there was evidence at last of movement and life.

How quickly she moved herself over it again, lest some sudden rush of spray or splinter of rock might chill or crush the eggs. Then, out of sight beneath her – urgent, desperate, infinitely strong yet tiny and weak – she knew life was there at last, and the chick was free. And some softening movement of her wings, some subtle change and heightening of her posture, told Finse that now the moment was come to Cuillin at last.

He, for his part, relaxed a little, his wings hanging just a shade lower, gazing at the billowing spray below them, and at the distant

Gap through to the main part of Romsdal. And he was thinking what this chick might one day be. A creature like himself, to fly to the wind and sea; a creature to spend its life in search of true flight; or one perhaps to wander, as its mother had done, wander the years alone, wander the dark sea, wander and struggle for a destiny no eagle would choose to share . . .

Struggle, urgent and pushing struggle at her belly, the soft feathers parted, her legs entangled with a breaking shell and tiny life. Struggle, and then stillness.

Then she did look, moving to one side to see, and saw her first young lying in her nest, one foot still caught in the broken shell, a wing so small that a single adult talon was bigger, a neck as frail as a flower's stem, a gawky, mucky head, and eyes bulging, closed and pale. Beak open and breath as urgent, in and out, as the flight of eider wings ahead of an enemy. It lay so exhausted from the struggle to break free that for a moment she thought it dead, and pushed at it with her beak, softly but urgently, until it stirred and moved as if in pain, and fell still again . . . breathing, breathing. And she snuggled it amongst her feathers, waiting for it to move again.

It. A male—like Finse. Like Waulk once had been. Like Clew. Like her lost brother Torrin. A male to fly and guard and seek and help give life.

Then she, who had been so strong at different times, realised she had never felt as strong as now—her posture part of the protection that the earth itself gave to life; her pride the pride of one who has made life, by Haforn's grace.

In the hours of waiting for her first chick to revive to a point when he would thrust up his head and demand, and demand again – and demand a thousandth time what she could give in food, and things to learn – she watched the billowing spray of the Storrin, as Finse had done, and thought a thousand dreams. Of how, one day, this male of hers would fly across the sky . . . as in her mind's eye it flew to a sun-shaft on a rocky shore, or stooped a thousand feet on to a fish beneath a wave, or fought a fight for territory and won.

The place where this mighty eagle fought and flew was Skye. The lochs and moors over which its bold shadow fell were known to her by name better than the environs of Romsdal—Kilmaluag, Duntulm, Waternish and Neist, lochs Bracadale and Ainort, Brittle and Scavaig. And then on he flew across the length of fair Coruisk, with the dread slopes of Sgurr Alasdair of the Cuillin for his left wing, and Bla Bheinn and its rugged top for its right. This great eagle – which lay at that moment under her belly, scarcely able to breathe, and quite at a loss to lift its gawking head – this stranger did deeds above the Cuillins which no eagle ever dared. He overflew the sleark. He gazed down into the Cleft of Straumen—where an eagle can fly, but from which he can never escape. He wanted prey? He found it. He sought out territory? It stretched before him. He sought a mate? She came. The reverie put joy into Cuillin's great heart, and the long years of shadow seemed suddenly light to her . . . as she stared out at the Storrin Gap and thought of this eagle, sent by Haforn, blessed by the Weir.

She stirred and looked again at his tiny form. She saw his breathing was a little less desperate, and marvelled at the delicacy of the tiny talons, and the beautiful curve of the beak, grey with youth and not a trace of yellow on it. She allowed herself to exchange a glance with Finse, and let him know her joy, and he ruffled and stamped and looked this way and that, to show he cared and was prepared soon to be busy, and was just waiting to see that his Cuillin was all right.

At which she smiled to herself—thinking that the eagle she had released from her mind into the winds of Skye looked rather less ancient and tatty than her mate Finse, whose feathers were now particularly bedraggled from the never-ending spray of Storrin.

'But if you have just half the grace and wisdom of your father, then I will be well pleased,' she whispered.

A tremor, a distant shaking from the centre of the earth itself—and the second egg was living, too. The first movement and she knew it was on the way, and would hatch out in three or four days. Well, her work seemed as if it was just beginning . . . and she stayed quite still and staring, her moods as fickle as a wind in summer. Will they have to suffer as I have? Will they have to fight through the years without a mate? Will they have faith and courage to survive?

She asked the questions of the sky above and the clouds, and the cliffs at her side, and it seemed they answered her with shadows and with unseen places round corners she would never reach. Her young were born of the Doom and part of its words. They would have to carry on the fight that she and Finse and Clew had fought alone so many years.

And beneath her the first-born stirred again. Mizen, Weever, Clew . . . we shall need you now. She looked round fearfully at Finse, as if she might see a shadow on him—one she had seen before, across a previous mate. And she called out a name. 'Waulk, Waulk—*tha cunnart ann!*' A despairing cry of warning that had her great wings spread out above—as if he was still flying towards that cliff from which they shot him down into the water below.

Then Finse turned and flew over to her, perching near, and

calling her name, 'Cuillin, Cuillin, I'm here, I'm here.' For she seemed racked by some memory, and was speaking again in her old language, words he could not understand but which seemed to warn him of some danger.

And she looked fiercely, angrily, at him, fixing him with a gaze that would have withered any other eagle but him. And she said urgently, 'They will not die. They will live and fly—as the Weir said my dream must live. They will carry it for me, Finse, for by it will Romsdal survive the Doom that comes. They will live, Finse. They will . . .' She fell quiet, and he stayed for a while until she was herself again. But when he returned to his stance, he stared for a long time at the Storrin and it seemed to him that its jets and spurts and dark racing shadows were beaks and talons, a raging wall of them, and each one threatened his young. And where would they find the strength to survive—where finally would it be?

There were things that Finse had not told Cuillin, things which had occurred in the last few days, but he did not want to trouble her with. There were more sleark inland than ever before; some had even come within sight of the Storrin. Sleat, too, was about, up in the Romsdal cliffs, here and there—a distant turn above a cliff; a sudden glint of talons on the edge of a precipice. He and other Hardanger eagles, hard and dark, watching and waiting for the Fremmed's brood.

In the fjord, too, with the coming of spring, boats and humans were seen more frequently than ever. Not just at the seaward end, but at several points along the great fjord itself, where a mountain road cut down the steep valley. The Storrin itself was inaccessible to man, but the waters immediately in front of the Gap were not; and Finse had watched the ominous signs of their encroachment this spring. Shouts, shots, always noise, these were the warnings that men were coming up from the south.

He quickly forgot these fears, however, when Cuillin moved again hours later, and he shifted a little closer, to catch sight of the first chick—a male! He felt a pride—and marvelled, as so often before, at its frailty and hopeless weakness. A few moments more and he would fly out of the Storrin's cliffs to seek prey.

'Look! Romsdal! Oh, it *is*!' And Mizen flew on faster, over the sea cliffs they had taken for their route, with Weever to one side and Clew to the other, as the distant, familiar entry to the great fjord rose into view. The evening was still, and a pale moon was forming over to the east. A little above it a star was already showing, even though to the west the sky was light with day, and the sea aflame with early-evening sun. The fjells had lost their snow early, and it lay now only in north-facing pockets below them to the left; while skerries and tiny islands dotted the sea to their right, and sea-birds wheeled and darted among distant cliffs.

'Fly lower,' ordered Clew. 'Take a route of shadows now, among the turns and twists of ground. Use the darkness of trees and overhangs . . .' For he had noticed that Mizen and Weever – unused to the need for care now that Romsdal was in the talons of sleark and Hardanger eagles – tended to fly as if the whole sky was theirs. As it had been, in the north. But it was the sight of boats bobbing in the sea, and smoke along the coast, which had them taking cover—though they could not believe that this beautiful, peaceful sky and land was any less theirs now than it had been when they were juveniles.

'You only see the Hardanger eagles when they want to be seen, and I have learnt their evil ways,' Clew added darkly.

Whether by chance or respect for this warning, they did not see any other eagle as they came into the main entrance to Romsdal, flying halfway across the great fjord before turning from the sun to face inland, where Storrin lay out of sight.

'We'll stay here until early morning,' said Clew, leading them to a skerry—the very same they had used when they were juveniles together, and whence they had watched Cuillin arrive on her flight across the dark sea, half an eagle's life ago. Then the sky had been cold and dark and heavy with a dangerous wind; now its light was warm and fresh, and the world seemed still.

'Look!' called out Mizen as they settled down and drank in the beloved sight of their native territory. 'Look!' And two new stars shone now near the brightening moon, and Clew felt a shiver through him as he saw them, and he knew. They were not too late, but their task had already begun. With each day that passed he sensed even more that his own mission was special and dangerous. For his brother was the Weir, and his father the mate of the Fremmed, and he himself once the guardian of her territory . . . and all these things somehow gave him a special responsibility.

'Give me strength,' he sometimes muttered to himself in the silence of night, speaking to the stars, and through them to Haforn. 'Help me!' For he was beginning to feel a direction in his life, and to understand that the years of waiting might soon, after all of it, have a purpose. At such moments did he call for help to the stars, and wonder what it was he should do, and what was guiding him.

Weever saw it, Mizen sensed it—the change in Clew. He was thinner than they remembered, and suddenly more aged than they were. He flew with simplicity and strength, yet seemed over-conscious of safety, and wary of the unknown. Sometimes he merely followed them, other times he boldly took the lead—as he had done the moment they came near to Romsdal. Often he took a stance by himself and remained in a deep silence—very like his old father, Finse. Sometimes, after these broodings, he spoke with a quiet wisdom that had Weever respectful and Mizen a little awestruck, for it didn't seem like Clew talking but some ancient wise eagle. So it happened that first evening in Romsdal, as the light began to fall.

'Can you sense the peace in the air, and the danger?' he asked. 'It is there. Cuillin has young now, and soon, in some terrible way, we will be needed. We have come in time, and with the Weir's blessing. But the dangers here have deepened, and the Doom seems nearer. See . . .' He was looking through the dark light towards a distant shore where a bare fire burned at the water's edge, and the sound of men's voices rose. 'See how the humans have come—each year further and deeper into our territories, never to be stopped. They drove the Hardanger eagles here, and now they may drive all of us out. For *this* is the Doom.' They fell hushed and silent, thinking of his words, and while Weever looked about him and about again, and Clew thought of the tasks ahead, Mizen wished that morning was here so she could fly inland and perhaps catch sight of Cuillin after so long.

Morning came, and with its first light Cuillin left the nest—letting Finse take over for a while. A week since the first chick had come forth, and now the second was out as well, and their demands ever more insistent as they craned and pecked at bare air, seeking food, and food, and more food. Tiny fragments of food at first, one to each, always starting with the elder chick, for he came first and his was the right to live. All eagles know that the first-born lives if all else fails, and his or hers is the right to kill the second if food is in short supply. When the second had lain limp and still, the first had pecked at it, even though he himself could barely raise his head. Yet some instinctive inbuilt rivalry had him pecking hard, to win food from it and stop it growing. Trying to kill it.

'Always the same,' Finse had said reassuringly. 'However good the food supply, and this year isn't bad, the first-born tries to kill the second. They often succeed. But don't worry, Cuillin. One will survive.'

Some distant memory came back to Cuillin of her sibling brother on Skye, and how she had shared the nest and fought and tussled with him. Food must have been good then for they both survived, until the men came and shot her father, and broke the neck of her sibling who had not quite learnt to fly as she had, and so could not hide among the cliffs as she had done.

Returning to the nest she watched the struggle between her two—knowing she must never intervene. It was the way of eagles. As long as the parents provided enough food in these first few weeks, the second, smaller one – a female in this case – would survive and then be strong enough to hold her own. She would eventually become bigger, and then woe betide her brother! Well, there was plenty of food out on the fjell, and neither sleark nor Hardanger eagle seemed to disturb them—preoccupied as they also probably were with their own young.

The names for them were easy, and came to her soon after the female's arrival, as she dreamed that she was in the ancient, most exalted Skye eyrie, above Cuilce . . . and she remembered the view across Loch Scavaig to the south . . . and her father's words came back to her . . .

This is your homeland, this your eyrie,
This is the place where the ancient ones flew.
Here did she fly, the one who made us,
Haforn flew here, and saw all these things.
To your left wing lies Coruisk,
To your right Cuilce. Seven peaks for the left,
And seven stones to the right.
To the south lies Rhum of three peaks, named
Ruinsival, Ainshval and Trallval,
And somewhere lost now, the peak of Askaval.

Askaval, the male! But the female? What would be her name?

Then she remembered the tale of Mourne of Ireland, who flew over the sea to Skye, rather as she herself had flown the dark sea to Romsdal. Mourne who was alone for so many years; Mourne who found a mate at the end of her life. Mourne, mother of many, that made the eagles of Skye. A fine name.

'And what kind of names are those?' said Finse, who had never heard anything like them.

'Names of my language,' said Cuillin. 'One is a lost peak on a distant island, which could once be seen from the sacred nesting site of Loch na Cuilce. The other is the name of an eagle who flew over the sea to Skye.'

'Ask-a-vaell.' Finse struggled with the name, unable to pronounce it with the same soft lilt as Cuillin did. He had got so used to her accent that he rarely noticed it, but it occurred to him now that her voice was very beautiful, deep and soft at the same time.

'Askaval,' he said again, rather nearer the Gaelic version. 'And Mourne . . . mmm, well, I suppose they'll do. Bit grand for chicks of a few days old, aren't they, who can't even hold up their heads for more than to take food or peck at each other?'

'Well, I was their size once, I suppose, and I'm named after not one peak but a whole range of them,' said Cuillin.

'All sounds a bit extravagant to me,' grumbled Finse, shaking his feathers out in a vain attempt to make them look smooth and complete. 'Ought to stick to a practical name like mine. Finse! Sensible name that.'

With that he flew off again to find food, and scout about over the fjord and see what the morning had brought. The morning brought death, sudden and cruel. The wings of Haforn opened out and hid the sun, and in the darkness old Finse died.

They had camped on the edge of the fjord, seaward of the Storrin, and the night before they had lit the fire that Clew and the others had seen. One man, a boy, a gun apiece, a dog, a silent boat. Up the fjord they had gone before dawn, silent in the shadows where the water ran by the fjord edge and cliffs rose steeply, up towards the awesome and legendary Storrin, where no boat had ever been or man climbed. There, it was said, had eagles been seen circling high over the waterfall, going back and forth among the high cliffs, probably with young. Some hunted such eagles for the bounty, five krone for an adult, two krone for a young one, for it was known they destroyed livestock, and in 1876 hadn't such a bird taken a baby child? Well, it was a good story. But these were from Oslo, and came for the pleasure of it. You need a break from the city when spring first comes—stretch your legs, sleep under the stars, wake with the dawn. Or before it, if you want to get an eagle in your sights.

So, up to the Storrin they went, hiding before first light, within range of the very Gap itself, where winds blew spray all the time and the water boiled out of sight behind the bluff of cliffs.

First light: grey. Second light: haze and a shaft of sun down the length of the fjord.

'Don't move. Stay still. You never know what you'll see in a place like this,' said the man.

A raven above them, worried by something he could not see, and curious, as all Corvidae are. Black wings and a broken flight and the raven's seen them, and a hand reaches out to stop a younger hand at a gun.

'No point in shooting ravens, lad. No one wants them. Anyway, they're harder to get than any bird I know. Deceptive buggers they are, twisting and turning through the sky. No, wait for something better.'

The eagle came with the sun, tentative at first from an age-old caution—so just a show of beak and wing in silhouette at one corner of the distant cliff.

'See it? Something's there.' And the dog was alert, its eyes to the sky where the eagle had been.

Minutes later the eagle was back, more of it this time, and then suddenly all out, full in the sun, a sea eagle over the cliffs of Storrin, and a gasp from the lad.

'It's huge!'

'Not as big as its mate. That's the male. The female will be bigger. Probably out to get prey for young. She'll be guarding the nest, but if it's up in that lot, we've no chance of getting to it.' They looked again at the forbidding cliffs and the spray roaring in the Gap.

The eagle turned in the sky far above them, and well clear of the cliffs, its primary feathers curling up with the air at its wings, and the sun catching the brown and grey feathers of its back, and seeming to make its great white tail nearly transparent. They lay quite still, the boat well hidden, their guns ready.

Finse was wondering where the raven was, the one which often flew about the crags to his left.

Finse flew nearer, circling away from the cliffs to enjoy the sun. Down in a shallow dive to flush the raven out, until suddenly, too late, he saw them there, humans and boat. A dangerous glint in the shadows. He was round and sliding at an angle through the air, so fast that his wings made an audible sound over the fjord—which had a herd of reindeer up on the fjell, hidden behind the cliff, turning and running from some sixth sense of danger. But no raven, and Finse knew that he had read that sign wrong and should have taken warning from the raven's absence. The raven had taken cover.

Even as he slid rapidly through the air, Finse knew it was too late. He was too near, and the men were up and moving and he exposed.

He had been shot at before, and heard the pellets whistling in the sky and known they were death. He had seen other birds caught when he was on the wing nearby, or watching from a shadow. He had seen them fall and flutter to the ground or sea.

The whoosh of death, when it came, was black and total: no gasp, no last cry, no final thought, except that the waters of the fjord were swinging black and closer, and he unable to raise his old wings any more, and Haforn was taking him for her own, and

what were those strange names of his last-born? Mourne and . . .
Ask-a-val . . . May Haforn give you strength.

Clew heard it, and Mizen and Weever, and there was terrible fear
among them as the shot echoed from far away, up near Storrin.

Cuillin heard it, and knew, and a terrible despair came over her.
She could not see anything, but heard some distant cry that called
out 'Askaval!' beyond the Gap, and she raised up her wings to the
sky, calling out his name—her Finse. She knew him dead, and
from that moment death began to take her, too. And if she had not
had her young there beneath her, she would have forsaken common
sense and flown out to the fjord to find her mate in death, and let
them shoot her.

Aiman and Hild heard it, and many other eagles. A gun, a shot,
death from men in the upper reaches of the Romsdal where the
Fremmed lived.

Sleat saw it, and was pleased. He had seen the fire the previous
evening and, ever cautious, ever wary, had watched the night
through and seen the slinking of a boat and heard the wooden
knock of oar on hull and, though not knowing what it was, knew
it sounded unnatural. And he had stayed on the far side of the fjord
and followed the sound up towards the Storrin and watched as the
first sun came, and seen the raven flutter out and dive back in for
fear. Its movement directed him where to look, and after a careful
search he saw them, hidden underneath the cliff. So he waited, safe
so long as he didn't move. Finse often flew out at dawn: Sleat knew
that because he had watched from the shadows day after day to try
to work out the route he took from inside the Storrin cliffs, where
Cuillin and he must now have young, judging from the frequency
of trips which Finse had been making. And since he had not seen
Cuillin fly out for a few days, he concluded that the grubby little
chicks had arrived.

Suddenly, Finse flew out into the sun—and the men moved and
shot him. He fell with barely a flutter into the waters of the fjord
below, a sorry mess. Sleat could quite clearly see the blood in the
water, swirling at the surface for a few moments before thinning
out in fronds. Well, Finse had gone to Haforn—may Haforn rest
his soul. And now Cuillin was in a nicely vulnerable position; not
that Sleat could reach her where she was, or try to. It would simply
be a matter of waiting, until need for food for her young drove her
out, and then he would take her—with the help of a few others
who had not bred this year, females mainly, who would be willing
to give a little of their time to see the so-called Fremmed to her
death. Then her young would die alone.

Sleat slunk away over the cliffs, a movement too subtle and swift for the men below to catch more than a glimpse of. Anyway, the sun did not seem to know how to catch Sleat's wings or talons.

Then he was gone, and the men had the fjord to themselves, to take the boat into the deep water and collect the floating body of the eagle before it sank forever without trace.

★　★　★　★　★

One afternoon that spring, the same that he first met Peter Conan, Jim MacAskill Stonor – as he now boldly signed himself on his school exercise books – was hop-stepping up New Street into Middle Street, on his way home after school. Step forward on the left foot, swing the right foot forward, hop once on the left foot, place the right foot on the ground, swing the left foot forward, hop once on the right foot, place the left foot on the ground again, and swing the right foot . . . and your bod-ee moves with a rhyth-mic lilt and your feet feel good as your satchel bumps at the small of your back, and the houses pass up and down and around, and the kerbstones pass under your hop-stepping feet.

Peter had taught Jim to hop-step and Jim had a special game with it in New Street, where the old worn granite kerbstones up the short street had a special magic for him. He found the ones on the left-hand pavement were the ones he liked best, and after school, once spring arrived, they were in the afternoon sun. There were forty-nine of them, or was it fifty? *That* was the question. The daily question. Because the stones were cracked in places right through, so that instead of being regularly spaced at intervals of three feet or so, they were sometimes three feet, sometimes two, and occasionally barely one. To add to this irregular confusion, the stonemasons who had originally laid them two hundred years before – long before the tarmac that now spread across the road between them – had found occasional pieces of granite which were longer than the others, and in places wider as well. All of which meant that if you hop-stepped your way up the street at a regular pace and tried to count the number of kerbstones at the same time, the number, when you got to the top, was never the same as it had been the afternoon before. Forty-nine was about par for the course.

That afternoon after school, having made his rhythmic way up New Street (and come up with a total of only forty-eight) and then along Middle Street to turn up seaward into Compass Street, Jim saw an alien bicycle propped against the wall of Number 11. It was a man's cycle with a crossbar, and it was black and old-looking, with a workman's box on the back. There was some wood tied along the crossbar with twine. As he got nearer, Jim saw that the back gate into the boathouse was open, and as he reached it he heard a man working in there.

Jim looked round the corner and saw – for the first time – Albert Chandler, carpenter and cabinet-maker. Mummy had got him in to mend the trapdoor through which coal was poured into the cellar. The trapdoor was quite near the street, but the light in the boathouse wasn't working so it was all a bit murky in there: boxes, beams, grubby walls and bits of old rope hanging from the beams. There was a man in there all right, working near the floor.

Jim entered the house by the front door and Mummy gave him one of her teas: runny orange marmalade which hadn't set properly, white sliced bread, tea-leaves floating in the cup, no saucer. She was in a hurry. She put it on the old oak table, without a cloth, and Jim sat looking at the grime between the sections of the table, grease and grey bits, and at the carving on the edge which Frank had once done with his penknife. Mummy was putting little green plants into a glass bowl, working on a newspaper on the table, but the black earth had spread beyond it on to the surface.

'You can take a mug of tea out to Mr Chandler,' she said.

He did, carrying a bowl of sugar in his left hand, with a teaspoon in it which Mummy had used for stirring the tea, so it was staining the sugar it was resting in.

'Hello,' said Jim politely to the man. 'My mother said you might like a mug of tea.'

'Thank you,' said Mr Chandler. He was down below the cellar entrance, the boathouse floor level with his shoulder. At the moment the trapdoor was propped against the wall behind him, tied there by a piece of wire which hadn't been there this morning. There was a red note-pad on the floor, and Mr Chandler had a pencil behind his ear, and a carpenter's white apron with a pouch pocket in front.

'Do you have sugar?' asked Jim politely.

'Two teaspoons,' said Mr Chandler. 'Please'—adding the last word as if in response to Jim's politeness.

As Jim adjusted to the gloom in the place, emphasised by the bright sun in Compass Street, he saw that Mr Chandler was taking measurements. He was whispering to himself.

'Nineteen and a half, mmm . . . thirty-eight or thirty-nine . . . that'll be the best part of ten feet of two-by-one, mmm . . .'

He measured again and stood looking at the trapdoor behind him, and finally reached out and took the pad and wrote something down.

There was a curious, peaceful slowness to his movements, like the tide of the sea coming in. He didn't seem to mind Jim watching.

Having finished his writing, which he punctuated by licking the pencil, he put the pencil back behind his ear, placed the note-book in a pocket in his overalls and, with a movement surprisingly agile for a man of sixty or so, he levered himself out of the cellar, and he was up.

'Thank you, lad,' he said, taking the mug of tea and sipping it. 'Mmm, that's good, that is. Very welcome indeed, so you say thank you from me to your mother.'

Jim took this as dismissal, but as he turned to go, Mr Chandler – seeming to address him though speaking to the boathouse in general – said, nodding towards the trapdoor, 'That's a good piece of work, that is. Knew how to make things a hundred years ago'.

Jim looked anew at the trapdoor, now that it had professional approval. The hinges were all rusted through, and one was broken so that the door was hanging from the wire Mr Chandler had temporarily fixed it with. The hole into the cellar was rectangular, and sloping slightly inward to direct the fall of coal, and it was rimmed by dark, rotted wood, grimy and black with coal-dust. The door itself was simple plank-work with cross-planks to keep it strong and firm, but these had warped away to such an extent that this was one of the first jobs Mummy said needed doing.

'If someone falls down that trap and breaks a leg, I'm liable,' she had complained. 'It's the sort of thing a husband should be able to mend, but Liam was never any good at that sort of thing, even if he was here to do it.' She had said this to Granny on the stairs, and Jim heard her. She added. 'I'll get a man in to do it.'

Looking at the trapdoor now, and standing near the man she had got in, Jim was still wondering why it was 'a good piece of work'. It looked a mess to him. It took him nearly a decade to find out the answer, and it was Mr Albert Chandler who taught him.

'Jim!' She was calling—there was a job to do, like there usually was after school, when all he wanted was to go up on the front and see where the sea had got to. He started to walk past Mr Chandler towards the street, to sneak away out of earshot, and therefore responsibility. The house was all right, but not when she was in it—which was most of the time.

'I expect you'll be wanting to take this to your mother,' said Mr Chandler firmly, seeming to stand in his way. Defeated, Jim scratched his leg and, pretending to peer down at the suddenly irksome and boring trapdoor and muttering 'Yes', he took the mug and went slowly back towards the kitchen. Mr Chandler smiled: he knew boys.

Jim found himself looking with some interest up Compass Street the following afternoon, a Friday, to see if the bike was there again.

But it wasn't. He was – for some deep reason he didn't understand, or try to – disappointed. But his hopes rose suddenly when he saw there was a neat pile of fresh wood, with a nice clean smell, along the alleyway floor, and the weekend promised something a bit different, because Mr Chandler, it seemed, was coming in to do the job on Saturday as he couldn't fit it in on Friday.

One way or another, Jim spent a lot of time in the boathouse that weekend, his excuse being that his mother had promised to let him paint it with whitewash to brighten it up a bit, so he was put on to scraping what he could off the walls, subject only to him not climbing on to anything but an old chair, and being generally careful and keeping out of Mr Chandler's way. The scraping soon got boring – and hard work – but Jim stayed on, nonetheless, because Mr Chandler had about him a curious order and peace which Jim liked. He had brought his tools on Saturday morning at eight o'clock sharp, and Jim took him out a cup of tea to which he said 'No thank you'—he didn't want one quite yet, having just had breakfast, but one at eleven or thereabouts would be welcome.

Mr Chandler's tools were in two boxes, one big, one little, both worn and old. They had 'AFC' painted on them in gothic letters, black with a highlight of silvery gold. They had leather handles like Granny's suitcases, and there was brass on them. They each had a lock, and at the sides there were little latches so that if you carried them they didn't fall open if the lock was undone.

Inside the big one, which was the first Mr Chandler opened, there were all sorts of things Jim had never seen before. The most exciting, the most memorable, and soon the most hankered after, was a brace—with a big round wooden handle on top where you put your palm, and a wooden handle in the elbow where you gripped and turned it. It was much worn and very old-looking, and had an air of careful oiling and harmonious handling such as Jim had never seen in any of the rusty old tools that congregated in the cupboards, or under the kitchen sink, in his own house. There were six drill-bits to go with it, each carefully placed into special slits in the box and ready for use. There was a gimlet, with a lovely polished wooden handle, a bradawl, and a countersink with a fat knobbly handle for the very core of your palm, and chisels and a wooden jack-plane. There were little bottles of screws, some brass, some steel, and other bottles with nails in them; and yet more with mysterious round washers and angles and things. About them all there was the smell of wood and oil, and the feel of deliberate assembly, as if each one had a role to play on the field of carpentry battle, and each knew what its role was. And if the pin-nails were but the privates, and the screws the platoon leaders, then surely the generals were the marvellous brace, and the great jack-plane with the curving wood handle that cried out to be held.

'Now, lad, I'll tell you something once, and I hope you never need to be told it again. You don't leave your tools by themselves. They have a habit of walking. They go off and they don't come back, or if by chance they do, they usually look very sorry for themselves indeed. Now, what's your name?'

'Jim.'

'Right, Jim, now listen to me.' Mr Chandler's voice had become deliciously conspiratorial, and Jim looked up at him with wide eyes and a terrible seriousness. 'I've got to get on me bike and go down to Union Road, where I live, and get me saw-horse, and I want you to stand guard over these tools, which I'll close up anyway, and not let anyone touch them whoever it may be. Right?'

Jim nodded eagerly. He would fight off whole armies of tool-stealers, if need be. He would not budge an inch.

Mr Chandler smiled and his whole face wrinkled and seemed to glow. 'Good lad,' he said. Then he went through the door, disappeared to get his bike, and then reappeared.

'All set?'

Jim nodded earnestly.

'Right. I'll not be long.' And off he went.

Jim stayed firm, and it seemed that suddenly Compass Street was beset by hordes of potential tool-stealers, fifth-columnists and enemies. Sirens as well, because he heard two boys at the top of the street shouting that there was something to see on the beach, something interesting. Yet Jim stood firm. Then there was Mrs Angel from next-door, asking if Mrs Stonor was in, and Jim saying yes she was but he couldn't leave the boathouse, and did she mind knocking on the door, which she did rather, because it meant climbing the two steps and her legs weren't made for that any more. Then Granny came out of the front door with the stick she carried now – he could hear it tapping on the marble at the door – and he knew she would ask him something and he might have to move. She came to the boathouse entrance and peered into the murk.

'Jim?' For some reason he did not answer, though he was only five feet away, and stood stock-still staring at the silhouette of his grandmother, and at her face all puckered up as she peered into the dark. She moved away, muttering slightly, and looking at the pavement before each step; and that was the moment he realised she was getting old. She didn't seem quite the same as the Granny who sat in the new room she had below his own in Compass Street, and reach out an ordered hand for the teapot or, with her glasses firmly on her nose, held *The Times* before her and read him bits in the evening, before bed. It wasn't Granny who stood puzzling at the alley doorway, but an old woman, and he wanted to run out and say, 'I'm here really, Granny. It was only a joke!'

After fifteen minutes or so he relaxed and peered down at the boxes. It was then he saw the initials on them and wondered what they stood for. He got the Albert wrong, thinking it was probably Alan, but he got the Frederick right. He looked down into the cellar below his feet, all dark and coal-dusty and rather spooky. The light from the street fell bleakly into it, lighting a strip of the old flagged floor beneath the trapdoor, from which the coal had been brushed away to give Mr Chandler room to work.

'Hello!' The voice was high and jolly, the face long and nervous, with thin eyebrows which moved up and down when the mouth talked. There were glasses over the eyes, which caught the light outside in their thick lenses. The hair was thin and wavy. The jacket was tweedy and there was leather at the cuffs and elbows. The shirt was coloured, the tie woollen. The grey trousers were bicycle-clipped.

'You can't touch Mr Chandler's tools,' said Jim, rather desperately, because this particular enemy had not only stopped and seen him, but had stepped inside.

'Ah! I thought so. Number 11 isn't it?'

'Yes,' conceded Jim.

'Is Albert here this morning?'

'He'll be back any moment now,' said Jim, almost cupping his hand to his ear to indicate that Mr Chandler was now clanking along on his bicycle, with a saw-horse on his shoulder—so don't try any tricks with the tool boxes.

'Now, do you think, young man, that you can give him a message, a simple message, an important message for some?'

'Yes,' said Jim, relaxing.

'Jolly good.' There was a pause, quite a long one, while the man thought, scratching his right ankle with his left shoe. 'Tell him that choir practice is at 5.15 today and not 4.45, because I have to go and see someone in St Michael's, Upper Walmer. Got that? Jolly good.'

'Who are you?' asked Jim.

'Roberts of St George's Church. Albert will know.'

The man was gone, leaving Jim relieved, and enlightened about the first initial of the box. Albert Chandler.

Then Mr Chandler came back and work on the new trapdoor began.

In May of that year, two months after the move to Number 11,

Margaret Stonor was taken ill. She banged her leg moving a wardrobe. There had been no one to help her and Jim wasn't much use, being only seven, and though she didn't show the pain at first, in the next few days it did not get better. The bruise turned bad and the veins on the side of her leg were affected, until one morning her whole leg ached so much she could hardly walk.

She said nothing to her mother, or to Jim, whom she packed off to school as early as she could. Michael, thank God, was off her hands at Betteshanger school, Frank was now doing a job in London before going to university in October, and Oliver had opted to be a boarder for his last term at the Grammar School.

Even so, it seemed to Margaret Stonor that getting Jim's breakfast that morning was one of the hardest things she had ever done. She gave him a bleak smile when he left, and when the door was shut and she was sure he wasn't going to come back for anything he had forgotten, she sat down at the folding oak table in the kitchen, the one the boys had cut with their penknife, and cried. She cried for more than the pain in her leg. She cried for the strain of the past six months; she cried because she felt suddenly old; she cried because the dream that had been Compass Street was turning into a nightmare, with bills to pay and extras she had not forseen; she cried because the house was a mess and she did not have the interest to do much about it any more: it *bored* her. Four boys, each demanding, each selfish, each taking effort and what little money there was, each one draining her. She cried because she was in pain and terribly tired now, and in need of the holiday she had never had, not for years, not since before the war when she and Liam had taken their bicycles and cycled along the coast to Brighton and back.

But finally, her forehead on the table, one hand clenched in her lap and the other at her hair, she cried because she was alone and there was no one to put his arms around her and hold her close and say to her that for a moment, at last, after so many years, yes, my dear, my darling, my own, you rest now and I'll take care of things awhile. She cried because of that.

When she had stopped crying and it was nearly 8.45, she put on a coat, and looking like death with the pain of each step, she walked the mile along the front, past the Royal Hotel and then past South Street, to where Dr Lessing's surgery was. Despite her pain she went reluctantly; indeed, she had already put the visit off a day or two. For Dr Lessing gave of his time, his advice, and his kindness about as willingly as a miser gives money. He was a grey, arrogant man, with a Hitler moustache and thin lips, who had seemed to regard her visits over the past few years – when she had suffered so much from the menopause – as the whining bleats of an inferior race. She had, for a long time, believed him. Anaemia, too little rest, too much pressure—'We've all suffered these past few years, Mrs Stonor, you know. All of us'. She had believed it all, and slowly the suffering had gone, and he seemed to be right. She had not seen him now for over a year. Well this, at least, was surely more specific.

He sat as usual at his desk in the corner of the consulting-room, with a green garden behind him. He did not look at her when she came in, gazing instead at the record card. His hair was very short, and there was a sort of angry pallor to his skin that made you want to leave the room and have a cup of tea and a biscuit and recover. For once, for a change, the symptoms that had been so apparent before the visit to his surgery did not disappear miraculously in the leather and polish of the waiting-room, then finally die before his unpleasant, arrogant gaze. As she looked at his bent forehead and grey jacket, she was very conscious that she still felt ill, tired, and in pain.

'What is it, Mrs Stonor?' he asked tersely, looking up with no interest at all.

'I bruised my leg a week ago and it has not healed, I'm afraid. It hurts quite a lot, especially at night.'

'Better show me, I suppose. Take off your shoe and sit on the couch.'

'Shall I take off the stocking, Dr Lessing?'

He looked up at her, and then at the leg. There seemed to be a slight sneer about his face.

'If you wish,' he said.

And that, suddenly, was it. She was suddenly, blindingly en-raged. Liam, her boys, her mother . . . all of them: they took from her and never gave. The people over in Betteshanger at that tawdry little concert, when the mothers were so self-congratulatory about little Johnny's bloody awful playing, and she had felt so ignored and out of place. It was their indifference and selfishness she saw in Dr Lessing's weary, uninterested gaze, and her father's contempt for women in general, and his daughter in particular, which she heard again in those words: 'If you wish'.

Various things happened to her. Her eyes widened behind her glasses, and then narrowed. Her hands began to work at her worn handbag, playing at the tear in the strap, which would break soon. Her chest began to heave as her breathing wobbled out of control. Her mouth opened and tears began to come.

And if Dr Lessing looked at her with the confidence of a man who had seen it all before, and was about to see confirmation of the emotional dislike he had of the women who made up most of his practice, and most of whom had no common sense, his confidence was about to be shattered.

For Margaret Stonor did not give way to tears, though God knows the pain in her leg was even worse now. The customary look of unctuous abjection which she showed in his consulting-room, which had given way to one of anger mixed with self-pity, now changed again into a look Dr Lessing found very hard to cope with: contempt—and the anger a parent feels for a child who has let her down badly. The tables were suddenly turned.

To her surprise Margaret Stonor heard her voice coming out strong and under control.

'That was not very kind, Dr Lessing.'

'I . . . well, Mrs Stonor . . .' he began.

'I am very tired and in a lot of pain. I probably should have called you on the phone and demanded that you came to see me, but I did not because I do not wish to cause a busy man extra inconvenience. It was very painful getting here. I have been under a lot of pressure in the last few weeks. In fact, Dr Lessing, in the last few years, as your records ought to show, I have had nothing but indifference and palliatives from you, and you have made me feel that all of this' – she waved about in a general way, to take in her body, her need for a doctor, and the last few years, all at once – 'is the self-indulgence of a stupid little woman.'

'Mrs Stonor, I really must . . .' Dr Lessing made an attempt to regain control of the situation by putting an army major firmness in his voice, while beginning to rise from his desk. It failed. Mrs Stonor was relaxing into the chair which, for the first time in years, was beginning to feel comfortable.

'Dr Lessing, you have skills, or are meant to have skills, which I need. Part of those skills ought to be an appreciation of the fact that it doesn't help anyone to make your patients feel small. I am not small, Dr Lessing. I have brought up four boys single-handed, I have put a roof over their heads, I have suffered a great deal at the hands of my father and my husband, as you probably know, and I have survived. But this morning I could hardly make breakfast for my son Jim. I am *ill*, Dr Lessing, and I want to be better.'

He was now standing upright, and whatever reaction she might have expected he did not give. Instead, he stood there, his mouth slightly open, his eyes fixed on her, with a curiously contradictory set of emotions crossing his face. Anger and outrage certainly, but hurt pride and annoyance as well. There was a touch of pomposity to the mute mouthings, and a hint of defensiveness she had seen lately in Oliver, as he began to grow into a man. But something deeper than that was struggling to express itself, something far more important and weighty, and as she saw it first in the distance, and then right across his face, she felt a wild disbelief. It was comprehension. Somehow or other she had made herself understood. Dr Lessing *understood*.

She slumped now in her chair and began not to cry, but to weep—deep sobs a thousand tired years old, which spoke of nights when the boys were so young and waking up and Liam not understanding or seeming unable to help, lost in his own world as he was. Those long years before she met Liam, when she felt like a nothing and believed that she had not got married because no one could possibly want her. Years on years on years of doing other people's bidding, and frustrated of doing her own.

For a moment, as the tears wet her cheeks and she put her hands to them, and then flustered in her bag for a hankie, she felt inclined to say 'I'm sorry', but as the words hovered on her puckered and distorted lips, she decided she did *not* feel sorry and in fact, if anything, felt enormously relieved.

Dr Lessing, obeying instinct and forgetting habit, for women had broken down quite regularly in his consulting-room, neither said 'There, there' nor got up and patted her clumsily on the shoulder. Instead he sat staring at her, and looking nearly as terrible as she did.

'I'm sorry,' he said, and he said it with such enormous difficulty that she felt admiration for him. 'What you say . . . what you said . . . well, I wonder if you understand how trying this job can be sometimes, and how silly so many of my patients are. Silly, Mrs Stonor. I have been under strain, as you have, for many years. But there it is. I'm tied to the job for a few years yet, and must try to be patient.' He smiled a little wryly, the first smile she had ever seen from him which had genuine human warmth about it, and then he said something which was to give her more cause for thought than anything anyone ever said to her in those bleak years which were the fifties. 'You know, Mrs Stonor, Deal is a very small and petty world, and yet I sometimes think that if I could come to terms with it, and with the hopes of mine that have died here, as perhaps some of yours have as well, then I would be able to go out into the world with my feet firmly on the ground. Sorry, I'm just thinking my own thoughts'.

Margaret Stonor shook her head sympathetically. The man was not only human but he was even just a little bit likeable.

'Now, Mrs Stonor,' he said, and as one equal to another, 'I think I'd better examine you. Please be kind enough to take off your stocking, and if it is not too painful, to lie on the couch. We'll see what the damage is.' He turned on a light, felt her leg here and there, asked her where the pain was – though it was so obvious when he pressed at certain points that not much asking was needed – and very gently bent her leg to see how that affected things.

'Thank you,' he said finally. 'That will do. Now put your stocking back on and sit down again, please.'

He went back to his desk and wrote things on her card. When she had sat down again he looked full at her.

'Mrs Stonor,' he said, gently but quite firmly, 'you are not very well. The immediate condition you have is known as thrombo-phlebitis, and commonly as phlebitis. Basically it is an inflamed vein, though in your case we're talking about veins in the plural. I'm sure that the knock you had caused it, or at least triggered it off. But you are tired and very run down, and that doesn't help. Now, are there stairs in your house?'

'Well, yes,' she said. 'Quite steep ones. Spiral . . . you know, North Deal.'

'Yes, yes, I do. Compass Street. Yes I visited Number 5 there last year. Well, you can't climb stairs for a few weeks.'

A look of alarm came over her face, and a thousand buts to her lips, but he raised his hand off the desk and continued: 'I know, you have a thousand responsibilities. Well, now, I am not going to try and persuade you that you need a rest, or use arguments like the fact that you can't meet your responsibilities if you are unwell, because knowing you, Mrs Stonor, I don't think they'll work. I am, as your doctor, going to *order* you to rest. The condition you have is potentially very serious indeed, since it can lead to pyaemia, which is a form of blood-poisoning. It can also lead to clotting, and though that is highly unlikely it is something I have to consider, even if you don't really need to fear it. Even so . . .' and he stopped and thought, a hand hovering in the air, and then he got up. 'Will you excuse me just a moment.' He went to the door and called out for the receptionist, and she heard whispering between them—a whispered order and whispered acknowledgement, and one word slipped through: 'Ambulance'. She was to go home in an ambulance. And now she did feel ill and tired.

He came back into the room, closing the door, and as he went to his desk, he briefly rested his hand on her shoulder in sympathy. 'You know, Mrs Stonor, I was once very tired and under pressure—or stress as we prefer to call it. I tried to go on, too long, doing too much. I . . .' and words failed him, and they stared at each other again, and somehow she knew that the reason he was in Deal was somehow connected with his 'failure'.

'Let me see,' he said, becoming more businesslike. 'You have your mother living with you, and young James, who must be eight or so now. And Michael's at Betteshanger . . . Mmm, not as bad as it once was, but still a handful. Is your husband cooperative?'

'I can't let Jim look after himself, and my mother's really got very shaky now and she can't . . .'

'How are you off for money?' Her look was enough to tell him. 'Savings? All gone in the house purchase, I expect.'

'It isn't that . . .' she said.

'There's someone I know, a very good sort, who would certainly help out with the house and meals and things. And though she would expect to be paid, I don't think it would be too much.'

Hope glimmered on Margaret Stonor's face, fortified by the thought of bed, at last, after so many years. Just to rest.

'There's a little money put by. I always kept a little because my father . . .' and it was her turn to smile wryly. 'Well, you know, a rainy day . . .'

'The rainy day has come, Mrs Stonor. But you'll manage,' he added firmly. 'Her name is Mrs Frewin and I will ask my reception-ist to contact her. Can your mother answer the door? Good. Then you'll not need to get out of bed once you're home.'

'I have a spare key she could have . . .' And they talked about the details. Dr Lessing would come that afternoon and give her various medicines and rubs she would need, and to check that everything was as it should be. She was to trust Mrs Frewin implicitly. She was to do nothing for herself, and certainly not climb up and down stairs. It was a mercy the bathroom was on the same floor as her bedroom. She was—and she had reason to remember this advice in the weeks ahead—to face the fact that no one else in the house would like it: Jim, her mother, or her husband if he came by. Few relatives could cope with the illness of one of their own. Most important of all, she was to let go, and see that other people did the work. And those were his last words to her as she got into the ambulance, feeling rather afraid and very tired, as he repeated again, 'Now, let go, have a rest, and try your best not to worry. And most important of all, Mrs Stonor, when you begin to feel fitter you will, believe me, be at your most vulnerable, so stay in bed and continue to rest until I say you can get up.' He patted her arm and smiled again briefly. And an avuncular ambulanceman sat her down in a special chair in the ambulance, and with a 'Won't be long before you're home now, love', he closed the doors and they were off.

It was finally Mrs Frewin who made it possible. Margaret's mother was not pleased—though she could not deny the existence of the ambulance, or of the uniformed ambulanceman. The doctor was to come that afternoon, it seemed, and Margaret to stay in bed forthwith. And shopping to do, and Jim to take care of, and all manner of things . . .

'Mother!' Margaret Stonor said wearily, 'Mother, please! I'll just go downstairs and sort things out.'

'But the doctor said . . .' began her mother irritably.

And what you're saying and what you're doing is going to make it impossible for me to stay in bed and relax and sleep, and my leg hurts, and can't you see I'm tired, and just once, just for once, I want to be the one who's cared for without being made to feel guilty and spoilt and indulgent.

The doorbell interrupted her thoughts, half-spoken, which were leading to tears again; and her mother hovered nastily at the bedroom threshold.

'All right, I'll answer it!' shouted Margaret Stonor wildly, levering herself painfully out of the bed into which the ambulance-man had insisted she get before he left the house.

'Now, my dear, don't be silly,' said her mother and went downstairs.

A suddenly still room, voices downstairs, and heavy, nearly tearful, breathing and she was pulling the sheet straight and turning to face the door as strange steps came up the old staircase outside the door. And before she could properly straighten her hair or even wipe her eyes of the tears, there was a knock at the door and it was opening.

'Hello, Mrs Stonor. I'm Grace Frewin, and Doctor Lessing told me you weren't well . . .'

Margaret Stonor's mother appeared at the door.

'My dear, this is Mrs Frewin and . . .' and her mother was beginning to take over as she always had, and would now, and she was not going to be able to rest, and would be made to feel that it was her fault this illness, just when things . . .

'A body doesn't get better by talking too much,' said Mrs Frewin very firmly to Margaret's mother, 'so begging your pardon, and I know you won't mind my suggesting it, but' – and for Margaret Stonor, listening to her mother being cut short and taken charge of, a lifetime hung in that 'but' – 'I think it would be a good idea if you made a nice pot of tea for Mrs Stonor.'

Her mother opened her mouth and then closed it, because Mrs Frewin had turned her ample back on her and was halfway into the room towards Margaret Stonor's bed, saying, 'And anyway, there are one or two things we will need to discuss alone.' And the 'we' was exclusive.

As her mother disappeared from view – whether to her own kitchen or downstairs, Margaret Stonor did not know – the feeling of relief that had begun to overtake her in Dr Lessing's consulting-room now redoubled in strength. Mrs Frewin was an ally, and on her side. She too, it seemed, understood.

'Well now, Mrs Stonor,' she began, 'I'm told you're feeling a bit poorly and need a rest'—and the tears started again. Sometime or other her mother was back at the door, but Mrs Frewin intercepted her quite firmly, took the tray of tea things, and closed the door on her with a bright 'Thank you!' Then, as Margaret Stonor dabbed at her nose and eyes with a hankie, Grace Frewin poured her the first cup from thousands of pots of tea the two women were to share in the years ahead.

Though she was only a year or two older than Margaret Stonor, Mrs Frewin seemed, in the nicest of ways, much older. Much wiser, certainly, though her voice had the country twang of East Kent to it, and the nearest she had ever come to a book was *Woman's Weekly*. Her arms were large, her back broad and straight, and her hair brown and short with touches of grey in it. Her cheeks were plump, her eyes warm and smiling, and she was the kind of woman who quietened excited noisy children, or loutish drunken men, by sitting quietly or getting on with her ironing until some sense of shame made them stop. And whatever the Japanese tea ceremony might be, and she had never heard of it, 'a nice cup of tea' was Mrs Frewin's effective answer to all the world's hurricanes and stresses. A pipe burst and the plumber not yet here—'Have a nice cup of tea and don't think about what you can't mend'. Everyone tired from clearing out the cellar, and Jim and his friend Peter having been ever such good boys, helping since eight-thirty this morning—'Have a good cup of tea and two biscuits'. Liam MacAskill the worse for drink, and wet through and cold; well, Jim's abed and Granny's listening to *Friday Night is Music Night*, and Margaret Stonor's in London again—'Come in, Liam, and have a nice cup of tea.'

That first cup of tea was one of the very few that Mrs Frewin ever had anywhere else but the kitchen, and she sat rather uncomfortably on Margaret Stonor's armchair near the window, refusing to sit back in it. There was a job to do and she was going to do it, and she hadn't come here to sit and relax. On the other hand, there was certain information she needed, like did the old lady eat with the family (no, except at weekends sometimes, as she has her own flat), and where were the cleaning things (broom and brushes halfway down the cellar steps on the wall; other things under the

266

scullery sink), and what time did Jim come home (4.30–ish), and what did he have for tea? It all seemed a bit haphazard.

These matters sorted out, and a second cup of tea drunk, and the doctor coming at 3.30 that afternoon before Jim came in, Mrs Frewin (please don't mind calling me Grace but I will call you Mrs Stonor, if you don't mind) said she must be getting on, and she would see that Mrs Stonor was not disturbed again till lunch in an hour's time, so she could rest in peace.

And rest she did, slowly. In the days ahead she learned to trust Grace Frewin implicitly and, by some alchemy of good nature and shared experience of motherhood, Margaret did not feel in the slightest bit guilty about the bustling, cheerful efficiency of the home-help she so suddenly found herself landed with.

The medicaments that Dr Lessing gave her made her drowsy, and the first two weeks of her illness passed as a half-awake period, when time and images ran into themselves as she lay in bed, with the door closed. She was too tired to read, and there were only noises off to stir her. A distant door opening, the patter of feet, a shout in the street, the sea – not so loud as on the street side of the house, but a presence all the same – and a dog barking in a garden.

Her leg worsened and became so sensitive to touch that the doctor arranged for a special bed hoop to be brought round from the Hospital, to keep the sheets and blankets clear of it. Sometimes, especially in the early morning, the leg seemed to burn and throb with pain—and she alone, so alone that she wanted to cry out in the still night. Such suffering, and no one to listen or to hold her or to tell her she would be all right, except the doctor, who came every day in the bad period.

Drugged, very tired, suddenly free of daily details, her mind and imagination seemed to take on a will of their own, and to wander down paths and across fields, splash into streams and climb over barbed wire fences that she had never crossed before. Sometimes feelings seemed to become places, and places to be people, and people to become carousels which turned and turned before her gaze, so she saw colour and mirrors and sudden laughter where before there had only been black and white.

'Oh, I'm sorry, I'm sorry . . .' she found herself saying once because she remembered something Liam had said about suffering in the First World War among soldiers he had seen in hospital, and she understood now it was of himself he was talking, and now it was too late to tell him she understood.

'Do you remember that holiday before Frank came, when we cycled along the coast and you began to talk to me at last about Skye. And I told you so badly about what I thought I was, and you said something in Gaelic, and that was the first time I knew you spoke it? Do you remember? That was the best time, wasn't it, before the children came? And on the road to . . .'

'Mummy, Mummy, Mrs Frewin said to bring you a cup of tea.' She smiled weakly at him from a distance, and acknowledged it with a nod, though she didn't speak. And he backed out of the room as if there was something there his very breathing might break. Poor boy, he must be feeling rather lost.

Frank and Oliver, Michael and Jimmy; they seemed to come in twos, and neither pair of the four brothers seemed to mix. The older boys took things from the younger ones, and she was too tired to protect them much. Liam no good, drinking and whining on about how awful the English were. Frank and Oliver came all right, but she was younger then. A gap, a relief, health coming back. And then the terrible fear that a third was on the way, and all because of Liam one night when she didn't want him, smelling like that, and, worse, pathetic. Crying. Not a man. And Michael so painful, such a terrible, terrible birth, and she vowing never ever to have another; never again to let Liam *have* her. The revolt beginning with the tedium of Michael's nappies, and his whining at her breast which didn't want him, and the doctor telling her not to be silly now; he was a nice baby. Bugger nice babies. Then just once more, at Christmas for God's sake, and that's what it took for Jimmy to be coming. Oh Christ, I hate you! She knew before he even finished off pathetically inside her: she *knew*.

'He'll not have your name,' she had said, cold and never, ever warm to him again. In the Hospital she said it: 'He won't have your name'.

'His name will be James after my father; MacAskill after you; but finally, and for always, Stonor, after me. That's his name, Liam, do you understand? And when I come back, you will never, ever sleep in my bed again. Do you understand?' It had been said histrionically, and Liam had thought it was a bitter, daft woman he had gone and married. But she never slept with him again. But then, he didna want her.

Now she lay in bed again, infinitely weaker than then, and sobbed for the terrible lonely pain on Liam's face and in his eyes. The return of the lost look she had seen in them at the start, when they first met in Deal in the thirties, when she was barely more than a girl. A man then who didn't scare her like her father did.

Everyone was against it: change the boy's name from his father's? If her own father had been alive then, it would never have happened. But somehow or other she was able to face the others, and one by one defeat them by pure stubbornness—like she later

268

did over the house, until Mr Wittle, the solicitor, got the papers. And through a combination of scorn, anger and timing, she got Liam to agree.

Poor Liam. Poor lost man. Why was she crying for him?

Jim downstairs now, *thunk, thunk,* probably banging that pen-knife of his into a piece of wood in the boathouse, pretending to be whichever Indian it was who threw a knife in the serial at the Saturday-morning pictures. At least he could play in peace, now that the big boys were nearly gone. Now that they weren't in that terrible house at Beach Close where everything was wrong. The big boys rebellious and bullying, her mother imperious, withdrawn and rarely smiling; and Jim with his eyes wide as saucers—like in the story she remembered as a child, and never seemed to have time to read to them. The two little boys . . . and some memory of them, standing together near the sea, came back; on their feet old worn plimsolls, round their middles cast-off bathing trunks, red and sagging. Michael pale, never brown from the sun; Jim brown, fine golden hair on the nape of his neck—and somehow she never could go to them as she wanted, but if she did, it was Jim she went to, not Michael; and Jim who got the bowl with the last of the cake-mix in it to scoop out with his finger and sit smiling at the kitchen table. Or rather was it Jim who put himself there, and Michael who did not? Their eyes were looking up at her, and was she to be trusted by them, and envelop them in protection when she was so tired, so worn, and had no help to give? Would time show she had failed?

★ ★ ★ ★ ★

Cuillin stared down at the two of them, each pecking feebly at the other, and knew she would have to leave them at last. Three days since Finse was dead, and the last of the food gone, and that eked out too long. But three days for ones so young was important—and one of them, at least, might survive now, despite the wet cold in the weather.

She flew off suddenly, not looking back, only knowing she must find prey as soon as she could, and bring it back for them. She must find food for herself, as well. Nothing could harm them here but the cold, but there was an urgent swiftness about her dangerous flight away from the Storrin, through the tangle of cliffs and falls where the wind could topple an eagle and plunge her into the foam in a second.

It would have been easier if she could use the fjord, where eider were, but that was where Finse had died and she had the sense not to try it. So she veered south over the fjell, where she might find pine-marten or dead reindeer, or press on to one of the lesser fjords. There might be ptarmigan or willow-grouse now—the young of them weren't much, but they were easy to take. So she followed a low flight line over hummock and dale, hoping to surprise something, but always conscious that behind her at the nest were two young, still far too small to fend for themselves—and one of them, Mourne, the female who had come second, already weaker for the sudden loss of food. Her brother Askaval was beginning to take it from her, and there was nothing Cuillin could do to stop him.

Back near the Gap of Storrin, taking a rest after seeing her fly over the fjell, Sleat rose high in the air, and through the veils of foam from the fall he caught clear sight at last of the nest, far out of his reach. There were two young there, just two. He could not kill them directly, but if he could arrange to harry Cuillin sufficiently, they might keep her off the nest for long enough for the two to become one—and that one to start to die from cold.

While seaward, three eagles watched and waited: Clew, Weever and Mizen. They had tried pressing inland to the Storrin, but the Hardanger eagles were about, and there were signs of sleark, and they had been driven off, though not without having had a glimpse of the nest site, as Sleat had done. There they had seen Cuillin feeding young, and knew her to be safe. No sign of Finse, and neither Mizen nor Weever dared put into words what Clew, now dark and silent, so obviously feared.

'We will watch and wait and soon we will know what to do. But if *only* we could get nearer, in safety . . .'

'As long as she's on the nest and able to feed them, even if she is . . . alone, then she will not want us to interfere. It is her territory—and anyway, what eagle can ever get into the Storrin?' finished Mizen, rather miserably.

'I might again. I did before, but . . .' and Clew remembered that terrible flight, when only the arrival of Finse and Cuillin had saved him, and he feared in his heart he could not fly there again. He did not have the power. So they waited, uncertain and miserable.

* * * * *

The film flickered on through the night, mute because neither of them had hired earphones. As they talked, hunched near each other in their seats by a porthole window, they caught occasional disconnected images from what was obviously a formula chase film. A car skidding round a corner with a door hanging open; a woman screaming and grabbing a child; a tough guy on the parapet of a building—their shouts and their mouthings grotesque in the silence;

their full-colour frenzy a contradiction to the dark light and still earphoned heads in the seats of the jet.

What Jim Stonor had been telling Judith was so deep to him, so beyond the normal barriers of what two people who barely knew each other talked about, that their touching seemed unimportant, and was nearly unconscious. He held her arm or hand, and she sometimes reached out to his cheek and face, or put her lips to his ear or neck, comforting rather than sensual.

'It was about then . . .' he began again, but stopped.

'It was about then,' she repeated firmly, for she had found he needed prompting and encouragement.

'It was some time then. I'm not really sure if it was *then* but in that period. Well, it might have been later, come to think of it, because of the weather. Autumn probably . . .'

'It was about then,' she repeated with a slight smile.

'You've got to understand what it was like. I hated her being ill and the house dead like a mortuary. Granny changed then, and with Michael gone it was as if I was in that old house alone, wandering, with no one to care. It was the beginning of being lonely. Well, there was Albert Chandler, thank God, and Peter I suppose, though our real friendship came later . . .' She felt the suffering come back again, that terrible deep shake to his body, and she moved even closer to him. She felt she had never been so close to anyone before, and as he talked and felt his way through it, she did the same, though often she found her feelings were for the other people he mentioned and not himself. She had to make a picture from the scraps of colour, half-forms and masses, an incomplete composition, and the picture kept changing, deepening, altering as she found herself looking at it first from one angle and then, suddenly, from another.

'Well, I don't know if it was then or not, but for some reason I associate it with that time. Do you know, I never mentioned it to anyone, though once I tried to tell it to Peter but . . .' and he was beginning to cry.

'*What?*' she said, and as he turned to her to tell her, she wasn't sure from the way his mouth was whether he was smiling at her sudden exasperation, or suffering from what it was that happened so long ago.

CHAPTER ELEVEN

February 1955

I T was a Sunday, and it was, in fact, nearly three years later. Jim was ten, and though Mummy was better now, she was forever changed. She was distant and preoccupied, and it was as if the energy that had carried her through four children had run out a few years before the course was complete, and the last two, Michael and Jim, had to fend for themselves.

Jim did not much like bringing his friend Peter back to the house because, by contrast with Peter's it was so messy and uncomfortable. He had reached the age when he was beginning to feel self-conscious, and he was aware that Peter's mother's carpets and tables and cups were less shabby and more prepossessing than his own. He did not yet see that there were pluses along with the minuses, and one of them was that Margaret Stonor was beginning to live, at an age – nearly fifty now – when so many women were beginning to die.

For one thing, she had started drawing again, and painting water-colours, and the wooden Reeves box her father had given her when she was sixteen was now out of the attic and in her bedroom. She did not yet sketch much, and in truth she had found it hard, months hard, even to get going.

'I had such a facility for it once, Grace,' she said to Mrs Frewin over one of her consoling cups of tea, 'but I'm really afraid now. I know I'll never do it as well as I did before I got married.'

The world seemed to have stopped for her then, at marriage, whereas for Mrs Frewin it seemed to have started, so Grace had trouble understanding this. In fact, Margaret Stonor was rather a mystery to her, because she did not seem to have the normal feelings women have; she did not much like her children, for example, and certainly didn't give them much time. But Grace Frewin overlooked these failings, which would have prejudiced her against other women, because the plain fact was you had to admire Margaret Stonor. She was clever, for one thing, and willing to pass on information which Mrs Frewin never knew existed. She owned her own house, for another, and had struggled hard for it with a courage and sacrifice Mrs Frewin could understand. She was willing to tackle new things, too, like this drawing business she had been on about. Furthermore, when Grace finally cajoled her into

272

showing her a few of the sketches, they were good. Why, she could *recognise* Jimmy—it was him to a T.

'Oh, and am I really *that* plump,' she said with a great laugh at another sketch, 'because if I am, there's no harm in my having one more Rich Tea biscuit, now is there? Won't make much odds will it!'

That particular Sunday, Mrs Stonor was away. On the Saturday morning she had taken a suitcase and, with a careful calm that did not fool Jim, had gone off to London on the 8.00 am coach to see 'a friend'. Unlike Mrs Frewin, Jim did not understand the import of 'a friend'. However, he was conscious that it was not 'a friend' in the same way that, say, Peter was a friend, or Mr Chandler was a friend. This friend wrote letters from Spain and had strange writing which addressed Mummy as '*Señora*'. This friend was a correspondent she found through an international club. This friend, sight unseen, had made Mummy go out to Chapell's and buy a new dress in the January sales. This friend might or might not detain Mummy in London overnight, which was why she had gone to suspiciously long lengths to set his mind at ease in case she didn't get back until late Saturday, or possibly – 'If the trains are not running at the right time' – on Sunday. Granny would look after him. Granny would be there.

This friend had somehow communicated to Jim, via Mummy, the knowledge that out in the big wide world there was something that made people nervous, ruthless, selfish and greedy and which left him feeling very shut out, as Mummy went out of the house at 7.40 am sharp, without looking back, and her hair neater than he remembered ever having seen it. And new shoes with funny heels, too. That wasn't Mummy going out of the door and leaving him in the house alone with Granny.

Whatever mood it left him in caused him to do something as uncharacteristic as Mummy was doing. He said to Mrs Angel next-door, 'Can I come to church with you tomorrow?'

This was not just a random request, but the impulse for it would have been beyond Jim to work out. His mother never went to church and never sent her children to Sunday School. But Mr Chandler, with whom Jim now often 'worked' – pretending to be his apprentice, much to Albert's enjoyment – had occasionally talked about the choir he sang in at church, and had extolled the virtues of his favourite musical instrument, the organ, which Mr Roberts played. Contrariness, curiosity . . . and one other emotion, and a subtler, deeper one – kindness – prompted him to ask Mrs Angel.

Jim did not know it, but his coming to Number 11 had brought

273

a smile to Compass Street. Most of the houses were occupied now by old people whose children had gone. Only Mrs Grimmond, opposite Number 11, had children, but they were nearly adults, one boy being a trainee postman, the other working over at Betteshanger Colliery and already engaged to be married, though only eighteen.

Jim was the only youngster there, and eyes behind many a lace curtain in Compass Street, and in Middle Street, watched his progress through the months and years, as he was heading off to the front with a hand-line and a stone weight he had rigged for fishing off the shore, or bouncing a tennis ball back and forth along the kerb, or fetching something for his Mum.

None more so than Mrs Angel at Number 9, who often sat near the entrance down into her basement flat and liked to see his tousled hair and tanned skin, and scratched legs below his shorts. A ragamuffin like her own daughter had been before the war, in the twenties—when that Liam MacAskill, Jim's father, had first come to Deal.

Jim was a good lad and didn't mind doing an errand for her now and then, and anyway the young rascal would scamper off the other way if he had more important things to do of his own. But often enough he was at a loose end and seemed happy to be given something to do, even if it was just a little piece of cheese she sent him for, which was all she could buy out of her pension; just a little piece. And Mr Allenby, at the corner shop, knew what that meant: an appreciable slice of his business was from the old dears who lived thereabouts, for whom a visit to his shop in the week and church on a Sunday were the only social contact they got, now their children were gone, and far away. Any excuse to come in for a chat—and buying a little something was their way of keeping their pride so they didn't have to say 'I'm lonely and I've just come in because there's no one to talk to and the house is dark and dreary'. Sending Jim like that was Mrs Angel's excuse to have *him* to talk to for a bit.

Mrs Angel was one of those who went to church on Sundays, the 10.30 family service. It was her big thing in the week now, apart from collecting the pension on a Thursday—and the same pale, withered faces, untouched by loving hand or lips, which queued up at the Post Office then, also congregated in church on a Sunday. Blue felt hats, winter coats; summer hose stockings, and fingers with worn gold rings which fretted at the prayer-books. Some kind of pride kept them upright and separate, and put a half-smile on their haggard lips. Some eyes were prying to see what the others were wearing; some bitter with age and pain; some so very lost now. Each one terribly conscious of their isolation and loneliness, and knowing that this was the one time in the week when they could come out in safety and alone and not be seen to be alone, and stand together (though isolated) and go through the ritual of God. The church on Sunday was an escape from the empty rooms that waited for them when the service was over and they trekked their slow and rheumatic way back to the solitary meal that waited for them at a table that once, long ago, had been filled with people and bustle, and a dish of roast potatoes, and the fragrance of Yorkshire pudding and roast, and Brussels sprouts. All faded now to a photograph or two on the mantelpiece above the fire that was too much trouble to light. Still, if they were lucky, there might be a letter to prop up there, from a daughter or a son, far away. The young didn't seem to stay in Deal.

So this Sunday was a very special one for Mrs Angel. Jim Stonor had said to her, quite out of the blue, 'Can I come to church with you tomorrow?'

'Of course you can my dear, oh yes!'

When Sunday morning came, Jim woke up regretting his impulse. But the discovery that Mummy had indeed not returned yet, and had stayed overnight in London, somehow renewed his desire to go off to church. Granny, who was in a funny, tight-lipped mood, told him to put on his school uniform—a penalty he had not thought about when he rashly made his request. He lurked about in the boathouse through the morning, playing with some rusty tools in the chest of drawers there, and rather dreading the approach of ten minutes past ten, when he had promised to go and knock on Mrs Angel's door.

The weather was cold, grey and wet, and the sea had a scurrying roar about it which told him that pebbles were being shifted and there might be good beachcombing later.

They went to St George's, and the service was long and incomprehensible, and Jim sat on the hard wooden pew not knowing where to put his hands when he had to pray, nor ever quite certain at which point to stand up or sit down.

But there was a part he remembered: when Albert Chandler came out from the choir-stall and read a lesson at the lectern. Only slowly did Jim register that the lectern was of wood, and the wood was carved, and the carving was a great eagle whose outstretched wings held the Bible from which Albert read.

The reading was from Luke 22, the institution of the Last Supper. Albert's voice was so warm and kind, so different from that of the crabby clergyman who took the service, that Jim almost understood what he was saying.

'*And he took the cup and gave thanks and said Take this and divide it among yourselves For I say unto you I will not drink of the fruit of the vine until the Kingdom of God shall come . . .*' And Jim stared at Mr Chandler transfixed, for his eyes seemed to be upon him and the church had fallen away and it was a voice he loved and knew. Though he still could not understand all the words, yet the images they made in him were powerful, and before them, powerful and strong, it seemed to him that an eagle flew, whose eyes had been carved to be angry but whose wings had been made to support. Between each word, between each syllable, a thousand images came and went, and each seemed to drive itself through him, forcing passage to his arms and hands, and he wanting to reach them out and touch something, as Mr Chandler's touched the eagle's wings . . .

A Christmas meal with the family: his mother at one end of the table, nearest the kitchen; Daddy, his father, known as Liam MacAskill, at the other, not quite there and yet making an effort to be jolly and join in, making such an effort; and the boys big and bold; and the red and green and silver of the Christmas crackers on the table in front of him . . . Daddy came and told him a story about eagles one year, and the curtain was fretting at the window and he was frightened, so he didn't want Daddy to go from the dark room, and Daddy stayed talking to him and teaching him to fly with an eagle's wings . . . Michael alone on the beach after he came back all hurt, and Michael turning into Daddy on the beach, alone, standing at an angle to the wind . . . and Jim was angry because Mummy wasn't there yesterday or last night; because she had gone to London and done something without any of them, and he felt alone like Daddy was . . .

Mr Chandler's voice drew him gently back from these dark thoughts and images and whirlpool feelings, as he continued: '*And he took bread and gave thanks and brake it and gave unto them saying This is my body which is given for you: this do in remembrance of me. Likewise also the cup after supper saying This cup is the new testament in my blood, which is shed for you.*' The reading ended.

As Mr Chandler returned to the choir-stall, the vicar began the rituals of wine and wafer before the altar.

Somehow Jim no longer saw him as he was before, but rather as some embodiment of the idea that the reading – and Mr Chandler's rendition of it – had put into his mind . . . As the vicar's hands reached up above the altar in supplication to God, offering the silver chalice and blood-red wine before he took of it himself, Jim's hands felt as if they, too, were reaching up, high above him, offering. He had indeed done the same thing himself, but on the beach and before a great and empty sea, and in his hands had been wet sand and shingle, and he had let it trickle and tumble from between his separated fingers, down his arms, all cold and shivery. Was that how the vicar felt?

Beyond his hands then, and beyond the vicar's now, and once more beyond the walls and windows above the altar, and out over the Deal sky where the winds blew so fresh and carried the salt and spray of a grey Lenten sea, an eagle flew out for Jim. Its body and wings and head were carved wood of which the sap had long ago dried, but its heart was a blood-red wine. Take, eat, this is my body which is broken for you. This do in remembrance of me. And as he sat trapped in the great church, trapped by ritual and centuries of incantation and little action, this particular service no more than half-complete, his feet ached to run on the Dunes and his hands to reach out and shape the sky. Then the eagle spread its wings and they gained life, and the eagle which his father had called Cuillin led Jim out at last and into the sky.

* * * * *

Cuillin was weak now, and tired—for the loss of Finse had imposed a terrible strain on her. The world was empty, the world was lost, and she had only the insistent demand of her young to give her a purpose for living. She must now not only try to keep her young warm in the swirling wet damp of the Storrin in March, but also frequently leave them, in search of food, out there where Hardanger eagles and humans waited to attack and kill her.

She saw both, and she saw sleark, yet she flew swiftly and low across the fjell to take lemming and ptarmigan to feed herself and the two young. But for none of them was there quite enough, and inevitably it was Mourne, the female, born second, who suffered most. For Askaval was stronger than she, and as the days went by, he grew relatively even stronger, able now to seize what food there was first, and to fight off her feeble efforts for a share, by pecking at her viciously, and driving her into a distant corner of the nest. Her weak voice became yet weaker and more pathetic, and her neck, which was frail and unprotected by feathers, was red and sore from Askaval's pecking, and her breast scratched from the vicious scrabbling of his strengthening talons.

Cuillin saw this struggle with sadness and despair, for not only did she know she could not interfere, but, worse, she knew she did not have the strength to find more food than the little that, day by day, she was able to bring back to the nest. Each trip back was yet harder, for the route was difficult even for a fully fit eagle to fly, and she dreaded the secret cliffs and falls where wind and spray reached out to push her off her flight-line and down into the depths of the thundering Storrin.

Yet every day, sometimes more than once, and clasping some morsel to give to them both, she would turn back from the fjell towards the first dark cliff that marked the beginning of the route into the Storrin. But each time its dark, sheer face seemed more daunting and more dangerous than before.

Askaval at least was beginning to talk now, and to him she said softly, 'Try and be patient. Try and understand . . .' But he only cried out for more food, and turned on his sister and raised his beak at her and hurt her, and left her crying and struggling on the far side of the nest. For the food was his, and he could claim it, and by ancient right of preservation Cuillin gave it to him, knowing it was only the surplus bits that now kept Mourne alive.

To add to her sense of doom and uncertainty, the sound of gunshot echoed occasionally among the hills, and the knocking of oar on rowlock—for the hunters were still about; though quite where it was hard to say.

Unknown to Cuillin, and unseen by her, Weever and Mizen and Clew had several times tried to reach the fjells above the Storrin, for they sensed she needed them and might be willing to let them help. For though the territory was hers, surely she might accept Clew or Weever as an aid. But their attempts failed, for the Hardanger eagles controlled all the flight-lines to the Storrin now, and seemed to act in concert to stop intruders laying wing across the inner fjells.

Once Clew found himself face to face with Sleat who, guessing the purpose of his flight, called out, 'If you are trying to help Cuillin, your intentions are good, for she is dying slowly and her young with her. Finse is already dead. Oh! Didn't you know? Well, well . . .' And Clew might have tried to fight him, had not other Hardanger eagles made an appearance, and females at that, and Clew was forced to retreat. As he did so, Sleat flew for a few moments beside him, saying darkly, 'After all, it was Cuillin the Fremmed herself who said where the Romsdal eagles should fly, and where those of us from Hardanger should roam. You see, it is by the Fremmed's own dictate that we cannot let you through. Nor can we help her—for is she not the Fremmed, and in the direct care of the Weir, and of Haforn the Great One? But never let it be said that we have harmed her or her young in any way, for we have not.'

'Yet you will not let us help her.'

'Ah . . .' Sleat sighed and affected sadness, and Clew was forced to turn away, as the other Hardanger eagles hovered threateningly near, their talons eager to strike him.

The days wore fatally on, until it was the final trembling cries of Mourne, now only a day or two from death, that drove Cuillin to try yet again to raise her wings to the wild wind and point her beak forward. Too weak almost to lift her head now, yet Mourne suddenly felt a terrible fear, and raised herself one last time and called out into the air. For long moments she held up her head, the cry as loud as she could make it, and her mother turned and looked down at her from above, two great eyes filled with compassion.

Then air rushed past and the nest rocked, and Cuillin went forward into the void and was gone, and a terrible, desolate light replaced the comforting dark where she had been. Before Mourne weakened, and her head fell back among the nest sticks, she saw her brother's fierce face frowning at her, his beak all ugly and open, and moving over towards her again.

'I haven't any food,' she cried, the world dark because she had closed her eyes on it, and she could hear him hissing as he came across the nest again, to peck at her neck and breast and aching head. Her wings were too feeble now even to try to ward off the blows.

Yet she called out 'Cuillin'—for that was the one name she could remember her father Finse saying in the distant past. 'Cuillin, Cuillin, Cuillin!'—and her eyes opened to her brother's blows, which came down on her from the cliffs and the wind and sky. But she knew Cuillin had gone, and could never help her now.

When Cuillin returned to the edge of the Storrin with what small prey she had managed to find, she stared into its treacherous depths and knew in her heart that she did not have the strength to return. She was too weak now, and her wings seemed to be failing.

Yet she seemed to hear them calling to her and to sense, which made her agony worse, that among the dark shadows of the fjordside cliffs the Hardanger eagles were watching. And that Sleat, after all, was going to be proved right. For how could she be the Fremmed if she did not have the strength to feed and raise her young? So she dithered on the cliff-edge hoping the winds and spray inside the Storrin might subside and give her passage through.

The day progressed to a cold afternoon and the threatening snow never came, just a wild bluster to the air which kept any sensible eagle grounded. Cuillin rested, but as the hours passed, she did not seem to gain strength, but lose it. Sometime then she let slip the prey she had found, and it fell into the void below. And all the time she felt her young calling, and could see them shivering in their cold nest, suffering from the loss of her protective warmth, wet from the raging spray of the Storrin. Soon to die.

She felt, she knew, they would not survive the long night that was coming. So once more she tried, taking a slow flight at the route, forcing herself into the wind, trimming her wings and straining, pushing, straining to reach the very . . . and then a rush and a whirl and a terrible plummet and she was turning out of the danger, defeated and beaten.

Then, no longer cautious of Sleat or the humans who might be down among the scree of Romsdal fjord, she turned off to the left, for there was one other chance and that was a flight through the Gap—the Flight itself. She had done it once with Finse, by the grace of Haforn, but she might yet again. Up she circled, wings pulling and straightening in the awkward wind, and conscious, the higher she rose, of the evening approaching from the north-east. Higher and into a final gyre, before turning on her side, head down and tucking her wings behind her, dropping into a stoop, down into the rushing wind, heading for the Gap below, with the raging spray and water beyond . . . Through the sides of the Gap she would go and up, up and on, up to reach her young. She had no food with her. There was no hope. Yet so great was the need to get back and comfort them that she simply drove on.

Lower, lower, the water's surface approaching faster and faster, and she began to pull her wings open, as Waulk himself had taught her so long ago, curving through the air, the wind raging in her feathers as she opened her wings to arc out of the very nadir of the stoop and turn its power up, and through the Gap. Flattening now, and a terrible pain at her shoulders and in her breast as the muscles strained to stop the fall and turn its power upwards. Flattening out, under control, one last effort to turn up, one moment of absolute stillness at the bottom of the curve. And as she hung there, her wings up and her head pointed towards the Gap of Storrin, a shot rang out down the length of the dark fjord, and there was a flash of fire among the shadows. Panic and pain in her breast as its echoes rang around the fjord, then another shot, and then more pain, and the flight-line destroyed as she wheeled away to the right, her leg caught by shot and bleeding terribly, her breath gasping and her mouth awry with pain; her right wing in pain as well.

She then turned back towards the very edge of the Gap itself and hovered there, searching for a gap in the spray, to see just for a moment, for one last moment, her young—Askaval and Mourne. And for a moment she did see them, or imagined she did—so near, so near, yet forever now out of her reach. Then the wind blew again and the spray billowed forth, and the sight of them was gone.

'Then you protect them, Haforn,' she cried out, 'You who have driven me so far into loss and suffering. You protect them, for you made them and they are yours. One for your right wing and one for your left. Take them now or help them, for they are all I have to give.'

And it seemed that her voice echoed about the great walls of the fjord, louder and deeper than the gunshot sounds. Her calls engraved themselves on the very cliffs, and travelled the length of the fjord so that eagle after eagle heard them and ravens fluttered and scuttered at their posts . . . and Clew and Mizen and Weever started at the thunder that seemed to come from near the Storrin, and their eyes began to search the dull sky.

Cuillin turned then, her strength not yet gone, and in anger and despair she dived towards the place where the gunshots had been fired, and where she could just make out the dark gunwale of a boat. Her right leg and breast were dead to feeling now, as heavy as stone, and her right wing felt weak, yet she dived with talons out and did not flinch at the sight of a man and a boy who stood staring from the shadows—the man with a gun raised now towards her. Down she flew at him, past the point where she could turn quickly up and away without a dangerous flapping and stalling of flight. Down and on towards them, until the air seemed to scream with the sound of her, and she to fill it with angry cries, and her talons seemed to grasp out at the very air where they stood.

Then she did turn away, cutting sideways, the power of her seeming to stop the very wind itself as she headed back towards the centre of the fjord, away from the Gap, away from the Storrin—away from her young, whose lives now rested in the grasp of Haforn. She expected a third shot but none followed her. She flew heavily west, seaward, towards the point where she had first reached Romsdal—to the west, where the dark sea lay, west towards her homeland. West to Skye. She was going home.

She looked worn, not old; tired, not beaten, and though her right wing was stiff and slow, yet there was a power about her that increased in majesty as she made her progress down the great fjord. And the very air seemed to still before her.

To her right and left, among the clefts and falls of the great walls of Romsdal, eagles turned and saw—Hardanger eagles who might easily have attacked her. Behind her a sleek, dark eagle skulked along in the shadows, watching her progress, willing her death, but making no move. For what eagle would dare make a move against one that flew with Haforn's strength in her wings—who flew like the Fremmed of legend and Doom? As they watched, it seemed some ripple of warning spread over the fjells towards the sea; and Romsdal eagles that had kept to their territories for weeks now turned towards the distant fjord, as if told by some premonition that they should be there. They called to their mates and turned in flight, beating ever faster towards the deeps of Romsdal, for there they were irresistibly drawn. One by one they came, from north and south, from the smaller inlets, flying swiftly now towards the great fjord itself, lining its routes, peering towards the darkness of the east, where the Storrin lay and from where they had heard gun sounds.

On Cuillin flew, weak but steady, an eagle near her time, an eagle who has given all her strength and leaves the land for other wings to fly its heights and depths. Her right wing ever more painful, her head ever more rigid with the strain of flight, her purpose ever more resolute. She was setting course at last for a lost home she could never reach; for she came from Skye and spoke its tongue. The lilt of its winds and the towering of its ranges were in her flight, and only the hope of it now – across the dark sea which once, when younger and stronger, she had been able to fly – kept her surging westward down Romsdal.

Ever since the sound of that first shot, and then the second, echoed and re-echoed down the walls of Romsdal, Mizen had been uneasy and distraught. She kept peering inland towards the Storrin, too far to see, even on a clear day, from the skerry where she rested with Clew and Weever, and quite out of sight as darkness came in from the east. At the sound of it she had startled, and the old look of fear and concern had come over her face, and she had hopped into the air and circled uneasily and settled again, only to fly up once more.

'It's Cuillin. I *know* its Cuillin, and we must go to her. We must fly there . . .' and she had looked beseechingly at Clew and Weever, who stayed still and cast down, upon the silent rocks. Only a few feet beneath them the evening sea ran up and down untidily, a grey wave breaking here, or a cold froth of foam withering on a clump of barnacle and seaweed over there—all black and wet. The tide was high but turning back. As it went out, the light on the westward sky would fade.

'There's nothing we can do at the moment,' said Weever. 'We might try at dawn to go up to the Storrin, but the Hardanger eagles . . .'

They both turned automatically to Clew. He had been silent all day, silent for several days, in fact, ever since that first shot, when the ravens rumoured that Finse had been killed. They had made repeated attempts to fly inland, but Sleat and his eagles had stopped them. Only three of them: how could they take on the might of the Hardanger eagles now?

But then the very air seemed to hum with change, and they all felt themselves drawn up into it, so that which amongst them first leaned forward into the growing breeze, and which first took off into flight, none of them afterwards knew. The three of them flew slowly forward, with the light behind them, searching the murk ahead for a clue as to what was coming. They could feel the company of other eagles near them, and a sense of tension and excitement growing which was nearly unbearable, so that a strange moan of expectation seemed to be in the air. They flew—and yet not far. For the wind was growing stronger, and whatever it was that was coming was heading towards them . . .

It was Mizen who first saw the steady seaward beat of Cuillin's wings, dark against the deeper dark of inland cliffs, advancing towards them over the grim waters of the fjord.

'Cuillin,' she called out, flying up towards her, 'Cuillin!' and there was agony in her wings and on her face, for Mizen could sense the suffering that Cuillin bore as she flew so painfully onwards.

'Oh Cuillin!' As Mizen called her name again, and drew in just a little below her, Cuillin wavered for a moment, turning her head down towards her before pressing on towards the sea. Her flight said 'Come with me, Mizen . . . Fly with me now . . . Help me, help me,' and Mizen fell into steady flight below and beyond her, and soon Weever and Clew joined them. It seemed to the many who watched from the shadows that the three friends were supporting Cuillin, and helping her forward, yet it was the pattern of *her* flight they took up, and her strength that their wings echoed.

'Cuillin, stop and rest, and perhaps in time . . .' but Mizen spoke the words unconvincingly, for now they were so close to her they could see the blood still fresh on her side, and understood that the wound was too terrible to heal. Already her wing-stroke had stiffened, and was no longer smooth, pulling the whole of her body off-balance, and causing her pain.

'Fly lower, Cuillin, fly lower and take lift from the sea winds,' said Weever, for she had taken a line just slightly below the level top of the fjell, but still far above the waters of the fjord. A seaward wind down the fjord would give lift and aid to an eagle who took a lower flight, just above the waves, where there would be turbulence. But Cuillin pressed silently on, for the line she was taking was the finest line down the fjord—higher, and she would lose the majesty of the fjord cliffs; lower, and she would be lost in its dark depths. She knew too that lower down one mistake, one slipstream awry, and she would be plunging towards the waves without the strength to recover.

Clew stayed silent and watchful, for he was still her guardian and even now he feared that Sleat or the Hardanger eagles might come. Nor did he seriously consider a different flight-line, because he knew her too well and understood the power of the line she had taken. It was the one that all those who saw her now would best remember. She was flying a dream for them, she was heeding the Weir's command to make a dream of a place across the dark sea. She was making something for all of them to remember.

'There are two of them, and their names are Askaval and Mourne. Askaval is the first-born and the stronger. Mourne is almost dead now . . .' she whispered the words to them in pain. And they had to fly closer to hear them above the sound of wind in their feathers, and with each word they could hear the suffering in her voice, and it was almost too much for Mizen to bear.

'Listen, my friends, who have given me so much. Listen and remember . . .' And as she spoke they crossed over the rocks on which Cuillin had first seen them, so many years ago; and they veered slightly southward on a direct course for the open sea, beyond the furthest skerry. 'I was not able to return to my young, for my strength was gone and I could no longer fly the Storrin winds. You, Clew, have been there, and you must find the way back and lead the others there. You, Mizen, must protect them, teach them, rear them as your own. You, Weever, will help her, as I know you have for so many years. You'll find the best places for food on the fjells, and when the humans go, as surely they must, you'll hunt prey in the fjord, in places Clew knows of. The three of you will rear them, one for love, one for learning, one for living, each of you with the pride an eagle can show. I have given their lives to Haforn to protect, and I trust her. You, in your turn, must trust them, whatever they do, whatever they are—always trust them. For their burden will be far greater than any I have known, and the courage they will need . . .' And she stopped speaking, and all four of them flew on in silence towards the distant horizon.

'She is flying . . .' began one who watched.

'Back to her homeland . . .' said another.

'Watch now the Fremmed, the great one called Cuillin . . .' said a third.

And they watched and they waited, for the end was not yet.

Below them the sea was cold and grey, and as they flew out over it, it roughened with the wind they rode, and white mares' tails of foam ran across its surface. At the same time, flight became harder, for the wind was straight and slightly down-graded, so that they had to beat up more frequently to gain height, and each time they did, they could hear Cuillin's breath more harsh and painful. Yet at last she managed to speak again.

'All are now beginning to understand that the Doom is slow and subtle and not easily seen. It will take years yet to be completed, and you three will feel a heaviness come to your wings and an ageing dryness to your feathers, before it finally arrives. But then, when you seem to be growing weak, will you be most needed. For what you do then will be remembered most, so now you will do Haforn's work, and bring life to the young I leave you. Trust them and teach them . . .'

'Which one of them will lead us?' asked Clew.

At this, Cuillin turned to him almost angrily before flying on. 'They are both my children. Both will lead you . . .' but then her voice softened, as if she was sorry she had shown anger, and she whispered, 'but one of them, one of them . . .' and her voice was gone in the effort of flying now, in the final effort to reach the edge of the dark sea that would take her back to Skye.

'One of them will what?' asked Clew.

'I don't know,' she whispered. 'I am not sure. Teach them both all I have told you of Skye and its language. Repeat it again and again and let them hear it. Tell them its places I have spoken of—Coruisk, Loch Scavaig, the holy nesting site of Creag, Loch Cuilce, the terrible Cleft of Straumen . . . Teach them so that both will know it, for one of them will lead the Romsdal eagles there, and save them from the Doom that will come. Teach them the old things I taught you . . . And you, Mizen, teach them to have courage, and to love, and to fly with trust in Haforn. And you, Weever, teach them what you know of water, of sea, of land, and of sky, of how the winds bear to north and south, and where the prey goes. Teach them and show them, that they may choose those things they need when the hour comes . . .'

The wind was strengthening, the sea getting rougher, and they were approaching the skerries furthermost from the land. They were already further west than any but Clew had ever been and, once past the last skerry, they would be further than that. Other eagles could still see them, for those that nested out on the skerries watched in wonder, though most knew what it was they saw. The Fremmed dying—a legend being born.

And some wiser eagles whispered to their young, though most were far too young to understand, 'You are blessed, my love, for the shadow that passes over you is that of an eagle in true flight. She is the Fremmed, called Cuillin, the Great One, who came from a land where eagles once roamed, and where the waters are soft and the winds fair and the prey good. A land they call Skye . . .' And as she flew past them, the dream Cuillin had long fretted over making began to be born.

Until at last they were on the edge of the open sea—the wind turbulent and the waves driving high, and the sky's brightness reduced to a small gap on the furthest horizon to the west, with black cloud lowering on either side of it.

'Leave me now,' whispered Cuillin, 'for the way is too far for any but me now . . . Leave me.'

'But, Cuillin . . .' cried out Mizen desperately.

'There was a time before when you did not want me to go,' said Cuillin, 'and yet I was safe then. Trust again now, Mizen, and pass on that trust to my children. Their need is greater than mine, and the danger they are in is far greater, too. Go to them now, for you have seen me back to the edge of the dark sea. Leave me now.'

And her voice became hard and strong, and all three of them understood it was an instruction, and began to fall back—first Weever, then Mizen . . . until only Clew remained at her side.

'Tell me what you will teach them. Repeat to me the names one last time,' Cuillin whispered.

So Clew, the last one still with her, began to repeat the names she loved: 'Coruisk, Loch na Cuilce, the holy nesting site of Creag, Loch Scavaig, the mountains of the Black Cuillin which are called . . .' The words were strong and clear, and slowly Cuillin pulled ahead of him and away, carried forward by the names she loved so well, into the last of the light that remained to the west, over the dark sea. Until the sunset began to fade, and her flight seemed to grow greater across the sky . . . as the winds around them and the sea below grew wilder, and the light so poor that between the moving sea and darkening clouds they found it hard to make her out any more. Nor could they tell if the wings that they seemed to see in the sky were really great clouds, dark and powerful, which now rose high in the sky to the right and to left, as if a great eagle filled the sky with the flight of night.

While deep inland, among the cliffs of the Storrin, darkness had fallen and a nest lay still and silent. Sometimes some lost light in the sky caught at the billows of spray rushing past, and turned them into shapes huge and menacing. The night was cold and growing colder, and Askaval had stopped calling out in the darkness for Cuillin; and Mourne lay quite still. She could no longer raise her head, and buried deep in the nest though she was, there was no escape for her from the cold that slunk its way among the sticks and debris, or from the moist winds that whipped at the top of the nest above her.

She was chill and lost, and the hunger had gone now to be replaced by the first stage of death: a feeling of lightness which knew no pain, in which the mind is clear but the body weak, and growing weaker. She could see great shapes above her, of white wraiths on darkness, and a racing nightswept sky. And the roar of the Storrin was cold and horrible.

Even then she called out sometimes – barely more than a whisper – for help from her mother, for food. While far, far, on the other side of the nest, her great brother Askaval looked about him in growing terror, for he was not the strongest now but the only one: his father a fading memory, his mother never coming back, and night nearly fallen. And the only sound to give him comfort was the call, so weak, of his sister Mourne.

Then, as some great shape or other seemed to rise high above them, a sudden, terrible loneliness came over him, and he called out again—but not for his mother, nor for Finse his father, nor for Haforn, had he known her name. But for the only one there who could touch him and make him feel life. He called out to his sister. And in the chill darkness he crawled the difficult way over to her, his talons caught among sticks and debris, his head seeming heavy, his beak questing forward. Mourne heard him and cowered away, fearing his coming, knowing that surely now he would kill her. But when his beak touched her head in the darkness, it was not with anger or violence, but gently, like the touch of her mother, and she felt his body come against hers, and felt his stronger wing about her, his head next to hers. She felt the warmth of his protection against the great and angry world around them. Then she felt safe and unafraid, and did not want her brother ever to go away again; while Askaval whispered, 'It will be all right, it will be all right,' to comfort her—and to comfort himself.

* * * * *

The church service was finally reaching an end. The best bit for Jim was when Mr Roberts played some final music, more or less cheerful, on the organ, and he enjoyed the sound of it, and the sudden relaxation he felt in himself and the congregation. He dutifully followed everyone else down on to the prayer cushions for a final shutting of eyes and clasping of hands at his face, and then he was up and sitting next to Mrs Angel, and looking around.

She beamed contentedly and enjoyed nodding to Miss Someone, and Mrs Someone-else, and the Mr and Mrs Whatever-their-name who had a curiosity about Jim in their eyes. Then Jim accompanied her out of the church and back home.

The truth was that for all his outward show of politeness, Jim was feeling lost inside. He wanted the wind to blow on his face and the roar of the sea to drown out whatever it was that was troubling him—and that was the imminent return from London of his mother. Something would be changed now, for ever, and he was afraid. He felt cast out. He felt rejected. The service, and all those people joining in something he could not understand, made him feel even more so.

Ever polite still, he accompanied Mrs Angel home and had to accept a cup of tea before he could escape.

He did not see the gentle smile on her face as he went back up her alley and through the gate on to Compass Street. She was thinking that when she got her pension on Thursday, someone at the Post Office would be sure to ask who was that with her, and she would say it was her next-door neighbour's son and he sang some of the hymns and I think he quite enjoyed it, though he didn't look very happy at the end.

'But you know what little boys are, or perhaps you don't! We sang one of my old favourites, *Oh God Our Help in Ages Past*, which is a funny thing to sing, when you come to think of it, becaue He's our help now, too, isn't he?'

As Jim slipped back into the boathouse he saw the black wing of a taxi coming round the narrow corner of Compass Street. It was his mother. He pushed the metal gate of the boathouse to, in the hope that she would think it was locked, and use her key on the front door. His heart was suddenly beating fast as he feared she might see him. He didn't want to see her. He felt funny and angry, and ready to skulk unseen and unheard.

Through the bottom of the gate, and from the darkness of the boathouse, he saw her feet in the new shoes get out, and heard the swish of her dress. The feet stood by the taxi for a moment, and he heard her saying, 'There you are,' and a man's voice saying, 'Thank you.' Then she said, 'Goodbye,' in a light voice which was part of the mother he didn't know or like. The feet walked away up the pavement towards the front door, and out of sight. The door closed. Then, without really thinking why but only wanting to get away, Jim opened the boathouse door, turned left down Compass Street towards Middle Street so that he wouldn't have to pass the front-room window and perhaps be seen, and started to run. Right along Middle Street, past Griffen Street, past Exchange Street, past Alfred Square where smugglers' tunnels had been discovered by workmen under the street, and then right up Capstan Row to the front. As he reached its end, a fresh north-easterly hit him and whipped at his hair—what the barber had left of it. He turned towards the Dunes. He usually wore a windcheater for walks, but he had gone to church in school uniform and a blue belted raincoat, and the wind now plied between its big round buttons and pulled at its collar and sent cold to his chest and swirled the tails of it up behind him. Above him, close in, was a great sky of racing, tumbling, angry cloud.

He walked on fast, bent forward, moving with a terrible energy, looking ahead into the wind with his eyes watering. He looked older now than he had in church, older than his ten years—and no one to reach out to him. The church service perhaps, or Mrs Angel's sitting-room all cold and lonely, the desolate beach . . . something had brought him to the very edge of a terrible angry desolation. But it was his mother he ran from, and wherever it was she had been. The world she had gone away to enter was too big, too vivid, too real for him even to imagine. Its language was violent and its forces far, far too powerful. And, yet, from where did the energy come which drove him now so far along the front towards the Dunes, and which had him beginning his own terrible entry, if not from the same terrifying place?

A greeting at a railway station, shy and sure, between a man and a woman who had never met but knew each other from letters written in lonely rooms—it would be lost on the wind where Jim was. A walk along a windswept Thames Embankment, a visit to a museum, a touch of a hand on an arm and a sudden aching need, and a look, and laughter still shy—what place had they on a lonely seafront?

And a soft-lit candle at a dining-table, a smile across, and simple assurance with a waiter, a taste of wine and food that would have fed all the children for three meals during the war. A tie well knotted at a white shirt collar, and the mouth of Ramon and the lips of Margaret, and she wondering whether she'll be on the train or will he want her, desire her, as she was beginning to desire him?

A little boy walks with the strength of a man, and Sandown Castle approaches—and up it into yet stronger wind, and a hand to shield his face as he looks out to the Dunes, wild and grey, the hummocks of sand and grass quite deserted; and then the great bank of shingle, and below it, half-hidden, the sea raging and falling, surging up and back, up and down, great tongues of water shooting up the round, brown pebbles which the sea had left there and might take away today.

But what does a boy know of the hand at the base of the brandy glass, and the eyes of Ramon as they look at the dress that covers the breasts of Margaret; or of the broken English that whispers words that say 'You're staying, tonight, are you not *Señora*?' And she laughs as a cover for her nervousness and need, and they go up by a gilded lift where the air's quite still, to a room with a brown leather case open by a wardrobe, and curtains that half-cover a window that looks at the Thames by night.

'There's a gale blowing,' she says.

'A gale?' asks Ramon.

'Storm, strong wind, rain.'

'*Si*, a storm. Poof!'—and his hands express the thought and hover near her and reach out for her and his body is against hers and it's happening, what started with a letter in a lonely bedroom in Deal, with just Mother reading upstairs, and Jim asleep long ago at the top of the house in the room he shared with Michael, before Michael . . .

'My name was Mrs MacAskill but I changed it back to Stonor, my maiden . . .' Cross out maiden because he won't understand it, whoever it is I'm writing to . . . 'my name before marriage. I have four children, Frank aged nineteen and at university, Oliver aged seventeen and a half and just finished school, and already living away from home, Michael aged eleven, and Jim aged nine . . .' No cross it out and start the letter again because it doesn't sound right. It's not what I am.

Jim Stonor started to plod along the high-tide mark carved out only an hour before by the sea, leaving Sandown Castle and Deal far behind. He came to a cluster of white cuttlefish shells, and he picked one up and smelt it, dug his nail into it, and threw it forward into the wind to watch it caught up and carried bouncing back along the beach, yards behind him. There was a lot of wood, much of it tar-covered, and he stepped carefully to avoid it, for if it got on your shoes, especially school shoes, you could never get it off.

There was a plank from a box, with writing on it, part of a word: Thierry. French. Tangles of fishing-line and round broken cork floats from fishermen's nets. The beach here had a slighter slope than nearer Deal, and so the sea had receded further from the high-tide mark, a widening expanse of wet shingle sloping down towards it. Occasionally there were lumps of battered wood, or a piece of sacking, but for the most part the shingle below the high-tide mark stretched empty and free; and even in the heaviest storm this part of the beach betrayed no other sign of flotsam—only the shiver of a piece of seaweed or the ripple of water caught in one of the bigger, weathered flints. From a distance it was still and bare and bleak, and it calmed Jim to walk along it or venture nearer the surf that died up its slope. He glanced behind him occasionally, just to get a reckoning on how far he was from Sandown Castle, or to look at the footmarks he left in the shingle, which were his and no one else's, and from which he got the same pleasure as walking across virgin snow. Ahead, in the distance, stretched Sandwich Bay, on which a couple of bait-diggers were working. While out to sea, and heading for their colony beneath the Dover cliffs, two cormorants flew atop the waves, now visible and racing, now seeming lost forever as the grey sea between them and the shore heaved high and hid them from view.

He saw a wartime girder sticking out of the shingle, and went down to it in the hope of finding some tackle on it. Nothing. It was ten feet long, and he worked it loose and levered it up on one end until it rose vertical above him, then he pushed it gently into the wind, which it slowly cut through before thumping back on to the shingle. It left wet rust marks on his hands. There was a wooden box there, a beer-crate with 'Shepherd Neame' on it. He picked it up, walked down to the sea past the girder, and tried to throw the box out into the waves. But the wind got into it and snatched it out of his fingers, bruising them, then dropped it back a little way along the beach. He went to grab it again but a big wave was driving up towards him, higher than the girder, and he turned to run up the beach. When he looked back, the wave had driven the box back up the beach, and it was lying across the girder.

He walked back up towards the high-tide mark at an angle, an old sewage pipe, where you often found tackle, ahead of him, awash with sea-water. He would look at it on the way back. Ahead, some hundred yards on, a black clump of seaweed flapped in the wind—except it didn't flap right. He walked towards it. It wasn't seaweed. It was a cormorant, and it had seen him and was trying to get away, but it couldn't. It was hurt.

He stood looking at it and saw that its body was heavy with tar, and one of its wings was bent back and broken. That was what was flapping in the wind. The bird stared at him warily. It was black and glossy, where not tarred, and the white patch below its bill was all mucky from where it had vainly tried to scrape the tar off its body. Its tail was quite big, and caught in the pebbles behind it, and its scaly grey feet were loose and floppy over the pebbles they pushed pathetically against. Its bill was long and yellow and hooked at the end. It just stared and stared.

He put a hand out to it and it hissed, its mouth opening pink as it tried to back away, the broken wing sagging, and revealing, to Jim's horror, a deep wound where it joined the body. It was hanging on to the body only by skin and white tendons. The tar was all over both wings and under its belly, and the white patch under its thighs was stained like the one on its face. Jim tried to coax it again, saying something into the wind, but the creature pulled painfully away, always looking at him and never anywhere else. He felt huge there, standing on the beach, and was conscious that he might look very menacing to the cormorant. So he backed away and squatted to lessen his size, then studied it. What to do? Without help the cormorant would die. He must pick it up and take it somewhere for help. And without further thought he took off his school raincoat, all blue and clean, and held it out towards the bird. The wind flapped the coat forward, the bird hissed and darted its head, Jim lunged towards it to gather it up, but the bird, unerring, caught his hand painfully in its bill and let out a guttural cry. It left white excrement on his coat.

One of the bait-diggers would know what to do. He rubbed the muck off his coat with seaweed, put it on him again, and headed off towards Sandwich Bay, going down to the sea-line because the sand there was firmer than the shingle above, so he could make faster progress. As he splashed his way along, one of his shoelaces worked loose, and flapped along getting wet and sandy.

A man's bicycle was up on the shingle bank, leaning against the end of a groyne. Its owner was on the sand, back to the wind, pools of water in front of him where he had dug in his fork and turned out the wet sand. There was a paint kettle, all rusty, at his feet, and he was putting the long lugworms into it as he found them. His fingers were stained yellow from their guts, when his fork had cut them in half by mistake.

'Mister, there's a . . . There's a bird back there, all tarred over. I tried to pick it up but I couldn't.'

'What is it?'

'A black bird bigger'n a gull. One of those you see flying out at sea.'

'Cormorant,' said the man, straightening up. 'What's wrong with it?'

'It can't move. Its wing's broken—torn here,' and Jim pointed to his shoulder.

The man looked at him for a moment, then down at Jim's grey, woollen school socks, and at his shoes all wet and salty from the sea. Then at his face.

'I seen you North Deal way, haven't I? Beachcombing?'

Jim nodded, serious.

The man said nothing for a moment, but leaned a little on his fork, and looked back the long way Jim had come, and then down at his own great hands.

'Son,' he said finally, 'there's nothing you're goin' to be able to do for that bird you've found. She'll die. Starvation, weakness, the gulls'll get her. The kindest thing with a bird that's tarred bad is to kill her.'

He looked at the lad. Tough little monkey who played around on the beach. Threw stones at seagulls probably, like he had once done, and now he was worried about a bird which could not be saved. The bait-digger had seen worse things on these beaches, worse things out at sea in the war. Jim stayed silent.

'Sorry, son, but there's nothing I can do, nothing anyone can do. It's nature.' He started digging again, but not so abruptly that the boy was excluded. Jim waited.

The man expertly caught a lug by its tail as it disappeared into the sopping sand in the hole he had made, and gently pulled it clear. 'They break in two if you're too rough with them,' he said. Jim stared.

'Sorry, son, but its best to put it out of its misery.'

Jim turned away with a 'Yes, mister', and started back along the beach. The wind came now from behind him, its sound much quieter in his ears. But then the whole beach seemed quieter as he was almost bowled along it by the wind. He walked up to the high-tide mark to make his progress slower, because he didn't want to go back there, to where the bird was, but what the man said was right. It was his responsibility because he had found the bird. A resolute coldness started to come over him, and a steadiness in his walk which was not there before.

When Jim, finally reached the cormorant, it turned round painfully to face him, dragging its torn wing behind.

It hissed automatically at the human. The world was closing in on it. It was going to die.

Jim stared at it—and the tar that had caught among its feathers, and the flexing of its foot, and opening of its bill, all etched into him. And its eyes remained staring at him for a lifetime. When it hissed, something moved back and forth in its throat. When it fell still, its good wing sagged. He saw for the first time that its mouth was tar-stained inside as well.

He took off his coat again, but slowly now, and coldly. He was going to kill it, because otherwise it would die painfully and there was nothing he could do to save it. He held his coat by the collar in one hand, and put the other hand behind it. He flexed himself ready, and the next time the bird stopped hissing at him and fell back waiting, at that moment he knelt down swiftly and, with a crunching of shingle at his knees, he threw the coat over the bird. It struggled, but he put his hands firmly on either side of it and tightened them round it to smother its movements, until it fell still in his coat, and he could feel the lightness of it under his hands, and the power of life in it.

Strangle, that's what they did with chickens. He felt a hand into the coat and cleared its head. He was still kneeling over it, and could feel the power of himself, the strength and the life in his legs and arms and, most of all, his hands. He caught the bird by the neck, and the neck was like a living thing all on its own: it was soft and smooth and very strong—with the frailest of throbs to it. Jim couldn't strangle it because the head turned to stare at him. So he put a knee on its body beneath the coat, to hold it down. He held the neck with one hand and he reached out for a large sea-rounded flint with the other. He arranged the head across another big stone, and pushed his hand higher up the neck to stop it moving. The bird merely hissed, and its eyes stayed open. Jim was quite calm, because there was no other way to do what he was going to do. He took aim at it like when he and Peter exploded pistol caps between pebbles, feeling the weight of the stone poised in his hand, then he smashed the flint down on the cormorant's head. It thunked, and there was blood on his left hand. Then he did it again, to be certain, and the cormorant's body quivered and went limp. Then, letting go, he stood up and pulled his coat away from it. It lay dead and suddenly small, and Jim stood looking at it dispassionately but breathing heavily, the stone still in his hand. He dropped it on the shingle near the cormorant.

His coat was wet from the stones and covered in blotches of tar and white bird shit. But he put it on against the wind, uncleaned this time, and stood staring, first at the bird and then at the sea. The desolation he had felt earlier, when he first left Compass Street, came back trebling and quadrupling—because in his hands he could feel the life of the bird still, and the fear in it, and the terrible resignation, and the lost hope, and he wanted to reach out and touch something to rid himself of the feeling. He thought of the man's fingers pulling the lugworm out of the sand; he thought of Mr Chandler's hands and fingers on the eagle's wings of the carved wooden lectern in church; he thought of the hands of Mrs Angel giving him a cup of tea. His hands felt heavier than theirs.

He was alone on a deserted beach with no one to see nor anyone to care, but a man digging bait far away, and a herring-gull hovering now down by the shore.

The gull flew differently from a cormorant, *with* the wind rather than cutting across it, its wings flexing to stress and plying with pressure, while the cormorant's would have been stiff, like others he had watched as they flew over the surface of the sea. He wanted to cut a line through the wind like the cormorant; he wanted to make a mark on the beach as black as the cormorant. He hated whatever it was, of which he was a part, that made him kill it. Its life ached terribly in his hands, and he felt dirty, filthy, like the muck on his coat.

He stood staring across the shore, and his eyes fell on the box he had earlier tried to throw out to sea, and the girder near it. Then on the line of sand that was exposed now, and the waves beyond it, and the sewage pipe all rusty brown, and he started down the beach without thought or reason, but with something he had to shed which hung heavy on him.

His hands took up the girder and he dragged it the seventy feet over to the great pipe. Then he fetched the box, and took it to the pipe as well. He went to the high-tide mark and searched for the piece of driftwood with letters on it, which he had seen earlier, and some seaweed. His eyes scavenged the flotsam on the shingle, searching for objects with no clear link between them except that his instinct sought them, and when he saw them his mind or eye seemed to devour them: a tin, new and shining, and some wire, and a length of rope. The piece of wood. These he took and put by the pipe. He stood looking at them, casting his eyes back and forth, and then standing back and looking at the site he had chosen, and the line that the sea's horizon made against it, and the wet shine of the grey sand stretching away, and the way the wind ruffled the pools of water in the rippled surface of the sand. Then at the great black pebbles, and the limpets encrusted around the base support of the pipe.

He stared and thought and felt the materials for only seconds. Then, when he started to move, he hesitated not once, his movements fast and resolute, the thing he was making growing smoothly from his hands. First the girder heaved up and tilted against the pipe, so it towered above him. Then the base of it pushed into the shingle and sand so it stayed in one place. Then the rope tied to the girder and hung loosely across to the pipe. Then the plank with its lettering pushed between the pipe and the girder, whose weight kept it in place. Then round the other side, and the driftwood piled up against the pipe, weakly mirroring the girder on its other side. All of it wet and salty and battered by wind. Then the open side of the box over the end of the pipe above him, so it swung a little in the wind, to and fro, and his feet nearly slipping off the curved, wet, smooth surface. Then him back down on the beach and walking away to look, and then circling round it all, and checking. And he finally putting the shiny tin inside the lower end of the box, from which, as the box swung in the wind, faint glimmers came which were echoes of sky or the shine of the wet pebbles at his feet or of the angry pools of water in the sands.

He did not go back up to get the bird because it was dead, and whatever it had been was gone. But he thought of it as he stood on the beach, his black school shoes among the wet pebbles, and what he had made for it seemed the very centre of earth and sea and wild air: it was a memorial like the ones in St George's churchyard.

James MacAskill Stonor, ten years old, turned back to look at it occasionally as he walked home along the beach, because it was different from anything he had done before, and it was his. He hoped no one would touch it until the sea came back in. Until then it was his, and the cormorant's thing, and he had made it with his hands and they didn't ache now and he felt better. When he got back to the front again, the beach was still deserted except for what he had made, his first sculpture, which would stay there moving slightly in the wind, and shining where the tin was, until the dark sea came in again and took it away.

CHAPTER TWELVE

'Now, as to your questions about the flight with him back to England from New York in 1974, I think what happened was in retrospect quite predictable. He had spent a hard three years in New York, doing a job he grew to dislike and which left him creatively frustrated; he had had a relationship which opened doors all over the place but left him standing helpless on several thresholds each of which led to terrifying possibilities. And he was flying back because his father was very ill—in fact dying. There was a strained family background in which Mrs Stonor had virtually thrown his father out of the house, and yet he still lived nearby and saw Jim from time to time, and I think there were many elements in his relationship with his father which he had never discussed or resolved, which mattered deeply to him.

'He started the flight hating his mother and loving his father. He ended it feeling rather differently. He was a lonely, sensitive, tough little boy living with an eccentric and highly talented mother who was absorbed in her own fight for identity long, long before the Feminist Movement started. At the same time he loved his father deeply—and you cannot understand his art without understanding something of the imagery and loves which his father passed on, in his own curious way. So Jim was caught in the middle . . .'

—Letter from Judith Shure to Marion Poyser, of the Museum of Modern Art, New York.

August 1955

THAT summer, after months of effort, Margaret Stonor finally rediscovered her ability to draw and paint again. With Frank off to Cambridge University on a scholarship, and Oliver set to go to London University, and already off her hands because he was living with the Clowes in Upper Deal, and Michael still at Grammar School in Sandwich, and Grace Frewin staying on after her illness to 'do' for her, because she wanted to and liked the house, even if she disapproved of Mrs Stonor's mucky ways . . . Margaret had time at last. Jim kept to himself, upstairs or out on the front, playing with his friend Peter Conan. Her mother was always a trial but she was used to that now, and they kept out of each other's way. In fact, they all kept out of each other's way, except for meals, since Granny coped less well on her own now and came and sat with them.

Time! Time to potter in the garden and watch the flowers grow.

Time to turn out old letters and clear up attic trunks. Time to sit late at night sometimes and listen to her house – and no one else's – and touch its panels with worn hands that had always been made to feel clumsy and unkempt. Time to read again the books her father had forced her to read, and learn the love in words his coldness nearly killed.

> Love bade me welcome; yet my soul drew back,
>   Guiltie of dust and sinne.
> But quick-ey'd Love, observing me grow slack
>   From my first entrance in,
> Drew nearer to me, sweetly questioning
>   If I lack'd any thing.

The love George Herbert wrote of was the grace of God, but her soul had long ago drawn back from that. Nor did she admit of another, simpler love with the men she sometimes saw: Ramon in London twice a year, such good times—and someone new over in Thanet. The love she sought, and perhaps after all it *was* the grace of God, was rest and peace from a turmoil and insecurity that had racked her ever since her father first summoned her into his study and fixed her with a stare from eyes that did not envelop her in love. For she was just a girl, without even the grace of grace, but clumsy and heavy-footed.

Yet those hands that were so clumsy could take up a pen or pencil and draw a fluent line, and *had* once upon a time, before she married Liam. She began now to draw again in earnest, with more and more success, until she gained confidence and the sketch-pad she had bought was no longer a thing to fear but a thing to take up and open. So Jim got used to seeing her with it and, already keen to draw himself, followed her example, and did not feel embarrassed doing it.

One day, that summer, she knew she was ready to look at some of her old work, though not quite strong enough to do it on her own. The removal men had put cases of old things not immediately wanted down in the cellar, and she knew perfectly well which case it was, and where the key was. It was in the tiny drawer of the only good piece of furniture she had, the little dressing-table mirror of polished mahogany, with drawers, in her bedroom.

'Come on, Jim, you can give me a hand.'
'But I'm just going cycling with Peter.'
'Well, I can't move it on my own.'
'But he's waiting for me.'
'Now?'

'Well, almost now.'

'When?'

'Four o'clock by the Lifeboat Station.'

'It's not two yet.'

'Oh, crumbs, I don't . . .'

'Come on.'

So down into the cellar they went, and Jim helped her pull out the trunks and cases until the big brown leather one was easy to get at.

'This one's locked,' said Jim.

'How do you know?' asked Margaret Stonor, surprised.

'Me and Michael once tried to open it,' he lied. It had been Jim alone, looking for a disguise for charades.

'I've got the key,' she said.

'Gosh! Do you know what's inside?'

'Come on, we'll take it upstairs and open it. But first we'll take up these other things as well.' And taking the opportunity of his labour, they carried up a couple of other cases holding clothes, and some out-of-date encyclopaedias she had never found space for upstairs, and which would decay in the damp cellar. All good stuff for a jumble sale.

The sun was shining into the garden, through the window, on to the old brown carpet in the sitting-room. There they put the case, and Jim wanted to open it straight away. She let him, hiding her nerves behind his innocent enthusiasm. She had not opened the case for twenty years. 'What's in it?' he wanted to know, like a child with a present before the wrapping paper's off.

'Drawings,' she said, 'and paintings I did before I married your father.'

'Oh,' he said disappointed.

'Well, if you expected gold coins . . .'

There really were cobwebs round the locks, and a sense of dust and age over the case; and he pulled the lid open slowly, as he saw adventurers do in films about treasure. And she thought to herself that he must be growing up at last: he was developing a sense of humour.

The drawings were in a folder and there were lots of them, all sizes. A chair in sunlight (Father's study chair), an old casement window (the Rectory drawing-room), a hand, a landscape (Folkestone Downs), a harbour ('That's Dover,' said Jim. 'Gosh! Did you do that?'), a boat. Liam, or LHM as she had put at the bottom of it.

'Who's this?' he asked.

'Your father,' she said, and sat looking at it and at Jim's bent head, and saw him staring at it and silent.

'Daddy?' he said finally. She looked down at him and nodded, then she looked at Liam's face.

'But he's laughing,' said Jim.

'Yes,' she said, 'Yes, he did then.' And she took the precious drawing from his hand and held it a little closer for a better look, and found herself caught between wondering how she had had the skill to handle water-colour so lightly and well, and where it was the man she had known – who was Jim's father – had really gone.

'Mummy?' Jim was looking up at her from where he was sitting on the floor, and she kneeling above him, and she knew what he wanted to ask and why he couldn't, because a child does not have the language. He wanted to know where the young man who laughed had disappeared to, and from where the old man who didn't had come.

One day she might try to tell him, if she ever found a simple answer. But the laugh was not typical, which was why she had drawn it; for it was the sun shining for a moment from the face of a man who had been hurt even more than she. He by war and loss of his homeland Skye; and she by shyness, plainness, the arrogant pity of her father, and her own crippling lack of courage. She never really knew how they had even talked, except . . . and as she knelt there with Jim, so many years later, she had a sudden insight into how that day, when she did talk to him, a revolution had started. The one that ended with her here in this house now, without Liam Hugh MacAskill, but with a garden, if only tiny and untidy, of her own.

It had been 1931 and she was twenty-five. She could hardly bear to think of it—the shy and clumsy creature her parents had made her. Her father was a guest celebrant of Holy Communion for the Remembrance Day service at St George's, Deal, and they travelled over from Folkestone in his second-hand Ford. It was she, Margaret, who had gone with him, because Mother had a duty to perform in Hastings with the Women's Institute, and of course Father had to be accompanied. She sat with the congregation mouthing the service automatically and going through its meaningless rituals, thinking that the coat Mother had made her buy at the Dickins & Jones 'Economy Week', for eighty-four shillings, did not fit and she felt uncomfortable. The man sat to her right just in front of her, and there was no reason she could think of for noticing him. He had thin hands, and when he sat back on the pew between prayers or hymns, he put his hands on his knees and fretted them. His hair was reddish-crinkly and he was perhaps ten or fifteen years older than she. He looked terribly sad, and she remembered that he

300

had stared for much of the time at the window above the altar as if, like herself, he was not really taking part in the service. The church was quite full, and a number of men wore uniforms with war decorations, and a few women wore nurses' uniforms. Most people were wearing cloth poppies. She was not listening much to the service and was thinking, as very often before, that she would have liked to draw, for there were so many good subjects, and all sitting still. She had suggested it once, but Father had been quite shocked. In a church? *That?*

At eleven o'clock the church clock struck ponderously above them, and they began the two-minute silence in remembrance of those slain in the Great War. The man stood to attention, his fists properly clenched and pointed: he had been a soldier. He wore a dark suit and a white shirt, but somehow did not look quite comfortable. Probably second-hand clothes.

Her interest in him was dispassionate and analytic, because it could not be much else. She felt too plain, too old now to marry, and though she harboured occasional romantic dreams and fantasies – ones tinged with bitterness now – the stage they were cast on was set far away from the coastal towns of East Kent. She was afraid of men, as she was of her father. They were bigger, they were stronger but, above all, they were free, and moved in a world where she could not go. She would have liked to have been held by one, though – just once – but not like Johnnie Falk tried to in 1924, when he suddenly attempted to kiss her. There were times since, however, when she wished she had let him. It occurred to her only very slowly that men, those few she had met who were eligible, were afraid of her because she was the Reverend Stonor's daughter, and because she looked so desperately serious and had a brain.

This man did not have wife or child on either arm, and there was just something about him that made him a good subject.

The two-minute silence ended in rustles and coughs as the vicar of the Parish, knelt down in his robes, and started on the prayers for the peace of the World. '*Almighty God from whom all thoughts of truth and peace proceed; kindle we pray in the hearts of all men the true love of peace . . .*'

The reading was the usual Matthew v. 3: '*Blessed are the poor in spirit for theirs is the kingdom of heaven . . . Blessed are the meek . . .*' And I am one of the meek, the downtrodden, the lost ones, the peacemakers, and I do not feel blessed, Margaret Stonor was inclined to think to herself at the sound of these familiar words. The man she had been watching appeared to follow the service in only a partial and disheartened kind of way. He had a prayer-book open, and it was only when his attention seemed to return to the window above the altar that she noticed, with a start, that the book was not that of Common Prayer, but that of the Church of Scotland.

Her father started the sermon in his usual cold and authoritative manner, choosing to augment the basic text from Matthew with a passage from Psalms—the Old Testament being more suited to his spirit when he was concerned with themes of peace and war, remembrance and just revenge. The heathen avenged, the kingdoms were moved; he uttered his voice, the earth melted. The Lord of Hosts is with us; the God of Jacob is our refuge.

'For today is a special day, when all of us, of whatever sex or age, do well to pause and remember the men who fought for us in the recent Great War . . .' It sounded good, but somehow unreal, coming from him who had never once set foot on foreign soil during the war, nor done more than impatiently counsel the wounded and sick and shocked who returned to his corner of their homeland field, and found things not the same.

'I remember an old soldier I met, who survived so many of the worst battles of the war, saying that at the end of it he did not bear grudges against the enemy. You know, this is not an easy thing . . .' And Margaret found herself drawn back to the man, who now sat staring up at her father, and she saw, but did not want to see, that his head was shaking very slightly and his hands were forward now on the pew in front, and clenched white and tight upon it. He was listening to what her father was saying, listening but not agreeing with it.

Normally she kept her eyes low during one of her father's sermons, because she did not much like the searchlight sweep of his gaze across the subservient and trapped congregation, and the ghastliness of him gazing at her with the words of God and Christ in his mouth, rather than some domestic instructions delivered over the breakfast table. Now, however, she started listening, too, and as she did so, she stared up at him. And when his gaze swept towards her, and on to her for a moment, for once she did not flinch. The gaze swept on and the words continued, but now she herself looked around the congregation, at the people there, and saw them not as subjects to draw, but as the people they were. Mothers and fathers, soldiers and nurses, people who had seen the war and its effects, and surely suffered so much, so very much. Couldn't her father *speak* to them and reach out to them and say . . . and her head dropped, for the words in her mind were those she most wanted to hear for herself: '*I care for you, and love you, and come unto you, for you are not alone though you cry in the wilderness.*'

The sermon over, the Communion started, and the man stood up to let another pass out into the aisle. He did not join the communicants. And suddenly, with her heart beating wildly, Margaret decided that she was not going to join them either. And as she decided, the man turned for a moment towards her before sitting down, and she saw that he looked terrible and lost, and she felt, she wanted, she desired to reach out to him, whoever he was, because he needed it, like she did.

The wickedness of her thoughts then escalated rapidly, for when the service ended, and in a mood of defiance and general bloody-mindedness, she dared to address him at the church door: 'I noticed you were reading from a Church of Scotland prayer-book . . .'

'Aye, I was, and I do. Not often, mind, for I'm no a regular at this kirk but I like to go on Remembrance Sunday, for it's the day I think of my parents.'

He began to walk away, like men did, and Margaret, desperate now that he shouldn't, made some more polite conversation, walking along with him as if she was leaving the church and not waiting for her father, as surely she should be, and must.

'Are you . . . I mean, do you live here then?' It was the best she could manage.

'Aye, its my home now. Since the war nearly, Mrs . . . er . . .' He hadn't even noticed her ringless left hand.

'Miss,' she said with a smile, and the wickedness continued, for she did not follow it with her name. She had no wish for him to know.

'Oh, aye. Sorry,' he said.

There was a silence between them but he didn't move this time.

'It wasn't like he said it was, you know,' he said suddenly. 'I dinnae think he ken's much of the war that was.'

'No?' she said, leading him on so terribly.

'Nae, it wasna like that.' And there was such loss in his voice and his eyes were suddenly so low, that despite herself and all her fears she moved just a fraction closer to him saying, 'I understand,' because she believed she did.

'I lost friends in ways you cannae imagine. I killed men who were no more than boys with my ain hands. The kirk doesnae comfort me nor wipe the tears frae my eyes.'

She did not know what to say.

'I'm sorry,' she said.

'It's no your fault, lass,' he said and then, miracle of miracles, the man smiled at her, really at her, and said, 'Ye're a lot more comfort than that foolish sermon, stopping and talking a while.'

'Margaret!' Her father, berobed, was there with them. Stern.

It was then, as her father looked at the man who was talking to his daughter, that the man laughed. Quite openly and quite loudly.

303

Just for a moment he laughed, and the terror Margaret felt was gone, because he didn't mind that she had led him on without saying who she was. And he, too, understood.

'Will you introduce me to your friend?' her father asked acidly.

'She cannae do that for she doesnae know it,' the man said, 'but my name is Liam Hugh MacAskill,' and then, turning away from her father quite deliberately, almost rudely, he said, 'And it has been a pleasure talking to you. I hope . . .'

'Yes,' she had said, 'Yes?'

'I hope we may meet again.'

'So do I,' she said, and she dared to look at him boldly and directly, and his stare and his humour were what were at her side to give her strength each time, in the days that followed, she began to quail before her father's growing fury that she had decided, quite irrationally, or rather for reasons he would not understand, never to take Holy Communion again.

It was that laugh of his then that she had really drawn, though it had only been possible after he, Liam MacAskill, did indeed meet her again, and together, on bicycles, they began to explore a strange and treacherous land of delights in which they both felt like ageing strangers. And though he had many disadvantages – as no doubt she had in his eyes – he had one inestimable virtue: he was not afraid of her father. And, even more surprising, her father seemed marginally afraid of him.

'Mummy, Mummy . . .' and Jim's voice brought her back from the past into Compass Street, as he drew her out of her absorption with Daddy's picture into what he was interested in. Until he lost himself in other things, and she went off into the kitchen to make a nice cup of tea for them both—with just the same spirit of hope and recovery, prosperity and cheer, which Grace Frewin often invested in cups of tea.

When tea was ready she called out to Jim to come and get it, but he never did; and by the time she thought about it again, it was getting cold. She went into the garden to do some weeding and saw him through the drawing-room window, lying on the floor with all her drawings spread out in front of him, his head supported on one hand, flicking through them. Later she looked again and he was still there, but now the drawings had been abandoned and he was reading, and that surprised her. He very rarely did. In fact, he found it difficult still, even though he was ten—and it worried her, since her other boys had all started to read when they were quite young. She looked closer to see what he was reading, and saw it was a children's book she and Liam had bought for Frank when he was six.

'Mummy, is this going to a jumble sale?'

'Well, I thought it ought to now. No one wants it any more and there's so much we don't use in the house, all piling up.'

'It's good, this is.'

'Well, we'll keep it then, for the time being.'

He was there for an hour, until he had to go off to meet Peter, and it was long enough for her to do a quick sketch of him, which she later worked up with water-colour, and she wrote along its bottom edge: JIMMY—AGED TEN. It showed a cast of sunlight, spreading the shape of the window, all angles and glass panes, across the brown carpet and on to the pages that he was looking at.

That day Jimmy stepped forward into a new world where the sun did indeed shine, and where he became a glutton, eating, grabbing and taking. The book he had taken up was Volume VII of Arthur Mee's *Children's Encyclopedia*, illustrated on nearly every page with pre-war graphics, duotone drawings, maps, and reproductions in blue or brown sepia of 'the World's Greatest Paintings and Sculptures'.

What had caught his attention to start with was the regular group of stories, retold by Mr Mee himself, under the general title *The Great Stories of the World that will be Told for ever*. Borrowing generously from Brothers Grimm, Perrault, Aesop, The Thousand and One Nights, Greek myths and Roman legends, plus tales from China and Japan, the book began to transport Jim away from the small world in which he had so far lived, and take him into the bazaars of Baghdad, the grim forests of northern Europe, the court of King Arthur, and on to the decks of the ships of Columbus and Captain Cook. Columbus wore a mauve cap and had a dagger hanging from his belt. King Arthur had a beard and a kingly crown, and Japanese heroes wore black pyjama things and had slit eyes.

These places became more real to Jim than school or church, and the people in them quite as real as Mr Chandler, Mrs Angel, Granny, his mother and his father, and those few adults who entered his life.

There were sections of the huge ten-volume encyclopedia whose words he habitually ignored, but whose pictures he looked at long and hard, losing himself in them.

As he leafed through the pages, in the weeks and months that followed, he began to register the paintings and sculptures that Mr Mee had insisted should be illustrated in his great work. Their effect was cumulative rather than immediate, and it was only after passing by Rodin's *Thinker* on many occasions that Jim finally stopped and stared at it; and only slowly that he registered the immensity of the pyramids and Egyptian sculpture, and the delicacy of the objects found in Tutankhamen's tomb.

Many of the paintings were of child subjects, and of no great interest to him. But Mr Mee had a love of the pre-Raphaelites, and though Jim did not take in their names, he liked the detail of their paintings, a hand at a piano, the tress of a woman's hair, the doubt on a face, and it was these he began to copy. So, before ever he registered the artist's name, he copied Millais' *Knight at the Ford*, Holman Hunt's *The Hireling Shepherd*, and Landseer's *Monarch of the Glen*. Sometimes he would do outline drawings of Greek lions, or try to reproduce Leonardo's *Mona Lisa*, or get in a tangle among the arms and hands and legs of Rodin's *Burghers of Calais*.

Often, when he had finished, he would turn the pages and ask himself, as Arthur Mee asked, questions like: How can we measure a country? Does the Earth ever bump into anything? . . .

Mr Mee was a patriot and Christian, and no opportunity was missed to drum home the magnificence of the British Empire and the virtues of the Christian life, the two of which were linked in some mysterious way. But these earnest messages were lost on Jim, who was free to move on through the pages in a way he was not free to do in class. So he wandered at his own pace, reading a moving story there, and copying very carefully an Uccello or a Michelangelo here. It never occurred to him that the pictures that absorbed him so much might actually exist, and since the reproductions were in either blue or brown monochrome, he could not know that their originals were in colour.

One day he was lost for a while among the 'Varied Products of the West Indies', until, getting bored, he turned the pages to find himself, with a shock, in 'Nature's Wonderful Living Family in Earth and Air and Sea: The Day Birds of Prey'.

A great buzzard, with wings as wide as the page itself, stared out at him. He turned on to the sepia pictures of exotic raptors: Pondicherry Vulture, Ruppell's Vulture, Imperial Eagle . . . and on to the fabulous Lammergeer Eagles. Then Merlin preparing a meal for its young; a Harpy Eagle; and a White-tailed Sea Eagle, just like that. He stared at it for a very long time, his eyes lost on the fuzzily-reproduced head and massive wings. It was in profile and was staring, cheek by beak, at the Harrier Hawk. Its eyes were fierce, and Jim immediately made a drawing of it, only bigger, like it really was. Its tail was white and big, and hung down the rock it was perched on. Behind it a great waterfall fell over a cliff, white and hazy.

He took the book upstairs for Granny to see, and she said, 'Well, my dear, we had better read what it says, hadn't we? But you read to me for a change, because I'm finding it harder to see small print like this.' So he sat next to her and read.

'The British example of the sea eagles is the white-tailed eagle which builds nests on craggy peaks remote from the haunts of man. Shepherds tell eerie stories of the experience of lambs with these bold harriers of the coasts. We still have our own sea eagles unless Fate in the form of a ruffian with a gun has slain the last we possessed. One read, indeed, that the sole survivor of the great beauties, which from time beyond count had built and bred in the Hebrides, had been shot. But as a tiger appears in India wherever tiger has haunted before, so eagles come back to the eyries of other eagles. We must hope the same in regard to this grand creature which formerly gave romance to the north of Scotland . . .'

He fell silent and Granny peered at the picture, holding it away from her at different angles but unable to make it out.

'Well, it just shows an eagle,' he said finally, 'with a great waterfall going down the mountain behind it. Look, I've drawn it bigger.'

But she couldn't seem to see it. He saw then, for the first time, that she was very old now, and not the same as when she had first come to live with them. When he moved now her eyes didn't follow him, so she was beginning to go blind. And though her pose in the chair was peaceful, she picked and worried at one of her thumbs with her old grey fingers. The room was quiet but for the rustle of the sea filtered up the narrow street outside. He sat and looked at her as she slowly gave up on the picture of the eagle, and he understood that she, like Daddy who had laughed and no longer did, and like Mummy, like all of them, was subject to change.

He had once come into her room and found her sitting in her chair with the picture Grandfather had given her in her hands. So he got up now, took it from the bedside, and without saying anything put it into her hands, which stopped fretting, and she held it close and felt it. It was a funny thing that the grandfather he knew through her was very different from the one he knew through Mummy. Strange, too, that Granny seemed so different to him than she seemed to Mummy—so much nicer to him. She relaxed with the familiar picture in her hands again.

'James,' she said, 'I'm afraid I wasn't able to see your picture of the eagle so very well. You may describe it to me, if you like . . .'

And so it was, that summer, and always using the *Children's*

Encyclopedia, he began to describe the pictures in it to his grand-mother, so that she might enjoy them through his eyes. 'There's a man.' 'What sort of man, my dear?' she would interrupt, forcing him to really look. 'A man with a beard who's quite old . . .' 'How old?' And she made him use his eyes as she once had used her own.

But the first picture he ever described this way was not one of the Old Masters, or the New Impressionists, but that poorly repro-duced picture of a sea eagle, two inches by one, which was perched on a rock somewhere in northern Europe, and behind which a great and terrible waterfall was falling down.

'Now, can you try and tell me what time of day it is in the picture, my dear?'

★ ★ ★ ★ ★

It was dawn, and Clew had taken a stance at the very edge of the only possible entrance into the Storrin, apart from the Gap itself. Mizen and Weever perched ten or fifteen feet away, the one looking anxiously at Clew to see what move he would make, while the other peered about him into the moist morning gloom, certain that they were being watched by Hardanger eagles or sleark, or likely both.

Yet they were not in such danger as they might have been. For when they had returned from the sea the night before, after taking their terrible leave of Cuillin, they had found a great gathering of Romsdal eagles at the entrance to the main fjord. Most were juveniles, but there was a welcome scattering of adults among them. Clew had addressed them, saying, 'Cuillin, the Fremmed, has gone as suddenly as she came. She is flying back to her own home called Skye across the dark sea . . .' And many were the mutterings that it was impossible, where she was going, and she would surely die, and Clew did not doubt that they were right. She had taken her last flight, and somewhere in the sky or sea she had flown to the wings of Haforn. Yet though he knew this to be so, he insisted, 'She has flown back to Skye—and has left us all the task of protecting and caring for her young.' And this news stopped their muttering short, for many did not know she had young, and most were staggered to learn that she had left them, even though so terribly wounded. No eagle ever leaves its young.

'She was the Fremmed,' cried out Clew, 'and her young are of Haforn, and by her blessed. Cuillin has left them for us to protect, for from them will come great things, and an inspiration that will bring us hope and courage. Even now will it start, for I ask you all to accompany Mizen, Weever and myself back up into the depths of Romsdal, where Hardanger eagles and sleark fly, so that we may have the protection we need to go to the aid of Cuillin's young.'

They all looked at each other and then up towards the darkness of Romsdal, and were silent.

'She flew its length, wounded in wing and side, steadily and with courage, and she turned her young over to Haforn's protection. Each one of us flies in the shadow of Haforn, and yet long have we turned our backs on her. Yet which of you who saw the Fremmed make her final flight down between the cliffs of Romsdal will take a stance apart from us and say, "She did not fly with Haforn in her wings"? Let any of you who think this come forth now and show yourself.'

His voice thundered around the great fjord, but not one eagle moved. All stared. All waited. All began to have a hope.

He began again, very softly. 'She came here with only courage in her wings, a stranger, a lost one, the last of her race. She taught me her language; she taught Mizen and Weever how to fly a true line. She took a territory in the very face of Sleat and the Hardanger eagles, knowing that if she held it – and I had the honour of helping her do so for many long years – then time would perhaps bring courage back to you of Romsdal who deserted her. She stopped us destroying each other in a feud between fellow sea eagles, so there might be enough of us left to fight the Doom when it came. Now men have come to the very foot of Storrin itself, and they have killed Finse, my father and her mate, and mortally wounded Cuillin herself. The Doom will come with them, and her departure is the warning and the proof of this.'

He fell silent, and one of the bolder eagles among them called out, 'What must we do now? Where should we fly, Clew? Tell us.'

'We must fly eastwards to the Storrin, even though it is now dark and the winds are dangerous. We must fly to save her young. We must resist the urge to fight the Hardanger eagles, for they are of our kind. We must fly steadily and as one, and if there are any who feel weak or begin to doubt, remember the flight of the Fremmed you have seen and let her great power bless your wings.'

So it was Clew led them back to the Storrin, and Clew who, the following dawn, bravely made passage through the Storrin cliffs and winds, praying to Haforn for guidance, and found a route through a chimney of rock which led to where the two youngsters lay.

There they were, hidden among the sticks and sinews of an ancient nest, Cuillin's young, beneath a great wet overhang, the Storrin to their right-wing side. They lay prone among the sticks, their necks stretched out in the final stages of defeat, their puny feathers sodden and limp, their bodies grey and still. They lay together as one, over to the far side of the nest, as if they had crawled there together for comfort. Clew landed at the edge of the nest, folding his great wings into his body and looking down at them despairingly, a fish still in his talons. He dropped it into the nest and side-stepped over to them carefully. He bent down to look at them, his great beak just a little open, and he nudged first one, then the other. They were terribly cold, and did not move. He came above them and settled his wing and side over then, and whispered gentle words such as every eagle knows to speak to young when they are stricken. No movement. He looked up from the nest and into the wild sky of Storrin in terrible despair, and cried out, 'Help them, Haforn, for they are Cuillin's young, and the young of my father Finse.' And looking down at them again, he whispered, 'They are my own siblings, my half-brother and half-sister.'

None can say how long he nestled them before some tremor among their tiny limbs, some surge of warmth, told him they were not yet gone. He whispered, he blew and he coaxed; he said they were eagles to live, not nothings to die. Their mother was the Fremmed and they would live, and by Haforn's own talons he would help them . . . and they stirred. First one and then the other, torn out of the chill and into the world again, with a great eagle's talon to stub their beaks on, and a mass of feathers to warm them and struggle through, out into the light. And food. First for one and then the other: Askaval first and little Mourne last.

'What are your names?' asked Clew.

'My . . . name is . . . Askaval . . . and she is . . . Mourne. My father was Finse and my mother is Cuillin of Skye.' And Clew could have laughed to hear it, for Cuillin had already begun her work on him who was the stronger, the better survivor.

'Where is she?' asked Askaval.

'She has gone back to Skye, and left you in the care of Mizen and Weever, and of myself, Clew, your half-brother.' But Askaval stared at him with a directness astonishing in one so young, until Clew found himself saying: 'No, that is not true. She has gone now to join Haforn. She is dead.' For Askaval looked like an eagle who could only ever want to hear the truth. Then Askaval blinked and shook his head slightly, and moved closer to Mourne—as if to say that, if Cuillin was dead, then it was his job to protect Mourne, his sister. Clew was surprised at such strength in one so weak and helpless and there came to him the first understanding of the nature of the eagle he might now be nurturing. Even so, the fact that there seemed to be no sibling rivalry between the two puzzled him, since

310

Mourne had signs of wounding on her head, where Askaval's beak must have battered her. Some eagles never lost these scars all their lives, the feathers growing awry, as they did on the head of Mizen. But now Askaval seemed especially concerned for the safety of his sister.

The day passed, and the two began to grow stronger, astonishing Clew by their rapid recovery. There was enough fish for a day, and some for him as well, and he decided to stay and not risk leaving them until he was sure they would survive until Mizen or Weever could find more food.

Come dawn, however, Clew returned to his companions. Tired, and his feathers wet and cold with spray, he quickly told them all he had seen, and that the two young were still alive. And, after resting a while, it was time to show Mizen the difficult route into the nesting site—and she followed him nervously but with determination.

As Weever watched them go, he had never felt so alone, for he could easily guess the danger Mizen was flying into. She was not and never had been a strong or sure flier. But an hour later – an hour that seemed several years to Weever – Clew was back.

'She's safe and sound and taking care of them!' said Clew, and if there had been several terrible moments, when the wind had sucked at Mizen's wings and she had nearly gone off-balance, he did not immediately mention it. When he had regained his strength he would lead Weever back, so that all of them would know the route and could fly it—though he had his doubts as to whether Mizen would ever be able to fly it in complete safety.

So, in danger and with courage, the nurturing of Askaval and Mourne was begun, by three eagles whose names even the Ravens now respect. On flight after flight, Weever and Clew brought food through the treacherous deeps of the Storrin, each taking turn to watch over the entrance and find prey.

Mizen took over Cuillin's role willingly, for she had not had young of her own that year. She now believed that had been the will of Haforn, and she entered into the job of nurturing the two of them with a serious concern which was typical of her. Her great wings seemed forever half-open over them, as if she feared some imminent attack on their young bodies, and her head darted this way and that, constantly on the look-out.

She felt it necessary too to talk to them as she felt sure Cuillin would have done, and as soon as Mourne was strong enough, she began to tell them stories, some true, others somewhat fanciful, of the things that Cuillin had done, and of how she had come to love Finse, their father.

'Cuillin was called the Fremmed, which means the stranger, because she flew from a distant place where no other Romsdal eagle has ever been, but where the winds are good and the waters warm and the fish plentiful . . . Her flight was like nothing any of us will ever see again, for her wings were huge . . .'

'Bigger than yours?' asked Askaval, for he could not believe that any eagle could have bigger wings than Mizen.

'Bigger and stronger,' said Mizen, peering out into the wild air around them, as if she could see Cuillin out there and was describing her for real. 'And one sweep of her wings carried her further than the eye could see . . . She flew north one year to see the Weir, whom I've told you about, and I was there, with Clew and Weever, and she outflew all of us, and when we grew tired and weary, why, she turned back for us and urged us on . . .'

So, story by story, Mizen gave them impressions and images neither could forget, though they reacted to them very differently. But it was wise Clew who first noticed how very different the two of them were. Three weeks had passed and they were both sitting up now, with vigour, and the down on their bodies was giving way at last to the pale grey fluff of feathers. And though Mourne was just beginning to catch up with Askaval in size, yet he was still by far the stronger, and was careful to protect his sister and make sure she had her share of food.

Askaval had asked about Romsdal and Clew had described it to them: the great cliffs, the deep, still water, the islands at the mouth of the fjord, green now with the beginnings of summer.

'I would like to go there now!' declared Askaval eagerly.

But Mourne merely bowed her head. She did not seem to have the same interest in things as Askaval, and often fell silent as if she had some burden on her wings.

Flying. It already nagged at Clew and worried him that these two would have to learn how to do it here, where even a fully mature eagle had great difficulty. What a place for a nest! He dared not think about how they were going to get the two of them out of the Storrin in safety, or what would happen when, as he surely would, Askaval learned how to fly before Mourne and wished to leave her while he tried his wings.

This was a worry of Mizen's too—as Weever noticed. Because, with all the other young she had reared, she had talked of their first flight with hope and promise in her voice—for then they would be free. And with a bit of care in the first few months, when they would have more to learn than perhaps they realised, they would be safe. But this time, with these two, she never mentioned flight, and when inevitably Askaval started to ask 'When shall I fly?' Mizen shushed him, saying, 'Soon enough, my dear, but not for a while yet.' Then she would look around at the Storrin and down at the raging white spray far beneath, among sodden black cliffs and cascading falls, and then back at their young fledgling wings, and she would wonder how they could ever manage here, and how they would survive. It was stressful even for an adult like her to stay on the edge of the nest site in such winds.

The weeks turned to months, then summer came over the fjord, bringing with it peace and light, though the latter only barely penetrated the Storrin directly. Yet there was a sense of calmer warmth, and the waterfall itself, now that the worst thaws of spring were over, was beginning to slacken slightly, and the winds about it to abate as well. Sometimes a shaft of sunlight would penetrate the gloom of the great cliffs and fall on the white water of the fall itself, and suddenly it would sparkle with grace and beauty. Sometimes now, also, the eternal mist and spray would lift, and from their nest Mizen would point through the Gap to the mighty view of Romsdal and its cliffs, and the route out westward to the sea.

'You'll go there one day,' she would say, but her reverie would be shattered by Askaval's increasingly strong-willed demand: 'Yes, but when?' He would raise his wings, now already filling out with feathers, and try to flap them as he had so often seen Clew and Mizen do. The more he did it, the more he dared to raise himself on his talons and feel the lift his wings were beginning to give him, and the sudden awesome lightness at his feet when the world started to wobble. Then he would settle down and fold them back, finding it hard still not to tangle one wing with the other, and failing miserably to fold them with the same grace as Clew.

His head was filling out too, and his gaze was growing fierce and proud, but with that touch of gentleness he had shown since Cuillin left.

As for Mourne, she was as large as he was now, if not bigger, and yet her whole body seemed gawky and unformed by comparison. And over her beak and on her forehead, where she had once been so viciously attacked by Askaval, the feathers were slow to grow and gave her face the strange look of one who does not trust the world. She, too, was beginning to try out her wings, though she preferred to do so rather more in the centre of the nest, for she had peered over the edge away from the cliff-face, and the steep drop into whirling nothingness had seemed to reach up to her head and made it swim, and she had imagined herself being dragged up out of the nest and over into the void. So she busied her wings in safety, not yet reaching up to the impossible sky, as Askaval was continually trying to do.

Seeing them both begin to try their wings, Mizen grew increasingly concerned, and voiced her fears to Clew, and later to Weever. 'I don't know how they can ever learn safely. The moment they try – and you know how hard it can be at first – they'll be grabbed by the wind, and though we'll be there with them, what can we do to stop them falling headlong, without the strength or skill to recover?'

Weever, normally so practical and confident, was worried himself, and could only say, 'Well, I reckon if we choose a quiet day and stay very close by them, and let them only do it when they're ready, *and* do it one at a time . . . they ought to be all right.' But he didn't sound convinced. Even after so many weeks of flying into the Storrin, he himself found parts of it quite frightening—and especially when entering into the chimney between the main cliff-face and the Great Pinnacle, as they called it now.

Only Clew seemed calm, for after a lot of thought, he had come to the conclusion that one way or another the two of them would be safe. For had not Haforn protected them thus far? Was not the great Fremmed's blood in their veins? Meanwhile, he tried to give Mizen confidence, but whatever he said she would still anxiously say: 'I just don't see how they will ever do it. Oh, it's so dangerous for them, and I swear its getting worse!'

★ ★ ★ ★ ★

One day a year or so later, Jim found Granny lying on the floor of her kitchen, where she had fallen down. Her head was on the lino, which was dirty, and her mouth was trying to say something but no real sound came out. Something was burning on the stove and that was why Jim had gone into the room, because he could smell it.

Seeing his feet by her head seemed to give her strength, and she pushed herself up as he squatted down to help her.

'It's all right, my dear,' she said. 'I'm quite all right. I'll sit down for a moment if you'll help me to my chair.'

He helped her to a chair in the neighbouring room, and when she sat down, he said, 'I'll just turn off the gas in your kitchen, Granny.' He knew she needed a moment to be alone, to put herself straight. For he knew she would mind being seen like that. He didn't like it either: something in his world collapsed seeing her there so weak, because she was Granny, and even if she was old she was stronger than anyone else in his whole life.

'Now you're not to tell your mother, my dear, on any account.'

A little later she explained: 'It would worry her, you see, and she has quite enough on her plate without this kind of nonsense. I just tripped, that's all—a moment before you came in.'

She stood up, or tried to, saying, 'You see, you see, I'm all right.' But her hand was shaking on the wicker chair, and Jim went to help her back down.

'Sit still for a bit, Granny,' he said. 'I won't say anything.' He knew it meant a lot to her.

But three weeks later she fell in the street, and Mr Allenby at the corner shop helped her home and told Mummy, despite being asked not to. Dr Lessing came, and said Granny had to rest. So Jim read to her, or they played cards, because she could still see the suits. She kept asking about Mummy, and Jim could sense she was frightened. That had something to do with her being angry, and with Mummy being angry too.

One day Mummy went off on her bicycle to Walmer, and came back with a form which she showed to Granny. Granny was going to go into a home for elderly people, a very comfortable home which she went to visit in a taxi in her best hat and coat. It was quite lovely and the people there were so very kind. Except Jim knew that Granny didn't want to go.

One afternoon he came back and ran upstairs, and Granny had gone. Her writing desk had gone, and the old carved book-case, and the wicker chair. He stood in the room with no expression on his face at all, just staring around, and his heart stopped still. His Granny had gone. He went into the kitchen, which smelled of her and her cooking, mince and onions and little lamb-chops. All her cooking things were there, and there was a row of jars full of jam on one of the shelves. Where Mummy had sent her she wouldn't be doing any cooking, or need jam. He went back into her room and opened the cupboard where her dressing-gown used to hang— blue with embroidery in red and beige on the front. It was gone.

But something was wrong in the room; something worried him. He couldn't bear the room or what had gone from it, so he went downstairs.

'Granny's gone,' he said to Mummy, who was in the kitchen by the fire.

'Yes, Jim, she has. To the old people's home in Walmer. I told you it was today.'

'I forgot,' said Jim. It had not been something he especially wanted to remember—nor she to remind him of.

'She was a danger to herself,' said Mummy. 'She'll be better off where she is. You can go and visit her.' But visiting Granny in a place where old people tottered about and stared vacantly wouldn't be the same as running into her room without knocking, as he had, and telling her things he had done. He wouldn't be able to sit with her now in his dressing-gown, by her gas-fire, and listen to stories about Grandfather.

Early in the morning, he woke suddenly and knew what was wrong. He crept downstairs to Granny's room, below his own, and turned on the light. It was cold and he stood shivering a little, still half-asleep, staring at the wall over the bed. Her little picture was still there. She had not taken it. She would have taken it if she had gone willingly—or if she had any hope. She was saying something terribly clear by leaving it there, and it was terrible to Jim to realise that. She was saying she had been sent away to die somewhere; and that wasn't a place she wanted her picture to be, because there was something important of her life inside it.

The door slowly opened and his mother stood there in her nightdress, hair wild, face grey, looking rather frightened. She had wakened and heard steps above her own room on the ground floor, light steps in Mother's room, sounds like Mother made at night when she got up to go to the toilet, or to sit by the fire because she could not sleep. But it was only Jim. Disturbed at Mother leaving, probably.

'Granny left her picture,' said Jim.

'Yes, I know, dear. And a few other things she'll need. You take them up to her tomorrow. She'll like that. Now off you go, back to bed. Go on!' So he did. But before he fell asleep, he thought it was strange to be alone in the house now, just with Mummy, and all those rooms empty, silent. First Frank and Oliver, then Michael, now Granny. Things had changed suddenly again.

Grace Frewin was busy in the kitchen taking the steak-and-kidney pie she had made for lunch out of the gas-oven. She was humming to herself and half singing, and ending the song with a sort of high-pitched harmony of ghastly dissonnance. Michael was in the front room facing the street, which had once been Margaret's room, and he was playing the piano. Jim was in the boathouse with Peter, playing darts. The two of them had been at Grammar School a year now. 'Them boys ought to be getting washed for lunch,' she said through the kitchen window, which was open on to the garden.

In the sun which had come with the first week of the summer holidays, Liam MacAskill sat supping a mug of beer. Grace had put a chair out for him, facing the sun, but he had a constant fear that Margaret, who was presently 'visiting London', would suddenly appear at the garden gate and their harmless deception be discovered. Margaret was really with a man she had met on a shopping expedition to Canterbury, and who worked for an agricultural machinery firm in Maidstone. She was 'visiting' him for the day.

Much as Grace liked and respected Margaret, she had taken pity on poor Liam MacAskill, who lived alone and did not feed himself properly. He looked pale and emaciated, and was to be seen up on the front in all weathers, sitting on one of the benches and staring out to sea, thinking about goodness-knows-what. Grace was one of those who believed that children needed a father, and these two boys especially, now that the older boys had left home for good. They had no one to look up to, apart from their Mum, and one parent isn't enough.

So now, on the regular occasions when Margaret was away, whether for a day or a night or two, Grace had taken it upon herself to invite Liam to stay for a meal and have a cup of tea. Or, as on this occasion, and it being hot, beer.

The pie was a big one. There would be Liam, and Jim, and his friend Peter, and Michael just back from boarding-school for the summer holidays. All three of them went to the Grammar School in Sandwich now, where Michael had boarded for three years but Jim and Peter went over on the train each day.

'Liam, you can get the boys and tell them it's time for lunch.' He did not stir, he did not even hear her, though he was barely four feet away. He was looking at the garden wall and thinking, his mouth set in that grin it went into these days, when you couldn't be sure if he was smiling or in pain.

The boys played a tacit part in the 'deception' of Liam's being there, by not saying anything about it. Michael barely spoke to him, but then Michael was Michael: he barely spoke to anybody the family knew. Not that he was shy, mind you, or backward; but he was silent. And he was pale. And he liked to do things his own way. Stubborn as a mule.

Jim seemed to like Liam, though he was wary of him. But they walked on the front together sometimes, and Jim told him about the things he was doing, though Liam never mentioned much of it to Grace. But if she said, 'Jim's done this, or Jim's done that,' Liam would say, 'Aye,' in that slow Scottish way of his, as if he knew already, and was weighing the matter up. 'Aye, I know that, Grace. The laddie told me.'

Michael was silent over lunch, and looked annoyed. He had angry red spots on his chin.

'Are you going to play that game *all* afternoon?' he demanded.

'Why?' asked Jim in surprise.

'Because it disturbs what I'm learning on the piano – bang, bang, bang all morning – that's why.'

'Why didn't you say, then?'

'I shouldn't have to.'

'Well, I won't be here this afternoon, so you needn't worry.'

'What are you doing then, Jim?' asked Mrs Frewin, hoping to switch the conversation away from what looked like an imminent argument, such as the two boys were always having when Michael was at home. She sometimes thought Margaret was actually right to send him to boarding-school.

Jim grinned. 'It's a secret,' he said.

'What, like little girls have?' sneered Michael.

Jim looked hurt and Peter pretended not to notice. Neither of them liked these quarrels Michael always picked.

There was silence. Liam MacAskill picked his way through the pie, bits of it sticking messily to his upper lip as he stopped chewing, sometimes in mid-chew, and stared out of the garden door. Then, for no reason, Peter started giggling and Jim joined in, encouraging him yet further by muttering between clenched teeth the word that currently made them both fall off their seats whenever it was spoken: 'Lugworms.'

'Children,' sneered Michael.

Mrs Frewin tried not to laugh herself, though they did make a funny lot, whichever way you looked at it.

'I walked on the Dunes yesterday,' announced Liam, stopping the giggling dead. They waited for him to tell them what happened, but he did not continue. He seemed to have finished telling them.

'I didn't have anyone to walk with, so I was alone,' he added suddenly, taking them by surprise.

Jim travelled away from them in his mind, to the Dunes, and saw his father out there alone, as he had seen him before. Something was wrong with Daddy, but he didn't know what it was. But Jim always spoke gently to him now, and tried to make sense of the things he said. Sometimes he wanted to put his hands on Daddy's face and feel how the eyes were, and the pulled mouth, and how those sharp, pale cheekbones, where the skin was shiny, flowed round towards the ears. He wanted to touch Daddy's hair, and his nose, and hold his head at front and back to feel its form and mass. He never wanted to forget Daddy, who seemed so often about to be leaving them and going on a journey.

'Where's Granny?' asked Liam suddenly.

'Why, she's been in the old people's home on Drum Hill weeks now, Liam. You *know* that.'

'Has she?' he said. He stared out of the window. 'I didn't really know,' he said, 'Not really. She'll be feeling lonely, so I'll go and visit her.'

Jim stared at him thinking, 'But Daddy and Granny don't get on'. She had never approved of him. She had caused him trouble. So why should . . .? And as he thought this, he saw a distant kindness in his father's eyes which he had not seen before, and which told him Daddy understood how Granny felt. There was a gentleness in Daddy's face, and Jim saw it was at the very heart of his father's nature, and that it was different from the strength that was in Mummy, and in Granny, too.

Sometimes these days, like now, Jim would find himself looking around the table, at Mrs Frewin, big and familiar, and Michael, strange and frightening, and his father, tall and thin, and even at his best friend Peter, who knew nearly everything about him, and he wondered . . . well, he wondered who they were exactly. He wanted to draw them, or make the shape of them, as if that might make them more real. He felt so distant from them at moments like that. But he wasn't afraid of Daddy any more, not now, because Daddy couldn't harm anyone, whatever Mummy seemed to think.

As for Michael, it seemed to Jim that he was in a different world now, different even from the one he had been since Mummy sent him to board at prep school, and continued him boarding when he went on to Grammar School.

He had more friends than Jim did, who only had Peter—but they were different as friends. They made quick jokes and laughed in a hard way in Michael's room, and Michael talked loudly to them. There was aggression in their talk, while in things he and Peter said there was sharing and deep trust. Usually they didn't need to talk.

Michael's voice had broken and he had grown taller, and was pale and spotty. He was clever and Mummy said he had a talent for music, so he played up on the stage at the Grammar School, a classical piece by Chopin, which he had practised at home till it drove Jim bonkers, and he had to go up and walk along the beach alone to escape it.

Peter was like Michael in some ways now, because he was clever, too, and won a prize for History at the end of the first year. He was in Upper Two next term while Jim was down in Lower Two. Also he was becoming interested in girls, and sometimes seemed to be in the same distant, adult world Frank and Oliver were in, which Jim couldn't even reach up to—but the same one as Michael was heading towards now. There was also something else in that world, which Mummy knew about, and it had to do with the way girls were when they walked in the street and boys whistled. It had something to do with that. Sometimes Peter seemed to move in that world, just for a moment, and Jim was afraid that he would lose him, and would try hop-stepping along the kerb so he could forget. And then his hands would ache and seek out a piece of paper or wood or something to hold on to and make something of, because those things out there were frightening and fascinating and it helped to put them down into something you could hold in your hand.

It was that afternoon that Peter introduced him to the ternery over in Sandwich Bay, along past the Dunes. Jim had seen the terns sometimes among the gulls on the beach, light and darting with sharp, bent heads and wings as delicate as sunlight on wind-ruffled water. Peter had become interested in ornithology and bird-watching, and he collected eggs. It hadn't been something he did with Jim, who didn't like the eggs, or taking them from a nest where they were so right and beautiful. The truth was that Peter wanted a tern's egg and didn't have the nerve to go to Sandwich all by himself across the Dunes, so he dragged Jim along.

The Deal dunes ended in a group of rich men's big houses, facing on to the great curve of Sandwich Bay. The sand of the bay extended on past them for three miles towards Pegwell Bay, but you couldn't walk further because there was the River Stour, muddy and deep, to stop you, coming out into the sea at a wild and desolate place called Shellness, which Peter and Jim had never reached. The beach there was said to be desolate and strange, with dunes and mud-flats, and the sea coming in at low tide from way out, nearly as fast as galloping horses. There were quicksands, and a girl was drowned there one year and never seen again.

The ternery was not that far along the beach, about a mile or so past the houses, with another golf-course just inland. Peter knew what to look for—a cluster of birds flying above a group of sandy hummocks, and squealing on the wind.

'That's it!' said Peter.

They lay in the dry, stiff grass and watched the birds like spies, heads low and bare arms touching, their legs stretched out behind them. Jim still in shorts, Peter in long trousers now.

They moved forward to see what they could see, and the terns flew more wildly, wheeling and diving in the sky, and Jim saw they were clustering towards them and beginning to dive down, one by one, letting out harsh cries as they did so. They didn't like them being there.

'Let's go back,' Jim said.

'Let's see if we can see a nest first,' insisted Peter.

They stood hesitating, glaring at each other, with the squealing

320

birds diving on them near enough for them to feel the air from their wings in their hair.

'I'm not taking an egg,' said Jim.

'Just let's see what we can see.'

'I don't like it here,' said Jim. He turned to go and his foot went into a scrape in the ground where there were empty broken eggshells, and there was a dry crackling as he broke them even more.

Nothing killed but he hated the sound. It was too late for eggs. He turned on Peter and lashed out at him with his fist. 'I don't like it here,' he repeated, and ran down towards the sea.

'I wouldn't want to harm them,' said Peter later, as they walked together along the edge of the waves, looking at things there: shells and lugworms' holes and cast-up seaweed.

'Look!' said Jim, and he pointed up the beach and over the rise of dunes to where the tern were still circling and wheeling, heads bent forward and wings so pointed and delicate. '*Look!*' They were beautiful.

Peter didn't need to say anything, and Jim didn't need to explain. They were friends. Peter suddenly jumped on him and brought him down on to the hard sand. 'Say you're sorry for hitting me,' he said.

'No!' said Jim. And a wave was coming in, fast as galloping horses.

'Yes!' shouted Peter above the wind, his hands gentle on Jim's shoulders.

'No!' said Jim, beginning to laugh and giggle.

'You better!' said Peter. 'The wave's coming in.'

'Hey!' shouted Jim, and suddenly Peter was pulling him up, and they were pushing each other up the beach and running away to avoid getting wet, laughing. And the sand he had been forced into was wet on his back, and sticking to the back of his head.

'I would like to see an eagle,' said Jim.

'Well, you won't here. There's only golden eagle now, and that's in Scotland.'

'Sleark,' said Jim.

'What?' asked Peter.

'Daddy calls them sleark. It's a Scottish word.'

'Oh,' said Peter.

'They live in the north now.'

'That's just what I said,' muttered Peter.

They both looked involuntarily over towards the Isle of Thanet, beyond Sandwich Bay, because that, roughly speaking, was north.

A cormorant flew out across the water and they watched it disappear down towards Dover. Jim said nothing.

They went back to pick up their bicycles and started off towards Deal, but Jim suddenly found he was alone. Peter had stopped to look back one last time at the circling terns. And Jim looked at them as well, and was glad because Peter was looking at them the way he did.

'There's no other colony of terns in East Kent. They're quite rare really,' said Peter.

'Then you shouldn't disturb them,' said Jim.

'No,' agreed Peter.

As they cycled home, Jim had an image in his mind of the angles of a tern's wings, different from gull or rook. And different from crow—the black birds which flapped ahead of them along the desolate paths on the Dunes, coming up from cover and then disappearing back into it. Or stomping about on the greens looking for worms and gossiping in twos and threes, whispering their stories of the things they saw. For they were of the Corvidae, the bringers of tales and legend, the disregarded birds that growing boys did not cycle miles to see. Yet they saw, and they whispered, and they spread their tales; and the ravens heard, far away among the cliffs and falls of moorland and mountain, and repeated their tales – where few men from Kent had ever been – up in the glen and the highland, over the loch and the kyle, and up among the pinnacles of Storr. Where the winds blow and the rocks fall unseen, except by the Raven of Storr. For in him are all things told, and he knows of the eagle, and of the boys who fight with love along the sands.

* * * * *

Time was passing. Askaval and Mourne were ready to fly, and even Mizen was beginning to take a stance some distance from the nest, so that the two of them might be encouraged to try their wings for themselves, and take a long, hard – and occasionally tottering – look over its edge.

There was a feeling growing among all of them that the time was now right to leave the Storrin. The place that had been a haven, first for Cuillin and Finse, and now in its own strange way for Askaval and Mourne, seemed somehow to be growing even more malevolent and eerie. The darkness of the place seemed blacker, the winds ever more vicious, the occasional sound of falling rock and ice avalanche more frequent. The waterfall itself, which sometimes in sunshine could look positively beautiful, seemed now to cast an even colder gloom over the whole place. Yet it was summer.

To add to this sense of foreboding, rumours were again rife among the Romsdal eagles of dangers beyond their main territories. The summer, it seemed, had marked the start of a renewed assault on sea eagle positions by sleark, who for years had remained quiet—only a vague and sporadic threat which expressed itself in occasional violence at particular nest sites, but violence which sea eagles too often came out of the worse.

It was as if the passing of Cuillin had left the sea eagles unprotected, and though the Romsdal eagles had united to bring Clew, Weever and Mizen in safety to the Storrin, now they were beginning to drift away again, and the Hardanger eagles were slinking back ever nearer. Clew, the only one to escape alive from direct attack by Hardanger eagles, was especially conscious of them watching and waiting. Sometimes, when he was hunting for prey across the fjell or down by some fish-laden lake, he would see, in the distance, the dark silhouette of a Hardanger eagle, watching. More than once he saw, or thought he saw, sleark and Hardanger eagles together, and the possibility that they might cooperate was so shocking to him that he never mentioned it, for fear that it would take Mizen and Weever's minds off the priority task of bringing Askaval and Mourne out of the Storrin alive.

There were other rumours more mysterious, and to Clew, who knew the Doom, even more ominous and significant. For one thing, eagles in the north reported strange discolorations of the sea over large areas, and the air full of a fine black dust. Migrations of the smaller birds past the northernmost sea eagle territories seemed distorted and half-hearted, and there were stories of a glow in the sky, and of boiling seas. Stories, up in the north, of another Fremmed—an old eagle flying south. A male who took stances by himself and watched from neutral territory, and then moved on. A swift flier and one who might be in league with sleark. Rumours of the kind which gather force when eagles flock together and feel they are under threat.

There was no denying that Askaval, and certainly Mourne, would find it impossible to cope alone with the winds of the Storrin. When they flapped their fledgling wings in its air, even the lightest winds were enough to whip at their feathers and send them floundering off-balance among the sticks of the nest. Askaval tried hard, facing into the wind as he saw the adults do, and spreading his wings low behind him, but even perched still and stiff, the howling winds seemed to flatten his feathers so that he looked as if he was already flying at speed through the air—not just standing still against it.

They decided to wait for a still day, so that Weever and Clew could take stances at the nest and stay on its void side as Askaval tried to make a small, quick flight—more a flutter than a flight. They would watch over him and be ready to dive under him and force him back to the nest if the winds began to make him flounder.

'It's the only way for us to do it, Mizen,' Weever said firmly. 'You leave the Storrin to us for a while, and go and occupy yourself with food or something while we get them out.'

The truth was that Weever thought it would be better without Mizen fussing about and putting even more nervousness into the two young ones, especially Mourne.

So it might have happened, but that Weever never got back into the Storrin. For as he bustled Mizen off towards the fjell, and turned back towards the Great Pinnacle, there was a sudden terrible roaring sound, and high above him he saw masses of rock slipping and sliding down the great cliffs towards the Pinnacle, a roaring even mightier than the Storrin itself. Then it was gone, but for rumbles coming from the chimney between the Pinnacle and the main cliff-face. Weever advanced warily, each wing tugged at by suddenly turbulent air, and needing to hold himself steady with all the concentration he had. He feared the chimney would be blocked, the route destroyed, and return impossible.

He was right, for when he reached the chimney itself, where normally the wind would have flung him straight at it, he now saw rock and ice debris loose and spilling from the gap, and the wind was changed so that it was all he could do to hover for a few moments before retreating, staring in despair up the towering cliffs above him. Behind was the maelstrom of wind which was the direct approach to the Storrin, round the outer buttress of the Great Pinnacle, and by which route Clew had never dared to go. Weever, ever careful, ever practical, turned to go back to the entrance stance, to work out a strategy. And he might, indeed, have made it, had he not seen a sight that took him off-balance and had him wheeling suddenly round and up, higher and higher, carried away from the Storrin but high above it, fearing that the very worst had happened, and that Askaval and Mourne had been killed.

Clew had been on the edge of the nest, preparing Askaval for his first attempt, and waiting for Weever to join them. Mourne was huddled pathetically in the nest, brooding on the terrible knowledge that if an eagle doesn't do whatever it is she is scared to death of doing, she'll be stuck doing something even worse—in her case staying in the nest while Askaval flew off to freedom.

But as Clew perched there, and Askaval stared hopefully up at him, a sudden roaring started. And before Clew could even turn

324

round, Askaval was crying, 'Look! Look!' in horror. Because beyond Clew, where the route from the Storrin really started, a great avalanche of rock was falling, grey and black and wet, and its edges were keeling over and seeming to bear down on the very spot where they were. The cliff itself seemed to be collapsing. In that moment the air around the Storrin was suddenly stilled, and so loud was the sound of rock that the waterfall itself appeared to be silent, and the whole balance of the place changed. Clew took the opportunity of the stillness to fly a little from the cliff to watch the fall, having realised that the avalanche, which was now beginning to weaken, could not make its way into the safe enclave where the nest was, for the cliff above them overhung, and if rock was going to fall from above, it would be well out from the face by the time it reached their level.

He had time to see – as Weever saw at that same moment, on the far side of the Pinnacle – that the chimney was now full of loose rock, and impassable. The avalanche stopped and a rumbling, petering roar from deep in the chasm below told him it was over. But as he tried to return the few yards to the nest, a sudden violent cross-current of wind battered at him, created by the rush of rock downward, and pulled him back towards the Storrin itself and inches past the edge of the nest. He tried desperately to reach out his talons and furl his wings to take a grip on the cliff-ledges, but the wind was too strong and he was forced to turn his back on the nest and face the terrible way he was going. He had been that way before, and the roar of the water that now formed a massive cliff of green-whiteness above him was a death-sound in his ears. But even as the first splattering spray began to drench him, and his wings grew heavy with its wetness, another shooting violence of wind took him, and he found himself almost literally plucked out of the depth and torn upwards in a rush and whirl, so that the nest site was spiralling away beneath him, and he was free of the threat of the water—but with the despairing sound of Mourne's cries in his ears. And she was not calling his name, but Cuillin's, and the weak cry became lost in the thunder of the water falling now far below him.

It was then that Weever saw him from the other side of the Pinnacle, and gyred round and up towards him—and saw the very depth of Clew's care for his two siblings. For before he reached near enough to Clew to call his name in that tumult of air, Clew had pulled back his wings for a stoop, his proud head bent forward, his eyes angry with courageous determination, his talons pointed downwards, and he began to drop back into the Storrin, towards the nest. And as he dropped with all the power he could, the wind from below seemed to rush upwards even harder, and he felt the power of his stoop weakening, and his body losing balance because of the low velocity, and he knew that he would have to try again from even higher.

Above him, Weever had seen the problem, and he was already circling higher and higher so that, as Clew gyred up again, it was Weever who tried the dangerous stoop down into the Storrin, down and down, wings back behind him, body feathers streaming, until the wind slowed him too, and he had to curl away to save his balance.

Then they knew that the winds were too strong. To make matters worse, the plume of spray above the Storrin had thickened and widened, and they could no longer see into the mêlée of rocks and crags that formed its depths. The nest and the two young were lost from sight, and Clew knew they would never get back that way.

They returned to the entrance, but as Weever had already found, that route was gone forever, and surely no eagle could ever fly back by the route round the outside of the Great Pinnacle!

As they settled down at the original entrance stance, Mizen flew in and they explained what had happened. And when they finished she said, 'Look what has happened to the sky!' And something had, indeed, happened, which in the rush of failed rescue they had not really noticed. The day had been clear and quiet until the rockfall, but now the sky was strangely ominous in colour, as clouds of mauves and greys built up high over the Storrin and the mountains behind it—just as on the day Cuillin and Finse had made the Flight into the Storrin. Rain suddenly began to fall, violent and hard, pounding down against the rock around them and changing its colour to grey-black, as rivulets of water began to course down the cliff-faces. The air was now heavy with driving rain, and the Great Pinnacle itself could hardly be seen through it.

'I'll try to reach them,' cried Mizen suddenly, terribly distraught. 'Let me try!' And had Weever not raised his own wings in front of her, and pecked at her quite powerfully, she would certainly have tried—and in that rain, and in that place, been killed.

The rain beat on, so loud that even conversation was impossible and they huddled at their stance, taking what shelter they could in the lee of the cliffs that towered above them.

Rain everywhere. Rain sleeking their head feathers and making them shiny wet; rain running down their breasts, at first turning just one part sodden but then spreading and turning all the tips of their feathers spiky with wet. Rain gathering in pools between their feet and causing them to move uncomfortably about to escape the cold of it.

'We stay quite still until it's over,' said Clew. 'They'll be safe enough for the time being. If they can't stand a bit of rain now, they'll never live to be eagles anyway!' Rain—a downpour which cast a pall of sullen stillness over the whole length of Romsdal, where trees and birds, waves and rocks, seemed covered by a grey, muffling wet that missed nothing.

With it came a gathering, unnatural dark and a stilling of the wind that had blown lightly before, except that high above them the sky seemed to be in a rage, and the air was charged with the violence of imminent lightning—which suddenly broke out across them in a deafening crack, as if the sky was breaking in three or four places at once. Then the sudden flashing light, which lit up the wet of their feathers and caught them gazing at each other, before darkness came again.

Then a flash of lightning over to their right, and the crack of thunder to follow it down, echoing all around and rolling across the sky, and among the crags and cliffs.

Then silence, and the gloom of a racing, maddened sky. And all were downcast before it, for each knew they were witness to change. This was not a normal storm: their very bodies and talons and heads seemed part of the forces about them.

'What's happening, Clew?' asked Mizen.

Whatever answer Clew started to give, his beak stopped still, for the fjord was bright with lightning and there, flying up the fjord, was an old eagle, sweeping below them from the sea and up towards the Gap.

The world seemed suddenly to tower all about them, and they to be nothing but frightened eagles in the grip of powers far beyond their understanding.

'It's the Weir!' said Clew with awe.

'But he seems so old!' said Mizen.

'It's the Weir come to guide the Fremmed's children. He has come for them—to help them.'

And Clew turned into the wind and rain and storm, and they followed him, flying down in a long descent to wheel right over the fjord and down towards the old eagle.

Or was he old? The thunder and lightning roared and flashed about him, and by its light he seemed a thousand different eagles all at once, his wings caught for a moment of clear view, dark against the darker rocks behind, and steady in the turmoil all about.

They followed the line that the Weir had been taking and found themselves in the centre of the storm, with the lightning and thunder all about them, and right at the threshold of the Gap of the Storrin. From there they could see – because the rain had stopped the spray from the waterfall – right across to the distant nest among the crags of the Storrin's side. When the lightning flashed they could see Askaval quite clearly poised on the edge of the nest, and the head of Mourne watching him.

'He is going to fly,' said Clew, who knew that he would—into the winds that were already catching at his tail and primaries, and had him unsteady on the edge of the nest.

So they crossed and wheeled and sought to stay near the Gap, to watch a young eagle making his first flight in hopeless conditions.

What they saw, when lightning flashes near and far allowed, was – or seemed to be – the shape of a great bird over the nest, though whether it was a raven or an eagle was impossible to say. It hovered there, seeming to talk to Askaval and Mourne, and then it turned away to the left towards the Storrin itself, whose falling waters were changing dark and light, the shapes of broken wings and thrusting talons. Into this dread fall the eagle – or the raven – seemed to fly and disappear, or rather become part of the raging might of the Storrin, tumbling into the water far below. Which was impossible—yet, as Clew watched, it seemed to have happened.

Long afterwards, Askaval affirmed that it *did* happen. For out of the darkness of their terror they had seen a great eagle come – though Mourne always maintained it was a raven – and it had spoken to them in a voice that was of rocks and water, sea and sky, and flowing with the strength of time itself. Whatever it was, it had told them that if they trusted in themselves, and bore in their wings the memory of Cuillin their mother, and Finse who had been their father, both of whom had trusted in Haforn the Great One—if they could trust, they would escape the Storrin in safety. And before they could recover their wits to reply, the shape above them swung over to the Storrin and was lost in its raging power.

'Don't try it, Askaval,' Mourne was saying, for she knew she wouldn't have the courage, though she was bigger than Askaval now. But she was not so strong, and never had been.

'But didn't you see there was an eagle here?' Askaval called out above the sound of rain and wind, and rolling thunder.

'I only saw a black wing against the sky,' replied Mourne.

'It was the Weir that Clew has talked about, and he told us to fly.'

'But I didn't hear any voice, only the roar of thunder and the hissing of rain against the cliff-face.'

'He said to try, and he would protect us,' cried out Askaval, bending into the wind, and tipping forward, just to try, and opening his wings a little.

'Askaval!' cried Mourne, for the wind caught at her brother, and suddenly his feet were off the edge of the nest and raised unsupported and hovering. 'Askaval!' she said with relief, as he came back down again with a thump.

'We've got to try, Mourne, otherwise we'll never get away. I don't think Clew or Mizen are coming back. They can't. Things have changed. We've got to try.' And his voice was trembling a little, because when the wind had caught him, and he felt himself free in the air, he could only see the terrible void below, where spray and water raged. And he had felt the power of the wind in his wings was far too great for him to control.

Mourne glanced up at him from where she was safely crouched in the centre of the nest. He was nervous! He was afraid, like once before, though she could only remember the feeling of it now—of him coming across the nest and shivering beside her. Well, he mustn't be nervous. Because he was Askaval, her brother, and he was strong, nearly as strong as Cuillin their mother had been. For him to be afraid and weak was for her world to collapse.

So she moved over to him and stood by his side, though she was scared to death, and said, 'Askaval, try, because it is our only hope.'

Then the wind seemed to clear ahead of him, and his feet to feel stronger, and his wings to open smoothly, and he leaned out into the wind, as he had seen Clew and Weever and Mizen do, and he pushed his head forward, and fanned his tail for balance—and he was into the wind. As it rushed full at him, he moved forward only slowly, only inches, holding his wings against it. Then the wind veered, and he was off balance in a second, wheeling right out over the void, with the Storrin off to his right, and the cliffs over to his left, and the Gap suddenly clear far ahead of him. Sliding through the air, the power of the wind in him, and his wings almost pulled off him through the strain of it. Then cutting back, and reducing its force as it slid over his wings, by folding them so they did not take the wind full-on. The world whirled about him, and he swung round again, the void below his feet and the nest ahead again, and Mourne was there calling, 'Askaval! Askaval!' and he was back, feet down, on its farther edge, head lowered to keep his balance, pecking at his breast feathers for a moment because he was an eagle now and did not like to look foolish.

He let out a cry and turned out into the wind again, only a few feet, and then back. And he knew *now* was the time to take Mourne out, while it looked easy, and before he went out into the full brunt of the wind, away from the cliff, and he lost control and might never be able to get back to her. For he knew already that the wind could defeat him if he lost concentration for a second.

'When you fly,' Clew had told him, 'take a line and observe where things are, so the shape of them helps you and you are not confused. A line is not a route but a purpose, an objective. Never fly without one, however unimportant the flight may be. Eagles often forget that.'

So now he turned and looked out across the Storrin, and decided to make a line on the Gap through which Cuillin had come. Whatever may have been said about its impossibility, that's where he would make for. For the waterfall to his right, and the cliffs and the void below, and the raging sky, where thunder rolled and lightning bit at the edges of clouds, all seemed to direct him there. He felt weak and powerful at the same time, and Mourne was depending on him as he, in a strange way, depended on her.

'Come,' he called out. 'Now!'

'I daren't,' said Mourne.

He grew angry. '*Now*!' he said.

But the void teetered far, far below her, calling up and pulling at her feathers—and yet she knew she would have to plunge into it on the wind, yes she would!

He went over and took a place near her, and without any warning brought his wing up behind her and she was over, wings open just like Mizen's, and he was there, just under her, to protect her, and he was calling out, 'Make a line on the Gap. The Gap!'

Clew saw them first, plunging down too fast, wings too far open to control, pulled down by the wind. Then he saw them wheeling round together, until Askaval began to slide sideways, talons grasping at thin air, and Clew heard him shouting instructions: 'Fly forward, Mourne. Fly now, because you can!' And he was pulling forward, but Mourne was slipping down. Then darkness, for the lightning faded.

When light came again, dimly from distant lightning, he saw that Askaval must have wheeled back down, and was now under Mourne by a few feet, and they were beating forward again. Desperate. Exhausted. Bludgeoned by the wind.

'They'll never make it. How can they make it?' cried out Mizen, the wind pushing her back and forcing her sideways out of sight.

Clew watched on, and he saw that Askaval could manage it, for his wings were strong and sure now, and he was urging Mourne forward, protecting her from the downdraught, leading her on complex tacks across the great void, with the Pinnacle towering above them to their left.

'Yes, yes, that's right,' whispered Clew, and Mizen muttered, 'He's going to get them both out. Just see him fly!'

For there was power and nascent wisdom in his flight, and caring for his sister as he did it. But none of them noticed that in Mourne's weaker wings there was power too, though covered in nervous frailness now. But she had the stamp of Cuillin in her wings: perhaps it was the way she tucked back her feet and talons, or a certain sense of purpose in her flight. But the Weir saw it, he who had flown to the Storrin to protect the Fremmed's young, and now perched unnoticed far below them all, near the water's surface, where once old Finse had taken a stance. He saw them all, the adults, including his own brother Clew, hovering anxiously by the Gap, and the two juveniles taking their first flight, and the sky low and grey above them all, and the towering of the rock. Askaval, Mourne, Clew, Mizen and Weever. Those were their names. He pointed his beak to the sky and watched. He saw them gain control of the winds, which were lighter after the rain. He saw them push forward, and Askaval seeming to encourage his sister on, and forward, until it was she who crossed through the Gap first, and he who came protectively second, and both of them heading down the fjord, away from the Storrin—and the three adults turning after them and calling aloud in the wind.

Then the Weir took passage into the Storrin, and it was as if its winds and torrents could not touch his wings, however frail they seemed with the grey light of age and wisdom.

CHAPTER THIRTEEN

Autumn, 1958

THE new boys, standing in miserable isolation on Deal station platform on the first day of the autumn term, made Jim and Peter feel slightly smug. They talked with exaggerated relaxation, Jim conscious that the new boys were watching, anxious, not sure whether to sit on the seats or stay standing like the older boys: the sixth-formers, who wore boaters, the fifth-and fourth-formers, and the third-formers like Jim and Peter.

But Jim was not quite as relaxed as he looked. He was wearing long trousers for the first time. Peter, who was taller, had started wearing them at the beginning of the previous school year. Jim didn't like them, and they made him stand awkwardly, and for the first time in his life he felt conscious of his knees. Knees are for getting dirty and cutting and grazing, not for grey material. Anyway, they weren't his first trousers but Michael's cast-offs, and they didn't quite fit round the middle because they were ones Michael got at the end of his third year. Mummy had pleated them at the sides rather crudely, and to make matters worse she had left it to the last moment and pressed them only that morning, so they felt damp and were slightly baggy at the knees as a result. They were also too long. So Peter had a good laugh – he always looked neat – and Jim felt uncomfortable, which was why he was joking in the faces of the new boys.

'Hello, Stonor, 'Lo, Conan.' It was Wright II, who was good at rugger. 'You in Lower Three as well?'

Jim nodded, conscious that Peter wasn't.

'Old clever-clogs here going to win a prize again this year?' Wright II looked at Peter, and Peter smiled uncomfortably. There was something he had to tell Jim.

A bell rang in the station.

'Just leaving Walmer,' said Wright. 'Be here in two minutes.' He strolled off down the platform. Peter looked across the lines towards the Dover College girls who were going the other way. Most of them went by bus from South Street, but there were usually a couple of stragglers, especially on the first day of term. Always more senior girls, for some reason. He had begun to notice girls—and there were other things that worried him.

'Listen!' said Jim and they heard the distant rumble and race of the steam train approaching, with the exciting metallic vibration that travelled ahead of it down the line. On Deal Station the down trains from London and Dover entered from under the road bridge at one end, the white steam suddenly held under the bridge and rushing out ahead of the engine, so the train made a dramatic entry through clouds of steam, with brakes squealing.

Mr Chandler said they were going to electrify the line all the way from London, so soon there wouldn't be steam trains any more. Jim thought of them and how big they were, and he couldn't believe that something like that could disappear.

They began to drift towards the platform edge.

'I'm leaving at the end of this term,' said Peter.

Jim stared slowly round at him, the rumble of the steam train louder in his ears, but the world suddenly empty.

'Daddy's being moved to London, and we're going to live on the far side of it, not in Kent at all.'

Jim still stared at him; he was being deserted.

'Oh,' he said. Then the train roared out from under the bridge, its bumpers red and wisped by racing steam, and he went right to the edge of the platform to watch its mass and shape grow rapidly bigger towards him until it was towering above him. As it roared past, pistons in and out, till the great wheels gradually squealed to a stop, he was lost in the noise and the racing harmony of the engine, and the rattle-tattle rushing of the carriage wheels. And doors beginning to open, and Jim stepping back and staring after the engine, last wisps of steam furling around his legs.

Peter watched him, Jim his friend, and he was more articulate and sensitive about what was happening. Jim standing there among the steam, his new school briefcase in his hand – because only first-years bothered with satchels – and his baggy trousers Michael had probably once worn; and his scruffy school jacket which would need a patch on the right elbow. Peter thought he looked like a new boy again, waiting.

It was the first time Peter knew he loved him, but if he had been asked, he would not have understood the question.

'C'mon, Jim,' he said, pushing forward for a door.

'Bags I the window seat,' said Jim.

That autumn was the last of their childhood friendship, and its minutes swept and scattered away as steadily as the ash-tree leaves that were first to fall on the mud of the rugby fields. Then the poplar, and the crinkly, rich-coloured leaves of sycamore in the gutters as they walked home on Wednesday after games, down the road to Sandwich Station.

They didn't see each other much during the day because they were in different forms and doing different things. Peter had different textbooks now for most subjects. Newer and better ones, which weren't dog-eared like Jim's. Peter was also in the school choir, in which Michael, who was a boarder, was now singing tenor. Sometimes after school the choir practised, so Jim went home alone, ragging along with the other boys from Lower Three, but not really friends with any of them. Ronnie James, who was good at rugger like Jim, was a friend of sorts, but he lived over in Margate and came in by bus. None of the Deal boys in Jim's year seemed to have the same interests as he did.

Peter had a new bike for his birthday, which was in October, and they went on a cycle ride all the way to Canterbury. Thomas à Becket was murdered there, and they followed his steps around the cloisters, stopping in the entrance to the chapter house as he had done, according to the guide, so he could say a prayer there. All the time the knights who were going to murder him were banging on the great doors, demanding entrance. Then the guide processed them round to where the cloister door enters the main cathedral, and he pointed to the very place where Becket was slain, one of his aides trying to stop the knights with a cross and being wounded in the process. It was the kind of thing they both liked, and Jim found himself in awe of the great cathedral, with its perpendicular columns which were so massive and yet so light, and the stone carvings over the door which he wanted to draw. It was the one thing he could do well—that and make up games in the playground for other boys to play, or win at conkers because his eye was so good.

But off the playground, and in the class, Jim was not a success. His work was untidy and undisciplined, his books a mess, his homework poor, and his results mediocre in an already mediocre class. Out of the thirty in the class he would come somewhere between twentieth and twenty-fifth for most subjects, dropping to a miserable twenty-eighth out of thirty for Mathematics, and rising to a best result of ninth place in Art. Crafts was his best subject but they didn't give places for that. How can you grade a wicker basket, or a tenon joint? Yet there he was best, best by far, but no one really noticed it or ever said anything.

To Margaret Stonor, who had already seen three boys progress well in the Grammar School, Jim's results were really no surprise. He lived in a different kind of world than they did, and was slower to talk, or understand humour, slower to go to the dictionary to pursue a word. And yet it seemed odd: he wasn't *that* stupid. And the Art result seemed oddest of all. With Frank and Oliver she had fought for their education, driving them on and giving them special lessons herself, and when that failed – as it invariably did, because they couldn't stand her trying to teach them during the holidays or in time off from school – she found tutors for them out of what little money there was. If people asked why she dressed badly in those years, and only had one decent pair of shoes, and that an old pair, it was because she spent what money there was from part-time secretarial and teaching jobs on the children.

By the time Jim was beginning his passage through school, she had changed and the fight had gone. And perhaps he wasn't so talented as the other boys were. Perhaps.

Yet she would watch him now, lost in the stories of Arthur Mee, or trying to draw something like the shadow of a tree on the garden wall, which was really very hard, just in pencil, and she would wonder why it didn't come out at school at all. Ninth in Art? She didn't believe it.

The art teacher was Mr Broughten, a Westcountryman who had nearly played cricket for Somerset. His main function was Games but he took the lower forms for English and Art because there was no one else, and because these subjects fitted in with his timetable.

Neatness was all. You got a mark off if an essay began too near the margin, or too far from it. Another mark off if you wrote your name instead of printing it. The end of the essay had to be ruled off neatly—another mark for that. Each spelling mistake was a mark gone, two if it was a simple word. Too few paragraphs or too many, and you lost more marks. A blot (and ballpoint pens were not allowed) or a smudge, and the already dwindling total of marks available to Mr Broughten's hapless class was plundered again. By the time you got to content, meaning, feeling or form, let alone style or observation, there were but five or so marks left.

Mr Broughten applied the same approach to art. Pictures had to be neat. Expression or impression were not good. Impressionism was acceptable in the Tate Gallery and on postcards, but, as Mr Broughten was inclined to say, 'Until you can draw a cube, a circle and a cone, you cannot start to experiment.' It was the nature of his classes that no boy ever did master a cube, a circle and a cone, and thus Mr Broughten was safe to impose his rule of tidiness. Chalk was not to be dropped on the floor, or else the culprit would stay in detention after school, which involved copying out *Daily Express* reports of how Somerset had fared in the County Cricket Championship.

Jim found these art lessons excruciatingly boring and did not bother much, but not so boring as two-thirds of the class did, so he came ninth. Snill, a snide, thin, wet little twerp, who had two school jackets and so was always neat and tidy, came top in both Art and English.

Margaret Stonor knew none of this for certain, until at last she got proof.

Jim had an art homework: 'My Pet'. You could use three colours. But Jim did not have a pet.

'Well, didn't you say?' she asked.

'Mr Broughten doesn't listen to anyone. He'd think it was an excuse.'

'Well it *is*.'

Jim looked stumped, and though he spent so much of his time drawing or looking at reproductions in Arthur Mee, he had no enthusiasm at all for painting a non-existent pet.

'Pretend you've got one. No one will know.'

'Wouldn't work. Can't draw something that doesn't exist.'

'That's what painting is, a lot of the time,' she said, pleased with the insight.

Jim still looked stumped.

'Well, isn't there something in the way of animals that captures your imagination?' she asked, and watched his gaze go automatically to the kitchen window and look at the branches of the apple tree, now bare of leaves and stark against the October sky. Yes, there was something, and it was an eagle, but he wasn't going to draw that for Mr Broughten. That wasn't for the likes of him. You protect eagles from people like him. Then a shadow flew across his mind, and an image came and, yes, there was something.

'Yes,' he said and cryptically at last: 'Might be something.'

She watched him go, and did not ask about it. He never, ever talked about the things he was about to do, only the things he had done—and then not much.

It was a cormorant he drew. Up on the beach where it had been looking at him, except this one didn't look with distrust like the real one had. He found a cormorant picture in Arthur Mee's volume, to check the way the beak was and the colour of the white on the face and the sides, but that was only for checking, and the picture he drew was free. He used black and white, tinging the background in grey, and with a hint of colour, orange, on the pebbles that ran down to the sea. It took him two evenings. In the distance was the rise of the Isle of Thanet, and the winds that blew across the sea were the winds he had often battled against up on the front, and the winds that his cormorant had known beating up the beach and swirling among the cast-up seaweed, the night before the day it died. But in his picture it didn't die, because there wasn't any tar now on its wings or body, nor blood where its wing had ripped.

He wrote his name 'Stonor' small along the bottom right. It balanced the picture that way.

Margaret Stonor approved and said he had done a good job, and he took it in to school, rolling it up carefully so it didn't get damaged. He felt better for making the picture. He had never worked so hard on a homework before.

Jim did not mention it afterwards, and it was only two weeks later that she remembered about it. After all, it had been a homework he had enjoyed, which was more than could be said for most of them.

'What happened to it?' she asked. 'You didn't bring it home.'

'No,' he mumbled. He didn't want to talk about it. She had seen that look before, successively, on Frank's and Oliver's and Michael's faces, and it meant 'Don't trespass here'. Sometimes she did, sometimes she didn't. This time she did.

'What happened to it, Jim? What mark did you get?'

'Didn't get a mark.'

'You mean Mr Broughten doesn't give marks for pictures done for homework?'

'Yes, he does, but not for that one. He said it was wrong.'

And he looked at her, waiting, and she saw in his look several things at once which had her instantly alert. For one thing, his look was rather accusing, as if she had misled him about the homework. But that was superficial. Beneath it there was a different, hurt look, of something he had lost, just like Liam sometimes looked. So like his father. And also there was uncertainty, and lack of confidence, and she understood that suddenly, over their old table in the kitchen, she had a crisis on her hands. Not one that would ever be remembered, nor one that was dramatic or obvious. But for Jim a crisis of trust in himself and in people around him.

'What happened exactly?' she asked, quietly.

'He crossed it out and said it wasn't a pet,' said Jim.

And he had, in red ballpoint pen, and had said a homework was to be done on the subject set. But he did this after holding the picture up and saying, 'This little boy hasn't even spelt his name out in full.' And, writing in large, crude letters along the bottom, so they cut through the beach and into the sea he put, 'James MacAskill Stonor'.

'This little boy,' he added sarcastically, 'has not used three colours as I told him, because he doesn't seem to remember what I told him, and what at least most of you have understood: that black and white and grey are not colours. If Stonor wants to enter the competitive field of wild-life drawing, then let him. But not, Stonor, for homework.' The voice was soft and sarcastic, and the sudden cut of the ballpoint across the face of his picture, through the body of the cormorant, was violent—and to Jim horrific. That was part of himself being murdered. He sat in the class stunned, and watched his work tossed indifferently back on his desk, before Mr Broughten moved on to someone else's homework.

'Right!' said Margaret Stonor when he had finished telling her. 'Right!'

'What are you going to do?' he asked, hopefully, because his mother was going to fight for him and that must mean it was okay. He hadn't been wrong.

'I'm going to go over to Sandwich tomorrow to see Mr Gower.' This was Jim's headmaster, and a man who had only spoken to him once, saying those familiar, disliked words: 'You're Frank and Oliver's youngest brother, aren't you?' Yes, he bloody well was, and his name also happened to be James MackAskill Stonor, and bugger the rest of them, except he didn't quite have the command of English necessary to express himself that way. So he had merely said, 'Yes, sir.'

Margaret Stonor gathered together some of Jim's drawings. Looking through them together for the first time, she was surprised at the range of his work and the relative skill. Most were derivative, many direct copies, but a few items were original. And though the line was often weak and confused, he was, by any standards, above average. He certainly deserved to be better than most in Mr Broughten's exclusive art class.

She rang Mr Gower's secretary and made an appointment for the next afternoon. Yes, it was important. Her name was Mrs Stonor.

Mr Gower knew of her because he knew the boys very well. Frank and Oliver had both done execeptionally well, one Head Boy, one a senior prefect and in charge of the school Cadet Force. Cambridge and London universities respectively. Bit of a gap to the next one down the line, Michael, who was also doing well—if anything, better then the others. Not so good at games though. Bit of an intellectual. Then James MacAskill Stonor. Brother? Half-brother? He wasn't quite sure. It was about James she wanted to see him, which wasn't surprising when you looked at his performance to date.

'Ah, Mrs Stonor. I'm very pleased to see you.'

She sat in his study, in an armchair, while he stayed at his desk. A high-flier by the look of it, she thought to herself, with a rather better-cut suit than Mr Martin, his predecessor, and a rather harder face.

The Times Educational Supplement was placed rather too prominently on the coffee-table near the sofa, where a parent might see it, and there were shelves full of books, and one ranged with the light-blue covers of back numbers of the school magazine.

She did not react to his blarney about Frank and Oliver, and got straight to the point.

What did he think, she asked, of Mr Broughten's teaching? It was not a question he expected. Mr Broughten was the games master and really taught other classes only on the side, especially Art—a subject which did not get people into university.

'Ah!' he said smiling in a wary way. 'Well you know I can't really answer that.'

'I'm not surprised,' she said, 'because you're probably as aware as I am that it's appalling.'

'English?' asked Mr Gower, rather caught out.

'Art,' said Mrs Stonor. 'Not normally a very important subject.'

'No,' said Mr Gower, dropping his noncommital pose and agreeing with her. Seeing her face, which was intelligent and searching, and clearly did not suffer fools gladly (and, though she did not realise it now, looked very like her own father's at its most severe) he decided honesty was the best policy.

'No, I won't pretend it is at the top of the curriculum.'

'Which means you put the games master in charge?'

'Well no, not exactly. Mr Broughten does have a diploma in art education, as a matter of fact.' He sounded as surprised as she looked, though her surprise was sarcastic, his genuine. Broughten, draw? Unbelievable. Finally he said, 'What exactly can I do for you, Mrs Stonor?'

The others, she said, had done well for the school. It was time the school did well for her youngest. Time someone took care. Time someone realised that he was not entirely untalented, at least in crafts and art. Time Mr Gower looked into the methods used by Mr Broughten, the master of neatness in drawing. Time someone encouraged Jim, not just in this subject but in others.

'He's not a dim boy, Mr Gower. I do realise that every parent who comes into this room believes their child is a genius. Well, I am a bit more practical than that. He is not as academic as the other three, and he is in a school where, rightly or wrongly, the academic standard is what matters, closely followed by games, and with a bit of soldiering in the Combined Cadet Force thrown in. I am afraid he will not do very well in any of them, though he might score a try or two for your second fifteen one day. But he is not dim, and he is getting a firm impression from your staff that he is.'

'Well, Mrs Stonor, I cannot speak for his art work, not having seen any, to my knowledge, but . . .' and his voice slowed as he trod carefully, 'there may already be changes in the pipeline in the whole arts and crafts field. More money now, you know. And I think the Ministry of Education is beginning to feel that it's an area which has been rather undernourished. It is quite expensive for a school that side, and good teachers are hard to get, though I think all in all, and with the means at his disposal, Mr Broughten does extremely well.' They looked at each other and both knew the other knew that neither believed this.

Mrs Stonor produced her trump card, the portfolio of Jim's work, and Mr Gower looked through it politely. It wasn't bad. In fact, he even recognised Deal pier and the school playground. An idea came to him. These things had to be done the right way. And there was a way.

'Well, I'll think about what you've said, and in my own way let your views be known in the right quarters. I'm sure you understand, Mrs Stonor.'

'I do,' she said.

'Will you have a sherry?' he asked. She was an intelligent and not unattractive woman, and fifteen minutes' talk with the mother of the two brightest boys in the school since the last war was worth having.

'Thank you,' she said.

He poured one and handed it to her. Then he leafed through the pictures and drawings again.

'Could I keep a few of them just to show someone who might be interested? It would strengthen my hand, you know.'

'Of course,' she said, sipping her sherry.

'Mmmm,' he mumbled looking at them. Yes, there might be a way.

A week before Guy Fawkes day, 5 November, Jim and Peter decided to have an 'M' night on the fourth. The derivation of the 'M' was unknown, murder perhaps, but Frank had held one once, and both of them were just beginning to have the taste for doing things other people didn't. They were beginning to revolt.

Jim had three shillings saved, and a shilling to come on the Saturday before the fourth. Peter had five shillings. Bangers were a penny each, jumping-jacks threepence, Roman candles sixpence or a shilling, depending on the size. Bangers were the best buy. You bought them at the sweet shops, and Mr Allenby at the bottom of Compass Street did a thriving business in them.

'We could get about seventy bangers between us, and a few Roman candles and things.'

'Have to have some left over for the fifth.'

'Jumping-jacks'd be good among the crowd at the Lifeboat bonfire.'

They grinned.

'What're we going to do on 'M' Night?' Peter asked the question. It excited him slightly and frightened him, too.

'We could put the Roman candles up on the front, on Seagirt, so people see them. That'd be good. And bangers through letter-boxes'n things.'

Seagirt was an old house, now no more than a concrete bunker, that abutted the sea-wall opposite Exchange Street.

They were up in Jim's room and spoke in low voices, huddled on the floor like conspirators. Peter got a piece of paper to write the plan down. 'M NIGHT' he wrote at the top. Then:

> Strategy: Murder and mayhem.
> Personnel: Peter Conan and James MacAskill Stonor.
> Time of rendezvous: 18.45 hours.
> Place of rendezvous: Deal Castle foreshore (behind bathing huts).
> Time of commencement of strategy: 19.00 hours.

He stopped and they talked more, the piece of paper soon forgotten in the excitement of the thrills to come.

Jim spent an afternoon, the first of many in the years to come, at Albert Chandler's house in Union Road, having asked his advice on how to make the guy.

He had taken a pair of Frank's old trousers, and found an old army shirt of his father's down in the cellar at Number 11. Mrs Chandler showed him how to make papier-mâché for the head, helping him tear up newspaper in her kitchen as she baked scones for a church meeting that evening.

Albert let him come down to his workshop in the garden to show him how to make a wooden frame for the body. It was the first time Jim had been allowed into the workshop or had seen the lathes and work-benches, and rows of polished old tools Albert used. There was a peace about the place, and a slowness to Albert's movements, which Jim loved. And, from that day on, rarely a week passed but he came out to visit Albert and give him a hand. Which was something Mrs Chandler liked to see, for in all the years of their marriage she had scarcely ever known Albert let anyone into his workshop, not even their own two boys who, he complained, would never learn that 'a tool's got to be treated with as much respect as a human being'. Now they worked in London with their brains and not their hands. 'A man loses touch with hisself if he doesn't touch real things like wood and that,' Albert would say to Jim.

Albert taught him a trick to make the guy burn better: he painted the frame with creosote, oily and smelling nice and acrid.

They mounted the finished head on the body and Jim painted it himself, marvelling at the way it took on life with each touch of his brush.

'That's almost too nice to be a guy, my duck,' said Mrs Chandler. 'Wasn't he supposed to be a rascal?'

However it was, Jim and Peter put the guy in an old pram and they wheeled it around Deal raising funds to buy more fireworks.

'M' Day dawned chilly and wet, and a dull wind swept in from the sea, flapping the rigging of boats against masts, and causing old-age pensioners to re-route their morning shopping along the shelter of Middle Street.

The rain stopped in the early evening, leaving the gound damp and shiny for a while, but becoming duller, the pebbles a little muted when Jim approached the bathing huts at 18.45 hours.

Jim approached their dark shadows cautiously, a blue bobble hat made by Mrs Frewin on his head, and half of the fireworks in a kitbag of Frank's over his shoulder. Without the bobble on his hat he might have looked like the commando he was pretending to be.

The shadows ahead moved, there was the crunch of shingle in the darkness and he whispered, 'Peter?'

Peter's head appeared, his face blackened with burnt cork like the commandos on raids.

'Mayhem!' he rasped. 'Say the answering password, Jim, so I'll know who you are.'

Ah, yes. Get it right. 'Murder,' hissed Jim into the night, as nastily as he could.

Their behaviour that evening was, by any standards, appalling. They lit fireworks and put them in letter-boxes, and two bangers together down the post-box of the main Post Office in Stanhope Road—disappointed that the ensuing explosion was so muffled. They set up three Roman candles on gravestones in St George's churchyard, lit the touch-paper and ran behind a wall, to watch in safety in case anyone came. No one did, but the effect was well worth it, as the tilted gravestones were variously lit red, green and white, the bare trees above them eerily bending in the wind, and the smoke wraithing in the lurid light across the graveyard. Thus emboldened, they set off for the seafront and there threw innumerable bangers down on to the shingle, where they fizzed and exploded in the shadow of the sea-wall. Then they let off six together, trying to coordinate lighting them so they all went off at once.

This failed, but the resulting succession of bangs caused a curtain or two to be pulled aside up in the houses facing the sea, and they lurked deliciously among the boats until the coast seemed clear again. Occasionally they heard other bangs in the distance, across the town, and knew they were not the only ones celebrating 'M' Night.

By 21.15 hours the sky was black but clearing, and stars were showing between runs of swirling cloud. Out to sea the yellow lights of boats moved slowly north and south in the dark, while to right and left the South and East Goodwin lightships sent out their regular, sudden shafts of light.

They still had plenty of fireworks left, preserved for the Assault on Seagirt, which was to be the finale of the evening, and so they decided to set off for the Dunes, itself an adventure at night. They went by bike, but without the lights on—Jim because his had none, Peter because that was the way commandos would travel.

The Dunes stretched away beneath them from where they stood on the ramparts of Sandown Castle. Down on the beach a fisherman sat by the sea-line, lit by an old oil-lamp on the shingle near his tackle-box. They watched him secretly, wondering whether to throw a banger in his direction and then run for it, but decided that might ruin their chances of a better bit of fun on the Dunes.

Jim, knowing the Dunes best, led the way, the sandy path between shingle bank and golf-course seeming mysterious and treacherous by night. Wind running in the long grass was danger, gorse bushes were German emplacements, the steeper dunes great obstacles to be crawled up. At one point a green came near to the path and the shingle, and its flag whipped in the night. A target. They set up Roman candles in the rough around it, lit them, raced back to the other side of the green, and when they went off, attacked the hole itself, hurling bangers ahead of them, and a couple of jumping-jacks as well. The flashes and bangs against the light of the candles suddenly giving the surrounding dunes a dramatic and lonely appearance.

'Pity we didn't have the guy here,' said Peter.

That gave Jim an idea.

'Let's burn it tonight on Seagirt,' he said enthusiastically. It was a challenging idea because it ran right against celebrating the fifth normally. It was the ultimate protest. Fawkes is guilty. Burn him a day early!

''Ere, you two, what the bloody hell do you think you're doing?'

It was the fisherman, come quietly over the shingle bank to see

343

what the noise was. In their drive for dramatic effect, Jim and Peter had created the perfect conditions for him to see them, for they were clearly silhouetted against the burning candles. Fortunately the fisherman did not play golf, or he might have been inclined to take each of them by the scruff of the neck and report them to the Golf Club—for the green was now a mess, with burnt butts of bangers all over it, and its smooth surface churned up by their heels.

'We were playing, mister,' said Jim, the automatic spokesman in this rougher type of confrontation.

'Well, bugger off, and don't do that any more,' the man said, and clipped each of them smartly over the ear to send them packing.

The incident upset Peter, who was terrified that he might be reported to his parents. But Jim seemed fired by it, for it meant they had been bloodied and could now counter-attack 'them' by the assault on Seagirt.

'Best not to do that now,' said Peter. 'It's getting late. I ought to be home as it is.'

But they did. Sneaking back down Compass Street for the guy and pushing him up on the front in the dark, like murderers bent on disposing of a body. Jim brought a tin of turpentine from the boathouse to get the fire going, and they approached Seagirt along the beach, having hidden the pram at the high-tide mark, by the concrete steps down to the shingle. Down here it was quite dark, for the light from the street lamps was cut off by the wall, and the shadow extended fifteen feet beyond it. They crept along, Jim carrying the head of the guy and Peter the body.

Peter still wasn't very keen and helped Jim rather half-heartedly, looking over his shoulder and up at the wall above to see if anyone was watching. Jim pressed on, knowing the route well. You could climb up Seagirt from the beach. It was perhaps twenty-five feet high, and some fifteen feet above the promenade itself—a relic of the time when a whole row of houses had stretched along the sea-wall itself. By now, however, it had none of the appearance of a house, having been converted into a gun emplacement during the last war. Since then it had been shored up with concrete after gales had caused it to collapse, the remnant castellations on its top now broken and dangerous. It was due to be demolished when owner-ship and responsibility could be clearly established. Meanwhile it was an eyesore, but a place of adventure for the few children who then lived in North Deal. It was about to have its moment of 'M' Night glory.

They heaved and tugged the guy up the side, Jim seemingly unaware of the danger of the twenty-five foot fall he risked at the top. But the familiar beach was below him, and the cold wind at his face, and in his pockets were bangers and matches. They were going to make a mark on the night.

'You watch out, and I'll fix it up,' ordered Jim, taking over completely. He settled the guy on one corner of Seagirt, facing towards the Royal Hotel, because it could be seen from there, but he kept it low until he had everything worked out. He put all the remaining bangers in the shirt pockets, down the trousers, and even inside the gloves. He tied the Roman candles on its shoes with fishing-line, because that's where it was going to start burning. He took the tin of turpentine and poured it all over the guy, till the air reeked with it. He worked quickly and methodically and in silence, with Peter peeking over the edge of Seagirt in growing terror. The Dunes was one thing, where no one could see you – until the fisherman caught them – but here, with houses overlooking, and *this* and the smell of turps. He wanted to go home. 'M' Night had lost its charm.

Jim, on the other hand, was growing increasingly excited. He was in charge for once, and imposing something on 'them'. It was going to be good. He took his time, working out just how to get the guy up into view at the last moment, before the final act of setting it on fire. He reorientated it so the wind would take the sparks from the Roman candles on to its legs. He was going to light the touch-paper on its feet, and then set fire to the arms. When he was ready, he told Peter to make his escape and wait down an alley across the road from the promenade.

Peter slipped over the edge and clambered precariously down the fifteen feet of brick and concrete. When he was gone, Jim took a last look round. Far across Sandwich Bay he could see the lights of Ramsgate and Cliftonville stretching out to sea. The Royal Hotel was all lit up as well, and he could see the lights of the Bosun's Mate two hundred yards down the front. The matches were in his hands, the stage was his, the moment his to decide. He pushed the guy up into the light, propped it up, and lit a match, shielding its flame from the wind with a cupped hand. No good, it went out. Quickly he held the matchbox close to the touch-paper of a Roman candle, and lit it. It started to smoulder. Then he lit a second and a third, all at speed. With a delicious, icy calm, he felt the power of his own self-control.

Then a final match to each arm, among the turps-sodden folds of the shirt—then he was gone, slipping over the edge and into the light, dropping down to the promenade and then over to where Peter was hiding.

They waited for what seemed hours, the face of the guy visible in the street-light but his body lost in shadows. Then one of the

Roman candles flared, a yellow one. And then a red one, and then the third one, also red, and the whole guy was lit up by their lurid light, and seemed no longer to squat there but to stand and stare over, insolent and scoffing, at the darkened houses of Deal. Behind it all the sea, swirling angrily on the shore hidden beneath the wall. Flames began to engulf the body.

'Cor!' said Jim, fascinated. But Peter wasn't really watching. He wanted to go.

'Come on, Jim,' he whispered, and he was off down the alley towards Middle Street where they had left their bikes.

'Stay and watch,' said Jim.

'We might get caught,' said Peter from the darkness. Then he was gone.

Then, suddenly the first banger went and a passing car stopped. And the guy's clothes started to flare and burn, and the face seemed ever more real by the flickering, windswept flames. Smoke billowed up into the night, its oily darkness caught by the last reds of the Roman candles, as more and more bangers exploded. As it burned more fiercely, doors opened along the front. People came out to see what was going on.

At first Jim watched from the shadows, fascinated. Then feeling clever and powerful, he wandered up into the light of the street, and stood by some grown-ups who had stopped there.

'It's Guy Fawkes,' one of them said.

'Funny place for one, isn't it?'

Jim stood there watching. The head he had made was still visible and unburnt, and one of the arms had just started to explode. The night was filled with flashing light, and the walls of Seagirt looked suddenly like a wartime bunker facing enemy fire—as, in the distance, the first sound of a fire-engine's bell could be heard. At first Jim didn't think much of it, but then it grew louder, and was coming up by the Royal Hotel and down along the front . . . and now he was afraid. They had come to put out the fire. Someone had called for them.

The guy's head started to burn just as the fire-engine pulled to a screeching halt, and great men in heavy, curved helmets clambered out. While some began to undo the hoses, two others approached across the promenade to have a look. It was so sudden, so dramatic, so magical to Jim, that so much could be started by so little. By himself. He stood glorying in his anonymity and his power. But far more than that, it was the spectacle of it, with light and sound and colour all at once, and the burning figure, which had transformed the boring reality of Seagirt. He had made a new reality, and it was one in which great firemen darted about with hoses and big leather boots.

The guy was now burning at its peak and bangers were still going off, so that with the sound of the engine, the chatter of people and the crackle of fire, he himself remained unnoticed. Just a boy, watching.

Then he saw his father. Liam MacAskill stood with a couple of people from the Bosun's Mate who had come out to see what the fuss was. Jim suddenly realised that Mr Chandler might be there, and he would know . . . but he wasn't. Just his father standing in the crowd, and staring at the flames and the bangs . . . and the figure burning in the flames—wearing an army shirt which had seen nights like that before, and had heard the screams of dying men and known the ricochet of bullets. MacAskill's hands were at his mouth and he was terrified and shaking.

No one but Jim seemed to see him. And the evening changed from excitement to horror for he understood something of his father then, seeing him so frightened. But it was only a game, a bit of papier-mâché and some fireworks. It wasn't something to be afraid of. As he started to cross the road to go up to his father and tell him, to comfort him, a hand smashed out of the darkness and knocked him sideways. The same hand grabbed his hair and started pulling, and he was crying and struggling, unnoticed by the crowd, pulled away and down a side-street.

'How dare you. How *dare* you!' It was Margaret Stonor. She had heard the engine, gone to see what was up, and caught sight of him lurking. She recognised the guy. How *dared* he do it!

Crying, humiliated, found out, and now frightened that she would tell, he was hauled back home. She viciously scrubbed his face and hands of the grime and tell-tale marks of fire and turps that were on them, then sent him to bed. She never did tell. Next night, November the fifth, he was confined to his bedroom in disgrace, only able to see the occasional rocket and distant glow of fireworks by standing at the window. But she never did tell.

But what he remembered most was the face of his father caught in the light of the fire and explosions he had started, up there on the front, lost and alone.

The last day of autumn term that year was 19 December, and in the final Assembly Mr Gower read out the names of boys leaving— mainly older boys who had places at colleges and universities. But he mentioned Peter. 'Greatly regret . . . who has done so well . . . we wish him luck . . .' Jim was standing next to Peter but they didn't look at each other. The Conans had already partly moved to their new house on the other side of London, and Mr Conan was overseeing the final bit of the move that very morning. He was going to drive over to school and take Peter up to London by car, following the furniture van.

That morning was a delicious one of packing books and checking registers and helping masters do the end-of-term things. Lessons were relaxed and you could play games in them, provided you were quiet.

Peter's father came after break and found them over by the dining-hall. Mr Gower didn't mind him leaving early.

'Time to go, Peter. Hello, Jim.'

'Hello, Mr Conan.'

Peter and Jim looked at each other awkwardly, not believing they were saying goodbye. Peter wouldn't be there in the holidays to go round and see, or to come down Compass Street on his bike, and round through the boathouse. Peter was going.

'Cheerio, Jim,' said Peter. 'I'll send you a Christmas card.'

'Okay,' said Jim.

Then Peter was gone and the people they had been playing with drifted off somewhere else, and the outside walls of the dining-hall seemed very bleak as Jim watched his best friend walk away. His big head was tilted to one side as he left, and he turned round to wave once by the school entrance. Then he was gone.

When the bell went for the end of break they all drifted back into the classrooms, and on every desk there was the clean, fresh, light-blue cover of the school magazine: Autumn Term 1958. Academic achievements, essays and poems by boys, and all the games results at the end. House news and scholarships. Jim went straight to the House Games section because he played rugger for the fourth fifteen and his name would be there: J. M. Stonor. Peter's was there as well because they played together: P. Conan. Peter's was in the Valete section at the front, so that was something. Other boys had their names in for different things, but not many in Lower Three—just Wright II because he played rugger for his house's third fifteen.

The magazine was for older boys who did things, and the upper forms who won the prizes, not for Jim.

'Jammy bugger,' said Wright II turning round to him and holding up the magazine. Jim stared and stared again. For there it was, a whole page, a complete, unadulterated, untouched page with his drawing of the playground. And his heart raced and he flicked through his own copy of the magazine, and read at the bottom of the page, and re-read, and read again, so he wanted to shout it out: '*A drawing of the school playground by James MacAskill Stonor, Lower Three.*' A ripple of interest went through the class and boys whispered, 'You never said,' and there was admiration and envy, and some pleasure, too, because the only other drawing was by Mattin in the Sixth Form, one who was known to be good. Jim had found a niche at last.

But he looked out of the window, because most of all he wanted to show it to Peter, and because his name, James MacAskill Stonor, was in print, upper and lower case bold, like Peter's had been for the History prize last term. He had done something to be proud of at last.

He sent a Christmas card to Peter and got one back from him, making his total three that year, excluding those from the family. One came from Mrs Angel next-door, with a five-shilling postal order, and there was a card signed 'Mr and Mrs Albert Chandler', which bore a picture of an old house all lit up with light and love and a warm glow of people inside, singing round a Christmas tree.

On Boxing Day, Jim went out on to the front, wearing the new Marks & Spencer pullover Mummy had given him, and wandered along alone. Frank and Oliver were home, but they were having an adult talk with Mummy in the sitting-room. Michael wouldn't talk to him, and was upstairs reading. Daddy and Granny had both been allowed into Number 11 on Christmas Day, but were gone now—one to her old people's home, and the other to the rooms where he lived, which Jim had never visited. He didn't even know where they were. Mummy had forbidden Daddy ever to take any of the children there.

The sea was calm and the air clear. A nice winter's day when two lads might take their bikes and cycle down the coast to Kingsdown and clamber up over the Royal Marine rifle ranges and find a few cartridges or spent bullets. Or crunch down to the sea and throw pebbles at a rusting tin can, or try to hit the seagulls who huddled at a distance on the shingle and who always seemed to know when a stone was coming and hop out of the way just in time.

Alone, on Boxing Day, these games were not such fun. Anyway, these days, with people around, he felt sort of awkward, as if they were watching him, and he felt very conscious of something like a new pullover. He pretended not to notice them and tried to look casual about what he was doing. Two girls walked past on the front, and he sort of looked at them and sort of didn't. Were they looking at him?

He couldn't seem to concentrate on throwing stones like he did last summer, because as he raised his hand he was conscious of it in the air. But he threw the stone viciously, not looking where it went in the sea. Where had Peter gone to? Mummy had said he could go and see Granny, but he didn't want to. He wanted to see Peter. He sent Peter a picture as a Christmas present, but Peter hadn't sent anything apart from the card.

The weeks passed by. Spring came, after so many storms had rattled his bedroom window at night, with him standing there looking out and listening to the running and the raging of the sea. Then, one morning, warm weather came back, and Mummy didn't have to light a fire in the kitchen grate. 'Time to go to school,' she said.

'I'm . . .,' and his voice wobbled.

She laughed. 'Your voice is breaking.' And she realised it was the beginning of the end of the childhood years in her home. Girls, and sex and posturing and idiotic moods and changes were all to come his way, as they had for the other three. But she could only think that the house that she had bought with such a struggle was beginning to be hers now, and times beginning to be easier. And when he was gone to school, she could sit and have another cup of tea and read the paper slowly.

'What?'

He sounded aggressive, and she knew it was because he was developing an adolescent self-consciousness.

'It's nothing, dear,' she said.

He stomped out of the kitchen to get his things for school. She had heard the stomping before, and this time, now she understood it, she could smile. Jim did not stomp quite so heavily as Frank and Oliver had done.

Stomp, stomp up the stairs. Silence. Stomp, stomp down again, and the front door banging without a goodbye.

'Oh, dear,' she whispered aloud to herself. She smiled just a little and relaxed. Mrs Frewin was coming today.

That evening Jim wrote a letter to Peter Conan.

'They are rebuilding the sea-wall so it's not straight but curves out and overhangs the beach. Also Mr Chandler says thay will demolish Seagirt. They're building groynes out where we used to beachcomb.' He drew a picture because that was easier. 'Granny isn't very well these days any more. Mrs Frewin sends her love . . .'

It was a long letter, with drawings, but Peter's answer was brief and scribbled. His writing was changing and getting harder to read. His mother had made him write it. He was enjoying school and had lots of friends. Jim left it on his bed and went for a walk along the front to see where they had invaded his beach, and were driving piles into the bare shingle and sand. The men had finished work for the day, and the piles formed stark and lonely rows down the beach to the low-tide mark, stretching all along the shore as far as Sandown and the very edge of the Dunes—to stop the seas shifting the shingle and eroding the sea-wall.

He stood down there in his invaded territory and looked south towards the wreck which lay a third of a mile offshore, opposite the Queen's Hotel. They were coming to blow up the wreck and it would be gone forever. But down here, among the wet round pebbles and sand, and by the already rusted piles, he was still free to wander and throw stones. Only now, when he climbed back up on to the promenade, among the houses and the people, he was in a world that was changing, lonely and comfortless. He was becoming conscious of when his trousers grew too short, and the way his hair curled untidily up at the back where the sea wind caught it, and that his world was different now, but he could not quite understand why.

★　★　★　★　★

Askaval and Mourne were 'immatures' now, the grey down of their childhood long gone, and the juvenile phase over, their feathers growing heavier and darker with the passing of the seasons. Mourne, the female, was the bigger of the two, but she was not so well-developed or self-assured as Askaval. His tail feathers were nearly all white now, and the years had brought him a confidence of flight and stance which gave him natural authority and grace. His beak had yellowed and he was nearly adult. Mourne still had a dark tail with only two or three lighter feathers. Her wings were ragged and awkward and her flight was erratic, though powerful on occasion.

They lived with a few other immatures and juveniles down at the mouth of the Romsdal fjord, in a neutral territory of skerries and cliffs and a few isolated beaches, and were visited on occasions by adults like Clew and Weever, who taught them things they ought to know.

Weever liked Askaval, and Askaval liked him. For though Askaval was already more knowledgeable about aspects of lore and language, in a way Weever would never be, for it didn't interest him, there was a strong bond between the two, born of the trials and troubles in the early months of Askaval's upbringing, first at the Storrin and then, after their escape, along the coast where Weever, in particular, looked after their physical welfare.

Weever got on with Mourne rather less well, for he had no patience with her hesitations and fears. That was surprising, for he had loved and cared for Mizen for years, and she was the same. But

Mourne did not seem to have Mizen's caring ways, being more preoccupied with some distant doubt and sense of failure in herself. As she approached maturity, she was, of course, bigger than Weever, but size did not seem to change her. She would become angry and bitter, and seemed unable to learn as naturally as Askaval did. You could show something to him one day, and he would be doing it the next as if he had known it for ever—but not Mourne.

Mourne was different. She was strong and – judging from the lines of her wings and beak and the turn of her talons – she was potentially a fine eagle, but her normal behaviour belied it. In her nature, which was quick and sarcastic, and in her personality, which was defensive and fractious, she was hard to like—and in the final analysis a disappointment for any who remembered the majestic maturity of her mother.

Yet Askaval never criticised her, or allowed any other eagle to do so in his hearing. He remained completely loyal to her to a point which mystified others.

But then there were things others did not know about: things *she* never talked of, and things *he* could never forget. For example, on the initial flight from the nest, when every eagle assumed it had only been by Askaval's strength and will that the two of them had survived – and that a miracle – he could not but remember, even from a haze of rushing wind and torrential sound, that it had been her faith in him that had spurred him on. If she had not been there to save, he would not have saved himself.

There had been other times, too. He had once got separated from all the others during a fruitless search for prey to the north, when, because of a sea wind, he found himself further towards the mountains than he liked to go, and alone. Suddenly two Hardanger eagles, females, appeared from off the fjell and bore down towards him, and with them came two sleark, the four together against him. He had been attacked before – what eagle hadn't? – but those were mock attacks and posturing, and he had won his reputation for strength and courage because he knew which were the bluffs to face out, and which the ones to yield to. On this occasion, when suddenly faced by four eagles, he was still young and inclined to battle it out. So he turned directly towards them with great courage and began to present a talon to the first that came.

Where did she come from then, his sister Mourne? She seemed to bear down from nowhere, from the sky or earth behind him, and overfly him swifter than he had ever been overflown by any eagle. 'Turn back, Askaval,' she had called angrily. *'Now!'*

Then she led him away back to the coast and out of danger, angry all the while, as if by endangering himself he had endangered her also. For all her bad temper then, he understood better than ever how deeply she loved him and how, in her strange and brittle way, she would always protect him, should he be in danger.

There was one other incident which, more than any other, sealed Askaval's mysterious loyalty to his difficult and prickly sister. One winter, four years after her escape from the Storrin, when she was still a juvenile, she became cast down by some strange gloom and despondency. It lasted for weeks while she skulked away by herself. Mizen was sent for, but could do nothing with Mourne, who even tried to attack her. Indeed, Mizen was quite upset, and it was all Clew could do to calm her down.

'Yes, but what would Cuillin have done? Mourne's over there among the cliffs eating nothing, getting thinner and more ragged by the hour, and the weather's worsening. She does nothing all day. What *would* Cuillin have done?'

Clew laughed. 'I hate to say it, Mizen, but I'm afraid Cuillin would have shown scant patience, and either left her to her own devices or given her a quick clip with her talons!'

But one night soon after this, Askaval woke suddenly out of a roosting sleep with a terrible sense of trouble and danger. He knew it was Mourne, and that she needed him.

The night was dark, a light and freezing blizzard running, and only some pale light from hidden stars or moon prevented an eagle from stepping forward from his stance and falling headlong into the dark void. But a bleak shimmer of sea, and a steep tumble of dark cliffs, gave him enough to fly on, and he turned north towards where she was. Urgent, urgent, a calling-out from her, and he felt a terrible sense of her despair.

How did he find her, up there among the cliffs? Neither sibling knew. But when he came to her, it was as if she expected him, and she did not look at him or talk. She was shivering and lost, and he remembered her as she had been in the nest when they were barely a few days old. So he went near enough to touch her, and let her feel his strength and warmth, so she would lose her fears through his presence.

'What's wrong, Mourne?' he asked at last, when dawn began to come.

'I don't know, but I was so frightened. So cold and frightened. It's going to come, it's all going to come, and it'll be much worse than it was in the Storrin. You nearly left me then. And when it comes, you'll leave me here, and I . . .'

'I'm not going to leave you,' he protested gently.

'You are. You are. It's coming, and it's darkness, and I know I won't have the strength to face it. Not like you or Clew, not like

Cuillin had the strength, and Finse. Not like Weever or Mizen. I won't know what to do, because you'll leave me, Askaval, and I'll be lost.' She was shivering and beginning to call out like a chick in terrible distress. And Askaval could feel her suffering as if it was his own.

'What's coming, Mourne? What is it that's coming?' Surely it was just her imagination, brought on by lack of food, and cold, or some illness that had come her way.

'I don't know what it is,' she said more calmly, 'but it's what Clew calls the Doom of Weir, which he says has already started. But even worse is coming, and I won't have the strength . . .'

'But we'll be here to help you fight whatever it is. The Doom is not one thing but many, and it is in us as well as out there' – and he indicated vaguely in the direction of the dark, dawning sea – 'and it's up to us to fight it.'

'It's not like the humans who come and shoot us, or invade our territories, or bring their boats into places where only eagles and gulls and eider have been before. It's worse than that, like a dangerous wind over which we have no control.'

'I know, Mourne, I know. It's why few eagles can take the Doom seriously. Because it isn't an easy thing like sleark or Hardanger eagles—something you can name and see and fight. It's vaguer than that.'

'If you hadn't come,' said Mourne eventually, 'I would have flown out over the sea and lost myself in its darkness. I was so frightened that I couldn't face what's coming. I don't have your courage, Askaval.'

But he understood very well that she did, for she had faced a dark cloud and looked at it, and suffered its coming towards her. She had not turned from it. She had the kind of courage other eagles see as weakness and fear, for she had seen how weak and vulnerable she was, and in calling out to him she had shown she knew her weakness.

Yet Mourne's fears of Askaval leaving proved correct, for two years later he took a mate. He had established a territory along the coast north of Romsdal in the winter months, and before any of the Romsdal eagles knew what was afoot he had accepted, and been accepted by, an older female of the new Hardanger generation that had been expanding coastwards. Her name was Ruann. A great and proud female who, like Askaval, did not see the reason for maintaining the old hostilities; those times surely were over. Of the Romsdalers, only Clew was truly sympathetic, for he understood best of all the need for unity among them all, if they were to survive the critical years ahead.

One day, soon after Ruann had come to Askaval's territory, but before they had made a full mating flight, Mourne suddenly appeared over his fjord.

'Hello, Askaval,' she called out, coldly. Her eyes sweeping the sky for signs of the Hardanger female. 'Alone, are we?'

She knew what she was doing. If the Hardanger eagle was serious, she was going to fly a challenge at Mourne, and as she probably did not realise she was Askaval's sister, it might all become very fraught.

'Why are you angry?' asked Askaval. 'It's right for me to mate this year.'

Mourne ignored him, turning up over the fjells and cliffs towards the end of the fjord where she suspected Ruann might be. She was right, and Ruann flew out from the shadows to meet her. She flew with maturity and strength, a surer flight than Mourne's, and for every twist and turn that Mourne made in anger and rage, Ruann met it with elegance and composure. Once their talons clashed, the sound echoing across the waters to Askaval, who watched helplessly. He could not interfere. It was not his right. He felt wretched, for he loved Mourne and understood her jealousy, but he was beginning to desire Ruann in a way that overrode everything.

Miserably he took off towards their rival tumblings in the sky, to fly a line between them and show them which one he preferred. But never did his wings feel so heavy. For he knew that Mourne was fighting for something she could never win, and he knew better than any eagle how lost she must feel.

His pace quickened, his flight became more decisive and he cut rapidly between them, drawing Ruann off with him in his flight, and isolating Mourne over the fjord, where she finally hung, staring with hatred and loss after him.

'You've become a Hardanger minion,' she called out. 'A discredit to Finse and Cuillin who flew out against that kind of eagle for so long. They will weaken you and change you, Askaval. You will be nothing.'

But the words were without effect, for Askaval now felt a greater drive than any sibling insult could weaken: a drive to mate and rear his own young, a drive finally to leave immaturity far behind.

So strong was this drive that when Mourne turned away, defeated and alone, flying disconsolately back towards the sea, he was glad to see her go. And he turned to Ruann and presented his talons for her to take in her stronger ones, for this was his territory to err in or to prosper over, and she would now become his mate. And calling to each other for the joy of it, they began to cartwheel down through the sky—as Cuillin had done once upon a time with Finse his father, who had mated with a fremmed. And was not Ruann fremmed, too?

If his mating with Ruann was a scandal to some, what Mourne did next changed other eagles' dislike of her to contempt. For she disappeared one morning soon after her tussle with Ruann, and none saw her until weeks later, when the grim news came out. She had been seen up near the Storrin, flying high and circling in the winds with the dark cunning eagle whose name was Sleat.

Even the ravens shuddered to see it, for they feared Sleat as much as any. Sleek he was and swift, older now and silent in his ways, his talons still sharp and yellow, his beak slim and pointed, his eyes cold as black ice in a glacier.

They saw him—and her. For he took her on the wing, high over the sacred Storrin, where Cuillin had flown, and Finse watched. He took her viciously to give her pain, so that her cries might be heard by many. And his beak crashed down on her neck, fiercely and painfully, and on her face already scarred by another frailer beak that had bullied her when she was young and dying. Sleat took her—and when he had, he made sure that Hardanger eagles visited Ruann, the wild one who had been difficult, to tell her the delicious news that Sleat had taken Mourne for a mate, and would let her humiliation be seen in the very place that Romsdal eagles held most dear: the Storrin. The Fremmed is dead—long live Sleat! The spirit of Mourne is weak—long live the pride of Sleat! The house of Cuillin is humbled—strength to the wings of Hardanger!

But Askaval did not seem to understand. For he was driven by such a power for making young and rearing that he did not care for Mourne now. She had gone too far—and surely the family of Cuillin was split forever.

* * * * *

Often, almost always now, Jim woke up feeling hard, his body racing one way and his mind another. After Mummy called him to get up, he turned on the old radio by his bed and when he was sure she couldn't hear the creaking of the bed, he would sometimes rub himself until he exploded with it.

But there was no one to talk to about 'it', no books to read. The jokes at school from other fifteen-year-olds were smutty, and he had to laugh as if he understood, when really he had no idea what they were talking about. Dictionaries in the school library did not help. *The Shorter Oxford English Dictionary* defined 'it' – masturba-

356

tion – as 'self abuse', and when he read that, he felt for the first time it might be wrong. Did it sap your strength, or give you boils on the neck like Watkins had? (Everyone said he did it all the time, and that's why his skin was bad.) Jim's skin was all right, except sometimes he went pale for no reason. His mother said that was because he was growing up.

His mother had a book called *The Family Doctor*, and this contained the first picture he ever saw of genitals, male and female. Except the photographs were sandwiched between medical abnormalities like 'A bad case of rickets in a boy from Nottingham', and 'Hare-lip before and after an operation of removal'.

He had better luck in the newsagent's, where he sometimes sneaked a look at *Health and Efficiency*, where girls and boys went out to play on 'a sandy beach somewhere near Ilfracombe'. It was all surreptitious and slightly silly, but the real thing, in the shape of the Dover College girls he passed each morning on his way to the station, was impossible to reach. How did you ever get to talk to them?

Some boys did. Some boys had kissed a girl already, on the lips. Some boys, boarders at the school, had done things with the housemaster's daughter which went beyond kissing. Jim had not even held a girl's hand.

Jim Stonor's behaviour at school now became increasingly brash and show-off, like others in his year who were near the bottom of the lower form. To them, Science was a write-off, English ridiculous, History boring, French and Latin a waste of time, Religious Knowledge a mockery because the class played up Mr Ennal who taught it. They seemed to be running all the time, not to keep up, for that they had failed to do, but so that they might not be totally lost.

He had begun the Fifth Year, with its dark threat of O-levels on the horizon, very seriously, trying to work harder and make sense of the material they gave him. He tried to keep his books tidier; he tried to keep his work clean; he tried, but failed. And failing, he slumped into brashness and bravado. Wright was always there to have a cheap joke with, and the others expected him to take the mickey when he could, and draw cartoons on the blackboard to embarrass the teachers.

To make things worse he sometimes heard from Peter—or about him through his mother who wrote to Mrs Conan occasionally. Peter was doing very well. He had taken his O-levels a year earlier, and passed nine, all with high marks. He was 'brilliant', and going into the Sixth Form. Peter himself never mentioned any of this, but his letters were different now, for they used words and language Jim couldn't always understand and which didn't sound like the Peter he had beachcombed with, and the one who had lain on his bedroom floor planning 'M' Night.

Several of the Lower Fifth teachers were poor and incompetent—different from the Upper Fifth ones, who assumed their charges would work. The Lower Fifth boys didn't want to work, and if they got through more than four O-levels apiece, it was a bloody miracle. A bad year, anyway, uncooperative louts most of them, like Stonor and Wright II. Clever, smug, skivers, so teach 'em by rote, feed them with notes on everything, and, with luck, enough facts might stick to scrape them through.

So, insecure, increasingly frightened of the O-level ordeal, badly taught, rarely encouraged, the Lower Fifth stumbled along its pre-set path of failure. And as the weeks of autumn term passed by, the early seriousness they had felt deserted them, because they were falling behind on all fronts again, and could never hope to compete in the open battlefield of public examination.

Autumn gave way to Christmas, and the holidays gave way to the start of a spring term. Snow settled on the shingle, and great grey sweeps of sea rushed up the beach at Jim's wellingtoned feet, and cut away the snow. There was wind in his hair, and he began long walks across the Dunes, and over the cliffs, and explored the dug-outs, and gun emplacements facing France, left behind from the Second World War. He began to cycle further from Deal – to Dover eight miles, to Canterbury seventeen miles, all round the Isle of Thanet thirty-five miles – and he was so full of energy and strength he would pound the pedals up steep hills and find himself sweating even in cold weather. The terns began to return to Sandwich Bay, their first grey fluttering of wings stopping him still on the sand below the shingle, to cup his hands to his eyes so he could watch without his eyes watering in the chill wind. He remembered being at that spot with Peter in a happier, more innocent year.

Other times he was cast down into loneliness and frustration, and always now – forever – he wondered about girls, and what it would be like to touch one, and be touched. At the end of the spring term they always had a school dance for Fifth- and Sixth-formers. The Dover College girls came over, but some boys had girlfriends to bring. They were the ones they had lip-kissed, and Jim was jealous. Stiles smirkingly announced that he had not only lip-kissed a girl he was taking to the school dance, but French-kissed her as well; and Jim looked out of the train window consumed by dark, despairing envy, but forced to snigger with the rest of them in that special way that established they had done it as well—or at least that they knew what Stiles was talking about. What is a French-kiss, wondered Jim? Perhaps Peter had done it.

There was one girl on whom his fantasies dwelled, and she came over the railway bridge on her way to the Dover College bus every morning. She had red cheeks and a clean look, and carried a leather satchel. She always walked with a friend. One day at the start of the spring term, Jim had noticed her staring at him. Since then, it had been her unsullied breasts and her tender lips that he had abused night after night in the secret orgy-house of his bed. He did not know her name until, in a roundabout way, he had asked Stiles—who seemed to know a lot. It was Stiles who had told him you did it from the front and not the back, which animals did. But you probably did it with the light out, so you wouldn't have to look at each other. 'It', however was the subject of curiosity rather than fantasy, because it was still so scarily horrific. Stiles's parents did it. Jim was never going to do it until he was married.

Stiles said her name was Christine King. Jim imagined her saying 'You may kiss me if you like', as Estelle said to Pip in *Great Expectations*, their O-level set book. And when he approached the station bridge in the mornings, his heart pounded, and he got ready for his morning glance at her; though on any day he caught her gaze, he looked away rapidly and pretended a fascination with the bridge's brickwork.

There was an alternative route to the station, over the footbridge behind the church. He took this on Tuesdays when he was kitted out in his khaki Combined Cadet Force uniform—the junior army organisation that was strictly voluntary, except it was known that Mr Gower did not give university recommendation to boys who funked joining it, so really it was compulsory.

Jim had one of those heads on which an army beret did not fit. It projected at the wrong angle, and when he looked at himself in the windows of Riceman's, the department store in the High Street, he knew he looked an idiot. Not wishing Christine King to see him like that, he took the long route on Tuesdays. His gaiters seemed to twist round the wrong way, so the straps were inside his ankle and not outside it. His boots, despite hard rubbing, did not gain the incredible shine that other, keener boys achieved. They used techniques like pouring on melted black shoe-polish and then rubbing it with the curve of a silver spoon. After that you were meant to spit on it, and rub it dry with a yellow duster. Jim had tried that, but none of it worked; also it bored him. So his boots were clean but dull.

The weeks of the spring term passed, and, with less than a month before the school dance, Jim began to feel desperate about the invitation yet to be delivered to Christine King. How to do it? How to go up to her? How to speak? How even to start? Then, somehow, it happened.

On the way home after CCF one Tuesday evening, as he was kicking his army boots along the pavement, Jim suddenly and terrifyingly became aware of two blue macs approaching him as he walked down past the Odeon in Queen Street, just beyond the station bridge. It was Christine King, and she was with her friend. Probably late back from school, like he was. He stared at her, his mouth opening, his throat withering into a desert dryness. To his simultaneous horror and relief, the friend sidestepped and ran past him, leaving him face-to-face with fantasy and reality all at once. This close, Christine had slightly piggy eyes, which right now stared at him with precisely the same helpless, excited fear with which he stared at her. And he confronted for the first time a mystery that was to trouble him in so many ways afterwards. Why is it that, at the very moment of arrival at a longed-for destination, at the moment when a dream is fulfilled, pleasure in it begins to wane? She did not look so good in real life as she did in his dreams.

'Will you come to the school dance with me?' he rasped.

'Yes,' she said, her voice strangling in her own tension.

He arranged to take her to the cinema that weekend, and on Saturday morning, and in a state of nervousness about the possibility of achieving the lip-kiss which was the evening's objective, Jim took a long walk along the front. It was a fine spring day, and the lifeboat was out, practising manoeuvres five hundred yards off the shore.

He came across his father by the Lifeboat Station, standing near the look-out tower. He was watching the lifeboat with one hand over his brow to shield his eyes. His father grinned at him from the distance he lived in, and pointed out to sea.

'Where are those binoculars I gave you?' he asked, rather accusatorily, as if he expected Jim to be carrying them right then. Jim was no longer afraid of his father, or embarrassed by his strangeness; and as he stood by his side now, looking out to sea, he felt close to him. He wondered how he lived, and what it was like to be alone. He wondered about the room he inhabited in a big house in West Street which he had never been inside. Sometimes he had stared at it, surreptitiously.

'They're in my room, Daddy, on the mantlepiece. I do use them, sometimes, to watch birds on the shore and things.'

360

'Good,' said Liam MacAskill. 'Been a long way they have—a long way.'

There was a thinking silence between them.

'Do you want them back?' asked Jim, suddenly aware that might be his father's meaning. Though he didn't want to give them back—but would if asked to.

'Och no, laddie, I wasnae meaning that. They're yours to dae as ye see fit wi'. Yours for all time, I dinnae want them back in this burgh!'

As he spoke, his voice thin and accented, Jim thought what a good voice it was, a good accent. He thought he wanted to talk to his father, because he was feeling nervous and at a crossroads. But he knew his father, Liam MacAskill, wouldn't want to talk, and would shy away from anything personal. He supposed his father had lip-kissed Mummy, but looking at him now, his lips thin and chapped, he could not imagine it.

So instead he said, 'Daddy, I told a boy at school you speak Gaelic. It's true, isn't it?'

Liam MackAskill nodded and smiled gently, still staring out to sea. Yes, it was true. *'Fhir a dh'imicheadh a maireach . . .* It's a dead language now,' he added, 'and the air in Skye is dead of the birds that flew there. I remember . . .' And Jim wanted him so much to continue, to talk to him, to share something of himself now at last—but Liam stopped short, as he always seemed to, shook his head a little and said, 'They're turning about now. Look, lad. Turning about and coming back to shore.'

And Jim watched the lifeboat out on the grey sea off Deal manoeuvring itself back to where it had started from, and said quietly, 'Goodbye, Daddy, I'm going to walk up to Kingsdown.' It occurred to neither of them that they might walk there together.

They both breathed with relief, and a shared joy and excitement quite in conflict with the clumsiness of which they had both been victims. Jim was thinking that he had now achieved lip-kiss and cheek-kiss together; Christine, that he had done it and it was over. She was like the other girls now. She had something to tell. But secretly both were wondering what all the strain and fuss was about.

On the pier afterwards, before they had their coffee and Penguin chocolate bars, they held hands, which was infinitely more exciting than the three more kisses they exchanged on the upper deck overlooking the lower deck fishermen. But already the excitement was gone. Kissing, lip or cheek, was not what Jim had expected. It left him feeling isolated, and Christine didn't seem to have much to say. They stirred their coffee and munched their Penguin bars in clumsy silence. She talked about television programmes and the school dance and he wanted to tell her about . . . well, he didn't know what. Outside her house they kissed one final time; and for a moment she put her hands on his neck and that was better than anything, because her hands were a woman's hands at last, and they came out of the dark night, from across the dark sea over which he was stranded, and for a moment he felt safe.

Judith laughed. Her own first kiss was at a party and was over before it started, and a total surprise. Jim smiled wryly, put his hand on her cheek, and kissed her—quite long, quite deep. Their eyes half-smiling, their bodies relaxed and tired.

'Like that?' he whispered finally.

'No,' she said, 'not like that at all.'

'Like this?' He kissed her again, and she, half-laughing, mouthed a 'No', and he felt her hands soft on his neck and in his hair. Beyond them, through the aircraft porthole, a dawn light was tinging the cloud base below them with red and gold.

The film was long over, people were up and down the aisle, some without shoes, to tidy themselves well before landing.

'This is the Captain speaking. Good morning. The weather in London is cold and rainy, with a temperature of twelve degrees centigrade, and fifty-four fahrenheit. We are just nearing the southern coast of England and will land in roughly twenty-five minutes, at 09.40 hours Greenwich Mean Time.'

Jim and Judith sat back in their seats, staring out at the clear sky and the cloud below. The laughter was gone, replaced by seriousness, and thoughts of Liam MacAskill dying.

Judith took toilet items from her flight bag, and got up to go to the back of the plane. Jim stared out of the porthole. Would Michael be coming down to Deal, as well? Away from the monastery? Assuming he *knew*—you could bet their mother hadn't told him. And Mrs Frewin wouldn't have known where to contact him.

The plane suddenly went into cloud, and the rising sun, and the view across a sky hidden from the ground was gone. The window now streaked with rain.

Michael, Peter, Gerald . . . where had they gone? Why had he ever turned his back on them? Below, for the briefest moment, a distant ground light shone up between cloud . . . a single light in the dark early morning of Hampshire, three years away, lost years which had aged him. He leaned forward to the porthole and watched the racing cloud as he felt the excitement of knowing that he was coming home again, and could begin to reach out to those who he had thought had turned their backs on him, but whom it was he who had left behind.

CHAPTER FOURTEEN

Deal, August 1961

J IM Stonor lay on the beach soaking up sun, wishing he had not asked Christine King to come to London to visit the National Gallery with him the next day. It was summer now, the long holidays had begun, and he was beginning the long wait to see if he had passed enough O-levels to get a place in the Sixth Form next term, and then study A-levels.

The relationship with Christine had faltered on since the school dance at Easter, maintained more by her than by him, because he discovered lip-kissing with her was not what he had expected, and she seemed silly sometimes. Alone he had desire, too much of it, but with her chaste hand in his, and her thin lips to his, and her thin body clumsily against his at the end of a date, his desire went. He wanted to feel her breasts, such as she had, but the desire seemed to go when confronted by her, and anyway he didn't dare. Life seemed easier alone.

Stiles got a job on deckchairs with the Town Council. Wright was working in a market garden near Eastry. Jim found he could earn money as a junior caddy on the golf-course on the Dunes. He got fifteen shillings a round.

He saved the money he made in this way, and wherever the idea of going to the National Gallery came from, it seemed a good way of using it. Jim thought he had asked Christine to come, but the truth was that she had really asked herself, and one way or another he'd got trapped. Anyway, he was beginning to like the look of other girls better.

The next morning, Christine King and he met at the bus station and boarded the eight o'clock coach to London. Her mother said that if they hurried, they would just have time to see the Changing of the Guard at eleven o'clock at Buckingham Palace. But it was really the National Gallery he wanted to visit, so by the time they got there it was nearly lunchtime. He was hardly talking to Christine.

Not that he had done much better on the journey. Christine made small talk, chatty talk, bright, nervous talk. When Jim was silent like he was being, she got nervous because she didn't know where she was. She didn't know, anyway—was he her boyfriend or not? He seemed strange and made her feel unattractive. She didn't understand him, and if her mother hadn't said there were surely other boys, she would have said it herself. As it was, in tiny revolt against what her mother said, she stuck by him.

Jim went quickly up the grand stairs of the National Gallery, deliberately making it hard for her to keep up—not wanting her there next to him, trailing pathetically along. He was struck deeply with excitement and awe, and surprised to find that it was so easy to get there. He looked at no plan or guide but simply entered beneath the great columns at the entrance, over the hushed and shiny floor, up some wide, red-carpeted steps, and found the scarlet image of Cardinal Richelieu staring down at him. Christine stood naggingly at his side, redundant. Up into a main gallery and some boring sort of medieval paintings he didn't like, except one where the colours of shining gold in a halo, and the rich cobalt blue of jagged angel wings stopped his breath. Christine twittered at his side, stopping and starting as he did, chaining him to smiles and words he didn't feel. Her eyes were piggy and her lips thin to him now, her bust more bra than bosom. She probably put cotton wool in them to make her breasts seem bigger.

Round a corner and the first real shock of many, many aweing shocks that day. Uccello's *The Rout of San Romano*, which he had only ever seen reproduced small, and in black and white. Great tilted white spears to the left; flying, curling pennants; a white horse like a rocking-horse with its front legs outstretched in the air; a bold, black horse on either side. Men with raised arms holding grey shining swords, and the cries of men dying, and the smell of horses, the run of blood and guts, and a body outstretched beneath a horse's hooves, its hand dead now, its fight lost.

'It's by Uccello,' said Jim, without looking at the notice by it, proud that he could identify it. He said the *c* as an *s*, all wrong, but he knew no better yet—and who would care before such towering strength?

He came across several other pictures he had seen before, in Arthur Mee and in other books, not small now or in sepia blues and browns, but in full and glorious colour, and in a size that often dominated him. He had learnt their composition, but now he learned of the importance of scale, and of colour, and of the different feel that an original painting has. It took his breath away. Round another corner and he found that Christine, hanging back to look at something else, was gone, and impulsively he raced on through the great square doors that separated different galleries, ignoring the pictures round and about until he hoped she might be lost. If he felt guilt, it did not last long, because he found himself before the face of a man which would in time become more familiar to him than Frank's or Oliver's, perhaps even than Michael's. Two self-portraits of Rembrandt were staring at him, aged thirty-four on one side, sixty-three on the other.

He turned away and saw Christine in profile in an adjacent gallery, looking away from him and seeming anxious. A coldness came over him, a kind of cowardice, hard and strong. He turned another way and walked through the gallery's door and headed as best he could towards the entrance hall, with no other plan than to get away. He felt a freedom without her chained at his side.

Pictures, pictures everywhere, until, turning yet another corner into a smaller room, he was stopped in his flight by his first major Impressionist painting. He stared and stared, and he saw a colour and light that he knew he had seen—that glistened and lit its way before him sometimes in high summer across the chalk downlands where the cornfields were; and there in the pebbles on the beach where striped towels lay. It was not a picture he recognised, or had ever seen; for anything later than 1850, and Courbet, was strange to him. It was Seurat's *Bathers, Asnières*, and its warm greens, blues and reds, its shimmering blue water, its strange lights and coloured shadows caught him and held him still. He had never seen it, but he knew that in a way he had—and had seen it many times. He wanted to reach out to its world. He wanted to touch it. He wanted to stand on the bank of the Seine and stare, as Seurat had stared. But, far more than that, he wanted to make it himself.

And with its colours in his eyes, and fearing that Christine would catch him at last – at this moment of all moments – he turned away from it, back to the entrance, and ran out through the Gallery's main swing-doors into the light and freedom of Trafalgar Square. Then, without a thought for her at all, and hardly a flicker of guilt, he crossed the square to look at the four great lions Landseer had sculpted for the base of Nelson's Column.

His freedom that day was forbidden fruit, stolen from a girl he no longer wanted, and the more magical and memorable for it. He had been to London before, for special treats, and had sat in Lyons Corner Houses long, long ago, when his father was more normal, on a visit to the Natural History Museum to see *Diplodocus carnegii*.

He found himself now staring down Whitehall, not knowing it was Whitehall, and from its furthest length chimed the sound of Big Ben, so he walked down to it. At its side the River Thames— and him leaning over the big, black balustrade and staring down at the river's dirty depths which swirled out from under Westminster Bridge. There the perpendicular architecture of the House of

Commons, so like Canterbury Cathedral, but gilded and shining, especially in the summer light.

London. His first appreciation of red double-decker buses approaching where he stood on a corner, then rising above him as they turned, with faces staring at him for a moment out of windows. London. And caught in a rush of people across a road. London, and Westminster Abbey, all gloomy, with him staring at the Tomb of the Unknown Warrior, unable to move. Then the sun shining and London again. Round its corners, past more of the Parliament buildings, towards an embankment park with people sitting lazily on chairs and lovers on the grass, the man's turned-up trousers pulled up his leg and white flesh showing. Her dress riding just a little high, and Jim wanting to look up her legs, but not daring as he passed them by. So, staring away, not seeing, but thinking of the girl there, wondering what it was like to lie like that with a girl on the grass. Staring ahead, not seeing, he saw only slowly the outstretched hand. Green and shiny. An arm, a body, five bodies, black or dark-green and still, casting shadows on themselves, and oh, he knew them, he had seen them so many times, and they were here in this city of sights, and he before them alone, having to share them with no one, and his heart beating fast as he stared and stared enthralled before *The Burghers of Calais*, the first Rodin he ever saw.

Jim Stonor stood before them where they stood forever chained together, beneath the House of Commons, one of the few replicas of the original commissioned by the town of Calais itself. He moved around them, staring up at the dark and shifting forms silhouetted against the blue sky and leafy trees above, changing always if he stood forward or back, or moved to left or right, dark tunnels between figures opening at his slightest movement, the gorges and clefts between them disappearing just as fast. A great foot to reach out and touch, his fingers to its toe; the hand he had first seen, stretched down and loosely open, and him touching it. The musculature of an arm and thigh and calf; so many of them there, and him unable to take it all in or grasp the greatness of it on himself. Auguste Rodin, the name cast deep into its base, like weathered writing—and he before it at last. He stood and stared and counted the figures, six in all, and behind him on the grass, a rook stopped and stared, from the family of Corvidae, of the crow and the magpie, of the raven . . . of the Raven of Storr, in whom all things are told. A boy of sixteen, lost in awe and a flight of joy before the slow discovery of his own soaring task. *The Burghers of Calais*, the Raven of Storr, in whom all things are told—a day in London, stolen from a girl who waited tearfully, then angrily frustrated, then miserably, at the foyer of the National Gallery where they sell the postcards.

Jim never went back. Nor did he go to Victoria Coach Station. He spent the last of his money on a train fare back to Deal, wasting the return part of the coach ticket. But it didn't matter; it never mattered. All that mattered, as the train swayed his head back and forth and he stared at the rolling chalk Downs he was beginning to love, blousey now with summer dryness, was the fantasy that filled him, that one day he, too, might have a painting hanging on a gallery wall, or make a sculpture like Rodin's, and that people would come and look at it and read his name: James MacAskill Stonor. That's what he wanted most of all, an impossible dream.

At home his mother already knew. Mrs King had phoned her. His mother seemed suspicious, and when he spelt out his story, he knew she knew he was lying.

'What really happened?' she asked, cutting through his wordy excuses.

'Got bored,' he said. 'She was so silly.'

'You can't do that sort of thing,' she said. But she said it without much conviction, and he knew that she understood why he had done what he had, and in one way even approved of it. He had preferred his freedom to what seemed the chains of a relationship, and so, so subtly, was a fatal pattern set.

* * * * *

The darkness that overcame Mourne in her years with Sleat was a strange, insubstantial thing, more murk than black. And at first so inarticulate was the feeling it gave her that Mourne could not even perceive that she might need to escape it. A distant ache.

Her territory was his, and that was from over the upper reaches of Romsdal to the Storrin itself, and from there over the southern fjells. The Storrin was out of bounds to any creature, for since the leaving of Cuillin and the escape of Askaval and Mourne, its waters had seemed to turn from white to raging grey, and its falls to be so violent and perverse that the permanent pall of spray over its deeps never lifted, even on the calmest day.

With the darkness came a tiredness, a weariness, and she seemed never to have quite the energy she needed to make the never-ending rounds of rearing young, seeking prey, hunting, killing, and waiting through the winter nights. The young she raised with Sleat over the years were competent, dull eagles, and they passed beyond her talons and joined the ranks of the Hardanger eagles whose serried, serious ways seemed dominated by Sleat. His guardianship of their territory was effective, brutally so, but strangely impersonal. He did it not for her, or their young, but for some inner purpose of his own to do with pride and unspoken show. His mate was Cuillin's daughter, his territory had been Cuillin's own, his eagles ruled the heartland of old Romsdal.

He did not allow her to speak of Cuillin or Askaval, and his talons struck her more than once in the early years when some slip of speech had her using some scrapword of the old language cited by Clew or used by Askaval. Though male and smaller, yet his strength of personality and his flight were more powerful than hers, and she was frightened of him. Yet, when he did fly, and when he flew for her, as he did in January and February at the start of the breeding season, then, despite herself, her spirit soared to see his wings so strong in the air, and she felt anew that strength that lay in hers, though for so many years it had lain hidden and unexpressed. Then she would fly with him, high over the upper cliffs of Romsdal, and eagles that watched would find their gaze involuntarily moving away from Sleat to his despised mate Mourne—who, for a moment or two, spoke a language in flight not seen since Cuillin and Finse. Then it was gone, and she taken, and Sleat's glinting thrusts of flight and speed overflew and enshadowed the brief glimpse of her majesty that seemed gone now, as if lost in the dark waters of the fjord.

Sleat forbade mention of Askaval's name by other Hardanger eagles, and in truth Mourne herself would not have wished to hear it. That life was past, it had never really been, and it seemed to her now that her brother was as proud and disdainful and distant as surely he had always been. He was not of her, nor she of him.

So, into the darkness the years passed on. Until, at last, Sleat himself grew weary of the triumph she had once represented, and began to enjoy taunting her and making mention of the very name of which he had forbidden utterance.

'Remember Askaval, do you? Want to go and see him, where he preens his wings down on the coast? Eh, Mourne, daughter of the one they called the Fremmed?' His voice was sneering, his talons fretful, his stance impatient and cruel, for it seemed that whatever he said she would not respond to. 'I'm told he says you're not fit to be his sister'—which was not true. Then Sleat would laugh, and cast his eyes on other females, and leave her alone. He would toy in the air then with female juveniles, grappling his talons with theirs, enjoying the power and clumsy potency of their youth—his eyes alight and cold, and cast back to Mourne to see her suffer.

Until, at last, a January came when he drove her off from upper Romsdal, off over the fjells, into another male's territory to let him take her if he wished. But none would have her, for she had been Sleat's and they were afraid. But taking a cue from Sleat, they mocked her, and false-grappled with her, laughing when she tiredly turned a talon on them.

Even the young she had had, the eldest of which were now matures, joined in the mocking, for Mourne was beaten, with bedraggled feathers and without place or hope, rejected by Sleat and unable to return to the Romsdal fold. So at last she became a vagrant, a wanderer, with other failed adults and juveniles, whose weakness of purpose or wing led them to collect together and prey communally on whatever food they could find in the neutral zones across the fjell, or by the lesser fjords, or along the outposts of the coast of Romsdal to south and north, drifting with the winds and rain, driven from place to place by other, stronger eagles guarding their own territories—outcast vagrants.

Wherever she went, other eagles seemed to know who she was, and she read in their eyes the contempt they felt that *she*, so bedraggled and pathetic, so lacking in pride, could really be Cuillin's daughter. For her mother had been the Fremmed, who flew with light in her feathers and pride in her wings, and whose stance was as solid as rock. And this daughter was the infamous Mourne who was taken by Sleat of Hardanger for mate and then rejected by him? She, over there, barely able to catch living prey, so tired was her flight, and making do with carrion. That one, Mourne? The ugly one with scars from her sibling who had tried to kill her in the nest?

She heard them, and month by month – in that first year of rejection by Sleat – the pride she had once felt in being Cuillin's daughter began to fade and her nature change. She began to believe in their contempt.

It was all the worse that others liked to talk of the doings of great eagles like Weever and Mizen, like Aiman who had attended the Gathering, like Clew the wise one, and like Askaval, son of Cuillin and worthy of her name. Askaval, the brave. Askaval, who flew true and taught others how an eagle should guard territory—with pride, with strength, with courage; but also with compassion and care. Askaval—the name became a trial and misery to Mourne, the more when she realised that other eagles spoke it to taunt her.

Until at last she was cast so low into her own darkness that she knew her only course was to leave Romsdal behind her, and to fly somewhere where she was not known, and could live free of the shadow that the wings of Cuillin cast across her. Such thoughts came at the end of the year, when the last migrants were flying south, and she knew she would join them and fly against her instinct. For south was where more humans lived, and where the sleark ruled now. South was nearer to danger and death. So she turned to slink away over the anonymous fjells, to the coast and down south. To be forgotten. To live another year. To die anonymously, as others did, where Cuillin her mother had never flown.

Another year, which one this time? Snow melting on the cornice at a cliff top, new plant growth showing green on brown, the waters of the Romsdal fjord blue for an hour or two after the long winter grey.

Clew stirred uneasily, and flew north to see Askaval. Soon Askaval and Ruann would mate again, and the year would start, and Clew would find it harder to talk with him. An uneasy year coming, to which the young can turn a blind eye but in which the old feel a creaking in their wings. Trouble in the sea. A grey cast to the sky. Cuillin's name fading now, her dream gone, and nothing done. Ships coming even earlier this year, up among the skerries and along the fjords. Lights and smoke to mar the snow. Shots and deaths with the coming of lighter days. Humans up on the empty fjells where they had no place to be, but would always be now.

Clew settled for a time and thought, and shrugged, and took prey at the sea's edge in that slow way of his. Not that he was old, just wise, and knew the worth of going carefully. So he went to Askaval.

'I've been thinking of your sister Mourne. Remember her?'

Askaval nodded and sighed. Yes, he did. She had gone to Sleat and been rejected by him and then become a vagrant.

Clew continued: 'I have had no reports of her, from north or south, or from the fjells. I thought perhaps that Ruann, with her contacts among the Hardanger eagles . . .?'

Ruann shook her head sadly. She felt no anger about Mourne, and knew more than any other eagle, more even than Clew himself, how much her mate Askaval cared for his lost sister. How often he searched the skies for her.

'This is going to be a hard year, a dangerous year,' said Clew. 'Perhaps the year we have waited for. I can see it in the sky and tell it from the sea.'

Askaval did not seem to be listening. He was staring across the small fjord which was his territory's heartland, across to its far side, which formed a black line of rotten rock against the plateau of snow behind it, white and thick, though marked on one side by the regular movements of reindeer herds down there for watering.

'I have never felt contempt for her,' Askaval said finally, 'nor even pity, though some might want to feel that. Only anger—and that because she has left me alone for so long. There was a time when we seemed able to understand what each was thinking without words being spoken. I often went across the fjells to her because I felt her calling. And sometimes she would appear in the air at my side, as if from nowhere, when I needed her. But in the years since Ruann and I matured, and she left the Romsdal fold for Sleat's company, I have never felt even the most distant call from her. I know she needs us, and yet she has cut herself off, so it would not be right to go and seek her.'

Clew nodded but said nothing. He understood that what Askaval said seemed right. But lately he had begun to think that he had been as guilty as the rest of them in simply waiting—waiting for the Doom to come. And not doing anything to confront it. Worse, he remembered making a promise to watch over Mourne, whatever might happen. Now he did not even know where she was. He was troubled, too, by other things.

'This past winter,' he started finally, 'I have talked to many eagles far and wide in Romsdal, and out over the skerries. Now, tell me, did you rear young last year?'

'You know we didn't,' said Askaval.

'And the year before?'

'A single one.'

'After two attempts,' added Ruann.

'And in your first years together?' asked Clew.

'Why, there was never any trouble then,' said Askaval.

'Yes, that is so,' said Clew. 'Yet this winter I have found, by talking to others, and listening to what the ravens say, and the hints an eagle can get from the migrations, that very many pairs have failed to breed. More, in fact, that I can ever remember. The winter was mild, fortunately, or else the population might have drastically continued the decline that has been going on through my lifetime.'

'But that's to do with humans encroaching, and nothing to do with breeding,' said Askaval.

'Is it now? Well, I'm beginning to wonder. A new generation of sea eagles along the coasts have got used to the idea that breeding is difficult. Eggs become addled, or shells are so thin that they break, or chicks are too weak to survive even mild weather, or eggs do not fertilise, or pairs seem unable to concentrate on guardianship, so that nests go cold and territories unoccupied. Have you noticed that the number of vagrants has increased? All this is quite separate from the encroachment of humans. When *I* was young there was no difficulty with breeding—extermination, yes; breeding, no. In fact, humans are becoming less trouble than they were. Cuillin herself was the last eagle shot in Romsdal, as I remember, though it's true that others have been poisoned near the towns. They may disturb us more, of course, but the killing is less.'

Clew fell silent and Askaval stared at him, thinking. At last he said, 'It's only an idea, just a thought, but . . .'

'Yes?' said Clew. Ruann moved nearer to listen.

'Well, I have wondered why the Hardanger eagles have bred so successfully over the years?'

'We didn't use to, from what I've heard,' said Ruann. 'Only when we came to upper Romsdal, where the food is good.'

'It's surprising how quickly patterns become established,' said Clew, thinking that the Hardanger eagles had not been with them for so very long. Thirty years, perhaps.

The Weir, through Cuillin, had warned them that the Doom would be a long time coming—and that when it did, they might not realise it had come. Not for some years . . . Ruann had said, 'Where the food is good'.

A terrible cold came over Clew, and suddenly he looked so stricken that Askaval came forward and asked, 'What is it Clew? What's wrong?'

'The Doom is about *extinction*, the end of our race,' whispered Clew. 'That starts with a failure in breeding, a slow imperceptible process which has now gone on too long for it to be reversed. Not enough of us left, you see; not enough with strength in them and life. If only I knew why the Hardanger eagles are more successful than we of Romsdal! If only I understood why you, Ruann, were so successful at breeding when you first came from them, but why, now that you live where we live you have started to have trouble rearing young! It could be the food, as you suggested.

'This is the Doom, you see, Askaval. This is what your mother tried to warn us of, except she herself could not have known. All she could do was to sow a dream of a place where it would be right for us to go. A place to return to, across the dark sea. A place abundant with prey and carrion. A place where the food would be good. The time has come for the waiting to stop. I am not so old yet that I can't make long journeys . . .'

'But where do you want to journey to?' asked Askaval.

'Not to Skye, that's for sure. That journey can only be made by an eagle with strength. That's for you, Askaval, one day for you.'

Askaval stared at Clew and knew it was so. Those past years with Ruann had been to gain strength, to learn wisdom, to learn so much of the legends and traditions which Clew and Mizen and strong Weever had taught him. One day, perhaps, he would know enough to make the flight. One day.

'Not yet,' said Clew, voicing his doubts. His talons grew

impatient. He stared out at the fjord. He moved his head uneasily this way and that. 'No. You two, rear more young, if you can, this year at least, and perhaps the next. No journey yet.' Then, impulsively, he turned to leave them.

'Where are you going?' called out Askaval.

But Clew was up and gone, impatient to be off, a new energy in his wings. His uneasiness was cleared from him, for the long years of waiting were over now, and there were things he had to do, and journeys to be made. And time was short. But he turned back to them before leaving.

'Askaval, yours is the burden of lower Romsdal now, for I am going far from here. So fly high over the seas and the skerries, and show all eagles here that you have strength and purpose, for in time they will turn to you as they have turned to me these past years. Do not let small things trouble you, but take strength from Ruann's wings, for she was sent by Haforn, and in time she will do Haforn's will beyond any dreaming we may have. Guard your territory. Watch and listen. Think and learn. Trust in Haforn with your eyes open and your wings ready, for Haforn needs thinking eagles now.'

Then he was gone, flying urgently away towards the coast—thinking that now, after so many long years, there was no time left for all that had to be done.

Mourne had hidden herself away far to the south, where none knew her. When asked where she came from, she lied that she came from somewhere far up north, a little island none knew; and gave herself a different name.

But she was made welcome all the same, and could not help noticing that the nearer she got to the bigger towns, and the busy shipping lanes, the more friendly the vagrant eagles became. The common danger they faced seemed to break down barriers. These eagles hunted in packs, like gulls—and felt themselves to be no better than gulls. They knew they were the least important of their species, the failures, and when they saw another eagle as broken and downcast as Mourne, they saw in her themselves, and they accepted her with a shared compassion. Sometimes, it is true, there were fights, but it was the fighting of frustration at what life had led them to and such moments soon healed over. In all her years till that time, Mourne had never known an eagle willingly give food to another, except a mother to her young. She had never seen friendship so easily shared, and mutual protection so willingly given.

The group she joined, nearly thirty in all, found most of their food near towns—at fish factories where the rejected offal was plundered by all sea-birds. Or they lurked behind the whaling ships and trawlers, whose crews felt no hostility to the great birds that swooped down from the cliffs to take the rubbish thrown overboard.

Here – unknown, unsuspected, unharried – Mourne began to find herself again. The arrogance of her juvenile days was gone, and also the impatience and wilfulness. She learned that there may be much that is good in even the humblest and weakest eagle. She learned, too, of the real gift that Cuillin had given all sea eagles, for even here the name of Cuillin was spoken. Younger eagles, still juveniles, spoke of her as if she was a distant legend so long dead that no living eagle could possibly have known her, let alone one who . . . Mourne shook her head, that was all gone now.

She saw then how potent was the dream that Cuillin had sown. For all of them seemed to believe that somewhere across the dark sea was a land without danger, where the prey was easy and the food healthy, and where the winter did not fall into never-ending nights. Often, of an evening, some would perch near each other for comfort, and stare at the stars or the lights of ships far out at sea, and say that there, far away, was the land where Cuillin flew once when she was young, and she had been a vagrant like them, a wanderer, a dreamer. Then they would shake their feathers with just a touch of pride and think that there was one great eagle who might have understood them and seen that, low as they were, yet there was pride deep in them still.

But there came a time, at the end of the summer when Clew left Askaval and Ruann to start his journey, that Mourne drew herself apart and fell into despair that she would have to live out another winter mate-less and without purpose. She took a stance among the cliffs and stared out at the western horizon, wondering what was her real task in life. Was it really to live here among lost vagrants? Then she would find herself drawn back among her vagrant friends, telling stories to them of things she had heard, about an eagle she had once known, a female, who had actually been up near the legendary Storrin and had met eagles who claimed to have seen the last flight of Cuillin. She would tell them, though it was only a story mind, that Cuillin had produced young, just one, a male, and his name was Askaval.

Then she would stop and say no more, and others would talk and share their hopes in the tales they told. In their dreams Mourne found she could lose herself, and not have to think of who she had once been. That was finished now. Then she went off alone again, among distant coastal cliffs—for what was the use of it all? It was on such a trip that she heard, to her alarm, that a great eagle from Romsdal had come looking for a female he had lost.

'His mate?' asked Mourne.

They shrugged. 'Said her name was Mourne, and we told him straight there was no eagle of that name around here.'

Mourne slunk away and hid herself again among the furthest cliffs. Her listlessness increased and she skulked in the shadows, watching the kittiwake and fulmar.

It was on such a grey day she saw him a little out to sea, flying slowly down the coast. An old eagle of wise flight, whose name she knew and whose name she feared. It was Clew. Did her fear make her move in the shadows, the sudden glint of her white tail show where she was hiding? Or was it instinct made old Clew turn towards the cliff? He glided into the darkness of the cliff and took a stance somewhere above her. There Clew fell into a deep silence, staring down at Mourne but saying nothing. She occasionally looked back up at him, before turning her head down to her breast.

'Why have you come?' she said at last. 'Why don't you leave me in peace here?'

Yes. Why had he come for her, and spent the past months searching the fjords and coasts, gathering a clue here and there, listening to raven and gull, and vagrant eagle, until he tracked her down and found her? He did not know—but he was wiser now, and listened to those things his heart and feelings told him.

Her forehead was scarred where Askaval had pecked at her when they were so young; her wings were grubby and tatty, her breast feathers marred by oil and tar gathered around the ports and harbours where she and the other vagrants fed. But, for all that, when he looked at her, he felt a sudden hope inside himself, and a resolution of the doubts and uncertainties that had racked him for so long.

'How is he?' she asked finally.

Clew came nearer. 'Askaval is well,' he said softly, 'strong and well.' He added softly, 'Come back with me to Romsdal. Come and live there in peace now. None will harm you.'

She shook her head violently and cried out: 'I can never go back there now. They will point at me and whisper that this poor eagle was Cuillin's daughter, and once Askaval's sister. I wish only that Romsdal eagles forget about me, and Hardanger eagles, too. I wish my name to be forgotten. I wish . . .' and she stared out across the sea.

'What do you really wish?' asked Clew, very softly.

She stared on in silence, the loneliness now redoubling inside her.

Before his gaze, which was gentle and loving and very strong, she could only speak the truth. What *did* she wish?

'There have been changes coming for years now. Once, with Askaval, I tried to tell him, but he did not really understand. I was afraid, for I knew I would not have the strength to face them alone. So I let my jealousy feed my fear, and I let my fear corrupt itself into anger, and I turned to Sleat—and all of that you already know. Then I came here, and found I have much to learn from those I once would have despised. Lately, I have sensed those changes more strongly, and I have known I cannot escape what they will bring.'

'You still have not said what you wish for yourself,' he reminded her gently.

'A territory,' she said promptly. 'A mate to care for. A good wind. A place where all eagles fly true. To have young again, and see them fly from the home territory, not caring if they are of Romsdal or of Hardanger, or any other kind, just that they know they are eagles.' She scuffed her talons on the rock and put her head on one side. 'Just a dream,' she added. 'None would have me now, nor would I offer myself. Those days are past.' She fell silent.

But Clew laughed at her melancholy for, despite her appearance, he knew she was still young. Mourne had lived in darkness and self-shame rather too long, and he did not forget his promise to Cuillin, to care for them both, Mourne and Askaval, and trust them.

'Do you remember your mother?' asked Clew.

Mourne was silent, thinking. She remembered how it was cold in the nest. She remembered she was alone and shivering. She could feel over her body the great spread of Cuillin's wings as she turned and flew away. She remembered how she knew her mother would never come back.

'Yes,' she said finally.

'And what is it you *really* wish—beyond those dreams you mentioned, which every eagle has?'

'To fly true, as she did,' said Mourne.

'Look at me,' ordered Clew.

Reluctantly Mourne did so.

'What do you see?'

'An eagle I am afraid of,' said Mourne. 'A wise eagle who flew with my mother. An eagle before whom I cannot lie or escape from truth. An eagle who will bring me trial and suffering.'

Clew flexed his talons on the rock, his head and eyes looking beyond Mourne and down at the sea, following the light of the sky on the waves.

'An eagle who knows me too well,' Mourne added. She said it with a hint of laughter, and she felt some burden fall from her wings.

And Clew then saw just a hint of how another eagle had once been. He saw the daughter of Cuillin, the Fremmed.

'There is no time left now,' he said. 'I have things to do, and I will need your help.'

'I cannot go to Romsdal,' protested Mourne. But he shook his head.

'Further north?' asked Mourne, disbelieving. Again he shook his head.

'Where, then?' demanded Mourne, now impatient.

'To the land of ice and fire,' said Clew, 'where the great Haforn herself was born.' Until that moment he had not known, but as he spoke the words he knew it was so. The hidden had become the obvious. 'It is where we must try to go,' he added.

'But I am weak, far too weak for a long flight. I have been ill too long.'

'I am no stronger,' said Clew, for before her humility he understood his own frailty. 'May Haforn give us strength.'

They flew past Romsdal in the dark of a winter's night, Clew leading on a route he had flown long before, and Mourne following in the path of their mother.

As they flew north of Romsdal fjord, she sensed in the dark that she was very close to her brother Askaval, whose territory was only a little inland from where they flew. She wanted to call out to him from her mind, as they had been able to when they were young: to tell him that the dark years were over, and her love and trust in him was deeper now than it had ever been. But she closed her mind to doing so, for she feared he would hear and follow her, and she was ashamed of the years when Sleat had taken her and held her in his power. So she flew on, following Clew northward.

While Askaval stirred suddenly at his roost to stare out into the winter night, Ruann nearby, and the fjord waters lapping coldly at the cliffs below. And he thought he heard his name called in the dark sky—and the sound of a voice he loved.

'What is it, Askaval?' asked Ruann, aware of his trouble.

'Nothing. Just a dream,' he whispered, but it *was* something. He sensed a grace come on him, and was thankful for the strength he had always possessed, and for the love that had always been given him. He felt the burden of leadership come on him and was grateful to Haforn that he had Ruann at his side. In the dark night, Romsdal and Hardanger eagle were one, and as one they could fight off the Doom or turn it to their favour.

He stared out westward into the darkness, at the presence he could sense, and he was filled with a joy and love for what he had, and for the challenge of the changes to come.

★　★　★　★　★

The same summer that Jim found himself running from Christine King and into a world of painting and sculpture, Michael, his brother, finally turned to God. He became a Roman Catholic—having fallen, without Margaret Stonor knowing, into the spiritual arms of Father David Cullock of Dover, whom he met through the Roman Catholic group at school. Michael was accepted into that church shortly after he had taken his A-levels. He took distinctions in all three, and was offered places at both Oxford and London universities—in one to read Theology, in the other History.

Margaret Stonor might have been delighted to see the third of her four sons so academically successful, except that she feared, with a cold fear that kept her wakeful at nights, the grip that religion had taken on him. She had seen it on her father, and on her father's friends and students. It might make them saints, but more often it made men cold, arrogant, pig-headed and, quite simply, wrong.

To Jim, Michael's growing obsession with religion was at once curious and scaring. Michael's room was Frank's old one, across the stairs at the top of the house. It was neat and ordered, and housed Michael's growing collection of books, almost all religious, theological, religious-biography, or religious-literary. This was in contrast to Jim's haven, facing on to Compass Street, which was untidy and full of junk—objects he had made or objects he had found. Cork floats from the beach, an easel he made himself from some wood Albert Chandler retrieved from a house demolition job, objects made of wire, maps of Kent he had found in junk shops and had stuck on the walls, and his wartime radio, big and cumbersome and made of brown bakelite, the worked gold cloth where the speaker was now pierced and frayed. And his ten-volume Arthur Mee *Children's Encyclopedia*, his fishing tackle and a few cheap art books.

Michael was grave now and rather dark, and he had his hair cut very short, which made him look ascetic. He also developed sudden obsessions, usually based on books he was reading about great Catholic figures. Over one lunchtime, when it was lovely and warm and the bees were bumbling about by the red-pink holly-hocks outside the garden door, and ants were crawling on the paving stones, he started telling the story of St Benedict, of whose Rule for monastic worship and living he now had a copy. The image of a man who retired to live in a cave for three years, in fact, rather fascinated Jim.

'Bet you wouldn't survive for long as a hermit on the Dunes in winter,' he said seriously. Michael took this as mockery and fell silent, hurt rather than angry, beatific rather than relaxed. Jim was conscious that his mother quickly changed the subject.

Frank, now an accountant, and an occasional visitor at weekends that summer, was brutal in argument with Michael, and evidently bored by his heroic ecclesiastical stories. He was also beginning to think about marriage and offended Michael by saying that he presumed he would not wish to be invited to an Anglican service. At this time Oliver was away in Germany for a year, doing a postgraduate course in languages.

Jim watched and listened but said little. Although Michael ignored him and never drew him into discussions with the various friends that visited that summer, yet still he felt closest to Michael and understood, better than Frank or their mother, the painful struggle for faith that was going on inside him. He disturbed Michael praying more than once, and sometimes heard him early in the morning, moving around his bedroom whispering words in an agonised voice. And Jim suffered something of Michael's own suffering on the path towards revelation. When Frank or their mother was hostile, however subtly, he understood Michael's hurt, and admired his strength of purpose in resisting them, even if he did not understand it. For though he felt a soaring of spirit at school services sometimes, and especially at Christmas in the anonymity of carol singing, he did not feel Michael's path to be the right one, neither for himself nor, indeed, for Michael.

Finally, towards the end of summer – and at the last moment as far as the university was concerned – Michael accepted his place at Oxford to read Theology, for Father Cullock said it had a very strong Roman Catholic tradition, and he would be in good hands there. The Church needed trained theologians, and God would lead him on the right path.

He left on a Saturday so he could have a weekend to settle in at Worcester College, and he packed two suitcases and put them down by the front door. Standing there, looking down as their mother was about to kiss Michael, Jim thought that he had seen him look that way before: rather frightened, rather lonely.

'I'll come down to the station with you,' Jim said impulsively.

'There's really no need,' said Michael.

'I'll carry one of the cases,' said Jim.

'Thanks,' said Michael.

They walked in silence down Compass Street, Michael looking back at his mother at the door, who waved for a moment but closed the door before they reached Middle Street. Down Farrier Street then, and over to St George's churchyard, the way Jim went daily to school.

'Didn't you want to look at the sea one last time?' asked Jim. That's what he would have done.

'I'll see it again,' said Michael. 'I'm not going forever, you know.'

But he was, Jim knew it. If he came back it wouldn't be the same; just as it wasn't the same ever again after he came back from that month near Canterbury with the tutor. They walked in silence, Jim finding the case rather heavy and leaning over on one side to counter the weight of it. But for all that, and though he was rather shorter than Michael, who was now six foot, Jim looked the stronger of the two.

There seemed nothing much to say.

'How's that friend of yours, Peter Conan?' asked Michael.

'Okay, I'spect. Haven't heard from him since last Christmas.' No, he had received a postcard from France.

'He was the one who was keen on ornithology, wasn't he?' asked Michael.

'This case is heavy, isn't it?' said Jim.

'It's got my books in it. You're not to touch the ones I left behind, or the record player. Mummy's going to send them on to me by carrier.'

'Okay,' said Jim. Such instructions went over his head: he had heard them all his life from one brother or another.

They said nothing personal to each other, but even so, Jim felt comradely walking next to his brother—and needed. Michael was cleverer than he was, and going to Oxford and all that, but sometimes, on the rare occasions when they had been out together somewhere, perhaps over Dover Cliffs or on the Dunes or on the beach, it was Michael who was the awkward one. In those places Jim was stronger. Jim felt that way now, as if the road to the station was a road to somewhere wild and dangerous, where, in a funny sort of way, he could help Michael put his feet down safely.

Michael bought his ticket at the station and they stood awkwardly on the platform together, looking around to see if the signal indicating the approach of the train was up; and, when it was, looking to see if the train was in sight; and when that happened, picking up the cases and walking a little way down the platform unnecessarily.

'I like the old steam trains,' said Michael. 'Really powerful they are.'

Jim nodded. He agreed. He didn't feel the same about the electric trains that were being introduced. He had talked to Michael so little over the years that he didn't even realise he agreed with him on that.

Michael got into the train, and Jim watched him put the luggage on the rack. He had a book all ready to read, an old one with red, shiny, hard covers, and a gold cross embossed on it, and he laid it on the seat. Then he came out into the corridor and opened the window.

They made small talk, meaningless talk.

The train started to move at last.

'Hope it all goes okay,' said Jim.

'It'll be all right.'

As the train gathered speed, Jim called out, 'Good luck, Michael, and don't forget to wave from the other side of the train!'

It was a game all the boys played. On the London line the track curved beyond the station bridge, and for a brief moment you could lean out of the train on its far side – if you got across the carriage fast enough—and wave.

Under the bridge, curving round the track, the opposite window opened and Michael leaned out to wave. Even from that distance Jim could see he wasn't smiling, and his face was very serious. Jim waved encouragingly, and Michael waved back until the train went out of sight round the bend. A raggle-taggle of Deal folk, mostly parents, walked quietly back along the platform, and out through the ticket barrier. The brightest and youngest people always left Deal.

CHAPTER FIFTEEN

JIM Stonor had scraped into the Sixth Form—as his headmaster, Mr Gower, put it in the brief ninety second interview which decided his academic future—with five O-levels, including Art. Mr Gower discounted the Art result, which was, in fact, outstanding, as being of no academic interest. Everyone knew Stonor could draw, but drawings do not gain university places. His A-level subjects were to be Geography, English and History.

The gods of Academe, the masters had long ago decided, had failed the Stonor family when it came to Jim. Six years at school, rubbing shoulders with a boy term by term, tells a master most of what he needs to know about him. An experienced headmaster can probably predict most boys' likely A-level results by the time they are thirteen, five years before they ever sit the examinations. But there are always some who change: neat boys, tidy boys, industrious, well-meaning boys who do well up to O-level, while application and memory are enough to carry a boy forward—until, in the Sixth, he has to start thinking more for himself, and becomes mediocre. Or untidy, individualistic, bloody-minded tearaways, who in the Sixth sometimes suddenly change their attitude and show a flair for thought, and a willingness to work, which give the lie to the previous years' waste. Perhaps it was not waste after all.

Jim Stonor fell into the latter camp in all but results: he was one of the ones who grew their hair long, turned up late some mornings, or who found excuses for not coming to the Combined Cadet Force in uniform, and attended the skivers' parade.

'Reason for no uniform, Stonor?' says Captain James, Commanding Officer.

'Got tar on it, Sir.'

'Tar, Stonor?'

'From the beach, sir.'

'How on earth did you do that? Show me it's been cleaned before next Tuesday, will you, Stonor?'

'Yes, sir.'

'At ease. Easy.'

It was a lie, of course, but Stonor's reasons were always better than most and indicated a certain imagination. Boys never understood that masters had heard it all before, until they, too, became masters, or started employing people, or became parents, or all three. Then they learned, if only in retrospect.

383

The enormity of A-levels did not hit Jim until the start of the year he entered the Sixth Form. But then, in that year, the enormity of a lot of things began to hit him. One was the reaffirmation of that fear he had felt when he said goodbye to Michael at the station on his way to Oxford, and Jim had realised for the first time that the secure life he led at home would soon disappear. He, too, would be on his own.

Another realisation was the littleness of the town he lived in and its limitations and enclosures. Even at his mediocre level of education – rushed essays, second-rate marks, passages of Chaucer poorly learnt at the last moment or climatic regions on the train to school – even with that he began to find he was streets, years, lifetimes ahead of Mrs Angel and old Albert Chandler in knowledge; and even of his mother, who had forgotten her history.

Had he been a high academic achiever, he might have been blinded into an arrogance about their lack of knowledge, but he felt too grubby in what few achievements he had at school, too low down in the B streams of his year's History and English sets, to believe that his knowledge made him better than they were. But he did seem to have learnt a lot of things they did not know. Yet when Albert talked to him of wood and tools, and showed him how to use a lathe or French-polish a surface, he sometimes wished he, too, could be so calm and sure. Often, too, he would have a cup of tea with Grace Frewin or Mrs Angel next-door, and get them to tell him about the last war, or about their childhood. 'It was a different world then, my love, different and more interesting in a way. Mind you, I'm not against change. That'll always be here, always. But there was time then, you see, time to stop and chatter about this and that; time to wander along with your Mam and play a game or two. That sort of leaves you when you grow up. In them days we had next to nothing, but we were as happy as the day is long.'

He listened to them talk and they didn't mind him drawing them, because they knew he was restless without a pencil in his hand and that sketch-pad at his knee.

That year was so strange, so wild in his mind, so hard for him to bear sometimes. He was a loner who was terribly alone, in a house that had empty rooms and a sense now of disregard, as if it was waiting for the very time – which Grace Frewin and Mrs Angel valued so much – to pass on by.

He was filled with rushing urges to do things, like cycle over to Dover on Oliver's old racer, pushing on the pedals as hard as he could all the way, sweat on his back and wind at his arms and cuffs, and running through his hair. Fast, faster, the pedals an enemy to push away again and again, and the handlebars to take the strain of each push, push, push, up the road to Walmer, or Drum Hill and out into the country at Ringwould, with the dead windmill on the right and the chalk all around, rolling subtly into vales of fallow ground and corn.

Swoop into the wind past the dog kennels down in Oxney Bottom, and then up another roll of chalk on the long run up towards the Duke of York's Military School, and into sight of the great ramparts of Dover Castle. No time to look. No time to stop. Driven by a demon pubescent energy. The steep one-in-four drops down into Dover town, with the bike going so fast that the frame itself shudders, and the back brake is too weak to hold the bike, so the front one goes on as well, juddering and racing, body falling ahead of the bike and the wind raw at his ears. Dangerous!

At the bottom of Dover hill, Jim would turn round, not bothering with the town, and start back up again, climbing the edge of the dry valley of chalk, sometimes too weak to cycle up it and forced to get off and push. Other times, his energy was so great he would madly cycle all the way up, to exhaust himself, his face contorted with effort, towards the top of the great hill, until at last the Castle came into view and the chalk flattened out, and then he was racing back down the dip slope, all the seven miles into Deal.

He would cycle to Canterbury in the same way, learning the grain and run of the country, and seeing how its autumnal browns and reds gave way to winter greys and blacks, before the first blue skies and green shoots of spring came back. Old-Man's Beard and rustling dead beech leaves, bright green holly and bundles of red berries, then the deadness of January, the bitter snows across the Downs, a bicycle wheel sliding away on rutted ice, before snowdrops again, and celandine, and the promise of a life not yet fulfilled. The terrible loneliness of spring and early summer days. The pulling of wild seas at shingle shores, where he stood in tar-marked wellington boots which were size nine now, shaving every morning, lip-kissed, knowledge-tried and knowledge-bound, unzipping his anorak open for the wind to cut into him and tussle at his throat. His writing stronger, his speech firmer but standing on an edge of a dark sea he feared and yet must soon start to cross.

Often Jim retreated into his own room at the top of the house, and closed the door on the little world he no longer much liked. He lay on the bed and switched on his old radio, turning the knob to run through the stations, to see what languages he could recognise. Michael and Mummy were very good at that: German, French, Italian and Spanish and Greek . . . And he could recognise all of them now, even if he could only understand a few of the words, and then mostly names—Londres, de Gaulle, Berlin, General

Franco . . . He would switch on the Short-Wave because you could pick up fascinating Morse signals, and sometimes ships talking to each other out on the Downs. He played for hours with the radio sometimes, especially at night when its distant variable signals and snatches of incomprehensible jabber were at their most mysterious. At night you could get Middle-Eastern music, and Radio Luxembourg was good then, and religious broadcasts for American servicemen in Germany.

That was how, too, he had first heard Bill Haley and Elvis Presley.

One day, as the set jabbered away, he slowly turned the knob, not to find a station that made any sense but to distort the sound and vibrations and lose himself in the distant world they came from. A snatch of a French song, summarily cut off. Morse at a high frequency. Turn on, and on, through a veil of signals . . . A distant male voice. Past it, then back to it again. A new language he did not recognise. He homed in on it, the needle of the tuning knob settling incongruously on Daventry, the wartime station. But it was a different channel, and this voice was not English, or German or French. He had thought it male, but the more he listened to it, or tried to, it came over as female. It seemed as if it was calling out from a distant, hostile place, entrapped by threatening radio signals, a voice in a wilderness place which needed help. It suited his mood. He listened, fabricating a fantasy round the lost voice that came stronger and then weaker, and then stronger again, as if rocked gently across a dark sea. He decided it was Scandinavian because it had rolling soft vowels and hard 'ck's' and 'rr's'.

He was interrupted by his mother coming up the stairs.

'Mummy, Mummy,' he yelled out. They still called her that, even Frank. 'Come'n'see if you recognise this language.'

She came in and settled on his bed to listen, some sheets over her arms. She frowned and strained to hear.

'I think it's Scandinavian,' he said to pre-empt her, and show that he might know.

She nodded. 'Mmm,' she said, 'I think you're right, dear.' Then after listening a bit more, her eyes softened and she smiled and got up. 'It's Danish,' she said, then frowned again. 'Unless it's . . .' She paused. He turned the volume up and the voice seemed to waver and hesitate, now loud, now soft, against the buzz and crackle of static, as if it came from far, far away across a grey sea falling into darkness.

'No. You know what I think it is,' she said finally. 'I think it's one we've never heard before. It's so like Danish, only older. I think it's Icelandic.'

386

He turned the radio up a bit after she left, and went to his school atlas and opened it at Scandinavia. With the sound of the distant voice calling for help, he stared, without really looking, at the map, his eyes travelling up the jagged coast of Norway until it reached an area boxed off at the page top, because the place it showed would have been off the map otherwise. It was Iceland. Then he turned to his old Arthur Mee encyclopaedia and looked it up. Geysers and Volcanoes and Glaciers. Then he started to read about Iceland as the lost voice on the radio came to him in his old familiar room with its call from over the dark sea.

* * * * *

Clew and Mourne had flown north, up the Norwegian coast—where Clew had gone once before with Cuillin, Mizen and Weever to find the Weir. Decades ago, that seemed, when they were all so much younger—younger than Mourne was now.

Then, he had flown urgently, led onwards by Cuillin. This time he flew very differently, for he was uncertain of his objective. And he soon found that Mourne was very weak and unable to fly far. She suffered aches and pains, and though her flight was clear, her stamina was poor. So they flew in short stages, a wandering sort of flight, making long stops along the coast for days at a time, while they found food and rested, and he watched the trouble and strain begin to lift from her wings.

It was the time of migration again, and they were going against the grain as sweep after sweep of sea-birds and duck flew past them southwards, until they began to thin out and the weather to cool as the days grew shorter into November.

Clew, who had spent so many years alone and was a natural solitary, found it strangely joyful to travel with Mourne. She was quiet company and spoke little, seeming to understand when he wanted to talk for a while, or fly away alone for an hour to hunt an unknown fjord in privacy.

One day, six weeks after they had first started on their journey, and still only two hundred miles north of Romsdal, he came back after a flight alone and found her stooping down into the sea to take fish. It was a grey day, and the coast behind her was dark. And though there was little colour in her feathers, because the light was poor, yet he saw that her wings were great and wide. And he realised that the eagle she was becoming, as health and purpose came back to her, had a strength and purpose very different from the one he had known first of all.

He watched as she folded back her wings and pushed down her talons, her head bent forward and her eyes fixed on a mullet or bass just below the surface, and then she dived swift and sure—seeming almost as powerful as Cuillin herself had been. As Mourne opened her wings and beat them out of the spray, a fish firm in her right talon, its tail writhing to break free, he knew she would soon have the strength for whatever it was Haforn would ask her to do. And he knew her strength would be part of all their hope and destiny.

One day when the weather had grown steadily colder and the air stiller, so that the sea beneath them was becalmed, and their flight slow, they came to rest at a place isolated from the towns and roads they had seen along the coast. It was a nondescript, deserted territory, with a few skerries offshore and a cliff full of kittiwake to scream and slide over the winds, and circle above them. It was Mourne who stopped there, and Clew took her lead. The air was heavy with cold, the cloud cover grey but high, the sea flat.

Clew did not like the place, for it seemed neither here nor there, a place of transit, unsettled. 'Let's go on a bit,' he said.

'This is as far north as we need go,' she said firmly, for she seemed to be gaining in strength and confidence every day.

Soon after they arrived there, a couple of juveniles came foraging down the coast, and seeing them, and since it was November and not a territorial time, came over to join them. They took stances some way off below them, though whether in deference to Mourne's evident size and strength, or to Clew's obvious wisdom, it was hard to say.

'Where are you bound?' one of them asked in the soft, gentle voice of eagles from the Lofoten Islands to the north.

Clew and Mourne stayed silent for a while, though Clew bowed his head just a little to acknowledge their presence.

'Far,' said Mourne, finally.

'We're going south to Romsdal,' said the other enthusiastically. Are you from there? You *look* like Romsdal eagles.'

'We are,' said Clew. 'Why are you going there?'

'Well, it's the place to go, they say,' declared one of the juveniles. 'Travel south. See the famous fjord. Catch sight of the great eagles there like Sleat and Askaval, son of Cuillin . . .'

'You've heard of them?' asked Mourne.

'Haven't you?' responded the juvenile. 'Anyway, things are happening up in Lofoten we don't like . . .'

'What things?' asked Clew.

'Strange lights over the sea to the west, strange colours at dawn. Strange discoloration in the water, strange things high in the sky. The old eagles in Lofoten say Haforn is angry.'

'But why go south?' asked Mourne.

'Well, we're not going north, that's for sure, and the winter's hard on us youngsters without regular prey-grounds. Look, if you're from there, why not travel back with us? If it's not too presumptious to suggest it! Surely you're not going north at this time of year?' They chattered on in the way immatures do, asking questions too eagerly even to wait for a reply, so neither Clew nor Mourne found they had to explain what they were about.

A day or two later, another juvenile deferentially joined them, and Mourne suddenly felt quite mature. They seemed in no hurry to leave, and eventually recognised in Clew a source of information and stories which they hoped to make the most of. At first he had been reticent, but really he had always been happy to tell others what he knew—and did so now. Though he was careful not to reveal who he was—not, for any reason, wishing to mislead them, but because he was genuinely modest and found it embarrassing when eagles stared at him in awe because he had been guardian for so many years of Cuillin's territory.

So he told them of Cuillin's flight north, as if it was a legend he had heard, and of the Gathering, and of the power of the Storrin. He told them of the mating of Cuillin and Finse, and of the birth of Askaval and an eagle called Mourne.

As he spoke, and the afternoon lengthened, he was very conscious of how closely Mourne was listening, and how moved she was. For he knew she remembered parts of the story, and now relived them, understanding them afresh and tending to see the light now as well as the shadows. Until at last, Clew turned to her and said: 'Mind you, my friend here knows more about Askaval and Mourne than I do, because . . . she knew them didn't you?'

'Well!' exclaimed one of the youngsters, 'That's a bit of luck', turning to Mourne.

Mourne cast a grim glance for a moment at Clew, who looked down at his talons just a shade embarrassed, yet she entered into the spirit of the exchanges between them, and told them this and that, trying to remember always to substitute a 'she' for 'I', when she spoke of herself in the stories she told. Though the air was still clear, the wind was worsening, coming in cold gusts off the land and driving westward out to the distant horizon. They moved a little to gain shelter from it, the kittiwake soaring up the cliff-face and into the wind, and then in great flashing circles round and out to sea, before diving low and coming back to the cliff. Below them, a little way out, flocks of birds still passed occasionally, the last migrations trying to make as much ground in the daytime as they could. And with them came solitaries, the odd duck or wader that had left its departure from a favoured ground later than other, less well-provided birds; or ones that were weak from injury or sickness, making their own way south.

Among them came yet another sea eagle, ragged-looking and old, which, seeing the small group of juveniles and vagrants in the shelter of the cliff, came to join them.

'Whither are you bound?' he asked, rather formally.

'Far,' they said, Clew barely looking at him.

'To Romsdal,' said the juveniles.

'Where are you from?' asked Mourne, cutting short her story out of courtesy to the old eagle.

'From the north,' he said, 'but please continue. Don't let me interrupt you . . .'

So Mourne continued to tell the story of her 'friends', Askaval and Mourne, and the youngsters listened enthralled, while Clew thought it good that she could tell it, and the old eagle eased himself into shadows and worked his beak through his feathers, preening them after his day's flight—but listening.

'So finally she left Sleat in upper Romsdal and flew south where she joined a group of vagrants,' said Mourne.

'What happened to her after that?' asked one of the juveniles.

'Well, I don't really know. I lost track then,' said Mourne.

'Oh!' said the juvenile, disappointed.

'She flew north,' interrupted the old eagle quietly, speaking from the shadows. 'She went on a journey of great courage, and started a flight over the dark sea. For her name was Mourne and she was the daughter of Cuillin, and that was her doom . . .'

His voice was gentle, so soft and rolling that it was almost as if it was not he who was speaking but a whisper of the wind around them.

The juveniles were fascinated by this sudden new information but Mourne and Clew were both struck dumb. Then Clew moved nearer to the old eagle, staring at him, yet not quite able to make him out there in the shadows, where the wind ruffled his feathers. While Mourne felt suddenly awed and frightened, for she knew the old eagle spoke the truth. He was telling her what would happen.

Then all of them fell still and quiet, and let the night take them into sleep, though the wind roared louder over the cliffs above them, driving westward, cold and freezing, out across the sea. Until, when dawn came, even the kittiwake were still, except for the odd individual who launched off from the cliff at the sight of distant day, up over its highest edge, and then let the great wind take its wings and drive it, arcing and cutting, round and round over the roughening sea, so that it was several hundred yards out before it was able to swoop down and start beating back over the surface.

Then the old eagle stirred, and his feathers, which had been tatty and ragged the night before, now seemed silvery and fine in the dawning grey light, and he took a stance near Mourne.

'Come now, Mourne, it is time to start, for the wind is strong and dawn is breaking. Come now, and trust in Haforn, to whose land you can make your flight. Wake now and come with me.'

So she woke, into the stillness of his presence, and saw he was an eagle like none she had ever seen, and one whose wings she could always trust.

'Who are you?' she asked, half-afraid and half-joyful.

'I am the one they call the Weir,' he said, 'and I am he who flew with Cuillin, your mother, who gave so much. She gave her strength to Askaval, her first-born, and to you, Mourne, her second. And we must leave now before the others wake, for otherwise my brother Clew will wish to come. His task is here with the youngsters, to lead them as he led you, to guide them, to give them love. So come now, and trust in Haforn.'

Mourne looked at him, and out over the great sea which seemed to stretch for an eternity ahead of them. 'But I have no strength to fly so far. I am not like my mother was, for she was the Fremmed, and had great power.'

But he ignored her words and turned towards the sea below them and opened his wings, and she found herself doing the same. Then he leaned forward into the void, and pushed off, turning back to face the cliff, to ride up its slipstream until he was nearly at its highest edge where the wind was blowing seaward, before turning back for her. As he came back, she pushed off to his side, and together they soared up the face of the cliff, until the great wind suddenly took their wings and they turned, as one, to fly westward. And the wind carried them forward faster and ever faster over the sea, making for Haforn's homeland.

As they left, the size and strength of them sent kittiwake flying and calling in alarm, and their cries woke up the eagle youngsters. And they saw, out over the sea, the female they had shared a stance with, and the old male, except that from this distance, in the dawning light, his wings seemed to be aflame with sky, and his flight was so true that it seemed the centre of the very sea and earth and sky together. Some instinct forbade them from waking Clew, so that when he finally stirred from a trouble-free sleep, he found that Mourne had gone, and the other eagle with her. And from the youngsters' description he guessed who it had been, and why the Weir had come. Then, rather thankfully, for a flight across the dark sea was not his way, not *today* at any rate, he told the youngsters that it would be a pleasure to lead them south to Romsdal, which was a good place to winter. Before they left, he spent a moment alone, to think about Mourne and the Weir, and to wish them well, and to pray that Haforn might keep the wind blowing their way.

Perhaps no flight in all the history of the sea eagles was ever of such importance as that of Mourne and the Weir across the dark sea to Haforn's land. Yet history in the making is rarely so dramatic as history told, and the truth is that the flight itself, aided all the way by strong winds from the hinterland of Scandinavia, was a long and tedious one. Yet had it been summer, it would have been achieved within a single span of daylight hours. It being November, however, darkness fell early, at a moment when Mourne was beginning to feel the strain of so many hours on the wing, even if the wind was so perfect that they were able to soar and glide most of the way. It was for just such a moment that the Weir had accompanied her, for she still had much to learn of endurance and stamina.

'We are well on the way and our direction feels right, so now we must trust Haforn and press on into darkness. Keep north of the setting sun, and trust your instinct.'

So they pressed on, after the setting sun had disappeared, on into darkness, over a grey-silver sea that stretched beneath them and beneath a black sky. Never once on that flight did Mourne think of what would happen if they failed to make landfall before they grew too tired to fly; though every eagle knows that fear only too well. A few minutes on the surface of the sea, playing a floating seagull, may be survived, but an hour or two, and an eagle's feathers are too waterlogged ever to fly again, and she dies by slow drowning. Never once did Mourne think of that, but the fear was always there. Until at last the air grew bitterly cold, and the following wind that had helped them began to die, and she found she was becoming more and more tired with the beating of her wings.

'Can you tell the air is different?' she asked Weir, excitedly.

'We're almost there. Press on now. Keep on . . .'

But 'almost' turned into an hour, and it was further into night before they saw, over to their right, a dim yellow light, and heard across the water the heavy, irregular ringing of a buoy bell. They headed towards it, and might have settled on it, but that they could make out, if only dimly, a darker mass rising from the sea, on which there were more lights. They had reached land. Towards it, warily, they flew, moving to the south of the lights and along the coast to find some hidden inlet among the cliffs, in which to take a stance until morning.

When it came, just another grey dawn, the Weir turned to Mourne and said: 'We are here, at last, and now we have our different tasks to do. I have my own search to make . . .'

And Mourne began to feel frightened of what he was about to say.

'. . . And you have yours. Only Haforn knows its full nature, and she will guide you, Mourne. There are other sea eagles here, but they are few, and far away across the land. Follow the signs their ancestors have left, seek out the Lomagnup, fly over the great ice, beware the fire and fumes, learn to trust your instinct and to feel your strength, which is great and growing. Try and . . .'

'But aren't you coming with me?' she cried out. He shook his head. 'At least part of the way?' she pleaded. 'And what is the Lomagnup?'

'You will know it—a cliff, a dark cliff. It is best you start out alone. Trust yourself and trust that I will find you again one day. And remember you have time, much time, for now . . . You will know finally where to go, and when to leave . . .' And then, quietly, as if she had always been alone, he was gone, and she began to search for she knew not what.

The land she found herself in was treeless and sparse. Its hills and mountains were, for the most part, of horizontal basalt strata, brittle and faulted, so that deep beneath their terraces steep runs of scree had formed. These cliffs on top of cliffs rose to flat-topped fjells which seemed more newly-formed than any she had known all her life before. It was November and there was snow about, but thin snow that only seemed to highlight the terraces and striations, fractures and clefts across the rising strata, by gathering along them, or avoiding them, where they were steep, so that there were long lines of white ice and snow between lines of black, bare rock above and below. While everywhere, more than she had ever seen, ran torrents and brooks, raging streams and angry rivers, white and foaming, and coursing their way down the terraces into the valleys.

There were few humans, and she could fly undisturbed for hours above wild, desolate beaches, or in the shadow of great rising cliffs so massive in height and length that they seemed to absorb and dwarf whole colonies of sea-birds.

The coast waters were rich in fish and in seal, and she took them with ease. No sea eagles; no sleark. But other raptors hung about: merlin, hawk, and gyr falcon, high and diving; while along the outwash plains of black sand-debris that had formed between mountain and sea, there were the brown, plump, spiteful Arctic Skua, mouths opening at her in distrustful hostility.

But November is not an aggressive time for birds, for the young are gone, and territory is less well guarded, or not at all, so though she scattered smaller birds, or caused them to mob her occasionally, and other smaller raptors followed her from afar out of curiosity, she was generally unmolested.

In the first few days she travelled far, back and forth, along the coast and inland, but gradually she slowed down. There was time, much time, and a peace came to her with the shortening days and chillier nights. It came on her unawares, until she found, to her surprise, that she was not lonely in this great empty desolate place, content to wander and let Haforn have her will.

She took a slow and meandering course westwards along the southern coast, keeping near the shore but investigating the higher terraces for signs of sea eagle, for she knew that remnant nests may remain visible for decades after the pair that made them have gone. In those first few days, which became weeks, she saw several definite ones, and signs of many more, though all so long deserted that only a few bleached sticks and fractured bones of prey remained. Many were scattered—perhaps by raiding ravens taking nesting material for their own sites, or by predatory humans from the farms that occupied the lowest valleys and fjord sides. It was desolate and strange to see such continuous evidence of eagle occupation along mile after mile of seacoast in a land now completely deserted of eagles. But that a few still remained somewhere, at least she knew was true, because the Weir had said it. More than that, there were the legends and stories told her as a youngster, which spoke of sea eagles still in Haforn's land, blessed eagles long lost and forgotten across the dark sea—stories she only half-remembered.

She did not venture far inland, no more than a mile or two, because the ground rose into low mountains, and atop the ground beyond them was the continuous grey waste of an ice-cap. Glaciers she had seen often enough, and small permanent ice-caps too, but never one as broodingly vast as the one on her right wing here, which seemed even more extensive the further west along the coast she flew. It spread inland out of sight, even on the clearest day, into a place where no creature could live. Where the mountains rose higher and more rugged, it sent huge tributary glaciers plunging between them, grey and mucky at their snouts where they carried the moraine of rock and soil before them. While from beneath them, running down towards the sea, came rivers cloudy with silt and mud, which meandered across vast deltaic plains of black volcanic sand–debris.

Distances here were illusory, for the sparse flat ground gave no sense of scale or distance. But her first sighting of Lomagnup left no doubt of its massive scale. From the first it was a vast dark wall blotting out part of the western horizon.

When she reached it, Lomagnup loomed as dark and massive as a convectional storm, so high and steep and gouged by gorges that its cliffs and rises made their own light, and carried their own grim climate. It was so long that a solitary bird, flying its length, seemed never to move far from the end at which it started. So the colonies of fulmar that drove across its face merely added to its sense of ungovernable size.

There was food in the shape of birds and rabbits beneath the cliffs, and the sea was near, so Mourne decided to winter there, for now the nights were dark and long and day seemed a thing forgotten.

The place at first unnerved her in its complex deeps, and she felt as if she was being perpetually watched by eyes unseen among the great cliff's crags. While in the whine of a wind on a winter night, she might fancy she heard the call of a female to a male, yet when she sought it out in the gloom, only an eddy of blizzard snow rose in her face, and tugged at her great wings.

Yet when spring began to arrive she became certain that there was another eagle there, and a sea eagle too. One day she had proof. As she rose on a wind, turning a corner of the great serrated cliff that banked higher and ever higher in lost terraces above itself, she saw, on a patch of wind-flattened snow turned to ice, the frozen impression of an eagle's talon. Not a falcon's, nor her own. Slightly smaller than hers, a male's, and worn old as time. The Weir's? Instinct told her no, and yet she climbed higher in the wind calling out his name and staring endlessly at the sheer falls of rock and gullies beneath her, from any of which she might be watched. She was not afraid, but full of awe, tense and uncertain, anxious for her instinct to be satisfied by discovery. She felt she was being tested and tried, but she did not sense the eagle nearby was hostile.

Then she had further proof. One day, at a hidden stance, low on the great cliff, her eyes caught sudden sight of a falling thing, turning and plummeting grey and red, from far over along the cliff—plummeting down on to the scree below. She leaned out into the air and wheeled over the object, the March wind driving in blusters against her wings. The thing she had seen lay clear on the snow, whose white it had stained red. It was the torn body of a mountain fox, torn not battered, its belly gone, its head half-crushed. A mountain fox on a sheer, inaccessible cliff, hundreds of feet up? No, it was eagle prey. She looked up immediately and caught a glimpse of a disappearing wing, and then she started on an upward flight across the face of the cliff, but a face that changed to gullies cut deep into the cliff, where she could never find the eagle that had dropped its prey.

One raging dawn, at the end of March, when the sea-birds were beginning to scream and nest for a new season, she woke suddenly, urgently, and almost cried out 'What is it?' as if some eagle had called her name.

Normally, in such weather, she would have stayed still – she had prey enough cached away near her stance – but now she flew out and up, instinct taking her towards the higher turrets of the Lomagnup, sleet driving in waves before her, catching on her feathers and making it hard for her to fly and harder to see. Ahead there were peaks of black rock, with tiny patches of grass showing now on little terraces where nothing but a sea-bird might settle. Past these and higher, into a bowl of rock from which, in the distant past, there had been a cliff fall whose remnants now lay spread out down the scree and over the black sand. Round this bowl, set hundreds of feet off the ground, now hidden from sight by the blizzards below, the cliffs towered higher yet. There she thought she saw, far across in the driving rain and sleet, a solitary figure of an eagle, old and bowed. Strangely black with deep-set eyes, and staring over at her.

'Do not come nearer, fremmed from afar, who has found sanctuary through the harsh winter months in these ancient walls. Do not seek to find me here.' The voice came over to her, though so distorted by the wind around the walls that it did not seem to come from the eagle ahead. Or was it an eagle? Was it not an ancient, weathered rock that the wind had shaped to seem something else?

'Long have we waited for your coming, fremmed. Long years of waiting. Now time has caught up with us, and time runs out. Do not fear the great ice-cap, for it protects the fire that first gave us life. From near the edge of its grey heartland, Haforn, the Great One, first came. Fear it not. Now you must fly over it, and then north-west to where the few remaining eagles live. Fly to them over the fires of the earth. Fly to them like an eagle. Take in your wings all the strength and wisdom you have known. For they are waiting for you, though they do not know it. For I have told them you would come some time—and you have. Fly to them proudly, for you are a fremmed, the one we have longed for.'

His voice was old like the rock around her, yet clear and as if worn to a simplicity by the storms of time.

'Who are you?' she called.

'They will give you my name. Let the storm abate, and then go, for spring is here at the winter's turning, and there is much you must do and far to fly.' He spoke as if he knew where she should go. And her eyes searched the great place for clearer sign of him— for she now saw the thing she had thought was an eagle was but a twisted rock with snow for the tail, and shadow for the eyes. Yet other places there seemed to hint at a presence, watching, half-seen, impossible to pinpoint.

'How can I trust you?' she called out, though in truth it was just to say something, for his voice was truthful, and the place so strange and powerful that it was hard to believe he meant her harm.

'As you trusted the Weir,' he said.

So he knew the Weir—who had perhaps been here before her, to warn him of her coming.

'Why can't I talk more to you?' she called out.

'Mine is the old way, the lost language. I am the last. Your wings will carry us forward, but first you must fly to the remnant of the eagles who once flew over Haforn's land. Tell them your story, give them hope, tell them of a dream you have, show them promise and give them courage, for one day soon they will need it. Sow a dream with them that one day you may harvest it. So now, prepare to fly. And remember there is little time, for the Doom has long come, the Doom has overtaken your friends and foes alike. Now you must fly so powerfully that time itself will stop in your wings, and you will conquer it in flight. So you must look and see the world you cross, remember it, feel it in your wings, for you must tell your offspring, and they must tell theirs, so that sometime the Raven will hear and all will know. Seek out the ones who dare to speak my name. Give to them your power.'

She went forward to the rock that had seemed to be an eagle, and at its base was the clear spoor of eagle: the drag of tail feathers, the marks of talons. She flew over to the edge of the great place, where she thought she had seen an eagle's wing in shadow, and there on the ground was a worn feather, fresh-moulted, grey and dry, the feather of an ancient eagle, older by far than the Weir.

So it was that Mourne of Romsdal, born in the Storrin, came to Haforn's land, and after wintering at Lomagnup, she flew north one spring day over Vatnajokull, Europe's largest ice-cap. There she came upon the ancient volcanic area of Grimsvotn, which thrusts up from beneath the ice and where the surface of the earth is so warm that ice never forms. But around it, endless stretches of snow and bleak ice glisten in low sunshine, or the wastes rage white with blizzards in a storm. Here, in these desolations, Mourne first saw the rising steam of fumaroles which drifted out over the barren stretches of ice-free rock, all yellow and red and grey and strange. The air choking and bitter with the smell of sulphur, which is the smell of the molten earth from which Great Haforn once came. Here she watched, alone in an ice waste, the sulphuric steam rising about her, feeling at her talons the eternal impermanence of the earth. Sensing that deep beneath her were forces so great that, should they erupt around her, their power would be a million times greater than even Haforn's great wings. Only by cunning, by courage, by stealth and in true flight, can eagle ever survive such powers—wary of land, forever wary of the sea, whose dripping grip will drown an eagle fool enough to let it take a hold. Over this strange waste at Grimsvotn she flew, over the ice again towards the mountains that rose at the perimeter of the ice-cap. Inland to the north-west. There she headed, just as the old eagle had instructed her, Mourne daughter of Cuillin, whom even the ravens praise.

They say she found a wild beauty up there where no creature runs and no bird flies, and a peace and a power came to her wings. They say she risked death by taking a stance in an overhang of ice turrets, so that she might witness the night fall, and dawn break, over a landscape of ice. There she waited for two days without food, watching the rise of light over deep-blue chasms of ice, and strange refractions of pink and green which shone on those rocks that broke through the pall of ice. Then, too, in the distance to the west, she saw a sleeping volcano, which must be Hekla, out of which in distant times the Great One, Haforn, came. This greatly awed her. Then, when she was ready, Mourne spread her wings and started a steady flight towards the mountains, over and past them, and on in the direction she had been told to go.

There in the north-west, where the spring comes sudden and clear, and the skerries along the coast are bright with sea pink, and alive with the call of oyster-catcher and redshank, and the evenings fall quiet with soft whimbrel calls, there she came at last and found a lost population of sea eagles. There, where the land is vast and deserted, a high dissected plateau of basalt, terrace rising on black terrace, with lonely lakes and drifts of frozen snow . . . there, where the fjords cut deep inland, she found seven pairs of adults, and another twelve juveniles. They were the remnant—all that was left. From north, from east, from south, their ancestors had been driven, shot on cliff sites, poisoned at skerries, disturbed by watchers, and killed by ignorance. Sharp-headed gannet, snub fulmar, fluttering tern and darting turnstone, they had taken over the territories lost. But sometimes, up in some lost height, where overhang or cliff-face had left a place unseen and untrodden, there a high-flying fulmar might see, or a falcon observe, the bleached bones and sticks that marked out the ancient site of an eagle's nest.

Mourne saw them before they saw her. Two females idling by the seaward rocks of one of the fjords. She was excited and full of hope, but as she flew fully into view and they rose up at sight of her, she thought she had never seen such resignation and bitterness in eagles' wings before. One was quite big and strong, the other rather weak in the way she flew, but both showed hopelessness in their flight.

'Call out your name and say whither you are bound,' said the larger one, speaking in a quaint old way the ritualistic greeting to a stranger, and doing her best to look aggressive. But Mourne felt that with one blow from her own wings this female would fall from the sky.

'My name is Mourne of Romsdal; I come in hope and peace.'

'Romsdal?' said the female in a suspicious, wary way.

Then Mourne realised that they could not possibly know its name.

'From across the dark sea,' she added boldly and with pride.

Both looked frightened, and at a loss. But the bigger female recovered herself and, trying to sound nonchalant, said, 'Then there will have to be a gathering to discuss your coming, to learn from you who you are and why you have come. In a day or two . . .'

'But at this time of year,' said Mourne surprised, 'when you are tending young and . . .?'

'Few young now. No young here,' said the smaller, rather pathetically. 'So it won't . . .'

But the other interrupted her: 'I will leave now and summon the Pairs together, and let Halldor Broken-Wing know, that he might come immediately. My name is Arngerd of Skotufjord and this is Thordis of Keflavik who will stay with you until the others arrive.'

With that the bigger one flew off, and Mourne could not help noticing that an aggressive urgency had come to her wings, an edge to the bitterness of flight she had observed earlier.

To Mourne's surprise, the moment Arngerd had flown off, Thordis began to circle round her, staring at her with fascination, as a juvenile sometimes stares at an adult of which it is in awe.

'Did the Fremmed send you?' asked Thordis eventually, with some distant touch of hope to her frail and feeble voice.

'The Fremmed?' asked Mourne, her heart suddenly racing.

Could they then know of Cuillin here? Had the Weir gone before her?

'You mean Cuillin?' asked Mourne.

Thordis looked blank.

'I know of no Fremmed,' said Mourne, 'save one who lived once years ago in Romsdal, and is gone now . . .'

At this, the hope that had come for a moment to Thordis's wings disappeared, and an even greater loss replaced it.

'Then the Fremmed is dead now, and his life did not find its fulfilment. The Fremmed is dead . . .'

She dropped down to a skerry, where Mourne joined her, and she seemed so lost that Mourne went close to comfort her. Whatever awe Thordis had felt was gone now in the gloom that cast her down.

'I came from across the dark sea, I came with the Weir. Do you not know of him?'

Thordis shook her head, her eyes lost in the grey sea beneath them.

'I flew along the southern coast to Lomagnup, and there met an old eagle, a male, and he . . .'

At this Thordis was transformed again, as suddenly as she had become depressed.

'But you said the Fremmed was dead . . .'

'Well if that's the Fremmed you mean, Thordis, he's old but very much alive.'

'Then *he* sent you here?'

Mourne nodded.

'Then you *have* come, as he said you would. Generation by generation he has said it, that you would come!'

'Who? Who am I supposed to be?' asked Mourne.

'The one from across the dark sea, the one who would find us, the one who would take one of us back to where the food is good and the wind is free, to where the winters are short and mild . . .'

'But I . . .' and Mourne's voice faded, for she had heard those phrases before—spoken by Clew and by Mizen . . . whispered by old Weever . . . a place where a dream was, a place called Skye.

'And how do you know of that place?' she asked, trembling.

'Why the Fremmed told us – or those who dared visit him against the wishes of the Pairs – and they told us. Legends of Loch Scavaig, of Rubh' an Dùnain, of Loch Coruisk, of the great Gars Bheinn where he was born and from where he flew, of the Black Cuillin.'

Then a numb silence came to Mourne, a stilling of all around her, as Thordis went on . . .

'For he was the last one, the lost one, who flew the dark sea as you have, and who came to Haforn's land to lead us back. But none would follow him, none dared, and he outgrew all he found here, and outgrew another generation, and then a third, waiting, waiting . . .'

'What is his name?' asked Mourne in a whisper. 'Tell me his name.'

'His name is Torrin . . .' and there Thordis stopped for she could see the look of surprise, of shock, of hope and of some deep urgency that came over Mourne's face and into her eyes.

'Torrin,' she whispered. 'Brother of Cuillin. Torrin who knew the legends, Torrin who was strong, Torrin who was bidden to fly north and find Haforn's land . . .'

Then both knew that some moment of history was being made there, and from it much would come.

'You must fly now with me,' said Thordis suddenly.

'But we are waiting for the Gathering . . .'

'The Gathering will bring you harm, for the Pairs are your enemies as they have been Torrin's. Halldor Broken-Wing will kill you. But there is a place for you to go; some eagles who have waited generations for you to come. I know them, and they trust me; though I was once of the Pairs. You must come now . . .'

'But I am tired from a long flight,' said Mourne.

'Now,' insisted Thordis. '*Please*,' she added in a pathetic plea. 'You must trust me.'

'Do you trust Haforn?' asked Mourne.

'Yes,' whispered Thordis. 'All of us who wait trust Haforn. It's the Pairs who have forgotten . . .'

'Then I will come,' said Mourne.

'Now,' said Thordis urgently, 'Now. Before they come back for you. *Now*!' and with that she flew up into a flight westwards.

They arrived at dusk near a great sea fjord, and Thordis left Mourne at a stance there, and went off to send word to 'them', whoever 'they' might be. She returned during the night, and at the first sign of grey day the first one came. Then a second, and soon a third, until there were twelve of them.

Mostly old, battered, mate-less; eagles of worn talons and dry feathers. But worse than that: eagles of aimlessness. They gathered on the shore as the flotsam and jetsam of a tired sea whose high-tide is past, and whose currents are running out. Yet for all that, there was about them a sense of trust and of purpose, as if life may have treated them badly, but by some quirk of faith they still trusted it.

So they looked at her, stared at her, watched her, gazed upon her great strong wings—with hope.

Among them were three or four younger eagles, all but one of them as defeated-looking as the rest. The exception was a male, no more than two or three years into maturity, who, though somewhat gaunt, was yet aggressive and strong in manner, and proud as well.

'His name is Bjorg,' whispered Thordis, 'and he is born of the Pairs. His mother was Thurid, last eagle to know all the names of those who settled in Haforn's land. But she died before Bjorg was old enough to learn the names and places where they settled.'

Thordis had already explained about the 'Pairs'—the six remaining breeding pairs who lived to the north and kept themselves away from the vagrants and old eagles whom they believed were sterile. Thordis had possessed the will and strength to fly north and win one of the males, after his mate had died, but she had proved sterile and drifted south again, after her mate was killed by Halldor Broken-Wing in a territorial dispute.

'Bjorg came south with me before he was mature, because this was his mother's last instruction to him. She said he would learn things of importance from us vagrants—and that he must trust Haforn to guide him aright. He spent a year away from us all, over in the south-east where you have been, and there he met Torrin, who told him to return here. But he will tell you of that.'

A hush came over the assembly and Thordis spoke briefly: 'Our time is short, for the Pairs are gathering, and will surely follow here. This great eagle's name is Mourne, and she has flown the dark sea . . .' at which an awed silence fell on them, and they stared even harder at Mourne, as if they could not believe what they were being told. When Thordis had finished, she asked Mourne to make them a telling of who she was, and where she had been, and of all she knew.

Then Mourne did so, beginning at the beginning with the story of Cuillin, establishing her own kinship with Torrin, and telling the Romsdal version of the Doom, and of the coming of the Hardanger eagles, and of the humans, and of all that seemed important.

When she had finished, there was a great silence among them, and looking at them one by one, Mourne could see that many there wished to speak but somehow did not have the courage. Until they whispered among themselves, and looked towards Bjorg, and he it was who spoke at last, to encouraging calls of 'Tell her of what you have seen. Tell her.'

'Know, fremmed, that I have flown to Lomagnup and talked

with Torrin, the old one, who came before any here was even born . . .'

The others nodded their heads, and Mourne could see that in him a part of them lived, as if they had forgotten the feeling of pride and courage, purpose and power, but in him they saw some echo of what once they might have felt themselves. For their hopes rested on his wings.

'He was very old, his voice frail as dry grass and yet sturdy enough to be heard through the grim winds that blow among the cliffs at Lomagnup.'

Mourne nodded, impressed by the way this eagle carried himself, and by the clear way he spoke. Then bit by bit, the story of Torrin came out.

For years after flying the dark sea from Skye, Torrin, the Fremmed, had stayed quiet, living at Lomagnup, a cliff deserted long before he came. He liked it, he said, because it faced out across the sea he had crossed, towards his homeland.

The years had passed and humans had come, and roads were built, so that steadily the eagles were exterminated—shot and poisoned, or so disturbed in their breeding sites that pair after pair failed, and the population declined. Until the only eagles that remained were in the north-west, where they were isolated from humans. But Torrin, the Fremmed, stayed in the south, fast in his cliff stronghold, and over the years he became a legend. Until one year he had flown over the great ice of Vatnajökull, after the earth had broken open at Gimsvotn, and ice had melted and water poured in great waves of violence down the valleys. At this time, too, Mount Hekla, birthplace of Haforn, opened again, and fire and smoke rose so high in the sky, and drifted so far on the winds, that even the eagles of the north-west knew of it. Then did Torrin fly north towards them, first to pay homage at Mount Hekla, and after that in obedience to some call of Haforn which he had read in the fire of the eruption.

He was appalled to find how few eagles were left even in the north-west, and he summoned a gathering on his own authority, and commanded them all to consider what would happen if the decline continued. He told them the solution lay in a flight across the dark sea to an island cut off from any mainland, where food was surely still good, and perhaps humans now less dangerous. But they laughed at him, saying that this new land might be worse than where they were now, and they would lose many in such a long flight; and what right had he, a fremmed, to tell them, who were Haforn's own, what they should do.

Yet some wanted to follow him, mainly the vagrants, and he

tried to lead them south. Then there was a fight with the Pairs, of which there were more than twenty then. The vagrants were routed and Torrin forced to flee south again.

They forgot him for a while, until a strange story got about that one among them, Thurid, Bjorg's mother, believed him after all to be right. She disappeared one spring, and it is said she went to him, and old though he was, older than she even, she told him the lore of the settlement of Haforn's land – and gave it to him for a safekeeping—for all the others she had taught it to had died. Then she died in her turn, and all this was forgotten.

'This Torrin spoke a dream to us, and it is one that has not died' continued Bjorg. 'I myself was not alive when Torrin came north, but when I first matured and failed to find a mate, I grew restless with the spring and secretly flew south to find him to seek his wisdom, which was not hard, for all know of the Lomagnup and his association with it.'

'Did you find him?' asked Mourne.

'Not exactly,' replied Bjorg. 'I saw signs of an eagle. I found his talon marks. I knew he was there . . .'

'And at last he spoke to you in a blizzard up among the high terraces, and still you never saw him?'

'Yes,' said Bjorg in wonder. 'It was so. How . . .?'

'I, too,' said Mourne with a laugh.

And for the first time she detected a touch of warmth about Bjorg's eyes, as he gazed back at her.

'He spoke to me and I asked him to teach me the lore so that one of the younger ones might know it, but he answered strangely, saying: "Go to a new land. Make a new lore. Remember the names of new eagles that settle, and their places." I asked him which land and he said: "My homeland, Skye. Make a new lore there. Go there." But I looked across the dark sea and I was afraid. Then he said: "Do not worry now, for the time will come, whatever the Pairs might say, when one of you shall fly. Be patient. Wait." So then I asked him again to teach me the lore, but he refused, saying I was not ready and it was better to fill my head with new names, new places, new ideas, than the old ones of the past. Finally I asked him why he would not let me see him, but only spoke from the shadows. He said he was old now and did not wish to be remembered as a dying eagle.'

When he had finished there was silence again, and Mourne sensed that they wanted to ask her something, but that none dared.

Finally one of the oldest there came forward, an ancient female whose feathers were slack, and whispered, 'They say that in the old days, before any of us were born, there were some who could fly great and special flights across the sky. Flights of welcome, flights of power, flights of joy. I remember my own mother telling me, and showing me a scrap or two of those flights . . .' and for a moment she raised one of her wings as if to try to hint at some old flight long gone from the skies. 'Well I was wondering if you knew any of them. Perhaps they fly them still in the land where you come from, this Romsdal place?'

'No, no, there wouldn't be time for that,' said Thordis, before Mourne replied. 'The Pairs will be coming . . .'

But Mourne understood the importance of what she had been asked, and one look from her silenced Thordis.

'It is true that the old eagles where I come from could make such flights. My mother Cuillin could, and I am sure that the Fremmed Torrin could, and perhaps still can. But for myself I . . .' and she hesitated, for who was she to talk of flight, who had fled from Romsdal and skulked with vagrants so many years? She was not a great eagle to teach others.

'I cannot fly such things . . .' she said quietly, and she felt a terrible dread, for she sensed that they wanted her to, and needed to see just once in their lives how eagles can fly if they have courage and pride.

'But you flew the dark sea,' said the old female.

'But that's different, that's . . .' and Mourne felt a surge of self-pity, for she knew she was not as her mother had been who would have known how to respond, and to give them all something to watch and live by. Yet as she stared out at them, she found that Bjorg was staring back, and in his eyes was a look more powerful than any eagle had ever given her for many years. It was a look that communicated to her an even greater sense of how important it might be for her to fly for them. 'You must, you must, you must,' he seemed to be saying. And she saw in his eyes not the defeat of an eagle population nearing its end, but the hope that lay in its ancestral beginning, the strength that made it fight and survive through the years, the faith and belief that had once made it great. 'On you we now depend,' his look seemed to say, 'In you I now trust.' Then she understood that he was pleading for himself as well, that she might show him what powers he could have.

So finally she said, 'Perhaps I can remember something of what great Clew told me of the famous Flights he saw—the Flight of Storrin, the Flight of Doom, and the Flight of Welcome that my mother flew when first she came to Romsdal . . . Perhaps there is something of that that I can fly for you . . .'

Then slowly, tentatively, and with a prayer to Haforn, she rose into the air above them, taking a line on the skerries where they had stance, and on the cliffs of the fjord about them, and on the spring sky of cloud and distant sunlight—a flight that cast her wings across the sky so that all could see its language and know that they were welcome to her heart.

High above them she flew, and so saw, before they did, the coming of the Pairs, resolute and angry and determined on a fight. Then did her flight change into a dark one of warning, one of foreboding, and her wings darkened the sky and cast fear into all who saw her, and kept them all at their stances even when the Pairs arrived.

Then realising the biggest male there must be Halldor, for his left wing was bent and crooked, she overflew him suddenly and totally, not once but three times, showing that an eagle may defeat another without once raising talon, but merely by the majesty and force of great flight.

Until she felt safe to fly for them all a Flight of Peace that seemed to calm the very waters of the sea about them, and say that eagles such as they had better not fight among themselves when the Doom had them so tightly by its talons.

She was about to take stance again when to her surprise Bjorg rose suddenly into the air beneath her and began, bit by bit, and at first clumsily, to mirror her flight. Then she understood how deep was his courage, for her flight would have been hard to follow even for eagles of Romsdal or Hardanger, let alone eagles who had lost touch with the language of flight for so long. Yet up he rose, and gyred beneath her, his wings seeming strong and swift, and she in great joy to see them, for it had been many years since another male had flown like this with her.

Then high above the skerries and the sea, they flew. And Bjorg said, 'My homeland is here and here would you be welcome. But I wish to make a new territory where no eagle flies, and its place will be over the dark sea, as Torrin has bidden me. I can promise you nothing but loyalty and courage, and the pride of an old race of eagles that is not yet dead. If I make passage to the south-east will you follow?'

Mourne laughed with joy and said, 'If your flight is strong and true, then will I follow, and if not, then I will show you where it went wrong!'

For the first time then, Bjorg laughed too, and led her down over the fjord where the others waited, so they might know it was he who would carry their pride and hope upon his wings, and follow this fremmed if she would permit it.

Then one by one, others flew up with them, soaring over those deserted skerries and calling out names they knew only by hearsay, until even Thordis joined them. Then they all began to say that if only Mourne would lead them they would follow her wherever she went, even across the dark sea to Skye.

But Mourne disappointed them. She could not allow them all to follow her back south on a wild scheme to overfly the dark sea and settle in Skye. Not that, not yet. If it was to be done at all, it was best to do it as Torrin had originally wished, with the Pairs cooperating, for then the chances of breeding successfully, if that was Haforn's will, would be improved. Nor had it ever been her intention to fly to Skye from Haforn's land—or, indeed, to fly to Skye at all. For that she would need Askaval's strength and wisdom and leadership if it was to be successful, and it was to him that she must first return.

Yet even so, as Mourne and Bjorg flew over the skerries of Haforn's land, they felt a bonding in flight together which neither had ever known. And finding it so unexpectedly that spring, as if it was a new colour in the sky, it changed completely their vision of the time to come.

To Bjorg, reared in the harsh climate of Haforn's land, where hopes were fading and eagles' wings hung low, it affirmed that his own private dreams, his belief that all was not over that might save his kind—the same belief that had driven him to find Torrin, the Fremmed—had not, after all, been misplaced. Doubt was replaced by purpose, vagueness by vision, frustration by faith.

While for Mourne, daughter of Cuillin, once mate of Sleat, and sister of the great Askaval of Romsdal, the horizon seemed no longer bleak or solitary, and she felt in her wings a new power from the knowledge she was no longer alone, which made her feel she might fly to greater heights and help other eagles regain the will to live.

So it was that Mourne and Bjorg finally left the north-west fjords, with the blessing of all the eagles of Haforn's land—including Halldor whom she had overflown. Thence they flew south towards the distant Vatnojokull, and if they took a long time, and often grappled high in the air, and roosted in secret stances to watch the setting sun and rising dawn, what did it matter? None could know.

Except that as their love deepened in those days of travel together, it seemed to Mourne less and less appealing to fly alone across the dark sea to her homeland, and more and more sensible to fly south together and try to make a landfall in Skye. For she had wandered alone long enough, and in those days of bonding flight and companionship she grew to love the presence of Bjorg at her wingside, or hunting on the wind across the valleys, or still at a stance with night above them, sharing a view of the same shining stars behind the drifting clouds.

They came at last to Lomagnup on a clear day in early May, and they overflew it for a long time together so that Torrin might see them and be drawn out of the upper terraces where he hid. They settled there, and stared towards the sea which lay miles across the outwash sands, now no longer snow-streaked but hard and black, or shining grey where the light caught the crystals in the sand. Here and there, isolated from each other, a few stray plants were beginning to grow: sea campion and tiny grass, and mosses among the rocks at the sides of the rivers that coursed from the great glaciers behind Lomagnup down to the sea. While on the screes below the huge cliffs, grass had taken over from the snow, and sheep were out for summer grazing, treading carefully the contours of the steep scree, and sending the occasional flurry of earth and rock down on to the black sand far beneath.

Mourne, once so certain, was now troubled over what to do. Her world here was secure, her love for Bjorg deepening each day, and his urgent persuasion that together they might make the flight to Skye was ever more appealing.

So, together they decided to consult Torrin, if he could be persuaded to talk to them, though in her heart Mourne knew that he would favour a flight to Skye, if all she had heard of him was true. Yet that would be enough to put a seal on her own longing to share a new life with Bjorg of Dyrafjord, whose wings seemed to shape the very sky for her.

An old eagle waited, an old eagle watched them. He saw their flight together and was glad to see life return to this ancient cliff where ravens gossiped in the night. He saw their love, in flight and at stance, and saw them join talons and tumble in the sky, and saw them mate where he had gone alone, forgotten, dropping hard-caught prey from ageing talons down on to the distant scree. He saw them and, with the wisdom of age, he sighed, for over them he saw that Haforn's wings were opened wide and her talons hanging, and it was the side of Haforn that is not light and shining, but dark and bleak, the colour of outwash sand on a grey, dull day.

So he prayed for them with old prayers, taught by his mother long ago in his homeland of Skye, that they would have the strength to survive, and to know the young they were trying to make, and others that Haforn's will might let them make. And he kept in the shadows of the high terraces so they might be alone in those few final hours that Haforn would give them. For time was not yet theirs.

Joyful, flying light as the froth of white on racing meltwater, Bjorg laughed in the air, and buffeted his Mourne with his talons until she turned on him and held him, talon to talon, and mantled her great wings over him so the very sky disappeared. And then he raised his head, and pointed his beak to the sky, and put his great talons to her back and took her, to the distant scream of kittiwake and fulmar wheeling in the cliff-side air. And her head came back to his and his softly down to hers, their beaks open to the sky, tongues red and tail feathers white as the life that plunged and raced between them. A pair so late in the season, whom the ravens might mock, but who to care, and who to stop them now? So Bjorg laughed and stared across the distant sea.

But Haforn turned her back on them and looked instead to the east, across the dark sea, to where Romsdal lay. And though not knowing why, Mourne was uneasy and moved away from Bjorg, her wings shaking, her heart beating.

For, weak at first, and then stronger, and then like some terrible pain that comes out of the night, Mourne heard and felt a call so numbing that she could not speak. But she rose in alarm from their stance on the cliffs, flying wildly across its terraces, letting out a sudden cry of such pain that, with one accord, thousands of stiff-winged fulmar took to wing, showering away from the distressed eagle, up into the sky, until she wheeled up higher than they, and circled over the highest peak of Lomagnup, her wings beating fast and irregular, her cries loud, her head forever turning and turning again to stare to the east where Romsdal lay.

Then, in alarm, Bjorg flew up to her, but all she could do, when he asked what troubled her, was to cry out, 'Askaval, Askaval, Askaval!' For she could feel him calling to her, as he had when they were young, but now his call was terrible to feel inside her, tearing at her from the east, and she knew he was in danger and in pain, and that now he needed her, and she must go.

Bjorg could not understand as she whispered again and again, 'I must go back. I must go now. I can feel his need. Something terrible is happening . . .' For all he could see was a calm May-time sea, and fulmar settling back at the cliff nests from which Mourne had disturbed them.

Thus, his triumph turned to disaster and his joy to sadness, for he had come so far, and now she was going from him.

And so it was. In minutes his world had changed. For Mourne could not wait, and no words could dissuade her, and all she could whisper was, 'Haforn will save us and bring us together again. Haforn will protect you whom I love with body and spirit'.

'Then let me come with you, to guard you back to your homeland in safety,' said Bjorg.

'No, no, Bjorg, I must fly alone. But I will come back, I will find you.' And she screamed out again the name of Askaval, her brother, who called her, for now he needed her, and her alone. And she called out that she was coming.

So, suddenly and terribly, Mourne left Bjorg, and he called after her in despair and incomprehension, yet even then loving her so much that he did not try to follow. It was the will of Haforn, the Great One, who had no wish to bring an eagle comfort or content, but only bind him to a wheel of hopeless duty and purposeless journeys, which in the end would break him. His anger was with Haforn, not with Mourne.

Then did Torrin come to him, for Torrin had known such a thing might happen, and came now to bring comfort. Out of the shadows he came, to show his old body, the feathers grey and lifeless, the wings torn and tatty, the beak now pale and cracked, the once-sharp talons worn to stumps that could not grip a stance nor hold a prey as once upon a time, they had.

'Bjorg of Dryafjord, who came to me once before, listen to me now . . .'

And Torrin tried to speak to him, the young eagle, who huddled in silent misery. But Bjorg did not listen and instead let his anger grow. Until, at dusk, when an eagle should stay still, he turned to Torrin and stared at him blindly, and said: 'I do not want your lore, or any sayings, or other eagles' help. We were going to Skye, over the sea, and I had found the strength and the purpose for the flight. It is still with me. If she returns, tell her she will find me there, for there she, too, belongs.'

Then he raised his wings into the grey air of dusk, turned his beak towards the distant sea, and took off into the night.

While Torrin called out: 'It is long. Wait till the dawning. Wait . . .' But Bjorg was not waiting.

Then Torrin cried out again, 'Watch for the South Star. Follow its line, and let the stars of Haforn guide you.' And after Bjorg was gone, old Torrin himself looked up at the night sky and stared at the stars, to where an eagle might see a greater eagle flying, and he whispered old words which his mother had once said for him—and which his half-sister Cuillin had once spoken with the Weir:

Feart fithich dhuit,
Feart fiolair dhuit,
Feart Feinne . . .

Power of the Raven be thine,
Power of the Eagle be thine,
Power of the Fiann.

For the Fiann are the spirits of Skye, who came from sea and sky
and land, who spin the spindrift on the sea, who weave the
goodness in the winds, who know the power of the rock and tide.
Had they not protected himself, old Torrin, for decades past? And
they would do so for a few years yet, until his waiting might be
over. Well, then, let this invocation go now after Bjorg, who had
love and strength in his wings, mingled with anger, too; and after
Mourne as well, his sister's child, who would bring honour to
those she served and led.

CHAPTER SIXTEEN

Deal, 1963

ONE morning, waiting for the train to take him to school, Jim Stonor, now eighteen and in the Easter term of his final year in the Sixth Form, heard from Wright that Stiles had done it. With a girl from Archery Square, Walmer, the previous evening, up on the Kingsdown cliffs above the sea, he said. Jim stole a look at Stiles, envious and disturbed. He grinned manfully with Wright but felt a raw jealousy mingled with fear. Stiles had done it—what Jim dreamed about and what made him hard in bed at night and in the morning. Stiles had gone forward to stand upright in a world he, James MacAskill Stonor, could only dream of, where girls wore bras and pants that might actually be seen and touched, and which were taken off. It upset him in all kinds of ways that Stiles had done it; just like it had when he saw a couple of them, Wright and that twerp Terman, kissing girls in the beach shelter opposite the Bosun's Mate—his shelter, his place. They were sitting in there doing what he wanted to do, and he walked by miserably, hoping he had not been seen alone.

The following Wednesday was the Combined Cadet Force Field Day, and they were to do an exercise over on Sandwich Bay and across the adjacent Dunes. Strict instructions not to go on to the golf-course of which Captain James was a member. They had briefings at the normal CCF Tuesday parade, at which the three masters involved and NCOs, like Swinnerton, School Captain, and Grant, Rugby Captain, and even lesser NCOs like bloody Stiles, ponced about looking important and wielding maps and batons.

On the day itself they were issued with three blanks each for their ·303s. Jim had done his best to look smart, but the beret was too tight around his forehead to make him feel comfortable, and the collar of his khaki shirt itched at his neck. They put on packs filled with sandwiches, thermos flasks, and empty cardboard boxes. These were to be filled with shingle from the beach to make them heavier and therefore more real. The pack had thin straps, and not for the first time Jim thought how inferior it was to the rucksack he used to carry his drawing gear and protective clothing when he went off into the country. The boots were heavy black leather, army issue, with metal studs, and inferior to the rubber Vibram-soled boots he had started to use: a pair he bought out of holiday earnings. The balance of the army boots was wrong, they were uncomfortable, and they did not grip well. The gaiters he had cleaned that morning were as uncomfortable as the rest of the uniform, while the heavy wide belt, with antediluvian buckles on it for attaching various of the pack straps, simply added to his sense of outraged bondage.

After mustering at 10.00 am sharp, the first hour of the Field Day morning was spent collecting and checking equipment. The only excitement was the arrival, in an army jeep complete with official driver, of an Observer, a captain, the real McCoy, complete with stars and a red flash on his shoulder and a yellow armband. He would decide who had won. Jim's squad were 'the Greens'; the enemy 'the Blues'.

The second hour was taken up in marching down the Sandwich Bay estate road to the sea, to establish camp on the Dunes past the holiday homes. There was a kind of pleasure in the rhythm of feet, and Jim marched the three miles watching seagulls hovering over the golf-links, and being watched by rooks that scavenged the grass at the road's edge or over on the greens, their black beaks up, their ragged black wings lugubrious in the cold, light March breeze. He noticed gorse in yellow flower, and some stunted daffodils on a ditch-side. The air smelt good.

Camp established, they had another briefing. Behind them was the sea. Facing it was the golf-course, to the north was Shellness. But to the south, ah, excitement; there was the enemy encampment. There were three possible routes they themselves could be attacked from—the seashore, the road they had just come down, the ditch along the golf-course. Platoons were deployed to guard these approaches. And a secret was revealed: there was to be a counter-attack to attempt to destroy the enemy's field guns.

Jim found himself lying on the foreshore among the sand-dunes, watching for the enemy, but in the certain knowledge that, unless they were completely daft, they would not come that way. Too visible. He wouldn't even have used the road or the ditches. He would have made a detour inland through Downs Farm, and then along the drainage ditches towards Black Sand Point, inland on the River Stour. Might get a bit wet but you'd be quite invisible. Having got that far, good soldiers who knew the ground could even make it to Shellness and back along the beach, the Greens' position encircled.

The tide was out and Jim spent a further hour and a half watching herring-gull and ring-plover down on the shore, the former stoic on the beach, the latter darting along with the run and lapping of the waves, and facing out each other in what might have been mating rituals.

Just before one o'clock, an attack took place over on the right, by the roads. Blanks were fired. Jim's platoon was redeployed over there, but as they ran across, a distance of two hundred yards, they were fired on from a position behind Bayview, one of the biggest of the empty holiday homes. Jim dived for cover and lay still.

A voice barked 'You're dead. You boy. *You.*'

Him. Jim. He was dead. Along with three others of his platoon. The Observer had spotted him and said that the course they had run had led them into a direct line of fire.

Feeling foolish, Jim stood up, as one of a group of walking dead, and crossed over into the enemy lines where they were jeered at by the opposition. Their status as dead was changed to that of prisoner, principally because numbers were so relatively few that the officers would have no one to play with if too many stayed dead. Also, it was deemed good practice for the Blues to have to look after a few prisoners.

'What do we do with our rifles, sir?' asked one of the dead-reborn prisoners, of Mr Perrin, the Geography master, who had done military service.

'Better hang on to it, old chap. Don't want to leave it lying around. Sand and muck, you know, gets them dirty.'

It seemed that someone had thought of a use for the prisoners, because they were suddenly taken by Mr Perrin on a forced march back up the road and north towards Downs Farm. Jim knew precisely where they were going and sure enough, after a three-quarters of an hour scramble, through scrubland and marshy ground, they came upon a huddle of Blue soldiers, including the big brass: Captain James the Commanding Officer, NCO Grant, and Romeo Stiles, who squatted on the dried mud at Black Sand Point. The prisoners, it seemed, were to help carry ammunition and stores across the Dunes to the beach up near Shellness.

It was on the march across the Dunes, carrying ammunition and keeping low in ditches, that Jim first saw the flutter of terns' wings in the distance. They were near the colony which he and Peter had come to see so long before. He had seen it often since, but always kept his distance in the spring when they were breeding.

A fear began to build up in him as the route they took headed inexorably towards the very heart of the colony.

Finally, he turned to Mr Perrin and said: 'Sir, we're not allowed to go that way. There's terns nesting there.'

Mr Perrin, along with Captain James and NCOs, was bent forward peering ahead to spot the enemy, although any fool could see that the enemy was not that close. There was a crackle of intercom. The hush of imminent mock battle. Jim's voice fell on deaf ears.

They approached nearer, the distant sound of sea coming to them on a light inshore wind; and the terns were beginning to rise and circle and flutter in alarm over the grass dunes ahead of them.

'Sir,' said Jim again to Mr Perrin, 'we can't go there.'

'Quiet!' It was Captain James's voice, urgent, excited, heavy with courage and seriousness, living again the wartime battles he had never, in fact, fought.

The men, the soldiers, the play-acting boys, had stopped to gather into a huddle. Jim noticed that Stiles and his mate, Playfair, had camouflaged their faces with burnt cork and put gorse into their shoulder straps to break their outline.

'Right, men . . .' began Captain James, and outlined an attack along the beach which he had planned and been living for days past.

At the end, Jim spoke up: 'Sir. I've been trying to say that you can't cross over that ground because there's nesting terns there.'

Captain James looked vaguely over his shoulder and then back at Jim, and then at his green flash. 'You're a prisoner, Stonor. We don't want your point of view.'

Jim found that his heart was beating faster and his palms sweating on the rifle he was still holding.

'It's National Trust ground, sir. It's not allowed.' Ahead of them the terns circled and squealed in the sky, in growing alarm at the disturbance.

'Shut up, Stonor,' said Grant.

Captain James was, in fact, rather thrown by this bit of information, but decided that, in war, civilian organisations had little status and he had no time to make a detour.

'Right, tread carefully chaps. Absolute silence. Watch that you don't make noise with your boots on the pebbles. Keep low or we'll be seen. The enemy is about a third of a mile to our south, roughly two o'clock, and I am pretty certain we've not been spotted.'

'Sir . . .' Jim began again, but he was ignored, pushed back into place by Mr Perrin, back at the tail of the line of boy soldiers.

The terns, now only four hundred yards off, grew alarmed again at the new movement from inland towards them, and wheeled and shrilled in the sky over their nests. And something in Jim, something that had grown taut and thin and terribly strained in the years past, something exacerbated earlier in the week by the story about Stiles and the Archery Square girl, that something snapped. Seeing the blundering 'soldiers' ahead of him, seeing what their boots

415

might do to vulnerable nestlings or eggs not yet hatched, he grew angry, terribly angry, and his mind began to race with icy coldness. He stopped still, bent down with the pretence of adjusting his gaiter, and let the last few go on. None noticed that he did not rejoin them.

A wind stirred in the grass where he had been, grass straightened up where he had passed by, and he was heading to the right, towards a bigger drainage ditch that ran obliquely towards one corner of the tern colony. Down into it, and he was able to stand up without being seen, though precariously because the bank was shelving, mud-caked on top, oozing underneath, and water, deep and black, down below it. He began to run forward as fast as he could, slipping sometimes in the mud, his legs and knees becoming covered thick with it, his boots a muddy mess, his rifle, which he held in his left hand for balance, messed with the earth and grass he clutched at sometimes to keep upright. As he ran he felt excited and determined. He felt a purpose, and he remembered running like this with Peter once, round a field nearer Deal to avoid a horse that seemed about to charge them. He felt his body and his mind stretching, and he remembered standing with Peter on the far side of the nesting ground from where he was now. If Peter had been there he also would have said they shouldn't go across the ground. Peter would have stood by him, to help stop them.

Ahead and above the terns screamed, and he turned up out of the ditch and, running very low, raced to cut off Captain James and his men.

He reached the fence where the Blues were to cross, half a minute ahead of them, and heaving with breathlessness, muddy, his beret awry, waited staring at the hummocky ground they were coming through. The terns were above him, still not quite diving as they would the moment he entered their real territory. His breathing slowed down, and he stood at ease, his gun held across his body, the muzzle pointing down. If they refused to stop he would stand up and hope to be seen, and so give their position away; if they still went on, he would climb up on the cattle trough and wave his arms in the air.

He leaned back against a fence post, very certain, his heart beating fast, but feeling calm.

First he saw their berets, blue-black against the sandy brown of the grass and gorse, then a flash of shoulder stripes, then a brass badge—no wonder soldiers in films blacked them out. Then they were approaching.

He was quite certain what he had to do.

'Sir,' he called out, 'you *can't* come in here.'

Captain James stared ahead in blank disbelief, and then shock crossed his face. He was confronting the first genuine mutiny in his brief and so far somewhat clerical military career.

'Stonor!' he cried, quietly so as not to draw attention to themselves. 'Get down! The enemy will see you.'

'Sir . . .'

Angry, indeed quite outraged, but increasingly aware that they might easily be seen by the distant enemy, Captain James called out, 'Don't be silly, Stonor.' He then turned to Stiles and said, 'Stiles, go and take his rifle will you, and make a note of his name.'

Stiles, looking both annoyed and aggressive, calmly approached.

'I'm not budging,' said Jim, a note in his voice that no one had ever heard before, including himself. It was utterly certain. He would rather have died than move.

'Oh yes, you bloody are, Stonor,' said Stiles, who was slightly taller than Jim and now moved aggressively forward.

Colour drained from Jim's face, but his arms felt strong and his legs were part of the very ground itself. He stood up slowly and held the rifle ahead of him, though with the muzzle still pointed towards the ground. The officers and cadets behind Stiles now piled up behind each other, staring.

'I'm *not*,' said Jim, quietly. And Stiles and he stared at each other, Stiles looking rather warily now at the rifle Jim held, and at his hands which looked big and brown and sure. Stiles backed away. 'Don't be daft, Stonor,' he said.

'Fuck off,' hissed Jim, raising his rifle. Stiles retreated.

'I don't think he's going to move easily, sir,' he muttered to Captain James. Behind the Captain, his slow brain registering the insult now being perpetrated, non-commissioned officer Grant saw what was happening and decided to take action of his own.

'Leave this to me, sir,' he said. There seemed to be a tacit understanding that the Captain himself could not sully his hands by actually laying them on Stonor. Wouldn't do at all.

All fifteen stone of Grant bore down on Jim. To him the position was now quite simple, and he knew what he had to do. He put his weight on his back leg, he pushed his left foot forward a little, he turned his rifle aggressively in the air. And before Grant could get near enough to touch him, he fired—the smoke and expulsion of wadding from the blank puffing over Grant's shoulder. Grant looked frightened and stopped dead. Jim stepped forward a pace, and taking the moment of surprise by storm he fired again into the air.

Tern flocked and screamed wildly above them all. The position was totally exposed to the enemy.

As the sound of the shot died down and Grant retreated several steps, Jim said very clearly: 'And if any of you try to come across here, or anywhere inside this fence, I'll bloody well bash you with this. Now fuck off.' And they did, with threats from the Captain, wild looks from Grant, and looks of amazement, surprise and delight from many of the cadets. As they left, Jim climbed over the fence into the terns' territory to follow them around the colony's perimeter, and none of them seemed to notice that his hands were shaking so much that he could barely hang on to the rifle. While over to the south, where the Greens were emplaced, the binoculars of the Observer also turned rapidly in the direction from which the shot had come, and the position of the Captain was publicly blown. And they watched a solitary figure inside a fence—from that distance he seemed to be herding them along outside it, his rifle held firmly in front—and a great cloud of terns wheeling and screaming in the sky above, their wings light and fluttering.

Expulsion hung in the air, black and sickening, and Margaret Stonor spent the following morning in Mr Gower's study, saving Jim – who had been ordered to stay at home for the day – from the grimmest punishment the headmaster could mete out. What she said, and how she said it, Jim did not know, but when she came back in the afternoon he learned that he was dismissed from the CCF, but would be allowed to stay on till the summer term and sit his A-levels.

'But put one foot wrong, Jim, *anything*, and you'll be out of that school.'

'Wouldn't mind if I *was* thrown out,' he mumbled defiantly. 'I was in the right, anyway.'

'That's not the point, Jim. If you threaten the system, like you have done, and make it look foolish, then it will destroy you. Don't you realise how dangerous what you did was? You could have blinded that boy Grant.'

'I aimed well above his head, and I am a marksman, according to them.'

He stared at his mother and she at him, until he smiled slightly and she too. He knew then it was like when Mr Broughten had marked down his art homework; she was on his side.

'I did warn them, Mummy,' he said.

'Well,' she said. 'Well.' And looking at him staring at her, smiling just a little warily, and at his hands on the table, she thought that when it came down to it, there wasn't one of her sons she wasn't proud of in some way. Perhaps, after all, she had not done such a bad job. Mr Gower had had the grace to concede that the CCF

418

should not have tried to cross that ground—and that fact had saved Jim.

'It's the last battle I'll fight for you,' she said.

'I know,' said Jim, getting up from the kitchen table and going to put more coal on the fire.

'Mr Gower wanted to know what you hope for when you finish school, assuming you get at least a couple of A-levels. I don't think he's going to give you much of a recommendation for university.'

'I don't want to go, anyway.'

'What *do* you want? Have you any idea?'

'Art college. It's the only thing I've been any good at.'

'Not much of a qualification, that. All you'll get afterwards is a job teaching art or as a commercial artist, you know. Advertising, that sort of thing.'

'It's what I like doing,' he said. 'I'm not academic like the others.'

She fell silent for a long time, thinking that university wasn't everything, after all. Jim squatted down by the fireplace staring into the swirling smoke and darting flames above the burning coal.

'Then do it, Jim,' she said. 'You'll survive.'

He stood up and turned round, warming his legs and behind against the fire. He was making a calculation in his head. There were ten weeks to go before A-levels. My God! But thinking of them; he felt the same cold calculation in the face of crisis and fear he had felt the day before when facing Captain James.

'Did Mr Gower say how many A-levels he thought I'd get?' he asked.

'One, possibly two.'

'Did he?' said Jim. 'Well, he's wrong.' He said it a little histrionically but, thought Margaret Stonor, watching him go up to his room to work, there was nothing wrong in that.

Jim seemed quiet and chastened after that. He cancelled an Easter holiday job out on a farm near Eastry, and got down to the hardest two months' work he had ever been through. Late nights and weekends, and April storms giving way to May calm down on the beach, without him seeing it. Sometimes, late at night, she heard him creep out of the front door for a few minutes' walk on the front, to stand on the edge of the sea-wall and stare out into blackness, watching the North and South Foreland lightships shafting their regular intervals of light around the sky, yellow and distant. Or watching a tanker's lights progress across the horizon. Sometimes then he would walk down the steps, on to the dark beach, sliding down the wet shingle banks to stand by the water's edge, out of range of the street-lights up on the promenade. If it

419

was past midnight, they were out, and he in blackness, except always there was just a trace of grey light from somewhere to light his way. He knew he would soon be leaving Deal, but in those late-night vigils, by a blackened, rolling sea, he felt stronger and more certain of himself.

The only interruption came in the Easter holidays when he went for interviews to Canterbury Art College, and to the London School of Art, to which he had applied, and from which someone called Harold Ginnan wrote to say he wanted to interview him. He took his work in a makeshift portfolio, and went up early one morning so he could visit the Tate Gallery first. Mr Ginnan seemed less interested in his work than what he had seen at the Tate. What gave him most pleasure?

Jim thought.

'The Matisse backs, the ones . . .'

Harry Ginnan nodded. He knew them.

'They were very good,' said Jim.

'Why?' asked Harry.

He watched the boy-man fumble for words, his hands opening expressively over the drawings he had produced – sea sketches, cottage interiors, a few portraits, very competent but a little cold – as he tried to say what it was about Matisse he liked. Christ above, Harry himself would find it hard to formulate an answer just like that, but an 'answer' wasn't what he was looking for.

Jim's hands struggled in the air to shape the words that did not easily come. Typical sculptor, thought Harry. 'They give me ideas for what I could do,' he said finally. 'Like the pre-Raphaelites once did,' he added cryptically.

'Do you know Degas' sculptures?' asked Harry. 'I mean, apart from the *Ballet Dancer* in the Tate.'

Jim shook his head and narrowed his eyes. 'I'll look them up,' he said.

'Yes, I think you might enjoy them,' said Harry, in a voice that told Jim that he had secured his place at the School. He could tell when someone was on his side. And soon he heard on formal headed notepaper that he was to start the following autumn term, a three-year course.

Back at home Jim returned to weeks of intense work for his A-levels. He did not draw or paint at all in those weeks. But the day after the last A-level exam, in the first week of June, he refused to go to school and instead took his rucksack and a board, and put on his walking boots, and walked the five miles across the Dunes to Sandwich Bay. He settled down among the matt-grass at the high-tide mark to draw the terns, whose flight now was freer and less hostile, for their young were fledged and were fluttering on the wind with their parents, nearly indistinguishable from them now. The colours there were the colours of a sand-dune summer, light greens, golden buffs, the yellow of gorse, with the high fluttering trill of the skylark in a sky of light blue. He felt such relief, and his crayoned drawing was light with the colours he saw. Though still, and for many years yet, he felt the need to draw the curling wing of a black rook, and its beaked head watching, of the race Corvidae, whose secrets he was beginning to know. Always watching they were, to tell it to the Raven, on the edge of his vision where he couldn't quite catch it. One day he'd go and find a nesting raven somewhere on the mountains and moorlands of north Britain where he had never been—up in the north-west of Scotland, where his father came from: in Skye, where the Raven was, and where the sea eagles had once flown. He could go there, he could go anywhere, so he stood up on the highest sandhill he could find, leaving his sketch-pad to flap in the wind while he stared out at the horizon all round him, first to sea, and then to land, and finally right up into the arc of the sky, with a sea wind blowing in his hair.

At the beginning of August they announced the A-level results. Jim had passed all three: Cs in Geography and English, but a B in history. Three! He stared and stared at the list they sent round, duplicated on a piece of quarto paper. STONOR, J.M.: 'P' in three successive colums. Wright only got one. Stiles three, Grant one, Mulligan distinctions right through, Condry two distinctions and an S level, Otford, Oppenheim, Morrow, Roskill, Simons . . . the familiar names dropping away into one line of 'P's against his own name. He had done it!

That Saturday, Stiles gave a party, his parents being away in Portugal, and after having shunted an aunt, who was staying, over to Canterbury for *Son et Lumière* at the Cathedral. Rid of her, he dared ask everyone still in Deal, and to his surprise, Jim found himself invited. Later, four of them, Jim, Wright, and two girls Carol – a friend of Christine King – and Sharon, walked down to the beach and along towards Walmer Castle. The air was heavy with full summer, and warm enough for shirt-sleeves. The more so because they had all drunk a little too much cider, and were giggling and daring with their hands. They rounded by the Castle and went up the lane to the Glen, a well-known lovers' spot where Wright said he had been for snogging sessions. Somewhere there, among the deep grass, their hands sweaty with heat and desire, the two couples separated, Wright with Sharon, and Jim with Carol.

Carol, her hair back-brushed and fringed across her forehead, her eyes made up and mascara-ed, her lips rather too red with lipstick, was wearing a traditional party dress, flared out and sort of silky. Earlier, on the promenade, when Jim first put his arm round her, he had felt her back slip sideways, back and forth, beneath his hand and the material together, as she walked along. It felt hot and good. They lay in the grass, trees somewhere just behind them, the spot rather self-conciously chosen. Earlier she had pressed her body against his, while dancing, and his hands had settled for a moment on her bum and then round her thighs. She didn't seem to mind. Now, lying next to her, his arm over her, he kissed her like he had never kissed Christine King, his tongue to hers and diving, pushing, yielding and playing, and her breathing different and more urgent under him, his thigh over hers and him not minding that she could feel his penis hard against her leg.

Her arms around him like he had dreamed, her hands on his shirt, her fingers at his neck, her hands sliding down his back and up again, her crutch pressing into his thigh. He went for her breasts and loosened, or tried to, the buttons down her front. She helped him. Her breasts were big and good, and the bra his fingers and face rasped into smelt of perfume. That was the first, the first joy of a body against his, legs to be opening, hands to be caressing, teeth to take and mouth to give, sounds to sigh and sounds to moan in the hair that smelt of good things; new, strange, urgent things, as the hands dared to travel down over the stomach, fingers trailing nearer her quim, as Wright called it, then round again over her hips and thighs and between them and up, daringly closer to the crutch that pushed; her hands down his hips now and suddenly across his flies, as she felt him and held him through his trousers, and he was sure at last and knew she might say yes, or at least not say no.

His hand on her stocking, then up it to where it stretched and finished in soft, bare flesh in the dark, where the dress had ridden high with the legs that pushed under him. Then migrating surely to a land they had never known, where it's warm and dark and the slide of knickers softens firmly, and the fingers push on under elastic into dark and delicious moistness.

'Have you done it before?' she whispered. Oh my God, yes, a million times, any girl I choose, me? Done it before?

'Yes,' he lied, as best he could.

'Don't finish inside me,' she said cryptically—him not having heard the word used that way before, but guessing what it must mean.

'No,' he said, his hand temporarily caught behind her back trying to undo her bra so he could get at her breasts. He gave that up and tried to take off her knickers, which is nearly impossible with only one hand when the girl's over seven stone.

'It's all right,' she smiled, 'I'll keep them on.' Disappointment. And he might have given up then but that her hands were at his flies and undoing them, and her hands were pushing his pants down over his penis, and her hands were sliding his own wet on him, and he was pushed sideways then by one of her hands against his thigh, so he was on her.

'Slowly,' she said. And she helped him into her, the knicker crotch pulled sideways and him never, ever forgetting the moment, the microsecond before, poised to enter before entering, the place that was really so small but felt, when he was there and moving forward and back, like a world bigger than any he had ever imagined.

'Slowly,' she said, 'only . . .' She gasped. 'Oh, yes,' she said, as he forgot the tightness of the knickers against one side of him, and he pushed in and out, her dress all undone beneath his half-open shirt, and her neck and cheek pushing and rolling against his mouth, and him gasping with her, his mouth open into her back-combed hair.

Her legs opened beneath him, her thighs opening up round him, her legs coming up over his, and he not knowing if it was slow or fast because, whatever he did he was hardly there, but pushing, the most of him, the rest of him forgotten, into a world that took him into an exquisite sliding darkness.

As he started to come, he reluctantly began to pull away, but her hands pressing behind him held him into her, and she pushing wider and wider under him, saying, 'It's all right, it's all right this week, it's all right . . . Oh, I like it, oh, I like, I . . .' And he came at last, after so many years, after nearly two decades, his mouth open to the grass and earth beneath her head, and smelling the crushed grass and fresh earth. So relieved, that he had done it! He had! He had done what he had dreamed of, and it was better than dreams.

Somewhere a car's lights lit the sky and trees above them, driving on the road on the far side of the Glen, and after several minutes they began to get up. Such relief flooded through Jim, and there was a smile on his face in the dark. My name is James MacAskill Stonor, he was thinking, and I've done it! They did not look for the others but walked back down to the sea holding hands, and his feet were on springs, his spirit racing. Carol looked a little dishevelled, and touching her now, holding her hand and putting his arm over her shoulder as he dutifully did, kissing her sometimes, he did not feel quite so racy or excited as he had before. Strange that.

He saw her home and felt rather guilty to find himself so strangely relieved to be rid of her. For now, as he bounded along the promenade past the Lifeboat Station towards North Deal, he wanted to enjoy the fact of what he had at last done.

He lay in bed finally, thinking of her hands at him, and his fingers at her soft moistness, and her body surprisingly strong and urgent round him; and the excitement he felt was stronger, far, far stronger than it had ever been before, even earlier that night at the Glen. So he lay there and took her again, even better as it seemed to him, and his sighs and renewed gasps filled the darkness of his old bedroom, in which he seemed to have lived for so very long.

Five weeks later he went up to London to go to art school, on the same train that Michael had left on two years before. His mother came to see him off. Carol had offered to come, too, but that was over now, and both of them relieved; though it was nice while it lasted. She didn't look much good in daylight, and didn't want to go walking in the country. He looked rather serious in daylight, and was younger than she had thought. She would escalate that moment late at night up on the Glen with others, but then it was not her first. Jim never would and never could forget it.

So it was Margaret Stonor who said goodbye to him, passing his portfolio up through the door of the train, and watching him walk round into the carriage and put his luggage in it, wearing the new tweed jacket it was right for him to have.

'Goodbye, dear,' she said simply. 'Good luck. And don't forget to write and let me know your address. And don't forget to make an arrangement with the bank's nearest branch so you can cash cheques. And . . .' And the train began to move, to take him to this new world, and she gave him a quick and final kiss, and him smiling and waving, feeling rather sick in his stomach to be going, but relieved as well.

When the train went under the bridge, he crossed over to the far door, pulled open the window and leaned out to wave at her a final time as the train turned into the bend. But she did not seem to know the game, because when he looked, he just saw her back disappearing through the ticket barrier. So he went to his seat and sat down to stare at the familiar sights of Walmer and Martin Mill stations, the rolling downs and the windmill near Ringwould, and the racing walls of the tunnel through into Dover and on, away from his home, away from the sea, away to the inland horizon he had begun to long for.

Meanwhile Margaret Stonor walked slowly back home, going by the High Street to buy something for lunch. The last of them was gone and her house would be empty. Those long years were finally over and she was free. She crossed the road by St George's to be able to walk by the chemist's, and see herself in the mirror they had outside the shop there. For a moment, pretending to be looking at the window display, she stared at herself. She was fifty-seven and there was time yet, plenty of time, before she was sixty. She could go on holiday, if she wanted to. She could take a job, if she wanted to. She looked rather tired and her hair was untidy as usual, and she was rather overweight. But . . . but she wasn't *so* bad. She had sent four boys out into the world, and had a house all her own. There was Martin Blabey over in Cliftonville who paid court to her; not quite Ramon, but she wasn't complaining. She stood irresolute with so many options before her, until finally, on impulse, she retraced her steps to Queen Street and, brushing her hair back a little with her right hand, she went into the hairdresser she had so rarely visited. Yes, they could fit her in. In an hour's time? Of course, madam.

Time for a browse in Woolworth's and Boot's, and a coffee in Riceman's. Then, after the hairdresser, she would go home and change, and if Grace Frewin was willing, why – and why ever not? – she would take both of them off for lunch.

'But where?'

'In the Royal Hotel!'

'Well bless me, Margaret. I can't go in these old clothes!'

So she quickly went home to change and rouge her cheeks, and the staff were pleased to have the custom of two middle-aged ladies laughing their heads off and having Cointreau, no less than two each, after the rice pudding.

And Margaret's youngest, Jim, got out at Charing Cross Station, London, where the people rushed and pushed, where black, shiny taxis crawled and pulled up outside the station, where advertisements for women's knickers escalated at you as you went down into the tube stations. And where he met other students who looked at him, as he at them, and said: 'I'm Gerald . . . Gerald Opie. Foundation year.' 'I'm Vi Clarke.' While he stood in the new groups, watching what the others did, taking in the grubby, exciting, strange studio walls and the paint-spattered floors of the School, and its new smells, until it was his turn to introduce himself.

'My name is James MacAskill Stonor. I'm from Deal in Kent.' As London, the great, strange city where you forget that you cannot hear the sea thumping on the shingle at night, nor get on Oliver's old bicycle and ride down to the Dunes, nor stand on the front and stare out to sea to clear the strain from your head . . . as London began to entrap him in its new excitement and made him suppress for years yet to come what he could never forget.

'We're here.'

It was Judith at his elbow, sitting down. She had a toilet bag in her hand and she had changed her blouse. London stretched out below them, though greyly because it was a drizzly morning. He could see a line of traffic, lights on, jammed on the M4. He could even make out windscreen-wipers going. The jet banked, the horizon tilted, the airport lights ran out to one side of the plane, and he caught a glimpse of them tilted out below him before the plane straightened out towards them, and with a juddering of engines dropped out of the sky and down at last towards the ground. The sudden sight of an airport coach at ground level, an executive jet and a man standing on its wing, and with a thump, thump, they were down, and he was home again.

They parted at the cab rank outside Terminal 2—she to take a cab to Reading where she was being met; he to go into London to get a train down to Deal from Charing Cross.

'You haven't even got my telephone number or address,' she said. 'You haven't got mine,' he answered. They exchanged scribbles: his on a torn-out diary page: hers on a neat piece of notepaper she had ready in her bag.

'Jim,' she said finally, 'you know I'm there if you need to call me.' He nodded. He suddenly felt very, very tired.

'You will, won't you?'

'Of course I will. Thank you for coming back with me. They held each other, he almost leaning on her, and she could feel the terrible tiredness of him, the long fatigue. 'Good luck,' she whispered.

He helped her into her cab, and before he closed the door, he leaned in and touched her cheek with the back of his hand, just to feel it again before she was gone.

CHAPTER SEVENTEEN

Aт Charing Cross he had half an hour to wait for the next train. He phoned his mother. 'I'll be down at about half-past two,' he said.

'All right, dear,' she said.

'How is he?' he asked.

'He's very weak, my dear. I'm glad you'll be here today.'

'Have you called the others? Frank and Oliver . . . and Michael?'

'We'll talk about that when I see you. Now you go and get ready for your train.'

Margaret Stonor put down the phone thinking it wasn't like her to say a thing like that. 'Go and get ready for your train', indeed! She was very tense and in a slight state of shock. Liam was in the front room facing the street, the curtains drawn and the window closed because it was cold outside. He was in what she called the guest bedroom, which used to be hers. She had had a sink put in it. She lived upstairs now, in Mother's old room. The boys' rooms upstairs were normally let, though there were no tenants at the moment.

Dr Lessing had arranged for a night nurse now, who came in at eight and stayed twelve hours until eight in the morning. Grace Frewin was coming in at lunchtime to take over for a while, so that Margaret could go and do some shopping. The doctor had said there was nothing they could do. It was a matter of time. He was not in pain. The doctor would come back in the early evening. Drugs would help slightly.

She went down the corridor towards the front door and quietly opened the door into the guest room. The curtains were drawn, so the room was dark, though a streak of light cut across the bed and over the rises of Liam's feet under the blankets. His breath was painfully strained, but frail and light. Sometimes he sort of groaned or hummed, a strange sound. He seemed to be asleep. She stared at his shape in the bed, unable to feel what she felt she ought to feel. Liam was dying. She could not seem to connect that fact with anything else. Liam was lying there dying, and she standing by the door, staring in the gloom, wondering what else she ought to be feeling. Well, she felt old, too.

'It was Jimmy,' she said. 'He's coming down to Deal to see you. He'll be here in two hours or so.'

Liam MacAskill heard her and moved his lips to say something, but it seemed awful hard to do it, and not much point just now. He could hear the sea on the shore up by the sea-wall, and wished the window was open so he could hear it the better. He was rather frightened because he could not move his feet, except his right one, side to side, side to side, and his fingers under the sheets. He was frightened, but Jimmy was coming, whom he gave the binoculars to. The sea was heavy, he could feel it, and he had left the window in his room open when it should have been closed. Mrs Hadden wouldnae have closed it for him. She hadna been to his ain room in ten years, the silly old woman.

'The wind is rising, close the window now,' he said.

Margaret pulled back the curtains for a moment and then let them fall. 'It is closed, Liam,' she said, in that voice of hers.

She hadna ever understood what he wanted, had the lourd lass he married. He was frightened, but Jimmy was coming back to his hame.

'Aye . . .' and his voice fell into a sigh and him to sleep, and Margaret to creep away, unwanted.

He was still asleep when Jim found him, two and a half hours later. He stood at the bedroom door, as his mother had, staring at the thin face and lank, greasy, pale hair on the pillow: his father. Liam was groaning in sleep, his breath painful to hear, and his hands were out now on the white sheet, the fingers quite still.

'Daddy?' Jim whispered the word, and tiptoed forward, peering down at the face. The mouth was open, his father's lips pale, and the lines down the cheeks terribly sunken. He was asleep, so Jim crept out of the room, but left the door open a little wider than his mother had left it, and went to join her in the kitchen.

'You do look tired, Jim,' she said.

'Jet-lag, but I slept on the train down. Have you called Frank and Oliver?'

She was silent. 'No,' she said finally. 'I saw no purpose in it.'

'For God's sake, Mummy, that's ridiculous,'

'Anyway, I'm not sure where to contact them now,' she added defensively.

'Michael?'

She nodded. 'I was not able to speak to him directly, of course, but I spoke to an abbot or someone. He said Michael was in Rome.' She raised her eyebrows in the air and just a touch of the old humour he always associated her with came back to her face.

'Well, he would be, wouldn't he?' said Jim ironically.

'They're going to let him know.'

'Let him know what?' asked Jim seriously.

'Your father's dying. Dr Lessing, my doctor – he didn't seem to have one of his own – says he's just very weak, failing, nothing much that can be done. He wasn't even sure that he'd be better off in hospital.'

'I wouldn't even have known about it if Grace Frewin hadn't . . .'

'This isn't the time, Jim. Not now . . .' An expression of pain went across her face, the old look that stopped a son complaining.

'There's a night nurse coming at eight o'clock. The doctor felt it best.' After a while she added: 'I'm glad you're here. But I couldn't have coped with the others.'

There was a call – a breathless, groaning call – and Jim started up.

'It's all right, he does that often. Go to him, dear, and see if there's anything he wants. Perhaps a glass of water or something, but only let him have very little.'

Jim was already halfway there.

His father was awake now, and trying feebly to adjust the pillows behind him with one hand.

'Hello, Daddy,' said Jim from the door, 'It's me. I came to see how you are.'

'Not so bright, that's how I am,' said Liam MacAskill. 'Help me, can you, laddie . . .'

Jim came to the bed and bent over to help him with the pillows. He didn't know quite what to do.

'I cannae sit up without your help, Jim.'

So he put a hand on one shoulder and the left hand behind his head to raise it a little, and ease his father up the pillows to be more comfortable. His body felt thin and strange, but not unpleasant, and Jim would have liked to kiss him on the forehead, but he didn't. It was like lifting a child.

He pulled a chair to the side of the bed and sat in it, and stared at his father, who was looking straight ahead.

'Turn on a light, Jim. I don't like this gloom.'

There was a bedside light, a green bottle with a plastic bulb-holder stuck into it, and an old plastic Woolworth's shade, scorched brown at one point where it had rested against a bulb that was too hot for it. Typical Compass Street decor. He turned on the light. As he walked round the bed and back to the chair, his father's eyes followed him.

'What did she tell you about me?' Liam whispered, eyes darting meaningfully towards the bedroom door.

'She said . . .' and he hesitated before the truth. But anything else before this old man he had never really known, but who was so much part of him, would be wrong. 'She said you're very weak. Failing. There's a nurse coming tonight at eight.'

'Aye, I am weak all right. I nearly died in the Great War, did I ever tell you that?'

'You hardly told me anything,' said Jim.

'No, I didna. I saw Neill Morrison of Lewis die, and Donald Wilson of Uist. We were friends. I saw Aonas MacEachlan also of Uist killed. They put me in hospital with gas and shock later on. I saw death then, Jim. A man will never forget that.'

Jim sat there listening. He understood there was little for him to say. He understood that his father needed him. But he felt restless and ill at ease.

Liam MacAskill dozed off for a few minutes, and Jim himself felt sleepy sitting by his father.

'I don't want your mother seeing to anything, fussing and that,' Liam said suddenly. 'You do it, Jim. You can do that. I want to be buried: I dinnae like fire, and never have.'

'Yes, Daddy.'

'Have you been to Skye, lad? Ever been there?'

Jim shook his head, unable to speak. No, he had not been there, or even to Scotland.

'It's a fine place to go, that's certain.'

'Why did you never go back, Daddy?'

'Too far, too painful. I left it in 1920 for the Remembrance Day burial in London, and I swore then I'd never go back. Did I never speak of it to you? There's moorland and mountain, loch and sea as fair as you've ever seen, nor will see elsewhere. But it was a bitter, lost place, Jim. I was best out of it.'

Margaret Stonor came into the bedroom with two cups of tea. Jim watched his father and even now, even here, he saw the look of distaste come over his face, and saw his mouth move into a bitter stance from which, had he been stronger, he might have said a sarcastic word: the anger that had separated them. If Margaret saw it she did not let on. She quietly put the cups of tea by the bedside lamp and asked Jim to help his father drink.

'There's no enough sugar,' said Liam, but when Jim started up to go and get some, Liam shook his head slighty, milky tea running down his chin, and said, 'Dinna bother her wi' that, it's nae worth it to me.'

Jim wondered how they had ever come to marry in the first place. They seemed to hold no love for each other.

Outside, the wind, which was gusty when Jim had arrived in Deal, now buffeted at the window and, though the windows were closed, the curtain stirred very slightly. Compass Street was full of old houses with sash windows which never quite defeated the Deal wind.

'It'll be rough tonight,' said Jim. He felt better for hearing the wind and finding that, after all these years away, he could still read the signs. It felt good to be home.

'Aye,' said Liam, and lay his head back and closed his eyes, suddenly very tired and feeling rather frightened. The fingers of his left hand fretted slightly at the sheet.

'Can I do anything, Daddy? Get you something?' Liam shook his head slowly from side to side, the eyes sunken and dark, the lids so thin that the shape of the eyeball showed through them. Jim wanted to draw him.

'I won't be a moment,' he said. He fetched the sketch-pad he had left inside his travel bag in the kitchen, and came back to sit in the chair. He started to sketch his father's head, not from any sense of curiosity or interest, but from a much deeper need to put outside of himself the terrible feeling of love and loss and suffering he was beginning to feel. He could sense his father was deeply frightened.

The room was quiet but for the sound of wind and rumbling sea up on the front—and the run of pencil across the cartridge paper.

For a moment Liam opened his eyes and stared slowly over at Jim, and then settled again.

'Your friend from London drew me once. Up on the seafront. Nice lass she was.'

'Judith,' said Jim.

'Aye, that'll be the one. Judith. Good lass.'

'I travelled back to London with her from New York.'

'New York?' Liam's voice faded. It occurred to Jim that he didn't realise he had come all the way back home from America. Jim smiled slightly: what did it matter anyway. Some journeys are easier than others. This one home had seemed so far, at the beginning, but now he was here within sound of the sea and listening to the familiar rattles and creaks of his home, why, the journey seemed nothing at all. It was where he had been that was far, far away.

His father fell into deep sleep finally, and late in the afternoon Jim left him, to go upstairs to sleep as well, jet-lagged and years tired.

He woke suddenly at the violent rattle of his familiar bedroom window against its frame, and lay for a few minutes very still, listening to the sounds he had missed for so long. He switched on a bedside light he did not recognise. The room had changed colour—the wooden panels a pastel beige now, and a new brown carpet on the floor for the tenants. But the old hardboard frame, to exclude draughts, still stood loosely in the fireplace, and was pulled to and fro with a slight clumping sound by the wind in the chimney above. He got up and washed his face in the bathroom through Granny's old room, which his mother had taken, then he went down to the kitchen. His mother sat by the fire, and oh, Grace Frewin was there, looking older.

'Hello, Jim,' she said, and she took him in her arms, him taller than she remembered, fatter round the face, but older looking and ill, as if he had suffered. She held him to her and patted his back. 'Glad you've come back,' she said. She smelt the same, of Woolworth's soap and chutney, familiar. She had not aged at all.

It was half-past eight and the nurse was in there with his father. He was not well—worse than he had been in the afternoon.

'But he seemed so . . .' started Jim.

The doctor had come and gone, and would probably return later that night, as he had another visit to make in Alfred Square nearby.

Liam's gasping breath came down the corridor to them, a sound that mixed with the scurry and sparking of the coal fire Grace had got going in the kitchen grate.

'I'll go to him,' he said. His mother seemed to be hovering, avoiding the fact of Liam's dying in some way. She looked pale and tired, her hair a mess. He was glad Grace Frewin was there at least.

'I'll make a nice cup of tea for everybody,' said Grace. 'I expect the nurse'll want one after coming out on a night like this.' Grace had arranged the back room overlooking the garden for the nurse, who said she really didn't need a place to rest, the armchair in the guest bedroom near Liam's bed would do. There was a feeling of change and suffering in the house; of waiting, waiting for an unknown darkness. The doctor had said it was only a matter of hours, but Jim did not need to be told. He could sense it.

'Have you heard from Michael yet?' he asked of his mother.

Margaret Stonor shook her head. 'I called the others,' she said. 'They're both coming tomorrow.'

'It may be too late by then,' said Jim curtly, and left the room. As he went down the corridor there was a loud cry from his father; and when Jim got to the room he could see why: he didn't like the nurse. A crabby, bossy-looking woman, inclined to say things like 'There's a good boy' to elderly, dying gentlemen. An 'I-take-no-nonsense' nurse, with a mean, overweening smile, and a white uniform. Jim did not like her.

His father had, indeed, deteriorated and lay now, the blankets lower than before and his pyjama button open as if he had been too hot, and exposing the grey hairs of his chest. His throat was long and thin; that part of his chest Jim could see was gaunt and bony and seemed barely to move when he breathed, though his breathing seemed hard and rasping to get out. His mouth was so dry, and his eyes were open and lost, in another place, and terribly frightened. His hands fretted still, more than before, the fingers stiff and tremulous.

'I'm James Stonor, his son,' he said to the nurse. She stared at him and mouthed something silently at him, but whatever it was – some instruction or other – he ignored it and went and sat by his father in the hard chair.

'Daddy, it's me, Jim.' He reached out a hand to his father's arm, and when he touched it his father's hand came up and found his own and gripped it tight between thumb and forefinger. The other fingers seemed to have lost their strength.

'Daddy, is there anything you want?'

Jim was conscious of the nurse. She was not looking, but was listening. He didn't like her.

'If there's nothing to do at the moment, I think Mrs Frewin has a cup of tea for you in the kitchen. Please do go and have it.'

His father's hand pressed on his own and his eyes opened and stared at Jim. There was the faintest and most distant glint of a smile, a look Jim had never quite seen in him before.

'Of course,' said the nurse, smiling unctuously, and with a 'He's been very good', she left the room.

'What have you been doing in America, Jim?' The question came out slowly, and took a long time in the asking. Liam was making a big effort to be sociable.

'Nothing much,' said Jim. 'I worked in an advertising agency for all the time I was there, and . . .' And he told his father softly, his father nodding sometimes and opening his eyes, but mostly lying still. Jim was conscious that it did not matter much what he said, but that he was there. The wind was a presence outside the window, powerful, and the sea rising and the room cold and hot by turns, for though there was a big dusty electric fire by the door facing the bed, occasionally little tiny gusts of draught would break through its heat. His father had some buttered bread on a side plate and a glass of water now on the table by the bed. There was a blue plastic transistor radio on the other side.

'Do you want the radio on?' asked Jim.

Liam shook his head to say no, he didnae want that. He didnae say what it was he wanted, but Jim knew, for as Jim sat there, with his father holding his hand and the wind outside, he remembered a time he himself had been frightened, in a storm in a lonely room, and his father had come to him and told a story. And remembering that and the comfort it gave him, he pulled his chair a little closer to his father's bed, so he could rest an elbow on it, and he said, 'I'm glad to see you again.'

'Aye, lad, and I am, too, to see you. You tell your friend at school that it's true your father speaks Gaelic, the old language. Tell him that.'

Jim nodded, unable to speak.

'I wrote you a letter in America, Jim, but I never sent it.'

'What did it say?'

'I thought you might be missing your hame, lad, where your mother and I raised you. So I said about the great sea and the things I'd seen on the Dunes, and the storms. I used to like talking to you and the others up there on the front, where the wind runs clear of the houses. Why did ye no come to see me where I lived down in West Street, in Mrs Hadden's?'

'I didn't think to go there. None of us did. We hardly knew.'

'Mrs Hadden who's got the shop in Walmer keeps that house. It's hers. She liked having me there. But I left the window of my room open, and she'll not have had the wit or strength to close it. She has a good garden. Didna know I like to garden, did you?' For some reason his father tried to laugh and started to cough, a terrible, desperate cough. Jim put his arm round his back and helped him to some water.

'When I had my attack the pain was wicked bad,' Liam said. He looked frightened again. 'My maither spoke the old language better than my father. She spoke in a lovely voice and told me stories. I should have gone back to her, to see her again. No courage in my life, Jim. Nothing to follow after that war, nowhere left to go. But I remember the names and will say them for you to show you I remember.'

And then he did, slowly and one by one, with a pause between each as if he was thinking of them as they were: Portree, Storr, the Quiraing, and the lochs that lie in the sun and are soft with dawn light: Brittle, Scavaig, Coruisk, and the Cuillins above them, Black to one side, Red to the other; jagged the one and worn smooth the other. The Isle of Raasay which on some days you, a bairn, can almost touch with your fingers, so close it seems by the light of the sun. Bla Bheinn, Sgurr Alasdair and Beinn Edra up past the Storr. Trotternish. MacAskills—watchers over the sea we were for Clan MacLeod.

'Did I tell you of the eagles I caused to be killed when I was no higher than the chair you're sat in?'

Jim shook his head, struck still by all his weak words.

'No, better not. Long time ago. I shouldna have given you the binoculars. I should ha' broken them on the stone step of the laird's house that spawned them. But I told you of the eagles, I remember doing so.'

'Yes, Daddy, I remember you telling me. I've drawn them sometimes since. White-tailed sea eagles.'

'Aye, lad, extinct to Scotland, but you'll find them in Norway and over in Iceland. I've read about them. You drew the last one for me.' Liam was remembering the drawing of Cuillin arriving in Norway which Jim had made when he was nine, after he was ill, but Jim did not understand the reference. He thought his father was meaning that the drawings and paintings he had made since then, more recently, were for him.

'I never forgot what you told me, Daddy,' said Jim. 'I made up stories sometimes like you did.'

'It wasna a story,' said Liam. 'It was never a story.'

'No,' said Jim.

'Did she get back to Skye, that strange one? The Fremmed? Who flew alone across the sea and who settled where none knew her?' his father asked. 'Did she fly back to her hame?'

Jim shook his head.

'No, it wouldna be possible after so long,' said Liam MacAskill. 'What happened then, d'ye know? Can ye guess? Did one of them gae back to her hame for her?' He sounded so frightened, so afraid of what might happen, and he held on to Jim's hand as if he was afraid Jim would leave the room. Once Jim had lain in bed so ill and so frightened, and he remembered again the blissful comfort of knowing his father would not leave him. So now, in his own turn, he stayed there and said, 'I'm not going, Daddy. I'm here by your bed.'

'You're a good lad. Then tell me, what happened?' asked Liam.

So Jim started to, in that downstairs bedroom with the wind down the old familiar street outside, because Liam MacAskill wanted to remember Skye where Jim had never been; but surely an eagle could go there, back across the dark and terrible sea which makes an eagle afraid. Jim told him, his father, how it finally happened.

* * * * *

Mourne flew steadily westward, through the night, driven by a growing sense that Askaval was in trouble and danger, and needed her. Neither tiredness nor doubt of arriving there worried her, for the need to get to him was so great that it masked out all other feelings. But halfway over the dark sea the wind from the south freshened and began to drift her a little more northward than she wanted to go, and she was conscious, from the rush and hiss of the water below, that there had been rough weather over the sea. As dawn came, she saw evidence of it: seaweed drifting far out, the flotsam and jetsam of wreckage, and near the Norwegian coast, when she finally reached it, rough seas heavier than the present southerly wind warranted, and ships anchored and battened down in the lee of the islands.

She recognised the lie of the islands and fjords from her journey north with Clew the previous winter, and with barely a pause in flight turned south along the coast to make headway towards distant Romsdal. She could no longer hear Askaval's call, as she had seemed to so terribly the afternoon before, but she felt a deep and aching need to fly south and find him. She knew he was in trouble.

Occasionally, mobbing sea-birds rose towards her in anger, for there were still many young at nests, and herring-gulls flocked and screamed along the gusting southerly wind, where they preyed at rubbish and fish carrion in harbours and along coastal jetties of fish factories. She saw a large, dead codling in the water, with a group of gull hovering and bickering in the air above it, and with one great swoop bore down through the lot of them, took it in her talons and rose again to surge through their flailing, mean beaks, hanging feet and beating grey-black wings, to press on and eat the food on the wing.

Further south, there was more storm damage. A group of humans struggled in a bay to pull in a boat that was drifting, capsized, in the rough grey sea. Further on, a whole mass of fresh, orange, drifting timber planks, cut and squared, floated loose in the water, fallen from a boat that had them too insecure on deck for the sudden storm that threw them overboard. Her progress was slow for the wind was difficult—not strong, so much as temperamental; the last throes of a great storm. And she grew more deeply worried and anxious and full of dread as she flew on, bay after bay, headland after headland, the great cliffs that heralded the beginning of the fjords now massing up ahead of her. She grew more and more certain that there was something amiss. Not just with Askaval, but with everything. The life along the coast below seemed muted and abnormal, sea-birds that would normally fly at her passing stayed huddled deep inside cliff terraces and clefts. Birds like turnstone and plover that might brighten up the shore and inlets and bays were gone, vanished; the beaches lorn and cold without them.

She could now see ten or twenty miles down the coast, nearly as far as Romsdal itself. It looked utterly deserted, not a seal to break its surface, nor a gull to soften its loneliness. Just the fall of cliffs into a strange sea, and a dull wind to fret at her eyes.

The heartland of Askaval's territory lay just a mile or two ahead of her now, inland by a small fjord's side, and she was now even fuller of dread, for no welcome sight of eagle wings in the sky rose before her. For surely had Ruann or Askaval been there, they would not have let her penetrate so deeply into their territory without coming to check her out. Surely, if they had young, they would be at the nest now, and . . . but perhaps they had failed this year. But then surely they would still be trying. It was not yet quite too late, not yet . . . The doubts, the hopes jumbled into a black fear in her as she drove on towards the fjord she had overflown only once before, but which she remembered so well. All the time she hoped one of them would appear out of the sky, or off the fjell, calling in alarm at the sight of her, so she could say, 'It is I, Mourne, and you are safe. You are safe . . .' But there was nothing in the sky but grey blustering clouds, nothing on the ground but moss and thin grass, and the green of gaunt conifers by a deserted fjord-side.

Then she was there, where her brother had based his years with Ruann, and there was nothing, no life at all. Her eyes searched the steep terraces running up from the ruffled waters to the scree, and then higher up to the cliffs, then moving round to an area of flat land on the far side, where reindeer came to take water.

Nothing. No life. Then she searched the upper scree and lower cliffs, beneath the overhangs, for a nest site and the tell-tale signs of fur, or scattered sticks, or . . . and she saw a black raven preying, toying at something off to her left, and rose quickly towards it. Last year's nest-site, perhaps, one of the secondary sites, perhaps . . . but she knew before she wheeled round to it and landed at its edge, that it was this year's. A half-eaten hare lay by the nest rim, its fur sodden from stormy rain. And inside, she saw what made her gasp in horror for what it must mean to her brother and his beloved mate: a grey chick, sodden and still, its down stuck together and lifeless in death, its thin neck extended pathetically over the sticks of the nest, as if it had been reaching towards the hare, whose flesh it was far too young to have the strength to tear. And its own thin flesh had already been torn by a raven's beak.

Something came to her then, another call, a cry from the south, but nearby, a cry in her heart that called her name: '*Mourne . . . Mourne . . .*' And she crying out into the sky and turning back towards the coast as fast as she could, and whispering again and again, 'Askaval, Askaval, I'm coming to you. I can hear your cry. Wait a little longer, just a little, and I'll be there . . .' And so she flew back to the coast and down the last few miles towards Romsdal. She saw its northern cliffs reaching steeply down into the sea, and the skerries in the centre of the fjord, and the distant southern cliffs. But the water between them and ahead of her was strange, its light abnormal for such a sky. She flew lower, towards the long beach before the entry to the fjord, her heart so filled with dread she hardly dared look, for now she saw life there, pathetic life, littered along the shore—desperate among the lapping waves of a sea that smelt sickeningly of humans.

Lower she went, lower still, until the unnatural colour of the water became dark, and she saw that the surface, for as far as she could see, was thick with black oil. Great rafts of it floated in and out with the waves and running tide, while out to sea lay a great slick, flat and oval, but whose tentacles spread north with the direction of the wind, and pushed inshore as if to encircle the beach and drown the sand and rocks and cliff-edges in ever more thick and shining oil.

Unbelievably, in this dreadful sea, birds still swam, or tried to. Auk and guillemot, their white parts stained dark, floated uncomprehending in the sea, trying to preen off oil from their wings and breasts with their great black bills. Some blinked in pain, appearing to have lost their sense of direction, for the oil stung their eyes and was beginning to blind them.

A group of eider, including young, drifted hopelessly inshore with the waves as they tried and failed to flap their wings with sufficient power to take them off the surface, the bright colours of their plumage – normally delicate whites and greens and blues and greys – now colourless and wan beneath the oil that clung to them. One had his wing raised at a curious angle, as if trying to free it from the black and sticky mess its feathers had become; another, a female, swam around in a circle about two young that floated, dead, in the filthy, swirling, glutinous water.

But it was the beach sloping down to the waves which most filled Mourne with dread. Its sands were black and shining with oil, and rocks above the sand were dark brown with it, up to where the high tide had driven it earlier. Seaweed, oil thick, hung down the rocks they clung to. A bottle lay mummified by oil; part of a lifebelt, red paint on it showing a white letter or two, but most of it oil-black. And birds lying on the shore, not dead but dying slowly with a black blindness at their eyes, and a terrible taste and painful stinging in their mouths; and the same desperate struggle to preen the enemy off their plumage—but that they weakened before its stickiness and vile, clinging stench.

Some lay in pools of oil so thick that only a head and beak showed, looking blindly up at the sky, beaks shiny with oil, too weak to open again. While others, still strong enough, called out for help that would never come their way. Mourne drifted slowly over this wasteland of dying birds, anger in her, and terrible, terrible fear, for the calling of her name from Askaval was still there, but weaker, growing weaker now.

She saw a gannet struggling on the beach, its legs in the air. It had somehow tumbled over in its plight, opened its great wings to push itself upright, and the oil on the sand had held one wing fast until, trying to push itself back upright with the other, that, too, was stuck, so it lay now on its back unable to raise either wing, its strong neck and pointed head straining up towards the sky, its legs tired from beating the air, its calls of pain weaker and weaker. Crucified.

She flew on over an oil-thick sea, closer and closer to the great northern cliffs of Romsdal, the beach still stretching grimly to her left. Near the cliff and not far from the beach beneath it, but before the entrance to the fjord itself, she saw a couple of herring-gull circle and then, as if they had seen her, turn away from the dangerous surface they were scavenging.

'Mourne, Mourne.' The voice was weak now. Where the herring-gull been she saw now something on the sea, something great and floating, something . . . and she cried out in fear and surged faster forward, her wings only inches from the heavy, black sea.

Nothing. The surface was flat with oil as she came to where they had been. Nothing, as she circled round again. Then something, something that would change her life.

For suddenly, out of the rolling blackness of the sea, turning slowly as if drifting, yet held high enough to suggest life still, bit by bit an eagle's wing drove up out of the waves, as if reaching for the sky. Then, like those grubby icebergs she had seen on glacier lakes in Haforn's land, it sank back again, and a talon emerged out of the water instead, and a surge beyond it, and straining, and black suffocating ripples, and the wing again: an eagle dying in the waves.

She stooped towards it, head down, wings hanging inches above the surface, and waited for the waves to raise the talon up to her, and when they did she gently took it and held it firm for a moment as the waves fell back again, so that his head was visible now, and his great beak, and all was black with oil, but for a tongue beyond a beak that opened out in agony—her Askaval. Her brother.

She beat desperately in the air to hold on to him, trying to raise him with her talons, but he was too heavy and the oil and the sea dragged him back, and she felt herself pulled back and down, the sea and its oil coming up for her. And, crying out, she had to let him go.

439

Then his voice, the voice she loved, saying, 'Leave me, leave me. Let me die alone.' And she crying out his name in anger and agony, 'Askaval!' into the cliffs of Romsdal above her that stretched higher and higher towards the sky which now rose forever inaccessible to him.

Yet her trying to raise him righted his body in the water, and with his wings spread out on either side of him, his head was above the surface and she saw his white tail feathers were also black with oil or tar. The whole of his head was oiled, and one of his eyes was closed with it, the other swollen. 'Leave me, leave me . . .' he whispered, for this was not a death for other eagles to see. But Mourne hovered over him, looked round to the shore, and saw that it was near enough to drag him there, and that the waves would help her. For if only she could save him from the water, then perhaps something could be done.

'It's no use, Mourne. I am lost now,' he whispered. 'I tried to save Ruann by dragging her from the oil but she was too heavy and I lost her, and I lost myself. Leave me here, and go instead to my territory and save my last-born. Save her . . .'

He did not know his chick was dead, killed by the rain that came after the storm in the night. Mourne dared not tell him. Instead, she stooped on him again, catching his body as gently as she could, and struggling to pull and heave him clear, to drag him over the surface of the sea which rose against her, tore at her, surged up to try and take her too. Again she had to let him go, and he sank once more, so she frantically stooped a third time on him, and dragged him further towards the beach; and then a fourth and a fifth time, until she was within reach of the shore.

'Leave me,' he gasped, the swilling oil and water choking back his words. 'Save yourself . . .' For her wings were already oil-tainted, and her leg feathers dripping black where the sea had surged under her. But now they had reached where the waves were breaking and driving up the desolate beach, and she held him again until a wave broke under her, and drove him with its oily brown surge up the beach, and him struggling with his wings to maintain balance, the dark sticky foam around him where he lay beached in the black sand.

She hovered over him, dropping down to hold him again, as another wall of water surged him further up the shore, and she held him fast against its retreat to the sea.

The tide was going out, leaving in its wake the oil and the dead, the oil and the dying. Huddled now, her great wings mantled over him gently, as if he was a chick to protect from life itself, Mourne tried pathetically to preen him, putting her great beak among his feathers to scrape away the oil that clung there. He was in terrible pain, and as she tasted the oil on her own tongue, she knew why— it was bitter and acidic, and it burned and left a nausea in the throat.

'Go now,' he whispered. 'Go and save my last-born . . .' But her look told him what he already feared, and with that the last of his will to live began to die.

'Askaval,' she whispered, 'Askaval, my brother.'

'You came back, Mourne. You heard my call.'

'Always, Askaval, always . . .' and she stared at him and he craned up to touch her, barely able to open his eyes now.

'*You* must lead them now, only you, Mourne. You have the strength, and they will follow. Lead them now across the dark sea where you have been . . . Lead them to Skye, away from this.'

'But you could not know . . .'

'Clew told me. The Weir warned me, told me this new Doom was coming, and I tried to tell them . . . Ruann and I tried to lead them, but none in Romsdal would listen. We tried to tell the Hardanger eagles, but Sleat ordered them to drive us away. And then the storm, and the oil with the south wind, and Ruann gone, and I torn between the nest and finding her. I knew she needed me . . .'

'I know, I know . . .' whispered Mourne.

'Lead them. Lead them . . .'

But still Mourne preened him, oblivious of the oil about her, at her wings and in her mouth, trying to save him, for this was not an eagle's death.

The ravens tell of her loyalty, of how, hour after hour, all through that day, she stayed with him, guarding him, showing her great love for him, for he was her brother, born of Cuillin, and he had flown with her out of the Storrin. She could not let him die so, in a sea of oil among stricken auk and guillemot and gannet and grebe, and all the birds of the shore and sea. Not there!

The tide went out, far out, leaving its wake of black desolation. And alone, along the shore from the south, slowly a human walked, staring at the dead and dying about him, walking slowly towards the great cliffs of Romsdal, taking notes, while out to sea the sky darkened and the sea whipped again with wind and rain across the skerries, and a new storm approached, a great storm that blackened the sky and tugged at the seaweed along the shore. The human came on, and Mourne saw him. She tried to drag Askaval away to hide him, but sand stuck to him, and small pebbles, and he was limper now, and dying. His breaths were short and his beak open, both his eyes closed and his words faint. 'Leave me now, for yours is the burden. You have the strength who once were so weak. You once gave me comfort, take it to them now. Give them your love . ...'

And the human was coming. A flash at his hands, binocular glass. The human was coming.

She wheeled suddenly up into the sky, angry, forbidding, huge in the gusting air, and drove down towards the human, stooping savagely at him, her talons outstretched. And the human stopped, and backed away, hands high, and she swung back to her dying brother.

Then some final anger, powerful as fire from the earth, surged into her, for the human was coming again, steadily towards her. Unstoppable. Dangerous. She stared wildly at the cliff above, at the rocks behind, and rose up frantically in the air, circling Askaval and calling out in distress as he raised his head weakly towards her, blind now and fading, the pain from the oil all over his body.

Out to sea, where the black storm raged, there was a flash of lightning among the skerries, and with its power behind her she stooped on her brother, for this was not the place for such an eagle to die. She stooped on him wildly, but her talons took him up gently, and his wings opened limply beneath her as she struggled up into the sky, carrying him with some great strength she found, taking him out towards the dark sea and the storm. And the winds caught her, and drove her up and wildly over the cliffs of Romsdal, the human watching, over the fjord entrance itself, and she beat seaward from there, with other eagles watching, seeing the return of Mourne, last daughter of the Fremmed, with the great Askaval gently held beneath her.

Out against racing cloud she flew, against ripping lightning, into a thunderworld of rain and wind and swirling darkness, out over the seas and beyond the skerries, her wings open and the wind of Haforn driving her.

Higher and higher, her beak open in anger, her wings ever stronger, until the great wind and racing darkness reached down from the sky and took Askaval from her, filling out his black wings again, raising his head, setting his talons true and strong, so that he flew again as Haforn wished it, and took an eagle's death within her spreading wings.

The ravens that saw it tell that Mourne flew in the storm for twelve long hours, tarred and torn, but never once in danger, her wings greater than thunder, her talons sharper than lightning. When a new dawn came, she returned, drifting over Romsdal, now torn and tattered, but stronger than any eagle that had ever flown there except Cuillin, her mother. Of none was she afraid, Hardanger or great female, immature or vagrant, but to all she said, 'Come, follow me now from this blackened place. Follow me over the dark sea.'

But even then they would not go, afraid still, for the Doom had made them weak and incapable, for that was the nature of the Doom itself. Humans had poisoned them, humans had weakened them, humans had shot them, humans had disturbed them. None in Romsdal had the courage to follow her.

But word of her call went out, up and down the stricken shore, and beyond it north and south, and she waited, for she was proud now, and she was an eagle to fly over the sea, not an eagle to tour the cliffs and skerries pleading with others to follow. If they had courage they would come. Nor, say the ravens, did she pray to Haforn, for she was filled with a powerful anger, nearly a hatred. For Haforn had taken Askaval from her, and that she could not forgive.

So she waited, certain that some at least would come, even if only one or two. Or else she would fly alone.

Three days, four days . . . five days she waited, down at the entrance to Romsdal, as rumours of what she was asking carried north and south, and pair after pair heard it and laughed, saying: 'She was the lost one, that daughter of the Fremmed, and we are safe here, even if the humans encroach and poison the water. Did we not survive this latest disaster? Will we not live through others yet? We are safe here. Ignore her.'

But there were some who heard, some who listened: worn eagles, tatty eagles, eagles without pride or hope, who scavenged the southern docksides, who preyed for carrion by the herring boats and shoreside factories. Some of them remembered a strange eagle who had come among them, who had foraged with them and was one of them for a time. Her name had not been Mourne, daughter of Cuillin, and yet had not that great eagle, Clew, come among them? Had he not asked for her? Had he not taken that other one away with him, the one who told stories of Romsdal, and wove dreams of Skye which none of them forgot? So they heard the new rumours and stared at the far horizon, and wondered if she and this Mourne were the same, and perhaps they could go with her, if she would have them. And on the sixth day the first came, tentative and diffident, drifting slowly along the outer shores of Romsdal, hardly daring to join the great one who was Mourne, proud and mature, strong of wing and firm of purpose. This old vagrant came and he took a stance near Mourne and said: 'They say

. . . well, some eagles I heard talking suggested . . . well, that maybe you were going on a journey. They said . . .'

'What is your name?' asked Mourne gently.

'In my own fjord down south they called me Reft the Vagrant, but I never go there now. Nothing there for the likes of me now, you know . . .'

And she looked down at his talons, an old eagle with barely pride enough left to raise his head and gaze at her.

'What is it you want, Reft?'

'Well, nothing much. Just to know what you're doing, I mean, well . . .' He stopped, and she waited. 'Well, I was wondering if I could come with you?'

Then Mourne turned and looked full at him, and she was deeply moved that a vagrant should come to her, for she knew how he felt, and what little he felt he had to offer.

'You see the far horizon, beyond the skerries, where the sun sets in the west?'

' 'Course I see it. I've often looked at it. They say there's a place there where the Fremmed came from.'

'It's far,' said Mourne, 'And hard. And of those that come some will die.'

'Well, I've flown a fair way in my time, and I don't suppose that'll be so much harder than some of the things I've done and had to do, nor some of the places I've been. But I've never done anything I'm proud of, not really—never even found a mate to speak of. An eagle's got to do something with his life, got to have a go. So if you'll have me, I'll come along with you.'

'I shall be proud if you'll accompany me,' said Mourne, 'for you have great courage to come here and offer. Far more courage than many others. Mine is the honour, Reft, whom they call Vagrant.'

'Right, that's settled,' said Reft, matter-of-factly, adding, 'I thought you wouldn't have the likes of me.' Then, after a moment: 'So when do we get started then? Might as well get on with it . . .'

Then Mourne wanted to laugh. Her spirits lifted, for he spoke as a vagrant did, with no nonsense about him. He would be a good companion.

Others came then, other vagrants, juveniles, old eagles who had lost their mates, tatty and worn, inexperienced and naïve, innocent and bitter. They came because they had a dream that over the horizon was a place that was better than they now had, and a great eagle had offered to lead them, and she had been a vagrant like they were, lost and rejected, and perhaps this was the one chance they'd ever have.

Until, after eight days, there were ten of them, as raggle-taggle a collection of eagles as Romsdal had ever seen all at one time. While established pairs came and watched from a distance, and laughed at the pathetic grouping. But none could gainsay that one among them, Mourne, born of Cuillin, was big and proud and strong and stole the mockery from an eagle's tongue.

'Well, Mourne. I reckon it's time we got going, since the wind's now right. Eagles get impatient . . .' Reft had become the voice of the others, and took some pride in his new-found role. Mourne was aware that he was no idiot when it came to survival, rough and worn though he looked, and there was something homely and tough about him that gave strength to some of the youngsters.

'I am waiting for some others, yet,' said Mourne.

'Well, if you ask me, about all the vagrants who've got the wit and courage to come are here already, so let's get on with it.'

But still she waited, for she trusted her instincts and knew that finally *he* would come.

And, finally, he did, over the horizon from the sea, an old male eagle, whose wise flight and leisured way brought a gasp of admiration from the others around her. Clew had come.

'I would have been here sooner, but . . .'

'I know,' said Mourne. 'The knowledge that you would come has been certain in me, and has kept me here. I knew you would come.' But even so, there was relief in her voice.

'Yes, well . . . it has been hard these days after the storm. The oil is bad on the skerries, and there were some eagles I had to help, old friends who were in danger . . .' And Mourne's heart filled with hope. For she would need experienced help where she was going, to help these youngsters and vagrants.

'Who were they?' she asked in a whisper.

'Oh, better let them speak their names for themselves. They'll be here soon enough, for I am not far ahead of them. Let them announce themselves. They'll want to come, Mourne. There'll be no stopping them.'

Then a whisper went about that others were coming, a pair, great ones, who were close to Clew, himself once guardian of Cuillin's territory after the great Gathering of many years ago. There was excitement among them, and a feeling of loyalty and purpose, for they were the few who were going, and each of them was glad to be there, even if secretly nervous and afraid. Except for Reft, who looked steadily and impatiently seaward, and filled them all with hope.

Shortly after Clew's arrival they saw a pair in the far sky, coming from the skerries, slowly, at their own pace, and they flew as great eagles do, with time in their wings. They were as old as Clew but

445

different. One, the female, flew high, her wings quite frail, and her head looking this way and that as if she expected some danger. The other flew beneath her, sturdy and strong, forging ahead; and it was hard to say which one led and which one followed, but together they made the sky and the earth and the sea seem a good place, a whole place, and the place where they flew the best place to be.

Then the vagrants whispered and muttered, and one said, 'That's Weever that is, famous as Romsdal itself he is . . .' and another declared, 'I'll bet you a whole herring that's Mizen, that female who cared for Askaval, now dead, rest his soul, and Mourne here, our leader. They say Cuillin loved Mizen and taught her to fly true.'

And so it was, Mizen and Weever filling the sky, and joining Clew and Mourne at last, at the skerry outside Romsdal fjord.

'Glad you didn't push off without us,' said Weever bluntly. 'Spot of bother with some oil . . .' and he looked at Mizen and Mourne saw that she was badly oiled on her right wing, and that even now it had only been partly preened and moulted away.

'Mourne!' said Mizen, but she could not say more, for there was too much to say and words failed her. An old female like her did not want to be seen crying in front of others.

'Oh, Mizen!' was all Mourne could say. 'Now we are ready!'

Then she turned to Reft, who had made himself scarce among the others, and called him forward, but he came rather reluctantly. He was intimidated by all these great eagles who only hours before had been just legends to him. By Haforn, legends don't *exist*. But here they were, looking at him, and he could stretch out a talon and touch them, they were that close!

'This is my friend and companion, Reft,' said Mourne. 'He was the first to come, and will always be honoured among us.'

'Now, for Haforn's sake, don't go on about it,' said Reft, very embarrassed. 'I only come here for the adventure of it. But I'll tell you one thing, if there's anywhere to be got to, across this dark sea we're all meant to be so scared of, these old wings of mine are going to get me there, and that's a fact!' And the others, including Weever and Mizen, nodded and agreed. He had spoken out what was in their hearts.

'Come then,' said Mourne, 'We will fly to the outer skerries, feed well this evening, and in the morning, if the weather is still good, we shall be gone.'

Then Mourne turned to Clew and said: 'You'll not come, Clew, for this is not your way. You are the guardian of Romsdal and will stay here. So give us your blessing. Pray for us.' Clew nodded, for she was right: his was not that way. It never had been. His only to see things right. His to stay and watch, and pass on his memories and dreams to others who came by, and teach his wisdom to the youngsters, so that in the years ahead others would know. But he could not speak, and merely watched them rise, one by one, and circle in the air, Mourne to lead them, Mizen to care for them, and Weever, as ever, to watch the ground and air and weather, and teach some of these youngsters, and the more daft vagrants there, a thing or two about knowing territory and making the most of it. And Reft, the best-natured side of courage.

Clew watched them, and saw Mourne circle one last time, and face up the dark interior of Romsdal to see her home fjord, where she had been raised, but from which she had been separated for so long. He knew then that she loved it, and hoped she would teach these others to love whatever place they found. Then she turned seaward, towards the outer skerries, and, like one huge shadow across the evening sky, their great wings took them beyond the arms of Romsdal fjord and out on the first part of their dangerous journey, to find a new home, where the food was good and the wind ran fair—and whose name was a dream called Skye.

* * * * *

Liam began to mutter and look fretful that he had left his bedroom window open and that Mrs Hadden would not be willing, or able, to close it; wasna the wind getting stronger?

'Shall I go and see to it, Daddy?' said Jim.

'Aye, lad, you do that for me. I'll rest easier knowing it's done. But don't worry Mrs Hadden about me. I wouldna want her to fret.'

The house was in West Street, opposite St George's churchyard, double-fronted and Victorian, with a great black door and a bell-push. It was in darkness, while the houses on either side had lights on. The street-lights were just on, too. Through the trees beyond the churchyard wall, Jim could see the west end of the church.

He pressed the bell-push, but if it sounded at all it was in some dim and distant scullery or kitchen at the back of the house, for he heard nothing. He thumped the great iron knocker on the door and, eventually, after the sound had died away, a sliver of light appeared at the letter-box and there was the sense of movement beyond the door. A brighter light went on. Chains, locks, bolts, latches and bars were weakly fumbled at by hands that seemed unfamiliar with them. There was a querulous muttering and breathing from beyond the door until, when all seemed undone but the door itself, a voice beyond it called out: 'Who is it?'

'My name is James Stonor.'

'What do you want?'

'I'm Mr MacAskill's son.'

There was silence. Eventually the voice, an old woman's, said, 'I can't open the door. You'll have to come round the side.'

So he did, and when he had stumbled over dustbins and past broken flowerpots, he came to a conservatory door which stood ajar, and he stepped inside. It was May, but he could smell the damp. The conservatory was dark and he knocked over a stack of flowerpots.

A light went on in the room against which the conservatory had been built, and Jim pushed open the door that led into it. It fell rather than swung open, since one of the hinges was so rusted that it no longer functioned.

'You should have used the kitchen door,' said the old, thin woman who now stood in the room staring at him.

In the stumbling darkness Jim had walked right past it.

'Is Liam dead?' she asked. 'Is that what you've come about?'

Jim shook his head, rather shocked, and stared at her. He knew her face, he had seen her . . . had spoken to her. Mrs Hadden! The woman who ran an antique shop on London Road, a sort of junk and antique emporium.

'He's not very well,' said Jim. 'He's been worried about his bedroom window. He says he left it open, and that you wouldn't be able to close it.'

'He's dying, isn't he?' she said.

Jim nodded.

'I don't know, I really don't . . .' muttered Mrs Hadden, pushing the fingers of her left hand through lank grey hair, and then shaking her head and adding: 'No, no, I haven't been up there to his room.'

'I'd better go and look,' said Jim.

'He doesn't like anyone going into his room. I never go. I haven't been there for twenty years.' She spoke of it, the place his father had lived in, as if it was a thousand difficult miles away, and not somewhere through the house above their heads.

'Well, I think he would be happier knowing I had been to check the window,' said Jim. 'Could you show me where to go?'

'Well, I don't know. It's not the way we . . . Well . . .'

But Jim advanced past her and towards the door leading into a corridor, and she followed behind him.

The place was so chaotically untidy, so piled up and choked with what seemed the contents of a thousand failed junk and furniture shops, that Jim had trouble picking his way along the corridor towards what he hoped would be the stairs. Old curtains were tangled up with broken chairs, piles of grubby books toppled sideways into Victorian washing bowls; five gross of white plastic combs had somehow enmeshed themselves among the delicate lace fabric of piles of off-white costume dresses that blocked the door of what Jim took to be a dining-room. Brass fireguards, a porcelain dog, carpets that had been rolled up and placed along walls, and then been trodden down by grimy feet to form raised walkways among the debris. A doorway into a kitchen so horrifically filthy that Jim could barely take in its details by the harsh light of the naked bulb that hung above them. A sink overflowing with mouldering plates, tins on tins of baked beans, mugs, cups, bowls, saucepans, casseroles, all used, all unwashed. A table on which there was no space to fit even a dirty teaspoon.

Yet, strangely, there was a fresh smell of freesias coming from the room, and as Jim passed it by, he caught sight of a vase of fresh flowers . . . no, *two* vases—one in the middle of the jumbled kitchen table, and the other on a huge dresser at one end of the room, with daffodils, forsythia and shop-bought freesias.

'I'm afraid you've caught me at a bad moment,' Mrs Hadden was saying behind him, fretting a little as she followed him down the corridor. 'I'm in a bit of a mess, rather a jumble, no time to tidy up, but what you see is about to be moved out to the shop. Really, I . . .'

They came to the foot of a wide stairway whose elegant banister was of polished mahogany; the lowermost portion of it, where it curled round to a full stop at the foot of the stairs, was draped over with off-cuts of white electric wire, tied together with twine.

'This isn't necessary, you know. I'm sure no window is open up there.'

But Jim, carried forward by the feeling that he wanted to get back to Compass Street but couldn't until he had closed the window, pressed on up the stairs, avoiding as best he could the piles of white catering plates that were stashed up its steps, each with the blue logo of *The Cliff Hotel, Folkestone* printed on it. Jugs, gravy boats, sandwich plates, twelve coffee pots, enough, in fact, to give breakfast to a roomful of hotel guests. At one point someone, either Liam MacAskill or Mrs Hadden, had knocked one of the piles of crockery over, and it had slid down the steps on to others and broken them. Bits of broken crockery cracked under his feet.

'I was about to clear that up,' said Mrs Hadden behind him. 'Most unsightly.'

At the top of the stairs he stopped, unsure which way to go. The hallway there evidently ran from the front to the back of the house. The end towards the street was as littered and overtaken by junk as

449

the rest of the places he had passed. But the corridor to his right, to the back of the house, was empty and clear. No pictures askew on the walls; no junk on the floor; no rubbish tumbling out of half-open doors.

'His room's down there,' said Mrs Hadden.

She sounded quiet and her voice broken, and as he looked around at her he saw that she was crying, her faded eyes and unkempt face very sad. She was biting her lips and looking up at him. 'That's where Liam lives,' she repeated. Then, as if she could not bear to see another person enter Liam's realm, she turned away and went back down the stairs into her chaotic house, and somewhere he heard a door shut.

Jim advanced down the clear corridor and opened a door. It was a small kitchen, sparse and neat. Not a thing out of place. He closed the door and went to the end of the corridor. It was a bathroom: green towel neat on a rail, a cork bathmat leaning against a wall, a toothbrush in a holder over an old-fashioned sink. A little window with a pattern etched on to the glass so it could not be seen through. A faint smell of no-nonsense, coal-tar soap.

Another door, and, opening it, he saw it was a bedroom, and from the echoing sound, a big one. An enormous room, with a great bay window, one of whose sashes was open and rattling slightly. His father's room. He felt around for a light, switched it on and stepped inside, feeling that he was trespassing in a forbidden land. The room smelt of fresh air. There was a desk, with a chair at an angle to it, as if someone had just got up from working there, and had not rearranged the chair. Over the desk were shelves full of books. One whole wall, too, was full of books. There was a gas-fire at one wall, and a single armchair near it, covered with a bright, woollen rug. A pair of slippers by the chair.

He stood in the centre of the room, conscious of the window being open because he could hear wind gusting in the trees out in the garden, now hidden in darkness, and could see the lace curtain shifting. He stared about him. There was an open box of filing cards on the desk, and more boxes against the wall nearby. By the window, mounted on a stand, was a small telescope with a stool beside it.

On the desk was a filing card and a pen, which, like the chair, were positioned to suggest that Liam MacAskill had been writing on the card only seconds before. Printed along the top was '*British Trust for Ornithology*' and below, to the right, in neat black ink: 'GR TR 382474'; a grid reference, and a place-name next to it. Printed in capital letters was 'FULMARUS GLACIALIS', and various dated entries

450

in different inks below it. The most recent read: '18.2.74. Breeding activity seen today above Kingsdown rifle range. A new site.'

The books seemed all, without exception, ornithological. *The Herring Gull's World* by Niko Tinbergen, *Seventy Years of Birdwatching*, by H. G. Alexander, *The Wood Pigeon*, by R. K. Murton . . .

Atlases, a run of thin white magazines, one of which Jim pulled out to see what it was: *British Birds*, Vol. XXIV.

There was about the books and the desk, and the whole room, a sense of purposeful order quite in contrast with any previous notion Jim had had about his father.

He had simply never known that his father's consuming interest was in ornithology. Jim opened one of the filing boxes and saw that the cards were thumbed and well worked, and stretched back over decades of observation and study. Entry after entry, year after year, herring-gull, fulmar, *Larus ridibundus, Larus fuscus, Larus argentatus, Uria aalge, Phalacrocorax carbo, Phalacrocorax aristotelis, Corvus frugilegus, Corvus corone Linn, Corvus corax*, the raven.

So, suddenly, in that abandoned room, his father, whom he had never really known, took on the form and substance of a person: a birdwatcher. And hours of time which had been a blank to Jim were filled up by the sense of industry and care the room projected.

Jim went over to the window and closed it, and pulled the latch to. Then he turned away, not wanting to see the rest of the room, only wanting to leave.

But he was stopped by the bed, a single, cast-iron affair, like a hospital bed, with a simple Indian printed coverlet. On the wall over it hung the only picture in the room. It was badly mounted in a thin, oak frame of Victorian date, one that Jim suspected had been found somewhere in the corridors of this great house. For a moment he did not recognise it. It was childish and simple, but when he started to read the writing along its base, he recognised it as his own. '*For Daddy, with love from James MacAskill Stonor*', it read, the words written in pencil—the '*Stonor*' a bit bent because he had run out of space. Above the words was the picture of an eagle: Cuillin. Young then, and flying over a grey sea near a windy coastline, arriving in Norway from across the dark sea.

Then he felt a terrible urge to get home, to be with his father again, not to leave him alone any more. And he went downstairs through the chaos of Mrs Hadden's house, to the kitchen, and she stared helplessly at him.

'I'll be in touch,' he said quietly. He was pale and his eyes tired and haunted, and he looked deeply troubled.

She nodded. 'You look like he did once,' she said.

Liam MacAskill was right: the wind was blowing up bad weather and things were going to crash and bang, and red tiles slide off old outhouse roofs, and milk bottles roll off untidy old doorsteps in the middle of the night and break in the gutters of North Deal.

At some late hour, perhaps nearer eleven than ten, Liam seemed to grow very tired, and Jim stopped talking to him in the low voice he had been whispering in for hours. The nurse had popped out for a cup of tea with Margaret, and Dr Lessing had come and gone, listening to Liam's heart and wondering what he could not really say: how long would the old man last? Through to dawn, at the most. But you never could tell.

Grace Frewin was also in the bedroom, watching from the shadows, for she more than all of them, more than the doctor himself, knew the end was very near. A body can't take such terrible breathing as that for very long; each breath was a pain to hear now. But Jim was there by him, bless the boy . . . the man, she ought to be thinking. As if he'd known Liam like a true son— not like the half-child, the half-father, which the terrible situation had made of them.

The window rattled suddenly with the wind outside, and so loudly that even Liam tried to turn his head towards it, and the fingers of his right hand fluttered for a moment as if trying to urge the rest of his hand to move.

Then he said: 'Go and close the window, laddie, for Mrs Hadden canna do it herself.' And as he turned to Jim again, his head lifted for a terrible long moment off the pillow and his mouth seemed to grow taut and stuck, as if struggling, and he stared up at the strange ceiling of a strange room that was not his own. And then the dark sea surged, and took him; and he died.

'Oh, Liam,' said Grace Frewin softly. 'Oh, Liam!' And she went to Jim, who turned to her from the chair he was in, and reached out to her, and she took him in her arms and felt his head in her bosom just as she had so often when he was just a little boy. And holding Jim tight to her for comfort, she stared down at Liam with such sadness in her kind face. But he would not have wished it otherwise, for though she didna know it, she was the only one in Deal he'd ever been able to call a friend.

PART III

'The Stonor Eagles'

CHAPTER EIGHTEEN

'The period after his father's death and up to the final resolution of his long and enriching relationship with Judith Shure marks Stonor's emergence as a major artist. In this exhibition, for the first time, the two different groups of works he produced in these crucial years – 1974 to 1984 – are shown together, and their links very clearly established. The series of straight figurative drawings and paintings of Deal and the people he knew there: *Albert* (No. 96), *Workshop* (No. 98), *Jamie Chunter* (No. 56), and the ironically titled *My Mum* (No. 86), contrast dramatically with the so-called secret paintings and sculptures of which *The Raven of Storr* (No. 54) was the great expression, and the notorious and controversial *Oiled Beach* (No. 112) perhaps the most famous. 'The first showing of some of these works side by side (Shure Gallery 1989), at a time when the artist's reputation for figurative work of exceptional skill was just becoming more widely known, caused a major controversy in Britain. It was the fact that the artist had been working simultaneously on works as seemingly tender and gentle as *Albert* and others as bleak, cruel and sexually powerful as *Oiled Beach* that offended many.

'But there are many precedents for such an artistic "double life"— with artists as diverse as Goya, Picasso, Klimt, Degas, and Britain's Lowry and Spencer having done seemingly contradictory work.

'In Stonor's case the difference went beyond the subject and into technique. The figurative, gentler work – with only one exception, the famous *Christmas Tree* (No. 60) – is in pencil or water-colour or tempera. This work is tight, controlled, craftsmanlike (as Stonor himself has put it) and carefully pre-planned. The "secret" works are usually charcoal or printwork or oil, the brush works much freer and wilder, almost as if done by a different artist. What this exhibition shows for the first time is how these two approaches found reconciliation through the period of great stress and development for the artist, of which he himself has written: "I was, or felt myself to be, journeying alone to the very gates of heaven and of hell, and to have no control or will of my own. It was a long time before I could bear to look at some of this work again. I was learning, learning, learning all the time, getting to realise how little I knew about technique, painting, sculpting, and, most of all, myself. In the tempera work I was trying to pin life down, my life, my perception of it, and say 'Look, look, this is what I see, share it with me. This is my town, these are its kerbstones, this is Albert, this Michael.' In the other work it was as if life had turned on me and pinned me down and said 'Look, look, and do not look away!' It was dark and frightening and I felt so alone. I said in that work things I dared say in no other way – dark and terrible things sometimes – about the people and the places I did not then know I

455

cared about and needed. *Oiled Beach* is the work which most of all expressed these feelings, and inevitably it is the one people remember and mention to me. 'How could you have done it?' they ask. They see it as a work of isolation and hatred, and perhaps only slowly come to see that it could only ever have been made with love. They see the darkness in it, and, as I did in my work after 1974, only come slowly to see the light.

' "We forget the fact now, but in the sixties and seventies so-called figurative-narrative, or illustrative work, was not something you were meant to do. Critics found it hard, sometimes impossible, to accept that I mixed such work – realist work – with abstract and conceptualist notions. *The Tanahorn Eagle*, for example, which was made in 1977 and placed on the Tanahorn cliffs in northern Norway in secrecy, with the help of two young rock-climbers, was in itself a straightforward sculpture of an eagle. But of course very few people could ever have seen it for real – they only read about it in the newspapers, and of the attempts of the Norwegian Government to remove it which resulted, as I knew it would, in its destruction. It was the *notion* of it that took off, not the work itself. It was an idea, for many a creative and wonderful idea. It was really conceptualist art. It was also a political act, because I believed that that would be an effective way of waking people up to what was happening to sea eagles.

' "But that was my only overt political statement, and after that I saw there were other ways of expressing my love for things – which finally is what good art is – and I turned to them . . ."

'The strong personal element in Stonor's work, at a time when many artists were seeking to remove such elements from their work, is the key to his successful reconciliation of seemingly contradictory elements in the Late Modern movement.

'This is why the death of his father in 1974 can now be taken as a key date in his development, and, as this exhibition is able to show, the progression of the eagle theme and motif through to 1984 is reflected both in the figurative work and the "secret" work. The surge of joyful, rich work that starts in 1985 was marked by another, happier, change in his own life and . . .'

—Marion Poyser in the catalogue for the New York Museum of Modern Art's Stonor retrospective, 1998.

A fortnight after the funeral, Jim called Judith Shure. He thought it was to tell her what had happened, but really it was because he was making decisions and needed to talk to someone whose horizons were wider than the Downs and the East Kent landscape, and who understood his need to make images. She came down a few days later on a Saturday, taking a train on a summer's day just as she had done once so long before. A girl then, a woman with decisions of her own to make now.

At the station they held each other like old friends, and she linked her arm through his as he led her down Queen Street, to the front.

'You look a lot better, Jim,' she said.

He felt it. So much had happened since he had come back, so many people to see and things to arrange, for the burden of making arrangements after his father's death had fallen on him. Frank and Oliver had come for the funeral, but finally not Michael. Albert Chandler came, now a lot older, and his friend L. C. Roberts, the organist, who played the music at the end of the service; and Jamie Chunter, and Sandy Watts from the golf-course. Grace Frewin, Margaret Stonor and Mrs Hadden, and that was about all . . . Jim told Judith about it.

'My father was quite an ornithologist, judging from the records he kept and the various articles with his initials at the bottom which he seemed to have published in various specialist journals. It's amazing. There's even correspondence from Tinbergen, the world expert on herring-gull, thanking him for information on the species and acknowledging his expertise! Extraordinary!'

Jim had found no names of anyone in Skye whom Liam had known, and Margaret Stonor knew none. There was no will and barely any estate: just a small Post Office Savings account, a few pounds in credit, probably all from the old-age pension. It seemed Liam's only expenses had been the three pounds he meticulously paid Mrs Hadden each week (all noted down in a rent-book kept by himself) and money for food which he cooked himself in the upstairs kitchen. He had evidently lived in West Street since 1949 when Margaret Stonor had asked him to leave the house in Beach Close.

Judith came for lunch to Compass Street, and his mother was soon showing her her water-colours and guiding her over the old house. Jim was acutely aware of the grubby tannin-stained teacups, and the jumble on the shelves, but somehow Judith didn't seem to see them, taking pleasure instead in the strange curves and angles of the spiral staircase, and in the sense of age and use in the worn panels and the lovely fireplaces.

'So many of these houses are being taken over as weekend retreats by London people now, my dear, as the old Deal people die off. When we first came here, most of the people in the street were local born and bred. Many still had at least some connection with the sea. But they've gone now, and the houses are being prettified and the old gas-lamps in the streets, which Jim can probably only just remember, have been replaced with electric ones.'

Jim watched his mother and Judith go out into the little courtyard garden, and listened as they talked about the apple tree, and different

457

kinds of apples, and the hollyhocks, and the toadflax which was beginning to flower on the walls.

Later, up on the front, Judith said: 'Your mother's quite different from what I imagined. Much . . . well, much nicer. Much more peaceful.'

'She has her dark side,' he said.

'So have you,' she replied. They walked along the front in silence until they came to some steps down to the shingle beneath the sea-wall, by the same shelter where once Judith had sat talking with Liam MacAskill. They both wanted to be alone for a time with their own thoughts. So Judith sat on the seat in the shelter while Jim went down the steps and walked over the shingle to the sea itself. He picked up a stone and threw it in a high arc over the water. It went so fast that it hissed into the sea with barely a bubble, and was gone. He threw another, and watching him her eyes grew gentle, for down there, literally at the sea's edge, throwing stones, he seemed at peace, a stone in his hand ready to throw, as he gazed out at the gulls over the waves. When he threw it, his legs and body and arms and head seemed to move united in an action he had done a thousand times before.

She thought of Patrick Chanay, who was in London now, and with whom she had spent the night. He was keen to marry her and she was wondering. Familiar, liked by her ageing father, older than Jim, completed and packaged in a way Jim was not, and might never be. She smiled a little, thinking that Patrick could never have thrown stones as Jim did, nor climb over the rusting iron of the groynes without wondering if his trousers might end up dirty. She wondered what it would be like to make love with Jim Stonor.

Jim turned back to the wall and stared up towards her. She looked away.

'What are you going to do now, Jim?' she asked, when he climbed back up the sea-wall steps.

He knew the answer. He had felt it building up for years, and had begun to articulate it with Patti in New York.

'I'm not going back to Stahl's agency. I'm staying here, for a time at least. I'm going to make images, paint and sculpt. Make things. *You* know, better than most.'

She nodded . . . she did know.

'How are you going to live?' she asked.

'I've thought about that, surprising as it may seem. I worked out that my total worth is around fifteen thousand dollars, principally money in Boston Trust. It's money I've saved over the last year or so—the result of things Patti said to me. She was right. She said I'd need it one day, and sooner than I thought.' He stood up again, restless, and looked up and down the promenade.

'It probably doesn't seem much to you, Deal. Just an old seaside town with the remnants of a fishing industry that died before the First World War and a golf-course, and a couple of big old hotels. As my mother said, the new money here is going into the old houses round this part, in North Deal, for weekend retreats. They come down and buy atmosphere. They like the old features: the fireplaces and panelling, the cellars where they find old fish-nets left rotting on the walls by seamen too old to go out any more, with sons who didn't care. They probably find short-pronged forks in cellars and wonder what they are. They've never seen a man digging bait with them. They come down in winter with their London clothes, and walking from the station, they wonder why people look so dowdy, in old anoraks and boots with socks furled over the top. Until they learn about the winds, and go and buy the right clothes. It's my home, Judith, but I know they have the right to buy into it if they want. My mother did in her day, though in a different way. She needed a roof over her head.'

Judith listened, as she had once listened to his father in the same place.

'Do you know, I went on the pier the other night and had a drink in the bar out there which the fishermen use. Most folk don't know it's there, so few strangers use it. But I went in there feeling a stranger myself. Look at these trousers – pants – American! Look at this haircut! West 50th Street! Look at these shoes: they'll not survive a winter's sea salt. I had a malt whisky from Islay they had in stock, and I thought of my old Dad. There was a young couple there, strangers prospecting for weekend property. We got talking—I think they thought I was new to the place. "Where are you going to buy?" I asked. "The conservation area," they said. "What's that?" It was new to me. They told me, and guess what? It's the area I was brought up in. It turns out that the Corporation have woken up to the fact that they've got an area of unique architectural interest which might get knocked down even more if they don't protect it.

'They were nice: young, bright, just a little brittle. He works for IPC Magazines; she's with a PR company. Media people. Friends of theirs have a place here already, in Golden Street. They said they were willing to pay up to twelve thousand pounds to get what they wanted, preferably somewhere in Middle Street, or on one of the side streets. Twelve thousand pounds! My mother paid eight hundred for the house in Compass Street! There's a deeper change in that than just inflation.

'We stood at the window in the bar, looking towards the shore. The Royal Hotel's lights were on. I said to them: "There used to be boats and fishermen north of it, on the promenade in the heart of the conservation area, until they rebuilt the sea-wall to protect the area, then they couldn't get boats on to the beach. End of fishing there."

' "Do you *know* the town?" they asked.

' "I was brought up here," I explained. They seemed quite awed to meet a real live local of their own age who spoke English. I think they thought locals had to be old and with seafaring voices. I told them about the beachcombing and how once there was a smell of boats and tar in the side streets. I told them I remembered a rowing-boat getting stuck trying to turn a corner between Middle and Griffin Streets. I told them about the storms, and how the windows rattled in the night, and herring-gull settled on the chimneypots, in regular, certain stances. Always one up on Spero, the guest house at the top of Farrier Street.

'They started asking questions, real questions, and their eyes lit up, and I suddenly felt like an old-timer, and I understood something I never knew: I have a place that's in my heart and body, whose images are a part of me so deep that I have been missing them for years. They asked me about the tides—didn't even know they come in an hour or so later every day. Didn't *know* it. Didn't know the black-headed seagulls lose their dark head plumage in the winter. Didn't know what a cuttlefish shell smells like or feels like. Had never been alone on a wild shingle beach in a storm. Well, I expect they've each got experiences I haven't, but talking to them made me see what I had, what I loved, what I turned away from when I went up to London to art college.

'They were a nice couple, but what they were buying into was a film set, a beautiful place, somewhere to talk about back in London, somewhere to have drinks in at weekends. Somewhere to go sometimes, and walk at night down Middle Street, loving the old doors I passed by unknowing as a boy, or going into the hubbub of the Ship or the Pelican, drinking, laughing, looking for local colour. I *know*: it's what I've done sometimes in other places. It's what people make a hobby of in certain parts of New York. It's what artists do in towns like St Ives in Cornwall.

'Well, I don't want to paint nostalgic pictures of Deal, or ones visitors and tourists might buy to remind them of a film set they cannot live in. As I talked with them, and stared ashore at my own town, I knew I wanted to spend time making loving sense of the material my home town had put into me.

'Yes, I *do* want to make pictures of Albert Chandler. But not because he's an old-timer of whom an image will be a trigger for nostalgia, but because I love him. Of the beach, because it was my land—it *is* my land. Of the gulls that give a shape to the sky here, because they made me look at them. Even if I didn't have that money saved – and it's not going to last that long at today's prices – I'd still stay here. There's nothing else I *can* do now.'

Judith got up from the seat and stood by him and he put an arm out to her, and then both arms round her and held her to him. 'We're friends,' he said, and she felt his body relaxed and tired against her. It was the first time he had dared say such a thing to anyone. He was coming back to a home he began to lose when Peter Conan left.

'Yes,' she whispered. 'Yes.'

'Well, friend, there's something I want you to see. Something to do with what I've been saying.'

'What is it?' she asked.

'Come and see!' he ordered. And they laughed, good friends.

He took her to West Street, explaining about Mrs Hadden on the way: 'She seems a bit vague, but it's a front really. She's no idiot, and although the house is a total mess, apart from the bit where my father lived, she seems to be able to find things when she wants to. She seems genetically incapable of doing the washing-up, and as I've been in a few times to sort out Daddy's things and I just couldn't stand the mess, I've cleared up her kitchen for her. I suspect my father used to do it for her before he fell ill, and it was only after that that she let it get so terrible. Christ, you wouldn't believe the mess it was! After my second visit she said something rather strange that . . . well, I'll show you first. You'll see.'

When they arrived, Mrs Hadden was somewhere deep in the overgrown garden, vainly pruning back the previous decade's weeds and overgrowth. Jim took Judith out to say hello, and then they went up to Liam's old rooms. All she said, as they passed through the damp and gloomy rubbish-strewn corridors was, 'What lovely proportions! Look at that ceiling, Jim. It's perfect! And I like the skirting boards—they're so big and well made!' He had to smile.

It was the bay window in Liam's great bedroom that she loved most of all, with its view out on to the great walled garden in which Mrs Hadden at that moment wandered about in the May sunshine, lost among her wild plants. There was a double-storey outhouse at the end of the garden, and beyond it the backs of the houses of Union Road, where Albert Chandler lived.

Jim sat at his father's old desk and waved a hand at the bird books. 'See what I mean?' he said.

Judith stared at the books, the box files and the journals, and nodded. It was of a piece with the man she had once met.

'What did you want to show me?' she asked.

'This,' he said quietly. 'The room, the house, the garden.'

Then she understood. He was trying to decide whether to live here for a while, to start his work here, where his strange father had lived. 'Mrs Hadden said she hoped I'd move back in soon. *Back* in. She said it twice.'

Judith looked around the room, and then went out to the kitchen and another room which was empty. She knew what *she* would do: make the second room a bedroom, make the present bedroom a studio because its light was good, change the wallpaper which was a bit dowdy and flowery, and then . . . but she stopped herself from saying it. You don't tell an artist what to put on a blank canvas!

Back in the big bedroom, her eyes cast about the room's details—the peeling wallpaper, the old paintwork, the raggedy carpet . . . so different from her father's house in Golders Green. There everything was perfect, expensive, beautiful, as it had always been. Someone, probably Liam MacAskill in some distant year, had painted this woodwork cream, and not too well. She was used only to having workmen come in and do it. Her kind came to houses like this and changed them – prettified them, as Margaret Stonor had put it – bought their way into a film set, as Jim himself had said just now up on the front. So why, suddenly, did she feel at home here in a strange room, looking out on to a garden so uncared for that her father, Max Shure, would not have tolerated it for ten minutes before he got horticultural specialists to come in and clean it up and replant?

'I would never have thought of living here, except that Mrs Hadden seems confused sometimes, and seems to think I'm my father and that I live here. And when I raised the possibility with her, she really got quite upset, as if she could not believe there was any doubt that I would.'

Judith went to the window and looked out. He looked at her back, at her arms, at the line of her legs beneath the expensive jeans she was wearing. Up at her dark hair which swept back elegantly and fell just a little short of her shoulders. He stared beyond her to the garden, where Mrs Hadden was now struggling to pin back a trailing rose on the wall of the outhouse. He felt at peace with the place, but restless in his heart, a good restlessness, which had him wanting to *start* now, after so very long. It was then he made his final decision to stay.

'And what are *you* going to do?' he asked Judith—which told her what he had decided.

But no, oh no, she didn't want him to ask. Not that, not now. She turned to him and said rather carefully, watching his face for any reaction, 'Somebody wants to marry me. Patrick Chanay, whom I mentioned before.'

There was no reaction.

'Have you seen him since you got back?' he asked. She knew what the question meant: it was the way he stressed the word 'seen'.

She nodded. Yes, she had made love to him. Yes.

He nodded, sagely, looking as Patti had sometimes looked: calm and wise. But he felt rather alone inside. He could not think of Judith with someone else; not that she had ever been with him. He could not imagine her making love. Well, yes he could, but he could not imagine her doing the little things, the silly things, the intimate things of touching and zips and buttons and nakedness that went before. He was just a little afraid of her, intimidated. Just a fraction.

While she, staring at him, at the way his eyes looked at her, and his strong hands resting on his father's desk, and his legs stretched out in front of him, she, too, was a little afraid. There were worlds in his face which he knew of and which she did not.

'Are you going to marry him?' Jim asked. His hand fretted with a filing card on the desk top.

She did not want to answer: she had been avoiding it for so long. She smiled wryly. 'Probably,' she said. Then, 'Yes,' she said, 'I am.' And she was. And at that moment something growing tentatively between them was blighted, withered; and each began to turn away to a separate world. One to a world that was familiar and secure, ordered in the best sense, and rich. While the other began to enter a world made of sky above a dark and troubled sea, where flight was the only survival. Each felt relieved, for though the options they had so unconsciously chosen seemed difficult – marriage and art always do – yet the world they might have faced together then was infinitely more forbidding. For it encompassed all they might have known. It had come too soon for each of them, though each was driven by a sense of age: Judith by the need to have children now and a settled life, Jim by the need for fulfilment in work.

'The time will come when you need a gallery and an agent, and so on,' said Judith. 'You know I'll always . . .'

'Yes,' said Jim, 'Though I thought that Max Shure only dealt with dead artists' work!'

'Father does, but I don't. He knows what he's good at *and* what his limitations are. That's why he's successful. He knows how other people can make money for him. It's a tough world, Jim, the galleries, the shows, all that. You're going to need help. You have no track record. No shows. No catalogues. No commissions. That eleven thousand dollars is going to run out quicker than you expect. You'll need money and guidance.'

He listened because he knew it was true, yet it all seemed irrelevant. It *was* irrelevant. There was only one course he could take, and that was to stay here and start working again. He also felt vulnerable. He had nothing really to show: barely any work.

'What are you going to do about the work in New York?' she asked.

'I don't want to go back. Not even for a couple of days.' She understood very well. His mind was off that now.

'Would you trust me to sort it out for you, Jim? I'll be in New York again shortly. We could always keep anything for you in the London stockrooms—we've already got *Portrait of Miss Campbell*.'

'That!' said Jim.

' "That" is a very fine work, and will one day be hanging in a gallery. "That", as you put it, is worth money. As a matter of fact, there's enough from what I've seen to include you in some kind of group show, say a Christmas show, just to test the market a bit and see how people react.'

'No thanks, I'm not ready for it. Anyway, I thought you Jews didn't celebrate Christmas.'

'Some of us do, I think.'

They laughed.

'Actually, my father never did, so none of us did. I always envied the girls at school who could, and got all excited about presents and Christmas trees. It was a rather gloomy day for us. Mind you, we had Chanukah, which they didn't.'

'You must have had a Christmas tree?'

Judith shook her head, smiling at his incredulity.

'Deprived!' he said. 'And I thought *I* had a tough childhood!'

Later, after jointly sorting out the rooms, Jim watched Judith talking to Mrs Hadden in the garden. It was warm and light out there, and he opened a window so that the air might circulate. For a moment Judith looked up at the sound, and he down at her, and just as something had withered inside them earlier, when, so subtly, she made her decision to marry Patrick Chanay, so now something else started up between them, something quite hidden, as they gazed at each other momentarily. Then she started talking to Mrs Hadden again and the sound of her voice came into the room. It was all beginning to start at last, and he knew even then how lucky he was to have as personal and trusting a contact in the gallery world as Judith Shure. One day she would be useful.

They had not moved the desk, nor the books, and he sat there again for a moment feeling comfortable in his father's environment. On a shelf a little above him he saw the five volumes of *Handbook of British Birds*, edited by H. F. Witherby, the classical ornithological text for the British Isles. He looked up sea eagle and found it under *Haliaeetus albicilla*. Turning to the page, the book opened naturally there, as if it had been consulted just moments before. The species was . . . *'reduced to one pair in Scotland (Shetland) which bred until 1908 when male was killed and subsequently the other bird (albino) of pair brooded on nest each year . . .'* and Stonor learned later it officially died in 1916. Yet his father had written in black ink in the margin: *'1917, January, Skye, Storr. I saw it.'*

Jim stared at his father's old writing. Eagles—why had they always obsessed him? *He* had never seen a white-tailed eagle in his life – only pictures of them, and museum displays. But now a surge of excitement came over him, and the urge to know about them, to go at last to their territories, to walk the mountains and moors where they bred and flew, to make images of them.

He put the volume back and stared along the shelf at other books, until in a corner near the wall, in the shadows, he saw that one row of books was supported by a piece of rock, raw rock. Black.

He took it off the shelf and held it. It was heavy for its size, and unlike any rock he knew of in East Kent. Not sedimentary but, by the feel of it, igneous. Volcanic. It had curious encrustations of white feldspar in it, and was rough, almost sharp to the touch. As he passed it from one hand to the other to feel it and get a sense of its form and mass, a small piece fell away in his hand. He looked closer at the rock and saw that it was brittle and cracked in places, without any obvious structure. It felt powerful in his hands, and had not the slightest sign of compromise with the elements on it, as the weather-rounded flint pebbles and smooth chalk he was used to had. It was from another landscape, another, wilder time. Why had his father kept it?

* * * * *

Far more than the sash windows of houses in a seaside town in East Kent rattled in the storm that blew up on the night Liam MacAskill died. More than milk bottles broke. More than old men died.

For the BBC weatherman's voice came out across the waves to

ships that already heaved with the wind and swell. Gale warnings: winds rising from Force Eight to Hurricane in Dover, Thames, Humber, Dogger and Fisher, all along the weather stations of the North Sea coast to Cromarty, to Fair Isle, to Faroes and to Viking, where the eagles flew.

A vicious early summer storm, of which the one that drove an oil tanker into Romsdal's coast had been the precursor. This storm hit the twelve eagles that finally set out with Mourne at midday, hurricane winds that came swirling in from the north-west and then veered with the passage of the depression back to west, to south; winds to scatter a group of eagles, and to drive any that were old and weak, or young and inexperienced, into the waves and spray-lashed swells below them.

Struggle as Mourne did, she could not keep them together, nor direct them forward to a place to re-group—for in the afternoon storm, visibility was poor, and no prospect of land lay forward or back, nor any easy sense of whether they were being driven north or south of their westward passage.

'Keep close by me,' she cried out above the wind. 'Weever, help them stick close, and you, Reft, encourage them forward.' But try as they did, the eagles began to scatter. Scalla and Eshen, both from the south, both old, could not keep up, and Weever, who dropped behind to help them forward, finally had to press on ahead of them lest he, too, lost touch with the others. While two younger ones, Sogna of Fjordane, and Veste of Smola, were driven southward in a sudden squall that hit them all, and were seen no more.

But somehow, Reft the Vagrant had the gift of encouraging the youngsters there – Fetlar and Aith, Regas and Ness – to stick close to each other and keep near Mourne, who pushed resolutely on, with Mizen just a little behind her, across the winds and driving rains, questing forward for direction, and backward to see that the others were nearby. While over the wind's violence came Reft's strong voice, shouting to one of the vagrants in words that encouraged them all, 'Keep it up, lad, and don't overstrain. When the wind softens, let its lull give you a break. Don't ask me where we're bound, 'cause I leave that to Mourne, but it's a better place than the one we've said goodbye to! Now push on and don't think about how heavy your wings feel.'

So on they went until, at dusk, Mourne realised she had lost four of the original twelve.

Dusk, with darkness coming. Unusually early for summer, but the driving cold and rain was heavy. Darkness and death, it lay grimly ahead of them and somewhere close behind.

Her own great wings were beginning to ache now, so how must

466

the others feel? To her left was Mizen, never complaining, wise in flight and strong, despite her age. Weever, too, who flew as he always had, like a sturdy youngster who would take no nonsense from the wind. And Reft, untidy, without pace or rhythm, ragged but experienced, and good to have near on such a flight.

Mourne noticed that two of the youngsters, Regas the male from the south, and Ness, whose wings were small for a female, stuck close together, flying as one. That was good to see. While Fetlar and Aith, male and female also, liked to stay as near to Reft as they could.

The darkness of evening fell into a wild and treacherous night. Mourne and Mizen, Reft, Fetlar and Aith, all managed to stay close together, near enough for their struggling wings to touch each other in the winds. While nearby, though unseen, in touch only through an occasional call, Weever led Regas and Ness, who were now weakening.

'Come nearer! Come nearer!' Mizen called sometimes to Weever, but she knew that he could not, without leaving the weaker two for ever.

Then suddenly, a light. It did not smell of land. Oil, waste rubbish, and the fretting metal cables on a ship. Not a ship. Not moving to the sway of the sea, but stolid and immobile. A massive, lit-up presence rising from the sea.

Reft had seen one far to the south of their homeland coast. A human place built out at sea, where ships came, and men-things that flew with a sound of an engine. Great circular legs down into the sea, taller than an island.

Caught for a moment in the lights, Weever saw the others and flew with Regas and Ness towards them, regrouping around Mourne, all battling to remain stable in the driving wind.

'We will have to stop and rest, even at a risk to our lives. Perhaps in the dark we will not be seen.' Around them, lit by the lights, now flew other birds of sea and land – gulls, flycatchers, warblers and blackbirds – wheeling and diving in the wind, seeming familiar with the place and using it as the eagles wished to, as a resting place.

Down at its darkest part they flew, where light glinted on wet metal platforms swept with spray. A sudden gust, a scream, a broken wing, hitting some unseen cable, and Regas and Aith were sliding away from them down towards the rising, raging sea, and the others unable to help, until they were lost in darkness and drowning sea.

So suddenly can eagles die. Shocked, wet, cold and tired beyond belief, the remaining six finally landed on the man-made thing that rose from the sea. Weever, Mizen and Reft took a separate stance from the others, down at the end of a deck: Fetlar and Ness stayed with Mourne.

There was a smell of humans but no sight of them. Other sea-birds roosting on the thing were the only sign of life. And the lights, flashing on and off, on and off, at the top of a tower above them; the wind caught in howls amongst the metal cables and metal plates.

Roosting and resting, a light opening, a man standing for a moment in the night and staring at the birds that had taken refuge from the storm on the decks of the oil-rig. A man who kept cards the same as Liam MacAskill had: records of things seen, weather endured, birds that passed by. He stared at the bigger, ragged shapes that roosted with the gulls and warblers, unable to believe his eyes. Great white tail feathers, the yellow bills, the great talons, tiredness hanging from their sodden feathers. His own tiredness replaced by excitement. He went away and roused another sleepy man, with oilskins over his pyjamas, to look and check and verify.

'What are they?'

'It doesn't matter what I think they are. Better you don't know. Just confirm what I'm going to report. Three of them. The heavy, yellow bill and the great tail feathers. White. Two bigger than the others. Look, dammit, *look!* It's important.'

'But they're just bloody birds, mate. Come on, get back in the dry . . .'

'The wings. Can you see their ragged shape?'

'Yes, yes.'

Reluctantly the second man agreed to what the first had seen and the first let him go, but stayed himself, for there was something he wanted to know. Something he had to see. If they were the species he thought they were, no one in British waters in his lifetime had seen what he was seeing now.

The night passed by, and he was wet and sodden, nearly dead on his feet from watching, but the storm was going and the dawn coming at last.

Then, one of the eagles stirred and shook out its wings, the great female, and he saw in the gloom another three further down the deck, hidden by the dark until then. They all shook their wings and the female looked this way and that, and seeming to see him, rose up into the wind – the others following – with a strength to handle the wind he could barely believe. For a turn or two they circled, and he stepped out fully into the wind, buffeted and wet, unable to keep his balance without holding on to a railing, but watching all the time to see which way they went. And all his life that man would remember the moment when those six sea eagles, the first he had ever seen, the only ones ever recorded in the oil-rigs of the North Sea, turned to continue their flight, turning to the west towards Shetland and north-west Scotland, where eagles had not lived for decades.

And he stood at the railing, high above the swelling sea, the wind at his chest, and in his hair, and watched them flying off into the dawn darkness, the light of day rising behind him. Sea eagles, returning to a land they had not been seen in for sixty years.

'I was only wondering, like,' said Reft, 'but how are we going to know when we reach Skye? I mean, none of us have ever been there, have we?'

'We can't be certain, not immediately,' replied Mourne, 'but Mizen and Weever heard Cuillin talk about it often enough, and you've heard Weever and Mizen repeat the names and the places. Clew often spoke to me as well, when I was a youngster. I think we'll recognise it.' Weever and Mizen nodded encouragingly. 'We'll find it, Reft, and when we do . . .'

'Yes, they say it's a place where the winds are fair and the prey easy,' whispered Reft, and stared from the stance they had taken on an island north-west of the Scottish mainland, and hoped it would be as easy as Mourne made it sound, and as wonderful as Cuillin's dreams had made it seem.

They were now among the skerries and islands of the Outer Hebrides, driven north-westward by the winds that veered round behind them on the second day. For a time they had stopped on Shetland – though none could be sure of its name – and Mourne had ordered that the two weakest, Fetlar and Ness, should stay there and rest, for they were near to death with tiredness, and unable even to hunt. Weever and Mourne had to find prey for them. Finally, Mourne sensed it was best they separate there. It would be safer in the long run to split up, and anyway, these two seemed to have an affinity for each other and, perhaps, by Haforn's will, might mate.

'We are surely not far from Skye now,' she told Fetlar, 'and as we are among islands we will be able to find each other easily once we know the lie of the seas. Skye is further to the east, but when we have found it, and some time has passed by, then we will return here for you.'

But they flew too far to the north, so they had to swing south with the awkward winds, keeping to the deserted parts of the sparse islands they crossed and looking, always looking, for an island whose sparkling lakes and rugged mountains would mirror the dream that Cuillin had made of her homeland.

They took their time, fishing in the seas beneath the cliffs, skulking in the shadows at the sight of boats, choosing early morning and dusk as the time to travel on. They found carrion on the moorlands where sheep lay fallen in gullies, and ailing birds made prey among the cliffs. It was all good land and the seas were mild and food-rich—but it was Skye they wanted.

Five days after they left their homeland, a morning came that was clear and fresh, and the seas seemed suddenly blue, and the cliff-side lighter. While up on the moors, which were softer than the fjells they knew, there was a green, and the sway of sedges and flowers among the rocks and peat bogs, and Mourne rose high, and Weever and Mizen followed; with Reft going off to one side, as he liked to. So it was together they saw, over to the east, towards the mainland they had avoided, the misty rise of steep and rugged mountains, to the south of an island that was bigger than any they had yet seen.

In its sides they saw small fjords – 'lochs', as Cuillin had called them – and along its coast a few small villages and a harbour.

'Too populated,' muttered Weever. 'That can't be Skye.' Yet when they looked in any other direction they saw no comparable island.

'Perhaps Skye is further south than we expected,' said Mizen.

'But that wouldn't fit with all the other clues that Cuillin gave us. The mountains are right, but if the Storr is there, it would be on the far side of the island from where we are, and so we couldn't see it. What do you think, Reft?' Mourne called out. Reft always spoke common sense.

Reft circled about and stared for a while. 'Well,' he said finally, 'What I think is this. The islands we've been over are too small and too dull to be the Skye that Cuillin came from. She never said there weren't any humans on it. I mean that's why she left it in the first place, wasn't it? So from our experience there's bound to be even more now. I reckon that *could* be Skye, and we're not going to find out unless we take a closer look. What's more, we're going to have to come to terms with the fact that wherever we go there'll be humans. I don't know what humans are, but they don't always cause our death. What about that place we got a rest on in the middle of the sea? Humans made that. Saved our lives, didn't they? They're not all badness.'

Mourne nodded, and turned towards the island, drifting north to where it seemed less populated. It was still very early morning, and there were no boats about. Just a solitary light moving along a road on the island where the darkness of night still lingered beneath the moors.

They rose higher as they came nearer, partly to avoid any conflict with the colonies of sea-birds on the cliffs, partly to get the best view they could. As they did, each of them fell silent, and an urgency came to their flying, and a sense of excitement. For as the dawn light came over the island, it fell gently into loch after loch, and the island stretched southward beneath them in pockets of green pasture, great spreads of brown and rocky moorland, and the lochs seemed like myriad wings of light spread into the misty distance.

Northward and higher they flew, and over towards the east they saw the edge of the island running parallel with the great dark mainland of Scotland, a dark sea channel running between. In the far north west of the island they saw a strange rise of turbulent cloud, and seas that threshed between great dark stacks of rock into a grim gorge in the cliff-side. No birds flew there and there was a grim forboding about the place. Even at a distance of several hundred yards they could feel an unsettling tugging and sucking of wind at their wings, and a will to go ever nearer, as if dank talons had gained hold of them.

'The Cleft of Straumen,' whispered Mourne. 'Beware.'

'Yes, I have often heard Cuillin speak of it and how it nearly took her into its depths from which there is no escape.'

Mourne shuddered and turned south to better light and fairer winds. As she did so the rugged mountains they had first seen that morning, now far to the south, seemed to rise majestically from the thin morning mist which skirted them, and began to catch the sun which lit their colours. Black and jagged to the west; pink and warm and rounded to the east.

Not one of them dared speak, though all dared hope that finally they had a sight of the legendary Cuillins. They flew round the northern end of the island and then swung southward, to follow the dark ridge whose gentler dipping side they had first seen from the west.

It stretched away ahead of them, steep and sheer to the east side, where the morning sun caught it, shallow and misty to the west. In parts it was high pinnacles and thrust forward, in others shallower, inaccessible, beaten back by the weathering of rain, wind and frost.

'The ridge of Trotternish,' whispered Weever to himself, daring at last to admit to the conviction that now powered his wings.

They swung over the ridge itself, staring down its twisting, rugged length, eyes alert for sleark which surely lived among these cliffs. Ahead the ridge seemed to buckle up and contort itself into a broken mass of dark recesses and drops. Eerie and dark, a place for flying carefully. Then, around the edge of a steeper rise in the ridge, the poke-up of a pinnacle, all on its own, rising at the base of the high cliffs: an outlier from them. They flew more urgently, dropping down to a hundred feet above the highest part. The grass at the base of the cliffs was rich green, and sheep walked there, with evidence of rabbit warrens. Dark pinnacles and cliffs, screes and hidden stances in a bleak and crumbling cliff that had the feel of a dead fire long burnt out aeons past. Then, round a cliff, in among the crumbles of a contorted, broken place, where the very heart might go still for fear—and up on the cliff-edge, and looking down, Mourne settled, then Mizen, then Weever, and finally Reft.

Not a word spoken between them, as they stared into the terrible depths beneath, where cliffs and pinnacles rose from grubby runs of black scree. Eyes trying to penetrate the dark shadows of the grim place. Somewhere, clattering rocks fell in the shadows, down and down beneath them, then out through a gulley and into light, sliding beneath the cliffs. Black rock, with no strata or obvious structure. Pieces of rock that caught the sun and swallowed it to nothing, where encrustations of feldspar glistened white and shining. Somewhere unseen, watching the rockfall, too, a claw scuttered and the voice of a raven croaked. Then another from some hidden place below them on the cliff. The Raven of Storr.

'You know where we are?' whispered Mourne.

The others nodded.

'Then praise the name of Haforn that has brought us home to Skye. Let the Raven see us overfly this place. Then south we must go, to re-possess the Black Cuillins where Cuillin flew, and to find again the ancient nesting sites so long deserted by our kin.'

They flew up out of the shadows of the Storr and into the light of a rising sun. And the Raven saw them go, and saw as well the slide and the slink of a sleark's dark wings as it followed them southwards, its eyes narrowed in hate. Until it veered down among the cliffs of Trotternish to find its own kind, and to gather its forces against the return of the sea eagle to Skye.

* * * * *

Jim's first summer in West Street passed quietly. He had no other wish than to work, and find again the skills and peace that had made him learn to draw and paint in the years before going to New York.

He had no grand design or overall concept to lead him forward; nor any desire to articulate one. He had no wish to talk with other artists, or renew those few friendships and acquaintanceships he still had in London. He wished only to be alone, and free to work; to eat and sleep quietly; to rest after the long hard years he felt he had been through.

He worked sometimes with old Albert Chandler, seventy-five now and retired, except for little jobs that came his way. Albert had been shocked when he first saw Jim at Liam's funeral, looking so pale and overweight, city-bound.

Jim had been restless then, and for those first few weeks uneasy and unsettled. Then Albert had asked him over to the workshop to help him do some lifting he was no longer capable of, and, from then on, Jim had made a habit of dropping by of an evening to draw Albert in his workshop, working at the lathe which he still enjoyed, or whittling away at something or other just for the sake of it.

'There's one job, Jim, which a man can reckon to call himself a carpenter if he can do perfect: make a cross tenon joint out of a piece of squared-off wood. Two by two, four by two, it don't matter that much. But you try making one perfect, and you succeed, and I'll say you've not much to learn!

'As for my old jack-plane you used to eye as a boy, well, hold it firm and look at the wood, and not at *it*. It's part of your arm if you use it right, a separate thing if you use it wrong, like I did in my early years. Quick to go blunt if you use 'em bad. As for chisels and the way they're kept, it's the easiest way to judge a good man, or a bad, by his chisels. There's a true sharp and a wicked sharp, and both'll cut, but one'll cut bad.

'I remember a job once, over Sandwich way. It was in a big farmhouse where the cattle-hand should've known better, when I . . .'

Those evenings, with a cup of old Mrs Chandler's tea and perhaps one or two of her scones on a plate, they'd sit and talk. Sometimes, when he came by, Jim would find Albert playing his old wind-up gramophone, with his favourite organ music, and just making a tenon joint, or fixing a chair. Listening and thinking, an old and happy man with strong hands and a true eye. Once Jim found – or rather tripped over – a set of old seventy-eights in one of Mrs Hadden's downstairs corridors, and took them over for Albert to play. Orchestral mainly, but there was a choral piece in there as well, a bit of the *Messiah*.

Albert held the records up one by one, as if they were as precious as a chisel, to let the light glance on them to see if they were scratched. Then Jim left him to play them, and chatted for a while with Mrs Chandler in her kitchen. It was a house he grew to love, and the things in it – and Albert and his wife – he drew and painted often, always using tempera which was an immediate medium.

473

One day that autumn, he finished a picture of Albert which he felt was completely right: the old man sitting in his workshop staring along the edge of a piece of wood he had planed, and the tools on a bench behind him, worn and old as Albert was, but still fine and true. Perhaps Albert was really a little older than he was in that picture, perhaps there seemed a little more vigour in his arm and look than he had then, but if it was so, it was because the eyes that looked at him and made his image had once seen him with the younger eyes of a boy, and it was an image not of a moment but of years—and years of love. Mrs Chandler's north-country griddle for the scones; the blue crockery displayed on the dresser shelves since 1923, when they married, the year Albert finished his apprentice-ship; the timber Albert kept in the covered arch between street and back garden. Jim drew and painted all of them.

That summer, Jim got to know L. C. Roberts as well, 'Elsie' as they called him, and they would share a drink or two up in the Bosun's Mate. They had a new organist at St George's now, and a new vicar, too, who did his best with a dwindling congregation and an ageing choir. 'Elsie' played sometimes, when the other man was not able to, just as Albert occasionally joined in with the choir, though his voice had nearly gone now.

Though Albert never drank more than a pint and a half, and that mild, Elsie drank rather more, and when he did, he would talk about past times in Deal, and yearned for the days gone by, before the 'townies' had bought up half of North Deal, and the regatta in the summer, with its famous galley race, was still a thing to remember.

'Not like that now, lad, when it's all watching and no taking part. Used to have bicycle-tyre races, and three-legged races, and egg-and-spoon races for the women, and we all went down to the beach and watched the young fishermen show their paces with their boats. Not any more. None left. Isn't that right, Jamie?'

'Aye, it's right enough, Elsie,' Jamie would agree, older now as well, his face even more creased with smiles; but displeased some-times when young mods and rockers tried coming in on a Saturday lunchtime to cause trouble. Sat in the ladies' seats they did, and wouldn't budge even if you asked them to. But Jamie only had to come out in front of the bar and glower at them, as once he had glowered at disorderly able seamen in the mess on ships during the war, and the youngsters soon left off their cheekiness.

Even so, the notion that seats should be kept free for the ladies was wearing thin. 'What ladies?' asked a mod one day. 'There's ain't none left, mate.'

They accepted Jim like an old friend who had been away for a while, in a place he shouldn't have gone to, and had now come back to his senses. And they asked him about New York, and London, and wanted to know what they were like to live in. As for his drawing, it was his second nature and they accepted it. They did not ask what he lived on, but assumed he had some kind of an income from some kind of part-time job in London. They liked him being an artist among them, knowing he loved them, though such a word was never spoken in the Bosun's Mate.

That first summer he was not lonely, but in a kind of daze alone, recovering. A convalescent from a life he had not liked. He rarely worked at night, but read a lot and delved into the more interesting of his father's books and journals.

He built up his studio piecemeal, and not in an expensive rush as he did the one at his New York apartment. He found a sheet of bevelled plate glass in the Deal Showrooms in Middle Street, which came from a butcher's shop up in Walmer, the woman said, and laid it on a table Margaret Stonor had no use for. It served as the ideal base for mixing paints and inks. In New York he had bought an expensive easel, but had rarely used it and, realising how limited his capital was, he now made one up, with Albert's help, from scrap wood. Paper and canvas were expensive, even more so outside London, but he used the best he could find—compulsively buying good paper when he was up in London for a day to see an art show or visit one of the museums.

Brushes, too, became a compulsive buy, and he would finger them with love, and they would seem passports to new work, new techniques, a fillip to encourage him on a grey day. But many went unused for months. He kept them neatly in jam-jars, and was meticulous about cleaning them except that, sometimes, when he was working very concentratedly over a number of days, he would forget a brush or two, and they would congeal and harden. These he did not throw away for they had a scouring, scoring sort of use. He put them in an old earthenware jam-pot, one of dozens he had found back in the fifties, when they moved in to Compass Street.

He had a sink installed in the studio, using the water supply from the adjacent kitchen, and eventually did what Judith predicted he would do—he made the smaller room his permanent bedroom. Nevertheless, he kept a big couch in the studio, partly because he liked reading on it sometimes, partly because he would lie on it and look at his work in progress and think. But also because there were some nights when, for no reason he understood, he liked to go to sleep in the studio with the feel and smell of his works and materials around him.

Perhaps, really, he just liked waking up to the view of the garden through the great bay window, in whose colours and changes he saw the slow passage of summer into autumn. Sometimes he would sketch the view, the sycamore tree to the right, the plum and apple trees to the left at the far end. Or else he made studies of the overgrowth of brambles and weeds that Mrs Hadden seemed positively to encourage, and the winding, secret paths she made through it all, to those few places where she still had the strength and patience to weed and hoe, and grow her private flowers, as she called them. These were the ones that she picked sometimes and put into vases in the kitchen.

The outhouse at the end of the garden was never opened, and he did not go into it. Its dark, cobwebbed windows, its rustily padlocked door, its slipping red tiles, became familiar and pleasant to him. He had no wish to explore it and felt, as he did with rooms in the house apart from his own and the kitchen (which, like his father before him, he kept clean and tidy for Mrs Hadden who seemed incapable of looking after it), that they were places Mrs Hadden had cut herself off from and left to themselves, and he would respect her wish. There was a rambling rose, several in fact, which had overtaken the apple tree and the outhouse building, and which in August had brought a splash of random colour to the view. It faded and began to shrivel in September, but a few of its small roses remained, soft pink-red, a joy to see from the distance of his studio window.

In September too, the shops filled with new school uniforms and student hardware like plastic rulers, slide-rules, and appealing soft green rubbers and pencil-cases, which brought to him that same sense of excitement he had once known at the feel of new exercise books at the start of a new school year.

As schoolchildren took to the streets again in the morning, and his own successors began their years of trailing through St George's churchyard, that other, powerful September change in Deal overtook the beach: the autumn equinoctial high tides came. Sweeping in and stripping away the pebbles, dusty with dark green bladder-wrack seaweed and cuttlefish shells; or leaving orange-boxes which had been dropped over the sides of ships passing by on the Downs, now half-buried in the shingle.

As winter approached, the sense of peace and quiet that enveloped him at first began to leave him, and he felt vulnerable and threatened by a darkness of images born of much more than the real things he drew. They surged towards him from over the sea, and though he wanted to make them, yet he felt he had no control over them, such as he had over a drawing of Albert, or an orange-box.

He tried then, for a few weeks, to make his way with the little social life of Deal, deserting the Bosun's Mate on the front for the Queen's Head in Middle Street, where the bar filled at weekends with the townies from London. There was a strong, gay element in this group, and the brittle chitter-chatter at the Queen's Head, the quick-eyed glances to see who was coming in, and who was going out with whom, reminded him of some of the better gay bars friends had occasionally dragged him to in New York. Their talk was of houses, of fireplaces, of decor, of people not present, of plays newly seen and films disliked. But though he tried, the smile on his face might have been fixed with hair lacquer, for all the real joy it showed. The Queen's Head was not for him.

But perhaps then, in that critical time, very few places or people would have been. For the eagles returning to his hands and his mind were beginning to fly their way into his work and confuse his home-based reality with a darker, richer vision.

If a time can now be set for the start of this renewed impulse, which had already had a brief precursor in New York, when he began the preliminary sketches for what was to become the *Raven of Storr* bronzes, which were finally only completed in 1984—it would be October of the year Liam MacAskill died.

It seemed to him then that Fate itself, or Haforn, or God, conspired to lead him to eagles. Though he knew even at the time that it came his way because he wished it so, yet letters he wrote then, and diary notes Judith Shure made, show that he also believed it could not be anything other than his destiny. So he accepted a reality and yet believed in a fantasy.

The reality presented itself in several ways. First, there was the visit he received in October from a Dr H. L. Osborne, then editor of *The British Journal of Ornithology*, and a world authority on raptors—or birds of prey. A brief letter from him addressed to Liam came in September: 'LHM: Would appreciate you reading the attached and making any comments you see fit. Sincerely, HLO.' The 'attached' was a note by an ornithologist in Norfolk on *Alauda arvensis*, the skylark, concerning nesting behaviour. It seemed Liam had been an expert on the *Alauda*.

Jim's brief, regretful note back brought Dr Osborne down to Deal a few days later, dressed soberly and knocking at the West Street door. He was about fifty, spare, tanned and intellectual-looking. He wore a collar and dark, sober tie, rather uncomfortably, and was quite patently distressed.

'Your father is a very great loss, Mr MacAskill,' began Dr Osborne.

'It's Stonor actually. Complicated family history.'

'Ah, yes, well.' He seemed lost for words.

'Did you know him for a long time?' asked Jim helpfully.

'Oh, no, indeed. You see, none of us knew him, to speak to, I mean, he was something of a mystery to us. Are you an ornithologist yourself, by any chance?'

Jim shook his head.

'So you're perhaps not aware of your father's work in the field?'

'All I know is what these books and records tell me . . .' Jim waved his hand at them across the room. 'None of the family knew him really, in terms of what he did, I mean. The first time I came into this room was the night he died.'

Dr Osborne eyed the books and file boxes and, though politeness seemed to indicate that he should remain seated, yet he was so curious to look at them that finally he said 'May I?' and got up restlessly, to stand closer.

He seemed excited, and in some slight awe, but it was some moments before he rather tentatively reached out his hand and took up a book. He held it reverently, opening it at the fly-leaf as if he expected to see the name Liam Hugh MacAskill inscribed upon it. Jim had already done the same thing and made a simple discovery: his father never seemed to put his name in the books. He never seemed to write his name down at all.

Forgetting whatever decorum gentlemen are meant to show in the presence of the deceased's son, Dr Osborne unbuttoned his heavy coat and went on his knees beneath the books to look at the filing boxes. He opened one at random and pulled out a card. He looked at it and muttered, '*Tringa totanus* 1931. 1933.' He put it back and pulled out another card, '*Philomachus pugnax*, 1948 . . .'

He stood up and turned to Jim, standing with his back to the books and looking rather like a lecturer. 'Your father was a remarkable man, Mr Stonor. Perhaps you don't realise what these cards represent.' He sounded protective of Liam, a little aggressive towards Jim.

'I have some idea I think, Dr Osborne, but perhaps you could tell me more.'

Dr Osborne sat on Jim's couch-bed and did so.

'My predecessor as editor of the *BJO* was L. M. Odham, a great student of the passerines. He died only last year, but I worked with him since 1950 and know the story. In 1928 there was something of a controversy going on about the length and number of primary feathers in skylark wings at different stages of their development. This had been rather a long-standing debate at a time when ornithologists were still concerned to describe the different species accurately. Well, Mr Odham had a letter one day signed simply

'LHM, Deal, Kent' and without an address. It made some categorical statements about primary length and first-year birds, which quite clearly established that the writer had made an extensive study of the species. But more significantly – though its importance was only realised in the context of post-war ornithological work – it suggested that perhaps it would be more interesting to discuss the relationship between the territory and song activity than plumage, and on these points the writer had a number of thoughts . . .

'The letter left Mr Odham feeling very frustrated, since he could not correspond with the writer to check on certain things which were obviously necessary before anything could be published in a serious scientific journal. I believe he made enquiries of correspondents we had then in Sandwich, which for some reason has always had a strong bird-watching fraternity, but no one knew who LHM was. Mr Odham passed LHM's comments on to the people who were most concerned with the issue, and the matter was noted, and for the time being forgotten. But eighteen months later, LHM sent another letter, this time to do with sea-bird migration, which again established that LHM had not only done an extraordinary amount of fieldwork, but was that unusual combination: a hard, meticulous worker with a creative mind capable of making intelligent guesses which set off whole new trains of thought. After that, the letters came regularly through the thirties, all from Deal. The day came when Mr Odham could stand it no longer and decided to track down his elusive correspondent. The full story would take a long time to tell, but it was not hard to read between the lines of your father's, LHM's, letters and work out from ordnance-survey maps the area where he did his fieldwork. It was in an area to the north of the town which no doubt you know . . .'

'The Dunes and Sandwich Bay,' said Jim.

'Exactly. Rather wickedly Mr Odham arranged for a couple of weekend field trips with friends based in Sandwich, and literally haunted the area of the Dunes near Deal hoping to track down his bird! Well, he eventually succeeded.'

Jim laughed. The thought of his father being pursued by eminent ornithologists over the Dunes was bizarre, to say the least.

'I'm afraid that at first your father was not pleased. But you know, when ornithologists get talking, barriers quickly fall – there is no better international language! – and I think Mr Odham threw out a few controversial statements about *Alaudia arvensis* which so provoked LHM that he finally agreed to set down his own findings in writing. But he also insisted – and Mr Odham was always quite meticulous about this – that his name should never appear, nor his articles be published except as material used by other people, and acknowledged as "LHM, Deal".

'That was the only time Mr Odham met Liam MacAskill, and his real name and address was known only to him, and subsequently to me. Bizarre, perhaps, but true. Needless to say, there are many, many workers who owe a great deal to LHM of Deal, as he is known, and would dearly love to have met the man. I think perhaps we realised what a great ornithologist he was when he sent us his commentary on one of the most famous studies in bird behaviour – in fact, a seminal work on animal behaviour as a subject – Tinbergen's *The Herring-Gull's World*. That work was based on years of student work directed by Tinbergen himself in Holland. LHM's commentary, which had already been prefaced by some remarkably far-sighted notes to Odham in the forties on herring-gull behaviour, was one of the very few at the time which took Tinbergen's work a little further in one or two directions—if only in the form of suggested answers to some of the problems he himself made clear were outstanding. Of course, the largest herring-gull colony in Britain is nearby, at Dover, and no doubt this is where your father formed his ideas.

'Since Odham's death I have been the person to maintain contact with your father, and I am sure you realise what a very great shock to me your letter was, and how sad I and many others are. Did you have no idea of his interests or work?'

Jim shook his head, stood up and went to the window. He had been deeply moved by what he had heard.

'You know,' continued Dr Osborne, 'I think that if Mr MacAskill had been willing to write up his work and ideas more formally, he might now be regarded as one of a select few of original amateur ornithologists—in the tradition of amateur history for which Britain is justly famed. With your permission I would very much like to make some comment in the next issue of the *BJO* to record our debt to him, and our sense of loss.'

Jim nodded and muttered, 'Of course, of course,' adding, 'But I think it best that his name be kept secret. It seems what he would have wished.'

Dr Osborne nodded in his turn.

'Tell me,' said Jim, 'Did he ever do any work on sea eagles?'

There was a dead silence and, rather surprised, Jim turned round to look at the other man. He sensed that the question troubled him in some way.

'Sea eagles? That's a strange question,' Osborne said carefully.

Jim Stonor had seen evasion before, around tables at advertising agency client meetings. He had not survived long in New York without being able to smell it. Dr Osborne was playing for time.

'Yes. Was he interested in the species, so far as you know?'

Dr Osborne smiled thinly. 'Yes, as a matter of fact he was. When Witherby finally came out with volume III of his monumental work . . . Oh, perhaps you don't realise: Witherby is the standard text on British birds—LHM wrote to Odham about the entry on the white-tailed sea eagle, *Haliaeetus albicilla*. It gave a date of 1916 as the last year when the species was seen. He claimed to have seen an isolated bird on Skye in 1917, January . . .' Osborne went on in this vein for some time. But there was a look about him which told Jim there had been more to his initial reaction than was now being revealed. This interested him.

As they talked about other things, the strain left Dr Osborne's face. Jim agreed that eventually the records and books might make their way to the *BJO* library for further study by someone prepared to do the work. Finally they went over to St George's churchyard and stood by the grave. Chaffinch and blue-tits were playing among the trees, and a blackbird hopped about the long grass among the gravestones. Jim agreed to ask his mother to provide any details she knew of dates of birth and so on, so that Dr Osborne could write an obituary.

Shortly afterwards Jim was again led towards sea eagles by a chance meeting, and though it seemed magical at the time that such things happened, he came later to see that it was inevitable.

He had become fascinated by artists who used light dramatically, studying the works of Goya and Rembrandt in the art books he had started to acquire obsessively when he made trips up to London. These trips were important to him, and were made spontaneously, whenever he felt the urge to visit the National or the Tate, or to go to one of the art shows, for the autumn season was then in full swing. Once he felt such an urge come upon him in mid-afternoon, and he set off without any plan, only to arrive, after train delays, when the gallery he wanted to visit had already closed. He came straight back—as night-life in London held no allure for him at all. Yet the trip did not feel abortive. He was restless these days, rushing off to do things that would take him away from the tyranny of his studio, then coming back with new vigour.

Judith wrote occasionally, and always briefly. He had had a few cards from France, one from Paris and then a couple from Provence, including one from Arles, Van Gogh's last real home. He guessed she was on holiday down there with her man, Patrick. 'Have you ever been here?' the card asked him. 'I'm sure you would

love it, Jim, and the food! All well. Hope your work is going well.'
Shortly afterwards she sent a Shure Gallery card inviting him to a
preview of some nineteenth-century water-colours, and adding
along the bottom of the printed invitation: 'The Hayward preview
is the same day. That's one you shouldn't miss.'

This was the Hayward Gallery's autumn exhibition of contemporary British painting, and impulsively he went up to see it one
afternoon, after putting in four hours' early start at the studio.

However, it was in the Second Gallery, studying a Craigie
Aitchison, that Harry Ginnan stood, a little thinner, a good bit
greyer, but his spirit seeming no less ebullient and full of cheer than
it had always been.

'I knew you were about!' said Harry, 'Judith Shure told me you
were back. Working down on the south coast, she said.'

They exchanged news, agreed that the exhibition was as disap-
pointing as annual shows of national work selected by a committee
usually were, and took a cab back to Harry's studio in Camden
Town.

The smell of wet clay, the clutter of modelling knives, a bent
screwdriver encrusted with plaster, a pile of shattered grey plaster
in one corner which looked as if a horde of students had taken
hammers to a group of busts—Harry's studio had not changed
much.

'Still teaching full-time?' asked Jim eventually.

'Part-time, two days a week. Sit on committees these days, my
services being much in demand by the ever-burgeoning industry of
art-education administration,' Harry replied. 'Actually, though we
all complain about committees, I rather enjoy them. I've a part-
time job with the Greater London Council now, sort of inspector
of art college inspectors. Now *that's* enjoyable.' Jim laughed and
Harry talked more, eyeing Jim carefully—the student he respected
more than any other for a quality he put into his work: a rigorous
quality.

'So what are you doing? Given up advertising agencies for ever,
eh?'

Jim nodded. 'Yup,' he said, falling silent immediately. Harry
was pleased it was so.

'How are you living?'

'Savings from the New York job. Reckon they'll last through
1975.'

'Really?'

'Well, *into* 1975.'

'Famous last words,' said Harry.

'I'm not going to give up,' said Jim, suddenly very serious.

482

Harry saw that he had aged, not just physically but spiritually. He looked tired, and his face was lean and a little pale. Around his eyes there were the beginnings of crows-feet, and there was a sense of struggle unfulfilled about him—a searching. He never knew why, but he felt love for Jim Stonor, and had done so ever since he made that maquette of the cormorant, or rather the cormorant's memorial, which he still treasured in his country cottage.

Harry offered Jim some coffee. While he was in the kitchen, Jim wandered restlessly around the studio. It was then that he first became aware that the Nature Conservancy Council was commissioning sculptures of endangered species, in association with a petrol company. He noticed a letter pinned to a notice-board – addressed to H. R. Ginnan, MBE, of the London School of Art – which listed the ten subjects, and asked for Ginnan's advice in seeking out different sculptors who might be asked to do the work. Jim cast his eyes down the list. The fourth species was 'the White-tailed Sea Eagle'. His heart raced. He wanted that commission— and said so.

'Well?' he asked Harry eventually.

'Do you know anything about birds?' asked Harry.

For a moment Jim was tempted to make the obvious joke, but the surge and power of eagles' wings was too strong for him, and instead he said: 'I know something about this eagle. In fact, I was talking to H. L. Osborne about it only last month.'

'Osborne?'

'Oh! Editor of the *British Journal of Ornithology*.' Jim gave him a vaguely surprised look in the way that Charlie Stahl had taught him, and which established that anyone who did not know Osborne of the *BJO* . . . well! Ginnan, however, did not look impressed, and the game palled immediately.

'I don't know much about sea eagles except what my father told me,' he explained. 'You see, he came from Skye, and claimed the last sighting of a sea eagle in Britain there—in 1917. He told me stories about them when I was a kid . . .' His words ran ahead of him and he pulled himself short. 'Look, is this commission up for grabs?'

'Jim, they're not looking for great original work but for zoologically accurate pieces in three dimensions, which anyone could recognise easily. Academic pieces. They want straight figurative sculptors. The only original thing about the commission is that they want a different sculptor for each species. Now that I do admire. And from a committee, too.'

'Would you put my name forward?'

'Jim, it's not my decision. I have to show them a portfolio of

483

some artists' work. And no doubt they're getting suggestions from elsewhere. You know. *Committees*. The money's not bad, though.'

'Harry, I *want* to do it,' said Jim firmly. As he stood there waiting, he seemed to Harry suddenly very young and vulnerable again—as he had been in that first interview at the London School. Something hung in the balance then, and though Harry knew that good art does not come from accident or circumstance so much as from pure hard slog and commitment, combined with a mad courage, yet there and then he felt himself to be in the right place to do something in favour of art's way.

'I'll send you the full brief, and you can come up with some ideas and roughs. There's no hurry, Jim. They'll not be deciding anything until after Christmas.'

The hope of this commission, after the visit of Dr Osborne and his curious reticence about sea eagles, now began a flow and surge of images in Jim's mind, images that hovered and flew just out of clear view, and caught him unawares in the middle of other work.

He was restless then and wakeful, and would lie in his bed in the great house in West Street, listening to the wind as he had done in Compass Street as a child, and thinking about those years. He was troubled those nights, and so lonely some days now that his hands could not work, nor his eyes see. He read Witherby again and again, until he knew its entry on *Haliaeetus albicilla* almost by heart. He ordered books on raptors from the Deal library and scanned their indexes for mention of sea eagles, though it was usually golden eagle – or sleark – which they dwelt upon.

It was in the course of this research that he again came across the name of H. L. Osborne, as author of a book, *Raptors of the British Isles*. This book detailed for Jim something he had not known before, and radically pushed forward the dark images that came when he thought of eagles. It seemed that since the mid-fifties European birds of prey had been at the apex of a food-chain of doom and death, whose poison was the pesticides used by farmers to increase production.

After nearly a full century of persecution, and ironically when conservationists were just beginning to win a propaganda war against destroyers of the environment and species, and to stop extermination of creatures like raptors, a new and unsuspected doom had arrived. In Britain, as Osborne's work noted, it had first been clearly observed in the failure of the greatest of raptorial flyers, the peregrine falcon, to recover fully from the official wartime policy of extermination executed because they preyed on carrier pigeons used for military communications. The cliff paths over

Dover, which Jim himself knew so well, had been stalked by marksmen who shot and killed the last pairs of peregrines to nest on the ancient cliffs. A brief period of recovery, and then, in the fifties, ornithologists noticed that the peregrine went rapidly into decline; and suspicions about a group of stable and persistent compounds called chlorinate hydrocarbons, which included DDT, dieldrin and aldrin, were confirmed by official enquiries. What was happening was that pesticides such as DDT, used against insect pests, and dieldrin, used in sheep dips, were being absorbed by earthworms or insects, which were then eaten by small birds and mammals, which in turn fell to the bigger birds of prey. The stable chlorinated hydrocarbons remained in the bodies of these raptors, gradually building up into damaging and lethal concentrations. Ornithologists noted disturbing symptoms: shakiness in birds renowned for their strength; loss of balance in creatures for whom perfect balance was essential; thinning and weakening of eggs among species already so hard hit by the predations of man that their survival was in jeopardy. Such reports came from all over Europe; and in Scandinavia, stronghold of the sea eagle, the species was going into such rapid decline that by the sixties food dumps of uncontaminated food were being provided for wintering immatures and vagrants, who fed on them in flocks sometimes as big as twenty or thirty. But in the southern parts of Norway, where predation by man was still a serious factor, the species continued to decline.

In Iceland the sea eagles' range had been steadily reduced to the isolated fjords and skerries of the north-west, and even there they were down to less than fifteen breeding pairs by the time Jim Stonor became interested. A population which – like the Condor in southern California – was probably too small to be viable any more. The Doom had come.

October passed on into a bleak and stormy November as Jim became increasingly absorbed in such reading and research. His interest in the wildlife along the seacoast of Sandwich, Deal and Dover increased, though it was not the time to see much of the sea-birds that frequented the shoreline in the spring and summer months: the autumn migrations were over, the new year yet to come. But he walked, and sketched, stood in the wet November winds, and watched the fall of dusk over grey and rising seas. He watched the herring-gull, as his father once had, and saw the Corvidae among the dunes and across the beach, preying on dead seagulls. But as he saw them, it was the bigger wings of eagles, and the shadow of the doom they faced, that stirred him and put the power and swirl of pity and a growing fear into the line and the colour of his work. It was in this period that he learned techniques of wildlife field-sketching – carrying minimum equipment, stalking, using natural hides – which was to find its fruition in the years immediately ahead.

All this time he searched for a clue or a lead towards the form that his proposal for the sea eagle commission might take. Doodling sometimes with simple line on paper, shading it with grey and black water-colour, trying to get the shape and mass of an eagle, but unable to find any form that satisfied him. The material of fact and imagination, and the skill of eye and hand and technique that he had already acquired, would not unite into a form he liked. He was beginning to feel an urgent need to observe sea eagles in the field.

Sometimes the frustration and the pain of the search was so great that he grew angry, and felt as dark as the image he seemed to wish to make. Then he would quarrel with his mother up in Compass Street, and refuse to go and see her for days; or he would walk past the warm-lit windows of the Bosun's Mate, muttering to himself that old Albert Chandler would have nothing new to say, nor Elsie anything other than organ music to talk about. He would eye women then, desiring them savagely, going to parties in the homes of people from the Queen's Head, or staring with hostility from the world he was putting himself in at the older, single women of which Deal, like New York, had an unusually high number.

What did he do, they wanted to know. What *was* he? He was an artist.

'Oh!' And the stupid ones would giggle, and say how exciting, and look interested-wary, while the few knowing ones would ask when he had last exhibited, and when he said never, their eyes would look around the busy room for some escape. A failed artist at thirty is nobody's idea of a partner.

Sometimes, though, in those miserable weeks when his head was full of the things seen out on the Dunes which filtered through his mind darkly, he would find himself with someone who fancied him and he would go back through the winding streets of North Deal to a cottage or artisan dwelling he had often passed as a boy, and creep up narrow stairs or into a tiny Deal sitting-room with a 'Shh!' for the children this woman suddenly had, and a 'What'll you have for a drink before?' And then reach out his arms and his body. Urgent, knowing, the overwashed knickers of middle-class, single mums, who had books on the telly and grot on the floor, and smoked as often as not, and fancied seventeen-year-olds on the beach in the summer. These few encounters only increased Jim's loneliness, and he began to enter into a desolate place which frightened him, where he did not want people, but from which he felt no wish to run.

It was a week or so after Guy Fawkes night that he received the invitation from Judith, in French, to her wedding. He barely looked at it, but propped it against the piece of rock his father had used as a book-rest and turned away to enter his work again. And yet what stark isolation glazed over his feelings when he saw that invitation, as a friend who might have been rather more stepped out and away from his desert world into one of apartments, and suits of well-cut grey and shirts of cuffed blue, with dinner parties at a long, polished table – grandmother's – and polished cut-glass, and a bathroom that was clean and warm and had the smell and the love of a woman about it.

Sometimes, for a brief moment, he had a wish to contact one of his London friends—Gerald Opie perhaps, whose name he saw in art magazines from time to time, or Vi Clarke, if he could track her down. Or he might take a fancy to write to Michael, who had written briefly after their father's funeral, but from whom they had heard nothing more. But in his heart he knew he wished to be isolated, not from any wish to throw himself into despair and gloom, but rather because he was entering a state of thinking about the motif of eagles, of which the stories he had told himself in the past, and which he now recalled, were really only a part. He was waiting for something, and it felt like a doom that was certain but unknown. He had to be alone when he faced it.

What kept Jim Stonor's feet on the ground in those months – when his mind and heart were reaching out beyond himself and the township he had chosen to work from – were small things. Mrs Hadden raking the last of the leaves from one pile to another in a garden he was growing to love; his mother making a fish pie for Sunday lunch; Albert Chandler closing his workshop door and walking up to the front with him for an evening jar. Elsie playing the organ in an empty St George's Church. The odd friend and acquaintance stopping in Middle Street for a moment or two and asking how it was going, whatever the 'it' was that Jim Stonor did in that great house he lived in with the mad old woman.

Christmas started to come, first in the shops with red and green tinsel, then in the newspapers with features on Christmas cooking, and suddenly into the Bosun's Mate where old Jamie Chunter put up the cardboard *Merry Christmas* sign, two feet wide and three feet high, which he had bought in Woolworth's in 1957. Some of the new tinsel streamers in plastic replaced the paper-chains of the previous year. His grandchildren were too old to make them now.

Jim saw Judith one day in London that December, ten days before her wedding. She looked tired but happy. She wanted him to go to Paris for the ceremony.

'You *could* come, Jim. From Deal, it's only two or three hours by boat and train. You could hardly live nearer to the Continent.'

But he shook his head. 'My French isn't up to it,' he said, and smiled, not looking at her.

'Thank you for your letter,' she said.

He had finally written, just a note of congratulation, and then several paragraphs about the work he was doing, and the meeting with Harry Ginnan and the eagle commission he hoped to get.

'You ought to have enough work for me to see already.'

He shrugged, and nodded. 'When I run out of money I'll call you,' he said. Then, 'I suppose your honeymoon will be a Christmas somewhere exotic?'

'Lyons, with Patrick's family. They have a family gathering. I'll be the newcomer. Then we're going skiing.'

'That'll be great,' said Jim. 'Great.'

'We'll be based in Paris, at Patrick's apartment, where I've been living for months now anyway. Mine's let. "Never sell property"—that's what my father always says, so I won't.'

'Well!' exclaimed Jim, searching for something bright to say.

They were not communicating very deeply, and there was an unspoken reticence in both of them, a distance not of unfriendliness but of intimacy unexpressed.

'At least you'll have a Christmas tree this year!'

'Oh no, I won't, as a matter of fact. He's Jewish, and the family is fairly orthodox. No Christmas tree.'

Her laughter did not extend to her eyes, which searched Jim's face, and in that little moment another image was born in his mind.

He left her for Charing Cross and the train back to Deal, and the new idea grew alongside his own despair at the Christmas he would have to have. With his mother, he supposed, in Compass Street, in a house that had once upon a distant time had a happy Christmas or two, until the older boys left and never came back, and the family began to wither. Granny drinking a toast of cider to Grandfather in her room, with all the family on Christmas morning. Daddy always coming in and sitting in a corner of the sitting-room during the present-giving, when Mummy read the labels out and you had to thank absent donors aloud before starting to strip off the paper. Mrs Frewin popping in with her own mince-pies on Christmas afternoon, and then a walk along the front. How many years like that? Five or six perhaps before the gloom of adolescence set in. Stockings which, however poor she was, Margaret Stonor always made for the children, though God knows there were grim Christmas Eves, when they were at last in bed, and she alone at a kitchen table or in a tatty drawing-room, with four stockings to fill and an assortment of little things to wrap: a school rubber, pencils, a plastic toy, a paperback for the older boys, a tangerine and toffees; wrapped up a little clumsily, put into old woollen games socks and tied with red ribbon, and she rustling about a sleeping house wishing there was someone to do the same for her. The night she climbed the stairs with four stockings in her hand and Frank was there on his way to have a pee—her 'Mother Christmas' cover blown, and he laughing in the way adolescents do, brittle and unkind.

Jim knew it, and remembered what sometimes she had told him. Those long years of struggle. He was learning to love what she had given them, in the loneliness of his own adulthood.

He remembered the Christmases in New York, so dreadfully false and miserable, without a family or English friends. Buying presents for people, presents that were far too expensive, for women usually, who didn't really care, or cared too much when he cared not at all. One as bad as the other.

That year, more than most in the previous ten, Jim would have liked to spend Christmas in company with someone he loved and who loved him in turn, but as the train rattled on into the black Kent tunnels, he knew that he couldn't expect two days of the year to be filled with love and family if the previous three hundred and sixty-three had been spent alone and isolated. To try, with his mother in a windy, empty house, or with one of his brothers who never phoned and never wrote – and with whom he himself did not communicate – was a pointless exercise which would leave him feeling depressed and have him entering a new year in dark gloom.

Yet how he would miss it, that dream he had not lived for over fifteen years, the stockings rustling at the bedroom door, the presents by a fire and a Christmas tree, the thanks to absent relatives!

It was these thoughts on that journey home, started by something in Judith and her lack of Christmas trees, plus the need to escape for at least a week or two from the dark journey into a new expression he was making, that gave Jim Stonor the impulse to make a work that barely anyone was to see for nearly two decades, but which, in the early 1990s, was to become the image many who never knew his name would grow to love: his *Christmas Tree*.

Amongst the junk in Mrs Hadden's house was a cracked wooden backgammon board, the kind with little brass hinges in the middle, which folds over on itself and forms a box to keep the pieces in. These had long gone, and the leather was peeling or torn right off the inside of the board. He noticed it that very night, on the way up to his studio, and filched it. It strengthened his idea. The following day he went to Woolworth's and bought the shining baubles and tinsel things that decorate a Christmas tree, and he hung them from a leafless branch of sycamore he cut from the garden tree. He had in his mind the famous *Wilton Diptych* in the National Gallery, which shows kings and a saint in the left-hand panel, and angels in royal blue and gold on the right-hand side. It, too, could be closed, for it was a devotional work of art for use when the King wished to worship away from the royal chapel. Jim's idea was not much different. In the left-hand panel of his diptych he painted the tower of St George's Church, angled and dramatic, against a blue night sky, more starry than any Deal had ever seen. And because it was meant as a decoration, and a celebration of a special time of year, he used fragments of mirror and glass in the sky, just as medieval craftsmen had used in decorated altar-pieces. Because of the lack of time, he used quicker-drying acrylic paints rather than subtler oil colours. Though less suitable for the left-hand panel, for the other one they were better, for it needed to be worked fast and spontaneously, with some degree of pre-planning, just as a Christmas tree is decorated.

For that is what the right-hand panel was: a Christmas tree in miniature, whose basic green of pine needles was overlain with a richness of colours and shining lights, of garish reds and tinsel greens, of golden angels and of silver foil, a tree whose baubles reflected a bright coal fire, decorated by excited, loving children who know that from somewhere, and very soon, such presents as dreams are made of will pile up underneath the branches they decorate. At its top, and from a tradition as old as any known at Christmastide, he placed a star of gold and silver, glass and shining paint, the whole built up into a rich and corrugated surface, so that it might catch the light—the paints mixed with a gloss medium to make them shine.

Then underneath, at the side of each of the two panels, he screwed in two small, hinged candle-holders of brass, similar to those on Victorian pianos, and fixed them so they could fold away inside the box when closed. To finish it he painted the outside in a gold lacquer paint, and for keeping it closed he affixed two brass hooks and eyes on the outer side. Then, finally, he painted in black, official-looking letters '*Not to be opened until 17 December*' – the day of Judith's wedding – '*and to be closed on the Twelfth Day of Christmas, 6 January.*' While above it, in bigger, warmer letters, he painted: '*Judith's Christmas Tree*' and in small silver letters, '*decorated by James MacAskill Stonor.*'

490

By the light of day, and in a cold room, it looked harsh and slightly vulgar, as a fully decorated Christmas tree might in July sun. But at night, with its two candles lit, and open on a mantel-piece, it shone and glistened in all the bright colours of Christmas, and somewhere in its heart it held all the yearnings Jim felt for a family Christmas of his own, where music played and each moment of the holiday is encircled with peace and love. It was his gift to Judith for the special Christmas just to come, and the many more to follow it. The symbol of a faith that was not hers, but part of whose ritual she might enjoy.

The making of it brought him the first sense of peace he had felt that hard year. The thought of her receiving it in Paris, surrounded by family and friends, carried him through the quiet Christmas he had in Deal that year. And something of what he had made then stayed with him long after this most famous Christmas present was quietly closed in a room he never saw, somewhere in France; and accompanied him in the hard years that followed.

* * * * *

Mourne, Weever, Mizen and Reft followed the line of the Trotternish escarpment on south past the Storr, exploiting the uplift of wind that flowed from the sea a mile to their left. The morning was sunny and bedewed, and heralded a day of high-rising white cumulus clouds and soft winds in the heath, and flushes of grass across the peat moors that fell gently westward from the top edge of the scarp. While, in its steep cliff-side below them, the sun was creeping among the dark wet crevices, where fern and alpine lady's mantle grew, and yellow rock rose, and caught at the red stems and white petals of starry saxifrage and bladder campion which grew among the shambles of the screes, while rabbits scurried in and out of the warrens that riddled the lower slopes of the screes, where well-established vegetation showed it was more stable ground. In one place they saw several rabbit carcases, eaten out and bleached by rain and wind. In another the white scatter of sheep–skin and wool, and a decomposed head: sleark or raven carrion, by the look of it.

While ahead of them, beyond the escarpment, the sky rose majestically, clouded and blue against the dark ground, lit by the lochs and lochans that seemed to cut in on all sides of this island. Along the coast there was much evidence of humans: roads, houses and, ahead of them, a town with a harbour. In the far distance, the mountains had clouded over, and only their dark bases remained in sight.

'Fly closely and be wary, though it seems quiet and beautiful.

Never forget that Cuillin was driven from this place, and there must still be many dangers here.' Mourne spoke out her instructions clearly, adding, 'These cliffs are as good a place for sleark as any I've ever seen; and obviously humans are thick on the ground.' She veered inland beyond the scarp's edge to where the moor spread out, desolate and peat-laden, until they were out of sight of the road that ran beneath. Here, too, there were sheep, though spread out more widely, with a lamb or two in tow. While off to the far west, where the moor lowered down into greener pastures, they could see heavy brown cattle of a kind they were not familiar with: long shaggy fur and straight, pale cream horns, long and sharp, with great heavy heads. Slow-moving and peaceful, they added to the strangeness of the place.

'Begging your pardon, but how can you be so sure this is Skye?' asked Reft.

'Well, if that wasn't Storr, then only Haforn knows where it is,' said Weever. 'But we'll soon know for certain. Twenty miles to the south are the Black and Red Cuillin mountains, and if clouds hadn't gone down on them, we'd see them clear enough by now. Never seen such a place for changeable weather as this. Westward it looks like a warm summer's day, south it looks like rain, and east there's a wind on the sea channel.'

Weever suddenly stalled and started to descend in that urgent way of his, which indicated that he had seen food. He was always the first to do so, having a natural eye for survival—though Reft was never far behind.

They found a lamb's carcase near a streamlet across the heather, and took stances nearby for a time before Weever ventured forth to feed on it, and the rest followed him in tearing off a piece of the thin flesh and hopping away to eat it alone. Until now the only bird life they had seen was the ravens in the cliffs and a few gulls wheeling over towards the sea, and a couple of grey heron in one of the lochs below the scarp. Over the barren moor there seemed little, but now they were on the ground, and no longer a threatening mass in the sky, the piping call of golden plover came over towards them, and somewhere nearby a nesting dunlin began its regular, deeper call; while some distant lamb called thinly and urgently for its mother.

When they rose up into the air again, the cloud cover over the distant mountains had lifted, except at their highest peaks, and beyond them they could see a spread of pale sea on whose horizon another island cut its profile.

'Look! Look, my love,' said Mizen to Weever. 'They must be the Black Cuillins!' And Weever whispered, 'Yes, yes, we are here.' Then each of them pressed forward over the moor to reach the

Cuillin mountains at last, which rose ever higher the nearer they got.

Higher, steeper, blacker and ever more jagged. Mountains to fly over in awe, whose winds an eagle must learn slowly. Mountains to honour. Opposite them were the Red Cuillins, softer and rounded and glowing pink, between them a deep U-shaped glaciated valley, in which a small river ran and where a small lochan shimmered with the whites and blues of the sky. Along the glen's length there were more sheep, while on the slopes above they could see the occasional movement of deer. A rich land.

Mourne slowed in flight, trying to control her excitement that soon, very soon now, they would be near enough to see the first glimpses of the fabled Loch Coruisk, and see the full expanse of Loch Scavaig, along whose cliff-sides the nesting sites of Cuillin and Torrin's parents had once been.

'We must be wary now, for surely sleark are here, and will attack when they see us,' said Mourne.

'They'll have seen us already,' said Weever quietly.

'Well, we're not going to skulk our way there, or creep in by dusk,' replied Mourne, proudly. 'Whatever we do, they'll object, so we might as well do it boldly. Remember this is our rightful place, once ruled by my own kin, and we will one day claim it back. But four of us is not a population. We must be bold but circumspect.'

So it was that Mourne, Weever, Mizen and Reft the Vagrant, flew at last down the great glen of Sligachan, nervous of the mountains on either side, from which they might be watched from a hundred places by the cold eyes of sleark. They flew at three hundred feet—high enough to give their flight majesty and power, but not so high that they could not dive lower and avoid a mid-air clash, where their low numbers and inferior manoeuvrability, away from sea-cliffs and changing air-currents, would put them at a disadvantage.

Mourne led them, pushing forward fast, until the ground below fell away to another valley to their right, which the morning sun behind them reached at the same moment they did, to cast their four shadows across it and down, deep down its boulder-strewn slopes and heather-grown sides—down to where the deep, glistening waters of a loch spread out, more beautiful than any they had ever seen.

They circled and stared, their shadows turning on the waters below, and they gasped in wonder at the sight. For though the loch was long and great, yet it was made to seem narrow by the sheer black walls behind it, and off to the north-west, where the loch cut into the very heart of the Black Cuillins, it was overhung by majestic, jagged cliffs, rising ever higher until they were lost in wispy cloud.

To their left it ran seaward, stopped short of the sea by a low rise, the ancient lip of the drowned valley from which the loch was formed. A short surging river cut the last few yards through the wall of this natural dam, and ran down over a sandy bay into the water of Loch na Cuilce.

'Well, there you are. Didn't I say we'd make it eventually?' It was Reft who said it, and celebrated with a ragged flight of fun and joy over the legendary loch. 'And I hope those sleark are watching, because these wings may be old but they've never felt as proud as they do now, and I don't mind who sees it!'

Though they were tempted to explore widely, to get a feel of the shoreline and mountains, yet all agreed it was best to stick together and go slowly, establishing a base not in Loch Coruisk, but further along the coast among the sea-cliffs facing out to Loch Scavaig, where they would feel more at home. After his initial flush of enthusiasm over Coruisk, even Reft was wary: he had lived too long not to know that sleark must already have taken such a prime site, and if individual sleark had not threatened them, then it must mean that some group attack was planned.

At mid-morning they saw boats on the loch, and took cover in the cliffs, deciding to keep to well-hidden stances and watch over the ground from a position of strength. As well as boats, they saw a few humans over by Loch Coruisk, and a single human with a dog walked the cliff edge above them. A seal swam in with the tide in the afternoon and basked near the shore, before slipping out with the tide again as the sun began to fade in late afternoon. Then they heard the haunting call of curlew from the shore, and answering calls from another bay that lay beyond the promontory opposite them. While out to sea in the south, a small island caught the last sun, turning golden from its daytime misty green and brown, blue and purple. This was probably the Isle of Eigg, which meant that Rhum, of which Cuillin had often spoken, would lie to the west, and out of their present sight.

A slow summer evening began to fall, and sounds took over from sight. The curlew and the piping oyster-catcher, golden plover on the slopes above them, and a hooded crow somewhere near. The urgent flap of shag across the loch below them, and another to a roosting point beneath the cliff-face.

'It's quite as beautiful as she said it was,' whispered Mizen.

'Aye, and the food looks good,' replied Weever, 'though I'd have to explore all over before I could be sure. But it's rich enough, and good in winter, too, I expect, being this far south.' These words were whispered a little nervously. For there was a growing sense of danger around them in the unknown straths and moors, and up in the gullies and clefts of the Cuillin—the sense of a marshalling of sleark.

The attack, when it came, was sudden and far more powerful than they might have expected. Sleark are better in open air than along a cliff-face. With a sliding swish, two sleark topped the cliff above them, wheeled round, and without hesitation, as if they had reconnoitred well, surged down towards Reft, who had taken a stance a little apart and slightly more exposed.

'Don't move,' ordered Mourne, 'for they cannot dislodge us.'

Reft's reaction was swift and loud. 'Bugger you, mate,' he cried out, and presented his talons to the air where the sleark had been. Then another pair came in, again from behind them, so they could not see the approach, their talons raking along the cliff-face within inches of where Mourne stood.

Then silence. Nothing. Tense, waiting, watching. Then, as dusk deepened towards night, and even the curlew fell silent, a sudden angry calling of sleark and a rush of wings and talons out of darkness at them, close enough to the rock-face to rasp viciously against it. And then an unearthly call of anger and threat before they were gone, unseen in the dark.

'Typical bloody sleark, that was!' declared Reft, when they were certain they were not coming back.

'Stay still and shut up,' ordered Mourne, angered by the attack. And so they did, all night, but barely rested before dawn.

It was the first of many attacks and scuffles between the sea eagles and the sleark, attacks which kept them out of Loch Coruisk, and on the seaward cliffs where they were safer.

'We'll steer clear of the Cuillins' heartland for now,' ordered Mourne, 'and wait until the winter, when territory will not be held so jealously, if at all. Meanwhile, do not provoke the sleark, nor invade their territory.'

They would proceed slowly, getting to know the shoreline south-west of Scavaig, and familiarising themselves with the skerries and islands that lay to the south along the coast. For safety, they scavenged and hunted together; territory would come later. But it was all rich in food, and felt good beneath their wings.

There were, they found, four pairs of sleark around the Cuillins, and there might have been a fifth on the promontory of Rubh' an Dùnain, but that a nest there, though fresh, seemed to have been deserted, and the eagles gone. Sheep and cattle grazed this section, and it was rarely walked by humans. But Reft disliked it. 'Something makes me uneasy over there,' he would say, while Weever mocked and said: 'At least there are no sleark there, and the fishing's good.'

'Well, I don't know,' said Reft. 'That pasture-land may look all right, but it's got shadows about it. I don't like it.' That was true in a way, for at its most seaward end there were traces of a long-abandoned human settlement.

'It's a change to see somewhere abandoned by them and not by us for once,' was Weever's reply.

'Watch for humans all the time, and get to know the places where they live and walk,' said Mourne, interrupting this wrangle. She was referring especially to the couple of crofts and a farm around Glen Brittle, beyond the mountain above Loch Scavaig.

'Our troubles will come next year, if Weever and Mizen breed,' said Reft one day. 'A nest is a target for everybody—humans, sleark, ravens, the whole bleeding pack of them.'

The summer passed into autumn, and that to winter. Stormy, grey, rainy weather, far milder than any winter they had known. No snow until late December, and that only a light powdering that served merely to delineate the falls and ridges of the Black Cuillins more clearly. It was then, when the sleark were less territory-conscious, they began to explore the mountains themselves, getting to know the steep-rising peaks of bare rock, too steep for flower or mammal. Tussling sometimes with sleark in great flappings of wings among the clouds and cliffs. Taking stances to stare into the valleys below, across an island that even in winter seemed fuller and busier with dangerous life than they had expected, and left them feeling uneasy, for all its beauty. Days of heavy rain when they were tied to their stances, missing the white stretches of fjells in their homeland, on which snow would long ago have fallen.

In those weeks of January and February, Mourne began to understand the immensity of what she was trying to do, and why this journey of theirs could only be a beginning. They would need more sea eagles to make it work, and luck and courage and endless patience, too. She knew that more of them would die, perhaps all of them finally. She knew she would have to dispossess the sleark of territory. She knew that humans would come and disturb them.

Yet for all that, she knew this was her place, and the food was good, and they should at least try.

In February, Weever started to stake out a territory on an island south of the cliffs, leaving the others on the mainland to continue their hunting along the coast, as he began to make what scrapes of nests he could from the limited shrubs and sticks he found along the shore. For on this part of the island there were no trees, and the few bushes and shrubs in the more sheltered clefts had no new growth, or even signs of any. The peaks were still snow-powdered and the sea still grey, and apart from resident oyster-catchers and gulls, there was little birdlife.

Mizen followed Weever over to the island, and Mourne and Reft watched their mating flights, whose patterns and rhythms cast the light of life over the grim sea. Perhaps they would succeed, perhaps . . . But somehow the vigour that had once been theirs was not there that spring, the exposure of the island too great, and the changes they had seen since flying from their home territory being too disturbing. After only two or three weeks, Mizen drifted back to the mainland and joined the other two, flying only occasionally over to Weever, who doggedly stayed where he was for a time. Mourne was disturbed to see how old Mizen seemed now, and tired. The adventure she had come on from loyalty to the memory of Cuillin had put her in a place that finally was not hers. Their journey was becoming a desperate nightmare.

A wet spring came, and spring gave way to the first days of summer, as the cattle and sheep began to go out into the hills again and the first lambs were born. They watched the lambing warily, knowing that it was both a time of danger, when humans were also abroad, and also, occasionally, carrion. The ravens here, they noticed, were bolder than in their homeland, mobbing lambing sheep and seeming to know that the best moment for attack on a lamb is at parturition, the moment it leaves the mother and struggles to find breath and life. Then, as it lay wet and flopping in a mess of bloody afterbirth, the ravens came low over the hills, croaking and diving, while the mother sheep watched out, ready to struggle up and chase off the Corvidae as best she could. Some lambs were too weak at birth to make the struggle, and their tiny mouths opened in silent, failing bleats, and their neck muscles struggled to support their heads, whose eyes were barely open. More than once they saw ravens go in for a kill on the moorland above the cliffs. A wheeling, blue-black, shaggy wing, a terrible call, and beaks flashing past a struggling mother to stab out the eye of a weakling lamb. Then another, and the bleats terrible, and the afterbirth red on a brown moorland or in a grassy covert.

Reared on fish and the seashore, the eagles did not try this tack, except once, and a fatal time it was. Mizen and Mourne came across a couple of raven at a still-living lamb they had taken, and, frightening off the ravens, took what they could. They did not see the human approach, and only the wary call of Reft saved them.

A sudden bark, a racing collie dog, the human coming over the ridge. Then ravens and eagles both were gone, but not before a shot was fired after them. Eagles killing lambs; his thought was wrong, but fatal. Strange eagles, big eagles, best not a word said, but the death deed already done. Do it the way they did in the old days long ago, when the MacAskill Clan still occupied the deserted peninsula of Rubh' an Dùnain—with a poisoned carcase.

So it was that Mizen was poisoned. And Weever crossed to the mainland to find her body, limp and wet after rain, her great, beloved head thrown back in an agony of death, her wings folded for ever, her tail feathers begrimed and dank. His mate, his beloved, dead.

'Come on, mate. Come and find food over the loch now, for there's nothing you can do, nor any of us. Come on, Weever.' It was Reft who comforted him, and Mourne who took a stance nearby to watch over him where he hunched among the cliffs overlooking Loch Scavaig. But he never seemed really alive again.

Three days later he, too, was taken—but shot, not poisoned. By a human not seen near the carrion he had left, for he did it by night and waited till the morning, watching over the sheep's body for the eagle to come, not raising his gun to the hooded crows but hoping – and rightly – that their commotion would attract an eagle. Weever, the careful one, the one who had seen so much and done so much, had not eaten since the death of Mizen, and disregarding the warnings of the others he went to the sheep boldly, as if he hoped to die.

The man who killed him looked long at his body in wonder, for this was not a golden eagle, nor any bird of prey he knew. Then, checking the hills to see if he was overlooked, he took a knife and cut off the head, and put the carcase under rocks on a forgotten scree below the cliffs, to rot. The head he wrapped in a cloth and put in a jacket pocket, with his dog excitedly running at his side and jumping at the smell of blood.

Strange times, dangerous times, and now just Mourne and Reft alone. Waiting, wondering, silent, proud.

They flew north along the western coast at dusk to find a place away from the mountains and humans, to give themselves time to think and recuperate. They disappeared from view, skulking, reconnoitring at dawn and dusk, ever more watchful—the last two of the twelve who had started out. And the Raven tells us that always, when Mourne began to despair, with wild thoughts of flight back to Norway, or north to Iceland, Reft would say: 'It took a lifetime coming here, and there wasn't one of us expected it to be easy. Until now I've always done the easy thing, gone the easy way; but in the end it left me nowhere. You led me here, Mourne, and here I'll stay, because something tells me this is a place for sea eagles to be. Weever and Mizen would have wanted you to find a way. The food's good, and the weather's mild, the winds as fair as any I've known. So, you trust Haforn like your mother did, and know that I'll stay at your side until the day I know you've done what you set out to do.'

'And what's that, Reft?' Mourne asked. 'I've almost forgotten.'

'Why, to see your own young, and Cuillin's grandchildren, fly out over Loch Coruisk again, looking as proud as they ought to, knowing who their mother is.'

So, vagrants both now, and without much left but the faith in Reft's wings and a belief deep in Mourne's heart that this was the sea eagles' place, the two of them saw the summer begin and discovered the reality of trying to live a dream.

★ ★ ★ ★ ★

The first months of the new year after he had made Judith's *Christmas Tree*, Jim Stonor turned further in on himself, and became even more unsociable than in the previous nine months. He was preparing final drawings and a maquette for the eagle commission he hoped to get with Harry Ginnan's help. But the real struggle in him was not so much with the work itself, but rather the dilemma he faced in his need to create an accurate representation of a species, but also to invest it with the idea of a species endangered by man and a changing environment. Throughout January and February he tried to reconcile the two, but became bogged down in a compromise solution which did not work.

It was on one of his regular walks along the seafront that he realised what, in retrospect, was blindingly obvious: there could be no compromise. The work he wanted to make – at that point a loose idea based on an eagle, hardly recognisable as such, emerging from a cliff-face – would not be accepted in its idea form by a committee wedded to an altogether more prosaic and conventional concept. His solution was pragmatic, and born of years of working on advertising agency presentations to clients. One of the tricks of the trade, with a client unwilling to take visual or copy risks, was to make a conventional presentation of draft work which the agency knew would be acceptable, but with provisos about having to 'see how it worked out', and maybe making a few changes on location, or at paste-up stage, and so on. Then, when the lead times for the campaign made it too late to change, present the finished work in the way it would have been presented originally, had the client been prepared to trust the agency more. Manipulative, dishonest, but it worked. He decided to produce a conventional work for the proposal, and keep the real work up his sleeve until he had had time to develop it, and soften up the committee.

One reason for this political approach was quite simply because Jim needed the money. His original $15,000 had disappeared rapidly: a car, the rent, materials and equipment for his studio, books of reference, his trips to London . . . they had all quietly reduced his bank balance. By March there was less than £1,900 left, and a totting up of material costs and basic living expenses alone showed he had only three or four months of freedom left. So he needed the commission money, if he was to get through the year.

In mid-March he finally made his conventional proposal, and remembering the importance of presentation, he had the accompanying outline professionally typed at an agency in London on special headed notepaper printed up for the occasion. His proposal was deliberately long, spelling out in detail the plight of *Haliaeetus albicilla*, and including as much ornithological and ecological jargon as he could muster. At his interview with the committee, a mixed bag of oil executives and Nature Conservancy Council professionals, he arrived neat, tidy and professional-looking, and made sure to let drop that although it would, of course, be a great privilege and honour to undertake the commission, he would have difficulty in fitting it into the work he was already committed to over the next eighteen months. He also made very clear that he had no intention of starting the work until he had a chance to travel to the species' present habitats, mid and north Norway, and north-west Iceland, on which travel the bulk of the commission money would be spent. It was a good performance, born of years of similar theatre in New York agencies, but though Harry Ginnan tipped him off that he had done well, he had to wait two months before getting official confirmation that he had been awarded the commission.

Towards the end of this period he heard from H. L. Osborne again. It was a brief letter with the spring edition of the *British Journal of Ornithology*, containing his father's obituary which still kept the identity of 'LHM' secret.

Dr Osborne wrote in his letter: 'We hope you feel the obituary is fair and acceptable, and I would be grateful if you could pass on the second copy to your mother, who has been so helpful. News of LHM's death has hit the ornithological world hard, and it is a measure of his reputation, and the slight mystery attached to him, that we have had a great number of letters from people who, one way or another, have been helped by his generous and always self-effacing work. Several of us feel that some sort of memorial is called for, and a little money has come into the office for this. However, there is the problem of anonymity, which you rightly raised in connection with the obituary, so we are in something of a dilemma over this. Your ideas would be most welcome.'

Ideas, images. From where, apparently so suddenly, do they spring? Not from thin air—but usually from months, sometimes years, of slog, and work, and thinking, and worry. So now, reading Osborne's letter in his studio on an April day, when eagles were around him in thought and image, did an idea suddenly bloom for a memorial for his father, which was also a response to the deeper unexpressed ideas work on the commission had engendered in him. Two Scandinavian names came to him: Varanger; Tanahorn.

Urgently he leafed through the books on eagles he had begun to collect; he muttered, and his eyes grew excited, and a restlessness came to his body and hands: Tanahorn; Varanger. He had read something of a nest site up there, in the furthermost north of Norway, finally abandoned in the fifties, the nest material still there when the observer inspected the site—but unused for years. Tanahorn and his father. An eagle to represent all of them, eagles that had died—like the Unknown Warrior of the First World War, who represented so many of the dead and the living: his father as well. An unknown eagle, cast in bronze, representing so many who had gone; his father, too.

Jim Stonor placed a sketch-pad on the easel by the window, rummaged round for a thick, soft pencil, stared for a while at the largest-scale map he had of Varanger, and then drew the plunging line of a high arctic cliff-side, rough and basaltic, fragmented and falling into its own scree at one side, and then plunging vertically into the sea. And on it, small but powerful, below a dangerous overhang, he boldly put an eagle at its stance. Staring, wings half open, perhaps about to fly. An unknown eagle that might have the power of Cuillin in its wings, and the wisdom of the Weir, and the love of Mizen and the sturdiness of Weever, and that caring warmth of Reft; and the courage of Mourne and the hope of Bjorg. He could not know then what powers would rest in its bronze wings and body.

But underneath the sketch he wrote boldly in capitals 'THE TANAHORN EAGLE'. Few would ever see it, but the idea of it, the impossibility of it, the courage in its making and placing would make it as well known in time as a *Guernica*, or Christo's *Running Fence*, up for a fortnight along twenty-five miles of a Californian landscape, remembered in pictures and film for centuries to come. *The Tanahorn Eagle*, his father's memorial.

A few days later, Jim called on Osborne in London, and though he did not then mention his idea for a memorial, he learned things that gave him the final impulse he needed to move from research and sketches to actually starting to make what became the Eagle Series. Using the opportunity presented by Osborne's letter, and already confident of having the commission, he asked him what he knew about the present status of sea eagles. As before, he detected the same reluctance to talk he had noticed in Deal, but he ignored it.

'There's a chance I'll be doing a sea eagle piece for a Nature Conservancy Council commission,' he said, taking a gamble. 'I'll need your help with contacts if you'll give it. It's what my father would have wanted, given his interest in the species,' he added, twisting the knife of sentiment and loyalty.

'As a matter of fact, I know you have the commission,' Osborne said, to Jim's surprise. 'Hubbard of the NCC told me. He's on our committee. He said your proposal was remarkably informed. You seem to know most of the prime nesting areas in Norway and Iceland. He wondered if you'd ever talked to me!'

'Petersen,' muttered Jim.

'Ah!' exclaimed Osborne, 'Petersen!'

A look of fellow-scholarship came to his eyes. Rolf Petersen, professor of ecology at a Swedish university, had written the classic text on sea eagles, including site markings for many of the birds along the Norwegian coast—a matter of concern for European ornithological officials who were now increasingly worried about the lengths to which obsessive egg-stealers would go to hunt down their prey. At least one Scottish golden eagle site had been raided because its nest site was too precisely located in a scientific paper.

'Your itinerary apparently takes in Skye, Mr Stonor. Why? Sea eagles have not bred there for over fifty years.'

'Personal reasons, and instinct. The fact is that my father created such a vivid image of it in my mind that part of the process of making this work must be to see where this species was last known in Britain. I was going to ask you for an introduction to anyone up there who might be prepared to hold my hand a little. I'm not an ornithologist.'

The same wary look came over Osborne's face again. Jim waited, saying nothing. The crux of the interview had come: Osborne would or would not help him.

'Well, I suppose I have to say something. You are putting me in an extremely difficult situation.

'From the research you have done you will be aware that we have an efficient body of amateur birdwatchers all over Britain, constantly on the look-out for unusual species to add to their lists, besides the normal sightings they would expect for their areas. You

502

may know about the "twitchers" who, the moment some rare vagrant is spotted, hurry off to wherever it has been seen – even right across the country – so that they can add it to their list. Their interest frequently borders on the obsessive, and in some cases it doesn't do much harm, but where a species is *re-establishing* itself, the disturbance they cause may be fatal.

'Also, there is a well-organised and totally ruthless group of egg-collectors in this country for whom eggs are prizes, in the same way as individual birds were trophies at the end of the last century. When the osprey began to re-establish itself in Scotland in the mid-fifties, for example, the first eggs they produced were, from the egg-stealing point of view, the ultimate prize. Their nest was raided several times, ruining their breeding chances. Only round-the-clock sentries finally made success possible.'

'What point are you making, Mr Osborne?' Jim was puzzled, but a distant excitement was building up in him.

'A year ago we received a call from the Royal Society for the Protection of Birds, which is the most powerful bird lobby in Europe, that vagrant sea eagles had been sighted by one of their members on an oil-rig in the North Sea. By God's good grace, the man wasn't a twitcher but a sound student of natural history, who properly understood the significance of what he had seen.'

'But haven't there been sightings of vagrants several times since the last war? The right wind conditions probably bring them over from Norway. Wasn't there one as recently as 1969, in Shetland?' asked Jim.

'True, but this was different. This was not a single individual seen only momentarily. Our informant observed six sea eagles of varying sex and age, resting for a period on an oil-rig. When weather conditions improved, they flew off to the west, towards Scotland.

'The RSPB wanted to know if they should publish this titbit, or was it best kept quiet. In view of the unusual number, we kept quiet. Nine months later, a group of ornithologists from Leicester University, doing a census of sea-birds on one of the more remote islands of Shetland, saw a pair of sea eagles apparently in established territory. The significance of this was not lost on them, nor the need for secrecy. One of these was a juvenile, and the observers were not there sufficiently long to judge whether they were trying to breed, though it seemed likely. The significance of this sighting can hardly be exaggerated, so we sent someone from the Fair Isle observatory to investigate. The fact that it was an isolated island made it very much easier not only to monitor, but also to keep secret. Well, the sighting was confirmed, but one of the individuals, the male, disappeared, probably dead from some unknown cause. The female was still there at the last report.

'Let us suppose that those two were part of the group seen on the oil-rig,' continued Dr Osborne, his voice now low and urgent. 'What happened to the other four? Well, we're not sure, but last month a group of geologists working ground in southern Skye came across the decapitated body of an eagle, and one of them had the sense to call a friend at Rhum, where there are ornithologists. The corpse was identified as that of a mature sea eagle, a male. It had been shot. Local sheep farmers, of course, deny it. The killing was almost certainly done by a shepherd worried about the safety of lambs, which eagles are said – wrongly, we think – to attack and kill.'

'Where was it found?' asked Jim.

'Just south of the Black Cuillins, on a moorland peninsula overlooking Loch Scavaig. A place called Rubh' an Dùnain.'

Jim went cold. The name was a childhood memory, a place mentioned by his father, along with those others, Loch na Cuilce and Loch Coruisk. Last home of the sea eagles of Skye.

'It seems, Mr Stonor, that the sea eagle is trying to re-establish itself in north-west Scotland, just as the osprey did in the fifties, and the avocet in the forties. It is hard to imagine the full significance of this development, or the enormous difficulties we will face in helping them to achieve what seems so impossible. The chance of survival is bleak, and some of the other species are in serious decline. In your own home area of Deal and Sandwich, for example, I doubt if the Sandwich Bay ternery will survive through to the eighties. The pressures of population are too great, and frankly the attentions of well-meaning but asininely stupid birdwatchers are sometimes criminally unhelpful. Now, the first clutch of sea eagles' eggs in Britain would be the greatest prize any egg-collector in Britain could wish for this century. It will be ten or fifteen years before we can know if we have been successful.

'I tell you all this for several reasons, but one is that if you go up to Skye and start ferreting around, you could do a great deal of damage. It is better therefore that you are given the right contacts up there, who will advise you how to approach your research.'

Two weeks later, Jim Stonor received formal notification that he had been awarded the commission, along with a contract and the promise of the first instalment of money on signature. At the end of May he had made his bookings for a journey of research and observation which would start in Skye and take him successively to Iceland, Norway, and Lappland. The cooperation that ornithologists were to give him in all three countries, combined with the risks he was prepared to take in pursuit of his work, was to produce the real material out of which the Eagle Series came.

The journey he made over the next twelve months, repeated more selectively in the three years following, are covered in Stonor's *A Sketchbook round the Northern Seas*, published in the late 1980s and in the wake of a number of successful natural-history artist books. Many of the drawings and water-colours he did in that period were 'art' rather than merely natural-history drawings, and the book represents the best link between his gallery work and his basic field sketch-books.

In June that year he camped at the Scottish Mountaineering Hut at Coruisk on Skye, walking and observing wildlife of the peninsula. In August he went by boat from north-west Scotland to the Faroes, and on to Iceland for a two month back-packing tour of the country, half of it spent in the north-west in the company of an Icelandic ornithologist.

This was followed by five winter months in Norway, at a field station in the north, ending with nearly three weeks' camping and walking in the desolate north of the Varanger peninsula in the spring of the following year, where the already potent idea of *The Tanahorn Eagle* took final shape.

In the course of such fieldwork, time takes a different pace than it does in normal urban life. The measurement of days gives way to the passage of weather. 'That was the stormy time' may refer to three days of gale. 'The time we sketched sea-thrift on the Bodo coastline' may refer to ten days of continual fine weather. 'Those dark weeks in Norway' may refer to nearly three months when the sun never rises.

Only four or five 'moments' during this year of travel and work, in which eagles became only a part of the visual research he did, though *The Tanahorn Eagle* was its immediate end-product, were to stand out at the end for Stonor.

On Skye, the first arrival at the Storr, crunching up the same screes his father had once climbed; and the arrival by fishing boat from Elgol to Loch Scavaig and its natural harbour at Loch na Cuilce, from where a short climb brings the first views of Loch Coruisk. In Iceland, there were the great glacier tongues of the Vatnajokull, and the dangerous climb, alone, up the screes beneath the Lomagnup, in which so much of his later Eagle Series was to be spiritually based. The *Cliff Bronze* of 1978 is only finally appreciated in its full scale by someone who has stood in the shadow of Lomagnup, as Stonor did . . . as Torrin did for so many years, and as Bjorg and Mourne were to do.

But always those that grew to love Stonor's work remember the name of the Tanahorn Cliff on north Varanger, to which he flew in a tiny eight-seater passenger plane, landing at a nearby arctic fishing port where ice flattens and stills the sea in winter; and even at the height of summer the ground is frozen beneath the shattered fragments that make it a rock desert, while snow lies unmelted in the shadows of the cliffs and in pockets on the undulating plateaux above them.

Standing there, at last, beneath a cliff that stretched sombrely ahead along the shore, he knew that few, if any, of those who would see his work could ever come there. They could not see, nor touch, as he did, the luminescent, grey Russian timber, bleached by sea and wind, which accumulated beneath the cliffs—piled so high that in places he had to clamber over it to make progress. Warm, tough wood, whose whorls were shiny and crystalline against the softer grey, wood to touch and feel, whose curves came from structure and weathering. Whose experience inspired other images and works inside him.

There he climbed the dangerous Tanahorn Cliff, his boots slipping on the scree, and then traversed a ledge five hundred feet above the sea, to a place from which, with ropes and help, he might reach the spot beneath an overhang where one day, when he brought it there, he would place *The Tanahorn Eagle*. Fragments of rock slipped beneath his climbing-boots, sliding over the ledge to spiral down to the flat sea below. Stonor lost his nerve and almost his life, and inched back off the crumbling face, and on up to the top, scared then of the tundra wastes of which the Tanahorn was the northern apex. Grey skies and bleak clouds where the Weir had flown, and Cuillin; and somewhere lower down the cliff, an abandoned nesting site overlooking a dead, arctic sea.

He took off his rucksack, took out a small sketching board and pad and some pencils, drank some coffee from his flask, ate a sandwich of sild and butter, and knew that he was at his journey's end. The eagles were gone. His heart, as theirs now, was in Skye. So now he could draw the scene without favour or sentiment. He paced the cliff-top, and made sketches, and leaned over the edge to take photographs from directly above the site where he would place the bronze. It had to be over the sea and not the scree, so that when it fell, as fall from these shattered, vulnerable cliffs it one day would, it would be gone for ever. Let the idea of *The Tanahorn Eagle* be a warning of what might finally happen to the sea eagle itself.

He had come from Skye, from the Faroes, from Iceland, from southern Norway and along the western coast. North was the Barents Sea. A year had passed by. Now, up there on the Tanahorn,

Stonor wanted to turn back for home and make the works which had been building up inside him for so long—and a life that touched the people that had touched him. Peter Conan, Gerald Opie, Judith Shure, Harry, his mother, Grace Frewin . . . they had all given him so much. Now he wanted to reach out to them and give back, again and again, the love and joy they had given him.

'What is true flight?' he whispered to himself into the arctic air, feeling foolish for talking aloud in such a place. It was the very question Cuillin had asked the Weir at that same spot . . . or perhaps it was at that moment in his imagination that she asked it. Whatever the answer was, he – like Mourne, like Reft, like Bjorg of Iceland, like Judith Shure – had yet to find it.

Three days later he flew into Heathrow, and instead of making his way down to Deal, headed instead for Ginnan's studio in Camden Town. *The Tanahorn Eagle* was not to be the commission after all. It was for his father's memory, and his own life, and he would make it later. Cuillin was the one he would make for them— though they would never know her name. Cuillin, who had travelled from Skye afraid of the dark sea to come—as he had been. Cuillin, who opened her wings wide over the sea at Videroe Cliffs on the Faroes, and wondered from where she would ever get the strength to push herself off for the start of her flight. Cuillin, who took a stance with the Weir on the Tanahorn, and dared begin a dream. It was her life and hope that his hands came out of the sky to make in clay, to be then cast in bronze, on that day in May 1976 when he came back to Ginnan's studio to begin his work for real.

CHAPTER NINETEEN

'It's not enough to make good work, an artist has to stand up in the marketplace and sell his wares, just like any other trader. And if he can't do it for himself then he'd better find someone else who can, unless he's going to starve. I nearly failed to learn that lesson. Thinking that the marketplace ought to come knocking on my door, all the way down in an obscure coastal resort on the south coast of England. Which has more to do with arrogance and cowardice than modesty, in fact, without exception, all the best and most successful artists of the twentieth century have been superb salesmen.'

—James MacAskill Stonor in an interview with Sally Beaman, London *Sunday Times*, 1987.

THE hardest and most challenging period of Stonor's working life as an artist was the two years following his return from north Norway in early summer 1976. Unknown, untried. Everything seeming to depend on a single small commission; and with financial worries and personal worries, he had to begin finding his own creative language.

Although the seminal work on the Eagle Series predates this period, it was during it that he produced two of the initial bronzes: *Eagle* (1976) for the Nature Conservancy Council, which was cast in November that year; and *The Tanahorn Eagle*, cast the following spring. Two bolder works, *Cliff Bronze* (1978) and *The Raven of Storr* (1983), were first begun in this period, either cast or modelled, to mark his move away from strictly figurative work.

Significantly, although he appeared to lead an exceptionally solitary life up to the end of 1978, when he begun *Oiled Beach*, one of his greaest works, it was in this period that he began to follow through the urge he had felt in Tanahorn to remake the friendships he seemed to have abandoned on his departure for New York at the beginning of the seventies.

It began closest to home, with his brother Michael. The first letter in a correspondence that was to affect both their lives so much in later years came soon after he returned to Deal and was working intensely on *Eagle*. It was prompted by Margaret Stonor, now seventy, being struck by a recurrence of the illness that had affected her in 1952, after the move into Compass Street.

'Although the doctor says it is not serious, provided she is careful,' Jim wrote to Michael, 'it has hit her hard as she cannot move from her bedroom for a while. She has, if anything, been more active than ever since father's death. She is a stalwart of the local artists' group (which I avoid like the plague!) and misses that very much. Mrs Frewin has been coming in, though she's getting on, too, same age as mother, which has relieved me a lot as I have to work, work, work all the time to finish a commission. I go round almost every evening, and she has been talking increasingly about the family, which she never did before. There's a lot I could say, but she was in tears about you this evening, feeling she never did enough. She would appreciate it more than you can probably imagine, if you could write something to her—even if only a note. Tell her what you're doing these days. In her low moments she feels you are lost to her, as if you were dead. Write something if you can.'

Stonor had little hope of this happening since, apart from a brief letter on their father's death, none of the family had heard anything of Michael for nearly eight years, though Frank's wife, Mira, always wrote to him at Christmas.

The answer when it came, a month later, postmarked Oxford, rather surprised Jim. He imagined that monks would write as churchmen sometimes spoke, beatifically removed from reality, rather than as the normal human being Michael now sounded: 'I was touched by your letter and understand better how she must feel, having myself been very, very ill last year. I have written to her. You sound as if the work you have chosen is hard to do and rather lonely, and that, too, I understand, as this life I have chosen has never been easy. It is a constant struggle with oneself to keep an open, unafraid prayer to God. As you will see from the address, I have moved to a monastery school near Oxford, where I am teaching history and English, and in charge of music. This is a great joy to me, as it has not been my lot to be involved with music for five years past. I missed it greatly but learned much about myself and my vocation in coming to terms with that . . . What is the commission you are doing? This must be a great thing for an artist to have.'

Simple as this letter was, Jim was deeply moved by it—and Margaret Stonor by the one she had received. Until then, neither had appreciated or admitted to themselves the loss in their life that Michael's departure represented. And in that moment, with the reading of his letters, the first part of the darkness of his leaving began to lift, and part of a greater darkness over Jim began to go as well.

He replied a few days later, late at night, as a relief from working all day, and it was one of many such night-letters he wrote to

Michael, letters which, in those years of isolated work, were to be his best and deepest conversation.

12 June: 'Summer is well and truly here, the sea sparkling all the way to Sandwich Bay, so it's strange that I am preoccupied with darker imagery when I am not working on *Eagle* . . . I am trying to do an hour's rigorous drawing each morning before I start serious work, taking as my subject the view from the studio window. My idea is that if I do the same thing each day, I will begin to see more—but at the same time there ought to be a gradual seasonal change to relieve the boredom . . .'

24 June: 'I should never had said I'd be bored doing it. Angry, fed up, exasperated with the fact that it is never the same, though I knew intellectually it wouldn't be, yet it still surprises me that it's so! *Eagle* going slowly and have discovered I have to make a booking, like going to the dentist, at the foundry. Harry Ginnan has suggested I commit myself to a date, then the deed will have to be done!'

5 August: 'Too good a day not to go swimming, so I went! Remember the pebbles round here? Sitting on the beach letting them fall through my hands, I realised that each one I felt and touched has a different feel, a different personality. Just like human beings. This amazed me and I brought three back and have them on the desk now, trying to decide what their personalities are! One's definitely grumpy and tired . . .'

30 August: 'I keep mentioning Mrs Hadden who, for all her eccentricity and wish to keep herself to herself, not only obviously needs someone around, but actually keeps me sane. She disappears on hot days and tidies up the front room, or rather un-tidies up. I have never seen over its threshold. We keep to our territories, the kitchen being our only communal place: she puts flowers in it, I tidy it. The other day I did a sketch in crayons of the vase of flowers she had put there, and substituted it for the real thing to see if she would actually notice. She said nothing, removed my sketch, and produced another vase. The flowers I pinched wilted up in the studio, and I felt very guilty and foolish . . . I enclose an ink sketch of her to give you some idea of what she's like . . .'

30 September: 'Storms, storms. Pebbles right across the front and down Golden, Silver, and Farrier Streets. I always love this time of year and *Eagle* will be finished in time . . .'

Michael's replies were irregular and generally brief, but he apologised for this several times, making clear that such letters must be regarded by him as a break from a different and more serious life with other demands on his time. In short, his letters gave a sense of reluctant restraint. He wrote:

15 August: 'It is perhaps a forgiveable complaint to make that no town in Britain is further from the sea than Oxford! Your description of the Deal seaside in this weather is positively cruel.'

26 October: 'By the sound of it, there is not much difference between the struggles I sometimes have with myself and my indulgent will on a retreat, and the struggle you are obviously having in these final weeks of making *Eagle*. I pray for you, Jim, because I know how hard it must be now. It will all be over by the end of November, when I hope to hear the casting has been successful. I wish I was able to write more . . .'

Eagle was delivered to Edinburgh in December, and first shown publicly the following February, in a period when Stonor, freed from the worry of it, and with the final payment for the commission received, was deeply involved with *The Tanahorn Eagle*, which represented an advance from the rather traditional – though thematically significant – *Eagle*. For this reason the goings-on with a few local journalists and oil and conservation officials in Edinburgh did not impress him. His sudden removal from his studio in Deal to the razzmatazz of the press launch simply left him cold.

But his disinterest went deeper than that. The previous month he had heard again from William Ferguson, the birdwatcher contact on Skye which Osborne of the *BJO* had given him, and the man who was keeping the closest eye in the field on sea eagle activity. Did he fancy a break from his garret, asked Ferguson, to give a bit of help with some fieldwork? The breeding season was about to start. Jim wrote back saying yes.

It was sleety weather, and a difficult drive from Edinburgh over the snowbound Highlands, but Skye was, as ever, milder than the mainland. But its moors were bleak and colourless, and the Cuillins shrouded in grey clouds of driving rain. Sheep huddled wetly in the lee of bridges along the roads. Skye at its worst.

Ferguson, a widower and ex-civil servant who had spent most of his working life in London, had retired early at fifty-five on a reduced pension augmented by a small private income, and lived comfortably, if muckily, in what had been his holiday home in Broadford on Skye, at the intersection of the only two roads on the island which led anywhere near the Cuillins. His contacts on the island were good, considering he was an incomer and more English than Scot, and he kept an eye on friends' holiday homes through the winter. He had several convenient bases all over Skye for the fieldwork he did.

His love of the island and its flora and fauna was enormous, and obvious from the clutter in his huge kitchen-parlour. It had a wide open fireplace on which he burned peat and coal and the driftwood he collected, all piled up at its side. Over the fireplace he placed the many postcards he received from naturalist contacts all over the world, and on the mantelpiece lay a pile of about-to-be answered correspondence. Books, maps, two sheep-skulls, boards with botanical specimens pinned to them, an old brass microscope, walking-boots and green waterproofs cluttered the tables, sideboard, dresser and the floor in the great room. He drank nothing but tea and a malt whisky made on the island. He cooked and ate well, and, indeed, there was a thick and bubbling Irish stew waiting for Jim when he arrived.

Ferguson's approach to fieldwork, like Jim's approach to his own field sketching, was meticulous and thorough, despite immediate appearances. The flap of his rucksack had sewn to it a list of essential items to aid his packing, typed on white paper inside a plastic bag to protect it from rain—compass, map, rations, thermos, water-flask, notebook, binoculars . . . a list born of frustrating omissions in the past. He was also rigorous in writing up his field notes at night, doing this wherever he was and whatever the conditions.

With whisky and a bowl of stew to hand, they sat on either side of the fire and chatted. Like many fieldsmen whose life is their work, Ferguson exuded peace and goodwill.

Suddenly he said: 'You never told me you were of Scots descent.' It was true. When they had first met Jim had not mentioned his father, or given any other name than Stonor. 'It's on your letter heading: MacAskill.'

Jim explained the background—and about LHM of Deal.

'Well, well, well,' said Ferguson slowly when he had finished. '*That* explains why Osborne was so helpful. He didn't explain to me, you know. Kept the secret. So you're LHM's son! What was he like?'

As Jim explained, Ferguson listened in silence, pouring Jim another whisky as he talked. Jim was conscious that Ferguson would trust him more because of the work his father had done. For the first time in his life he was conscious of Liam as an active influence in his life.

'Extraordinary!' said Ferguson at the end. 'And in all those records I wonder if he made mention of the position of the original nesting sites on Skye? It would be fascinating to know exactly where they were, though I have a good idea from what some of the old folk have said. But of course, none were skilled observers like LHM.'

Jim explained that Osborne would get someone to go through the files, but it would probably take years.

'What do you know about the MacAskills on Skye?' asked Ferguson.

'Not much. Do you know anything?'

Ferguson smiled. 'As a matter of fact I do. But it can wait. I'll take you there. That's the best thing. Tomorrow. Now, about the sea eagles. There was a sighting of a pair, a fairly mature pair, on the west of the island in November; and again in South Uist by one of the Rhum Conservancy people last month. No breeding or territorial behaviour—so probably vagrants. But, more interesting, and the real reason I wrote, is that a younger male was seen by a good friend who was fishing recently in Loch Scavaig, along the cliffs below Ceanne na Beinne, which I'm almost certain was the last nesting site on the island. The sighting was quite positive. That's near where the male was found decapitated last year. We're going to spend a few days in a bothy between there and Coruisk. You've got all your gear I take it?'

They drove over to Glen Brittle the following morning, and leaving the car with a farmer, they set off to walk over the moor and round the edge of the southern Cuillins towards Gars-bheinn, the mountain forming one side of Loch Scavaig. They walked easily together, Jim in climbing-boots and breeches, Ferguson in green wellingtons and with an old army anorak over several pullovers. Both carried rucksacks and binoculars. Neither said much, though Ferguson would occasionally halt at some animal spoor on the ground, and mutter to himself and point his stick.

The ground rose until they had a view south-west to the very end of the peninsula they were crossing. Beyond it, across ten miles of sea, was the Isle of Rhum, shrouded by cloud.

'Do you see the point at the end of this peninsula?' Ferguson asked. 'It's called Rubh' an Dùnain, which in Gaelic means something like 'the promontory of the small hill'. The eagle's body was found some way above us . . .' He raised his stick, '. . . and it's over the cliffs here that the sea eagle was seen this year.'

Jim stared silently over the wet moor, the wind cold on his face and the straps of his rucksack heavy at his shoulders.

'I wonder if my father ever came here?' he said, finding it hard to believe that the old man whom he had known in Deal had ever been younger, and stood somewhere near where he stood now, his eyes screwed up against the wind.

'Oh, I think we can go further back than that,' said Ferguson quietly. He thrust his stick into the ground a little in front of him and leaned into the wind, staring towards the end of the peninsula.

Black rocks and skerries there were white with driving waves. He slowly looked round at Jim. 'This is what I wanted to show you. I thought you might be interested. I'm absolutely certain your father came here.

'The MacAskills are one of the oldest families on Skye, and it's said that when they were driven out of Ireland, MacLeod of Harris gave them lands in Skye. What you're looking down at now is the last MacAskill stronghold on the island. It was abandoned less than a hundred years ago, and if you go down there, you'll see the field boundaries are quite clear, and the walls of two of the houses still stand. That's where your ancestors come from, and I'm sure your father would have come here at some time. There's still a fort down there—a chamber cairn really.'

He seemed to realise how affected Jim might be by what he had said, for he stepped back a few yards and pretended interest in some lichen on a rock, leaving Jim to stare at the little bit of moorland and deserted rocks where once his ancestors walked, and which his own father must have explored.

'You know,' he said eventually, when he trusted himself to speak with a firm voice, 'I think my father was afraid to come back.'

Ferguson looked at Jim, his eyes crinkled and warm. 'Yes, it might well have been like that. It was for many Scots folk who left,' he said.

'Well, now, I'm going to find a spot over in the lee of Cnoc Leathan and have a hot drink. Why not go down and have a look around. I won't come with you, if you don't mind . . .' Jim was more grateful than he could say that Ferguson was sensitive enough not to accompany him there—and that he was going to move out of sight of him, so Jim could feel quite alone.

'If a mist comes up, just follow the coastline round to Coruisk, and you'll find the bothy. It's a longer walk than it looks. Here, let me show you on the map.'

If the goodwill and understanding of William Ferguson was a major factor in Jim's discovery of Rubh' an Dùnain that morning, the sense that he was returning home on his father's behalf to his ancestral home was what made it so emotional and significant for him.

Each step along that primitive path brought Jim nearer to a spiritual home which his father had deserted, and always missed, and whose loss had hung like a cloud over him and his family. As Jim came over a final rise which gave him a full view down on to the ruined hamlet beneath him – grass-covered stone walls enclosing a sheep or cattle field, ruined houses and remnant outlines of more, the ghosts of vanished people – he stopped, and his eyes filled with tears. He wished then that he might have had his father with him, to speak Gaelic and to explain the many things he did not know, nor ever would. To bring alive the history that was lost among the broken stones and among the heather and grass that bent in the wind about him; and which whispered in the sea below the cliffs.

Yet whatever had been lost, Jim began then to understand what it was he had been given in the eagle story. The last of a race leaving its ancestral home with a dream of coming back one day, when Haforn, or God, would make it possible. A terrible sadness, Liam's sadness, projected into a story for a little boy who, he would never know nor dare to hope, might one day stand where their kin had stood, and weep as he did for a home they had to leave. As so many had wept in the Highlands, for the homes their poverty and their landlords drove them from, and the vales and straths and burn-sides they would never know again.

If Jim sometimes felt foolish that morning, stumbling about the walls and stones of Rubh' an Dùnain, crying, he did not care. He felt the burden of his father's loss lifting from him, and that same sense of light come to him which had come in such a different way with Michael's letters. It was all of a piece, and he knew his life was changing and deepening—and that his work must as well.

He ate an early lunch among the ruins, staring at the sky reflected in the lochan near the shore, thinking and not sketching. Indeed, he made no drawings at all that day, but thought instead of the tough and sometimes bitter life his ancestors must have lived, and that what he had now was a better lot than theirs. Not a better life, perhaps, for that lies with the heart and not with circumstances; but a better *lot* than this bleak place.

He thought of what the eagles were, of what their story had become. He thought of the life and emotion he had put into it, and still put in it, and knew then very clearly that often he had turned from life to live in this story. But had *he* shown the love or the courage or the purpose of Cuillin, or Clew? What of him was there flying with Mourne? Or with Reft, a vagrant as he had been, as so many were; as his father was.

How long he stayed there, he did not know, but suddenly he knew it was too long, and he must trek north and find Ferguson at the bothy by Loch Coruisk. But first he made his way round the lochan to the furthest promontory, and then back along the cliffs to the Dun itself—now little more than a few rocks.

Then up the slopes and away, to turn once more and look back and think about what he knew in his heart: that he could never return and see it that way again, or with such power. He would come back again, that was sure, but never as he had that day.

Then, for him standing there, the strangest thing of all, and something that was to haunt him for years yet to be fought through, was the sudden realisation that in those few hours something of the eagles had begun to go from him. Their power over him, as his over them, was slipping. It was a moment's insight which would take much work and suffering and joy finally to make clear. But he saw then that the story was coming to an end, and would leave him one day, and that when it did, if he had not learnt – as an eagle should – to fly true, to fly as Liam never did, then he, too, would be lost in a world he did not have the courage to touch with love.

Stonor's stay with Ferguson on Skye that week passed without sight of sea eagle. The weather was too wet and bleak to see much at all. But on his return to Deal, work on *The Tanahorn Eagle* immediately began, without any reference to previous sketches and drawings he had made. For on Skye he had touched something of his father's, and therefore his own, roots which made it possible for him to invest the wings and head and feathers of his new work with that eternal loss that lies in any vagrant heart, eagle or human.

Six weeks later, Jim heard news from William Ferguson that pushed him even deeper and more urgently into his work. The first positive evidence for sixty years that a breeding attempt by sea eagles was being made in the British Isles had been confirmed. The site was not on Skye, but forty miles to the south-west, in a tiny island of South Uist, an island which has many similarities to the islands off the north-west coast of Iceland.

* * * * *

Again and again Reft had spoken words of encouragement to Mourne, but through that January and February she had grown increasingly despondent—as once she had in south Norway, before Clew found her. She took very hard her sense of guilt at having led so many across the sea and seen them lost, especially Weever and Mizen. She felt she had betrayed the faith and trust that Clew had put in her. In vain Reft declared it was not her fault, and that there was not one of them would have turned back, even had they known what to happen.

'Well, it's not exactly what we expected—I mean, there's a lot more humans here than I imagined. But as I said at the beginning of it all, you can't keep clear of danger all your life. If humans are the Doom, then it's best we face the fact. I reckon the carrion and prey we've taken here is cleaner than that in the south of our own homeland. Also, the place looks bloody marvellous: I've never known such a beautiful winter all my life. No snow to speak of! As for the winds here, well, they can't be beaten . . .' So he did his best, but still Mourne was cast down, and it was only slowly that Reft began to realise that it was for mating and for young that she craved.

Well, he wasn't going to be the one, not him, Too much of a wanderer and too restless to stake out territory, and all that nonsense. But still . . . And they say, when they speak of Reft, that he took a stance by himself on a cliff on the island of Uist, and spoke the shortest prayer to Haforn ever known to be effective. 'So far, Haforn, Mourne's come a long way for nothing. So why not give her a chance for once? If an eagle's got to suffer, let it be me 'cause there ain't much I haven't seen in that way.'

The way they tell it, the very next day, over the isles to the south of Uist, they saw the distant silhouette of a soaring eagle whose beak was strong and whose tail was white, and whose flight pattern was unmistakably that of a male marking out territory.

Some say that Reft saw him first, others that Mourne's instinct drew her that way. However it was, it was Reft who stayed still and Mourne who circled nervously above him, staring again and again at the distant eagle whose flight, on her rising into view, had gained a pride and urgency that none could mistake.

'Well go and get on with it then,' said Reft finally and a little grumpily, for he had said plenty of farewells before, and he knew that the sooner they were over, the better. This was just another one. This was not a moment to stay and watch. This was Haforn's will.

'Stay and see what eagle it is,' said Mourne, still hesitating, hardly daring to hope that her heart's deepest yearnings might soon be satisfied.

But Reft left her there, not looking back, and wandered north along the ragged coast of Uist where the diver and the greenshank call, and the wet peat bogs cast lonely shadows. He would endure them if only Mourne might find her way, for she was a good eagle who had given him more than she would know.

As the eagle gyred on the sea wind, a weak sun caught its back each time it made its furthest turn, and in wonder Mourne whispered a name she had tried to forget but never could: 'Bjorg . . . Bjorg . . . eagle of Iceland . . . beloved partner I thought I'd lost.'

Then, as she advanced over the spring-blue sea, her flight began to soar over skerries and islands up into the sky to join him. While there he flew proudly, not looking at her, as if pretending it was only an hour since they had parted so suddenly and inexplicably in the shadow of the Lomagnup.

They began to fly again as one, casting their shadows on the rippling sea below, and across the heather and thrift of the skerries. Gull and tern saw them, seal watched them as they circled higher round each other, their great wings curved up to the sky, their primaries out and rippling, their great tails white as snow; their talons sharp.

Yet still Bjorg refused to look at her, except for sidelong glances at her wings to trim his course with hers, and keep their rising in the sky patterned to the sea and islands far below.

For a year he had searched, staying too far north amongst the Orkney Islands, and later in Lewis to drift among the Outer Hebrides, searching the wrong places, without the same clues that Weever and Mizen had received from Cuillin.

A year alone, in which the young Icelandic eagle had matured and grown stronger, more powerful and certain of himself. But always angry, too, that she had left him at a call he could not understand, for she was his love, and for him there could only ever be her; no call could be more powerful than that. So he had travelled the islands a long year through, steering clear of the place he did not know was Skye because it looked too overrun with humans—especially as he was used to having hardly any beneath his wings. A year passed and February came, and a terrible, unfulfilled urge to mate and make young. Then he remembered what his mother, Thurid, had once told him: 'You're a male, and your lot is always to find territory first and a mate second. Mark out your ground in flight, overfly its limits, make yourself known, and as sure as the arctic sun will one day shine again, a female will find you.'

So it was, and he flew now over a territory that might be a bit loose and ill-defined for his taste, but at least he had his beloved Mourne at his wing, and driving him on. He was still angry with her for having left him so long, so he would not look at her or say her name—not yet.

Higher, and higher, until their great wings were but dark specks circling in the sky, until at last they touched cloud, and the sea beneath them looked flattened, and the islands like feathers on it. Then, swiftly, unexpectedly, angrily, he turned to her and presented his talons, and took hers with an audible rush of wind to his wings, and he swung forward and down and pulled her up and over, then rushed her under him, so that the sky was the earth and the earth an arcing sky above them, and over again and down ever faster, cartwheel-falling, and his talons painful on her in an anger that turned, with their fall, into a passionate strength that forced him to cry above the sound of rushing wind on their bodies. 'Never again will you leave me, for my love is your love, my place is your place and my territory yours. Where the sea wind catches your wings, there will mine fly. Where your talons take up prey, there will mine dive. Where the cliffs rise and the sea threatens, there will our wings go together, stronger for being two eagles flying as one. And where our love is, there will our young be, and your need will be mine and mine yours, and our youngs' needs will be forever ours.'

As he spoke he grasped her talons yet tighter, and though she was the bigger, his was the power and control that plummeted them downwards, until the cartwheeling sky and sea bewildered her, and she relaxed into his power, letting him take her, as she had taken him once over the Lomagnup, pulled down and ever downwards through the air. Until the sea rose faster towards them, and she grew afraid, and began to struggle to free herself but found that her strength was gone, and he held her fast, over and down and over again, and down. The waves suddenly near, the cormorants on the island near enough to count, the cormorants flying away in fear, and she calling out, 'Bjorg! Bjorg!' and screaming this time, 'Bjorg!'

And he crying out 'Yes!' and releasing her so late that, even though her wings were open wide and her tail fanned to slow her fall, her outstretched talons splashed hugely on the surface of the sea, and her wings had to beat it vigorously into spray before she rose up again.

'Yes,' he called out again, 'My name is Bjorg and I am your mate, Mourne, daughter of Cuillin. And let every male beware my wings and talons.'

So did a pair of breeding sea eagles finally return to the waters of the Hebridean islands.

Their first nest that year was little more than a scrape on one of the most isolated Uist skerries, well away from the summer ships that plied the routes to the outer islands. But it was badly judged as a site, and with a storm that accompanied the neap-tides in March, the sea flooded out the two eggs that Mourne had laid.

A second site was found on higher ground near the little isle of Flodday, but when they came, the eggs were sterile, and so in vain did Mourne try to brood them: lifeless they were, and finally abandoned. Then she blamed herself for this, and he protested it was his fault for failing to find a better site sooner, and together were they thrown into despair. But always their love for each other was strong, and each setback was a trial to face and conquer, from which their love grew even stronger. For to her he was the finest male that ever flew, as strong as Askaval, as cunning as Weever, and one day, perhaps, as wise as Torrin. And for him her wings held all the beauty and power that he imagined to be in the wings of Cuillin, and she one day would have the wisdom of Thurid, whom he had held in awe and loved.

* * * * *

It had been on the journey to Edinburgh with *Eagle*, before he proceeded to Skye, that Jim had first heard the name of Anthony Cunliffe. He was an acquaintance of Harry's, no more than that, but Harry felt he might now be what Jim Stonor needed.

At that time Cunliffe had a small print gallery in Camden Town, which had done very well, and he was looking for a way of expanding out of prints into original contemporary art. He had an option on a gallery closing in Bury Street, W1, and was in the market for artists who were not well known, and therefore wooable, but who were at least semi-figurative since, in Cunliffe's opinion, that was the way art would go in the last quarter of the twentieth century.

'He's tough, Jim. A very good businessman, and ambitious . . . which may be just what you need,' said Harry.

Mrs Hadden did not have a telephone, so Cunliffe wrote a letter, but Jim was too deeply involved in the *Tanahorn Eagle* project to be bothered to fix up the meeting he requested so that he could see some of Jim's work. However, he did not like to seem too negative with a friend of Harry Ginnan's, so he wrote back briefly saying a meeting was out, but that the Shure Gallery on Cork Street held some of his work, and no doubt they would show it to Cunliffe. Reading this, Cunliffe smiled at the naïvety of it, for galleries show unexhibited work to each other about as willingly as stags swap hinds, but he had done a favour for Max Shure once, and used that as his 'in'. He was not over-hopeful anyway; he had not been impressed by the eagle commission Stonor had done for the Conservancy Council—rather too staid for his liking.

If Judith Shure had not been in Paris, it is unlikely that Cunliffe would ever have seen Jim's work. But Max Shure, now ageing, couldn't give a damn, and seeing it, Cunliffe knew he had found a potential winner. Two groups of work impressed him: one was the *Portrait of Miss Campbell*, and related sketches, which he realised at once was a major work. The second group, and more significant in the longer term, were the sketches in a portfolio for what was obviously a sculptural work or works to do with eagles and ravens.

The power, the movement, the sense of scale, showed Stonor to be a far more original and profound artist than *Eagle* itself suggested. Harry Ginnan was obviously right: it had just been an academic piece done for money.

Ignoring Jim's discouraging letter, Cunliffe went down to Deal to track down the artist, and so became involved in *The Tanahorn Eagle*, one of the few British-inspired examples of conceptualist art to gain international recognition in the seventies; and also the single work which, more than any other, established the reputations of both Stonor and Cunliffe in the international art world.

What Cunliffe saw in Stonor's studio was the nearly complete clay maquette of a sea eagle, and it was a major advance on *Eagle*, so recently shown. Its lines were infinitely freer, the working of its head and wings so sensitive yet sure that it seemed almost to lift off the studio floor. While somehow in the extremities of the eagle were the workings of some notion of a cliff-face, broken and sheer, a terrifying world of danger and void, from which the eagle sought escape. The piece carried a sense of doom.

But far more significant to Cunliffe was Stonor's plan for the piece. 'It's a memorial, but it doesn't matter to whom. Say for eagles. Say for the many species *we* have killed. It's an "unknown eagle". Unlike the one I made for the Edinburgh site. I am going to take it to a place so remote, so dangerous, that few people will ever see it before it crashes into the sea below. And it will, because the cliffs I'm going to install it on are too fractured and friable to hold it for long. Then I want the world to know about it.'

As Cunliffe listened to Stonor, he seemed half-mad—a man who had been alone too long. He stood before his work holding forth about it, and though not tall or broad, yet the way his arms and hands hung at his sides, or gesticulated at the work, was almost too massive and brutal for Cunliffe. His own energy hid itself behind gallery accounts, Pierre Cardin shirts, and dinners in north London homes where the talk might be about art and artists but no clay, nor paint, nor ink ever begrimed a fingernail; nor passion spilled a cup of coffee on the carpet—as Stonor, talking vigorously, kicked a forgotten mugful across the studio floor, spattering its contents on a far wall.

For his part, Jim was unimpressed by Cunliffe, who was too smooth and clever for his taste. Still, he seemed to know something about art, and after he had gone, Jim admitted to himself he had rather enjoyed talking about his work to someone who seemed to appreciate it. Also, Cunliffe had made him realise that if *The Tanahorn Eagle* was going to take off as he intended, he would need to get the publicity right.

In the event, it was through one of the media weekenders in the Bosun's Mate that Jim made contact with freelance nature photographer, Vernon Herbert. He fancied a trip to Tanahorn, and would record the event while doing other work. So he, Stonor and Richie Hughes, a freelance writer on expeditions and an experienced rock-climber, finally took *The Tanahorn Eagle* in a van by ferry over to Bergen, and then up twelve hundred miles of Norwegian coast to the fishing station at Berlevag. From there they carried it along the shore to Tanahorn, a trek of some twelve miles. In extremely difficult weather conditions they succeeded in installing it beneath the overhang Jim had attempted to climb to before. They used a hand rock-drill and expansion bolts to fix it in place, and then camped at the site for two days while Vernon Herbert completed his photographic and film record of the piece.

There it might have rested, but that Jim's instinct about the potential of the concept proved right. Late that summer, the attention of the Norwegian military authorities was drawn to the piece, which was uncomfortably close to a missile-tracking station to the west of Berlevag. Bureaucracy took over. The installation was deemed unsafe. Worse, it was unauthorised.

A small article appeared in the London *Guardian*: an official complaint had been made to the Foreign Office about a bronze eagle placed by a British national on a dangerous cliff-face, which might affect NATO defences; the military authorities intended to remove it. It provided the classic silly-season story in Fleet Street, and both the *Guardian* and *The Sunday Times* interviewed Stonor. On a hunch, a BBC film crew, then completing work on a documentary about the Lapps, stole half a day off to film the offending statue's removal, in the company of Norwegian newsmen equally short of good stories, especially from the far north.

The two army rock-climbing experts attempting to remove it bungled the job, and instead of the sculpture being safely raised to the top of the cliff, the BBC brought home perfect shots of the dislodged eagle slipping and falling five hundred feet down into the cold Barents Sea. That summer, the destruction of a British work of art by foreign officialdom highlighted eccentric British artistic enterprise, and drew to the work far, far more attention than it might have received if it had survived. Pictures of the sculpture ran in several dailies, and the BBC used its film in a late-evening arts programme. Stonor, an obscure artist working in a seaside resort, became, for the moment anyway, a public name.

In the same apparently arbitrary way, the American sculptor Carl Andre had suddenly become a name in Britain a few years earlier, when the Tate Gallery made a controversial purchase of a collection of prefabricated bricks, a superb but misunderstood minimalist piece. In Stonor's terms that piece, which received widespread negative publicity, was more conceptualist than real, since for every one person who ever saw it, there were probably a thousand who knew and talked about it. Like any other concept, from democracy to tyranny, Andre's work attained an existence and reality quite separate from its physical presence. So, like Che Guevara a decade before, *The Tanahorn Eagle* took on an existence in the moment of its destruction, and Stonor's hope for the piece began to be fulfilled.

A few days after the BBC arts programme, Anthony Cunliffe contacted Jim again, by telegram, and offered to run an exhibition of works associated with *Tanahorn*, and other items, in October, as the autumn launch of his gallery in Bury Street. Jim said yes. He was beginning to want to come out of the cold. And anyway, he owed Mrs Hadden rent; had needed to borrow money from his mother to cast *The Tanahorn Eagle*.

That same autumn, before this first show, he met Judith Shure again on a trip to London. She saw some of his work and made some sales of his drawings through a friend's gallery, and not her father's. She took no commission for herself, and parleyed down the friend's commission to just cover costs. Jim gave the friend a small painting – *Tanahorn Study* – with the words: 'Don't sell it yet. It'll be worth a hell of a lot more in five years than it is now.'

'Brave words, Mr Stonor,' said the friend.

'True ones though. You'll see!'

This bravado was meant for Judith's consumption, for her obvious success, her growing maturity, and her strength made him feel uneasy and grubby. She now had a son, Philip, and told him bluntly she was trying for another child. 'I'm thirty-four, Jim. I don't want to be an ageing mother.' A son, children, domesticity, a house with the sound of a family in it, where the carpets were fitted, and shoes had a proper place, and shirts did not clutter the bottom of cupboards.

'How *are* you, Jim?' she asked then, just as she had in New York; and they smiled, for it was a joke between them. He always told the truth.

'Broke. Tired. Frightened at what I'm trying to do . . . Excited by the Cunliffe show . . .'

'If you need anything, you know . . . I mean . . . *advice*. Its a shark's world you're entering.'

He shook his head. 'You've got me started selling pictures. But money isn't really the problem'—and he looked away, his eyes seeking an escape, in a way they had when once they had been so close on a flight from New York.

'How do you survive it?' asked Jim, after a pause.

She didn't answer but instead interlocked her fingers, and gazed at them. 'I don't know if I do really. I thought that when I married and had children, it would be a completion. Well, I don't know what I thought—something to do with being safe and secure, I suppose. Patrick's very kind, you know. I'm very lucky. There's a nanny for when I go on trips, everything. But . . . well, have you noticed any change in yourself since you got back from America, since you moved into your thirties? It's as if I never asked myself anything before, in the sort of life I lead: about the fact that three people were killed in a terrorist bombing in the Champs Elysées last week, or the sense of arrogant irrelevance in so much work I see among European artists, or the economic decline which has hit the stock-markets, and is obviously going to stay this time . . . Well, people laugh if you talk about it.'

'Do you know my chief memory from walking the coastlines of northern Europe?' said Jim. Judith shook her head. 'Plastic bottles and containers,' he said. They both smiled warily.

After a meal together, Jim walked her over Hungerford Bridge to the National Theatre, where she would be meeting a friend for the evening. She took his arm and they stared down at the running grey waters of the Thames, and what each thought, neither dared start to say. And whatever play she saw that night, the actors seemed merely empty figures on a derelict stage; while the only station sign Jim was conscious of on his train journey home was the stark, drab one that said DEAL.

The newspaper stories on *The Tanahorn Eagle* brought a letter from Gerald Opie. They met for a meal one evening a few days later, in London, and Gerald brought his wife Nina. Gerald was as tall and gangly as ever, but like Jim, had aged a little. His hair was a little thinner and higher on his forehead, and his eyes more smiling and wrinkled, his voice just a fraction more measured. But his language and his manner had not changed. He was now a senior member of the Royal College staff.

'Well, you old bum, why didn't you get in touch before? You've been back in England for more than three years, according to Judith Shure.'

'Oh, you know . . . trying to find myself, trying to work,' said Jim flippant-seriously.

''Course I know, silly sod, but now you've got a lot of talking to do. This is Nina.'

'I have, as they say, heard a lot about you,' she said, stretching out a hand, executive-like.

''Fraid I don't know a thing about you,' said Jim.

They all laughed, and as they did so, Jim and Nina eyed each other shrewdly, and each seemed impressed by what they saw. In her neatness, smallness, obvious incisiveness, and general solidness, Nina was a total contrast to Gerald. 'I am his measure of common sense,' she said later that evening, 'and he is my measure of creativity.'

'Rather too much common sense and rather too little creativity,' grumbled Gerald in reply.

Nina was evidently no fool, and Jim was not surprised to learn that she did not merely 'work in computer programming', as she first put it, but in fact ran her own computer software house in Islington, near where they lived. They had three children, and Gerald, with no embarrassment and much pride, produced a photograph of them.

'We've a portrait drawing of Gerald you did in that flat you shared, and it gives me great pleasure,' said Nina, to switch the conversation to Jim. Jim had done so many at different times that he could not remember that particular one. Indeed, he made one now, doodling on a white paper napkin that came with the bread basket on the restaurant table.

'Picasso used to do this, and pay for his meals by signing them and giving them to the patron. Do you think I could do the same?' he said.

Nina took the sketch from him with a smile. 'You can give it to me,' she said, 'and I'll pay for the meal.'

Jim laughed. He was growing to like Nina. She had wit.

'Sign it, please,' she said. So he did.

He told them something about his work, but little of it very personal, for he and Gerald had never talked in that way about things they made. Their talk was either joky, as light relief, or technical and about what Ginnan had once called 'cooking'—the technical process of producing a finished work. Jim said he was beginning to foresee problems in casting *The Raven of Storr*, which was growing bigger in his mind, at the South London Foundry, so Gerald suggested some other places to cope with something as large and fine in detail. They removed more napkins from under the bread, and sketched round Jim's ideas, their old familiarity returning.

He told them, too, about the drama of erecting *The Tanahorn Eagle*, and was pleased at Gerald's grasp of what the project was really about: 'Frankly, I almost cheered when I first saw the press cuttings. Of course, the newspapers *would* get it wrong. Nobody in their right mind would believe that you produced the sculpture to be *viewed*—a fact which even one of the art magazines ironically got wrong. The whole thing is conceptual, of course . . .' he turned to Nina, adopting a slightly lecturing tone, but Jim could see she didn't mind and, if anything, understood better than he did what *Tanahorn* was about '. . . where you create an "art" idea so potent that it grabs peoples' imagination in some way, and makes them recreate a new work in their minds. Christo's just done it with *Running Fence* near San Francisco: twenty-five miles of a white curtain cross country. Marvellous! Though hardly anyone in Britain understands what it's about yet. You need the back-up of video or film and stills, of course, to get the idea going, but the real work is done by the audience, who never see the real thing. That's why I'm all for Andre, like it or not.' (And Nina clearly did not.) 'The image Andre created has remained more potent in people's minds than your average Cézanne or Monet, which the same people may describe as great art!'

'I was still in New York when all that blew up,' said Jim, 'but I've seen the piece and I think it's rather good. But then I like his work. Have you seen his pieces in wood?'

Gerald nodded, but continued his theme: 'I think *The Tanahorn Eagle* is really a propagandist piece in the sense it seems to be more about the notion of man protecting the environment – or not, as the case may be – than about art as such.'

'Ah, but that's what I dislike about a lot of stuff showing now: it's about the way we *ought* to see rather than what we see. If I seem traditionalist, it's because I want to show people my vision in a language they can respond to. I don't think I'll do another conceptualist piece, but the ideas it gave me will occur in other works. Like *Raven*, for example . . . But with that I've still a long way to go.'

Gerald nodded.

'Anyway, sculpture's been too concerned with making something to look like something else, rather than to exist in its own right. I want to make *things*, not images. That's why I enjoyed the Hayward's "Condition of Sculpture" exhibition a couple of years ago . . . Did you see it? Because it was a show of *things*. But the trouble with things, combined with too much talk, is that they tend to end up very cold and cerebral, especially in the face of a move away from sentiment and narrative and the human figure, which is so fundamental to a lot of modernism. Did you see the Phillip King Arts Council exhibition? Needless to say he's a St Martin's man, friend of Caro, and he uses a lot of steel. Very good indeed, but *cold* in my opinion. Caro's cold, too. Warmth isn't fashionable at the moment, which is why everyone's so bloody rude about Hockney, except of course the general public, who quite rightly love him. The man's got heart . . .' Jim stopped talking and thought of the love and warmth implicit in all the work he most loved: Hockney, or Picasso, or Miro, or Wyeth, or Rothko in the States. He wanted that warmth and joy in his own work and vision.

The preparation for the Cunliffe exhibition involved more work than Jim had expected. It was not just a matter of packing some works into a pantechnicon heading for London. Cunliffe wanted to show a good few of the eagle works—drawings and sketches for the now famous *Tanahorn* piece, the few finished oils Jim had, the *Tanahorn* maquette; and some of the best drawings from Deal, which he described as 'bread and butter' pieces. Not all of these would be exhibited, but Cunliffe wanted material at hand to show potential buyers who like to feel that they were being shown something others have not seen.

'Selling pictures is no different from selling anything else, except that the reasons why people are prepared to pay what they do are frequently obscure or unexpected, as you'll soon find out,' he explained to Jim. 'We have some important decisions to make about pricing, but I'd rather wait until I've seen all the work together and assessed its overall impact. In a mixed-media exhibition like this, with small drawings alongside bigger works, the trick is to get differentials right, and not underprice the small works because of fears of overpricing the big oils. The sculptural work is easier.'

In the event, the prices he suggested seemed to Jim outrageously high, except that he was beginning to see that the costs of mounting an exhibition were considerable. Quite apart from fixed costs like gallery space, which was expensive since Cunliffe had now acquired a gallery in the heart of the West End, a major cost would be the catalogue, on which Cunliffe set much store. 'It's not just a sell for you, but one for my gallery as well, and it's going to be good. I'll send someone down to do an interview piece with you, which will establish you personally, and your ideas. Colour is tricky, but luckily most of the major eagle oils are virtually monochrome . . . don't you *have* colour? But the tempera Deal pieces like *Albert* will be lost in black and white . . .'

Cunliffe visited the Shure Galleries again to go through the work Judith had rescued from Opie's old flat, and from New York, and Cunliffe wanted to show *Portrait of Miss Campbell*.

Some instinct told Stonor to resist, and he did. 'The Campbell portrait is not for sale,' he said firmly, in a voice that Cunliffe respected.

'Brave words,' said Cunliffe, in a voice Jim might have feared.

So, annoyed occasionally, excited often, increasingly apprehensive about the show which would involve him in some socialising of a kind he had seen at previews as a student, and which he disliked, Jim waited for the show to open.

But when it did, it was all something of an anti-climax. Apart from the preview party at which people did everything, or very nearly everything, but look at the works, the gallery was nearly empty on the three occasions that Jim visited it during the four-week run.

'Wonderful! It's going very well,' was all Cunliffe would say, and it seemed true. Because of the Tanahorn story at least two major newspapers, which might not otherwise have mentioned it, did pieces complete with pictures of one of the bolder sketches of the original sculpture. All the art magazines covered it, and two London radio arts programmes did interviews, and even a BBC producer looked in at the show.

'It all adds up to public awareness and interest, and makes it easier for me to build you a reputation and, frankly, a market,' said Cunliffe. But he was reluctant to talk about sales or, more to the point, likely money in Jim's hand. And Jim was reluctant to trust the red stickers that did appear on most of the drawings and three of the oils, since he had seen one on *Workshop* – one of the major tempera pieces – on the preview night, and discovered that it was a lie: it was Cunliffe's way of suggesting there was already active buying interest. Judith had been right: galleries were where sharks swam. There were times when he wished it was Judith, and not Anthony Cunliffe and his willowy and too well-spoken assistants, who was dealing with his work.

One of these occurred on the final day of the show, when he came up to see all his work displayed together for the last time. Cunliffe himself was away in Bristol at an Arnolfini preview.

'Well, how have sales gone, then?' Jim asked Carole, one of the two assistants. She smiled in that superior non-committal way – of which she and her colleague were such mistresses – as if Jim had made a tasteless joke. Then she said, 'I'm sure Mr Cunliffe is pleased, Mr Stonor.'

Disgusted, Jim wandered round his works, among the two or three people there on that occasion. Whatever the truth, and he assumed that the large number of red stickers was generally a good sign, he felt suddenly deeply depressed. Perhaps Carole was the trigger, but the reasons lay far deeper than that. Despite all the talk, all the good words written, the glossy catalogue, the hype, Jim felt a desolation about the whole thing. Of all the things said and the people spoken to, from Cunliffe downwards, or upwards, somehow no one had spoken to Jim himself, not really spoken about what mattered to him. The images he had made were stared at, reproduced, discussed, even occasionally bought; but those feelings Jim had when he had stood with the eagles in Iceland and Norway, when he worked in silence in his studio with old Mrs Hadden out in the garden, feelings of being on a difficult and isolated search—no one had been able to share these with him and tell him they understood. Except Michael in a letter received just before the show opened, wishing Jim luck and saying it must be hard to see so much work together. At the time Jim had smiled. Hard? Triumphant, rather. But that had been an artist's fantasy. The reality, as Michael said, was *hard*. Hard to feel, as he did, that his work fell so short of what he had tried to make.

He had turned to take his leave of Carole at the desk, steeling himself to smile at her, when she said: 'One gentleman came in two days ago, who was most insistent about knowing your address. Of course I explained it's against gallery policy . . . you know . . . to protect you from people . . .' she lied. It was really to prevent any possibility of non-gallery private sales at lower prices. Cunliffe wanted all of his fifty per cent.

'Who *was* he?' Jim asked.

'Well, I have his name somewhere. I said I'd pass the message on . . .' She looked on her desk but, despite its extreme tidiness, did not find the note she had made. 'Well, as a matter of fact, he bought something,' she said smugly, 'so I'll have his name and address . . .' She produced a receipt book and leafed through it, stopping at a stub and showing it to Jim.

'P. J. A. Conan,' he read out, his mind blank for a moment—then he read no more. It was Peter, his oldest friend. He read on in silence: an address in Cambridge, and the title of what he had bought. It was Number 43, one of the few water-colours, and a fine one. A study of the ternery over Sandwich Bay, called simply *Terns*.

Peter! Oh how he had missed him. And later Jim sat in the train staring out of the window at lights in the night and remembering.

It was on that same journey that he first read, in the late news column of the *Evening Standard*, of a major oil-spillage disaster on the north-east coast of Scotland. A tanker called the *Marie Joseph* had collided with a smaller vessel in heavy seas, and two massive oil slicks were drifting towards the coast.

He could easily imagine the scene, having seen smaller oilings on the Deal foreshore—and on his Norwegian tour: a beachful of dying birds. He stared at his dark reflection in the train's racing window; he thought of Peter, his oldest friend, and what he had once meant and must mean again; he thought of Judith, who knew so much but whom he had so rarely seen since New York; he thought of a pair of sea eagles trying against odds too great to think of to raise young in the Scottish seas; and a grief and a desperate isolation came over him, a reaction to the draining weeks past.

Perhaps it was then that the elements came together as one, and the first terrible images of what was to become *Oiled Beach*, the huge triptych that consolidated his reputation as a major artist, first began to take shape. And whose price, when the Museum of Modern Art in New York bought it at auction in 1996, would be one of the highest ever paid for a living artist's work.

* * * * *

The departure of Mourne and the others for Skye had had a profound effect on Romsdal. The sight of them swinging out to sea had been seen by many, Hardanger and Romsdal eagles alike, and though they outwardly scoffed, yet in the weeks and months that followed, they could not but marvel that such a ragged bunch of old vagrants and young untried juveniles, with only Weever and Mizen along to give them any substance, had somehow managed to look so heroic, so proud, and make the rest of them seem has-beens.

The difference between the two groups had begun to blur with new generations, as the ever-strengthening Hardanger eagles had spread and inter-bred into the coastal skerries.

Mourne's flight was a source of pride to the battered Romsdalers, and a source of envy to those of Hardanger, yet somehow the shared regret that they who had watched had not had the courage to join in, put among them all a common sense of something missed, and made their wrangles seem as nothing against the horizon of the sky and sea.

So it was that one day a Hardanger eagle flew slowly out of Romsdal fjord and across the island waters, quite unmolested and came to the territory of Clew, wise eagle—eagle who, when he was young and strong, was guardian of Cuillin's territory.

'You are welcome,' said Clew gently to the Hardanger eagle, for there is no fear in an old eagle at peace with himself. 'Why do you come?'

'Well, it's Sleat. He wants you to come up to the Storrin and see him', said his visitor, adding: 'If you don't mind, that is.' Clew could not help smiling, for times had changed, and increasing security had brought ordinariness to the once proud Hardanger.

Then Clew followed the messenger, watched by many of Romsdal, and all knew that day that a change was coming over Romsdal once more, and it had to do with Sleat, the strong one, whom all feared.

Yet an awe did finally come over Clew as he advanced inland and the darkening cliffs loomed close on either side as he reached the Storrin, for it was years since he had heard or been near the waterfall, and its roar seemed even mightier with the passing of time. It was years, too, since he had seen Sleat, whose first arrival there, at the Gathering, he remembered so well.

'Wait here,' said his guide, leading him to a stance near the Storrin, at the very place where the famous Gathering had taken place. 'He'll come soon.'

There Clew waited, watching the spray that drifted out of the Gap, and unable to believe that he himself had once flown through it and helped raise Cuillin's children within its now inaccessible walls.

It was an hour later that Clew saw the distant dark shape of an eagle flying steadily towards him from off the southern fjell across the fjord. It was the flight of a tired eagle, tired not from journeying over land, but tired in spirit; an eagle, it seemed to Clew, which has become wearied by questions to which there seem no answers.

And as the eagle crossed the cliffs towards him, Clew saw clearly what he could not have believed moments before, that this tired eagle was Sleat of Hardanger, the most powerful male eagle of his generation. Once he had flown with many colleagues at his wing-side; now he came alone, with a desolation to his flight that made Clew want to reach out and comfort him, even though he had dispossessed them all.

'Welcome, Clew of Romsdal, Cuillin's friend, welcome,' said Sleat taking a stance near Clew's, neither higher nor lower. 'Welcome!'

He stayed silent for a while, staring at Clew and over towards the spray at the Gap of Storrin. Slew studied his wings and the line of his back, and saw they were as sleek and powerful as ever. The ageing was in his stance and in the gaze of his eyes, and sadness clung about his talons.

'You wanted me?' said Clew.

'Yes, and I am glad that you have come. What do you know of the flight of Mourne over the dark sea?'

'Of its outcome, nothing, but of its genesis much,' answered Clew. Then he told Sleat how he had sought and found Mourne in the south, and of her journey north, where they met the Weir, and her flight to Iceland, Haforn's land. Then of her return. The rest Sleat knew.

'She was my mate once, was Mourne, bleak years ago when I was different from what I am now,' said Sleat. 'She was the only mate I have known who could overfly me.' He fell silent again, and Clew was surprised to hear him say this, and that he seemed to be thinking of her still. Had he not driven her from Romsdal?

But when Sleat spoke again, it was of something quite different: 'When I first came here I knew no fear. I was young and strong and found I could lead others and make them do my will—as I still can. But I knew no fear, nor had I suffered. I saw my home fjord of Hardanger overtaken by humans and sleark, and knew no other desire than to bring those that were willing and strong enough up north here, to where I thought the sky would be safe. I was contemptuous of the Romsdalers, and saw them as weak and broken and willing to compromise, and that up here, by the Storrin, we of Hardanger might find a home.

'So it was, Clew, and we stayed those years through with only Cuillin and yourself to stop us advancing southwards to the coast. Do you remember?'

Clew nodded, and Sleat whispered, 'Those long years waiting for the Doom.'

'But that surely was our belief, not yours?' exclaimed Clew. 'Only we who lived by the Storrin believed in the Doom.'

'I wanted to destroy Cuillin,' said Sleat, 'and bring evil on all of you. I tried to make a pact with sleark, but their words were as cunning and slippery as their flight. I wanted to rule the whole of Romsdal, but its secrets were too great, and always there was the Storrin whose sounds at night spoke words that struck fear even into the heart of a young ambitious leader who thought himself fearless. Many times I wanted to attack you all, and might have done so but for the whispers I heard in the Storrin's roaring, that it must not be so. My fellow eagles tried to persuade me to let them attack, and hard it was to stop them sometimes, nearly impossible. Indeed, they killed some here and there—killed them when the Doom of man was coming on us, and all our kin under threat. Do you remember the night Cuillin was shot?'

Clew nodded again, unable to speak. Tears were in his eyes.

'Yes, I too remember. I saw it from where we have now taken stance. Over near the Gap, it was. I saw her shudder with the shot, I saw her turn, I saw her flight, whose pain would have had all other eagles falling into the waters below. But she had such strength and courage that she turned on the humans – over there – and flew at them. Then she headed down the fjord towards the west, towards her homeland horizon—and for the first time I saw true flight. Not the flight of pride and war which I had flown, nor the flight of widsom which Finse your father knew. But true flight, of an eagle who sees the sky and the earth clearly and without fear, and has the courage to fly always towards truth.

'After that I tried to turn away from what I had seen. So many wasted years followed then, so many. I took Mourne for a mate, to mock her and Cuillin and all of you, though sometimes, when we flew a mating flight, there were echoes of great Cuillin in her wings, and I was ashamed and afraid.

'Finally, I drove her away, mocking her for failing to produce young one year, but I missed her ever after, and was cold to the other mates I had. Bitter and cold.

'When she returned at last from the south, I flew along the shadows of the fjord to watch her. I was pleased when at first none came. Then when that vagrant Reft joined her, I laughed, for I said to myself, that he was all she could attract now. But . . .' He stopped for a moment and stared away, and Clew knew it was difficult for him to continue, and he understood the courage needed to say what he had.

'But in truth I was envious of those that came to her. They had a courage I did not.

'Always I seemed unable to escape the Storrin, which at first I had feared, but whose roaring I now began to long for. I flew to its edges and stared into its depths, and felt its winds. I knew I never would have the courage to fly among its cliffs as Cuillin had, or you and the others that protected her young.

'No, I could not find that courage . . .' And Clew began to understand what Sleat's life had been, and how much he had misunderstood him. An eagle born into prejudice, and who was needed to safeguard his kin from extinction in Hardanger, with the gifts and strength to lead, and to help prevent the bloodshed that had never quite taken place. And the insight to let his followers, once so hostile to the Romsdalers, begin to mix with them, to see the divisions blur, to understand that the Hardanger pride was a lesser thing than the life and spirit of all sea eagles, which the Doom threatened with extinction. And then, finally, growing older but still a leader, to dare ask himself questions few eagles even know. How could he, Clew, help Sleat find the answers?

'What eagle was Cuillin the Fremmed—and what was it she gave to Mourne that she should have the strength to make a flight across the dark sea? Who was she, Clew? For ever in the dusk, when the Storrin roars, her memory haunts me.'

Then Clew told him of Cuillin, as he had once tried to tell others, Askaval and Mourne included. He spoke of the dream she made, and of how Mourne had made a flight to live it.

'But what of Mourne now? Have you heard nothing of what has happened?'

Clew shook his head.

'You eagles of the islands and skerries may hear more of her than we. Let me know if news comes. And fear no more my eagles, for the task I set myself is complete. My eagles are safe now . . .'

'I fear for Mourne,' said Clew, 'and for the others. Twelve of them left here, but how many survived the dark sea? And what dangers do they face in Skye, and taking territory on it? They will need Haforn's help. All my life I have waited and watched, and taught and seen youngsters grow to maturity, and I always knew Haforn would go with them if they tried to fly true. But now I fear that even Haforn cannot help them.'

'Sometimes I have wondered if some of us should follow the way Mourne went,' said Sleat, 'But none of us have the knowledge. Only you knew Cuillin, among those who are left . . .'

Clew shook his head. 'Haforn will tell us what to do—or the Weir will show his wings again, and guide us. Try to trust in Haforn, as I do. And wait. Do not fear the sounds of the Storrin, for only eagles with true courage can hear them. Seek patience. Give guidance to your own eagles when they need it . . . and trust the winds and skies and cliffs, for of them Haforn was made. And let there now be peace between those of Romsdal and of Hardanger.'

*　*　*　*　*

Jim Stonor did not contact Peter Conan until two weeks later. He preferred to phone rather than write, and finally overcame his natural nervousness one evening. Their conversation was stilted, each finding the other's voice so different now that they did not recognise each other at first. They exchanged news and agreed to meet in London, neutral territory. But a date was awkward: Peter was a lecturer at Cambridge University, and it was a busy term; Jim wanted to go north and see the oil devastation following the collision of the *Marie Joseph*. They agreed to phone each other nearer Christmas, when things might be easier.

Jim decided to take a rest from his studio after the exhibition, and catch up on some museum and gallery visiting, also some reading he had not done. He needed time to think. His work was deepening, and those dark themes that had been like wraiths on a far hill for so long were now storm-clouds coming closer. Perhaps for this

534

reason he became interested in Goya again, and arranged to have a private viewing at the British Museum of Goya's *Disasters of War* etchings, made in the 1820's in the wake of the French invasion of Spain.

Perhaps no single period of studying another artist's work was to have such a profound effect on him as those two hours with the terrible depictions of the mindlessness of wartime horror, in which no one is innocent.

'*Why?*'—a man being garrotted at a tree. '*And nothing can be done*'—a blindfolded man being executed, the guns but barrels thrust in from the edge of the image. '*This is how it happened*'—the sacking of a monastery. '*What more can one do?*'—French soldiers castrating a Spanish peasant.

Their truth, combined with the ironic titles, presented a depth of vision that made Stonor see how pitiful and facile was the reaction of his own generation of artists and photographers to similar atrocities in Vietnam and Uganda. Blinding, torture, weeping for life destroyed—it happened now. Torture in an East End garage in London. A hot iron on a baby's genitals. It happened *now*.

The following day he travelled to north-east Scotland, and was shown the oil devastation by a representative of the Royal Society for the Protection of Birds. No words could describe the horror of the beaches he saw, or the oiled wings and desperate eyes of dying birds. But the press photographs failed here as well—just as the war photographs of Vietnam. The 'spirit' of it all was not in photographs. Stonor stayed in Scotland for less than a day. He had seen all he needed to.

It was on the journey home, on the M1 north of Sheffield, halted by a fatal car accident, that his controversial series of etchings, *Disasters of Peace*, was really begun. The accident had happened seconds before he had arrived; indeed, the same car had overtaken him too fast in the outside lane. No police, no ambulance, nothing but a couple of cars already stopped, and several more slewed across the road. Broken headlights, flashing indicators, a smashed windscreen, and a man's head thrust through it, blinded by his own blood. Another man by him, in a dark suit, crushed and huddled into death by a door whose edge thrust through his stomach.

Jim stared, as others stared. Hysterical voices screamed and shouted. Flashing lights. And struck cold by it all, he went back to his car, took out his sketch-pad, and stood on the hard shoulder drawing it, detail after detail, until the police moved him on with a curse.

Before the crash, the place must have seemed peaceful: two

horses in a field nearby, a superb rise of hills rolling up into the distance, and a clump of trees with a farmhouse tucked into their solid protection.

He produced the etching in the print department of an art college in Canterbury, and called it *They do it every day*, because they did— the police and the ambulance men who tried to sort out the mess. It was the first of thirty-seven etchings, done over a period of over four years, all based on things he had seen or feelings felt. Some were within his everyday experience. His depiction of oiled birds, for example, was based on a small slick on Sandwich Bay a year later. His extraordinary image of old people in an old folks' home originated in the TV lounge of the home where his grandmother had lived her last years and died. His obesity image – *She's starting a diet* – was based on someone seen the following summer on Deal seafront. Not all the images were as real as the first one, for he had realised that realism or photo-realism did not quite tell the truth. A camera has no heart. For some he enlisted the cooperation of friends and of the authorities: his three etchings on the theme of terrorism followed nights in casualty wards in a London hospital. *Children aren't what they were—this one survived* showed a child's legs being blown off in Oxford Street.

He spent a grubby Christmas that year with a woman he met at a party in Deal, in December. At their first meeting she had come back through the junk of the corridors of Mrs Hadden's house, up the stairs, and taken off her clothes with a joke about models. He had her, or she had him, but whichever it was he did not like it there. That house was a sanctuary. So he made love to her angrily, and if old Mrs Hadden heard much sound from rooms that had been silent and tidy so long, she did not say. But this new temporary girlfriend had a way about her legs and breasts that reminded Jim of Vi Clarke so long before. She was the first woman he lusted after since he returned to Britain.

They went to the cottage of a friend of hers in Lyme Regis, just to get away, and spent that Christmas at parties, in bed, and finally, on the twenty-seventh, in a foursome with a middle-aged couple from Exeter. It was a turn-on, but sometime late in the evening Jim surveyed the scene, replete and tired, and wondered if it might make a 'Disaster of Peace'. It was just not his idea of how Christmas should be spent.

He came back from Dorset a week later to find that Mrs Hadden had started to tidy the house for real. She had hired two men to do it and to throw the rubbish into a skip. There was something strange about it, but she said nothing. It took the men just two days and eight skips to clear the clutter of over thirty years. Only later did Jim learn that her premises in Walmer had been bought by the Council on a compulsory-purchase order. Mrs Hadden no longer had a shop, so the junk had no place to go now, though for years it had not gone there anyway. But *having* a place to go, or something to do, may be infinitely more important for a person than going there or doing it. Horizons keep people more alive than pavements do. Mrs Hadden now lived entirely in the front room, into which the men had moved her bed from upstairs, and a wardrobe, and the suddenly empty, clattering house disquieted Jim. He was filled with a sense of foreboding which certainly found its way into the etchings he was making, and the sketches he was just beginning for *Oiled Beach*.

One day at the end of January, after a morning of silence, Jim found Mrs Hadden dead. She had died in her sleep. Her room was immaculately tidy except for an old blue dressing-gown that had slipped off the foot of her bed and on to the floor. On the mantelpiece, stuck on some cardboard and propped up against the wall, was the drawing of flowers Jim had once made for her as a joke, substituting it for the real things.

Within a month, the solicitors acting for the executors of Mrs Hadden's estate – a cousin and a nephew living in Birmingham – had given Jim notice to quit the West Street house. The crisis quickly resolved itself into another, more practical one: was he willing to pay the £18,500 which the executors were advised was the market price for the property? He had better decide quickly, as there was a buyer prepared to pay cash.

Jim did not have the cash, nor even the deposit or regular income needed to get himself a mortgage. Cunliffe was unsympathetic. He still had not paid Jim most of the money arising from sales at the autumn exhibition, as he said the figures 'still had to be worked out in detail and final costs processed', and there was a painting on which a buyer had defaulted, for which it was not worth suing . . . But Margaret Stonor, a regular saver throughout her life, even when money was down to shillings and pence in the early fifties, was able to offer him a £1,000 loan. She remembered her own financial struggles to buy the house in Compass Street. While to Jim's immense surprise, his brother Frank wrote offering a loan of £5,000 and to act as guarantor for a further bank loan if it was needed. 'Enjoyed the exhibition' was virtually all his brief letter said.

But it was Judith Shure who really made it possible for Jim to keep West Street. They met in February at the Hayward Gallery, where a major retrospective of Dada and Surrealism was in progress.

Jim thought she looked tired, more wan than when he had last seen her. Something in her eyes had gone, and when he embraced her at the entrance, she seemed almost to lean against him as if she had not rested for a long, long time. But she said she was well, and happy, and content, and that business was thriving, and Jim put her tiredness down to the journey from France. As usual, Patrick was not with her.

'He doesn't really like me coming over here at the moment. He's very French, and he likes his woman in the house. But my father's been ill and a gallery business goes downhill very quickly if it's not run personally. It's that kind of trade . . . Anyway, building the French gallery has been enormously rewarding. I wish you'd come and see it, and the children. The nanny looks after them perfectly well when I'm not there.' She sounded just slightly guilty. 'Now tell me all about the show in the autumn. I couldn't come over for it after all, but my father went and I had the catalogue sent to me . . .'

Jim described it to her, and eventually got on to the subject of money, and Cunliffe's failure to produce anything but a small interim payment.

Judith's expression changed from mother, wife and friend, to businesswoman. It was the subtlest of things, but in it Jim saw again her latent strength and drive.

'You've got a contract I take it . . .' but her voice faded as Jim shook his head. No, he hadn't.

'Well, it was a matter of trust, really. I mean, he was recommended by Harry Ginnan, and everything seemed . . .' he said weakly.

'It always does,' she replied. 'You *need* a contract, and not just any contract, because there are all sorts of problems between gallery and artist. For example, what's your cover if pictures get damaged during the show? What happens if there's a default on payment?'

'Damn it, Judith, I'm an artist not a bloody lawyer! I expect him to sort that out . . .'

'It may not be in his interests to sort it out.'

Jim began to feel foolish and to bluster a little, but in his heart he knew she was right. And the fact was he did now need money and help which he wasn't getting. He explained the problem about West Street.

'Well, that's ridiculous,' said Judith, colour and a fire returning to her face. 'My broker would get you a loan in ten minutes. You're not just a poverty-stricken artist working in a garret, Jim Stonor.

You're on the threshold of being one of the few international artists of your generation. You may not think it, Cunliffe may not say it, the critics here would laugh because in Britain they're mostly unbelievably negative about their own nationals, but I *know* it. How much do you need?'

Jim opened his mouth and started to say 'Well, I'm not sure . . . It's hard to say exactly . . .'

'How much?'

'The house is going for £18,500 but I think they'll reduce it by a thousand for a quick sale. I've raised £6,000 from the family, so probably about £12,000 or so, with legal costs.'

'I'll lend it to you.' They stared at each other and Jim instinctively refused. Their relationship must not be a business one, for that would fetter something far more important, and far more valuable. He shook his head.

'The Shure Gallery will lend it to you.' He shook his head and smiled.

'All right then, Jim, I'll offer you £13,000 for your *Portrait of Miss Campbell*, which I was glad to note was not for sale at the Cunliffe show.'

'It's worth more,' said Jim laughing.

She laughed, too. 'You're right, as a matter of fact, or it very soon will be. Look, I'll tell you what I can do, and what you'll surely find acceptable. I'll talk to Anthony Cunliffe while I'm here. There may be a few things I can say which you wouldn't be able to. You know—as one gallery owner to another. And I'll get my broker to phone you. He's very good and you can trust him implicitly. His name's Beckmann. If Cunliffe offers you a contract, don't sign it until your own lawyer has seen it.'

'I haven't got a lawyer,' Jim said.

'Surprise, surprise,' she said, and she wrote down the name of her own in London.

Whatever it was that Judith said to Cunliffe, it must have been tough and to the point. A letter reached Jim less than a week later with a substantial cheque and, to Jim's surprise, some guesstimates of likely income over the following twelve months, with dates of payments and a contract. Jim sent it to the lawyer Judith had recommended. In the same week he had a call from Beckmann, who made raising a mortgage sound as easy as buying a pint of milk. The crisis subsided. Two months later, contracts were exchanged and West Street was his.

It was strange to Jim to become owner of a house in which he had been tenant for so long, and whose rooms, apart from his own, he had never really entered. There were two days towards the end, distasteful days, when the relatives came down and earmarked what furniture and effects Mrs Hadden had not sent to the rubbish dump in the weeks before she died. The rest, and there was not much, they said Jim could have if he wished. The main item was an old upright piano, with an inlaid design of flowers in walnut wood in two panels on the front, and a piano stool with music stashed away beneath the seat. He played a few notes which were tinny and out of tune, but as they echoed around the room and out into the empty, carpetless corridors, Jim felt a sudden unbelieving delight that this place was his own. The French windows out on to the old garden, and the ancient dresser in the kitchen, the wonderful mouldings and roses in the front room and hall . . . all were his. He had a place to call a home.

That same evening, he walked round to Compass Street and fetched his mother back with him, and made her a meal of chicken and salad, with a bottle of German hock she liked, and they sat in the kitchen and celebrated. Nobody better—for he remembered so well her own emotion and pride in becoming a home-owner when he was a boy.

For her, too, it was emotional, for she had never been to West Street where Liam had lived, nor spoken to Mrs Hadden, though they knew each other by sight.

Liam's books were still up in the studio, along with Jim's work, which had now spread out into the front bedroom facing on to the churchyard of St George's. The room had been taken over by clay and wire.

In the main studio, Margaret Stonor reached out a hand to Liam's books, and sat in his chair and, seeing the piece of rock that Jim still kept on the desk among his own artist's clutter, she said softly, 'Why, I haven't seen this for a very long time. Such a long time. It came from Storr on the island of Skye'.

'How do *you* know?' asked Jim, surprised.

'There are a lot of things I know.'

'Why didn't you ever talk about them? Why didn't you tell us what happened?'

'There's nothing much to tell, really, that you don't already know, and those things are best left behind people . . .' But Jim could tell she wanted to talk, just as she had done since she had been ill the year before. So he went back downstairs, fetched a couple of glasses and the remainder of the hock, rummaged round in the dresser for a couple of candles, and brought them back up to the studio. His mother was still at the desk, holding the piece of basalt from Storr. Jim poured some more wine, lit the candles and turned off the light. Virgin and unfinished canvases were stacked against one wall, and an easel stood empty and awkwardly by the window whose curtains were open on to a dark garden. The floor was a mess with clay and some powder paint, but he had long ago removed the carpet and replaced it with veneered hardwood blocks. The walls, clean and empty in Liam's day but for the picture Jim had drawn as a child, were now cluttered with different pictures and sketches which Jim had pinned up to look at. His own drawing was still there somewhere, but submerged.

'My treatment of Liam must have seemed hard to you children,' she said eventually.

'Yes, it did,' he admitted honestly. 'He seemed so harmless.'

'Well, you know I *was* hard. I was. But it took years for me to become like that.'

She fell silent and Jim said, 'Did you know about his birdwatching?' to encourage her to go on.

'Good heavens, yes. Of course I did. It was his only passion. And in a way it was what broke us up, though that really happened before you were born. Perhaps you never realised how damaged he had been by his service in the First World War. *I* never realised. He must have been such a fine person before he went, so strong. A man who knew moorland and mountain from childhood, who saw life in a way I never did. Life in the open. Sometimes in the first years I knew him you would see him as he must have been then, just for a moment, laughing and happy—whole. Then the shadow would come over him again, and a terrible oppression, and for days he would be unlivable with, dark and silent and bitter. Yet here was a man who gave me life, without whom I would be a spinster now, I suppose, without Compass Street, or you and the others, without the joy you've all given me. He gave me the strength to break away. So I loved him and felt I must always help him, and for years, those terrible years when you children were young and he was so useless, I did try to help him but his moods and silences got steadily worse. Do you know what he used to do when we argued? He would take his binoculars and go off on long walks and look at birds. He was utterly meticulous and had a room which he allowed no one to enter, where he kept his records and books and journals, at which he spent hours. He complained bitterly that I was not interested, but if I tried to show interest he became secretive and possessive of his knowledge. I came to hate those binoculars.'

'I've got them now . . .' said Jim.

'I know he gave them to you. I rejected him when you were born—well, when Michael was born really. But he loved you both in a way he hadn't the older boys. I remember finding him in your nursery staring down at you, and if I had been different and more confident, and less tired and angry myself, I would have understood he wanted to hold you, and I would have known how to help him. But I wasn't perfect, Jim. It became a fight between us as I began to grow, and my own horizons to expand, starting with you children—and Compass Street was the symbol. Bit by bit I found my identity. While he, poor man, unable to say what he really felt, or to cope with children and a family life, a real family life, retreated into all of this . . .' and she waved a hand at the books and desk.

'How did you know about Storr?' asked Jim.

'He told me. He picked up this rock on his last day on Skye. On 9 November 1920 . . .' Then she told Jim about Liam at that 1920 Remembrance Day, and of his coming to Deal, and their meeting years later in St George's, across from West Street, of which she had talked occasionally before.

'It's hard for you to believe, I know, but his war experience had hurt him, made him bleak and bitter and unable to see the good in anything. All he seemed able to do was to watch birds through his binoculars and note down their behaviour. But it was easier doing that than changing nappies and getting up night after night. It's a way of cutting yourself off from reality.'

'Not always,' said Jim, thinking of William Ferguson.

'In his case it was. Anyway, there were too many occasions when he let me down on vital things: looking after you and Michael, for instance; failing to meet Frank off a train once when the boy was too young for that. Forgetting the fireguard by the coal fires. Things you don't allow, with children. And I hardened and got tougher. And he retreated more . . . And when I insisted that your name should be Stonor and not MacAskill – which was all part of me finding myself – that was when the break really happened. But it was some years before he left home. He should have gone sooner. And I began to breathe again, and not worry all the time about his need, and the great well of loss and sadness in him which I could never satisfy. And slowly, in those years, the guilt I felt for failing him began to lift as one by one I achieved things on my own. Pride came back, pride I had never had, and the guilt began to go. You cannot carry others all your life. I had myself and you children to think of.'

She was silent again and her eyes a little tearful, and her hands played at the rock on the desk. And then Jim realised that his mother still loved Liam in some deep way, and he understood it had been a sacrifice she had made, not a desertion. Through long years she must have tried and tried to help him, and it must have taken great courage for her to turn away finally, admit defeat, and start to build her own life alone.

'He was an ill man in some ways, but none of us knew about psychology and mental illness then. You know, there was a night during the last war I always remember. At the beginning of it he worked with the Observer Corps in Dover—typically he said it gave him a chance to study herring-gull! It was in the early days, before you or Michael were born, and the big boys had been evacuated to Devon. Well, you know all that. There was a heavy raid on Dover, and I don't know what happened exactly, but he came back here quite late at night in what I now realise was a state of shock. At first I didn't understand and tried to give him something to eat, and there was this strange knocking or shaking sound, building up. It was his legs shaking against the table. Then his hands. Then his whole body seemed to go into what I think is called rigor, and he kept saying over and over again, "I can't stop, I can't stop, I can't stop".

'Well, it did stop finally, and I got him to bed, and he was calm in a way I never saw before or since. It was then he told me something of what he had been through in the First World War, and strangely enough about an incident in his childhood when he had taken a landowner or someone on Skye to where eagles were nesting.'

'Can you remember what he said?' asked Jim.

'Not much. He said it was the last breeding pair on Skye, but of course that's not true. I mean, there are lots of eagles up there.'

'Golden eagles, not sea eagles,' Jim murmured.

'Well anyway, he felt terribly guilty about it, and somehow it was mixed up in his mind with the death and destruction he saw in the war afterwards. It was as if the one made him guilty of the other.' There was no anger or bitterness in any of the things she said, not even about the long years being left alone with four children. Only compassion and love for a man she still felt she had failed. But one of them had needed to grow to survive—and it had been her.

A few days later, Margaret called round again at West Street. She had a package of things under her arm, wrapped in brown paper and tied with string.

'I've been sorting things out. I want to get straight now, and I think it's time one of you boys took these. They're Liam's things. You can decide what to do with them, yourself.'

She handed him the package and he opened it on the kitchen

table. Inside there were some documents and two thick, tatty note-books with writing Jim could not read.

'He gave them to me just after we married and asked me to keep them somewhere safe. They're what he called his *War Diaries*. They're in Gaelic.'

Jim riffled through them and thought of that desolate peninsula of land where he had stood with William Ferguson, and the ruins he had explored alone. Gaelic, an old and dying language, but one his father had spoken. He remembered the rare occasion he heard his father speak it, and understood then to what a different world he had come in Deal. How often must he have wished to go back to his home, and what guilt and alienation must have kept him apart from it!

Jim sent the diaries to Ferguson, thinking that if he could not translate them himself, he could find someone who would, and perhaps somewhere in them would be the clue Ferguson had hoped for, to the sites of the old sea eagle eyries on Skye.

Neither Mrs Hadden's executors nor her solicitors had ever mentioned the outhouse at the bottom of the garden in West Street, but it was clearly marked on the contract plans, complete with a back entrance on to a public right of way at the rear of the garden.

Jim broke into it the day after the sale was completed, and found himself in an empty two-storey building like a storehouse. Any hope that there might be some romantic find of forgotten antiques or things of value was shattered. The rooms were quite empty, but Jim saw immediately the building's potential as a sculpture studio. Immediately his ideas for *Cliff Bronze* and *The Raven of Storr* expanded, and he began to think more seriously about them, then and there. In fact, planning of both had been going on for years – *Raven* originally started in New York – and the happy chance of having a private place to actually make them brought the date of their completion forward.

This was to be the year in which Stonor made works which formed the basis for a significant part of his future reputation. While the passionate interest in etching steadily continued, with more additions to the *Disasters of Peace* series, he began the first detailed work on the panels that would make *The Raven of Storr*. His idea was to make a piece that would literally engulf the viewer, as the walls of the cliffs and pinnacles of Storr engulfed a climber. It had started as a single piece, but as he began to sculpt and model the detail of its walls, the piece became ever bigger in conception, until it eventually comprised five separate, free-standing structures, interlocked with each other visually, but with enough space for the viewer to walk between them. The surfaces would have the dark, absorbent colour of basalt mixed with feldspar, but their details would be those of ravens, hundreds of ravens—hints of beaks and hints of claws, and the jagged poke of feathers, and the glint of black and shining eyes. The external faces of the piece would be smooth and reflective, to catch a sense of sky and water. If Stonor had ever suspected how many years *The Raven of Storr* would take, and the technical problems he would have with it, he might never have tried to create it. But then, Rodin might never have started *The Gates of Hell*, from which so many of his best pieces came, had he known he could never complete it.

At the same time as starting *The Raven*, Stonor began *Cliff Bronze*, a much smaller and less significant work, which was completed that year and cast in late summer.

Judith's broker deliberately secured Jim a larger mortgage than he needed to leave him with sufficient funds to make some improvements to the house. Whatever Jim's ideas may have been, they did not finally run to putting in new kitchen units, or laying fitted carpets throughout, or any other conventional home improvements. Instead, the kitchen remained old and the corridors uncarpeted, for he impulsively spent the money demolishing the internal walls of the garden studio to give himself more space. He had the floor boarded, because he liked the feel and sense of wood at his feet, and painted the walls white himself. Perhaps it was standing there that one day he stepped back and looked up the fifteen feet or more of wall, and knew quite clearly how he wanted *Oiled Beach* to be. And though it was *Cliff Bronze* that he was most preoccupied with, and *The Raven* he kept returning to, panel by panel, it was *Oiled Beach* he was thinking of throughout the weeks when he made *Cliff Bronze*. Jim frequently found that when one work was over intellectually, with only its form to be finally finished, he would be working on something else in his head. In those years the sculptural work was often a medium to keep his hands and body busy while he mentally worked on something pictorial.

Jim brought a cassette/radio into the studio and played music, often unconsciously, as Albert still did when he went into his workshop. Albert liked the organ; Jim liked choral music because its rhythms and melodies seemed to free his mind to play with ideas.

It was on such an occasion, one weekend, when the garden studio was full of the choral drama of Janáček's *Glagolitic Mass*, and Jim's hands seemed to be at a cliff-face, while his mind was cast adrift on a sea before a great and terrifyingly oiled beach, that Jim

545

heard a knocking sound above the choirs and the waves, and the door into the studio swung open. A man stood there rather awkwardly, a little taller than Jim, with dark hair on a big head that leaned a little to one side, and stared at him with a slight smile. Jim, who had been bent forward at a bench, slowly eased himself upright and dropped his hands to wipe them on the cloth that he had tucked into his overall pocket.

'Hello, Jim,' said Peter Conan.

'I'll turn off the music,' said Jim.

There are some friends, perhaps only one or two in a person's life, the depth of whose absence can really only be felt when they return. For their love is a trust so deep, so bound in time and shared experience, that even after decades apart it continues where it left off. There is little awkwardness, no silly words, no try-out conversation.

Now, in that moment, each found the other was such a friend, and knew they could never again be apart so long. Each wondered how they had let the years slip by.

'Well, I wasn't going to go on waiting in Cambridge the rest of my life,' said Peter.

'Don't like phones,' said Jim.

'Nor do I,' said Peter.

'Come on,' said Jim, and he took Peter up the garden, to begin to show him something of the life he'd made.

They arrived finally in Jim's upstairs studio, now becoming relegated to a store-room for canvases and a place for Jim's books, and they ate some beef sandwiches Jim put together, with a couple of mugs of lager.

'I'm not alone in Deal,' said Peter. 'I brought my wife Annie.'

'Congratulations,' said Jim with a laugh. 'Where is she?'

'As a matter of fact she's on a day trip to France with the children. We came down last night spontaneously, because of the good weather, and we're staying in the Royal Hotel. I didn't have your address so I went to see your mother first thing this morning, and Annie thought it would be a good idea if I saw you alone with so much to catch up on, and the girls wanted to go to Calais. So I ferried them to Dover and here I am.'

'You look older!' said Jim.

'You've got a beard! You hardly even shaved last time I saw you.'

It was nearly twenty years. Peter was now a lecturer in economics at King's College, Cambridge, where he'd received his degree.

'You're coming to have dinner with us tonight at the hotel,' Peter said. 'Annie wants to meet you.'

'What does she know about me?'

'Everything I know,' said Peter quietly. Jim understood. Those years along the seafront and over the Dunes, 'M' nights and conkers and bicycles and rugby fields—those years now lost. Peter must have talked of them to his wife Annie, as Jim had talked of them to Judith.

It was several months before they talked about it all fully, and Peter came to hear about the nature of loneliness in his friend that he had seen so clearly at the exhibition he visited in London at the Cunliffe Gallery.

'It was just a chance. Annie happened to see your name in an art magazine, announcing the exhibition. It was extraordinary for me to see those drawings and painting of places I knew, people I knew just as well as you.'

They were silent, each staring into their beer, with so many things to say and feelings to express. So much living to get on with.

'I could see the loneliness in your work, Jim—shades of your father,' said Peter eventually. 'Why do we humans have to suffer so much?'

It was the first time in four years of work in Deal that anyone had ever said anything to him about his art which showed they understood. Perhaps only Peter Conan could have said it; indeed, perhaps he alone understood better than Jim himself what he was saying in all those images. Jim gripped his mug and stared at the floor, his mouth trying to say something, but he could not trust himself to speak. For if only one person understood, just one, then he was not alone, and the relief of the discovery made him want to cry.

What ground they covered that afternoon! Talking and exchanging so much news that sometimes they stopped each other short and said that, for God's sake, there was plenty of time, they didn't have to say it all now. So they stopped talking and walked up to the front, and then along past the Coastguard Station, and on to Sandown Castle to look at the Dunes. Then on to the Dunes, because they couldn't resist them, Peter's town shoes covered in sand. Sea-holly was beginning to sprout along the shingle edge, and the skylarks were trilling for spring above them.

'*Alauda arvensis*,' said Jim.

'*Sterna albifrons*,' responded Peter promptly.

'What's that?' asked Jim.

'Terns,' replied Peter, and they both laughed at a shared, unspoken memory, in the way only old friends can.

If the rediscovery of Peter Conan was to help put love and joy into

Oiled Beach, which Jim began working on in earnest soon after his visit, the death of Albert Chandler put the anger and the pity. For the most brutal face of the bitter violence that had been building up in the streets of Britain's cities all that decade finally made its way into the tatty, gale-blown High Street of Deal.

It happened over Easter, while Jim was away staying with Frank and his children near London. He had taken Margaret Stonor, and it was in the nature of a family reunion for a family that was beginning to come out of the years of darkness. The siblings were beginning to talk to each other again.

A week later, Jim returned to Deal and found a note on his door from 'Elsie' Roberts. It said simply: 'I'm so very sorry I was not able to contact you. Albert has died. Please come and see me.'

On the evening on Easter Sunday, after the six o'clock service, Albert and his wife and a few others had been leaving St George's and were standing opposite the chemist's. Four abusive youths had crossed the road and come along the pavement and shouted at the church-leavers to 'fuck off out of our way'. Albert had gone forward to remonstrate with them, and one of the youths had butted him in the face, and Albert fell to the ground. Another kicked him hard before they all ran off, laughing and jeering.

Albert had never regained consciousness and died the following morning. The flowers on his grave were already wilted and rain-bedraggled before Jim returned.

After seeing Elsie Roberts, Jim went round immediately to visit Albert's wife. The moment she opened the door, her old arms were out to him, and in truth it was she who comforted him in his sorrow and impotent anger, as much as he did her. All they could do finally was ask 'Why?' and repeat those precious remembrances of times past which mourners must always talk through before they start to live again.

The police had found the youths and they had been identified. They would probably receive a suspended sentence, or perhaps a period of Borstal. It seemed irrelevant when set against what they had done.

Mrs Chandler's kitchen was as it always had been, tidier and cleaner if anything. It was she who made a cup of tea for Jim, and who took down one of her blue and white tea-plates to put some biscuits before him, as she had done so many times before.

'No scones, my duck. I've not baked since it happened.'

Then she did weep, for herself, and for old Albert. And Jim held her as once Judith had held him, and in her weeping he understood something of himself.

'The boys organised the funeral . . . well, they did it all.' But the boys, it seemed, had done much more than that. 'They went into his workshop and took what tools they could because, well, they said it would be best, since they were here, and that.' Jim could scarcely believe it. Didn't they know what the workshop had meant to Albert and must mean to his wife? Couldn't they imagine? Couldn't they have waited? 'It doesn't matter. It's over now,' she said. 'Anyway, I *thought* they would. Something told me. Not one of them respected or understood his work. Don't work with their hands, you see. Often asked their dad to lend them tools and he wasn't very willing—said he needed them. So before they came . . . well . . . you come with me, Jim.'

She led him into the front room, a formal dining-room in which they rarely entertained, with a polished oak table which Albert had made himself.

She pointed to a cupboard built beside a chimney-breast next to the fire. 'I put it in there and covered it with a blanket so it wouldn't be found.'

Jim opened the cupboard, took away the blanket, and in the dim light saw Albert's big wooden tool box with the letters 'AFC' on the top.

'You take them, Jim. He would have wanted you to have them, now wouldn't he? I know he would.'

He held her to him and she wept again, saying, 'Why? Why? Why?' because she didn't understand. He could not explain.

Later, he took the box out of the cupboard and found it was heavier than he remembered, so how had she carried it? But he could imagine it. Shocked, enraged, driven by a power far beyond her normal strength, she had needed to do something in the hours afterwards, to express her feelings—for the same reason he once made the cormorant's memorial down on the beach by the Dunes. He could see her going down into the empty workshop where she so rarely went, taking Albert's great box of tools – the bigger of two – a box he made for his apprenticeship, and dragging it up the garden and hiding it. She was giving him the most precious things Albert ever possessed.

'You'll take care of them like he did, because you understand,' she said with certainty. 'He always called you his apprentice, you know, Jim. So you make good use of them.'

'I will,' he whispered.

Jim took the box of tools home to West Street. Then he went into the garden studio, dug about among his cassettes for some Bach organ music, and turning it up loud, he took out the tools and looked at them one by one. He ran his hands over the great wooden jack-plane, and felt the handle of the brace. He held the chisels to the light as Albert often had done, and idly pushed the bradawl into the top of his bench. Then, with hands that moved as sure as eagle wings across a sky, he took some pieces of oak which he had found inside an old picture-frame, and with chisel and mallet, and his mind always a blank, he made a perfect cross tenon joint. When afterwards he looked at it, he smiled, as Albert would have done to see it. He cut three ends short and equally, and left a fourth twice as long to make a wooden cross. He bevelled its corners, smoothed and then waxed it. Then he wrote a letter of his grief and anger to Michael, asking if he understood or could explain how God could let an old man die like that. And with the letter he sent the cross, because Michael had known Albert, too, and in its making and sharing all of them might join their grief.

Nor did Stonor stop his carpentry there. In the same burst of energy he made the great bulky frames he needed to take the three canvases of the *Oiled Beach* triptych. It would not be as he had first conceived it – a simple beach of oiled and dying birds, figurative and literal – but a beach along whose stretching length images of all the things he loved and cherished would suffer as if besmirched by oil.

Five long, dark months it took, a summer of darkness in which, as he worked at the great canvases, only slowly did the joys in his life, the loves and friendships, begin to shine through and turn the work from bitterness to tragic compassion for all he had lost in Albert, and all he felt the world had lost.

In Jim's concentration, *Oiled Beach* began to need to be as big as the great abstract expressionist canvases he had first seen in New York, nearly ten years before. But whereas they stretched length-ways on either side of the eyes' view, his stretched upwards, almost out of sight, forcing the viewer to raise his head and look. He would set it resting on a gallery floor and tilt it backwards, and he made the frame so that it was wider at the top than at the bottom, to give a sense of stretching space. Albert was there, and Mrs Frewin, his brothers Frank and Oliver, the yellow-horned poppies on the Dunes, the pink sea-rocket besieged by oil, and somewhere, somehow, the soaring song of skylarks, strangled short. Michael was there, and Peter, and Peter's children; and Margaret Stonor . . . image on image of something beloved, dying or destroyed. Not a literal painting of an oiled beach, but a beach that rose from a wooden gallery floor as shingle, into images whose tension lay in the meeting of dark blue sea, and a once-clean shore, both set against an eagle's sky. Cuillin was there, and Finse, Mizen and Weever, dying Askaval and rising Mourne. Image on image to live and regret, to fear and reject, finally to face and accept with love.

Turning from this as yet unfinished central panel, Stonor began work on the left-hand panel which was tall but not so wide, and which he planned to open towards the viewer like one side of a three-part mirror on a dressing table. It was a mirror image of the central panel, but that the light and the colour and the joys were blanked out with black paint—a panel of darkness. Then, in the last two months he started the right-hand panel, an opposite mirror-image of the central one—but here was only the colour and joy of all he loved. It was a panel of light to set against darkness, and between them both was the ambiguity of feeling which he had first faced with the oil-bound cormorant as a boy. To kill a thing he wanted to love. To see death in the oil, but feel life in the hands that killed.

He finally came back to the central panel, and in two days' working he moved across its face with a palette full of the colours of light, and it was if a sun had risen in his soul.

When he finished, he found that the summer was over and autumn well under way. Trees in his garden that had been in green bud when he entered his studio were losing their leaves when he came out. He was tired beyond fatigue, benumbed—and he went to stay with Peter Conan in Cambridge. They gave him a room and let him be, to wander about the town and into the bookshops, and listen to the students arguing in pubs. Young . . . so brittle and young.

He sat then by a fire in Peter's study, and they talked deep into night. The children woke him sometimes of a morning, with coffee they had made themselves. He played the ogre to them, yet one who bought them things and taught them to draw; and Annie Conan watched the greyness leave his face and laughter coming back. And sometimes, when he and Peter were together in another room, she heard their laughter and thought it not much different from the children's, just deeper, that was all.

CHAPTER TWENTY

'I argued in the catalogue that, like Picasso, Stonor's sculpture often tended to be made when he was under pressure of some kind. As if he needed a three-dimensional medium to project his stress into. I applied this thesis only to the Eagle works because after that the sculpture changed as the man himself seemed to. Of course the last sculptural work in the series was not in the catalogue, as he only brought it with him on the eve of the exhibition. This is not only his profoundest statement on the eagle theme, but I willingly concede that it is a joyful work as well, and not an image of dark stress so much as joyful enlightenment. So much for thesis, you might say! But I prefer now to see it as the natural transition to his post-1984 works, a start rather than an ending.

—Marian Poyser in an interview in *Art in America* in 1999, reviewing the retrospective of James MacAskill Stonor's work at the Museum of Modern Art, New York.

S TONOR went into a period of intense and contradictory work when *Oiled Beach* was finished, as he had done after the first Cunliffe exhibition. Far more often than before he began to visit and stay with friends and family, making paintings and drawings of things and people he saw and found pleasure in. Increasingly he began to bring images of children into his work, yet secretly he worked on more of the *Disasters of Peace* etchings, which at that time no one saw. They were his secret catalogue of horrors experienced, and marked clearly and profoundly his growing interest with, and concern about, the society of which he was a part. Indeed, they mark his emergence into a world beyond his own life and his studio, his home-town and his friends, and in their sardonic humour, black tragedy, fierce horror, and frequent pessimism about mankind, show the side of Stonor he himself found hardest to face.

The darker abstractions of *Oiled Beach* continued as well, but now they were found in his restless search for an image of an eagle that seemed to struggle and escape from the clay in which he worked. Sometimes a wing, sometimes a talon, often a head thrusting up from the beach. There is no record of how many studies were made, and certainly he destroyed some, and it was only when Anthony Cunliffe pressurised him to produce more material that he agreed to cast any at all.

552

Only his letters to Michael tell of this struggle and his slow understanding of what it was he sought.

15 November: 'I spend hours in the garden studio, sometimes getting freezing cold, playing around with clay and trying to make God-knows-what. Something to do with eagles, I suppose. But that sense of them leaving me, which I first got to know in Skye last year, is coming back stronger and stronger. They've often gone from me and I can't reach them, but I try to find them with my hands. It leaves me feeling so frightened. In some ways I need them, Michael.'

12 December: 'I had an idea about these things I'm making, most of which I'll destroy before I ever cast them, but I'm almost afraid to mention it. An eagle's head came out of my hands, the beak dripping back into the clay, the eyes half-formed, the struggle as fierce as fire on your face. I wanted to call it *Haform*, Michael, but I don't dare. I wish, like you, I could say "God".'

At the same time Stonor was making calmer, more joyful work. Indeed, his portrait *Judith with Her Picassos* was begun within days of this December letter to Michael when, impromptu, he took a ferry over the Channel and went to see a major Picasso retrospective which had just opened at the Grand Palais in Paris.

'We always meet at exhibitions,' he said to Judith, who met him there. 'Am I going to see your family, now I'm here?' He was staying the whole weekend.

Judith's smile faded. 'It's better not,' she said. He must have looked hurt and surprised for she added, trying to be flippant, 'French men are notoriously jealous, you know.'

'Don't be so bloody ridiculous. What's your Patrick got to be jealous of? Me?'

'No, Jim, not you. Not really you. England, my home, my family, my almost-everything, over which he does not have control . . .'

'But . . .'

'Every marriage goes through bad times, and this is ours. It's not a good moment for James MacAskill Stonor, artist, an old friend of Judith Chanay née Shure, to come and see our apartment-home. Frankly, life's too short, and I wouldn't want to impose that scene on you.'

Still, they went round the Picasso exhibition laughing, as the French did, at so many of his jokes, nearly crying at his tragic images.

A little later she added: 'But at least you can see the children.'

'You should bring the children here tomorrow,' said Jim, 'because there'll never be another exhibition of Picasso's work like this in our lifetime.'

'They're only babies, Jim. Just a little young!' But she did bring them—wheeling Lucy, the younger, in a buggy; and letting Philip, the four-year-old, walk.

Philip called him 'Monsieur Jim,' and held his hand. And when Jim asked Judith which of the smaller sculptures or ceramics in the gallery she would most want to take home, she smiled and waved at the two children and said: 'Those are my two Picassos!' And so Jim made his portrait of the three, and would have sent it to her but that he thought her husband might not like the idea, so he put it in the downstairs back room of his house, where the piano was, and which was the only homely, comfortable room in the whole place.

The truth was that, since Mrs Hadden's death, Jim found his house was often a lonely and irksome place to be. He had not realised before what a comfort another person is, even if only an old and eccentric one whom he rarely saw or spoke to. There had even been something comforting in clearing up the mess she made in the kitchen, and certainly there was pleasure in the vases of flowers she had left there. Often now the house seemed grim and sombre as he walked up West Street towards it, wishing, especially after a period away, that he might see a light in one of the rooms, or smell something cooking in the kitchen. It was for this reason more than any other that he began to visit friends and stay long periods away from Deal, and two months' working at Harry Ginnan's studio in London while Harry was abroad.

Money was now less of a problem: Anthony Cunliffe was having no trouble selling Jim's work, and indeed was steadily raising the prices. There was continual pressure on Jim to produce figurative work, since it sold so well, but Jim resisted that. He made what images he wanted to make. But he cast some of the 'Haforn' series, as he was beginning to call them, to keep Cunliffe at bay.

At the same time, there was Arts Council interest in a four-man exhibition to tour eight provincial galleries, the common theme being wildlife drawing and printwork. The name of Stonor was beginning to become known, though Jim himself kept clear of the London art scene.

But he conducted a few special classes under Gerald Opie's wing at London art colleges, and booked to run some weekend courses with the Field Studies Council two years ahead, in north England and Scotland, under the general heading of 'Field Sketching.' His lonely years seemed behind him.

Yet often, back home in Deal, he would be cast down again in one of his darker frames of mind, and then, after having made a new *Disasters of Peace* etching, he would wander into the garden studio, take up some clay, and begin again the search for an image that expressed the longing for a peace and truth he could not yet seem to find from eagles.

Only rarely in those months, which began to fade into years, did he seriously think that what he needed was a woman (if not, perhaps, a wife), and that only when he was lonely. He would spend months on end celibate and then, usually after a hard spell of work, seek out sex, often with women he had known before. Only slowly did the pleasure he saw in Peter's children, and Gerald's as well, become a fantasy he projected into his own home; but that would only be for a short while, for he had seen the tiredness in the faces of young parents he knew in Deal, and dreaded the disquiet it might bring to his own life. He had never loved that intensely . . . except perhaps for Patti in New York, all those years ago.

'I don't have the right sense of responsibility,' he would say disarmingly to Annie or Nina when they asked if he was ever going to settle down. But their hopes rose when, in the summer of 1980, a girlfriend moved into West Street. He claimed she was a lodger, but she was sharing his bed and tried to make a sort of life with him. She left before the year was out, and all that Peter and Annie remembered of her was a weekend they came and stayed and nothing was right, and Jim retired to the bottom of the garden and let them sort it out. Perhaps he was right: he did not have that kind of responsibility.

Taken together, the works made in those years seemed confused and sometimes weak when set against the achievement of *Oiled Beach* and *The Tanahorn Eagle*—with the exception of the *Disasters*, which no one had seen. Perhaps, finally, it was the etchings which those years were about, and not the eagles, which seemed to have left him searching for an image he could not find.

Then, in the spring of 1981, the shadow of Haforn's wings fell over the Hebridean islands, and she proved an angry and demanding God.

William Ferguson had regularly kept in touch with Jim since the sea eagle pair's breeding attempt in South Uist. The second year nothing had happened—or if it did, it went unobserved. In Ferguson's opinion they had been too much disturbed by fishing vessels and early sailing activity in an unusually good spring. In the third year the male drifted north along the coast of Harris and attempted to establish a territory patrolled by golden eagle. Eggs were laid, but the pair was constantly disturbed and harried by other birdlife, especially the golden eagle, and the nesting proved sterile.

This year they had moved yet further north, settling into what seemed to be a pattern of vagrancy, and the male had finally overflown the territory seaward of Callanish, site of the most famous stone circle in Britain after Stonehenge. The site itself was superb, a small sea island off a coastline inaccessible by road, and Ferguson heard of it through coastguard contacts who had been briefed on what to look for.

He set up an operations centre in Kirivick, north of Callanish, and once the female started brooding, established a twenty-four-hour guard near the island. Because of the danger of disturbance, critical at a time of breeding and raising young, there were no guards on the island itself. But radio alarms were fixed under cover of darkness, and the pair was constantly, under surveillance from a hide three hundred yards away.

Of this Jim as yet knew nothing. A blanket of secrecy was put on the operation, though inevitably locals on Lewis were informed and involved. Local boats avoided the islands and skerries near the site, and the sea eagle pair was left to fly and feed, hunt and display and, finally, to brood by themselves.

The nest itself was on a rocky platform beneath a low bluff halfway down a shallow cliff-face. A colony of shag occupied a rocky ledge not far off to one side of it. Gulls were active over the cliffs from mainland colonies. So Ferguson and his watchers waited, finally catching sight of the first of a clutch of three large white eggs on the morning of 2 March. The pair were unusually attentive to the nest and the eggs, more so than they had been in previous attempts. Those in Britain's ornithological world who were in the know waited and held their breath, as they had done twenty years before when the osprey tried again to breed on Loch Garten, in north-east Scotland.

Incubation of sea eagle eggs takes about forty days, and Ferguson's team began its long watch, knowing that, isolated and undisturbed though the site was, it would be difficult, if not impossible, to keep its location secret. For not only was there the small but very active egg-stealing fraternity, but also a trade in chicks of birds of prey among hawkers and raptor fanciers. Servicing these groups is a small and expert coterie of fieldsmen in whom all sense of responsibility towards their prey is overridden by a simple desire to beat the system. The very fact of its uniqueness was what made the sea eagles' nest so fatally attractive. Ferguson hoped that the egg-stealers or hawkers would only find out about the pair when it was too late for them to raid the site.

But on 9 March that year, a small paragraph appeared in a Scottish newspaper which told readers that 'For the first time in over seventy years sea eagles, once common all over Scotland, may again be seen along our coastline. A major operation by conservation organisations to see that a pair who have tried unsuccessfully to breed for the last three years is now under way in north-west Scotland, and there is hope that they will succeed'. No mention of a site, no hint that eggs had been laid, but the report was enough to do the damage Ferguson feared.

The press article was sent the same day by a Scottish egg-collector to an address in north-east London, and two days later, two men – one a former sergeant in the British Army, the other a school physical education teacher – methodically packed a car with climbing gear. In addition were binoculars and a full set of 1:25000 ordnance survey maps of the north-west coast of Scotland and the Hebridean islands – already creased and marked from use – and four thermos-flasks without glass inside, but lined instead with cotton wool. There were also some sea-fishing equipment and a small net with a special attachment which made it possible to fix it quite firmly to the head of a harmless-looking fishing-rod. They drove to Edinburgh, where the journalist writer of the original story was bribed . . .

Two nights later, at just after four in the morning, when the sea was choppy, a drizzle was running on gusty wind, and visibility was nil, the radio alarm sounded in the hide on the cliffs north of Callanish and William Ferguson began running with a colleague to a boat on the shore below the hide.

*　*　*　*　*

With darkness and the sound of sea about her, Mourne brooded at the nest, the eggs warm and round beneath her, cocooned in a layer of moss and heather, and some of last year's dried fern that Bjorg had found. Though she could not see him, she knew he was nearby, watching into the darkness as she did, listening for danger.

Bjorg was restless: she could hear his talons at the rock and sometimes the shudder of his wings against his sides as he shook himself to keep out the cold and drizzle. Suddenly the sound of wood on rock, and Mourne froze, desperately alert. An alien presence nearby. Then she heard Bjorg fly noisily up, and the desperate harry of his wings, a sudden wheel of them above her, and a warning call. She heard human steps on the rock below, and scree slip.

Wind blustering, and her eyes fierce and yellow into it, feathers mantling, aggressive and the eggs so vulnerable.

557

An artificial light bobbing below and an urgent voice, and the human was moving more quickly and less carefully up towards her, while Bjorg circled frantically above. The human climbed nearer, something clattering at the rock by his hand, and she agonised between flying to attack or staying and protecting what they would destroy. The light shone on her, the nest was suddenly harshly alight, and her great wings opened and she stormed forward with talons out calling in anger and fear, and rising above the human, striking at air with her talons. She did not dare fly so close as to strike for real.

The human shadowed over the nest, moving slowly now and gently, and she and Bjorg successively dived at the shape in the air, anger in the sound of their call and their wings. A gloved hand moved among the moss and fragments of the nest, there were shouts and lights on the beach of the bigger island opposite, the sound of an engine, a call from below the cliffs, and the human was swinging back down to the beach over the rough but easy ground, running. A curse, the sound of metal on wood, an engine in a boat—and they were gone.

Before the other humans came, Mourne soared back to the nest and settled at its edge. Two eggs were gone, the third smashed where it had been dropped on rock nearby. Bjorg calling hopelessly, and she joining him, and they circled and called until dawn as other humans came, and lights shone on the plundered nest. They stayed near the site for weeks after, feeding and hunting and hopeless, and whatever Bjorg tried to say, Mourne could not be comforted, and in truth nor could he. He cursed the wings of Haforn that she had brought such sadness to them both.

Until a day came, a spring day of lovely light, when the Hebridean islands stand proud off a sparkling sea and the white of the waves is as white as can be, when Mourne said: 'We have been wrong, Bjorg, to try to breed among these smaller islands, hoping to stay clear of humans. In my heart I have known this is not my place. My mother flew from Skye, and it was to Skye she wanted us to return . . .'

'But we've talked of it before, Mourne. There are too many humans there, and even less protection. If they reached us here, so far from roads or houses, what can we hope for over there?'

'You've never been, Bjorg, so how can you know?'

It was not quite true, for although he steered clear of Skye, and rarely even ventured on to the seas nearby, he had once flown near it. He had seen the human signs. Why venture there?

Yet strong as Mourne was, and angry now, she would not want to fly without him, and so they drifted along the coasts of the

Hebrides, their chance of young gone again, waiting and hunting another year out, but finding a happiness in each other that would have soared higher now in the making of young.

It was Reft the vagrant who helped to change Bjorg's mind, and finally set them on a flight to Haforn's will. Some time, late that summer, over good waters and in a fair wind, Reft came back as suddenly as he had left, and together they soared and circled over the islands.

'We have failed in what we tried to do, Reft. Sea eagles can never return here, for their will and their strength is gone,' said Mourne, telling him despairingly what had happened. She told him, too, of her wish now to return to Skye, but of Bjorg's great doubt.

'Trouble is,' said Reft, 'there are too few of us to make it work. Even if you succeeded in raising young, then how long do you think they'd last alone? How soon before *you* were shot or poisoned, or the young taken? One pair is far too few. Two eagles can never make a population. If some of the others had survived – Weever or Mizen – why then we could establish ourselves and take territory, and there would be enough of us to start again . . .'

He fell silent and they circled down to a cliff-side and took stances near each other to watch over the sea. Eider were plentiful and food was good. The day was clear, and across the sea they could see the jagged, beautiful peaks of the Cuillins.

'You know, Mourne,' said Reft, 'when I look at that island I say to myself what I said when we first came here: it's a dour place and always was, not to possess, mind, for we can never do that, but to live in like those others do—the sleark, the humans, the bloody sheep. I've been thinking this last year or two that I fancy going home, just for a while. Now, if I was to say to them in Romsdal, doing nothing, that you were holed up in the Cuillins needing help, well maybe I could get a few more to come back. Just a few. I mean, *I* came, didn't I, and I'm not much?'

Then he turned to Bjorg. 'Of course, there's no good even trying that, if you're not willing to go with her, because she'll only go where you do. It's got to be Skye, you see, because they wouldn't wear anythin' else. But if I thought you were there, I would try for you—though I couldn't promise anything.'

Bjorg stared at the Cuillins and then at Mourne, and then at his talons. He was proud and strong and did not bend easily, especially to another male. He did not like another male ever being near Mourne. But he remembered old Torrin on the Lomagnup, and how he had stared and stared across the sea as if, somehow, one day, he would will that Skye might be overflown by sea eagles again.

'Well, all right, I don't mind taking a look again,' he said at last. 'Just a look. But we'll go the way I lead,' he said, 'and we'll explore the island thoroughly, starting where I arrived at the place Mourne says is called the Cleft, because it's not a place you'll find humans.'

So they flew over one evening to where the sky swirled and was troubled by the cross-currents of air above the violent sea between the stacks of the Cleft, in which no sun ever shone, and only wet wood and dying creatures found a home. The Cleft was a black ghost in the line of towering cliffs along the coast.

They stared into its depths from a safe distance in the sky, but feeling the air sucking at them, as it had at Cuillin once when she was young.

'Well,' said Bjorg finally, 'So long as there's nothing worse than this place, I reckon we'll survive. But I don't reckon this'll do for a nesting site!' And with a laugh that told Reft that his offer was being taken up, Bjorg circled away and began to search along the coast.

'Well, then, I reckon he'll have a go at finding somewhere, though between ourselves, Mourne, I don't think you'll find anywhere better than down near Loch Coruisk. But don't tell him that, Mourne, because I don't think he'd have a sense of humour about it until you've had young. Nothing more serious than a male who's trying too hard! Do you ever want to go home, then—back to where you come from?' Reft asked suddenly. 'Do you reckon it was all a mistake?'

Mourne dared to think again of Romsdal, and the great sweeping coasts she had grown up with and loved. 'Yes,' she whispered, 'Yes, I do think of it. I feel about it as Cuillin must have felt about Skye. But an instinct makes me feel we should be here, and trying, because there is a peace on this island, and light and winds and so much that all of us need. May Haforn protect us, Reft, and may her power grace your wings especially.'

'Well, I hope it does, too—believe you me. I don't fancy the flight back, but it's a strange thing, when you've done something once it never seems so bad. Only thing is, though, that living as I have, I don't ever remember going backwards before. Still, there's a first time for everything.'

'I know,' said Mourne.

'Well, I'll be off.' Then, with a laugh and a couple of farewell circles in the air, he was gone, and Mourne turned to follow Bjorg on his careful search for breeding territory for their next year on Skye.

* * * * *

Inevitably the 'Callanish Eagle', as two London tabloids dubbed it, became a major news story after the disaster off Lewis. The wandering of the pair and their drift over to Skye was followed by reports and photographs with the same avidity that Fleet Street had once followed the saga of Goldie, the golden eagle that escaped from London Zoo. There was a superb syndicated picture of the female at stance on the coast of Skye, 'mourning her lost young' as the *Daily Mirror* put it. Outrage, shock and dismay was the general reaction of the public, and Anthony Cunliffe, always with an eye to good publicity for his artists, got Jim Stonor into a hurriedly-created BBC documentary on the plight of the species trying to re-establish themselves in the British Isles, in which Jim was interviewed standing on the edge of the dramatic Cleft of Straumen, talking about his own obsession with the sea eagle, and the film cut to show clips of his sculpture *The Tanahorn Eagle* falling into the Norwegian sea.

But the tragedy and publicity had one good effect. A special appeal was quickly mounted by conservation bodies – a 'Help the Sea Eagle Return' fund – money that William Ferguson and his team would, if the opportunity ever came again, use to make a sea eagle breeding site impregnable.

To Jim, the renewed interest in his eagle work was welcome, though he found it irksome to be interviewed about works of art that, for him, had finished. It was his irony, as it is for all great artists, that he only found himself being asked about works which he had completed and passed by, to become preoccupied by new and different problems and work.

Annie Conan had her third child that autumn, of which Jim became godfather, and he found himself strangely affected by this, as for the first time in his life, he actually started looking with interest at a baby: Andrew Timothy Conan. He seemed to Jim the best baby in the world.

For most of this year, Michael did not write to him: he had gone back to Rome for a period of new training, and later into retreat. But, in October, Jim heard from him again: 'My retreat was interrupted by illness which I could not fight off and it has made me rather weak and upset. The trip to Rome was perhaps rather a strain after all, and in a gesture which is the nearest we ever get to a holiday, the Abbot has asked me to go for a period to a school in north England, which is temporarily without leadership. It has good music, I am told, so that is a blessing! This music business is rather an issue with us now, and many communities have changed in response to changes inspired by Rome. I have been very tired,

Jim, and somewhat depressed. Your letters have been a great joy to me over these months. Please forgive my failure always to reply.'

Despite Michael's problems about finding time to write, he managed to do so again two weeks later, and three weeks again after that, from the north: 'I have perhaps not said before how much the cross you made has come to mean to me. It was almost the first thing I unpacked here. It is rather a mystery to me that something made personally in this way, which is symbolically no different from what I might call an institutional cross – like the one I had on the wall over my bed before – should contain so much extra spiritual meaning. This has worried me. But it is very simple and beautiful, and a link with many things I have grown to appreciate more since I have been away from them, though my family and my home is in Christ's love.'

The letters now became more discursive and brief, but more frequent, and Jim slowly began to see that Michael was searching for something with the same helplessness he himself sometimes felt. In the letters there was a sense of an agony deeper than even Jim himself had known, and a curiosity about things he felt that Michael dared not be openly curious about. A sense, finally, of entrapment, of a need for escape.

It was against his background of struggle sensed in someone who mattered increasingly to him that he had a call one day from someone else who mattered: Judith Shure. She was in London, and her father had died.

No, there was nothing Jim could do, and it had not been unexpected. She sounded distant and over-controlled, and whereas Jim might once have let it go at that, now he was not willing to do so. Gradually, over the months, he had felt his own strength building up, and his feet more solidly on the ground. He had the strength now to do what once Judith had done for him.

'Is your husband with you, at least?' he asked.

'Well, no . . . he's coming over for the funeral on Thursday. He's not able to before then. I can cope, it's quite all right. There's an uncle here, and his wife.' Judith was an only child and her mother had died years ago.

'Who's helping you?' he asked, as gently as he could.

There was a very long silence. She was crying.

Then: 'There's no one, Jim. There's no one really.'

'I'm coming up,' he said firmly.

'No, Jim, it's not necessary. It's not . . .'

'Now!'

She had no one! But he—he had so many, and they included Judith.

There was a hush about the house, a sense of shock. Curtains were drawn, and though Max Shure's body had been removed by the undertakers, he was still there in almost any direction that Jim looked. The shining grand piano he must have played; a wooden box of cigars on a table; the pink pages of three unread *Financial Times* of recent dates. While on the walls were paintings and drawings and, most especially some superb early nineteenth-century water-colours, of which Max Shure had been one of Britain's greatest collectors.

To Jim it was a kind of wonderland, and he understood now what a gift of knowledge and culture Max had given his only daughter. In one room he came upon a set of original colour-printed relief etchings by William Blake from *Songs of Experience*. 'Love seeketh not itself to please,' he read, '*Nor for itself hath any care; But for another gives its ease, And builds a heaven in Hell's despair*'. He remembered how Judith, then hardly more than an acquaintance, had entered his world at a critical moment of change and loss, a world of dark seas and loneliness that, judging from her home here, must have seemed alien and incomprehensible.

Now, on her father's death, he reached out to her all the love he had to comfort and support her. Such moments in a life, when people are themselves and all guards are down, are rare, seen perhaps only at moments of birth, or joy, or loss, or death, as now. Then may the deepest bonds be made, and evermore may those who shared those days know they mean to each other something that cannot be broken. So was it with them now.

They talked deep into the morning, as Peter and he had sometimes talked, and she told him of her father, and memories of her mother and things he had never known. And finally, sometime when the loss had begun to ease with talk, she spoke of her husband frankly to him for the first time, and of a life without love or, it seemed, passion. It was the rich, successful desert life her group and generation knew so well, a life of things and things to do, mistresses and lovers, and rendezvous to which a husband turns a blind eye, as he goes about his own.

There was not one word of blame in all that Judith said, and there were times when, for a moment, it might have been his own mother's sadness he heard when she talked about Liam: the same sense of failure to make something work that should have.

'There,' she said finally, 'That's how it is and I'll sort it out.'

'I'll stay until he comes on Thursday,' said Jim.

And in that hushed and curtained house, with a garden like a new-mown park, and relatives and friends beginning to come, so many, so voluble, so kind and Jewish, and alive, he envied a little her grace and full life as he watched her cope, but understood why she might envy him. No, not envy. Pleasure in a different person's joys.

Then, moment by moment, born over the years, they fell in love. The uncle, Jack, a man of seventy-two, and his wife Lotte, seemed pragmatic about him being there, and let him draw them with a grace and ease that made him wish for a home where such people came. He gradually realised that none of them talked of, or much liked, Patrick Chanay; and Uncle Jack's son explained frankly that there never had been much love lost between Patrick and the family.

'A cold man, you know. Never relaxes. Not like you or me, who sit here in a house where Max has died and talk in the way *he* himself would want. Monsieur Chanay could not do that, I tell you. Patrick and Judith?' He said no more, but shook his head from side to side and pursed his lips in a way that would have had Jim laughing, had the circumstances been different.

On the morning that Patrick was to arrive, the Thursday, Jim held her to him to say goodbye. Then he stepped back and looked at her. She was dressed in grey, with a white blouse fastened with an ivory brooch her father had given her, and he noticed for the first time that among her hair there were a few strands of grey. Just a few.

'I love you,' he said slowly, and she gazed down at the garden path in front of the house for a moment and coloured slightly before looking up at him again. 'It's a different world, all this,' he said, waving a hand up at the great detached house, 'and I'm glad I've seen it now, before . . .' Before it ends? 'Good luck,' he said finally, and he smiled again, and walked away, knowing that she would watch him go until he had disappeared from view. And that she would stand there seconds more, and be smiling, for he had come to know her now. And it occurred to him, as he walked away, that never once in those years, not once, had he ever thought of her as Judith Chanay: to him she had always been Judith Shure.

Now the shadows on Jim's life, so long so dark, began to fall away. He made *Haform* then, two great wings that were strong as rock but curled in the detailed primary and secondary feathers to a sense of watching care. No body, no tail, the head a tectonic thrust from a molten earth, but talons sharp, and the great wings that would stretch across a studio floor and then a gallery – and finally into so many people's minds – as a symbol of the caring power of an eagle god flying the Nordic night and encompassing its days.

A lightness came over him in those months, a certainty. And the fear he had first felt when eagles began to leave him in Skye he now understood for what it had been: man's oldest fear, the fear of standing alone and being truly what one is—which may not finally seem very much. Most strange of all to him then was the knowledge that it was his love for Judith, so far so slightly expressed, that gave him this sense of certainty and strength. He *trusted* now, though if it was Haforn or God, or just himself, he did not quite know. And, trusting life, he started walking free.

He began to talk more openly of eagles now, and sometimes told the stories to Peter's older children, as once Liam had told them to him. Sometimes they would get him to illustrate them as he talked, because they knew in their hearts it was easier that way; and they would watch as his pencils made up great cliffs and towering waterfalls, and magically made marks which made an eagle live.

So it was in Peter's home he began one day to draw Sleat for them—but now somehow it was not right. Once it would have been easy, when Sleat was young and cold and fierce, with eyes that glinted from enshadowed cliffs. Easy to make that! But now Sleat was old, old like Clew, and like Clew he waited for something that puzzled him and which he needed an eagle's courage to face.

When Jim returned to Deal after that visit to Cambridge, he could not get on with other work he had been doing, and instead toyed for days with drawing Sleat. He found, as he had found with the making of *Haforn*, that it was only in his garden studio, with clay in his hands, that he began to come nearer to the form he sought. Until, at last, out of the clay and from his hands, a form that was barely an eagle any more, but a searching and despair, a desperate hope, an abstraction of what *Sleat* must become, began to grow and shape itself and live.

★　★　★　★　★

Sleat of Hardanger had left Romsdal. Soon after his talk with Clew in the shadow of Storrin, the restlessness he had then expressed made him want to turn in flight and head south-west over the fjells towards the coast. He told the younger Hardanger eagles that he was leaving, and was not surprised that some seemed glad to see him go. There seemed no need of his kind of leadership now, for they had all settled down, and his silhouette across the fjells made them a little restless these days.

He had drifted southwards, month by slow month, coming closer to the fjords of Hardanger, his home territories. Of his battles then with sleark, and later with illness and hunger in a harsh winter, little is told. But he suffered along those shores, as Mourne had once done, and learned to be afraid. Like her he sought anonymity, so what eagles, least of all the vagrants he met, would have thought this tatty, bedraggled stranger from up north could be the fiercesome Sleat? None.

He heard one day among the vagrant gossip on the shore that excitement had come to distant Romsdal, and a gathering had been called.

'Not for the likes of us, mind you,' one of them said to him. 'That's for the high and mighty eagles who have territory and young and mates and all. Don't see any of them coming down here now and getting themselves grubby robbing the fish stations for food. But see one gathering and you've seen them all. Nothing ever comes of them.' Under cover of darkness, Sleat flew north again, swiftly now and surely, and with a power and certainty to his wings that none of the vagrants he had come to know would have recognised. Sleat of Hardanger flew again. But it was a different Sleat than had flown that way a decade before. Wiser now, with strength and far more control.

When he reached Romsdal, and flew inland between its walls, there was no doubt that something had happened. Eagles were gathered near the Storrin, but only as he came closer and they parted on seeing him, did he see a sight that might have made him laugh. For there amongst them all, and next to Clew, and looking not only untidy and unkempt but decidedly bemused and annoyed all at once, was Reft, the old eagle that had flown with Mourne.

Reft was, in fact, fed up. He had hoped to sneak among the Romsdal skerries, say his piece to Clew, quietly enlist his aid, and some of the young eagles, and then be off again, no questions asked. But before he knew where he was, or had time to shake the sea salt from his wings, the whole bloody lot of them were flying about and more or less forcing him up towards the Storrin for a gathering. To make it worse, he was going to be the Eagle of Honour. Him! Reft! Who didn't like crowds!

Anyway, he didn't fancy getting done over by those Hardanger eagles, and in spite of all the reassurances Clew made – and even the sight of a couple of them doing their dark and heavy best to look friendly and pleasant – he did not feel at his ease. The opposite, if anything. To cap it all, that cunning Sleat wasn't around—no doubt waiting to make an appearance just when it suited him.

But the moment Sleat came all changed, and for the first time in his life Sleat knew the silence of eagles in his presence which was born not of fear and awe at his strength, but of respect at the old wise powers they now saw in his flight and stance.

Then, when Sleat settled beside Clew, and the two were together as one, they knew that Romsdal itself was now one, and the eagles there united. They marvelled, too, at the difference between the two old leaders: one gentle and quiet, whose wisdom came from thought and wise stance; the other strong and sure now, however vulnerable, which came from a life of action reviewed and flight that had been questioned and refined. A leader for peace, a leader still for war: both equal before Haforn.

Reft told them all he knew and had seen, and cast them into despondency with his tale. Only two survived, apart from himself. Just two! And Bjorg and Mourne seemed without much hope of making young or, if they did, of surviving without help.

'Thing is,' said Reft finally, 'that I couldn't let it stay like that. I thought, well, you know, that there might be some round here would want to give them a helping wing. I know it seems difficult, but look at my old wings! I've made the flight over the dark sea twice, haven't I? It's like anything else: seems hard till you do it. So I came back to ask for your help. One thing's certain, I've never come back to the same place before, and now I'm here I know I want to get off again. I'm a vagrant, see, not a gatherer!'

There was a roar of support for what Reft had said, but as it began to fade, Sleat's voice broke across it all. 'It would seem easy now for some of us to gather together and make the flight over the dark sea. I know there are many who would say yes to that now, and start right away . . .' and many did, indeed, call out their willingness '. . . but this is no more a matter of heroics than it was heroism that made a group of Hardanger eagles gather about me so many decades ago, and follow me here. That was a matter of survival, and it is survival that Reft's courageous return must force us to think about now. The odds against the success of Mourne and Bjorg are so high that none of us must think that whatever we do will lessen them greatly. We know now that the Doom is in humans, and in ourselves as well. Reft has made clear the danger they face from sleark. But beyond those fears is the problem of finding the strength within themselves to hunt and protect and trust in the life they are trying to make. There we cannot help them.

'But perhaps with thought and planning and a realisation of some of the strengths they need, we can ourselves make a contribution. They need support. When I came here I was ruthless and hard and proud and unkind; but we made a place, and by Haforn's grace and your good sense, who are gathered here now, and that of your parents who have gone, we made a peace. We have put the Doom at bay. We have found our strength.

'Now we must help Mourne and Bjorg, and romantic heroism is not what they need but common sense, fearless strength, and a ruthlessness in establishing territory. There we can help them . . . Some of us must go.'

As he said this there was a sigh among them, and cheering broke out. 'I do not think that many of us should try, but five or six perhaps—to help Mourne found a better base from which a future generation can grow. Young eagles, some of Romsdal, some of Hardanger, so that our unity may fly the dark sea. Eagles willing to sacrifice their lives—while those that survive may never see this home of theirs again. They must be led by one who fears not death nor loss of home; but trusts that Haforn will lead him.'

Then Sleat fell silent, and stared over at the great Storrin Gap through which he had never been able to fly, and all knew which eagle there would lead the few over the dark sea. It would be Sleat himself. It would be his recompense to Cuillin for the harm he had once caused.

Then Clew spoke. 'There is a time when things are right to do, and right to seek. Reft wants to leave now, but do not go yet, my friends. Not yet. We will know when it is best, and in the time before we do, the many who want to go now will reduce to a few who *know* they must go, who have the strength of wing and character that Sleat will need at his side. These eagles will have to be patient, and you others who clamour now for flight, go back to your territories and think what you may lose, and ask Haforn for guidance.'

'That's all very well,' protested Reft, 'but what about Mourne? While we're hanging about here looking at our talons and thinking fine thoughts, what about her and Bjorg? They need us now. I mean . . .' and his voice began to sound just a trifle guilty, 'It's a bit of a while since I left. Well, I didn't exactly come straight here, if you know what I mean. I hung about Shetland for a while, and having heard about the Faroes . . . You know how it is: once a vagrant always a vagrant.'

'Precisely,' said Clew. 'You needed time to summon up strength for the flight back here. So do we need time now. In the light of the sky, in the strength of the rock, in the roar of the Storrin, and with the grace of the Weir who first led Mourne over the dark sea, we will know when to go.'

So it was that Sleat, and Reft, and all the eagles of Romsdal began their wait, and in the months that came began to decide which of the many would finally be the few.

*　*　*　*　*

A year or so after her father's death, Judith quietly left Patrick Chanay, taking the two children back to England with her, and returning to live in her family home in London. Perhaps finally the decision was provoked by the need for someone experienced to run the Shure Gallery in London, as it was beginning to lose its strength without someone capable to lead it. However it was, she left and began to make a different life for herself.

It was two months after she first came back that she first brought the children down to Deal to stay with Jim for a weekend. He was so concerned that the house should at least be comfortable for them, that he got old Mrs Frewin, who still went to Compass Street twice a week, to come and help him sort out a few things.

'You haven't even got enough decent beds, Jim!' she declared. 'If the boy is seven now, as you say, he'll probably want to sleep separate from his sister. Boys like a room of their own. *You* did! As for the kitchen, and I'm not being hard, it needs a good clean and polish, and a bit of fresh air. And the front room with all them drawings and brushes and Lord knows what! I don't know, I just don't know!'

'Well, don't involve my mother, that's all,' said Jim.

Mrs Frewin laughed loudly. 'Your Mum? She wouldn't be so daft. Got plenty to do without worrying about you and what goes on here.'

Beds meant blankets, blankets meant sheets, and somehow, that weekend, the house took on a new shape. He had always made do when Peter and Annie came, and they brought bedding for the kids. But Judith would be without help, and he wanted to make it easy for her.

She came, and the children ran about the house and into the studio, and though Judith was tired and still under strain, she relaxed as she had not done for months. Philip no longer called him 'Monsieur Jim,' but Lucy did, her little voice serious and determined.

Jim had planned to have supper alone with Judith on the Saturday night, after the children had gone to bed, but there was a knock at the door and old 'Elsie' Roberts stood there, looking dishevelled. He often popped by now, because he still missed Albert on a Saturday night, when they had always had a drink or two.

So he came in and joined them, and played tunes on the piano for the children, and somehow stayed on for supper and a chat, before he finally left.

If they had wanted each other then, content with a day happily spent, they might have taken each other. But it was not like that. It was to be slower and surer than that, though they held each other after the old man had left, and moved about the kitchen with an easy grace as they cleared up.

'The children seem very balanced, very stable,' said Jim.

'Well, they haven't seen much of their father these last two years, and whatever else you might say about Patrick, he's not one to throw things and be bitter. Frankly I think he's rather relieved, if anything. I don't think he realised what marriage or commitment is, what sharing is. So I think the children will be less affected than they might have been with someone more loving. The important thing is that they continue to know they're loved.'

In practical terms Judith had no problems. Half the Jewish community of Golders Green was falling over itself to help; the Shure family had no shortage of kind friends.

A few months after they had left him, Patrick Chanay went over to London and tried to reconcile himself to the change while spending Christmas with his children at Judith's family home. Jim spent the holiday alone, but spoke to Judith and her children on the phone. As he put it down, he thought that was no way to spend such a loving holiday. It was a time to be with your own, and Judith was becoming that to him.

She came down more regularly after that, weekends of snow and gales, days of warm fires as Britain settled into a hard winter; weekends when Jim took Philip and Lucy for walks across the snow-covered Dunes and watched them trying to get the hang of the old brass binoculars that Philip had ferreted out of a drawer in his bedroom. He did not bother to say whose they had been.

The house began to take on the feel of Judith, whose eye for some things left Jim's far behind. One weekend that winter she might bring down a rug for the hall, another time some lampshades which seemed just right for the back bedroom; a third time some table-cloths because the kitchen table was all very rustic but lacked a certain clean domesticity. Normally she was careful never to leave things in the bathroom – a flannel or a bar of soap perhaps – as if that was too much of a statement of invasion. But once when she did, a small bottle of Chanel Cristalle, Jim was glad to see it there, and to have its perfume in his house.

They did not become lovers. For although they were close, closer indeed than either had ever been to anyone else, yet to Jim, at least, making love with Judith would have been a commitment far deeper than with anyone else in the past. Indeed, in those months, he occasionally slept with other women he knew, but infrequently and with less and less pleasure. Which puzzled him and left him annoyed with himself. Secretly, perhaps, he knew he was on a threshold, or a stance over a void, and dared not yet make a starting flight that would commit him to unknown depths, or soaring heights.

And they might well have become lovers. At the end of January they stayed with Peter Conan at a cottage on the Hampshire coast, and Annie put them together in the same room, thinking that was how they would want it. It was more the children's reaction Judith was worried about than herself—or putting pressure on Jim he might not like. But somehow they left it, and came to bed finally together, arms out for each other and as close as many lovers ever are. As they talked, Judith whispered, in case the walls were thin, that he and Peter were like two children the way they chattered on, leaving sentences half-finished, as if they knew what the words would be and had no need to say them.

'We're friends,' said Jim, simply.

'I wish I had a friend like that,' said Judith.

'You have,' whispered Jim.

Then they might have made love, but the time was not yet right, and they fell into a sleep deepened by each other's warmth. And when the children woke them up in the morning, not one of them seemed to mind that Jim and Judith were together there. Any embarrassment was theirs.

They slept together at Jim's house after that, just sometimes, for comfort and friendship.

Jim steadily continued to develop and work on the original idea for *Sleat*, and also the final panels of *The Raven of Storr*—which he began to find a millstone round his neck, now it was nearly completed. If he needed to be quite alone, as he sometimes did when Judith and her children were visiting, he would go down to the garden studio and turn on some music loudly, just as Albert Chandler used to do, and no one would disturb him.

But once, and only once, they did. It was Judith, braving the February freeze to knock on the studio door.

'It's the phone, Jim, for you.' She added, 'I think it's important.'

'Who is it?'

'I think you had better go and deal with it, Jim.'

So he did, feeling rather put out, and rubbing clay off his hands as he walked up a snow-covered garden.

'Hello! Jim Stonor. Yes?' He said impatiently.

'Hello, Jim.' The voice was thin and distant, rather lost, and for long moments Jim did not recognise it, and there was a silence. He started to mouth 'Who?' when the voice started again.

'It's Michael here. Hello?'

Michael! Oh Michael! The pips went just as Jim started to speak, but more money was inserted and the voice came over again.

'Hello?' As if not used to phones.

'Yes, Michael? It's Jim.'

'I'm in Oxford at the station. I'm . . . I've left the Order.' Jim had never heard anything so final in his life. 'The final leaving was sudden, just a matter of two hours,' said Michael.

'But I didn't know . . .' began Jim. Didn't he? Those letters, those questions, that entrapped voice—writing from a wilderness he also knew.

'Can I come down to Deal, Jim, to your house?'

The voice was shaking and so lost, and Jim's eyes and face so full of shock and care, that Judith came and put a hand on his arm, and one arm round him.

'Of course you can, Michael. Of course you can. Have you money? I mean . . .'

'Yes, yes, I'm all right. I'm in a state of shock, I think, and very tired. It's been so long coming, and now all so quick.'

They talked a few minutes more, and Jim gave him directions about trains to Deal. Michael's voice sounded so tired that all Jim finally said was, 'Come, there's a place for you here. You know that.' Some instinct told Judith it was best not to stay. Michael would be tired and perhaps not easily able to deal with children and someone he did not know.

So Jim went alone to meet Michael at the station, with a house ready and warm for him, and food prepared. The train stopped and the doors opened, and Michael MacAskill, in a dark raincoat and grey trousers, and with hair shorter than Jim remembered, and a pair of glasses Jim did not know he needed to wear, stepped down slowly on to the platform, carrying an old brown leather suitcase of the sort found in junk shops such as Mrs Hadden had once run. The two brothers advanced on each other, and Jim did what he had never done with any of his brothers, nor could have done even a few months before: he took him in his arms and hugged him. And, doing so, he was rather surprised to find that Michael was thinner, even smaller than he was, and yet he had always seemed the bigger one. Then Jim took the suitcase and led Michael over the railway bridge, down through the ticket barrier and across the station forecourt, and turned towards West Street.

Time now to see the rest of the winter through and sit by fires in his house and talk with Michael as neither had talked before, and walk over the cliffs against cold winds, and pull on gloves and woolly hats and watch the white snow fall among the trees of St George's churchyard.

A winter to take things slowly and watch the snow freeze on the ground, and hoarfrost rime the fallen sycamore leaves among the brambles in the garden, and icicles point their serried tips down from the northern gutters of the house.

Those first few days Michael seemed tired and benumbed by the change that had overtaken his life. He said very little—and nothing at all about his departure from the Order. He spent hours in his room, sleeping or reading, and went for long walks with Jim over the chalk cliffs towards Dover. He did not even go to visit their mother.

Jim understood. Michael needed a breathing space, and when that was over, he would begin to live his life again, and would be ready to start going out into the world.

One day, as Jim was sorting through some work up in the 'old' studio – his father's former bedroom – he heard Michael trying to play the piano. But it was somewhat out of tune, so Michael spent the afternoon tuning it, note after note. And occasionally Jim heard him humming as well, amid a sudden run of notes and chords, snatches of pieces he must know by heart.

There was a silence and the tuning and humming stopped. Then Jim heard him run through all the notes of the piano. Perfect.

Then quite suddenly Michael launched into a brilliant and exciting piece of Bach. It was so beautifully played, so committed, that Jim simply stopped what he was doing and listened. From Bach, his brother moved on to Beethoven, and from Beethoven to a piece by Chopin, though he seemed to know it less well, and stopped to repeat a run several times before seeming satisfied with his mastery of it, and finishing the piece. His playing was fast, alive, and joyful.

Jim knew he was listening to Michael rejoining a world he thought he had left forever. When the music finally stopped, Jim heard him at the front door, going out. And he knew he was going to visit their mother.

A couple of weeks later Judith came down with her children. Michael seemed a little wary of her at first, perhaps a little shy, but spent much time with the children who, once they discovered he would play the piano for them, would hum everything from French nursery songs to television jingles, and get him to play variations of them. That weekend Michael began to laugh in a way Jim had never seen since childhood.

Whatever Michael and Margaret Stonor talked about when they met again, Jim did not know. Both assured him separately that the meeting was successful, but neither seemed anxious to expand on that.

So Jim decided to invite their mother over for supper, on the next weekend Judith came down, but found Michael noticeably ill at ease. He made a rare visit down to Jim's studio and peered about silently. Then he tried to settle at the piano, unsuccessfully. He ended up teaching young Philip gambits on a small pocket chess-set.

Margaret Stonor arrived promptly at 7.00 pm, having refused any suggestion that she should be collected. She wanted to walk, she insisted, and at seventy-nine she was indeed looking remarkably fit. Her previous week had been spent on a sketching course in East Anglia with a group of old-age pensioners, and she had brought her portfolio along for them to see.

As she went through it with Judith, Michael hovered about a little uneasily, as if unsure of his role there. Her water-colour sketches were sure and easy, observations of the people on the course rather than of the trees and leaves and buildings they had been told to paint.

The children came in to say goodnight and, curiously, though Margaret was not outwardly warm to young children, they seemed fascinated by her. For she drew a little cartoon for them, and told them a story.

Later, after supper, and sitting by an open driftwood fire, Margaret Stonor suddenly said, 'You know, thinking of you all, I haven't done such a bad job really.'

'We agree,' said Michael, shouting a little because their mother was getting a little deaf and often forgot to put in her hearing-aid.

'I made mistakes, of course. *You'll* make mistakes, my dear,' she added, turning to Judith.

'I probably already have, Mrs Stonor,' said Judith.

'What mistakes were you thinking of, Mother?' asked Jim, realising there weren't many who could ask their mothers such a direct question with any chance of a frank reply.

'Not worth going into, most of them. But I blamed myself for Michael,' she said—as if Michael wasn't there.

'What—becoming a priest?' said Jim.

'It's not *natural*,' she said, with a look of distaste and her hands fidgeting now, in her lap. 'It wasn't right. Well, we've spoken about that now, and I'm not going into it again.'

Later, the two brothers walked her home, and stood for a while afterwards on the seafront, staring out at ships' lights on the dark horizon.

'What was all that about?' asked Jim.

'When I saw her a couple of weeks ago I'm afraid I accused her of the kind of things children do accuse their parents of . . . But my outburst didn't last long. Do you remember the move to Compass Street?'

'When you were sent away?'

Michael was silent, staring ahead.

'What happened, then?' said Jim softly, 'You never did tell me.'

'I didn't really tell anyone until I saw Mother the other day. Except when I spoke about it to a kind old priest, not long before I decided to leave the Order, and somehow the anger left me—or I left it. I grew up overnight.'

Jim remained silent, waiting.

'The family I stayed with were disciplinarian, to say the least of it. I was so homesick that I cried continually, and the father caned me to make me stop. Night after night he did it, until I did stop.'

'Why didn't you *say*, something?'

'I don't know really. I was afraid that if I told Mother, she'd tell him, and then he'd do it more. He said I should be grateful to them for taking me in, and not make them feel bad by crying for my home.'

For a moment Jim felt very sad at the thought of Michael, so young, so vulnerable, crying for a mother who could not hear, and when she could, did not seem to listen. *He* could have borne it better than Michael, for he had always been stronger.

So now they stood together and let the past slide away. Until Jim smiled in the darkness and said, 'I can jump further over the sea-wall than you can, Michael!'

And Michael said, 'It's the kind of daft thing you always could do better!'

Thus they passed a winter to end the long bleak journey that each of them had made—Jim, Michael, and Judith too.

It was the beginning of a stay that was to last over a year, and with the coming of Michael into a life that had expanded and deepened with Judith and the children over the previous months, Jim Stonor's work on eagles began to come finally to its natural end. His work now was becoming lighter and fuller of colour and joy, and the bronzes of *Haforn*, and *Sleat*, and those earlier works of *Eagle* and *The Tanahorn Eagle* began to fall behind him. In a few short weeks then, as Michael told him all about his decision to leave the Order, and of the long and troubled discussions with his superiors that led up to it, Jim finished his work on *The Raven of Storr*. Although it had not yet been shown in its entirety, already, to Jim at least, it seemed redundant and past. A work which soon others would write about and celebrate, and some would find a fear within its towering, frightening walls and recesses. But to him *Raven* was over.

Significantly, too, he made no further *Disasters of Peace* etchings after Michael returned, and the collection lay untouched and unseen until Judith herself first saw it in the autumn of 1984.

But long before that, in the bitter February that Michael returned, the Callanish Eagle came back into the newspapers.

★　★　★　★　★

Winter—and winds across Romsdal that left black ice on fjordside cliffs, and drove the reindeer down to the valley, trekking through the wastes. While on the fjells, blizzards howled among stunted birch and shrub, drifts of snow burying rocks and streams and tiny lakes, and leaving the ptarmigan and willow grouse to roam the wastes, and die for want of food.

Hardanger? Romsdal? What is one name or another against the winter night, where day lasts only a few brief hours, and then but a distant shining in a driven cloud?

Eagles. They shivered at their stances in the cold that put ice on their talons and a shine on their beaks, and rimed their feathers where they dragged in snow. The inexperienced began to die, or fled to the skerries hoping for respite there, but found that ice was settling on the sea. Only further out, where the currents flowed, would the ice not come.

Slowly, then, the fjords began to ice over; spreading out from ragged edges, crackling in the night. And eagle fought with eagle for scant, living prey, itself desperate for food.

Out on the skerries, old Clew saw the scavenger eagles come, the vagrants who had territory no more, but tried their luck where humans were, or moved across his territory to find the surface fish, or carrion seal, or stricken gull.

One day, if day it was when the light was violet as early evening, he flew inland and up the frozen fjord, where only the scutter of raven made a sound, and the fall of ice on frozen rock. Only the whisper of wind in cold-dry snow. Then further on, and only the Storrin's roar to break the deathly calm, but muted now, beginning a slow death in ice as well.

From off some hidden stance another came, old as well, but sure, and flew at his side without a word to say. Sleat and Clew.

They took a stance near the Gap of Storrin and waited there as night-time came, and a cold as cold as either had ever felt. Old feathers fluffed to keep them warm, and necks retracted, and stomach feathers tucked over talons to stop the cold from creeping in too far.

Not one word said, but who needs words when they can hear the Storrin trying still to roar through ice? Never in living memory had ice stopped the Storrin, but instinct had them both there then, waiting as they had waited for over a year since Reft returned. Waiting. Dark night fell. Then a light, distant but changing, casting

576

a vector across the sky, ragged and hanging and shining at its edges, flowing across cloud, through cloud. Light that cast no light at first—but a light. And their eyes opened into the stark cold, watching it in wonder as it swung over the great fjord and changed to flowing cloud that flew full of light that brought a peace and awe that was an eagle, old and worn and nearing death. 'Look!' Clew wanted to shout. 'Look!' But no voice came from him, and he could only stare in wonder and feel a hope and know at last the time had come. Then, beneath them, the whisper of the grey feathers of an eagle, familiar as a brother or a friend, flew on and upward, and just for a moment, the great rising, iced-up walls of the Gap were lit before it disappeared towards the Storrin's deeps.

Sometime in that long night, the roar began to thin and weaken and the spray that had cast thick ice on the inner walls of the Gap ceased, and only tinkles of sound now, echoing quietly among the great cliffs of Storrin. Then dawn and great Clew whispering, 'The time is come, Sleat. Now you must go.'

Instinct brought them then, one by one, of Romsdal and Hardanger, four males and three females, young and resolute. The Few. What power or force in that dark night had told them, no one knew, but days and weeks past they had felt the need, and in that night of freezing doom they knew theirs alone was the task. So they came, some over the fjells, but most slowly up between the ice-drowned cliffs.

They took their stances with Clew and Sleat, near the Gap, and stared through it at the towering snow-bound cliffs and frozen gullies, where the wind had died and only stillness fell. Distant ice-falls echoing about them like thin-voiced thunder; strange cracks and slides up in the cliffs beyond.

One more came then, Reft the Vagrant, slowly and tiredly circling above them for a while, the only movement.

'Now is the time,' said Clew again. 'Now, fly across the sea. For in the weeks to come your strength and courage will be needed over there. But first yours shall be the honour of flying through the Gap, and seeing what not one of you will ever forget.'

So they followed Clew, all but Sleat who would not go, and flying beyond the Gap, pushing on and round the bluffs of ice that overrode the overhangs of cliff, they flew into the great frozen well which dropped far, far below—not into spray, or rushing white water, or terrible deep-green flows, but down to a frozen sea of ice that seemed forever held in a stricken suspense of waves and eddies, flows and shoots, not one of which could move.

Then up they looked, up a towering slope of ice, up past a nesting site so hallowed that some of them dared not look too close, up at the Storrin, frozen in its massive movement downwards. Overhung, overshadowed, a vertical river of sheer ice. Wings and beaks and white wings that soared forever into frozen stillness.

They stared and circled nervously; and slowly, one by one, they saw that through the Storrin, from behind its icy walls, it seemed as if an eagle stared. Great as Haforn, its body white, eyes great pools of darkness, and wings caught in the ice as if raised up and seeking to escape. An eagle bigger than any ever knew, trapped and waiting.

'Now make your flight and trust in Sleat, whose wings will guide you to your destinies,' cried out Clew. 'Remember what you have seen in this hushed and holy place, and know that what you see will never be like this again. Know that the Weir came to bless your flight.'

So they turned to go, out of the Gap, and Sleat flew down to join them from his stance, with Reft at his side, and they turned to fly west, over the grey fjord, leaving the Storrin frozen and solid still.

Then Clew flew up the Storrin's full height again, and watched a final trickle of water at the top, coursing clearly down over the icicles, shining and thinning and glazing until it, too, became ice, and the Storrin hung quite still.

Three hundred miles further south, across the dark sea, encompassed by the warm Gulf Stream, Skye's winter was not so bleak or harsh as that Romsdal suffered. But it was exceptional. Snow had fallen early on the Cuillins, giving them a stark white beauty scarred and blackened by the dark crevices in the gabbro rock.

In January, snow had come to the glens and swathed them heavily in white. A thaw, and then light snow again, and the beginning of the freeze. The moorland north and west of the Cuillins became bitter and bleak, and had it been stripped of heather and raised a thousand feet, it might have been the fjells that Mourne knew and loved.

The cold worsened, and verglas built up on cliffs and screes, first to windward, then on their lee: a shining ice that gave no talon a hold.

The sky seemed darker that year, too, and the nights longer. But Mourne felt released and lightened, and flew with Bjorg, along the coasts of Skye, excited and invigorated by the chill.

'This is the last year, my love,' she said. 'This is our chance. Haforn has sent a winter we are used to, and in it we shall have a strength when others weaken. Prey will be easier to find, and the enfeebled sleark, harried by cold they are not used to, will not want to attack us so much.'

They had searched the island for over a year, and Bjorg's fears were right: the island was busy with humans. So it was doubt, fear and uncertainty fighting against desire, love and need. Until at last it was Mourne who took the lead over territory. 'We have searched and sought for too long. There is only one place for us here, and that is where Cuillin was born in the ancient nesting sites beneath Gars-bheinn, overlooking Loch Scavaig, within sight and sound of Loch Coruisk, near where Mizen died and Weever was shot.'

'But that's a dangerous place, exposed, hard to defend from sleark, accessible to humans.'

Mourne did not listen, but skirted the Black Cuillin from the west, and soared over Loch Brittle, and then round and over Rubh' an Dùnain, whose ruins were black-patterned lines across a snowy moor at whose rocky edge great winter seas drove up and crashed.

They flew together up the coast, with the rugged hump of Gars-bheinn ahead to their left, and the narrow landward end of Loch Scavaig ahead, the rises of the inner Cuillins beyond it, where the great stretch of Coruisk lay.

'How will you know these ancient sites?' asked Bjorg.

Mourne turned to be nearer the side of Gars-bheinn, where it fell down towards the sea. 'This is the southern end of the Cuillin ridge,' she said, 'and from its side an eagle may see the quieter waters of Scavaig, and watch the heavy seas run in. When we of Romsdal first came here, we sought shelter further down the coast, but found we were on dead ground which sleark could approach unseen, to harry us.

'Now, do you not think the wise old sea eagles would have chosen a better site than that for their nesting place? A site that is protected from above by rising, jumbled ground on which the winds are difficult and fierce; and which commands views over sea to left and Loch Coruisk to right? And towards which the approach is over an open stretch of sea?'

She stared meaningfully at the great slope of Gars-bheinn's side, and circled there, her eyes criss-crossing the cliff's shadows and rises, seeking out a likely site.

'And do you think the most ancient site on Skye, the last to escape the human doom, would have been easily accessible to them? Remember how they climbed the short cliff where we made our previous nest and how easy it was? But this face here is complex and steep, and more complex as we fly nearer to it. I feel at home here, among places of which my mother once spoke. Search these great cliff rises, Bjorg. Find a place, and trust in Haforn to guide you.'

So it was that Bjorg tracked back and forth across the eastern face of Gars-bheinn, judging his line on the islands that lay in the waters of Loch Scavaig. He was tired, and nervous of the place, of sleark in the heights above, or watching from across the loch, and the ground was unremarkable if steep—bluffs and little cliffs, and overhangs, higher and higher, rising steep to the top of Gars-bheinn. Mourne took a stance among the snow on one of the skerries, and watched her love soar up across the mountain's side, searching back and forth with a thoroughness far greater than she would have had. She saw him stall and circle, she saw him swoop, and then she saw him land and disappear.

Instinct made her rise and circle then towards where he had been, higher and higher, so the island she had been on now seemed but a gull upon a sea. Where had he gone? A call, a moving wing, and there he was, in a place beneath an overhang, protected by a complex of small cliffs. It was a secret spot, in shadows, but well placed for views to north and south, and east over the waters. While being on a slight bluff in the cliff, it had a place, a few yards from its centre, where an eagle might stand and see the cliff-face above quite well.

But Bjorg was not looking at that, nor even nervous now. For at his talons, where he had taken stance, was a stick, and another, bleached and ancient. And at Mourne's talons she saw the fragments of bone. It was an ancient nesting site, and it felt secure and safe, and good.

Then Bjorg raised his head and opened his wings, and thrust out into the air before them, and turned in a great celebratory wheel to the south, and she watched him as he dropped height towards the cliff line, and out of view. But back he came, eagerly and sure, carrying in his right talon a stick of birch. The first.

'Here is our place,' he said, 'which we have sought and we have found together. Here we shall raise our young and, by Haforn's grace, this time we shall succeed. And the stronger the cold winds blow, the more the ice, the more the hardships, the stronger shall I be in guarding this site and hunting prey, and making this place fit for the first of a new race on Skye.'

For a month they flew back and forth over Loch Scavaig, bringing sticks and moss and heather for the nest, and flying glorious mating flights over the south side of the Cuillins and the peninsula south-west of Gars-bheinn, all the way down to Rubh' an Dùnain.

Because they started early, they took the sleark by surprise, and the pair that might have nested somewhere near their territory moved west to the far side of Loch Brittle. There were skirmishes sometimes, but Bjorg's strength was great, and the aggressiveness he had once shown in his own homeland came back renewed. Ravens harried them, but both would laugh and turn their talons on any raven that dared come too close. While with each deepening of the weather into a long winter, they seemed to gain strength and determination. Until at last, in mid-March, perhaps a little later than in other years, a single egg showed, and Mourne settled down to brood it, staring fiercely down at the lochs and mountains of her mother's own ground, as Bjorg began to watch and guard the long wait through.

Twice they were disturbed by humans. Once a boat came from across the sea loch at dusk, and quietly put metal things about the cliff-side. Bjorg attacked one of these objects but his talons could not get a grip on it, and it smelt harmless and had no life. Another time, two weeks into the brooding, Bjorg was scouting out above Gars-bheinn and saw two groups of humans camping on the moor, their tents dark squares against the snow. Then lights at night there sometimes, and sounds of human voices. But instinct said they were harmless, and soon Bjorg took no notice of them, for he had much to do in finding food, and keeping their territory marked out with flight, to warn off any sleark.

* * * * *

If William Ferguson had hoped that the Callanish Eagle's next breeding attempt could be kept a secret, he was mistaken. But this time he was well prepared. Because of the extreme vulnerability of the site, at a place known to generations of walkers and climbers – indeed, within two miles of a Scottish Mountaineering Club hut – he realised that word would get out, and the site become known. So, pre-empting this, the conservation bodies of the British Isles involved in the sea eagle operation, combined together to hold a press conference in Portree on Skye, and later in London, which gave the fullest possible briefing on what was happening. The exact site was kept secret, but it was not hard to work it out, and Ferguson knew this. He hoped that full public knowledge and involvement might alert people on Skye to the potential threat from egg-stealers and naturalist vandals. He realised, too, that there would be some residents in Skye who would be hostile to the return of the sea eagle, and might do their best to destroy its chances. The hope was that full press coverage might not only create public interest, but also dispel myths about eagles causing damage to livestock, the farmer's main fear. On the whole the campaign worked, and national interest in the mis-named Callanish Eagle began to grow.

The atmosphere on Skye was soon similar to that on the south-east coast of Britain at the start of the Second World War, when the spy scares were at their height. Any stranger, especially one in a car, was eyed suspiciously all over the island; and there were random checks of unfamiliar vehicles on the ferries from the mainland.

Ferguson's operation to protect the pair was centred on the mountain hut at Coruisk which, though not within sight of the eyrie itself, was the best access point for boats, and within walking distance of vehicle tracks made by the army, who suddenly decided to do a small winter survival exercise for SAS men conveniently near enough to keep an eye on Gars-bheinn, with a radio link to Ferguson's operation centre.

There were three known attempts by egg-stealers on the nest. On successive days at the end of March, when the brooding was nearly halfway through, two separate cars were stopped after a tip-off to the Skye police, in which a total of three men and a woman were found with equipment such as egg-stealers normally use. Then, on 9 April, a call for a mountain rescue team went out from a climber returning from a day's ice climbing in the Black Cuillins. He had seen two climbers in difficulty near the treacherous ridge of Sgurr nan Eag, which leads south, if a climber happens to be going that way, to the top of Gars-bheinn. The weather worsened and a blizzard blew up. Two days later a mountain rescue team brought down the bodies of two roped climbers who had fallen fifty feet into a deep gully on the side of the Sgurr, and died of exposure. They were both properly equipped and evidently experienced, but they had failed to leave any note of their movements with the police, as winter climbers should, which was surprising since one was a former British Army sergeant with great climbing experience. What rescuers at first could not understand was why each carried an additional thermos-flask without a glass container but lined with cotton wool. They came from a north London suburb, and police investigation revealed that in the spare bedroom of the ex-soldier's house was one of the most complete collections of birds' eggs ever seen in private hands. It included clutches illegally taken from a Scottish osprey nest site, several from peregrine falcons, one of avocet, and two large sea eagle eggs. There were detailed record cards for each clutch of single eggs, giving date, grid reference, time and other technical information, which left no doubt about where the sea eagle eggs had come from.

In the early morning of 20 April that year, the field telephone rang in the Coruisk hut, and woke Ferguson. It was Roger Ruthven, aged twenty, a good climber and very experienced ornithologist, who had been doing his spell of watching the site from a hide well above sea-level on Gars-bheinn.

'Hello, is that you, William?'

'Aye, it is. Problems?'

'No, I don't think so.' The lad sounded excited. 'I think they've done it,' he said finally. 'I'm almost certain I saw a chick's head a moment ago. I think they've made it.'

'You're meant to be an ornithologist, not a bloody radio commentator,' said Ferguson. 'What have you seen?'

There was a long silence, but the line stayed open and crackling. Then the lad's voice came back, controlled but ironic. 'At 07.54 hours today on the eastern-facing slopes of Gars-bheinn on the Black Cuillins of Skye, the first official confirmation was made that a pair of sea eagles have for the first time since 1908 bred within the British Isles. There, that do you?'

Ferguson laughed and whooped with joy. 'Don't forget the grid reference and the weather conditions in your final report,' he said. Then he added: 'Well done, you lucky bastard. That's a sight you'll never forget.'

'It's beautiful, William,' said the lad softly down the line. 'It's got me hooked for life. Come up and see.'

But before he did, Ferguson put through three calls on the special land lines the army had laid. The first was to the Press Association in London, making a prearranged announcement. The second was to Dr H. L. Osborne, chairman of the liaison committee of the conservation bodies for the return of the sea eagle, which funded the operation. The third was a telegram to James MacAskill Stonor in Deal, Kent, whose *Tanahorn Eagle* had done so much to draw public attention to the plight of the sea eagle. It read simply: '*07.54 hours Gars-bheinn. Success. Ferguson.*'

* * * * *

Success in breeding—but what of survival? For now, as she stared down at the chick beneath her, Mourne knew that the hardest time was coming. The finding of food, the wait as the chick grew, the worry, the tiredness.

Sleark seemed to know, too. Perhaps the pair over Brittle were failing that year and so were more aggressive; perhaps instinct told all sleark around the Cuillins that their territory had not merely been invaded but was now under permanent threat.

The attacks began. One after the other, hour by hour, day by day, they came. Diving at the sea eagles' site, harrying the male when he hunted for food, stooping on the female when she left the nest, pressurising them all the time, until the tiredness in Mourne and Bjorg became a fatigue, and the fatigue a greyness in which all feeling began to go and their single chick became a growing burden.

The chick was a female and they called her Hekla, for that was the place in Bjorg's homeland from where Haforn was said by legend to have come; though in those first weeks nothing could have looked less like a volcano than little Hekla, who was too weak to raise her head for long, or do much more than flap her vestigial wings and roll over on her side.

Now, in those first few days, Mourne realised that the Doom had fully come. Now they must fight, now survive. Though April was nearly done, the winter was getting colder and ice still lay on the lochans over the moors. Sensing their weakness, the sleark attacks renewed, getting especially bad when one or other of them left the nest for food. It was at such a time, when Mourne was at the nest and Hekla still far too weak to tear meat off the prey they brought, that Bjorg was attacked over Loch Brittle and harried by three sleark. They drove him steadily over the sea, forcing him south and blocking his desperate attempts to get back to Mourne. While at the nest site itself, others renewed their assault, great powerful talons and beaks filling the sky above the nest. Then, in that desperate hour, Mourne was caught by the talons of one of them, and her eye was suddenly pained beyond belief, so that she fell back in the nest with blood over her beak, unable to see. Struggling then to regain strength, and only instinct making her mantle her wings to protect tiny Hekla from the slearks' questing beaks and vicious talons, she heard the strangest sound. A sudden rushing, and sudden silence; then a stillness over the lochs. Then the sleark above retreated, calling angrily in the wind, turning away from her, letting her live, letting Hekla survive that hour.

But why? Another few minutes and Mourne could not have survived. Why had they left?

She peered northwards over Loch Coruisk, grooming her head to clear the blood from her wound, and trying to make out whatever it was that had caused the sleark to turn away and head towards it. Then a group of gulls and three cormorants, down on the rocks below, suddenly and noisily rose into the sky, the cormorants shooting away over the tops of the waves, the gulls wheeling round and then scattering out of sight.

Then she looked north again, and saw the sky darken with eagles, great sea eagles whose wings loomed as menacing as the ridge of the Black Cuillins, and moving surely towards Garsbheinn, with a flight she knew. So she whispered, 'Reft. It's Reft . . .' and her heart filled with pride and relief to see them bear down on the sleark and scatter them, talon to talon, as if they were no more than dark spray lost on the wind.

Reft . . . and others she did not know. But some seemed like Romsdalers. She could not know then that among them had been one she once knew and feared—one whose name was Sleat.

But that was not the time to hear the telling of how old Sleat had given them the strength to cross the dark sea, binding them together in safety and loyalty as once – so many years ago – he had led his own kind out of Hardanger with a ruthless courage and intelligence for which Mourne might soon be thankful. But he was too old to survive the dark sea, and somewhere over it, when the Shetland islands were drawing near, the great wings of Haforn had broken through the sky and taken the burden of flight from his ageing wings.

Of this Mourne could not know, but she saw the sky over Coruisk clear of sleark, and she whispered to Hekla, 'Watch now, my love, for these will be your skies one day, and they will be safe for you. There one day you will fly, and there you will hunt—so watch now.' But Hekla was too young to understand, and instead pecked hungrily at the prey in the nest, and wondered why her mother's face was torn and bloody, and what it was she was whispering about.

Bjorg survived the attack, and the others spread their strength over the Cuillins, harrying the sleark, fighting battles, so diluting the strength of the sleark that Mourne and Bjorg were left with time to cherish Hekla.

In mid-June, Hekla began to flap and waddle a short way from the nest, though always with Bjorg or Mourne nearby, for they knew that sleark would kill her if they could, as their great hissing wings and fierce, treacherous eyes stooped and shadowed sometimes over the site, frustrated not to be able to get closer.

By August she was flying, though timidly and unable to hunt well for herself, and relying on Bjorg for food. While Mourne, still badly troubled with her eye, was finding it all she could do to find her own food. Now Hekla was at her most vulnerable, from raven and sleark and humans, too, and Mourne knew she would be lucky to survive through the autumn. The winter had gone, the months had flown, but the toll on all of them had been severe.

Yet Hekla did survive, and began to grow and gain character, strong and determined like her mother, and aggressive like Bjorg. An eagle a parent could trust to grow alone.

Mourne would tell her some nights of her ancestors, of Cuillin, and Finse, of Mizen and Weever and Clew, and of the courage and flights that brought her to the side of Coruisk and Scavaig.

But Hekla was not interested in such old tales. Her pleasures were in flight and hunting now, soaring along the cliffs and exploring the islands as autumn advanced. Until a time came when she stayed away for days, and was proud and fierce and thought her own thoughts at stances of her own.

Then Mourne knew that her job was done. They had returned. Still vulnerable, still weak, still needing courage, sea eagles on Skye and the islands nearby would take years yet to establish a life. But a start was made, and she could let others take the burden now. She was tired and ill, too, weakened by the injury to her eye which had not healed, and troubled her all the time. Bjorg was forced to watch his once graceful mate seem to flounder and grow nervous at the winds, and hesitate over living prey at sea, and seek instead the easier food of carrion. She was losing judgement of distance and depth.

They flew more separately now that breeding time was done, but he would watch from a distance, as others did, and feel a grief that Hekla's mother had, after all, been caught up by a doom.

While to Mourne herself, the rest of them became a nuisance, and she sought out a place to be alone, and when they tried to come near, she would present her talons to them and call aggressively for them to leave her be. Had she not done her duty? Had they not taken enough of her strength?

So sea eagles returned to Skye. Some took a territory over on the islands west of Uist, others explored Rhum and Eigg. Reft wandered far and wide along the shores, wondering why he could never settle down. But always he would be drawn back to the Cuillins and seek out Mourne and Bjorg, and watch over them, afraid in his heart of the winter to come. He could see Mourne was tired and ailing now, and even he could not get near her before she drove him off. Him! Reft! Who never harmed a flea!

'She's ill, Bjorg, and troubled, and she feels she's done her bit. It would help if that Hekla of yours was a bit more friendly, but you know what the young are like: prickly and selfish, and self-seeking. Not like us!' It was true enough, and an eagle as experienced as Reft knew that when a serious injury occurs, an eagle retreats until it recovers . . . or until it dies. No eagle likes to be crippled and make a fool of itself in front of others when it can't seem to judge landing at a stance, or misses one too many prey. Best leave well alone.

That autumn three eagles came over the dark sea from Iceland and brought news, bad and good. Old Torrin was dead, or disappeared at least. But the harsh winter had helped rather than hindered breeding, and nine pairs had young. Some sense of strength had come back, and after rumours of what Bjorg had done, vagrants wanted to follow him south to Scotland and see the place that Torrin had come from.

Bjorg spent days talking with them, drifting on the wind, and somehow then lost touch with Mourne, for it was the weakest time in a pair's year, when they may spend days or weeks apart. When he returned to their territory in December, he found she had gone, and in her place was Hekla, proud and strong. She mantled when he came near.

'Where's Mourne?' he asked.

'Gone. This is my territory now.'

Anger at her rudeness and conceit overcame him and he stooped on her suddenly, talons outstretched, and was glad to see her retreat and frightened.

'She *has* gone,' muttered Hekla, in a voice rather less certain than before. 'She said that I should stay here and watch over the site, and keep off sleark. She said winter was coming again, another year, and no eagle was to seek her.'

'Where did she go?' asked Bjorg, appalled.

Hekla shrugged. 'North, I think. Along the coast. Up there somewhere.'

Mourne had gone north slowly. She had missed Bjorg, and was so cast down with pain and doubt about her strength that she believed he had turned away from her, and gone to seek another mate.

She had drifted along the coast, her head always aching with pain and her vision distorted when she tried to look straight beneath her. She had lost herself among the cliffs. Then one day she had seen a cloud, a swirling cloud, and tired, so tired, tried to overfly it, only to find her wings pulled down, the darkness and drear depth beneath her coming near, and she unable to prevent a downward spiral. Wings so weak, her sudden fear so great as the sky darkened, she fell into shadow. Cliffs rose above her, and the wind sucked her down towards the roaring and the rushing of the sea that crashed between the stacks and at the great rock-falls at the bottom of what she knew was the treacherous Cleft of Straumen. Then, taking a slippery stance, she tried to fly back out, but the winds were too distorted and strong, and it was all she could do not to be taken by the sea beneath. Spray caught her at high tide, her feathers were drenched, and bit by bit she began to grow cold.

There was food there though, cold dead birds that had been sucked in as she had. Some were living, too. She could feed, and dimly, far above her head, see the sky and sun. But ahead was only the devouring, grey sea, rushing between great narrows and surging up towards her. She would open her wings and try again and again to escape, but she had not the strength. And as the drenching cold seeped in, and night-time fell, she began the fatal thought that after all, it was an out-of-the-way place where a tired eagle who had done her duty could quietly ask that Haforn take her to her wings.

* * * * *

It was December, and the shops in Deal were bright with Christmas things. Jim Stonor and Judith, hand in hand, with the children at their sides, were doing final shopping for things they would need for the holiday. They had decided to have Christmas at West Street, and open the house to quite a crowd of people. Peter and Annie and their three children were coming in a couple of days. Michael was there, of course, and Margaret Stonor would come on the day itself, along with Mrs Frewin, and 'Elsie' Roberts, and Albert's wife, all of whom were at something of a loose end.

So now Philip had charge of two very large boxes of crackers, and Lucy was carrying a huge bag of chestnuts, while Jim and Judith were trying to decide whether to buy any more last-minute stocking presents now, or break for some coffee up on the front.

It had been a happy year, marked by a second major one-man exhibition in London in the autumn. Jim had finally broken with Anthony Cunliffe, though amicably, and the Shure Gallery held the first exhibition of modern art in its history. Then there was the breeding success of the sea eagle pair on Skye that year, and the arrival of more after unusually harsh winters in their home territories had apparently driven some younger vagrants over the North Sea; these factors had given Jim's show an intrinsic news value. For the first time, American galleries and museums had shown real interest in his work, and a show was planned for New York the following year.

It was at the Shure Gallery show that *Disasters of Peace* was first shown in its entirety, and featured on a television arts programme. Within the first ten minutes of the half-hour programme, twenty-six phone-calls of complaint were received by ITV, and three of fierce praise. Stonor had once again made art controversial. It seemed indeed that etchings could be more effective than photographs in telling passionate truths. The edition of the etchings being limited, two museums made immediate purchase of the complete set: the British Museum acquired one, and the Museum of Modern Art in New York the other.

Yet, sitting with the children in a busy coffee shop on Deal seafront, with day fishermen vying for tables with Christmas shoppers, Judith was aware that eagles were not quite done. That period of retreat and retrospection that followed one of his shows had come on him again, and sometimes at night in their room he would be up at the window staring out, listening to the wind. And once he found himself waking from some troubled dream, almost a nightmare, which he had sometimes as a boy, running up a shingle beach, and the form that was coming from the sea was behind him, and the shingle so heavy at his feet and wellingtons, and him unable to escape; him unable to reach up his arms as wings to the sky and fly as an eagle should to escape the thing that came.

Judith knew of this and other shadows that clung about him still, and just as he respected her for what she did, and trusted her to run her business for herself, so she trusted him to make his work the way he must.

They returned home from the Christmas shopping to a pile of mail. There was a card for Jim from William Ferguson, bearing news of the eagles. 'Flock feeding on Rhum at a special food dump showed two matures not seen before. One pair over at Lewis; and the chick now full grown, still hanging around Gars-bheinn. Report of a female, suspected to be the mother, caught in the Cleft, which means she has little hope. But a marvellous year overall. Hope to see you up here, Jim, if you can drag yourself away from your comfortable studio.'

Jim spent the afternoon in the garden studio getting cold and increasingly depressed. He knew his mood was caused by the card, and the image of the Cleft suddenly huge and fiercesome in his mind. He would have gone up to Skye then and there if it had not been this time of year—not because he could help, but through some need in himself to witness something.

He was troubled all evening, and took a walk along the front, leaving Judith and the children with Michael to make chestnut stuffing. He was worse than troubled: he was suddenly bereft. The Christmas lights in the trees in windows of old North Deal mocked him, and he could hardly bear to see the crowds at pub windows, laughing and shoving in the warmth inside.

He stood outside the Bosun's Mate, unable to go in. He went further along the front to Compass Street, and hesitated before his mother's door. He could not go there either.

He returned home then, walking angrily and powerfully, his hands restless at his sides, as they had been often in the past before he worked.

It was Judith who told him he must go, though it was mad to go then, in winter weather. But she alone could understand.

'Peter won't mind. He'll just think you're daft, that's all,' said Judith. 'And Michael's here. Leave in the morning early, go slowly, and pray that the weather stays mild.'

He packed the car with gear he had not used for over a year. Boots and rucksack, anorak and waterproofs, and a bivouac tent for safety. Rations and a small gas-stove. His field sketching things and a sleeping-bag. And he left before dawn, driving steadily to London, and then on, sleeping in the car at Carlisle. Fourteen hours to William Ferguson's home, door to door.

Ferguson had gone. Left for Christmas, destination unknown. Jim had not even thought to telephone. But he knew the way in, and slept until another dawn in the spare room he knew so well. Then he drove up through Portree, along the grey moorland road, along the Trotternish peninsula, which looked as sullen as he could remember, past Storr, past the Quiraing, and then up to the north of the island until he reached the section of road nearest to the Cleft. There he got his gear together and walked the three miles across open moor to the cliffs, and then along to the great dismal Cleft itself. Standing at its edge he took out his binoculars and searched the base of the cliff. She was there, clear enough, huddled and wan at a stance not far above the high-tide marks and the reach of the waves. Once found she was easy to locate again, for jammed in the rock near where she perched, her great head staring at the sea and only moving very occasionally, was a great chunk of grey, bleached wood, which caught what little light there was.

He stared down at her. It was, as Ferguson had said, a nearly hopeless situation. No boat would reach her through the narrow stacks and heavy seas that rushed up at her periodically. And to climb down would be a major feat which few on Skye could manage. So he sat there all day, witnessing her end, watching her occasional movement of wing, or hobble from her stance to peck at some carrion fish. Exhausted, she was past care or hope. Dying—and he to witness it.

Dark fell, and instead of going back to his car, he bivouaced. It was mild enough, gusty and a little wet, but not too cold. He lay in his sleeping-bag listening to the great sea beneath the cliffs, and the wind in the heather running against the tent. Thinking of an eagle who had come across the dark sea, made young, and waited now, as he did, for something that had no name they knew.

* * * * *

Some time at dawn, as grey skies over grey sea began to lighten, the shape of an old, slow eagle skirted along the southern coast of Uist and then crossed the sea to Skye, searching. Seeking out an eagle.

Long had it searched, and many bays and cliffs and clefts and stances found, some with eagle roosting through the night.

An old eagle, grey and almost seeming beyond flight, and yet, when it flew, the light of dawn seemed to be with its wings and light upon its tail, and it flew as powerfully as the strongest eagle. It was the Weir.

Reft was half-asleep and half-awake, and wholly troubled. Restless through the long mild night, waiting for something he could not put a name to. Until he saw, at dawn, a shape and a shadow of wings and a lightness near him, and heard a voice that said: 'Go to Bjorg now and tell him what he must do. Go to him, Reft, for you have strength in your good wings. Go to him . . .' and the voice became the wind at the heather on the moor, or the fall of spray upon a rocky ledge. So Reft did, and found Bjorg and said: 'I don't care what Mourne thinks or does and doesn't do, Bjorg, but you know where she is as well as I do. You're her mate, and so what if she didn't want you after the autumn, when she fell ill? So what if she went off by herself? You go to her.'

If Bjorg hesitated to do what really he wanted to do, the care and love in Reft's voice was enough to make him want to go now, now the end must be near—to be close to her and give her comfort.

And was it Reft's voice then, or the wind at the cliff-side, that whispered again, 'You go now, Bjorg, and help her. For she who has helped so many cannot die like this. Go now with courage and face what Haforn decrees. Trust in your wings. Give her the faith to trust in hers. So go now.'

So Bjorg went, flying slowly north throughout the dawn, then more swiftly and ever more urgently, until he came to the Cleft where the winds blew. He took a stance and saw her in the early half-light, her wings huddled down and her tail stained with oil and muck from the Cleft's messy rocks.

'Mourne!' he called out into the wind. 'Mourne . . .' But the wind was violent and gusting there, and she did not hear or look up towards the sky.

'Fly now for her, fly a flight for her that she may see you,' something whispered to him, but he was afraid, for the winds were too strong there, and might pull him down. 'Fly . . .' Then he did, casting himself powerfully over the void of the Cleft, cutting his dark wings across the light of the sky, and beginning a flight of love and comfort for her, high above where she had taken a stance to die. Until she seemed to sense him there, and looking up saw him high above, caught in the winds that sucked and pulled at him, her love. And she knew the language of his flight, and feared for him there, for he did not have the strength. 'Leave me here,' she called. 'Leave me . . .'

He could not hear her words, but seeing her calling, came lower, not thinking of his safety, lower still, and she began to call out frantically: 'No, Bjorg, not here. Leave me! Leave me!' But the wind was sucking at his wings now and he was nearing her and wanted to hear her once again.

Then from the shadows of the Cleft, or perhaps from where the spray drained off the rocks as the seas rushed in and out, an old eagle's voice spoke and said: 'Fly up to him, Mourne. Fly up now, for you have the strength still. Your mother made a flight once into winds too strong for an eagle's wings, and she survived. It was true flight she made, true flight . . .'

'But I can't fly true. I have never flown true,' Mourne whispered to herself. 'I can't, I can't.' Yet Bjorg was sinking fast now, the pattern of his flight destroyed before the winds as he began to sink beneath the line of the cliff, and into the Cleft itself.

'Go back. Go back,' she called, as she heard his frantic calls.

'Fly up to him and help him now. Fly with him as Cuillin your mother flew with Finse. Fly true with him and give him strength, or he will die, Mourne, he will die.' The voice of sea, or the wind at bleached wood.

'I can't,' she whispered, but her wings were opening and the sea was rushing, and she was pulling at the air, opening her wings, pulling them down and heaving herself up and struggling. 'I can't, I can't,'—as slowly, very slowly, she raised herself into the wind, and inch by inch through driving spray that filled the air, her wings so heavy, she rose up towards the distant sky.

'Mourne,' he called, 'Help me. Help me . . .' and then ever stronger, ever surer, ever more true, she flew up with the strength of a thousand eagles into the wind, into his call, towards the light that had seemed so far, into the great sky, to make it hers.

'Come, my love,' she said, 'Follow my line of flight. Cut through these winds . . .' And slowly they made a line to destroy the great winds of the Cleft, rising into early winter sunshine, their shadows across the heather, skirting across the moor and rock, across the cliffs, and their shadows falling on to the distant sea.

'Why did you come for me? Where are we going?' called out Mourne.

'Home,' he said. 'Home across the dark sea. Home to where food and health returns. Home where you belong. To Romsdal, to the fabled Storrin, to the place you've missed and nearly died for.

Your work here is done.' So they flew south to Loch Brittle, round to Loch Scavaig, up towards Loch Coruisk, past Gars-bheinn, the true flight of great eagles. It was a flight that stopped sea eagle and sleark alike who saw and marvelled at it, a flight that a young, still unsure eagle saw and recognised for what it was, and was proud to know her parents could fly true.

'Watch and remember,' each one who saw it said to those nearby. 'Remember. For this is true flight that we see, the only flight for eagles across a conquered sky.'

Then Mourne and Bjorg turned from the Cuillins and flew north, taking a line on the Trotternish ridge to fly away from Skye and over the dark North Sea.

While an old, worn and tatty sea eagle, a vagrant whose name was Reft, watched after them and groomed himself, thinking that it was time he was moving on now and there was a place he had not been to, and that was where Haforn was said to have been born, the land of ice and fire.

He wasn't so old that he could not make another flight over the dark sea to see this place Lomagnup, which Bjorg and Mourne had told him about, where an old eagle called Torrin lived so long. As for the other eagles there, up in the north-west, it sounded to Reft like they needed a dose of common sense and inspiration, such as an account of all that had happened in Skye would give them. And there being no time like the present, so far as Reft was concerned, he gave up trying to make himself look tidy, and took off into the wind, to begin a slow and leisurely flight up towards Shetland, and from there out over the northern sea.

* * * * *

Jim Stonor woke long after dawn, when cloud had cleared and a pale sun lit his tent. He climbed out of his sleeping-bag, put on his boots and anorak, and went to the side of the Cleft. The eagle had gone. The piece of wood which had marked her stance was there—but she had gone.

He stared. Letting the binoculars drop to his side, he stared down into the Cleft. Then, at last, he knew what he must make, and what he would need, and where he would find it.

He packed his gear and drove south again on the Uig road, and down to Loch Brittle. He walked the path to Rubh' an Dùnain and searched the shore there for a grey, bleached piece of timber. Small enough to carry, but big enough to make the carving that he must finally make.

He took it back to Ferguson's house, and using the odd hammers and chisels and knives he found, and without stopping to rest, he cut the wood and worked it, quickly, violently, powerfully, his face pale from the effort, his hands chapped and scratched by the wood. Then he sat and stared at it for a while. Then he cut one final thing, at its base, with a sharp knife—a shape, barely more than a shadow of something. Until it was done.

Then he phoned Judith in Deal. 'I've finished,' he said. 'I've finished.' There was a long silence between them.

'When are you coming home, my love?' she asked.

'Now. Soon. I'll have a rest. I'll have a bath if Ferguson's got such a thing as hot water. But soon.'

He arrived back in Deal in the late afternoon of Christmas Eve, coming along the Dover Road and driving down the front. He had phoned again from London and she knew he would soon be home. He stopped the car and walked up to the sea. There were lights along the pier, and the Royal Hotel was lit up and festive; while several houses had left their curtains open so their Christmas lights showed.

Yet Deal, like the eagles, had gone from him. It was the people not the place that mattered now. He went down the familiar steps in the sea-wall where long ago he had first met Peter Conan, and walked down wet shingle to the sea. He felt light and festive, released from burdens decades old. He let the sea wash up towards his feet in the dark, only the white foam catching light, the rest all black. Then he turned to walk back up the shingle, to go through the old streets and join his family and friends. At the high-tide mark on the shingle bank beneath the great sea-wall, he turned and looked over the sea that was lost in night at the lights far off on the Goodwin lightships. And he picked up a pebble from the shingle, a big one, and pulled his arm back. He threw the stone, arcing into the night, over a dark sea that held no fear for him now.

Judith sat by a great and roaring fire in West Street, with Jim's brother Michael, Peter Conan and Annie, and the five children. There was a snakes-and-ladders board on the carpet, recently abandoned. Michael and Peter stood with backs to the fire, warming their legs, and Annie sat beside them.

All were gazing at the big cardboard box at Judith's feet, tied together with fraying red twine. It was worn and tatty, with French printing on two sides, as if once it had been used for supermarket goods, and had then found a happier, more beloved use as perennial storage for those special Christmas things – old decorations, fairy lights, silver angels, artificial snow – which every family should have.

But the Christmas tree was already decorated, standing in one corner of the sitting-room, its red and silver baubles reflecting the light of the fire.

'Open it! Open it! Oh, come on Mummy!' Lucy was pleading, laughing and eager, and then saying to Andrew, 'You wait and see!'

'What is it?' asked Peter, very curious.

'It's something Jim made for me a long time ago . . .'

'Don't *say*, Mummy. It's a surprise for Andrew.'

'I wasn't going to, my love,' laughed Judith, cuddling Lucy to her. 'Anyway, I'm not going to open it, not even the box, until Jim's here, because he's going to light the candles this year. Or maybe he'll let you light them, Andrew, because you're the youngest here, and so the most special!'

'Light what?' Andrew asked, not really understanding, but as excited as the others. 'What do I light?'

Peter poured a drink for the adults, some sloe gin that Annie had made that autumn, and allowed each of the children a small glass as well, because it was nearly Christmas. As he stoked the fire, Michael put on a record of Christmas music. Songs from the King's College Choir of Cambridge. And the harmony of the ancient carols, rich with a distant echo among the well-worn wood and towering arches, filled the excited sitting-room, and seemed to add a depth and special brightness to the warmth of the fire that shone in all their eyes.

Suddenly they heard keys at the door, and the door opening, and Lucy and Andrew bounded into the corridor, shouting excitedly, 'He's here! He's here!' And they heard Jim laughing as they came together into the sitting-room.

'Now what's all this about?' he asked.

'Mummy said we could light the candles when you came.'

Jim looked for a moment at Judith, who looked at him across the busy room, and what they said silently then had taken years in the making—and spoke of love.

'I don't think we can keep them waiting any longer, Jim,' she said with a smile.

So he sat on the sofa next to her and took the box up on his knees, the two children rising with it to get a better look, and Philip rather more serious to one side.

'I wonder what's inside?' Jim said with a smile, opening it slowly.

'You know. You know already,' said Philip. Jim nodded, and said nothing.

Then he took out the wooden box, and read out what he had

once so carefully printed out in paint: *'Judith's Christmas Tree: Not to be opened until 17 December.'*

'Well, that's long past!' he said, 'so I think we can open it now.'

'I think Andrew wants to,' Judith said softly.

Then Andrew took the old backgammon box and, with Judith's help, tilted it against the sofa, facing the fire.

'What's in it?' he kept asking.

'You'll see,' said Lucy, giggling.

He struggled a bit with the two brass latches, then suddenly opened it out like some great and magical book.

As he did so the two images inside came into view. The picture of St George's church on a starlit night on the left-hand panel; and the Christmas tree on the right. And the flickering flames of the fire caught the tinsel and glass and corrugations of light that Jim had so carefully worked into it.

'It's a Christmas tree!' said Andrew excitedly, reaching out his right hand to touch its lights, as if he could not believe they were only an image. But the other children – and adults – merely stared in awe at what Jim had made. And Judith reached out a hand to touch his.

There were two fresh white candles already in place on each panel. So Jim set the whole thing up on the mantelpiece, and opened out the candle-holders.

Then he struck a match and lit first one candle, and then the other, his face lit up as he stood back with the others to stare at their soft light—and the flickerings of colour and reflection on the sky, and church and the Christmas tree.

'Time for some carols of our own,' declared Michael finally, turning the record-player off, and leading the way out to the dining-room, where the piano was.

So they all trooped out, laughing and chattering, until only Judith and Jim were left, standing by the fire, its glowing flames warm at their legs, the candles of the Christmas tree glimmering at their hair. And as the sound of the piano came to them, they held each other close, to whisper the words of love and blessing they had found beyond the dark sea.

CHAPTER TWENTY-ONE

April 1998

MARION Poyser ran her hands over the head and wings of *Eagle*, the first sculpture Jim had made in the series and said, 'It's a pity the public aren't allowed to touch them.'

'You're right,' said Jim. 'And if I ran a museum, I'd let them do what they liked with sculptures. You can't really do much damage to bronze or stone. In fact, if anything, I think Rodin's *Burghers of Calais* in London is enhanced by the fact that so many people have worn away the outstretched fingers of one of the hands. It gives the sculpture extra life to know that people need to touch it.'

Lunchtime had passed by, long before, and someone had brought them in some sandwiches and coffee. There had been so much to talk about, and so much about the eagles she had not known.

'One reason why I never worked with steel, and probably never will, is because I don't like the feel of it, and I don't think anyone else does,' he said. 'It's a cerebral kind of material.'

'What about wood?' she said. 'You've rarely used it, though you probably know more about it as a material than most sculptors.'

He smiled, walked across the gallery, and picked up the bag containing the small item he had brought to New York with him, the one he said was his final piece. She had known he would eventually get back to it, and smiled a little at the sudden way he did. He always liked theatre.

'Well,' he said, 'this is wood, though hardly what you'd call a carefully carved piece. But it's the last one, and the only one I think I'd never sell or part with.'

'We've put a stand ready on the wall, just as you wanted us to,' she said. 'All measured to the right height and with the right spotlight, according to your instructions. The spot's already on.'

She pointed to the stand that projected from a wall at one end of the gallery by the doors leading into another room.

'The security men will make sure it's fixed properly overnight. Will it stand of it's own accord for now?'

'Oh, yes,' said Jim, and without more fuss he took it out of the bag, unwrapped some rough brown paper from around it, and placed in on the bracket. He stepped back, stared at it, reorientated it slightly, and then seemed satisfied.

'There we are. Your exhibition's complete,' he said with a smile.

It was pale grey wood, bleached by the sun and a thousand seas, a vagrant piece of driftwood that had drifted over the dark sea and come to rest near the ruins of the last MacAskill stronghold on Skye.

It had been carved savagely, crudely, sometimes violently, with rough chisel and knife, but into a thing of such gentleness and power that Marion Poyser could only stare mutely. It was a head. The head of an old man, a young man, the eyes of a boy who searched the horizon. It was Stonor's head . . . no, it was Liam MacAskill's. It was both of them in one form, subtle and changing like *Oiled Beach*, and shifting as you looked at it. Its eyes were cast up towards a sky, and the sky was so powerful in the eyes that Marion herself almost raised her own eyes to see its blue and clouds and running winds.

She looked for a moment at Stonor and he whispered, 'Look again. Look more closely. Look at the thing that people forget in sculptures, and see what you see.' Then she looked at the sculpture's eyes, and his mouth, and then down to his neck and where the wood was left almost untouched to form a natural base. And she stared, and looked up to see if something had got between the light of the gallery and the form he had made. Then she gasped in wonder, for by some magic of cut and scoring, some fractional hint of shape, some turn and twist of the whorls in the wood which Stonor had seized upon and used, it seemed that there, across the base of the head, was the subtlest hint of the shadow of a great and powerful sea eagle's wing.

Then she looked again at the eyes and knew that they saw across the great sky an eagle in flight; and its flight was true.

* * * * *

Old Clew, his feathers tatty and dry now as once his father's had been, had stared at the stars all night. Strange lights in the skies above Romsdal, winter lights, and stars as bright as a young eagle's hope. Night faded into dawn, and dawn changed slowly to a clear winter morning such that made an old eagle want to fly out across the waters of Romsdal and up towards the Storrin, taking his time as he did so because the wind was fresh and the day good.

For months now a great peace had been with him and a sense that finally all was well. The Doom, whatever it had been, seemed past, its shadows clearing onto a different world. Humans were here now in Romsdal, down by the coast and along its gentler slopes, and the coastal fjells cut by their tracks and roads. Eagles had learnt to avoid them, taking territory on the outer skerries, or finding some inaccessible coastal cliff or lakeside scree to make a nest at, and take stances to watch over growing young.

And though there were still stories of poisonings and shootings, why they were rare enough now and no worse a hazard than many others. But the weakness of the recent decades, the failure in breeding, the decline of the population, that had gone now. That had been the Doom.

Plenty of young juveniles about now, though more timid than in the old days, keeping themselves to themselves. They watched eagles like Clew in awe, as if they were from a great age past, and sometimes Clew grew exasperated that they did not see *that* age was now, in *their* wings. Not his.

Why, they spoke of Cuillin as if she was a god second only to Haforn, and Finse as if he too flew at Haforn's side. Well, perhaps they were right. But Clew was less sanguine about hearing Mourne spoken of as if she was a legend who had gone from them to a dream, because she was still alive, she *was*, though none of them had had word of her. But Clew could not help thinking sometimes that it would be good to have an eagle like her around Romsdal now, to show the youngsters how to fly, to give them a lead, to link the old like him with the new like them. To show them pride and courage, and tell them of the world beyond Romsdal.

There were a couple of juveniles now, down on the skerries at the entrance to Romsdal, where once he had foraged with Mizen and Weever when they were very young. The same place from which they had watched in such fear the historic arrival of Cuillin from across the dark sea.

Well that was past now and he had set course today for Romsdal's depths to fly up to the Storrin and stare at its great grey swathing depths.

And so he might, enjoying the image of his shadow sliding along the fjord waters beneath him, had not some sudden movement of alarm between the youngsters below stopped him and had him circling. They were staring out to sea towards the western horizon, but peer as he might his old eyes could see nothing at all but sky and winter sun. Yet they stared and mantled and then stared up at him, their wings fluttering in alarm and their heads moving.

They stared up as if they expected him to give some lead, but for what, he could not say . . . unless, unless . . . and the western horizon lightened before his aged gaze and his heart filled with joy and his great wings opened yet wider, for he saw a great eagle coming, who flew as Cuillin once had, from off the dark sea. And at her side was a male, a fremmed, not one of Romsdal.

They came steadily, with tiredness and pride in their wings as if they had flown a great way.

'Mourne! It is Mourne, daughter of Cuillin, returning to Romsdal . . .' He whispered the words. Then he called out in a voice that carried out over the fjord to north and south, inland and seaward, 'See, it is Mourne, daughter of Cuillin. Now fly up to welcome her, for she flies with courage and truth and has brought a fremmed for us to honour.'

Then high above the entrance of Romsdal old Clew began to fly a flight that Mourne's mother had taught him, a great flight, a flight that heralds a new start, a new beginning. He flew for all to see, but especially the youngsters who never saw the like before. He flew a Flight of Welcome such as once, had he known how then, he would have flown for Cuillin. He flew it now with pleasure, joy and wisdom, for he could see that Mourne was returning, and her task in Skye was complete. Great Mourne, born in the Storrin, watched over by the Weir, sister of Askaval, was coming home. And Clew opened his great wise wings across the sky to welcome her.

*　*　*　*　*

Marion Poyser stood before Stonor's last work in silence, the images of eagles and flight and Romsdal fading from her mind where, for a moment, they had suddenly been so strong. She looked around the gallery and stared at 'The Stonor Eagles' as if all were her friends and had something of her in them. Then she looked round for Jim Stonor to tell him that for a moment she had been there with his eagles, really there, and that after so very long she understood. She had seen his eagles fly, and in seeing them they had become a part of her.

But when Marion Poyser looked for Jim again, he had gone, into the next gallery which showed the work he had done after 1984 – which was work of colour, of light, of people and of life, where no Storrin roared nor wind howled across a black cliff's face. A different world there which was rich with love and life.

Publisher's Note

Readers of THE STONOR EAGLES who would like more details of William Horwood's other work should write to him at PO Box 446, Oxford, OX1 2SS

Acknowledgements

My first thanks to John Love, who has been in charge of the Nature Conservancy Council's Sea Eagle Project on Rhum, N. W. Scotland, who gave me great help and encouragement in the early stages of writing this book. If sea eagles finally re-establish themselves permanently in the British Isles it will be due primarily to the years of work he has given to them.

The main academic source on the species has been the *Handbook of the Birds of Europe, the Middle East and North Africa*, chief editor Stanley Cramp (Oxford University Press, 1980), whose authors will know where I have used artistic licence: any errors or omissions are entirely my own.

Many individuals have helped with ideas and research. My special thanks to Gerald Searle of the Royal Society for the Protection of Birds; to Roy Trollope of St Martin's School of Art, London; to Janet Tod, Sue Wolk, and John Sharples; and Anni Haugen of Reykjavik, Iceland. I was advised on the Gaelic by Donald Meek of the Department of Celtic Studies, Edinburgh University, to whom I am very grateful; and I acknowledge once again the Scottish University Press for permission to quote from Alexander Carmichael's *Carmina Gadelica*. I am especially grateful to Peter Lavery, my editor at Hamlyn, for patient help with a difficult text and, once again, to my typist Marjorie Edwards for her unfailing professionalism.

Any marginal changes in historical chronology or fact in this fictional story are entirely my own and were made for personal or artistic reasons.

Bestselling Fiction

☐	No Enemy But Time	Evelyn Anthony	£2.95
☐	The Lilac Bus	Maeve Binchy	£2.99
☐	Prime Time	Joan Collins	£3.50
☐	A World Apart	Marie Joseph	£3.50
☐	Erin's Child	Sheelagh Kelly	£3.99
☐	Colours Aloft	Alexander Kent	£2.99
☐	Gondar	Nicholas Luard	£4.50
☐	The Ladies of Missalonghi	Colleen McCullough	£2.50
☐	Lily Golightly	Pamela Oldfield	£3.50
☐	Talking to Strange Men	Ruth Rendell	£2.99
☐	The Veiled One	Ruth Rendell	£3.50
☐	Sarum	Edward Rutherfurd	£4.99
☐	The Heart of the Country	Fay Weldon	£2.50

Prices and other details are liable to change

ARROW BOOKS, BOOKSERVICE BY POST, PO BOX 29, DOUGLAS, ISLE OF MAN, BRITISH ISLES

NAME...

ADDRESS...

....

....

Please enclose a cheque or postal order made out to Arrow Books Ltd. for the amount due and allow the following for postage and packing.

U.K. CUSTOMERS: Please allow 22p per book to a maximum of £3.00.

B.F.P.O. & EIRE: Please allow 22p per book to a maximum of £3.00.

OVERSEAS CUSTOMERS: Please allow 22p per book.

Whilst every effort is made to keep prices low it is sometimes necessary to increase cover prices at short notice. Arrow Books reserve the right to show new retail prices on covers which may differ from those previously advertised in the text or elsewhere.